THE INVISIBLE SPY

CHAWTON HOUSE LIBRARY SERIES: WOMEN'S NOVELS

Series Editors: Stephen Bending
Stephen Bygrave

TITLES IN THIS SERIES

FORTHCOMING TITLES

Eliza Haywood,
The Invisible Spy

Edited by

Carol Stewart

Routledge
Taylor & Francis Group

LONDON AND NEW YORK

First published 2014 by Pickering & Chatto (Publishers) Limited

Published 2016 by Routledge
2 Park Square, Milton Park, Abingdon, Oxfordshire OX14 4RN
711 Third Avenue, New York, NY 10017, USA

First issued in paperback 2016

Routledge is an imprint of the Taylor & Francis Group, an informa business

BRITISH LIBRARY CATALOGUING IN PUBLICATION DATA

Haywood, Eliza Fowler, 1693?–1756 author.
The invisible spy. – New edition – (Chawton House library series. Women's novels)
I. Title II. Series III. Stewart, Carol (Carol Ann) editor.
823.5-dc23

ISBN 13: 978-1-138-23555-7 (pbk)
ISBN 13: 978-1-8489-3441-2 (hbk)

Typeset by Pickering & Chatto (Publishers) Limited

CONTENTS

ACKNOWLEDGEMENTS

First of all, I would like to thank Gillian Dow, who allowed me to extend my Honorary Chawton House Library Visiting Fellowship, giving me access to the resources of the University of Southampton. Ros Ballaster, Moyra Haslett, Kathryn King, Manushag Powell and Ian Campbell Ross responded generously to my call for help with Haywood's Catalogue: I am grateful for their suggestions and advice. Mark Pollard, of Pickering & Chatto, was encouraging and supportive. Miss Christine Reynolds, Assistant Keeper of Muniments at Westminster Abbey, gave a comprehensive answer to my query about the tomb of an English princess.

INTRODUCTION

The Invisible Spy begins with a playful account of how an unknown author's identity might be constructed by curious readers:

> I have observed that when a new book begins to make any noise in the world, as I am pretty certain this will do, every one is desirous of becoming acquainted with the author; and this impatience increases the more, the more he endeavours to conceal himself. – I expect to hear an hundred different names inscribed to the Invisible, – some of which I should, perhaps, be proud of, others as much ashamed to own. – Some will doubtless take me for a philosopher, – others for a fool; – with some I shall pass for a man of pleasure, – with others for a stoic; – some will look upon me as a courtier, – others as a patriot; – but whether I am any one of these, or whether I am even a man or a woman, they will find it, after all their conjectures, as difficult to discover as the longitude.

If we accept as truth an anecdote in the earliest biographical account, Haywood's identity was a mystery she took care to preserve. In David Erskine Baker's *The Companion to the play-house* (1764), we read that 'she laid a solemn Injunction on a particular Person, who was well acquainted with [her History], not to communicate to any one the least circumstance relating to her'.[1] That injunction was evidently obeyed. Despite her prolific career, Haywood left little trace on the historical record. We know only that by 1715 the woman who later informed a potential patron that her maiden name was Fowler, appeared as Eliza Haywood in the cast list for the Smock Alley theatre in Dublin. The identity of her husband is unknown, but we glean from her letters that the marriage was 'unfortunate', and that Mr. Haywood died suddenly, around the same time as her father. She turned to writing to support herself and two children, the eldest of them being 'not more than 7' in 1729. Haywood reveals little about herself in her work, but then self-revelation or confession was not generally the early eighteenth century mode. The author disappears behind a neutral 'polite' style – erotic scenes notwithstanding – constructing personae as the occasion requires. In *The Female Spectator* (1744–6) she is a gentlewoman of unusually liberal education with youthful follies now behind her, who could be single, married or widowed. For *The Parrot* (1746), she is an East Indian bird of many languages. The Haywood of *Epistles for the Ladies* (1749) takes on the voices of numerous correspondents.

Spying was a device she had used before, most notably in *A Spy on the Conjurer* (1724), albeit with less *élan*.

Published in November 1754, *The Invisible Spy* is the last major work by Eliza Haywood (*c*.1693–1756) appearing in her lifetime. Only her conduct-books *The Wife*, *The Young Lady* and *The Husband*, all from 1756, post-date it, with the last of these published in February, just after the author's death. Sales show *The Invisible Spy* to have been a popular work: seven editions of the *Spy* in English between 1755 and 1789, and six editions in German, translated by August Gottlieb Meissner, between 1791 and 1814. Critical reception was mixed. For the *Gentleman's Magazine* the book contained 'some natural pictures of life, and some extravagant pieces of grotesque, neither of which have any striking excellence, but amuse, rather by the variety of images which they represent, than the manner in which they are drawn. There are many exceptionable incidents, sentiments and expressions in the work; yet there are some lessons which every reader would do well to practice'.[2] It excerpted from Book VI the story of Matilda's abduction from the masquerade and subsequent rape as offering, presumably, an example of the latter. The *Monthly Review* had little by way of comment, noting only that the anonymous work 'seems to be a production of a female pen, which for a course of years has often entertain'd the public'.[3] It provided the story of the funeral of a lap-dog at the home of Lady Marvell as a taster. 'Displeasing', was the laconic verdict of Lady Wortley Montagu (1689–1762), recorded on the title page of the first volume of her copy of *The Invisible Spy*.[4] In a letter to her daughter, she wished that there had been a key to the work, particularly the mock 'Catalogue', in Book VI, Chapter iv, for 'I know not whether the Conjugal Happiness of the [D]uke of B. is intended as a Compliment or an Irony'– a thought that may well be echoed by the editor.[5] The identification of the objects of Haywood's praise or sarcasm by their initials and a cryptic line of text is an inexact science.

Even with the growth of interest in Haywood in the last twenty to thirty years, *The Invisible Spy* has not attracted sustained attention. It has not rewarded readings of Haywood that see her earlier, more racy novellas as liberating or proto-feminist. In 1985, Mary Anne Schofield judged that 'the tales [in *The Invisible Spy*] become attempts to recapture the excitement and expectations of Haywood's earlier romances, and they fail horribly'.[6] The 'spy' persona has intrigued feminist scholars interested in women authors' self-fashioning, without necessarily producing detailed readings of *The Invisible Spy*. Juliette Merritt has looked at Haywood's persona in *The Invisible Spy* as a form of rhetorical positioning, but has little to say about the tales that comprise the book itself.[7] Political readings of Haywood have begun to proliferate, though these too have had little to say about *The Invisible Spy*. The most recent contribution is Kathryn R. King's important and well-researched *A Political Biography of Eliza Haywood* (2012). King argues that beginning in 1740s, Haywood wrote 'often and consistently' as a Patriot. Patriotism was a programme informed and shaped by the writings of Henry St. John, first Viscount Bolingbroke (1678–1751) in *The Craftsman* (begun 1726), *The Idea of a Patriot King* (1749) and elsewhere. Beginning in the 1720s, Bolingbroke wanted a campaign that would unite the fractured opposition to Sir Robert Walpole. To that end, he developed the idea of a 'country' party that would form an alternative to the corruption of Whig values supposedly represented by the court. In Bolingbroke's vision, distinctions between Whig and Tory had been settled in 1688, and the real choice now was between a self-interested and self-serving court, and those who would uphold the virtues of independence, selfless public activity and liberty. By 1737, the figurehead of this programme of national renewal was Frederick, Prince of Wales (1707–51). The mutual antipathy between George II and his eldest son made Frederick's cause a vehicle for widespread distrust of the House of Hanover, with Leicester House the focus for politicians hoping for position when Frederick became king. Patriotism, so understood, could encompass dissident Whigs (usually meaning out of place Whigs), Tories and even Jacobites.

King's study ends with reflections on Haywood's persona in *The Invisible Spy*, but the political contextualisation she argues for is illuminating in terms of a reading of the work. This is a narrative grounded in a specific time and place, and written from a Patriot perspective. George II reigns, and the narrator hints at his loyalty to Hanover rather than England: 'the king was lately return'd from visiting his German dominions'. Such is the pervasive power of self-interest that British politicians follow him there in the hope of preferment. Frederick, Prince of Wales, has lately died, but such is the indifference of the town that the event only serves to remind one fashionable lady of the dress she wore to court when the period of mourning was over. Colley Cibber's birthday ode for the king is an example of sycophancy and subservience. Anyone thinking of offending the ministry would do well to remember the powers it has at its disposal. A young lady remarks that she likes plays well enough, but 'there are others so cramm'd with the words Liberty and Public Spirit, that they are quite surfeiting'. 'When there is too much of these things, madam, the Licence-Office knows how to correct them', is the author's dry return – a reference to the Licensing Act of 1737. Gentlemen in a coffee-house discuss their opposition to the Marriage Act and the Jewish Naturalization Bill of 1753 – issues to which I will return in a moment – and one warns his companions that if they are overheard, members of parliament might prefer to avoid elections altogether and vote to keep themselves in power for seven, fourteen, twenty-one years or *ad infinitum*: an allusion to the Septennial Act of 1716, which extended the life of parliaments from three to seven years and helped to ensure the dominance of the Whigs. The people would not bear it, remarks one: indeed they would, returns another. However tenacious the British people of earlier times might have been in defence of their liberties, those living now will give up their constitutional rights without a fight. Only the electors of Westminster, who sponsored their own anti-government candidate, stand as an example of independence. The perceived dominance of self-interest and corruption in public life; the danger posed to the liberty of the British subject by an over-mighty executive; the need for frequent elections; warnings to a credulous or supine electorate – all of these positions and attitudes are recognisably those of the Patriot opposition.

The work belongs to a late phase of Patriot writing, with the Opposition cause now being taken up by John Russell, fourth Duke of Bedford (1710–71). In 1744, under the Pelham administration, Bedford had been first Lord of the Admiralty, and then, in 1748, secretary of state for the south. However, he had an uneasy relationship with Henry Pelham (1694–1754) and his brother Thomas Pelham Holles, duke of Newcastle (1693–1768). Tensions between Bedford and Newcastle surfaced in January 1750 in the struggle over the Bedford Turnpike Bill: Horace Walpole described them as 'on the brink of declaring war'. Bedford had put forward a bill for the repair of a road between Knotting in Bedfordshire and Market Harborough in Leicestershire, but it was defeated. Turnpikes are an issue touched on, somewhat ambiguously, in *The Invisible Spy*. Bedford was eventually manoeuvred into resigning over the dismissal of his protégé, Lord Sandwich (1718–92). By then he was at the head of a faction that became known as the 'Bedford Whigs'. *The Invisible Spy* takes the same side as Bedford on two significant measures brought before the House of Commons in 1753. Hardwicke's Marriage Act – after Philip Yorke, first earl of Hardwicke (1690–1764) – was designed to curtail the practice of clandestine marriages, that is, those frequently carried out in 'liberties' outside the jurisdiction of the Church of England, without banns being read or one or other spouses being resident in the relevant parish. It also made parental consent legally necessary for those under 21 years of age. Bedford argued that 'clandestine marriages ... are marriages of love and more likely to be productive of useful subjects than the prudential marriages made by parents'.[8] Haywood's story of Miss Hasty, who to pre-empt the passing of the Marriage Act proposes to, and marries, a haberdasher's assistant, is clearly designed to serve Bedford's cause. The aim of the Jewish Naturalization Bill was to allow Jews born outside England to naturalize as British citizens without receiving the sacrament of the Lord's Supper. This was simply a modification of existing naturalization law, and any foreign Jew seeking naturalization would still have had to obtain the passage of a private Act of Parliament.[9] Naturalization would have permitted Jews property and trading rights. Bedford paid James Ralph, a journalist whose name often appears in connection with Eliza Haywood, to attack the Jew Bill in *The Protester*. *The Invisible Spy*'s satirical representation of Jews and Jew Bill supporters, as well as a 'goatish Jew', serve the same purpose, and will strike the modern reader as proof of ugly anti-Semitism on Haywood's part. However, it is worth bearing in mind Thomas Perry's caution that 'most of the ostensible anti-Semitism of the clamor [against the Bill] was aimed wholly at the Court politicians, and was surely understood in that spirit. ... [I]n opposition writing, 'Whig' and 'Jew' [were] almost interchangeable.'[10] The occasional nature of this sort of work is underlined by the contrary position that Haywood seems to endorse elsewhere, in *Epistles to the Ladies*, where we find Alinda writing to Euphrosine that 'those who place so much Merit in the *Ceremony* have little of the *Spirit* of Religion in their Hearts – They go to the *Protestant* Church, the *Popish* Mass-house, or *Presbyterian* Conventicle, because they have been accustomed to it ... and for the same Reason might have gone to the *Jew*'s Synagogue, for aught either they or I know'.[11] We might clear Haywood of anti-Semitism, but she was evidently writing for Bedford, paid, or in hope of payment. The author explains at the beginning of Vol. 4 that she had planned for *The Invisible Spy* to appear in the winter of 1753/4: it would then have come in time to influence the election of 1754.

The setting for much of the narrative in *The Invisible Spy* is also politically loaded. We are reminded that we are in the parliamentary constituency of Westminster.[12] Characters go to Westminster-hall, Westminster Abbey or Westminster school; among other locations in Westminster are St. James, Covent Garden, St. Clement Danes, the Strand, Scotland Yard and Clerkenwell. Westminster was the scene of hotly contested elections from the beginning of the eighteenth century, frequently marked by violence and disturbance on the streets. Turnouts at the poll were high. The franchise in Westminster was unusually broad, extending to all 'scot and lot' tax payers, meaning those who made a contribution to community costs such as the poor rate. Although the western parishes of Westminster were the home of the élite, the electorate in the Middlesex parishes of Clerkenwell were tradesmen and luxury craftsmen who had the vote. The latter, in particular, are given sympathetic treatment in *The Invisible Spy*. The basis of the Independent Electors of Westminster, an association formed to co-ordinate opposition to the court in 1741, was trade, but it provided a focus for some disparate social groups, down to, and including, unskilled labourers, and disparate political allegiances, including Tories and Jacobites, or crypto-Jacobites. In 1749, the court candidate Granville Leveson-Gower, Lord Trentham (1721–1803) presented himself for re-election. The court faction did not anticipate any difficulties, but in the event, a combination of factors produced a turbulent, and violent, contest, one still resonating five years later. Trentham's Tory father, Earl Gower (1694–1754), had caused resentment among his former allies by crossing to the court. Trentham did not bother to present himself to the electorate for renomination as a candidate. His patronage of a group of French actors – presented in Haywood's 'Catalogue' as 'An Exhortation to Hospitality to Foreigners, even tho' it should happen to be destructive to the Liberties of the Natives. – By L— T—, as he deliver'd it at the Hay-Market. Bound in the French Taste' – caused a riot. Trentham refused to use his influence to obtain a pardon for Bosavern Penlez, a thief singled out from many under the rarely-used Riot Act for his part in the sacking of brothels on the Strand. Penlez's execution, a little more than a month before the election, was deeply unpopular.

All the power of the court was brought to bear on getting Trentham re-elected: 'treating', meaning the spending of large sums on entertaining voters at hostelries; artificially enlarging the electorate to include well-disposed voters; and straightforward intimidation. In May 1750, Trentham was declared elected by a majority of 170 votes. Petitions were drawn up in protest, alleging bias on the part of the returning officer: the enquiry was frustrated. Instead, supporters of the Opposition candidate, Sir George Vandeput (*c*.1717–84), were charged with misconduct and intimidation. Alexander Murray (1712–78), brother of Lord Elibank and Jacobite earl of Westminster from 1759, was charged with using threatening language to the High Bailiff and confined to Newgate prison. Brought before the House to receive sentence, he refused to kneel, and was recommitted for contempt. The Sheriffs of London released him at the end of the parliamentary session, and it seemed possible he would be imprisoned again. As he drove to his brother's house a crowd gathered with a banner proclaiming 'Murray and Liberty'. The Commons offered a £500 reward for his recapture, but he fled to France.[13] These are the events alluded to by Haywood as 'the fate of M—y'. The penalties for speaking out against injustice are, I would argue, in Haywood's mind when she prefaces the story of Deidamia and Meroveus with reminders of the need for the 'Government of the Tongue'. Deidamia's harmonious marriage to Meroveus is destroyed when her friend Eutracia reveals that he has a mistress. When Deidamia confronts Meroveus, he rejects her brutally and immediately, and blames her for contriving her own unhappiness. Haywood had personal experience of the dangers of opposition: in 1749 she was held in custody and examined over her alleged part in the distribution of the seditious pamphlet, 'A Letter from H— G—, Esq.'. Another reason for invisibility, perhaps.

The Invisible Spy is, arguably, a reply to the social pamphlets of Henry Fielding (1707–54), who had been a ministry writer since 1745, if not before. Readers of *The Adventures of Betsy Thoughtless* (1751) might remember Haywood's interruption of the narrative for a seemingly gratuitous swipe at her contemporary and one-time employer:

> There were no plays, no operas, no masquerades, no balls, no publick shews, except at the little theatre in the Hay-market, then known by the name of F—g's scandal-shop; because he frequently exhibited there certain drolls, or, more properly invectives against the ministry: in doing which it appears extremely probable, that he had two views; the one to get money, which he very much wanted, from such as delighted in low humour, and could not distinguish true satire from scurrility; and the other, in the hope of having some post given him by those whom he had abused, in order to silence his dramatic talent.[14]

Fielding had once been an Opposition writer himself. In essays in *The Champion* (1739–40), plays such as *Pasquin* (1736) and *The Historical Register for the Year 1736* (1737), and in *Jonathan Wild* (first published in the *Miscellanies* of 1743), he had satirised 'the great man', Sir Robert Walpole. However, Haywood's charge of double-dealing is borne out by Fielding's own words, and by contemporary documents. His poem *Of True Greatness* (January 1741) was written in praise of

George Bubb Dodington and dedicated to him as a man whose honour and principle formed an obvious contrast with the false greatness of Walpole. However, when the poem was republished in the *Miscellanies*, the Preface to it defended the author's own suppression of anti-Walpole writings, a service for which he acknowledged that he had accepted money from the Minister. By 1741 he had definitely reached an agreement with Walpole. A letter from Thomas Harris to his brother James, both of them friends of Fielding, notes on 5 December 1741 that 'Our Friend F—g is actually reconciled to ye great Man, & as He says upon very advantageous Terms'.[15] Ten days later he published 'The Opposition: A Vision', a pro-ministerial work which can confidently be attributed to Fielding as he acknowledged his authorship of it in the Preface to the *Miscellanies*.

In 1749–50, Fielding was appointed magistrate for Westminster and Middlesex, aided in the property qualification needed for the latter by none other than the Duke of Bedford, who was then still in office, and a Lord Justice. In that capacity, Fielding was responsible for the conduct of investigations into the abduction of Elizabeth Canning (1734–73), a case that was one of the century's most fiercely debated *causes célèbres*.[16] In January 1753, Canning went missing for twenty-eight days and then reappeared, claiming that she had been held captive in a brothel in Enfield Wash, eight or so miles north of London, owned by Susannah Wells. When she refused to become a prostitute her stays, she said, were cut off by the gypsy Mary Squires, and she was locked in an attic. Eventually she had managed to escape through a window. Fielding was approached by Canning's solicitor to assist in securing the conviction of Wells and Squires, and he took evidence from Virtue Hall and Judith Natus, two lodgers in Wells's house. Hall confirmed Canning's story, and in February 1753, Squires was sentenced to be hanged and Wells to be branded on the thumb and imprisoned for six months. However, three erstwhile supporters of Canning who were disturbed by contradictions in her account approached Sir Crisp Gascoyne, Mayor of London (1700–61). Hall's evidence was inconsistent, and under re-examination by Gascoyne she recanted. Witnesses testified to seeing Mary Squires in Abbotsbury, some one hundred and fifty miles away, at the time of Canning's supposed kidnapping. There were irregularities in the taking of testimony from Hall and Natus. In March 1753 a warrant was issued for the arrest of Canning on the charge of perjury. It was at this point that Fielding's *A Clear State of the Case of Elizabeth Canning* was published. In it, he defended his 'Protection of injured Innocence' – Canning's – and the manner in which he had taken the testimonies of the supposed witnesses. *A Clear State* was an early contribution to the controversy that occupied newspapers and pamphlets from February 1753 to late 1754, with opposite sides being taken by 'Canningites' and 'Egyptians', the latter being supporters of the gypsy Mary Squires. Haywood, like many another participant in the controversy, pours scorn on Canning's story, and she paints her supporters as Presbyterians, nonconformists and Methodists. This was not the case, though the link had been made before: it was reported that while in Newgate, Canning associated with Methodists.[17] Possibly Canning's mother was a Methodist.[18] By the time *The Invisible Spy* was published, Canning had been taken to live in the household of the Revd. Elisha Williams, a man sometimes described as a Methodist, in Wethersfield, Connecticut, a fact that might have lent some credibility to Haywood's case. However, by representing Canning's supporters as nonconformists, Haywood was implicitly connecting them with the Whigs, and thus implying that the administration was responsible for injustice.

Malvin Zirker argues that pamphlets Fielding produced between 1749 and 1753 on such matters as the justice of the laws in *A Charge Delivered to the Grand Jury* (1749), a defence of the reading of the Riot Act and the execution of Penlez in *A True State of the Case of Bosavern Penlez* (1749), and the reasons for an increase in crime in *An Enquiry into the Causes of the Late Increase of Robbers* (1751), all implicitly supported the Pelham administration. They were certainly conservative in nature, being defences of the political *status quo* and a clearly defined social hierarchy. Fielding's pamphlet on Penlez can also be read as a piece of electioneering in its own right. The peruke-maker was hanged on 18 October, 1749, but, anticipating the outcry that might follow, Fielding had the Penlez pamphlet ready in September 1749. Yet he withheld publication until 18 November, just four days after Trentham announced his candidacy.[19] In *An Enquiry into the Causes of the Late Increase in Robbers*, Fielding identifies the growth of luxury among people of the 'lower sort' as one of those causes. In this instance he was articulating the prevalent view. Luxury, and the threat it posed to the stability of the state, was also a common theme in Patriot writing, wherein it was agreed that 'the labouring poor had become so licentious as to be no longer manageable'.[20] Fielding's cure is to limit and restrict the 'Diversions of the People', and make sure that price of tickets for such polite amusements as the opera remain high enough to exclude the tradesman or the mechanic. The author makes it abundantly clear that he is not about to criticize the gentry or the nobility, even if they do set an unfortunate example: 'I aim not here to satirize the Great, among whom Luxury is probably a moral rather than a political Evil ... Pleasure always hath been, and always will be, the principal Business of Persons of Fashion and Fortune'.[21] The tales in *The Invisible Spy* take a different view. In stories like that of Melissa, who becomes hysterical when she finds that another lady has the same fabric for her dress, she focuses on the wastefulness and conspicuous consumption of the upper ranks. The extravagant funeral of a lap-dog is another indictment of upper-class luxury. In *The Invisible Spy* it is the young and innocent country couple who are corrupted and ruined by the fashionable masquerade. Although she may not have intended it, Haywood's take on luxury puts her in some radical company, namely that of Jean-Jacques Rousseau, who, while working through the classical indictment of luxury, produced a critique of inequality and the *ancien régime*.[22] For Fielding, gaming is 'the last great Evil which arises from the Luxury of the Vulgar' and another cause of the increase in robbery. Again he is at pains to confine his remarks to the 'inferiour Part of Mankind' – 'I am not so ill-bred as to disturb the Company at a Polite Assembly'[23] – and his remedy is to more strictly enforce the laws, some of them dating back to Henry VIII, that prohibited the lower ranks from play. Gaming is a preoccupation of *The Invisible Spy* as well, and while Haywood might have been no more in favour of a promiscuous mingling of ranks than Fielding, her gamblers are predominantly the gentry and the nobility. One remedy is an increase of female agency: Charlotte saves her indebted lover from the card-sharps by posing as a man and threatening them with arrest.

It could be argued that the political context outlined above still fails to engage with the stuff of the narrative, its seductions and arranged marriages gone wrong. What, say, has the story of Alinda's corruption by her clerical tutor, Le Bris – a graphic account of what we would now call sexual grooming – to do with Opposition politics? Or the story of Flaminio, who believing himself to have been visited by the ghost of a woman he long ago seduced, intends to place his daughter in a nunnery in an act of expiation? Here, Opposition writing becomes a vehicle for potentially radical thinking, often feminist in nature. In these stories, the sins of the fathers are visited upon the children, whether in the case of Alinda's father, who kept her isolated and uneducated, or the perverted cleric, or Flaminio. The old order is rotten. Cleora's jealous husband Aristus would keep his wife virtually imprisoned, and in the end his jealousy drives her into the arms of her former suitor Leander. The story ends with them living, unmarried, in Paris. Socially sanctioned relationships like marriage tend to produce misery. The subsequent anecdote about a pair of sisters, Celemena an obedient and Flavia a disobedient wife – the obedient wife comes off best – seems to balance this sympathetic account of wifely suffering with a vindication of submission. However, in the course of their conversation Celemena reminds Flavia of their humble origins, and their good fortune in marrying well-off husbands: wives, good or bad, are always dependent on husbands.

This edition makes available a work by Haywood that is significant not only in terms of the author's *oeuvre*, but also in terms of Patriot writing as it evolved over the course of the eighteenth century, and informed women's writing. Kathryn King has pointed out that *The Female Spectator* argues for the political rights of all tax payers, not just property owners.[24] *Epistles for the Ladies* (1749) makes women the agents of national renewal. In *The Invisible* Spy, relations between the sexes play out the dynamics of power, with women who think and act independently pointing toward a more just and happier society. Haywood's last major work deserves the attention her other late works are now receiving.

Notes

1.   D. Erskine Baker, *The Companion to the play-house*, 2 vols (1764), vol. II, *s.v.* Heywood, Mrs. Eliza.
2.   *Gentleman's Magazine*, December 1754, p. 560.
3.   *Monthly Review*, 11 (December 1754), Art. lxi, p. 498.
4.   P. Spedding, *A Bibliography of Eliza Haywood* (London: Pickering & Chatto, 2004), p. 580.
5.   *Complete Letters of Lady Mary Wortley Montagu*, ed. R. Halsband (Oxford: Clarendon Press, 1965–7), vol. III, p. 89.
6.   M. A. Schofield, *Eliza Haywood* (Boston, MA: Twayne, 1985), p. 102.
7.   J. Merritt, *Beyond Spectacle: Eliza Haywood's Female Spectator* (Toronto: University of Toronto Press, 2004).
8.   Cited by M. J. Powell, 'Russell, John, fourth duke of Bedford (1710–1771)', *Oxford Dictionary of National Biography*, Oxford University Press, 2004; online edn, May 2008 [http://www.oxforddnb.com/view/article/24320, accessed 18 Nov 2013].
9.   See T. W. Perry, *Public Opinion, Propaganda and Politics in Eighteenth-Century England. A Study of the Jew Bill* (Cambridge, MA.: Harvard University Press, 1962), 31–44ff.
10. Perry, *Public Opinion*, p. 74.
11. Eliza Haywood, *Epistles for the Ladies*, introduced and annotated by C. Blouch, ed. A. Pettit and C. Blouch, in *Selected Works of Eliza Haywood*, 6 vols. (London: Pickering & Chatto, 2000), vol, 2, p. 114.
12. For the account of politics in the constituency of Westminster at mid-century, I am indebted to N. Rogers, 'Aristocratic Clientage, Trade and Independency: Popular Politics in Pre-Radical Westminster', *Past & Present*, 61 (1973), pp.70–106.
13. H. Douglas, 'Murray, Alexander, of Elibank, Jacobite earl of Westminster (1712–1778)', *Oxford Dictionary of National Biography*, Oxford University Press, 2004 [http://www.oxforddnb.com/view/article/19586, accessed 14 Oct 2013].
14. Eliza Haywood, *The History of Miss Betsy Thoughtless*, ed. B. Fowkes Tobin (Oxford: Oxford University Press, 1997), pp. 45–6.
15. Cited by F. Ribble, 'Fielding's Rapprochement with Walpole in Late 1741', *PQ* 80:1 (Winter 2001), pp. 71–82.
16. For the account of the Canning case, I have drawn primarily on M. Zirker (ed.), *An Enquiry into the Late Increase of Robbers and Related Writings*, The Wesleyan Edition of the Works of Henry Fielding (Middletown, CT.: Wesleyan University Press, 1988), pp. xciv–cxiv, but also on J. Treherne, *The Canning Enigma* (London: Jonathan Cape, 1989) and J. Moore, *The Appearance of Truth. The Story of Elizabeth Canning and Eighteenth-Century Narrative* (Newark, DE: University of Delaware Press, 1994).
17. See Zirker, *An Enquiry*, p. xcix.
18. M. Battestin with R. R. Battestin, *Henry Fielding: A Life* (London: Routledge, 1989), p. 570.
19. M. Battestin, 'Fielding, Bedford, and the Westminster Election of 1749', *ECS* 11:2 (1977–8), p. 165.
20. J. Sekora, *Luxury. The Concept in Western Thought, Eden to Smollett* (Baltimore, MD: Johns Hopkins Press, 1977), p. 65.
21. Zirker, *An Enquiry*, pp. 77, 83.
22. See J. Jennings, 'The Debate about Luxury in Eighteenth- and Nineteenth-Century French Political Thought', *JHI*, 68:1 (2007), pp. 79–105.
23. Zirker, *An Enquiry*, p. 94.
24. K. R. King, *A Political Biography of Eliza Haywood* (London: Pickering & Chatto, 2012), pp. 124–5.

SELECT BIBLIOGRAPHY

Primary Sources

Bysshe, E., *The Art of English Poetry*, 2nd edn (1705).

—, *The British Parnassus*, 2 vols (1714).

Complete Letters of Lady Mary Wortley Montagu, ed. R. Halsband, 3 vols (Oxford: Clarendon Press, 1965–7).

The Correspondence of Horace Walpole, 48 vols, vols 13–14, ed. W. S. Lewis, G. L. Lam and C. H. Bennett (New Haven, CT: Yale University Press, 1948); vol. 20, ed. W. S. Lewis, W. Hunting Smith and G. L. Lam (London: Oxford University Press, 1960).

Enquiry into the Late Increase of Robbers and Related Writings, An, The Wesleyan Edition of the Works of Henry Fielding, ed. M. Zirker (Middletown, CT: Wesleyan University Press, 1988).

Erskine Baker, D., *The Companion to the play-house*, 2 vols (1764).

Haywood, E., *The History of Miss Betsy Thoughtless*, ed. B. F. Tobin (Oxford: Oxford University Press, 1997).

—, *Epistles for the Ladies*, introduced and annotated by C. Blouch, ed. A. Pettit and C. Blouch, *Selected Works of Eliza Haywood*, 6 vols (London: Pickering & Chatto, 2000), vol. 2.

—, *The Female Spectator*, ed. K. R. King and A. Pettit, *Selected Works of Eliza Haywood*, 6 vols (London: Pickering & Chatto, 2001) vols 2–3.

Hervey, J., Lord, *Some Materials Towards Memoirs of the Reign of King George II*, 3 vols, ed. R. Sedgwick (1931; New York: AMS Press, 1970).

Locke, J., *Some Thoughts Concerning Education*, ed. J. W. Yolton and J. S. Yolton (Oxford: Clarendon Press, 1989).

Memoirs of Laetitia Pilkington, ed. A. C. Elias, Jr, 2 vols (Athens, GA: University of Georgia Press, 1997).

Secondary Sources

Banks, S., *A Polite Exchange of Bullets: The Duel and the English Gentleman 1750–1850* (Woodbridge: Boydell Press, 2010).

Battestin, M., 'Fielding, Bedford, and the Westminster Election of 1749', *ECS*, 11:2 (1977–8), pp. 143–85.

Burns, R. E., *Irish Parliamentary Politics in the Eighteenth Century*, 2 vols (Washington, DC: Catholic University Press of America, 1990).

Findlen, P., Roworth, W. W., and Sama, C. M., (eds), *Italy's Eighteenth Century: Gender and Culture in the Age of the Grand Tour* (Stanford, CA: Stanford University Press, 2009).

Gerrard, C., *The Patriot Opposition to Walpole. Politics, Poetry and National Myth, 1725–1742* (Oxford: Clarendon Press, 1994).

Halsband, R., *The Life of Lady Mary Wortley Montagu* (Oxford: Oxford University Press, 1960).

Harris, R., *A Patriot Press. National Politics and the London Press in the 1740s* (Oxford: Clarendon Press, 1993).

Jennings, J., 'The Debate about Luxury in Eighteenth- and Nineteenth-Century French Political Thought', *JHI*, 68:1 (2007), pp. 79–105.

King, K. R., *A Political Biography of Eliza Haywood* (London: Pickering & Chatto, 2012).

Lang, A., *Pickle the Spy* (London: Longmans, Green and Co.,1897).

Langford, P., *A Polite and Commercial People. England 1727–1783* (Oxford: Clarendon Press, 1989).

McLynn, F., *Charles Edward Stuart: A Tragedy in Many Acts* (London: Routledge, 1988).

Merritt, J., *Beyond Spectacle: Eliza Haywood's Female Spectator* (Toronto: University of Toronto Press, 2004).

Miers, D., *Regulating Commercial Gambling. Past, Present and Future* (Oxford: Oxford University Press, 2004).

Moore, J., *The Appearance of Truth. The Story of Elizabeth Canning and Eighteenth-Century Narrative* (Newark, DE: University of Delaware Press, 1994).

Muse, S. V., 'Eliza Haywood and the Jew Bill', *Notes & Queries*, 57:1 (2010), pp. 105–8.

Newman, A. N., 'Leicester House Politics, 1748–1751', *EHR*, 76:301 (1961), pp. 577–89.

O'Donovan, D., 'The Money Bill Dispute of 1753', in *Penal Era and Golden Age. Essays in Irish History, 1690–1800*, ed. Thomas Bartlett and D. W. Hayton (Belfast: Ulster Historical Association, 1979), pp. 55–87.

Outhwaite, R. B., *Clandestine Marriage in England, 1500–1850* (London: Hambledon, 1995).

Oxford Dictionary of National Biography

Perry, T. W., *Public Opinion, Propaganda and Politics in Eighteenth-Century England. A Study of the Jew Bill* (Cambridge, MA: Harvard University Press, 1962).

Phillips, R., *Putting Asunder. A History of Divorce in Western Society* (Cambridge: Cambridge University Press, 1988).

Probert, R., *Marriage Law and Practice in the Long Eighteenth Century* (Cambridge: Cambridge University Press, 2009).

Ribble, F., 'Fielding's Rapprochement with Walpole in Late 1741', *PQ*, 80:1 (Winter 2001), pp. 71–82.

Rogers, N., 'Aristocratic Clientage, Trade and Independency: Popular Politics in Pre-Radical Westminster', *Past & Present*, 61 (1973), pp. 70–106.

Schofield, M. A., *Eliza Haywood* (Boston, MA: Twayne, 1985).

Sekora, J., *Luxury. The Concept in Western Thought, Eden to Smollett* (Baltimore, MD: Johns Hopkins Press, 1977).

Spedding, P., *A Bibliography of Eliza Haywood* (London: Pickering & Chatto, 2004).

Stone, L., *Broken Lives. Separation and Divorce in England 1660–1857* (Oxford: Oxford University Press, 1993).

Treherne, J., *The Canning Enigma* (London: Jonathan Cape, 1989).

NOTE ON THE TEXT

The copy-text for *The Invisible Spy* is the first edition, dated 1755, held in the British Library, shelfmark 12612.d.14. The first edition has the author as 'Exploralibus', but this was corrected to 'Explorabilis', meaning able to explore, in the second edition. The version in the first edition has been retained. The first edition was also misbound, with almost all of Vol. II appearing as Vol. III, and vice versa: this has been corrected. Punctuation of speech has been modernized, and the 'long s' replaced with 's'. Haywood's variable spelling has been retained, but 'Doriman' and 'Dorimon' have been regularized as 'Doriman'. Typographical errors have been silently corrected. Internal page numbers in the list of contents for each volume have been updated to correspond with the pagination of this Pickering & Chatto reset edition.

THE

Invisible Spy.

BY

EXPLORALIBUS.

In Four Volumes.

VOL. I.

LONDON:

Printed for T. Gardner, at Cowley's Head, near St. Clement's Church in the
Strand.
M,D,CC,LV.

CONTENTS

TO THE

First Volume.

BOOK I. CHAP. I.

CHAP. VIII.

BOOK II. CHAP. I.

CHAP. II.

CHAP. III.

CHAP. IV.

CHAP. V.

CHAP. VI.

CHAP. VII.

CHAP. VIII.

CHAP. IX.

THE
Invisible Spy.

BOOK I.
CHAP. I.

INTRODUCTION.

To the PUBLIC.

I Have observed that when a new book begins to make any noise in the world, as I am pretty certain this will do, every one is desirous of becoming acquainted with the author; and this impatience increases the more, the more he endeavours to conceal himself. – I expect to hear an hundred different names inscribed to the Invisible, – some of which I should, perhaps, be proud of, others as much ashamed to own. – Some will doubtless take me for a philosopher, – others for a fool; – with some I shall pass for a man of pleasure, – with others for a stoic; – some will look upon me as a courtier, – others as a patriot;[1] – but whether I am any one of these, or whether I am even a man or a woman, they will find it, after all their conjectures, as difficult to discover as the longitude.[2]

I think it therefore a duty incumbent on my good-nature to put an early stop to such fruitless inquisitions, and also at the same time to satisfy, in some measure, the curiosity of the public, by giving an account of the means by which I attained the Gift of Invisibility I possess.

Know then, gentle reader, that in the former part of my life it was my good fortune to do a signal service to a certain venerable person since dead: – he was descended from the ancient Magi of the Chaldeans,[3] inherited their wisdom, and was well versed in all the mystic secrets of their art: – besides his gratitude for the good office I had done him, he seem'd to have found something in my humour and manner of behaviour that extremely pleased him; – he would often have me with him, and entertain'd me with discourses on things which otherwise I should not have had the least idea of.

But it was not long that I enjoy'd this benefit; – he sent for me one day to let me know he was much indisposed, and desired I would come immediately to him: – I went, and found him not as I expected, in bed, but sitting in an easy chair; – after the first salutations were over, and I had placed myself pretty near him; – 'My good friend,' said he, taking hold of my hand, 'I feel that I must shortly quit this busy world; – the silver cord is loosen'd, – the golden bowl is broken, – every thing within me hastens to a speedy dissolution; and I was willing to see you once more before I set out on my journey to that land of shades, – as Hamlet truly says,

> That undiscover'd country, from whose bourn
> No traveller returns.[4]

As the remembrance of you,' continued he, 'will certainly accompany me beyond the grave, I would wish, me-thinks, to hold some place in yours while you remain on earth, to the end that I may not be quite a stranger to you when we meet in eternity. – I have no land, – nor tenements, – nor gold nor silver to bequeath, yet am not destitute of something which may be equally worthy your acceptance.'

Then, after a little pause, – 'Take this,' added he, giving me a key, 'it will admit you into a closet which no one but myself has ever enter'd; – I call it my Cabinet of Curiosities, and I believe you will find such things there as will deserve that name; – chuse from among them any one that most suits your fancy, and accept it as a token of my love.'

He said no more, but rung his bell for a servant, who, by his orders, conducted me by a narrow winding staircase to the top of the house, and left me at a little door, which I open'd with the key that had been given me, and found myself in a small square room, built after the manner of a turret: – all the furniture was an old wicker chair, with a piece of blanket thrown carelesly over it, I suppose to defend the Sage from the air, when he sat there to study; – near it was placed a table, not less antiquated, with two globes; – a standish[5] with some paper, and several books in manuscript; but wrote in characters too unintelligible for me to comprehend any part of what they contain'd: – just in the middle of the ceiling hung a pretty large chrystal ball, filled with a shining yellowish powder, and this inscription pasted on it:

The ILLUSIVE POWDER.

A Small quantity of this powder, blown thro' the quill of a porcupine when the Moon is in Aries, raises splendid visions in the people's eyes; and, if apply'd when the same planet is in Cancer, spreads universal terror and dismay.

I easily perceived that this was one of the curiosities my friend had mentioned, and a great one indeed it was; but as I had neither interest nor inclination to impose upon my fellow creatures, I judged it fitter for the possession of some one or other of the mighty rulers of the earth.

I then turn'd towards the walls, which were all hung round with telescopes, – horoscopes, – microscopes, – talismans, – multipliers, – magnifiers of all degrees and sizes, – loadstones cut in various forms, and great numbers of mathematical instruments; – but these, as I was altogether ignorant of their uses, I pass'd slightly over, 'till I came to a hand-bell, which having the appearance of no other than such as I had ordinarily seen at a lady's tea-table, I should have taken no notice of, but for a label prefixed to it, on which I found these words:

The SIMPATHETIC BELL.

The least tincle of which not only sets all the bells of the whole country, be it of ever so large extent, in motion, without the help of men to pluck the ropes, but also makes them play whatever changes the party is pleased to nominate.

Tho' I thought art could produce no greater wonder than this bell, yet I felt no strong desire of becoming the master of it; but proceeded to examine what farther rarities this extraordinary cabinet would present. – The next I took notice of was a phial, not much unlike those which are commonly sold in the shops with French hungary-water;[6] – it had this inscription:

SALTS *of* MEDITATION,

WHICH held close to the nostrils, for the space of three seconds and a half, corrects all vague and wandering thoughts, – fixes the mind, and enables it to ponder justly on any subject that requires deliberation.

This beneficial secret I also rejected, through a mere point of conscience, as thinking it would be a much better service to mankind if in the possession of the divines, – lawyers, – politicians, or physicians, especially the two last mentioned, as it might prevent the one from engaging in any enterprize they have not abilities or courage to go through with, and the other from falling into those gross mistakes they are frequently guilty of in relation to the case of the diseased.

I should have ruminated much longer than I did on the excellence of these wonderful salts, if another object had not suddenly catched my sight; – it had the form of a skull-cap, or such a coif as serjeants at law wear[7] when a new one is called up: – what it was made out of I know not, for I am certain it was neither of the silk, woollen, or linnen manufactory; – it was, however, of so light and thin a texture, that as it hung at some distance from the wall the least breath of air gave it motion, – it was fasten'd by a single thread to the ceiling, to which also was fixed a slip of paper, which contain'd these words:

The SHRINKING CAP,

WHICH put upon the head immediately contracts all the muscles and sinews of the whole body, so as to render the person who wears it small enough to enter into the mouth of a lady's tea-pot, or a quart bottle; but great care must be taken no accident happens to the vehicle while he is in it; for if it breaks during that time, the man will never more recover his former dimensions.

I hesitated not a moment to reject this, as it seemed calculated for no other purpose than merely to amuse and astonish, and could be of no real service, either to myself or any body else: – I should, perhaps, not even have thought of it more, if an accident had not brought it fresh into my head: – my readers can scarce have forgot, that about some four or five years ago the town was invited, in a very pompous manner, to see a man jump into a quart bottle on the stage of the little theatre in the Hay-market;[8] – on the sight of the bills I presently concluded that the person who was to exhibit this wonderful performance must certainly be in possession of my friend's shrinking cap; nor was at a loss afterwards to guess, why so illustrious and numerous an assembly, as came to be spectators, were disappointed in their expectations: – I doubted not, but second thoughts had reminded the man of the danger his bottle would be in from the waggish humour of some among the audience, and that an apple, or orange, or even a hazle-nut, darted from a judicious hand, might give a sudden crack to the brittle vessel, and so he would be compelled to continue a lilliputian for his whole life.

The next, and indeed the first thing that raised in me any covetous emotions, was the apparatus of a belt, but seemed no more than a collection of attoms gathered together in that form and playing in the sun-beams. – I could not persuade myself it was a real substance, till I took it down, and then found it so light, that if I shut my eyes I knew not that I had any thing in my hand. – The label annexed to it had these words:

The BELT *of* INVISIBILITY,

WHICH, fasten'd round the body, next the skin, no sooner becomes warm than it renders the party invisible to all human eyes.

A little farther, on the same side of the wall, was placed a Tablet, or Pocket book; which, on examining, I found was composed of a clear glassy substance, firm, yet thin as the bubbles which we sometimes see rise on the surface of the waters; – it was malleable, and doubled in many foldings, so that, when shut, it seemed very small; but when extended was more long and broad than any sheet I ever saw of imperial paper; – its uses were decipher'd in the following inscription:

The WONDERFUL TABLET,

WHICH, in whatever place it is spread open, receives the impression of every word that is spoken, in as distinct a manner as if engrav'd; and can no way be expunged, but by the breath of a virgin, of so pure an innocence as not to have even thought on the difference of sexes; – after such a one, if such a one is to be found, has blown pretty hard upon it for the space of seven seconds and three quarters, she must wipe it gently with the first down under the left wing of an unfledg'd swan, pluck'd when the moon is in three degrees of Virgo; – this done, the Tablet will be entirely free from all former memorandums, and fit to take a new impression.

Note, That the virgin must exceed twelve years of age.

I was very much divided between these two; – the Belt of Invisibility put a thousand rambles into my head, which promised discoveries highly flattering to the inquisitiveness of my humour; but then the Tablet, recording every thing I should hear spoken, which I confess my memory is too defective to retain, fill'd me with the most ardent desire of becoming master of so inestimable a treasure: – in fine, – I wanted both; – so encroaching is the temper of mankind, that the grant of one favour generally paves the way for solliciting a second.

While I was in this dilemma a stratagem occurr'd, which I hesitated not to put in practice, and found it answer to my wishes; – I took both the Belt and Tablet in my hand; and, having carefully lock'd the door of the cabinet, returned to the Adept;[9] – he saw the Belt, which being long, hung over my wrist, but not perceiving I had the Tablet, – 'The choice you have made,' said he with a smile, 'confirms the truth of what I always believed, that curiosity is the most prevailing passion of the human mind.'

'However just that position may be,' reply'd I, 'that propensity is not strong enough in me, to make me able to decide between the wonderful Tablet, and the no less wonderful Belt; – they appear to me of such equal estimation, that whenever I would fix on the one, the benefits of the other rise up in opposition to my choice; and I know not which of the two I should receive with most pleasure, or leave with the least regret; – I have therefore brought both down to you, and intreat you will determine for me.'

I soon perceived he understood my meaning perfectly well; for, after a little pause, – 'When I made you the offer,' said he, 'of whatever you liked best among my collection of curiosities, I intended not that your acceptance of one thing should render you unhappy through the want of another; – take then, I beseech you, both the Belt and the Tablet, – you shall leave neither of them behind you; – nor do I wonder you should desire to unite them; – they are, in a manner, concomitant; and the satisfaction that either of them would be able to procure, would be incompleat without the assistance of the other.'

Thus was I put in possession of a treasure, which I thought the more valuable, as I was pretty certain no other person, in this kingdom at least, enjoy'd the like; – after making proper acknowledgments to the obliging donor, I took my leave and returned home with a heart overflowing with delight.

I was not long before I made trial of my Belt, and found the effects as the label had described; I also open'd my Tablet, – spoke, and saw my words immediately imprinted on it; – I then procured some Swans-down, according to direction, and intreated several young ladies to breathe upon it one after another; but tho' I dare answer for their virtue, the favour they did me was in vain, – the impression remain'd still indelible.

Indeed, when I began to consider maturely on the conditions prescrib'd in the label of the Tablet, I was sensible that it was not enough for a virgin to be perfectly innocent, she must also be equally ignorant, to be qualified for the performance of the task requir'd; and not to have once thought on the difference of sexes, seem'd a thing scarce possible after six or seven years of age at most, and would have been as great a prodigy as either of those that had been bestow'd upon me by the Adept.

What would I not have given for such a one as Dorinda in Shakespear's Inchanted Island;[10] but such a hope being vain I was extremely puzzled, and knew not what to do; – at last, however, a lucky thought got me over the difficulty; – it was this: – I prevail'd, for a small sum of money, with a very poor widow, who had several children, to let me have a girl, of about three years old, to bring up and educate as I judged proper; – I then committed my little purchase to the care of an elderly woman, whose discretion I had experienced; – I communicated to her the whole of my design, and instructed her how to proceed in order to render it effectual.

The little creature was kept in an upper room, which had no window in it but a sky-light in the roof of the house, so could be witness of nothing that pass'd below; – her diet was thin and very sparing; – she was not permitted to sleep above half the time generally allow'd for repose, and saw no living thing but the old woman who lay with her, gave her food, and did all that was necessary about her.

I frequently visited them in my Invisibility, and was highly pleased and diverted with the diligence of my good old woman; – she not only obey'd my orders with the utmost punctuality, but did many things of her own accord, which, though very requisite, I had not thought of. – To prevent her young charge from falling into any of those distempers which the want of exercise sometimes occasions, she contrived to make a swing for her across the room, taught her to play at batteldor and shittlecock,[11] – to toss the ball and catch it at the rebound, and such like childish gambols, which both delighted her mind and kept her limbs in a continual motion.

This conduct, and this regimen constantly observed, maintain'd my virgin's purity inviolate, as I did not fail to make an essay in a few days after she enter'd into her thirteenth year, and the success of my endeavours made me not regret the pains I had been at for such a length of time.

Now it runs in my head that some people will not give credit to one word of all this; for as there are many who believe too much, there are yet many more who will believe nothing at all but what their own shallow reason enables them to comprehend: – well then, – let them judge as they think fit, – let them puzzle their wise noodles 'till they ake, – I shall sit snug in my Invisibility while they lose half the pleasure; and, it may be, all the improvement of my lucubrations.

But those who resolve to pursue me through the following pages, with an ingenuous candour, I flatter myself will lose nothing by the chace; – they will find me in various places, though not in so many as perhaps they may expect; – they would in vain seek me at court-balls, – city-feasts, – the halls of justice, or meetings for elections; – nor do I much haunt the opera or play-houses: – in fine, – I avoid all crouds, – all mix'd assemblies, except the masquerade and Venetian balls.[12] – I am a member of the establish'd church; but as I am not asham'd of appearing at divine worship, never put on my Invisible Belt when I go there. – I revere regal authority, but seldom visit the cabinet of princes; because they are generally so filled with a thick fog, that the christaline texture of my Tablets could not receive what was said there, so as to be read distinctly; – nor do I much care to venture myself among their ministers of state, or any of their under-working tools; the floors of their rooms, in which their cabals are held, are composed of such slippery materials that the least *faux pas* might endanger my Invisibility, if not my neck. – I should be more frequently with the military gentlemen, but that they are so apt to draw their swords without occasion, that while they think they are fencing in the air they might chance to cut my Belt in sunder; – and what a figure I should make, when one half of me was discover'd and the other was concealed. – I will not mention the consequences such a sight might produce in some of them.

But it would be of little importance to the public to be told where I am not, unless they also know where I am: – have patience then, good people, and you shall be satisfied.

Sometimes I step in at one or other of those gaming-houses, which are above law, by being under the protection of the great;[13] but I seldom stay long in any of them, as I can see nothing there but what I have seen an hundred times before in those lesser assemblies of the same kind, that have been so justly put down by authority.

Sometimes I peep into the closet of an antiquarian, where I find matter enough to excite both my pity and contempt. – What greater instance can we have of the depravity of human nature than in a rich curmudgeon, who, while he grumbles to allow his family necessary food, chearfully unties his bags and pours out fifty, or it may be an hundred guineas, for the purchase of a bit of old copper, – only because a fellow of more wit than honesty tells him it was found under the ruins of an ancient wall, where it had been buried ever since the time of Julius Cæsar or Severus?[14]

Sometimes too I amuse myself with turning over the collection of a virtu-oso,[15] where I am always filled with the utmost astonishment, at finding sums sufficient to endow an hospital lavish'd in the purchase of wings of butterflies, – the shells of fishes, – dried reptiles, – the paw of some exotic animal, and such like baubles, neither pleasing in their prospect, nor useful in their natures.

Sometimes I make one at the levee[16] of a rich heir, just arrived from his trav-els to the possession of an overgrown estate; where I cannot help trembling for the future fate of the poor youth, on seeing him besieged with a crowd of mar-riage-brokers, – pleasure-brokers, – exchange-brokers, – lawyers, – gamesters, – French taylors, – Dresden-milliners, – petitioning harlots, – congratulating poets; – in fine, with sharpers, flatterers and sycophants of every kind.

Sometimes I mingle in the route of a woman of quality,[17] – see who wins, – who loses at play, and in what manner ladies are frequently obliged to pay their debts of honour.

When I have nothing better to employ my time, I loyter away some hours in St. James's-park, Kensington-gardens, or at Vaux-hall, Ranelagh, and Mary-le-bon,[18] and am often witness of some scenes exciting present mirth and future reflection.

But my chief delight is in the drawing-room of some celebrated toasts, whence I often steal into their bed-chambers; – but don't be frighted, ladies, – I never carry my inspections farther than the *ruelle*.[19]

These are some few particulars of the tour I have made; – to give the whole detail would be too tedious, – I shall therefore only say, that wherever I am found, I shall always be found a lover of morality, and no enemy to religion, or any of its worthy professors, of what sect or denomination soever.

And now, reader, having let thee into the secret of my history, as far as it is convenient for me to reveal, I shall leave thee to enjoy the advantage of those discoveries my Invisibility enabled me to make.

CHAP. II.

Contains some premises very necessary to be observed by every reader; and also an account of the author's first Invisible Visit.

It was in the beginning of that season of the year which affords most food for an enquiring mind, that I had got all things in order to sally forth on my Invisible Progressions; – the king was lately return'd from visiting his German domin-ions;[20] – the august representatives of the whole body of the people were just ready to assemble; – Hanover had given back our statesmen,[21] and Paris our fine gentlemen; – the expounders of the law were hurrying to Westminster-hall, and those of the gospel to pay their compliments at St. James's; – the ships of war were mostly moor'd, and their gallant commanders had quitted the rough athletic toil for the soft charms of ease and luxury; – the land heroes, who having no employment for their swords had pass'd their days in rural sports, now hunted after a different sort of game at the theatres and masquerades; – frequent consultations were held at the toylets of the ladies, on ways and means to outshine each other in the circle; – former amours were now revived, and new ones every day commenced; – madam Intelligence, with her thousand and ten thousand emissaries, all loaded with reports, some true, some false, flew swiftly thro' each quarter of this great metropolis; and had every pore of every human body been an ear, they all might have been fully gratified.

But tho' I confess myself to have been born with the most insatiable curiosity of knowing all that can be known, yet I could never depend upon the credit of common fame for the truth of any thing I heard; – always remembering mr. Dryden's words:

> With wondrous art things done she magnifies
> Feigns things not done, and mingles truth with lyes.[22]

How pleasing therefore must this Gift of Invisibility be to a person of my inquisitive, and at the same time incredulous disposition; – a gift which enabled me to penetrate into the most hidden secrets, and be convinced of their veracity by the testimony of my own eyes and ears.

But besides the gratification of a darling passion, I had another, and much more justifiable reason for the value I set upon the legacy of my departed friend; which is this, – I have it in my power to pluck off the mask of hypocrisy from the seeming saint; – to expose vice and folly in all their various modes and attitudes; to strip a bad action of all the specious pretences made to conceal or palliate it, and shew it in its native ugliness. – At the same time, I have also the means to rescue injur'd innocence from the cruel attacks begun by envy and scandal, and propagated by prejudice and ill-nature. – In fine, I am enabled, by this precious gift, to set both things and persons in their proper colours; and not in such as either, thro' malice, or partial favour, they are frequently made to appear.

I should be sorry, however, if any thing I have said should give the reader occasion to imagine I am going to present him with a book of scandal; – no, – the secrets of families, and characters of persons, shall be always sacred with me; – I shall give no man the opportunity of indulging a malicious pleasure of laughing at his neighbour's faults; – my aim in this work is not to ridicule, but reform. – I would touch the hearts, not call a blush upon the face; – and as few people have errors so peculiar to themselves as there are not many guilty of the like, if the offender keeps his own council, he may very well pass undistinguish'd among the crowd of others equally culpable.

Let no one therefore pretend to point at his companion, and cry out, 'This is the man,' – on pain of provoking my Invisibleship to declare his own faults; but let every one who finds a disagreeable likeness of himself in any of the characters I shall draw, set immediately about rectifying the blemishes which give that resemblance; and, as I inscribe no real name to the picture, he may safely defy the tongue of censure.

Verramond is justly accounted one of the most accomplish'd gentlemen of the present age, – the gracefulness of his person, – the engaging manner of his conversation, – his fine address and uncommon capacity, make his company desir'd by all the young and gay part of the world, as his great learning and perfect knowledge of men and things render him the oracle of the more grave and serious; – I had frequently the honour of meeting him at several places where I visited, and found nothing in him which could in the least contradict those high ideas fame had given me of him.

It was therefore natural for me to take the advantage of my Gift of Invisibility, in order to view this great person in his most retired moments; – I mean, when he was alone, and divested of all those modes and ceremonies, which often disguise the real man, and shew him to the public far different from what he is.

Accordingly, the first visit I made in my Belt was to his house; – I slipt in as soon as I saw the door open'd, – went up stairs, and pass'd thro' several rooms till I came to that where he was sitting; – I found him with a book in his hand, on which he seem'd very intent; – I doubted not but it was a treatise of philosophy, or some other piece of learning or wit, suitable to the capacity of so great a genius; but how much was I surprised, when, looking over his shoulder, I perceived it was Hoyle's method of playing the Game of Whist![23] – He appeared more than ordinarily taken up with one page, for he read it over three or four times, then started up from his chair, and throwing the book from him in a rage, – 'Curse on this stuff,' cry'd he, 'it is good for nothing but to teach a man how to undo himself with more art.' – After walking for some minutes backwards and forwards in the room, with a disorder'd motion, he flung himself into his chair, and fell into a profound resvery, in which I knew not how long he might have continued, if he had not been rous'd from it by the approach of a person, who I presently found was his steward.

The business on which this man came into the room was no way pleasing to Verramond; but because I would avoid the troublesome repetitions of, – said he, – and reply'd he, – and resum'd the other, and such like introductions to every speech, I shall present all those dialogues, which are proper to be communicated to the public, in the same manner as in the printed copies of theatrical performances.

Steward. My lord, the several tradesmen, whom your lordship order'd to come this morning, are below and wait your Lordship's commands.

Verramond. I have no commands for them at present, so send them away.

Steward. Shall I bid them attend your lordship to-morrow?

Verramond. Aye, – to-morrow six months if you will; for I shall scarce have any business with them before.

Steward. My lord, I told them they should all be paid off this morning, – What excuse can I make to them for such a disappointment?

Verramond. E'en what you will; – if you can invent nothing better, you may tell them that you ly'd when you made them that promise in my name.

Steward. Your lordship knows it was by your own order I made them that promise; and that you sent me into the city yesterday for money, which I doubted not but was to make good what I had told them: – if your lordship please to consider it is now a long time since they brought in their bills, and they have had a great deal of patience.

Verramond. Rot their patience. – Do you think to make a merit to me of their patience? – Go, I say, send them away, and let me hear no more of them.

The tone in which Verramond utter'd these words was so austere that the honest domestic had not courage to reply, but left the room immediately, probably to receive no softer treatment below from those he was compell'd to disappoint, than he had just met with above for attempting to intercede in their behalf.

Lord Macro was presently after introduced; – the late sullenness of Verramond seem'd now entirely dissipated; – whatever was in his heart, in his countenance were only smiles, and he ran to receive him with open arms and all the testimonies of the most perfect satisfaction; – and yet, as I soon found by the discourse they had together, this very Macro, the night before, had won of him at play fifteen hundred pounds, which was the sum he had set apart for the payment of his creditors. – Their conversation turning wholly upon gaming, a subject neither entertaining nor improving, I shall give my readers no more than a bare specimen of it.

Lord *Macro.* My dear Verramond, I could not be easy 'till I saw you this morning. – I thought you left the company somewhat abruptly last night, and was afraid your ill luck had given you some chagrin.

Verramond. Not in the least, my dear Macro, – I never think any thing lost that a friend gains; but I remember'd that I had some letters to write, otherwise should have staid and trusted fortune with a brace or two of hundreds farther.

Lord *Macro.* As it is an honour to get the better of your lordship in any thing, so it will be no disgrace to be overcome by a person of such superior abilities; therefore I am ready to give you your revenge when you think fit.

Verramond. Nay, – as for that, Macro, it must be confess'd you know the game better than I.

Here follow'd a long succession of mutual compliments on each other's skill in play, of which growing heartily tired, I was beginning to think of leaving the place, and should have done so, if the appearance of the steward a second time had not made me expect some change in the scene; – his errand, and the success it met with, will not perhaps appear so extraordinary to those acquainted with the modish way of thinking as it then did to me.

Steward. Farmer Hobson is below, my lord; – the poor man has rode hard all night, on purpose to reach town this morning and lay his miserable condition before your lordship.

Verramond. Pish, what have I to do with his condition?

Steward. He says, my lord, that his crop prov'd so bad last year that he had scarce wherewith to stock the ground; – that mr. Hardmeat, your lordship's steward in the country, is very sensible of his misfortunes, yet, though there are but five quarters due, threatens to turn him out of the farm next week; – he therefore humbly hopes your lordship will take compassion on him, as he has six small children, and his wife now lying-in of the seventh.

Verramond. What business have such fellows to get children? – Does he expect my rent shall go for the maintenance of his brats?

Steward. He begs your lordship to consider, that for these eleven years he has rented the farm he has always paid your lordship honestly, and does not doubt, through providence, but to do so still, if your lordship is pleased to have patience till next harvest is over, and not ruin him at once.

Verramond. Let me hear no more of this stuff, – I leave all to mr. Hardmeat, he knows what he has to do, and I shall give myself no trouble about it.

The steward, with whose good-nature I was infinitely charm'd, had his mouth open to urge something farther in behalf of the distress'd farmer, but was prevented by a servant that instant coming in and presenting a letter to Verramond, who then bid him go down and tell the unhappy supplicant he might return home, for there was no answer to be given to his complaint.

Verramond would not open the letter he had just receiv'd 'till he knew who sent it; but on his footman's informing him it came from mr. Gamble, he hastily broke the seal and found the contents as follows:

May it please your lordship,

My ever honour'd lord,

Bridewell.[24]

I happen'd to be engag'd last night at a house where the constable with his possee made a forcible entrance, demolish'd our tables, put most of the company to flight, and seiz'd the rest; I was unluckily one of this last class, and committed to durance vile, as Hudibras says,[25] and your lordship will perceive by the date hereof.

A person here has undertaken, for a fee of five guineas, to procure my immediate discharge, and I do not doubt, by the method he proposes, but that he is able to do it. – I am not, however, at present, master of as many shillings, nor can any way raise the money he demands, having been obliged, the day before this accident befel me, to leave my watch, linnen, and best apparel at mr. Grub's, in trust for a small sum requir'd of me by the parish officers, on account of a bastard child,[26] which a wench of the town has done me the honour to swear I am the father of.

All my hopes, therefore, of getting out of limbo are in your lordship's generosity, which if you vouchsafe to grant me this one more proof of, I shall, if possible, be more than ever,

With the most profound duty,

Dear patron,

Your devoted vassal,

RICHARD GAMBLE.

P.S. I had forgot to acquaint your lordship, that I shall have need of more than the above-mentioned sum for discharging the fees of this cursed hole, without the payment of which I cannot be released.

Verramond hesitated not a moment to comply with this request, nor even whether he should exceed what was desired of him: – he drew out his purse, put ten guineas into the footman's hands, and order'd him to run directly to Bridewell; – Carry that money to mr. Gamble, with his compliments, and let him know he should be glad to see him as soon as he had recover'd his liberty.

Who will say now that Verramond is not liberal? – but alas, – How ill placed an act of benevolence was this? – was it not rather caprice than true charity, which induced him to bestow this money to save a common sharper from the punishment he justly merited; yet at the same time refuse to an honest industrious tenant a small respite of payment, tho' to preserve him and his poor family from sure destruction? – but Gamble was a necessary person at a gaming-table, – he was of importance to his pleasure that way, and the farmer, being only regarded for the rent he paid, when deficient in that, must be thrown out like a piece of useless lumber, and his place occupy'd by some one who promised to be of greater utility.

Yet do I not think such a conduct is always to be ascribed to the fault of nature, – Verramond has certainly the seeds of virtue and honour in his soul; but they are suffocated and choaked up by his immoderate love of play; – strange is it, that a man capable of thinking so justly, will not be at the pains of thinking at all, but suffer himself to be sway'd, by a darling propensity, to actions, which if he once reflected upon, he would be so far from perpetrating, that he would despise the very temptation of being guilty of.

I left him and Macro together; but, my Tablets being already full, I can repeat no more of their conversation that what my memory supplies me with, which is only that an agreement was made between them to try their fortune a second time at whist; but whether Verramond either recover'd or added to his loss the night before, I did not give myself the trouble to examine; nor, indeed, thought it worthy of any part of my concern.

CHAP. III.

Presents the reader with some passages which cannot fail of being entertaining to those not interested in them, and may be of service to those who are.

Among the numerous troops of British toasts, there are few who shine with more distinguish'd lustre, in all public places, than the beautiful Marcella; besides an exact symetry of features, a most delicate complexion, and a fine turn'd shape, there is something peculiarly enchanting in her air and mien; – I never see her without being reminded of the elegant description Milton gives of Eve in her state of innocence:

> Grace was in all her steps, heaven in her eyes,
> In every gesture dignity and love.[27]

She was married very young to Celadon, and tho' neither of their hearts had been consulted in the match, yet they had the reputation of living well together; – they behaved to each other with the greatest complaisance in public, and if any cause of discontent ever happen'd between them, both had the discretion to keep it extremely private.

I could not, therefore, expect to make any extraordinary discoveries in this family; – the door, however, happening to be open one day as I pass'd by, I stepp'd in without any previous design, and now I did so was rather excited by curiosity of seeing some fine pictures, which I had been told were in the house, than of prying into the behavior of the owners.

But it frequently falls out, that what we least seek we most easily find, and that those things which we imagine farthest from us are in effect the nearest; – in passing through the several rooms in this house I saw Marcella writing in her closet, and never was I so much amazed as now to find so fair a form harbour a mind capable of dictating these lines:

To Fillamour.

Dearest of your sex,

Thanks to the powers of love and liberty, that hated bar to all the happiness of my life is removed for a short time, – Celadon is gone into the country upon a party of pleasure, and this night is entirely my own; – if therefore no more agreeable engagement detains you come here between the hours of twelve and one; – I shall take care to send all the family to bed, except the faithful Rachel, who shall attend to admit you, on your giving a gentle rap against the shutter of the parlour window next the door; – let me know by the bearer, whether I may expect you, – though it is a blessing I scarce doubt of, if any of that affection be sincere, as you have often vow'd to

The believing,

And passionate

MARCELLA.

Having sealed this billet, she call'd her chamber-maid, and order'd her to send it, as directed, by a trusty porter; – then threw herself upon a couch, – took the novel of Silvia and Philander, – read a little in it, – sigh'd, and seem'd all dissolv'd in the most tender languishment, when her emissary return'd, and brought this answer to her summons:

To the charming MARCELLA.

Dear angel,

I AM at present surrounded with a great deal of company, and have no opportunity to thank as I would the kindness of yours; – I can only say, that nothing shall keep me from flying, with all the wings of love, to my adorable Marcella, at the appointed hour; – till then – adieu; – be assured that I am always,

With the utmost ardency,

Your devoted Vassal,

FILLAMOUR.

The fair libertine now express'd the highest satisfaction, and immediately fell into discourse with her confidant Rachel, concerning the manner in which this nocturnal guest should be conceal'd, and how neither his entrance nor his exit be discover'd, or even suspected by any of the family.

I had no curiosity to know any thing farther of this affair, so took the first opportunity of leaving the house, extremely troubled in my mind that a woman, whose beauty had so much attracted my respect, should prove herself so unworthy of it by her conduct.

With what boldness, said I within myself, does the lovely wanton run headlong to her ruin, fearless of guilt, and of the punishment which one time or other must be the unfailing consequence;

As if that faultless form could act no crime,
But heaven on looking on it must forgive![28]

I went home and got my Tablets clear'd from the impure contents of the above recited epistles; – I wish'd, indeed, to think no more of this transaction; and, to second my endeavours that way towards evening sallied out again equipp'd in my

Invisible Belt, like a true knight-errant, in search of such adventures as chance should present me with.

For the sake of amusement I stepp'd into a certain coffee-house, which I had been told was much frequented by the lower class of politicians; but either I was misinform'd, or none of those gentlemen happen'd to be there at the time I was; I found only a good number of jolly tradesmen, – honest, well-condition'd creatures, who see no farther than their noses, – take every thing for gospel that they find in the Gazette,[29] or is told them by their superiors; – are very far from wishing any hurt to the commonwealth, and not much nearer in abilities to do it any real service: – in fine, such as may be call'd real passives in human life, who are govern'd by what they think is the judgment of others, without making the least use of that with which God has endow'd themselves.

The king had been that day at the parliament house, being the first time of his going there since his return to England,[30] and on this joyful occasion artificers had thrown aside their tools, – shopkeepers had leap'd from behind their compt-ers to be spectators of the royal pomp; – all the conversation among the company I now was with, at least all I could distinctly hear, (for it must be observ'd there were many speakers at the same time) turn'd on these important points: – how well his majesty look'd, – what cloaths he had on, – and who were the noblemen that attended him: – one boasted he had been so near the state-coach that he could with ease have touch'd the king's garments as he stepp'd in; – another, that he had got into the guard-chamber, and saw the procession pass the whole length of the room; – a third, that a friend had introduced him where his majesty put on his robes and crown; – a fourth, that he had seen him seated on the throne: – in fine, there were several who had received honours that day such as had left a glee upon their countenances, which perhaps a statute of bankruptcy the next would scarce have remov'd.

But what most diverted me was a poor grocer, who, on being ask'd if he had seen the king, shook his head, and in a very piteous tone made this reply:

'Sure never any thing happen'd so cursedly unlucky; – just as I had taken up my hat and cane to go, an impertinent ill-starr'd customer came in for sugar, and oblig'd me to pull down half the loaves in my shop for her to chuse which she lik'd best; – then ask'd for spices of three or four different sorts; – then half a dozen of jar raisons and a pound of almonds. – I told her I would send the things home immediately to her house; but she would needs see them all pack'd up before she left the shop; – all this took up so much time, that before I had quite done the second guns went off; and I knew that if I ran that moment to the Park, his majesty would be at St. James's before I could get to Spring-garden gate.'[31]

A grave old gentleman, who all this while had sat mute in a corner of the room, on hearing what was said, rose from his place, and approaching the grocer with a sort of contemptuous sneer, address'd himself to him in the following terms:

'You have met with a very grievous disappointment indeed, mr. Fig; – it is not, however, without its consolations; – I dare answer the profit in the goods you have sold to that impertinent customer, will enable you to make a good pudding for your family next Sunday, which is as much, at least, as you could have got by the shew, even though you were to have been paid for your huzzas: – but if this consideration should seem too trifling, I can add another of more weight; – it is this, – by being hinder'd from running after the king's coach-wheels, you got something towards the payment of your share of the taxes for the support of his government; and this, as I take it, is the best proof that you or any good subject can give of your allegiance, except your vote and interest at an election.'

He said no more, nor waited to hear what sort of reply might have been made to his reprimand, but threw down two-pence for his dish of coffee and went directly out of the room.

Every one had stared all the time he had been speaking, with their mouths open as tho' they could eat him, though none had offer'd to interrupt him; but they no sooner saw his back turn'd, than they all at once burst out into a horse-laugh, and cry'd, – 'A grumbletonian, – a grumbletonian, – a malecontent, – a disaffected person I warrant.'

I had no inclination to be a witness what farther comments would be made on the old gentleman's behaviour, but follow'd his example, and left a company in which I found nothing capable either of improving or entertaining me; nor should I have made any mention of this incident, but to remind the populace how ridiculous it is in a man of business to run gadding after every public shew that presents itself, while the necessary provision for his family is left neglected.

From thence I went to the house of an elderly lady, with whom I formerly had been acquainted; she was at that time look'd upon as a pattern of piety and prudence: – fathers; – husbands, – brothers – all who had any concern for the virtue and reputation of the female part of their family, recommended her example for their imitation; – but at last, after a long series of the most laudable and becoming actions, she at once degenerated into the very reverse of what she had been; – fell into all the fashionable follies of the times, at an age when others are beginning to grow weary of them, and commenced a coquette at sixty-five.

I had been told such things, in relation to her conduct, as seemed to me too unaccountable to be believed; and was extremely sorry to find, in the visit I now made her, all those reports confirm'd by the testimony of my own senses.

This lady, whom I shall distinguish by the name of Lamia,[32] sets an high value upon herself for her great skill at picquet; – she challeng'd Grizelda, another antiquated belle, who also pretends to be an adept in that science, to play with her for an hundred guineas the first four games in six; – the other loved money, and, not doubting she should come off conqueror, readily embraced the proposal; and the night agreed upon between them for the decision of this event, happen'd to be that in which I went.

Grizelda came to the door just as I did, so I slipp'd in behind and follow'd her up stairs, where she was received by Lamia with the greatest politeness and shew of affection: – till supper was served up, the discourse between them was only compliments on each other's beauty and good fancy in the choice of their cloaths, which were indeed very elegant, and would have been no less becoming had time stood still in his course some forty or fifty years: – the cloth was no sooner removed than the card-table was call'd for, and orders given that whoever came that night should be deny'd access, both these ladies having their own reasons, as I soon after perceiv'd, that there should be no witnesses of what they were about to do.

The ladies sat opposite to each other, – I placed myself at the end of the table, that being between them I might have the better opportunity of observing what both did: – they were now very serious and attentive to the business they were upon; – play'd, or rather cheated each other with great caution; for I soon perceived that it was in this latter part of the art of gaming that the excellence of either chiefly consisted.

For a time each was so taken up with her own petite fourberies[33] as not to have leisure to observe those practiced by her adversary; – at last, however, Lamia having retaken in a card she had laid out, Grizelda perceiv'd it, and accused her of the change: – rage and disdain, on finding herself detected, made the cheeks of the other glow with a deeper scarlet than the carmine[34] had given them; and her eyes, even in despight of age, sparkle with fires which love and youth had never power to fill them with: – the other was no less enflamed; – but their resentment will best be shewn in the expressions made use of by themselves.

Lamia. I am surprised you can suspect me guilty of so mean a thing as cheating at cards; – sure you cannot think I value the trifle we are playing for. – What is an hundred guineas to me? – I regard an hundred no more than a pinch of snuff.

Grizelda. Madam, I value an hundred guineas as little as yourself; – but I hate to be imposed upon.

Lamia. What do you mean, madam, – do you say I have imposed upon you?

Grizelda. I say you would have done it, madam, if my eyes had not been quicker than your hands.

Lamia. Madam, I scorn your words; and if you were not in my own house should tell you that you lyed.

Grizelda. And if it were not in respect to your age, madam, I should tell you that you were a base woman, and had invited me hither only to cheat me of my money.

Lamia. My age, – good lack, – my age, – I leave the world to judge which of us two looks the oldest. – I beg, madam, you will not deceive yourself: – it is not your long false locks, hanging dangling on each side your face, that hide the wrinkles of it.

Grizelda. I wear no plumpers, madam, – Do you not remember when one of yours dropt out of your mouth at lady Betty's drawing room how all the company were frighted at you, and cry'd out you had lost half your face?

I started on hearing this reproach of Grizelda, being at that time utterly unacquainted with the meaning of it; – but as it is highly probable that a great many of my readers may be as ignorant in this point as myself then was, I shall explain it by giving a direction of the use and preparation of plumpers, as I have since received it from the waiting-maid of a woman of condition.

A sure way to help LANK CHEEKS.

TAKE a piece of the finest, cleanest spunge you can get, – cut out of it two small bolsters, and place them between your cheeks and teeth, if you have any, if not the gums will serve to keep them up; – on taking them out of your mouth, going to bed, throw them into a tea-cup of rose or orange-flower water, and let them soke all night; – this will not only cleanse them from whatever impurities they may have happen'd to have received, but will also give a delectable flavour to the breath. – Probatum est.[35]

These ladies pursued their mutual altercations for a considerable time, in a fashion which the intelligent reader may easily conceive by the sample I have given; – I shall therefore only say, that after having charg'd each other with all the vices and foibles that either of them could think of, they at last quarrell'd themselves into a reconciliation, – begg'd each others pardon, and went to play a second time; – then fell out again, and provocations on both sides being renew'd, and reproaches still growing more piquant, Lamia tore the cards and threw them into the fire; – Grizelda call'd for her chair and left the house in a great fury; – I gladly follow'd her out, being heartily sick of what I had seen between these fair, or rather unfair antagonists; but had no opportunity of getting away before, as the door had never once been open'd.

It was now near two hours past midnight, and I found more satisfaction in the thoughts of going to my repose than in those discoveries my Invisibility had entertain'd me with. – I was making all the speed I could to my apartment for that purpose, – but fate decreed it otherwise, and had contrived an accident which renew'd all my former curiosity: – in my way home I pass'd through the street where Marcella lived, and the sight of her house bringing fresh into my mind what the Morning had presented, I could not keep myself from stopping short to make some reflections on the conduct of that fair fallen angel.

'She is doubtless by this time in the arms of her beloved Fillamour,' said I to myself, 'and while revelling in the pleasures of a loose inclination, forgets all

sense of honour, – duty, – fame, and even what is owning to the merit of those
charms nature has endow'd her with; – and oh, – strange paradox of a vicious
flame! – renders herself cheap and contemptible in the eyes of the very man
whose esteem she most wishes to preserve.'

   How long I should have remain'd in this resvery I know not; but I was rous'd
from it by the sudden appearance of Celadon, who with a light carry'd before
him came hastily down the street and knock'd at his own door: – to see him
return at a time when I knew he was so little expected, made me not doubt but
that he had receiv'd some information of the injury done him, and came in order
to detect and revenge himself on the guilty pair: – I trembled for poor Marcella;
but what grounds I had to do so, as well as the event of this night's transaction,
must be left to the next chapter.

CHAP. IV.

Concludes an adventure of a very singular nature in its consequences.

THE anxiety I was under to know what would become of poor Marcella, immediately determin'd me to follow her husband into the house. – A man-servant
not having obey'd his lady's commands in going to bed, having something or
other wherewith to employ himself in his own room, on hearing somebody at
the door look'd through the window, and perceiving it was his master flew down
stairs and gave him entrance on the first knock.

   Rachel, who had been posted centry in a back-parlour, in order to watch the
break of day, and conduct Fillamour out of the house before any of the family were stirring, now come running out on hearing the street door open'd; but
scarce could an apparition have spread a greater terror through her whole frame
than did the sight of Celadon at this juncture.

   Rachel. Lord, sir, who could have thought your honour would have come
home to night?

   Celadon. I did not design it, indeed; – but is it so strange a thing that a man
should change his mind?

   In speaking this he was passing on, but she threw herself between him and
the foot of the stairs, and catching fast hold of the sleeve of his coat, prevented
him from going up, with these words:

   Rachel. Oh, dear sir, I beg you will not disturb my lady; – she is gone to bed
very much discomposed: – pray be so good as to step into the parlor, – there is a
good fire, – and I will go and see if she is awake, and tell her you are here.

   Celadon. My wife ill! – What is the matter with her?

   Rachel. I do not know, sir, but she was seiz'd with a sort of a – I can't tell the
name of it, – indeed not I; – but I believe it was something like a fit, – and so, sir,
she went to bed; but I will go and let her know you are come.

Celadon. No, no, – she may be asleep, and it would be a pity to wake her; – therefore I'll take your advice, mrs. Rachel, and sit a little in the parlour. – Tom, do you go to bed, – I shall not want any thing to night.

The fellow did as he was commanded; and I could easily perceive, by Rachel's countenance, that she was upon the wing to be gone too, impatient, I suppose, to apprize Marcella of what had happen'd, and assist her in contriving some means for concealing her gallant; – but whatever her thoughts were, Celadon had that moment got something in his head which effectually prevented any schemes she might otherwise have laid for securing the honour of her lady; – Tom was no sooner gone than Celadon took hold of both her hands and drew her gently into the parlour, with these words:

Celadon. Come, pretty mrs. Rachel, if I am so complaisant to my wife's disorder as to refrain going to bed to her, I think that I may very well be allow'd the pleasure of your company, by way of consolation.

Rachel. Oh dear, sir, what pleasure can you find in the company of such a one as I?

Celadon. As much as I can wish; – come sit down, – nay, you shall sit by me; – now we are alone there is no occasion for all this distance between us, – I have a great deal to say to you; – nothing sure was ever so lucky as my coming home to night; – all I could have found in the journey I proposed would not have afforded me the thousandth part of the satisfaction I now enjoy in this private interview with my dear girl: – in fine, I like you, – I love you, – and have long'd almost ever since you came into the family for an opportunity to tell you so.

Rachel. Lord, sir, how can your honour talk so, – who have so fine a lady of your own?

Celadon. I like my wife very well as a wife; but there is something in the tyes of marriage which quite suffocate and choak up all those desires which can alone give any relish to enjoyment. – A man goes to bed to his wife as he goes to court, because it is the fashion, and a sort of duty which is expected from him; and he cannot, without being ill look'd upon by the world, be dispensed from; but flies to the arms of his mistress as to a delicious retreat, the choice of his own fancy, and well stored with all that can regale the senses.

Rachel. Lord, sir, how strangely you talk to one! – I wish your honour would let me go up stairs to see how my lady does.

Celadon. No, indeed, I shall not suffer you to be so uncharitable as to run away and leave me alone here; – if my wife wants any thing she will ring her Bell, – in the mean time, let us make each other as happy as we can. – Come, none of this coyness; – let me tell you, child, that too much reserve in private with a man who loves you, and has it in his power to make your fortune, is as unbecoming as too much familiarity would be in public; – you may depend upon it, that whatever favours you bestow on me shall be return'd with others no less agreeable to yourself. – I know very well how a person of my station ought to behave towards one of yours in these cases, and shall act accordingly.

Rachel made no reply to all this; – but hung down her head and look'd extremely silly, – not that she wanted either wit or assurance on other occasions; but at present she was quite at a loss; and it must be own'd, indeed, that such a crisis afforded sufficient to perplex her on a double score; – first, – the improbability, and even impossibility there appear'd of concealing her lady's secret, which, if discovered, might prove of the most fatal consequence, had thrown her into, and still kept her in the utmost distraction of mind: – and, secondly, surprised at the unexpected offer made to her by her master, join'd with the uncertainty in what manner she should receive it, might very well put her into agitations, such as to render her incapable of contriving any thing on her mistress's account, or resolving what to do on her own.

Celadon, interpreting her silence as a half consent to his desires, began now to add kisses and embraces to his sollicitations; – the warmth with which he press'd her soon wrought the effect it was intended for; though I easily perceiv'd the most prevailing argument he made use of was taking out his purse and pouring twenty guineas into her lap.

The transport which sparkled in the eyes of this mercenary creature, on beholding the glittering bait, put me immediately in mind of what mr. Dryden makes Jupiter say in his play of Amphytrion:

> When I made
> This gold, I made a greater god than Jove,
> And gave my own omnipotence away.[36]

But it is little to be wonder'd at that a girl, such as this Rachel, should fall prostrate before that reigning idol of the world, who has for its votaries not only men of the greatest parts and abilities, but also too many among those who make the highest professions of honour, probity, and virtue; – nay, I am sorry to say, of religion: – daily experience, however, and a very small observation of the corruption of the present age evinces this melancholy truth. – But to return.

The amorous Celadon now finding her all dissolv'd, and soften'd to his purpose, proceeded to the greatest familiarities: – there was no bed, nor even couch in the room; but, – as the poet says,

> Many a nymph has on the floor been spread,
> And much good love without a feather-bed.[37]

So finding a scene was likely to ensue, which it was not agreeable to my inclination, or any was proper that I should be witness of, I withdrew into an adjacent parlour, which having a communication with this, and the door between them not being quite shut, I open'd wide enough to gain a passage, while the lovers backs were turn'd towards that side of the room.

Solitude, – darkness, and the profound silence of every thing about me, here contributed to promote the most solemn meditations; – I reflected on the extreme folly, as well as wickedness, of giving way to an inordinate gratification of the senses, and the certain danger, and almost certain infamy, which attends the doing so; – on this occasion several passages and accidents relating to many of my acquaintance occurr'd fresh to my mind; and when I remember'd how some, who had been endow'd by heaven and fortune with every requisite, excepting virtue, to complete their happiness, yet by the want of that alone had exposed themselves to a condition the most abject and contemptible to which a reasonable being can possibly be reduced, I could not forbear crying out with the inimitable Cowley,

> All this world's noise appears to me,
> But as a dull, ill-acted comedy.[38]

While I was thus ruminating, and wondering within myself what would be the consequence of this night's transaction, I perceiv'd, through the crevices of the window shutters, that the day began to break, and presently after heard a certain rustling upon the stairs; – it was occasion'd by Marcella and Fillamour, who, on finding Rachel did not come up as they expected, and the light was pretty far advancing, were creeping softly down, – the noise Marcella made in unfastening the chain that went across the street-door wak'd Celadon and Rachel, who it seems had both fallen asleep; the former, on hearing the noise, was running out of the parlour to see what was the matter; but Rachel prevented him, by saying she was sure it was only one of the footmen who went out more early than ordinary to the stable; – this excuse might have solved all, if Marcella herself had not unluckily been her own betrayer.

That lady, incensed beyond measure, push'd open the door of the room where I was, and rush'd through it into that where Rachel was order'd to attend, beginning to upbraid before she saw her.

Marcella. So, minx, – you have serv'd me finely; – it is almost broad day, – I have knock'd the heel of my shoe almost off, for I would not ring for fear of alarming the family, – I suppose you have been asleep: – this it is to place any dependence on servants.

Celadon, on hearing his wife's voice before she enter'd, had stepp'd behind a screen, either suspecting something of the truth, or because he was unwilling to be surprized with Rachel at that hour; and Rachel, doubly confounded between her lady's reproaches and the knowledge who was witness of them, that she was utterly unable to speak one word for some time, but shook her head, – wink'd, and pointed to the screen, thinking, by those significant gestures, to prevent

Marcella from saying any thing farther, 'till finding she was again opening her mouth, she recover'd herself enough to cry out:

Rachel, Lord, madam, – do not stand talking here, you will certainly get cold and make yourself worse; – consider you are half naked; – pray go to bed again.

Marcella. What does the wench mean? but I suppose you have been at the ratifie[39] bottle and stupified yourself, according to custom. – Well, 'tis your own loss; for I dare swear Fillamour would have given you no less a present than five guineas for your diligence, if you had come up as you ought to have done; – tis now quite light in the street, and a thousand to one but some of the neighbours may have seen him go out.

Celadon coming forward. So, madam, I find you have been diverting yourself, and Fillamour is the man to whom I am oblig'd for giving you consolation in my absence.

That person must know very little of nature, who does not easily conceive what Marcella felt in so shocking a juncture; – surprise, shame, and vexation for having thus foolishly exposed her guilt, quite overwhelm'd her heart – she gave a great shriek, and sunk, half fainting, into a chair; – Rachel ran to her assistance, and at the same time willing to retrieve, if possible, told Celadon that he must not take any notice of her lady's words; – that she went very ill to bed; – that she was delirious, and knew not what she said. – This, however, had no effect upon him, – he was too well convinced of the injury had been done him, and loaded his transgressing wife with every invective that a husband, in his circumstances, could invent.

But certainly it is impossible for any woman to behave with greater courage and resolution than Marcella now did; – she presently regain'd her spirits; and, after having made Rachel leave the room, a moment's reflection served her to reply to the reproaches made her by her husband, in these terms:

Marcella. Well, sir, I confess appearances are against me, nor do I wonder at, nor will resent the asperity of your treatment; – though guilty of no real crime, my vanity has led me into a folly which merits all you have said to me. – I have not, in fact, dishonour'd either myself or you, and my behaviour this night has only mortified the pride and arrogance of a man who would have rival'd you in my esteem and affection.

Celadon. So you went to bed to him, merely to convince him of your esteem and affection for me?

Marcella. Yes, incongruous as it may seem, I did so; – I had heard that the vain fellow boasted no woman could resist him, if once he had an opportunity to press his suit: – on this I resolv'd to give him one as full as he could ask, or man obtain, – I admitted him into my chamber; – nay, into my bed, – listen'd to all the arguments he could urge to work me to his will; and, when his whole stock of rhetoric, on that occasion, was exhausted, shew'd him that the wife of Celadon could love no other man: – I repulsed him in a manner which made him asham'd of his attempt; – but had he not been so, and had proceeded to gain by force those favours I refused to grant, Rachel was planted here, in order to come up to my assistance and prevent his efforts.

Celadon. Excellent, i'faith, – beyond imagination; – I have been told, indeed, that a woman need but look down upon her apron-string to find an excuse[40] for the most enormous crime she can be guilty of; but this of yours in such a one as cannot fail of giving a good deal of diversion in a court of judicature; tho' I scarce think it will save either Fillamour's estate from the penalty the law inflicts on an attempt to bastardize an honourable family,[41] or his throat from the justice of my sword.

The boldness of Marcella was not to be aw'd by these menaces; – she found he had too much understanding to be imposed upon by the shallow artifice she had made use of; that he now heartily despis'd her, and that she had no longer any measures to preserve with him; – therefore, collecting all the courage she was mistress of, she threw her eyes upon him with a contempt equal to that with which he look'd upon her, and made him this reply:

Marcella. 'Tis mighty well, sir, – you are at your liberty to make use of all the weapons you fancy are in your power for revenge; but I would have you remember, that whether Fillamour cuts your throat, or you cut his, and are hang'd for it, the matter will be of little importance to me: – and as for a court of judicature, I believe you will find it very difficult to make good any accusations you may exhibit against me there: – no one ever saw me in bed with Fillamour, much less can prove any criminal conversation[42] between us, so that the ridicule would turn wholly upon yourself; and, perhaps, provoke me, as I have had no child by you, to bring in a bill of impotency,[43] in which case I should have all my fortune return'd, – a thing your present circumstances would not very well bear, as some part of your estate is already mortgaged.

To all this Celadon was able to make no other reply, than that he stood amazed at her audacity; – that he found she was abandon'd to all sense of shame; that she was a monster of impudence, and such like; at which she seemed not in the least mov'd, but proceeded to reason with him in the same determin'd fashion she had began.

Marcella. Look you, Celadon, all the fury you can be possess'd of will remedy nothing; – let us argue like rational creatures: – whatever opinion we may have of each other, the only way to preserve either of our characters is to live well together in the eyes of the world; – I tell you that I am innocent, and it is for your ease and interest, as well as mine, that you should believe I am so; which if you do, I faithfully promise to regulate my conduct in such a manner as to bring no disreputation on myself or dishonor to you; – but if you fly into extremes you will oblige me to do the same, and what but our mutual infamy and destruction can be the end of such a contest? I leave you to consider on what I have said, and wait your cooler moments for an answer.

With these words she went hastily out of the room; – Celadon offer'd not to detain her, but continued walking backwards and forwards, testifying, by several disordered gestures, the inward agitations of his mind; – after some moments pass'd in the silent expressions of his rage, he call'd to the servants, most of whom were now stirring, to get a bed prepared for him in another chamber; but I am of opinion, that when he retired thither, it was less to sleep than to reflect how it would best become him to behave under the shocking circumstance he was now involved in.

Finding no farther discoveries were likely to be made at this time, I left the house on the first opening of the street-door and return'd home; where, fatigued as I was for want of rest, the astonishment I was in at the behaviour of Marcella would not suffer the least slumber to close my eyes.

For some days I was extremely impatient to know the result of this affair; but hearing no talk of it about town, began to conclude that the wife's arguments had prevail'd, and the husband had submitted his resentment to his convenience; – I soon found I was not deceived in my conjectures, for in less than a week I saw Celadon and Marcella taking the air together in their own coach, with the same appearance of serenity in both their countenances as if nothing of the adventure I have been relating had ever happen'd.

CHAP. V.

Contains the history of a distress, which, according to the author's private opinion, is much more likely to excite laughter than commiseration.

MELISSA, by all who know her, is accounted one of the most vain of her sex: – true, – she is so; – but then her vanity appears to me to be of a species far different from that which other women are ordinarily possess'd of; – her glass, whenever she looks into it, which is not seldom, presents her with the view of ten thousand graces; – she sees very well that she is handsome, – finely shaped, – and has something peculiarly engaging in her mien and air; – yet does she not plume herself on the perfections she is mistress of, or is at all thankful to nature for having bestowed them on her; – this some people at first may think is the very reverse of vanity, yet is it in effect the quintessence of it; – the case is, that she would be the only fair, – the only lovely, – the only Venus, – the sole object of attracting universal love and admiration; and every single charm she finds in any other face, gives her more pain than all those in her own can give her satisfaction.

Every little regard, or act of complaisance, paid to another in her presence, she looks upon as a kind of indignity to herself, and is a mortal stab to her pride; and, as it is impossible for her not to meet frequently with such shocks, she is perpetually racking all the invention she is mistress of to render herself more conspicuous, and to force, as it were, that attention which she finds her beauty alone is insufficient to excite.

I had heard at full the character of this fine court belle, – had been several times in her company, and seen verified all I had been told concerning the extravagance of her humour; – yet, I know not how it happen'd, but passing by her house, and seeing a good number of chairs and livery servants about the door, I stepp'd in and went directly up to her drawing-room, where I found her encircled by about a dozen persons of distinction of both sexes.

It was the evening before the birthday, and when I enter'd, the conversation among them turn'd wholly on the ode composed by mr. Cibber on that occasion,[44] most of them having heard the rehearsal of it; but soon after they fell on the more important subject of dress, – every one discanting on the fancies of all her acquaintance, finding a thousand faults, and no one thing to approve, each concluding what she had to say with an, – 'I wonder people of fashion can have such vulgar tastes.' – The gentlemen also, in complaisance to the ladies, affected to be connoisseurs in this point, and ridiculing all that were absent gave no praises but to the present, as will appear by the speeches made by some of them.

Beau Civet.[45] Indeed, ladies, I think dress is the only true touch-stone of a fine woman's genius; and she who is indelicate in that, igad, must be so in every thing else.

Monsieur La Mot. I have the honour to be entirely of your opinion, sir, – nothing can be more just than the observation you have made; – yet certainly an elegance of dress is a thing so little understood, that I believe out of this room there are scarce three women in the kingdom who know how to set themselves off to any advantage.

Melissa. As to that, monsieur, – a woman who is really agreeable need be at no pains to appear so; – but I detest every thing that is common; – I hate your gold and silver stuffs, – your brocades, – your velvets, – and embroideries; – you see them upon the backs of every one who has either money or credit to purchase them.

Lesbia. That is true, indeed, my dear; but if you exclude all these things, what in the name of wonder can a woman of condition find proper to appear in at court?

Melissa. Oh there are a thousand pretty whims; – Do you not remember, that on my first going to the drawing-room after the Prince's mourning was over,[46] I had a gause mantau[47] and petticoat, flourished with twenty different colours; – every one was charm'd with the oddness of the fancy.

Lesbia. Yes, I remember it very well, and that the weather being pretty cool you got a sore throat which confin'd you to your chamber for ten days afterwards. – For my part, I think one ought always to suit one's cloaths according to the season of the year.

Melissa. Then I suppose you will be draw'd forth to-morrow in some heavy brocade or other.

Lesbia. No, – I shall have only a rose-colour'd damask, flounced with a point d'espagne.[48]

On this, two or three of the other ladies gave a description of the habits they had prepared to do honour to the ensuing august day; but Melissa mention'd not a word of what she intended to wear, till being ask'd the question, she told them that she should have only a slight sattin, not strip'd, – not either flower'd in the loom[49] nor embroider'd with the needle, yet it would be such as she doubted not but would attract the eyes of the whole assembly upon it.

She had no sooner ended these words, than lady Twinckle, who had not spoke before, cried out, – 'Nobody can doubt the excellence of your fancy; – but yet, my dear, I believe I shall have the pleasure of dividing with you the attention of the company; for I shall have a suit of cloaths which will certainly appear the greatest oddity that ever was seen.'

Every mouth in the room, except my own, was now open to entreat her ladyship to give them some idea of this curiosity: – she had too much good nature to refuse their request, and presently made this answer:

Lady *Twinckle.* I will not be so vain as to assume the merit of the invention; – no, it was brought to me on the wheel of fortune, – a mere accident, – I only improved the hint, as you shall see; for I will send both for the petticoat and the piece of silk from which I took the pattern.

She said no more, but starting from her seat ran directly to the head of the stair-case, – called her servant, who was waiting below, and ordered him to go home and fetch the things she had mention'd; – as her house was no farther off than the next street, the fellow return'd immediately with them: – the bundle was no sooner brought into the room than she open'd it, and shew'd the company about a yard of white sattin, painted in water colours, with cupids, some flying, others standing, but all of them with their bows extended as if to shoot at hearts, which were every where scatter'd, in a careless manner, upon the piece.

There was no time for one syllable to be utter'd, either in praise or dispraise of this pretty fancy; – the moment lady Twinckle had spread it on a table Melissa sent forth a loud shriek, which, together with the exclamations that ensued, threw every one into the utmost astonishment.

Melissa. Confusion, – distraction, – is it possible! – What can this mean, madam? that piece of silk is mine, as well as the invention painted upon it. Pray how came it into your ladyship's possession? – But wherefore need I ask, – the case is plain enough, – that villain Pencil, after the handsome present I had made him for secrecy, over and above paying him for his work, has most cruelly betray'd me, exposed my contrivance to you, and ruin'd my design.

Lady *Twinckle*. I am strangely surprised; – sure this is the oddest thing that ever happen'd. – Indeed, my dear, I little thought that I was shewing you your own; – but I would not have you lay the blame on mr. Pencil; – upon my honour the poor man is perfectly innocent in what you accuse him of; for though I was at his shop one day last week, and bought a five guinea fan of him, he never once mention'd your name, or that he had been employ'd by you in any work: – but I will tell you the whole matter; – my woman, you must know, wanting something to new robe a gown I had lately given her, went among the piece-brokers[50] behind St. Clement's church,[51] where she made a purchase of this remnant; – on her bringing it home I was vastly taken with the whim, and resolved to have something like it for a birth-day suit; – accordingly I set a fan-painter to work upon the pattern, only directed him to make some few alterations, which you shall be judge whether for the better or not.

Melissa. Then it is by the mantua-maker I have been thus basely used. – I could forgive the wretch for stealing my silk; – I know those creatures make it a part of their trade to do so, and will rather spoil one's cloaths than lose what they look upon as their perquisites; and for that reason I always allow five or six yards more than is necessary; – but to be so hasty in the disposal of her theft, – to let what I had invented on purpose to be particular be seen in the shop of a common piece-broker, before I had worn it myself, is such a piece of impudence as deserves, and shall meet with all the mischief I can do her.

No reply was made to what she said; – lady Twinckle had by this time unfolded her petticoat, the sight of which sufficiently employ'd every eye and tongue in the room; – that lady had indeed greatly improv'd upon Melissa's fancy; for besides the ground of the sattin being all over frosted, as it were, with silver, the wings of the cupids and the barbs of their arrows were much better delineated, and the hearts dispersed in a more elegant manner; – Melissa, at sight of it, was ready to swoon, and the high commendations she heard given of it by the whole company increased her disorder. – Monsieur La Mot, happening to turn his head that way, and perceiving the confusion she was in, thought to remedy it by making her the following compliment:

Monsieur *La Mot*. Well, madam, whatever praises lady Twinckle may at first receive on account of this most agreeable whim, they will afterwards naturally recoil on you, as being the first inventor.

Lady *Twinckle*. Indeed I shall do Melissa the justice to acknowledge it.

Melissa. Oh, madam, your ladyship need not give yourself any trouble about the matter; for I shall neither go to court to-morrow, nor ever put the cloaths upon my back.

Lady *Twinckle*. I am sorry, my dear, to find you are so much disconcerted, especially as I know myself the innocent occasion. – But sure my having a gown something like yours will not hinder you from paying your obedience to the royal presence.

Melissa. Since I am so unlucky to be frustrated in my expectation, I do not chuse to appear in a thing so exactly of the same design, and so inferior in the execution, to that your ladyship will have on; therefore shall not attempt to divide with you any part of the attention of the assembly.

Lesbia. What a pity it is one has not the same liberty of going to court as to a masquerade, in an antic habit, – if so, you might have render'd yourself as conspicuous as a certain lady of our acquaintance did at the Venetian Ball in the character of Iphigenia.[52]

Here ensued a general laughter, and the conduct of that lady hinted at by Lesbia gave occasion to many sarcasms, which I forbear to repeat on account of their severity – Melissa, however, in spite of her known talent for satire, was entirely silent on the subject, than which there could not be a greater proof how much her mind was taken up with the accident that had befallen herself.

It required, indeed, no great share of penetration to discover that it was with the utmost difficulty this disappointed belle restrained her ill humour within the bounds of decency while the company staid; but they had no sooner taken leave than she gave a loose to all the agitations she was posses'd of, and burst into such extravagancies of grief and rage, that whoever had seen her, without knowing the cause, must have imagin'd some fatal chance had deprived her of all the friends and fortune she had to boast of in the world.

Awhile she wept, and utter'd the most piteous lamentations; – then rav'd and call'd hastily for the unlucky garment that had been the cause of her present woe; – she stamp'd it under her feet upon the floor; – then snatching it up cry'd, – 'The sight of it never shall offend me more;' – and with these words was about to throw it upon the fire; but her maid, who was a quick-witted sprightly girl, catch'd hold of her arm, and prevented her from doing what she design'd, with this Remonstrance:

Maid. Dear madam, do not quite demolish this pretty gown: – if you resolve never to wear it, you may make it into charming furniture: – besides, a thought is just now come into my head, how some part of it may afford you an ample revenge on lady Twinckle for stealing your invention.

Melissa. Revenge! – oh that it were in my power: – but tell me how, – by what means can I accomplish it?

Maid. First, let me know, madam, whether you can remember exactly the alterations made by lady Twinckle?

Melissa. O, yes perfectly well: – the sight of that detested petticoat, methinks, is still before my eyes.

Maid. Well then, madam, if you approve of the contrivance, I will take as much out of the tail of the gown as will make a robe de chambre[53] for the monkey; – you must give mr. Pencil directions to change the pattern just like lady Twinckle's; – if he sits up all night about it, a small present will make him amends; and I will undertake to run up the habit, and a head-dress and three double ruffles, time enough for Pug to make her appearance when the ladies are going into court.

Melissa. Thou would'st not carry her thither?

Maid. Not into the palace, madam; – tho' 'tis possible there may be as ill figures there; – but my intention is to attend lady Pug into the Mall, – saunter about with her in St. James's piazza, and towards the foot of the great stairs where all the company go up: – I warrant we shall have eyes enough upon us.

Melissa. Sure there never was such a charming plot: – dear girl, I could almost kiss thee for it; – to see the monkey below, and lady Twinckle above in just the same livery, – oh! it will be a lasting jest, and turn all the admiration she expects into ridicule; – but no time is to be lost, – let John run this instant to mr. Pencil's, and find him wherever he is; – a second disappointment would quite break my heart.

The waiting-maid flew to do as she was commanded, and I retired at the same time, smiling within myself to have seen how much it is in the power of the smallest trifle, relating to dress and ornament, to discompose a woman whose sole ambition is to attract public admiration.

I had the curiosity, however, to go the next day about one o'clock to St. James's, where I found the plot I had heard concerted was carry'd into execution; – Melissa's monkey, attended by her maid, were there before me; and certainly a more diverting sight could not be seen; – the girl had, indeed, discover'd an uncommon ingenuity in the management of this affair; – she had not only decorated madam Pug in all the punctilios of a fine lady, but also dexterously fasten'd the fore limbs close to its sides, to prevent it either from jumping or affronting its new quality by going upon all four; so that the little creature walk'd erect and stately on its hind feet amidst a crowd of laughing spectators, led by its careful conductress by a piece of broad white ribband fixed to the neck of the robe de chambre: – most of the ladies, and several gentlemen stopp'd in their chairs to pay their compliments to the burlesque belle; and no small notice was taken of the figures painted on the garment.

On this I could not doubt but the contrivance would have all the success aim'd at by Melissa and her maid, and was afterwards assured of it by a friend who was that day at court, and told me that a general whisper, accompanied with a sneer, ran through the whole assembly on seeing lady Twinckle's cloaths; – her ladyship, it seems, has since been made fully acquainted with the matter, and is so incensed against Melissa, that she will not come into any place where she is.

CHAP. VI.

Shews, that tho' a remissness of care in the bringing up of children, can scarce
fail of being attended with very bad consequences; yet that an over exact
circumspection, in minute things, may sometimes prove equally pernicious
to their future welfare.

VARIOUS were the reports concerning Alinda, both while she was alive and after her decease; but all the world could say with any certainty, either of her affairs or conduct, might be compriz'd in the following articles:

That she was the only child of a very eminent and wealthy merchant in the city, who, on the death of his wife, left off business, and having purchased an estate of near a thousand pounds a year in the country, retired thither to pass the remainder of his days, taking Alinda with him, at that time about ten years of age.

That through some peculiarities in his temper she was educated in a very odd fashion, – secluded from all conversation with the neighbouring gentry, and scarce suffer'd to speak to any one out of their own family.

That after his death, which happen'd in her seventeenth year, she return'd, with the consent of her guardians, to London, – lived in a manner suitable to her fortune, and had many advantageous offers of marriage, all which she rejected without giving any reason for doing so.

That at one and twenty she fell into a wasting disorder, which was judged to proceed rather from some inward grief preying upon her spirits, than from any distemper of the body; – it baffled, however, all the skill of the physicians, and she expired after a tedious languishment of near three years, leaving the possession of her estate to a nephew of her father's, who was the next of kin.

All these things, I say, were public; – but as to the motive which made her avoid listening to any proposals for changing her condition, or the cause of that melancholy which brought on her death, every one spoke of them as they thought proper, and according as the dispositions of their own hearts inclined them to judge.

Few, however, were charitable enough to put the best construction on her conduct; – some said she was a man-hater; – others, that loving the sex too well she could not think of entering into a state which must confine her to one alone: – those who entertain'd the most favourable opinion, imagined she had unhappily engaged her heart where there was no possibility of a return: – this last conjecture seem'd, indeed, most probable, and gain'd ground after she fell into that heavy languor which excluded her from all those pleasures she had been accustom'd to partake, and at length deprived her of life; – but all this, to make use of the vulgar adage, was speaking without book,[54] – my Gift of Invisibility gave me alone the means of penetrating into the mystery.

As I had been acquainted with her, and visited her while she continued to see company, I frequently sent, or call'd, to enquire after her health; – one day when I did so, a servant belonging to her kinsman and heir at law, came to the door at the same time, and we both received for answer, that she expired the night before.

The fellow ran directly to inform his master, to whom these tidings would probably be not unwelcome; and I went home, clapp'd on my Belt of Invisibility, and return'd in a short time to the house of Alinda; – the reader will perhaps wonder for what reason, and it is not fit I should keep him in ignorance.

There was a clergyman lived in the house with her, and perform'd the office of a chaplain; – he was a person who her father having conceived a high opinion of had taken into his family, and set over her in the manner of a preceptor, and he had ever since continued with her; I had several times dined with him at her table, and perceived he professed an extraordinary sanctity and the extremest regard for the welfare of his fair patroness; – and this it was that made me desirous of seeing in what manner he would behave upon her death.

I expected to have found him either in his own chamber, bewailing the early fate of so beneficent a friend, or sitting by her corpse religiously moralizing on the shadowy happiness of this transitory world; but after seeking him in vain, in these and several other rooms, at last I discover'd him in a closet, where I knew she reposited her things of greatest value; – he was busily employ'd in rummaging her buroe, from the little cell of which I saw him convey, as near as I could guess, between two and three hundred pieces of gold, and several bank bills to a much greater amount; – he then pull'd out a drawer which contain'd her jewels; – he first took up one, – then another, – survey'd them with a greedy eye, but laid them down again and shut the drawer; but, after a moment's pause, open'd it a second time and took out a ring set round with large brilliants, – 'I may keep this,' cry'd he, 'it will scarce be miss'd; – or if it be, I can pretend she made me a present of it in her lifetime, and nobody will suspect the contrary.' – Here he gave over his search, lock'd the buroe, put the key into his pocket, and went into his own room.

It would be hard for me to determine, whether astonishment or indignation was most predominant in me at this sight; – I wish'd never to have beheld it, or that I had been at liberty to pluck the sacred robe from off the back of that vile prophaner of his order; – I was going away with a mind more troubled than I can well express, when one of Alinda's maids came running into the room with a seal'd packet in her hand, and deliver'd it to this disciple of Judas Iscariot, telling him at the same time, that it had been found under her mistress's pillow just after her death; but that she had forgot in the hurry to bring it to him before.

He reply'd, with an affected indifference, that it was very well; – that he would look over the papers and take care that whatever injunctions they contain'd should be fulfill'd, – and with these words dismiss'd her.

The superscription on the cover of this packet was to a lady with whom Alinda had been extremely intimate, but had not seen for a considerable time, she being excluded, as well as the rest of her acquaintance, after she fell into that deep melancholy which ended her days; – the priest immediately broke the seal, and found a little letter to the above mention'd lady, – the contents whereof were as follow:

DEAR MADAM,

THAT I have not seen you so long has not been owing to want of friendship, but to a resolution of depriving myself of every thing that was agreeable to me in life; and that I do not now, in these last moments of my life, ask to see you is only because I would not tax your pity with the sight of so sad an object; – I am blasted, my dear friend, wither'd in my bloom, and scarce the shadow of what I was; the enclosed memoirs will inform you of the cruel cause, which I entreat you will publish to the world after my decease; – the shocking tale may perhaps be a serviceable warning to some parents as well as children: – I have given my cousin ***** orders concerning some things I would have done, among the number of which is, that he will present you with my hoop diamond ring; – I beg you will accept and wear it in remembrance of

Your dying friend,

ALINDA.

He started, – bent his brows, turn'd pale and red by turns, and seem'd in great confusion while looking over this little epistle; but all his emotions were very much increased on examining the papers that accompany'd it; – still as he read he tore the leaves asunder and threw them on the fire, which happening not to burn very fiercely, I was quick enough to snatch from the intended devastation and convey into my pocket, while he was taken up with the remaining pages, thought himself secure by the tale of his misdeeds being extinct in all devouring flames.

He had but just finished, when a servant came running into the room, and told him that mr. ***** was below, and having been informed that Alinda's keys had been deliver'd to him, demanded to speak with him immediately; – on this the artful hypocrite composed his countenance, drew every feature into the attitude of solemn sadness, and holding a white handkerchief to his eyes, went down to act the part he thought would best become him before the kinsman of Alinda.

I follow'd close at his heels into the parlour, where mr. ***** and two other persons waited for him; – he began, with well dissembled grief, to expatiate on the loss the world had in so excellent a lady as Alinda: and fail'd not, in his harangue, artfully to intermix some praises on himself, for the good principles his precepts had ingrafted on her mind.

Mr. ***** seem'd to take very little notice of all he said on this occasion and prevented him from going so far as perhaps he otherwise would have done, by telling him, in a very grave and reserv'd tone, that he was in great haste at present; – that he came thither only to give the necessary orders concerning his cousin's funeral; and that till the melancholy ceremony was over, he should put a friend in possession of the house, and whatever effects it contain'd; therefore expected the keys of every thing should be immediately deliver'd.

To this the parson reply'd, – that he had got them into his hands with no other view than to secure them for him, who had the undoubted right to all which his dear benefactress had been mistress of; – 'For indeed,' continued he, 'I apprehended some foul play might have been attempted, as at the hour of her decease she had none but servants about her, some of whom had been too lately taken into the family to have given any great proofs of their integrity.'

After this they went through every room, examining what was to be found; all which scrutiny, as yet, afforded the heir no reason for complaint: – on opening the abovemention'd buroe, and looking over Alinda's jewels, he miss'd not the ring he had been defrauded of; but when the other private drawers presented him so little of what he expected, he could not forbear discovering some suspicion, as it must be own'd he had sufficient cause; for the person who had been beforehand with him in the search, had left no more than eight guineas and one six-and-thirty piece in specie, with three or four bills of an inconsiderable value.

'I am surprised,' said mr. *****, 'that a woman of my cousin's fortune should leave herself so bare of cash; and cannot imagine by what means she dissipated so large a yearly income.' – 'Alas, sir,' reply'd the pretended zealot, with his hands and eyes lifted up to heaven, – 'it ought not to appear strange to you, that a lady of your excellent kinswoman's charitable and benevolent disposition should refuse nothing in her power, when the cries of distress and the moans of affliction call'd for her assistance. – If you would know in what manner she disposed of her money, enquire of hospitals, the prisons, and the necessitous petitioners that every day received their sustenance from her bounty, and you will find an easy account of her expences in her large and numerous donations.'

Mr. ***** only answer'd sullenly, that he should be better able to judge how he ought to think of the affair after he had spoke to her steward; on which the other clapping his hand upon his breast, was beginning to make many asseverations, that till that moment he never knew what sum or sums the lady had by her when she died, or had ever look'd, nor even entertain'd a thought of looking into any place where it might be supposed she kept her money. – I staid not, however, to hear what effect his hypocrisy produced, but went home, being impatient to see the contents of Alinda's manuscript.

CHAP. VII.

Will fully satisfy all the curiosity the former may have excited.

THE haste I made in snatching the following papers from the flames, happily preserv'd them so entirely from the destruction to which they had been destin'd, that tho' the edges were in many places much scorch'd, yet not a single word throughout the whole was any way damaged; and the reader may depend on having the story as perfect as if he saw it in the heroine's own hand.

Memoirs of the unfortunate ALINDA, *wrote by herself, and faithfully transcrib'd from the original copy.*

I AM sensible that many people have been very busy with my fame while living, nor do I expect to be treated with less severity after I am dead; – I cannot, however, think of an eternal separation from this world, without leaving something behind me which may serve to clear up those passages in my conduct, which by their being mysterious have given room for censure; and I do not this with any view of softening the asperity of the ill-natured for the errors I have been guilty of, or of exciting compassion in the more generous and gentle for my misfortunes; but merely to the end that if I am condemn'd, I may be condemn'd for real, not imaginary facts.

Sorry am I to accuse a father who so tenderly loved me; yet certain it is, that his over anxiety for my welfare has been the primary source of every woe my heart has labour'd under; and that by his mistaken endeavours to make me great and happy, I have been render'd the most miserable of created beings.

The fortune I was born to be possess'd of, and some natural endowments his affection fancy'd in me, made him flatter himself with the hopes of seeing me one day blaze forth in all the pomp of quality; nor could he endure the thoughts of marrying me to any man beneath the rank of right honourable;[55] and for fear any partial inclination of my own should disappoint these high raised expectations, he kept me from the conversation of every one whom he thought capable of attracting a heart unbyass'd by interest, and unambitious of grandeur.

Soon after my mother's death he quitted business, and retir'd to an estate he had some time before purchased in the country: – when we removed, I was too young to have any taste for the pleasures of the town, and regretted only the want of those play-fellows I had left behind; – indeed I wonder that I was not quite moped; I was suffer'd to go to no school, tho' there was a great one very near us; – never stirr'd beyond the precincts of our garden walls; – went not to church, because there it would have been impossible for me not to see and be seen; – no company visited us; for my father deprived himself of the pleasure of conversing with any of the neighbouring gentry, for fear that, as I grew up, I might take a liking to some one or other of their sons, none of whom he thought a match good enough for me, as they were not dignified with titles: – I had learn'd writing and dancing, but was far from being perfect in either; and my father, being unwilling I should be without these accomplishments, took the pains himself to set me copies to improve me in the one, and at length provided a master, too old and too ugly to give him any apprehensions, to instruct me in the other; – besides these two avocations, I had no amusement except reading, which, as I much delighted in, my father constantly supply'd me with such books as he thought proper for my sex and age.

Excepting some treatises of divinity, the subjects of my entertainment afforded little improvement to my understanding, they consisting only of romances, and some few very old plays; so that the ideas they inspired me with were as antiquated as the habits worn in the days of queen Elizabeth, and I was utterly ignorant of the modes, manners and customs of the age I lived in.

In this stupid and dispiriting situation did I pass full nineteen months; about the expiration of which time my father happen'd into company with a person who wears the sacred appearance of an Ecclesiastic; but is in reality one of those mention'd in holy writ by the name of wolves in sheeps cloathing; – his outward behaviour seems directed by the ministers of grace and goodness, while in his treacherous heart a thousand fiends lie in wait to bring ruin and destruction on the credulous listner to his wiles; – but before I procede in my unhappy story, it is fit I should give a more particular character of the wretch who has so great a share in it.

First for his extraction: – his father was a frenchman, servant to a person of distinction in Normandy; but having more ambition than honesty, found means to rob his master of a considerable sum and came over to England, where he set up for a gentleman and a most zealous Protestant, told a long plausible story of the great hardships he had sustain'd on the score of religion, and found here the same pity and encouragement as many others had done who fly here for an asylum on the same pretences.

Soon after his arrival he married a Dutchwoman, by whom he had a son who inherits all his father's virtues, and is the person whose story is so unhappily interwoven with my own.

Young Le Bris,[56] for that is the name of this worthy family, discover'd in his youth some indications of a good capacity for learning, insomuch that a certain lord taking a great fancy to him, sent him to Westminster school, and afterwards to the University, in order to qualify him for the pulpit, assuring him that he should not be without a handsome benefice[57] as soon as he should be fit to receive it.

But he had scarce completed his studies for that purpose, when all his present support and future expectations vanish'd on the sudden death of his noble patron, which was follow'd in a few months after by that of his father, so that he was left entirely destitute, his mother not being able to afford him the least assistance.

After many long and fruitless solicitations for a living, he was glad to accept of a small curacy in one of the remotest counties in England, where he resided several years; but was at last turned out on account of neglect of duty, and other misbehaviour; – he then came back to London, – gave out printed bills for teaching French and Latin at very low rates; but finding little encouragement that way turn'd Fleet-parson, earn'd a precarious sustenance by clandestine marriages.[58]

It was in these wretched circumstances that my father met with him, being in town on some business, and being told by some one, who it is likely knew no more of him than what he was pleased to say of himself, that he was a very worthy, tho' distress'd clergyman, made him the offer of a handsome sallary to come into his family, by way of chaplain; and, withal, to instruct me in the French language, and whatever else was fit for me to learn, or he was capable of teaching, – he readily embraced the proposal, and on my father's return came down with him.

My father presented him to me as a kind of Tutor, or Preceptor; – told me I must submit myself to his directions, – be attentive to all he said to me, and in every thing treat him with the greatest respect and reverence; – For, added he, it is by the lessons he is capable of giving you, that you alone can make any shining figure in the station wherein I hope to see you placed.

It will, perhaps, afford some matter of surprise that my father, who had hitherto preserved such an extreme caution in preventing my having the least conversation with any man, should now so strenuously recommend this parson to me; but it must be consider'd, that he was no less than six or seven and forty years of age; – that tho' not deform'd was far from handsome; and, besides, had a certain austerity in his manners which could not be thought would be very agreeable to youth.

It was, indeed, some time before I could be contented with the dominion given him over me; but my obedience to my father obliging me to behave towards him with esteem, custom at last converted that complaisance, which at first was no more than feign'd, into sincere: – a kind of affection, by degrees, mingled itself with the reverence I was bid to pay him; – I was never so happy as in the hours set apart for receiving his instructions; and the thoughts of the benefits that might be supposed to accrue from them afforded me less pleasure than the praises I was always certain he would bestow on my docility. – In fine, I not only lov'd the Teacher for the Precept's sake; but, as the poet says,

I lov'd the Precepts for the Teacher's sake.[59]

Nor is it to be wonder'd at that I tasted more satisfaction in his society than I had ever known before; – I wanted not ideas, tho' hitherto I had nothing to improve them: – I had been allow'd to converse with none but the servants, who could only divert me with idle tales of thieves, apparitions, and haunted houses; – my tutor, after having finish'd his graver lessons, would frequently entertain me with some extraordinary incident or other, either taken from history or romance; but, whether real or fictitious, I had sense enough to know were such as enlarg'd my understanding as well as charm'd my ears.

It is certain, indeed, that he spar'd no pains to insinuate himself into my good graces; and no less certain also, that the ungrateful design he had in doing so succeeded to the utter destruction of the whole happiness of my future life; and, at last, of my life itself, as will appear by these memoirs, which, while I am writing, I know not whether I shall have strength to finish.

I shall therefore reduce my unhappy story into as short a compass as I can: – in spite of the little amiableness this Tutor had in his person; – in spite of the vast disparity of years between us, I conceived the most tender affection for him; – alas I was then too young, – too innocent, to know what was meant by the word love, any farther than that love which we naturally bear to a father, brother, or some other near relation, – and thought not that what I felt for him was any more, or would be attended with any other consequence; and, as I apprehended no shame or danger in the kindness I had for him, endeavour'd not to put a stop to the growth of it, nor even to conceal it.

But Le Bris saw much better into my heart than I did myself, and dreading lest my father should be alarm'd at the too open fondness of my behaviour to him, began to treat me with less familiarity, and exerted the master much more than he had done; – this change both surprised and griev'd me; – I bore it, however, for two whole days, without seeming to take any notice of it; but on the third, being alone with him in his closet, where I constantly went every morning to receive my lessons, – 'What is the matter with you, my dear Tutor,' said I, 'I hope I have done nothing to offend you? – I am sure I would not willingly be guilty of deserving that you should frown upon me.' – 'No, my precious charge', reply'd he after a pause, 'it is not in your nature to give offence; but I would not incur your father's displeasure either towards you or me; – men are apt to be jealous of the affections of their children, and I am sometimes afraid that he should think you love me almost as well as you do him.' – 'Indeed I do so, – quite as well,' cry'd I eagerly. 'But why should he be angry at that, when he bid me use you with the same love and respect as I did himself?'

'People on some occasions,' answer'd he, 'will be displeased at a too exact performance of their own commands; and if my worthy Patron, your father, should happen to be of this opinion, the consequence would infallibly be an eternal separation between us; – he would drive me from his house, and I should never see my pretty charge again.'

'If you think so,' return'd I, 'though I hate all kind of dissimulation, I will make him believe I am weary of learning of you, and that I cannot abide you.' – 'Dear pretty angel,' cry'd he, tenderly taking me in his arms; 'there is no need of going to such extremes; – I would only have you behave with more distance towards me than you have done of late; and it will not be amiss if you sometimes complain that I set you too hard lessons; because if you should seem to learn too fast, he may begin to think there will soon be no occasion for a Tutor.' – 'Well,' said I, 'I will do every thing you bid me; for indeed it would almost break my heart to part with you.' – Here he kiss'd off the tears that fell from my eyes in speaking these last words, and I return'd all his endearments with the same affection as the fondest child would do those of the most indulgent parent.

It will, perhaps, seem a little strange that a girl turn'd of thirteen, as I then was, should think or act in the manner I did; but the way in which I had been brought up left me in the same ignorance and innocence as others of six or seven years old.

I obey'd his instructions with so much exactness, that my father was far from suspecting either my folly or the baseness of the person he had set over me: – the rest of the family were no more quick-sighted, nor it could not be expected they should be so; – our house-keeper, tho' a very good, was a silly old woman, and knew nothing beyond the œconomy of those affairs committed to her charge; – the maid who waited on me was her daughter, and had been bred to think every man who wore the habit of a Parson was to be worship'd; and the other servants were too seldom with us to have any opportunity of making discoveries.

I arriv'd at my fourteenth year, – my father kept my birth-day so far as to order something better than ordinary for dinner, and drank my health several times at table; – among other discourse concerning me, he said to Le Bris, – 'Well, Doctor, your pupil will now begin to think herself a woman, and I must find a husband for her who will be able to reward the care you have taken of her with a good fat Benefice.' To which the fawning hypocrite reply'd, – That the pleasure of seeing his worthy patron's daughter happy, would be to him the best benefice he could obtain.

Nothing farther pass'd at this time on the same subject; but the next morning, when I was alone with my Tutor in his closet, 'Do you remember, my dear miss,' cry'd he, with a very melancholy air, 'what your father said yesterday? – you will be marry'd soon, and I shall lose you for ever.' – 'Do not talk so,' reply'd I hastily, 'I do not want to be married; but if my father should compel me to it, all the husbands in the world should not make me forget my dear Tutor; – no, you shall always live with me; – I would not part from you to be a dutchess or a lady mayoress.' – 'Nor would I part from you,' said he, taking me in his arms, 'for an archbishopric; – and to be plain,' continued he, 'I have received letters since I have been here, with the offers of several great livings; but I have refused them all rather than quit my dear pupil.' – 'Have you indeed?' return'd I, hanging fondly on him – 'oh how kind you have been! – I should be the most ungrateful creature upon earth if I did not love you dearly for it.' – 'But will you always keep me with you?', cry'd he – 'As long as I live,' answer'd I. – 'Will you swear it?', rejoin'd he – 'Yes,' answer'd I, 'a thousand and a thousand times over, if you desire it.'

The wretch did not fail to take me at my word: – I bound myself, by the most solemn imprecations that words could form, that when I became mistress of my actions he should always live with me. – After this, the hours we pass'd together were employ'd more in improving the foolish affection I had for him, than in any lessons for improving my understanding. – My father imputed the slow progress I made in my studies not to any want of ability in my teacher, but to my own neglect, and often chid me for it, which I bore patiently, as I believed it the surest means of keeping my dear Tutor with me: – this he took so kindly, that he told me one day, he flatter'd himself I lov'd him almost as well as I did my father. – 'I hope it is no sin,' cry'd I childishly, 'if I love you quite as well?' – 'Far from it,' answer'd he, 'you are only his daughter by nature, but you are mine by affection; – you are the child of my soul, and therefore ought to love me better.' – 'I am glad of that,' rejoin'd I, 'for indeed I do love you a great deal better, – I am sure I do; for I don't feel half the pleasure when he kisses me as when you do; – and when you take me in your arms my heart beats as if it would come out.' – It will scarce be doubted but that he now bestow'd upon me those endearments I had declar'd myself so well satisfied with; and some minutes after, as I had turn'd to a looking-glass to adjust some disorder in my head-dress, he pull'd me to him, and making me sit upon his knee, – 'You are very pretty, my dear miss,' said he, 'and have no defect in your shape, but being a little too flat before;' – with these words he thrust one of his hands with in my stays, telling me that handling my breasts would make them grow, and I should then be a perfect beauty.

Not conscious of any guilt I was ignorant of shame; and thinking every thing he did was right, made not the least resistance; but suffer'd him, by degrees, to proceed to liberties, which, had I known the meaning of, I should have stabb'd him for attempting; but, as I have somewhere read,

> By no example warn'd how to beware,
> My very innocence became my snare.[60]

It will, perhaps, be supposed that the perfidious man did not stop here, but proceeded yet farther, to the utter completion of my dishonour; but I shall do him the justice to say he never offer'd any such thing; though I have good reasons to believe he was prevented only by his fears of the consequences that might have attended it, to the ruin of a design which promised him more satisfaction than the enjoyment of my person.

In the ridiculous way I have been describing did we continue 'till I was in my seventeenth year, about which time my father being obliged to go to London on a law affair, he left the sole management of the family, as well as of myself, to his favourite chaplain, 'till he should return, which he expected to do in two months.

He had not been gone full three weeks before a stranger came to our house on a visit to my Tutor; – he received him with great marks of civility, and told me afterwards that he was the land-steward of a nobleman who had sent him on purpose to court his acceptance of a benefice worth near eight hundred pounds per annum: – as I suspected not the truth of this I was terribly frighten'd, and cry'd out, '– Then you will leave me at last!' – 'It would be with an extreme reluctance I should do so,' reply'd he; 'but what can I do? – If I should hereafter be exposed to any misfortunes, how would the world blame me for having refused such an offer?' – 'What misfortunes,' said I, 'have you to fear? – I shall always have enough to support my dear Tutor.'

'My dear child,' resum'd he, 'you forget that when once you are married there will be nothing in your power, – all will be your husband's, who may take it into his head to turn me out of door directly.' – 'No such matter,' reply'd I hastily, 'for I will make him promise and swear beforehand to keep you always in the family.' – 'Few men,' said he, 'pay any regard, after they become husbands, to the promises and vows they made when they were lovers. – In fine, my little angel,' continued he, taking me tenderly in his arms, 'there is but one way to secure our lasting happiness, to which if you agree I will immediately refuse the great offer now made me, with all my future hopes of rising in the church, and devote myself eternally to you.'

These last words I thought so highly obliging to me, that I hung about his neck, kiss'd his cheek, and cry'd, I would do every thing he would have me; – he then told me that a writing should be drawn up between us, by which we should mutually bind ourselves, under the penalty of the half of what either should be possess'd of, never to separate.

On my ready compliance with this proposal he ventured to make a second, even more impudent than the first; – after seeming to consider a little within himself. – 'I have been thinking,' said he, 'that if the person you shall marry should happen to be of a cross, perverse nature, tho' for his own sake he not will drive me from his house, yet he may use me so ill as to compel me to go out of it of my own accord, – suppose, therefore, you should bind yourself by the writing I have mention'd, and under the same penalty, never to marry any man without my consent.'

'Bless me,' cry'd I, a little surprised, 'how can I do this! – you know I must obey my father.' – 'Heaven forbid you should do otherwise,' rejoin'd the artful hypocrite, – 'you may be sure I shall never oppose either his will, or your own inclination, in the choice of a husband; – what I speak of is only a thing of form, which, when shewn to your husband, will oblige him to treat me with gratitude and respect.'

I was entirely satisfy'd with this, and reply'd, I would do what he desir'd as soon as he pleased; – on which, – 'It happens luckily,' said he, 'that the gentleman who came here on the business I told you of was bred to the law, – I will let him know as much as is necessary of our affair, and get him to draw up a proper instrument.' – In speaking these words he left me and went in search of his friend, who at that time was walking in the garden, waiting, no doubt, his coming.

I had little time allow'd me to reflect on what I was about to do, – Le Bris immediately return'd, bringing the lawyer with him, – the latter of whom desir'd to receive instructions from my own mouth for what he was to write, and accordingly I repeated the sense of the obligation I was to lay myself under, leaving it to him to put it in such words as he should find proper; – if I had been mistress of the least share of common reason, I must have seen that all this scheme was a thing previously concerted between these two villains; for the Lawyer immediately pull'd out of his pocket a large parchment, with seals fix'd to it, and every thing requisite to make the instrument firm and valid; – but I was infatuated, – all my little understanding was subjected to the will of this wicked Tutor; – I gave an implicit faith to all he said, and paid an implicit obedience to all his dictates.

The lawyer took his leave next day, and nothing material happen'd till within a week of the time my father was expected home, when, instead of himself came the melancholy account that he had been seiz'd with an apoplectic fit, and tho' he recover'd from it, expired within two hours after; – he had made his will about a year before, by which he left me sole heir of every thing he was in possession of, except a few legacies, and in case his demise should happen before I was married, or of age, appointed two gentlemen for his executors and my guardians; – they both wrote to me, as did also my cousin *****, acquainting me that it was necessary I should come to London directly on this occasion, and each inviting me to their respective houses, which as they lived in different parts of the town, I was at liberty to chuse which I liked best.

My Tutor, however, dissuaded me from accepting any of their offers, and told me he would write to a friend in London to provide a ready-furnish'd house for my reception, till things were settled, and I should resolve whether I would reside in town or country; – accordingly he did so, and when we came within ten miles of London we were met on the road by the lawyer, who, as I have since discover'd, was his chief agent in every thing; – he conducted us to a house in Jermin-street, which was indeed very neat and commodious.

It was late when we arriv'd, but I did not fail to send the next morning to my two Guardians and cousin ****, who all came to see me the same day, and express'd themselves in very affectionate terms; – I presented my Tutor to them, as a person for whom my father had a high esteem, on which they treated him with that respect they supposed him to deserve.

I now enter'd into a scene of life altogether new to me; – several distant relations, whom I knew only by their names; and many other gentlemen and ladies, who had been acquainted with my mother, came to pay their respects to me; – all my mornings were taken up with messages and compliments, and all my afternoons with receiving and returning visits. – How strange was the transition?

– from being confined to the narrow precincts of a lone country mansion, I had now the whole metropolis to range in; – instead of the grave lessons of two old men, my ears were now continually fill'd with the flattering praises of addressing beaus; – instead of having nothing to amuse my hours, new diversions, – new entertainments, crowded upon each moment, and I was incessantly hurried from one pleasure to another, till my head grew giddy with the whirl of promiscuous delights.

As I was young, not ugly, and look'd upon as a rich heiress, proposals of marriage were every day made to me, all which I communicated to my Tutor; but tho' many of them were much to my advantage, he always found some pretence or other for refusing his consent, and I accordingly rejected them, to the surprise of all who knew me, and the great dissatisfaction of my best friends.

He was not, however, half pleased with the gay manner in which I lived, and as soon as the affairs relating to my estate were settled, would fain have prevail'd upon me to return into the country; but I had too high a relish for the diversions of the town to pay that regard to his advice I had formerly done; and, instead of complying with it, quitted the house I was in, hired another upon lease, and furnish'd it in the most elegant manner I could: – he grew very grave on my behaviour; but as I kept firm to both the engagements I had made with him, he had no pretence to complain of my actions in other matters.

For a time, indeed, my head was not the least turn'd towards marriage; – I thought no farther of the men than to be vain and delighted with their flatteries; – happy would it have been for me had I continued always in this mind; but my ill fate too soon, alas, presented me with an object which convinced me, that all the joys of public admiration are nothing, when compared to one soft hour with the youth we love, and by whom we think we are beloved.

I believe there is little need for me to say that this object, so enchanting to my senses, was the young, the handsome, the accomplish'd Amasis: – the world, whom he made no secret of the passion he prosess'd for me, was also witness in what manner I received it; – we appear'd together in all public places; – I treated him in all companies with a difference which shew'd the esteem I had for him: – my friends approved my choice, and the union between us was look'd upon as a thing so absolutely determined, that many believed the ceremony was already over, when, to their great surprise, they saw at once that we were utterly broke off, and in a very short time after, the ungrateful Amasis become the husband of another.

My tutor, on perceiving me inclined to favour Amasis more than I had ever done any of those who had hitherto address'd me, began to rail at him, and tell me a thousand ridiculous stories he pretended to have heard in relation to his conduct; – I still retained too much reverence for this wicked man to contradict what he said, but not enough to enable me to conquer my new passion; – I loved Amasis, and continued to give him daily proofs of it; – this so incensed him, that he told me one day, – that he wonder'd I would encourage the courtship of a man whom I must never expect to marry. – 'Why not, sir,' answer'd I, 'neither his birth nor fortune are inferior to mine.' – 'Suppose them so,' rejoin'd he, 'the most material thing is wanting, which is my consent.' – 'When I gave you that power over me,' said I, 'you promised never to thwart my inclination.' 'I did so,' reply'd he; 'but, to be plain with you, I then expected all your inclination would be in favour of myself.' – 'Yourself!' cry'd I, more surprised than words can describe. – 'Yes, Alinda,' resumed he, 'methinks the thing should not appear so odd to you; – call back to your remembrance the familiarities that have pass'd between us, and then justify, if you can, to virtue or to modesty, the least desire of giving yourself to any other man.'

Rage, – astonishment, and shame, for the folly I had been guilty of, so overwhelm'd my heart at this reproach, that I had not power to speak one word, but stood looking on him with a countenance which, I believe, sufficiently express'd all those passions, while he went on in these terms:

'How often,' continued he, 'have you hung about my neck whole hours together, and by the warmest fondness tempted me to take every freedom with you but the last, which if I had not been possess'd of more honour than you now shew of constancy, I also should have seiz'd, and left you nothing to bestow upon a rival?'

The storm which had been gathering in my breast all the time he was speaking, now burst out with the extremest violence; – I raved, and loaded him with epithets not very becoming in me to make use of, yet not worse than he deserved; – he heard me with a sullen silence; but when I mention'd the cruelty and baseness of upbraiding me with the follies of my childish innocence, he told me, with a sneer, that he would advise me not to put that among my catalogue of complaints.– 'For,' said he, 'the world will scarce believe, that a lady of fourteen, fifteen, and sixteen, had the same inclinations in toying with a gentleman as a baby has with its nurse'.

I would have reply'd, that the manner in which I was educated kept me in the same ignorance as a baby; but something within rose in my throat, stopping the passage of my breath, and I sunk fainting in the chair where I was sitting: – whether he was really moved with this sight, or only affected to be so, I know not; but he ran to me, used proper means to bring me to myself, and on my recovery I found myself prest very tenderly within his arms: – his touch was now grown odious to me, – I struggled to get loose; – 'Be not thus unkind,' cry'd he, holding me still faster, 'you once took pleasure in my embraces, you have confess'd you did; – oh then recall those soft ideas, and we shall both be happy.'

'No,' answered I, breaking forcibly from him, 'what then was the effect of too much innocence, would be now a guilt for which I should detest myself as much as I do you.' – 'I still love you,' said he. – 'Prove it then,' cry'd I fiercely, 'by giving me up that writing which your artifices ensnared me to sign, and cease to oppose my marriage with Amasis.' – 'No, madam,' reply'd he, 'if you persist in the resolution of marrying Amasis, half your estate would be a small consolation to me for the loss of you; and you cannot sure imagine me weak enough to resign my claim to the one, after being deprived of the other.'

I had not patience to continue this discourse, but retired to my chamber, where, throwing myself upon the bed, I vented some part of the anguish of my mind in a flood of tears; after which, finding some little ease, I began to reflect, that tormenting myself in this manner would avail nothing, and that I ought rather to try if any possible means could be found for extricating me from the labyrinth I was entangled in.

Accordingly I arose, – muffled myself up as well as I could to prevent being known, – took a hackney-coach, and went to the chambers of an eminent lawyer; – I related to him all the circumstances of my unhappy case, concealing only the names of the persons concern'd in it; – he listen'd attentively to what I said, and when I had done, ask'd me of what age I was when I enter'd into that engagement I now wanted to be freed from; which question I answering with sincerity, he shook his head, and told me that he was sorry to assure me I could have no relief from law,[61] and that the best, and indeed the only method I could take, was to endeavour to compromise the affair with the gentleman.

I return'd home very disconsolate, and was above a week without being able to resolve on any thing; but my impatience to be united to the man I loved, and at the same time eased of the presence of the man I hated, at last determined me to follow the lawyer's advice; – I sent for my wicked tutor into my chamber, – talked to him in more obliging terms than I had done since the first discovery of his designs upon me; but represented to him the absurdity of thinking of marrying me himself; – and concluded with telling him, that if he would cancel the engagement between us I would make him a gratuity of a thousand pounds, and also be ready to do him any other service in my power.

He rejected this proposal with the greatest contempt. – 'You are certainly mad, Alinda,' said he, 'or take me to be so; – a thousand pounds would be a fine equivalent, indeed, for the half of your estate, jewels, rich furniture, plate, and whatever else you are in possession of; to all which your marriage will give me an undoubted claim, and I accordingly shall seize' – 'Suppose I never marry,' cry'd I. – 'Be it so,' answer'd he, 'I must still continue to live with you; and what you offer for my quitting you does not amount to five years purchase of my sallary and board as your chaplain.'

These words making me imagine his chief objection was to the smallness of the sum I told him I would double, nay even treble it, for the purchase of my liberty; but he told me it would be in vain for me to tempt him with any offers of that kind; – that no consideration whatever should prevail with him to depart from the agreement between us, and he would always hold me to my bargain.

The determined air with which he spoke this, made me think it best not to urge him any farther at that time; – the next day, however, and several succeeding ones, I fail'd not to renew the discourse; but tho' I made use of every argument my reason could supply me with, – tho' I wept, pray'd, rav'd, – by turns cajol'd and threaten'd, all I could say, – all I could do was ineffectual, and the more I labour'd to bring him to compliance, the more stubborn his obstinacy grew.

To make any one sensible what it was I suffer'd in this cruel dilemma, they must also be made sensible to what an infinite degree I loved the man whom it was now impossible for me to be happy with, and both these are inexpressible; – I shall therefore only say, that I was very near being totally deprived of that little share of reason heaven had bestow'd upon me.

Amasis, to whom I had confess'd the tenderness I had for him, was all this while continually solliciting me to complete our union; – one day, when he was more than ordinarily pressing on this occasion, and my heart being very full, I cry'd out, almost without knowing what I said, – 'Oh, Amasis, you know not what you ask, when you ask me to marry you!' – This exclamation surpris'd him; but having begun, I now went on. – 'You expect,' said I, 'an estate of twelve hundred pounds a year; but I will not deceive you, you find me worth only the half of what you have been made to hope.' – 'When I made my addresses to the lovely Alinda,' answer'd he, 'I had no eye to the fortune she might bring me; – but wherefore this fruitless trial of my love? – your guardians have shewn me the writings of your estate, and I know to a single hundred what you are possess'd of.' – 'Suppose,' rejoin'd I, 'that I should have previously disposed of the one half of what otherwise our marriage would have given you?' – 'I will suppose no such thing,' reply'd he, 'it cannot be.' – 'It both can and is,' said I, bursting into tears, 'I have unwarily enter'd into an engagement, by which I forfeit the moiety of all I am mistress of, even to my very jewels, if every I marry any man, except on certain conditions, which condition I am now well assur'd I never can obtain.'

'Death and hell!' cry'd he, starting up in a fury – 'What condition, – when, – where, – to whom, on what account was this engagement made!' – Shame would not let me answer to these interrogatories, and I remain'd in a kind of stupid silence. – 'If by any artifices,' pursued he, 'you have been seduced to sign a compact of this wild nature, unfold the whole of the affair, and depend that either the laws or this avenging arm shall do you justice.' – I now repented that I had so rashly divulged any part of this fatal secret, – not but I should have been glad to have seen my wicked tutor punish'd; but I knew that on the least attempt made for my redress, he would infallibly expose the follies I had been guilty of in regard to him; and when compared to that the loss of Amasis, – my fortune, or even my life itself, seem'd a less terrible misfortune; – for this reason, therefore, I refused the entreaties of a beloved lover, and screen'd the villainy of a wretch who most my soul abhorr'd.

In fine, I would reveal no more than I had done, – Amasis left me in a very ill humour, and the next morning I received a billet from him containing these stabbing lines:

To miss ALINDA*****

MADAM,

I HAVE been considering on the amazing account you gave me last night; and as you refuse to discover either the person with whom you made this engagement, or the motives which induced you to it, can look on it as no other than a contract with some gentleman, once happy in your affections; – a second-hand passion neither suits with the delicacy of my humour, nor to encroach upon the rights of another with my honour: – I shall therefore desist troubling you with any future visits, but shall be always glad to hear of your welfare, which I despair of doing till you prevail upon yourself to be just to your first vows; sacrifice the affection you have for me to the obligations you are under to my rival; – I yield to his prior title all the late glorious hopes I had conceived, and wish you more happy with him than it is now in your power to make

 Your humble servant,

AMASIS.

Here ended all my hopes of happiness; – all the soft ideas of love and marriage vanish'd for ever from my breast, and were succeeded by others of the most dreadful nature: – for several weeks I abandon'd myself to grief and to despair; but pride at length got the better of these passions; and, to conceal the real situation of my heart from the enquiring world, I all at once affected to be madly gay, and ran into such extravagancies, as, without being criminal in fact, justly drew upon me the severest censures.

But nature will not bear a perpetual violence, – grief and despair were the strongest passions in me; – in the midst of dancing, drinking, revelling, tears were ready to start from my eyes, and sighs from my bosom, which, when I endeavour'd to suppress, recoil'd upon my heart, and shook my whole frame with the most terrible revulsions; – the marriage of Amasis seconded the blow our parting had given; – I could no longer dissemble what I felt, – no longer appear the giddy thoughtless libertine, but flew from one extreme to the other; – I now would see no company, shut myself up in my chamber, denied access to my best friends, and never went abroad but to visit the hospitals and prisons: – I never suffer'd Le Bris to come into my presence; and I believe, perceiving me so resolute, he would now have accepted of a sum of money to have quitted my house entirely; but I had now done with the world, – had lost in Amasis all I valued in it, and would not give the monster, whom I justly look'd upon as the source of all my misfortunes, any more than I was compell'd to do, – his bare board and sallary.

Behold, by these memoirs, the beginning and progress of my miseries, – the end is near at hand, – death is already busy at my heart, and allows no time to apologize for the errors of my conduct; – pity is all my ashes can expect.

CHAP. VIII.

*Contains a very brief account of some passages subsequent to the foregoing
story, with the author's remarks upon the whole.*

As I know very well that solidity has but a small share in the composition of the
lady whom Alinda had intended to entrust with the publication of her memoirs,
I thought the surest way of having the will of the deceas'd perform'd, was not
to trouble a person of her character with the perusal of them, but to take the
opportunity of my Invisibilityship to present them to the world myself, which I
accordingly have done.

And now, as I doubt not but the reader will be glad of being inform'd of
somewhat farther concerning Le Bris, I shall relate such particulars as have come
to my knowledge.

It must be concluded that this unworthy preceptor, in looking over the
papers of Alinda, had either not observed, or afterwards forgot, that the ring he
had just taken from among her other jewels was the very same mention'd in her
letter to her friend, otherwise he would certainly have had cunning enough to
have replaced it where he found it.

Mr. ****** soon recollecting what his cousin had said to him in regard of this
little legacy, and missing it from her other trinkets, made a strict enquiry what
was become of it: – Le Bris, having had her keys in his possession, was one of
the first interrogated, and on being so, boldly reply'd, that such a ring had been
bestow'd upon him by Alinda. – 'How can that be,' cry'd the other, – 'when but
three days before her death she bequeath'd it to a lady of her acquaintance, and
insisted on my promise of delivering it to her?' – 'She must then be delirious,'
said the parson; 'but however that might be, heaven forbid I should detain what
is even suspected to be the right of another;' and with these words presented the
ring to mr. *****, who received it from him without the least ceremony.

This affair, notwithstanding the hypocritical manner in which the ring was
return'd, gave mr. ***** room to imagine there had been some foul play in relation to Alinda's effects; – the steward prov'd, by his books, that he had paid into
her hands, a week before her death, two hundred and fifty pounds in specie, and
more than twice that sum in Bank-bills, being arrears he had receiv'd from the
tenants; – it seem'd unlikely to them that she could have disposed of the money,
much less have had any occasion to change the bills in so short a time; – orders
were therefore sent to the Bank to stop the payment of such numbers till further
notice; but the precaution came too late, – the person who had secreted them
had been already there, and converted all his paper into cash.

The heir, however, was confident that he had been defrauded; – he consulted
council upon it, who all advised him to have recourse to equity:[62] – whether Le
Bris had any hint given him of what was intended to be done against him, or
whether his own guilty conscience made him only apprehend it, is uncertain;
but be that as it may, he had not courage to stand the test of examination, –

he fled the kingdom, after having thrown aside that robe, which, had he been known for what he truly was, would long before have been stripp'd from off his sacrilegious shoulders.

But Providence would not permit him to enjoy his ill-got spoils, nor a life he had devoted to such wicked purposes; – designing to turn trader at Jamaica he embark'd for that place; – but the vessel being overtaken by a storm, was lost almost in sight of shore, and he with many other, perhaps less guilty persons, perish'd in the wreck: – this last piece of intelligence I received from his mother, who, tho' he had supported during the life of Alinda, to prevent being exposed by her clamours, he now left pennyless, destitute and starving, in an extreme old age.

Thus did the vengeance of heaven at last overtake the wretch, who, besides his other impieties, had been guilty of the most cruel ingratitude and breach of trust, in imposing upon the simplicity of a young creature committed to his care, and utterly destroying all the views of his generous Patron and Benefactor.

As for the unfortunate Alinda, tho' it is certain her conduct cannot be wholly justify'd, yet, according to my opinion, neither ought it to be wholly condemned; – it would be passing too severe a judgment, to impute the fondness she express'd for her wicked tutor to a wanton inclination: – if we consider the various arts of her seducer, – the commands laid on her by her father to love and obey him as himself; – the manner in which she was brought up; – the perfect ignorance she was kept in of the customs of the world, and how other young ladies behaved, we shall find that these are all of them very strong pleas in her defence, and not forbear pitying the mistakes of such artless innocence.

I wish as much could be alledg'd in her behalf on the score of her behaviour after breaking off with Amasis; – the excesses into which she ran, in order to conceal the disquiets of her mind for the loss of that favourite lover, too evidently shew that she sacrifized two of the most valuable characteristics of womanhood, – her prudence and her modesty, to one of the very worst, – her pride.

Nor can I offer any thing in vindication of the last stages of her life, – if convinced of her error, in being perpetually among a promiscuous unselected company, it was flying to an almost as inexcusable extreme, to shut herself from her best friends, and avoid the society of those whose conversation might have dissipated her chagrin, and at the same time improved her understanding; – to do this seems to me, I must confess, to have more the favour of despair, than of virtue or true fortitude.

There was, doubtless, a certain giddy propensity in her nature, which wanted to be corrected by reason, – example, – precept, – authority, and the rudiments of a good education, all which she was deny'd; and it must therefore be acknowledged, that both her faults and misfortunes were entirely owing to the caprice and credulity of her father, and the base designs of the person appointed to be her governor and instructor.

End of the First BOOK.

THE
Invisible Spy.

BOOK II.
CHAP. I.

The Author, by the help of his Invisibility, has discover'd such a contrast in the behaviour of two married couple of distinction, as he thinks would be the utmost injustice to the public to conceal.

Placentia, after a long and most passionate courtship, was at last wedded to Dalmatius; – she brought him an ample fortune, a very agreeable person, and an unblemish'd character; – she had studied all the duties of a wife before she became so, and afterwards practised them in the strictest manner: – whenever she found him gay, she heighten'd his good humour by her own sprightliness; and when sullen and perverse, as was too often the case, she endeavour'd to dissipate his chagrin either by playing on her spinnet or telling him some diverting story: – without seeming to consult his palate, she always took care to put such dishes into her bill of fare as she had perceiv'd he fed upon with most satisfaction: – whatever company suited his taste were sure to be often invited by her, and entertain'd with the greatest marks of esteem and complaisance: – her whole thoughts, indeed, were taken up with obliging and making him happy: – she had no will, – no inclination of her own, – both were entirely regulated by his; and, to add to all this, she was an excellent œconomist, understood the management of a family perfectly well, and knew how to make a grand appearance with less expence than some others are at who are accounted contemptibly parsimonious.

What would some husbands give to be bless'd with so virtuous, so tender, so endearing a companion? Dalmatius, instead of placing this jewel next his heart, hung it carelesly upon his sleeve; either not knowing, or not regarding the true value of it.

During the course of several Invisible Visitations I made at their house, never did I see him treat her in any degree proportionable to her merit; – when in his best humours he return'd the caresses she gave him only with a cold indifference; but when any thing abroad had happen'd to thwart his view, either of pleasure or ambition, no man could behave with more churlishness at home: – but the manner in which this couple behaved to each other will best appear from their own words, which I shall give a short specimen of on two different occasions.

They were to go out together one day, to call on some friends who were to accompany them on a party of pleasure, – the landau[63] waited at the door, – he had just finish'd dressing, and sent up to know if his wife was ready; – the message could be scarce deliver'd before she came flying into the room, on which the following dialogue ensued:

Placentia. I hope I have not made you wait for me?

Dalmatius. Not at all, – it wants some minutes of our appointment; but I know you women are generally so long in equipping yourselves, that I was willing to send a messenger to hasten you.

Placentia. I should know but little of the value of time, if I wasted much of it in dressing. – But pray, my dear, how do you like me to day?

Dalmatius. Like you, – that's an odd question; – why – as well as ever I did.

Placentia. I should be miserable if I did not think you did; – but I mean, how do you like my cloaths? – you see I am all in new.

Dalmatius. Are you indeed? I should have seen nothing of it if you had not told me: – I never mind what women have on.

Placentia. Then I am disappointed, my dear; for I assure you I consulted your fancy more than my own in the choice I made of this silk, as I have heard you say an hundred times, I believe, that you thought blue and silver the most agreeable mixture that could be.

Dalmatius. So it is; but it may not happen to become every body; – however, I must do you the justice to say, you look well enough in it, and I believe every body will think so.

Placentia. If you think so, my dear, it is all I wish.

In speaking this she took hold of his hand and kiss'd it with the greatest warmth of affection; – he return'd the favour with a slight salute upon her cheek, then looking on his watch, said he believed it was time to go, and went down stairs, she following.

The truth of the affair is this: – Dalmatius is not only vain and insolent in his nature, but also amorous and inconstant to an excess; tho' he no longer had any eyes for the charms of his fair wife, his heart was but too susceptible to those of other women. – Miranda for some time engross'd all his devoirs;[64] nor could her being married to the most intimate of his friends restrain him from making his unlawful addresses to her; nor the vow she had taken at the holy altar, deter her from gratifying an inclination he had found the way to inspire.

The husband of this lady is a man of so much indolence and so little delicacy, that he never gives himself the least concern about what pleasures his wife may indulge herself in, provided she offers no interruption to those he takes himself;

– there are some, indeed, who say that on their marriage they mutually agreed to allow each other a perfect latitude in this point; – but be that as it may, Miranda seems under no apprehensions of her conduct being called in question by him.

Her amour with Dalmatius soon became so notorious that it was in the mouth of every one; – Placentia herself was the last that gave credit to it; – that excellent lady would not suffer her heart to entertain ill thoughts of the man whom she was bound to love, nor could any thing but the testimony of her own eyes have convinced her of the guilty truth.

Miranda came to visit her one day when she happen'd to be abroad; but Dalmatius being at home the presence of his wife was little wanted; – she soon return'd, however, and being told that Miranda was above ran hastily up to receive her; but not finding her in the room where company were usually introduced, yet thinking she heard the murmur of voices very near, she stepp'd towards the place whence it seem'd to proceed, and peeping through the keyhole of an adjacent chamber, saw her husband and the lady in a posture such as could leave her no doubt of their criminal conversation.

The sudden shock at first transfix'd her feet; – but presently recovering herself, she retired from the guilty scene and went into her own chamber; where, finding her woman at work, she order'd her to go immediately down and forbid the servants to take any notice of her being come home: – 'I hear,' said she, 'that Miranda is below, and I am not very well and would not see any company at this time.'

The woman being withdrawn to do as she was commanded, Placentia threw herself into an easy-chair and fell into a profound resvery; – I was present all this while, but my Belt of Invisibility did not enable me to penetrate into her thoughts, till seeming as if determin'd on something she had been debating within herself, she rose suddenly from her seat and burst into these words:

Placentia. No, – he shall never know I think him false; much less that I have detected him: – reproaches would avail me nothing, and might harden him in his crime; – I am his wife, – we must always live together, or be subjected to the ridicule of a laughing and censorious world: – prudence, therefore, as well as duty, commands me to conceal the shameful discovery I have made; and rather endeavour, by added tenderness, if possible, to reclaim him, and oblige him to see I am at least as worthy of his affection as Miranda.

I left her in this resolution, and found that for several days she strictly adhered to it; excepting only that she could not so far dissemble her uneasiness as to be able to receive Miranda in the manner she had formerly done; she therefore desisted from making her any farther invitations to her house, and always excused herself from accepting any sent to her by that lady.

This was enough, however, to give the lovers some apprehensions that she suspected their intrigue; – but Miranda was of too vain and gay a temper to feel any inquietudes on this score; and the ungrateful Dalmatius, finding himself treated by his wife with the same love and complaisance as ever, gave himself not the trouble either to examine, or be under the least concern whether such a behaviour proceeded from her ignorance of his fault, or her discretion in over-looking it.

But the sweetest nature may be embitter'd by continual provocations; – Placentia, finding that all the efforts she made for regaining the affections of her husband were ineffectual, began by degrees to grow more remiss in her cares of pleasing; – not that she ever departed from the essential duties of a wife; – she only ceased the practice of those which, as the case stood between them, might justly be call'd works of supererogation.

Being to have a great route at her house, just as she was going to send cards to invite the company, Dalmatius came into the room, and having looked over the catalogue of names, on finding Miranda's not there, began with an unusual haughtiness to interrogate her on that occasion; and she, now, for the first time, reply'd to what he said with as much indifference as she had formerly done with submission.

Dalmatius. How happens it, madam, that Miranda is left out among the number of your guests?

Placentia. I had forgot her.

Dalmatius. It is well then that I reminded you; – but methinks a lady of her rank and character in the world might well have deserved a place in your remembrance.

Placentia. It may be so; – but one cannot invite every body.

Dalmatius. When any body is invited to our house, especially on these occasions, it would be the utmost absurdity to leave Miranda out; – therefore I insist upon her coming for your own sake.

Placentia. Oh, sir, you need not give yourself any trouble on that score, I am certainly a judge how to behave to my own acquaintance; – but if you are so desirous of having Miranda here to-morrow, the best way is for you to send a card as from yourself; – I doubt not but the invitation will be full as agreeable, and as readily comply'd with.

Dalmatius. You talk in an odd manner, madam; – and now I think on it, – I met Miranda the other day in the Park, and she complain'd to me of a strange change in you towards her; – that you have never return'd the last visit she made you; – have scarce spoke to her in any public assembly, and seem'd to shun her presence as much as possible. – Pray what is the meaning of all this?

Placentia. That, sir, is a question which perhaps neither you nor she would thank me for answering directly.

Dalmatius. I understand you, madam, however; – you have got notions in your head not becoming in you to indulge, nor worthy any endeavours of mine to expel; – I would only have you be wiser, and consider that of all domestic animals a jealous wife is the most contemptible.

He flung out of the room with these words, and all the tokens of disdain and indignation in his countenance, leaving Placentia in a confusion not easy to be describ'd; – I could perceive, however, by the gestures of that unhappy lady, that she repented having gone so far, yet knowing herself the only injured, could not yield either to recede from her resolution on the account of Miranda, or make use of any attempts to soften so ill-founded a resentment in her husband.

It is now said that his amour with Miranda is on the decline; – that a new face has utterly eclipsed all the charms he lately found in hers; and that Placentia has at least this consolation under her misfortune, to find that no one beauty has the power long to retain the heart she has lost; – so just are the poet's words:

> When fix'd to one, love safe at anchor rides,
> And dares the fury of the winds and tides;
> But losing once that hold, to the wide ocean borne,
> It drives at will, to ev'ry wave a scorn.[65]

Marriage, tho' a sacred institution, – tho' ordain'd by heaven to bestow the supremest felicity we mortals are capable of enjoying, becomes the severest curse, when souls ill suited to each other are join'd in its indissoluble bonds; and it too often happens, that those who by nature and education are qualify'd to give and receive the greatest happiness, are render'd the most miserable through the perverseness of a bad temper'd partner.

Montelion has been twice married; – he has experienced both all the contentments, and all the inquietudes of that state, with women of humours as widely different as light and darkness; – I had almost said, as heaven from hell: – his first lady, as she was excell'd by none in exterior perfections, so she was equall'd but by very few in the more valuable endowments of the mind; – his life, while in possession of this treasure, was one continued scene of harmony and love; but soon, alas, the blissful prospect vanish'd! – the fair, the virtuous, the tender Erminia died; and, to add to the misfortune of her disconsolate husband, left no pledge behind her of their mutual affection.

Though in that season of life when amorous flames are at their highest bent, those of Montelion seem'd all bury'd in the grave of his dear Erminia: – he remain'd for several years the lonely occupier of a widow'd bed; – at last, however, the ardent desire of having an heir for his estate got somewhat the better of his melancholy, and determined him on a second venture.

In the choice he made he consulted neither fortune nor beauty; – the one, indeed, he wanted not; – and as for the other, since his Erminia's death, all women were equal to him, and he regarded the lovely and unlovely with the same indifference; – he therefore marry'd Ferocia, merely because she was one of the daughters of a fruitful family, and likely to answer the only end which induced him once more to become a husband.

Every body was astonish'd at these nuptials, and much more so on the knowledge of Ferocia's behaviour afterwards; – but I shall present my reader with the character of this lady, as it was given by an impartial hand in a letter to a friend.

Ferocia, now the wife of Montelion, is a woman plain in her person, – weak in her understanding, – capricious and fantastic in her humour, – unpolish'd in her manners; – and, what is worse than all, insufferably vain and insolent on her new dignity, without one grain of true love or gratitude for the man who has raised her to it.

My Gift of Invisibility assisted me in proving the truth of the above in all its parts; – further I will not pretend to say; for tho' it is a vulgar Adage, that, 'Where there is no modesty, there is little sign of honesty';[66] and I have heard severe censures pass'd upon her virtue; yet I never could make any discoveries to her prejudice on that score, and am apt to believe, that the rampant airs she gives herself among the men, are, in reality, more owing to a hoidenly than an amorous disposition.

Montelion seems to see her behaviour in the same light I do; yet, for the sake of his own honour, cannot but wish she would act with more reserve. – They had not been married above three months when he was seiz'd with a fit of the gout which confined him to his apartment; – Ferocia came in cover'd over with jewels and blazing like a star; and, without expressing any concern for his indisposition, told him that she was going to lady Primwell's route; on which ensued the following dialogue between them:

Montelion. I flatter'd myself, madam, with having the happiness of your company at home this evening, as I am not in a condition to stir out.

Ferocia. Oh heavens! I should make the worst nurse in the world: What good would my staying do you?

Montelion. A great deal, madam, and I hope I need say no more to engage you not to leave me.

Ferocia. Indeed, my lord, I must go, I have given my promise.

Montelion. You will be easily excused; – nobody will expect a wife on a party of pleasure, when they know her husband is confined by pain. – Come, my dear Ferocia, you must not think that staying at home one night is an act of too much complaisance to a man who would refuse nothing for your satisfaction.

In speaking this he drew her gently towards him, and gave her two or three very tender kisses; but in doing so a little snuff he had between his thumb and finger happen'd to scatter on her glove; on which the started from him and returned his kind expressions in these terms:

Ferocia. Pish, how silly this is? – you have spoil'd my gloves with your nasty snuff. – Here John, William, run one of you to my dressing-room and bid Faddle bring me a pair of clean gloves in a minute.

Montelion. Don't put yourself into a passion, my dear, but sit down and resolve to oblige me; – I'll call for cards, and we'll have a game at picquet.

She made no reply, but hung down her head, and stood counting the sticks of her fan till Faddle came into the room.

Ferocia. Where are the gloves?

Faddle. Madam, I thought the fellow was mistaken when he bid me bring gloves, as your ladyship had just now a clean pair.

Montelion. Aye, mrs. Faddle, there is no occasion; rather get your lady's night-dress ready; for she has changed her mind, and does not go abroad.

Ferocia. Indeed I both must and will, my lord. – Do you imagine that because you are sick I must mortify myself, and be mew'd up with you till I am sick too? – No, – no, I am not weak enough to comply with so unreasonable a request; therefore adieu till morning, I shall scarce see you till that time, and hope I shall then find your lordship better.

She waited not for any reply he might have made, but flounced out of the room, follow'd by her woman. – Montelion soon after heard the footman call'd to attend her ladyship and the chariot drive from the door. – How would some husbands have resented such usage, even from the most lovely of womankind? yet Montelion bore it without any shew of impatience, from one endow'd with no charms to excite either love or respect; – his tameness, however, is not owing to any meanness of spirit in him, but rather to his good sense; – he does not care to have his domestic affairs become the talk of the town, nor to come to an open rupture with the woman he has made his wife; and having in vain essay'd all the means that prudence and good-nature could suggest, to bring her to a more reasonable way of thinking, he has at last given over the attempt; – seems not to regard whatever she does, but endeavours to lose the thoughts of his private disquiets in the toils of public business.

CHAP. II.

Relates a strange and most unnatural instance of bigottry and enthusiasm in a parent.

Nothing is so desirable as religion, – nothing so truly amiable as piety; – what blessings does it not diffuse to all who are within the reach of its influence? – from it all other virtues are derived, and by it alone are enabled to act with vigour; – yet how often have we seen this heavenly quality perverted into its very opposite; and, from the spirit of meekness, benevolence, mercy, charity and universal love, become the spirit of pride, contention, envy, hatred and persecution;

– like the arch-angel, who, standing nearest to the throne of glory, precipitated himself into the lowest hell.

Bigotry and superstition are the surest engines which the subtle enemy of mankind makes use of for our destruction; – all other crimes carry their stings with them; conscience reproaches us for doing amiss, and we fall not again into the like without extreme remorse and shame; but the man possess'd of this holy frenzy of the mind glorys in his perseverance, because he looks upon it as the highest virtue.

But this, indeed, is not an age in which errors of this nature much abound; – it has been much more the fashion of late years, for people to laugh at and contemn all the duties of religion, than to be too warm in the practice of any of them; – there are, however, some few examples of the contrary extreme, a melancholy proof of which I am now about to give.

A gentleman, whom I shall distinguish by the name of Flaminio, had attain'd to the age of 50, without having been known to be guilty of any one thing which could call in question either his honour, good nature, or good sense: – he had lived caress'd by his friends, respected by his acquaintance, and almost adored by his tenants and dependants; – he had one son and one daughter, and having lost his wife in bringing the latter into the world, he never ventured on a second bed, but laid out all his cares on the education of these two darlings of his soul.

Adario, for so I shall call the son, having finish'd his studies to the satisfaction of all those who had the charge of instructing him, in order to complete the fine gentleman, was sent to make the tour of Europe, under the care of a discreet and experienced governor. – Isabinda, the daughter, remain'd at home with her father, and being extremely beautiful, and mistress of every accomplishment befitting her sex and rank, attracted the love and admiration of as many as had opportunity to be witness of her perfections.

Being such as I have describ'd, it may easily be supposed, that, in a town like this, there were not a few who declared themselves her lovers; – Lysimor was among the number of those who had the least to fear, and the most to hope for, in his addresses to her; – he had an agreeable person, – was descended of a good family, and was heir to an estate adequate to his birth: – he had been fellow-student with Adario, and though, being some years older, he had left the University before him, they had always kept up a correspondence; – he was introduced to the acquaintance of the sister by the intimacy he had with the brother, who fail'd not, before he went abroad, to recommend his friend's pretensions to her in the strongest terms.

He it was, indeed, who alone had the secret to please her; – her young heart presently distinguish'd him from all his rivals; but her modesty and discretion would not permit her to give him any marks of the peculiar regard she had for him, till authoriz'd to do so by the person who she had always been taught to consider as the sole disposer of her fate.

Lysimor, who had also been bred in the most strict obedience, made not his court to Isabinda without having first communicated the passion he had for her to his father, and received his approbation; – the two old gentlemen had aftewards an interview on this occasion; and Flaminio, being perfectly satisfy'd with the proposals made by the other, readily gave his consent, on condition his daughter, whose inclinations he said he would never go about to force, should have no objection to the match.

The same evening, as they were sitting together at supper, Flaminio related to his daughter all that had pass'd between him and the father of Lysimor; and added, that he look'd upon him as a very deserving young fellow: – that his birth and fortune were unexceptionable; and that if she had no aversion to his person, he should be heartily glad of an alliance with him.

Isabinda blush'd like the sun just peeping from a cloud, on hearing her father speak in this manner, and could scarce recover herself from the glad surprize enough to tell him, that since he was pleased with such an union she should be all obedience to his will; – she said no more, but the soft confusion she was in, and the joy which she could not restrain from sparkling in her eyes, sufficiently testified how much her inclinations corresponded with her duty. – 'Well then,' resumed he, 'from this time forward receive Lysimor as the person by heaven and me ordain'd to be your husband.'

I leave it to my fair readers to conceive what delightful images must fill the mind of Isabinda, after this sanction to an affection which hitherto she had not dared to indulge, yet had it not in her power to subdue; – for my own part, tho' I was present during all the conversation she had with her father on this head, I left the house when she retired to her chamber, which she did more early than ordinary that night, I guess, to have an opportunity of giving a loose to the transports of her mind.

As for Lysimor, the joy he felt on being acquainted with what his father had done for him was very much allay'd by the perfect ignorance he was in of having made any impression on the heart of his charming mistress; – he went to visit her the next day, hoping, yet trembling for the event; but soon the lovely maid put an end to his suspense, by assuring him, that for his sake alone she could resolve, without reluctance, on changing her condition.

Not only the lovers themselves, but both their parents also seem'd equally impatient for the consummation of these nuptials; – a short day was appointed for the celebration; – the articles of settlement and jointure were drawing up, – new habits, – new coaches, – new equipages, – all necessary preparations were carrying on with the utmost expedition, when lo! – a sudden and unexpected storm bore down at once the pleasing prospect of their hopes, – for ever dash'd their expected joys, and spread a lasting scene of desolation and despair. – How vainly, alas, do we depend on mortal happiness? – the gaudy bubble fleets before us like the wind, – eludes our grasp, and mocks the idle chace, – as sir Robert Howard justly expresses it,

> Short is th' uncertain reign and pomp of mortal pride;
> New turns and changes ev'ry day
> Are of inconstant chance, the constant arts;
> Soon she gives, soon takes away,
> She comes, embraces, nauseates you and parts.[67]

Flaminio, from being the most chearful, good-natur'd man that could be of his age, became all at once transform'd into the most sullen, gloomy, and discontented; – from expressing the utmost eagerness for his daughter's wedding, he now appear'd wholly negligent of every thing relating to it: – when the father of Lysimor, and the lawyer employ'd to draw the marriage writings, went to his house, he order'd his servants to say he was from home; – made several tradesmen carry back the things he had bespoke for the solemnity; – and, in fine, put an entire stop to all he had been so solicitous in forwarding.

The father of Lysimor began to think himself affronted by this proceeding; and both the lovers were amazed and troubled beyond description at it; but tho' the young gentleman came once or twice every day to visit his dear mistress, Flamimio so carefully avoided his presence that he could get no opportunity of complaining to him, and Isabinda was too much terrified by the unusual austerity of of his looks to have the courage to open her lips to him on this score.

She was one afternoon alone in the fore parlour, waiting the approach of Lysimor, when her father, who was in a back room, call'd her to him; – she immediately obey'd, and on her entrance was accosted by him in this manner:

Flaminio. Well, Isabinda, I suppose you expect Lysimor here presently?

Isabinda. Yes, sir, – it is near the hour when he generally visits me.

Flaminio. His company may be spared at this time; – I have something to say to you, and would not be interrupted; – I have therefore given orders to the servants to tell him, when he comes, that you are gone abroad.

Isabinda. He will scarce believe that; – because I promised to take a walk with him in the Mall after tea; but if you require my attendance I will dismiss him the same moment he comes.

Flaminio. No, it shall be as I have said; – if you marry him you will have opportunities enough to see each other; and if you do not, it will be best for you not to have settled your affections upon him.

Isabinda. Sir, I should never have entertain'd the least thoughts of marrying either him or any other man without having first received your commands to do so.

Flaminio. However that may be, – events we think most near, are often the farthest from being accomplish'd; – and for that reason a young maid ought never to dispose of her heart till it is accompany'd by her hand.

Isabinda. I hope, sir, that Lysimor has done nothing to forfeit the good-will you once had for him?

Flaminio. No, no, I have nothing to say against the young gentleman; – and should still approve of him for a son-in-law; – but –.

Isabinda. But what! – I beseech you, sir, keep me not on a rack more cruel than death.

Flaminio. I am sorry to see you so much concern'd on his account; – I hoped to have found you more indifferent; but, since your inclinations are so deeply engaged, wish from my soul there were a possibility for your union.

Isabinda. Ah, sir, what prevents it!

Flaminio. A father's everlasting happiness or misery.

These words, the emphasis with which he utter'd them, and the horror that appear'd in his countenance, frighted the poor young lady almost into fits; – she started, – trembled; and, not able to comprehend the meaning of what she heard, the most terrible ideas came into her mind, and made her rather dread than wish an explanation.

She stood pale as a ghost, and motionless as a statue, while her father, greatly agitated, walk'd backwards and forwards in the room with irregular and disorder'd steps: – both remain'd speechless for some time; – at last, – 'I cannot as yet,' said he, 'bring myself to relieve the suspence I see you are in; but will do it soon; – retire therefore, my dear Isabinda, to your chamber,' continued he with a deep sigh, 'and invoke the almighty dispenser of blessings to give you that composure of mind, which can alone enable you to support chearfully whatever fate he is pleased to ordain for you.'

She went to her chamber as commanded; but whether to pray or weep I will not pretend to inform my readers: – I remain'd with Flaminio while he staid below, which was not long, then follow'd him up to his closet, where he shut himself in, plucking the door so hastily after him I had not time to enter; but, peeping through the key-hole, I saw he had thrown himself prostrate on the floor, with his hands and eyes lifted up to Heaven, seeming very earnest in devotion; – I left him in this posture, and return'd home much surprised at what I had seen and heard.

Impatient, however, to get some farther light into an affair which at present appear'd so mysterious to me, I went the next morning to Flaminio's house; – I enter'd Isabinda's chamber with a servant who was carrying in a dish of chocolate; – that unhappy lady was sitting leaning her elbow on a table and her head upon her hand, – her eyes red with the late fallen tears, and all symptoms of despair and grief about her; – but nothing being to be learnt here I went in search of Flaminio, whom I found in his dressing-room; – he was in a musing posture, but had a countenance much more serene than the day before; – I had not been many minutes with him before he rung his bell for a footman, whom he order'd to fetch Isabinda to him; – she presently came, and I was witness of the following extraordinary dialogue:

Flaminio. Sit down, my child; – I was to blame to leave you in the perplexity I did last night; but it was occasion'd only by my too great tenderness; – I could not easily resolve to tell you a thing which I fear'd would make you wish I had lov'd you less.

Isabinda. Sir, I have always look'd upon your paternal affection to me as the greatest blessing of my life.

Flaminio. I believe you have; and I had never any cause to think you did not return that affection with an adequate proportion of filial love and duty.

Isabinda. I flatter myself, sir, that no one of my actions has ever shewn the contrary.

Flaminio. None, indeed, my dearest child; – I ought not therefore to have doubted of your ready compliance in a thing on which my soul's eternal peace depends. – Tell me, my Isabinda, would you not willingly forego a trifling satisfaction to assure your father's happiness both here and hereafter?

Isabinda. I should else, sir, be strangely unworthy of the goodness you have shewn to me.

Flaminio. Well then, my dearest Isabinda, I will no longer hesitate to make thee the confidante of a secret which hitherto has never escap'd my own bosom; – it is a story will very much surprise thee; – but see thou mark me well, and be attentive to every particular I shall relate.

Isabinda. You may be certain, sir, I will be so.

Flaminio. Know then, that going into the country to take possession of that estate which you have heard devolved on me by the death of my uncle, I fell into the acquaintance of a young lady in the neighbourhood, called Harriot; – she was handsome, – I had a heart entirely free, and I became, as I then thought, violently in love with her; but marriage being a thing of too serious a nature to be agreeable to my inclinations at that time, the addresses I made to her were extremely private; – such as they were, however, they succeeded but too well; and, on my promising to make her my wife, obtain'd all the gratification my passion could require.

Having finish'd the business which had brought me thither, I set out soon after on my return to London; – Harriot took leave of me without much regret, being to follow in a few days, with her father and the whole family, the winter season coming on: – on her arrival she sent me immediate notice, and I provided a proper place for our private interviews, which were not seldom, my amorous desires being yet unsatiated.

Perhaps her youth, her beauty, and, above all, the extreme tenderness she had for me, might have engag'd me for a much longer time, had not the charms of your dear mother render'd all those of the whole sex besides contemptible in my eyes: – I ador'd her from the first moment I beheld her, – the flame she inspir'd me with was widely different from what I had ever felt before; marriage was no more a bugbear to me; – on the contrary, I burn'd, – I languish'd to be link'd in those glorious bonds with a person of such distinguish'd merit, and the means of attaining that felicity engross'd all my thoughts.

I now made a thousand excuses to avoid meeting poor Harriot, and when her repeated sollicitations drew me sometimes to her, my behaviour was so cool, so chang'd from what it was, that she could not but see into the cause; – in fine, she grew jealous, inquisitive, and soon discover'd my honourable attachment.

Tears, reproaches, and complaints, now furnish'd me with a pretence to quarrel; – I told her I would see her no more, and indeed she put it out of my power to break my word; for in three days after we had parted in this manner she died, – not without some suspicion of poison, as I have heard it whisper'd; – but whether she had recourse, in reality, to any such desperate method to rid her of a life she was grown weary of, or whether grief alone did the work of fate, I know not; but am but too certain, that however that might be, my ingratitude was the cruel cause, though she was too generous ever to declare it, and not one of all her numerous kindred or acquaintance had the least intimation of the intercourse had been between us.

The shock I felt on the first intelligence of this sad catastrophe is inconceivable, and would doubtless have made a lasting impression on me, if the progress I every day made in my courtship to the object of my virtuous affection, – the gaining her consent to be mine, – our marriage, and the hurry of pleasures attending that solemnity, had not too much taken up my heart to leave room for any other sensations than those of joy and transport.

Events once obliterated from the mind, by others of greater consequence to our happiness, seldom or never recur to it again: – a long succession of years pass'd over without any remembrance of the unfortunate Harriot; and it is but very lately that the thoughts of her have begun to trouble my repose.

But heaven would not suffer me to be always dead to a just sensibility of the crime I had been guilty of; – not many nights ago, whether sleeping or awake I cannot pretend to be positive, I saw, – at least I thought I saw, the figure of that injur'd woman stand by my bedside; – I heard her too, with a voice hollow, yet sonorous as an eccho, bid me repent, and attone for my past transgression – 'How shall I attone!' cry'd I. – 'Devote to heaven the dearest thing you have on earth,' reply'd the phantom, and in that instant vanish'd from my sight.

It is not possible for me to express, much less for you to conceive, the horrors I sustain'd after this amazing dream, or apparition, I know not which to call it; but am since convinced it was no other than my guardian angel, who, under the form of Harriot, instructed me how to attone for my crime; – and should I neglect or disobey his admonition, it would more than double my transgression and sink my soul down to the lowest hell. – 'Devote to heaven the dearest thing thou hast on earth,' the vision said. – Now what have I on earth that is truly dear to me, except your brother and yourself? – I have examin'd well my heart, and find that of the two you sit the nearest there; – it is you therefore, my Isabinda, that is ordain'd to be the sacrifice; – and, like faithful Abraham, I must submit to lay my darling on the altar.[68]

Isabinda. Oh, sir, you will not kill me!

Flaminio. Kill thee, my child, rather would I suffer this flesh of mine to be torn with burning pincers, – every limb dislocated, – my breast laid open, and my panting heart exposed to public view, than hurt the smallest part of thy dear precious frame; – no, – I mean to present thee a living sacrifice on the altar of piety; – to consecrate thee to the service of heaven, and to make thee, while on earth, a companion for the saints above; – in fine, my Isabinda, you must be a nun.

Isabinda. A nun, – oh heavens!

This poor young lady seem'd no less terrified with the word nun than she had been with that of sacrifice; – but my Tablets being quite full with the conversation already recited, and my memory a little treacherous, as I confess'd in the introduction to this work, I can present the reader with no farther particulars on either side; – all I can say is, that not all the obedience Isabinda had hitherto been practised in, nor all her father's authority, nor the arguments he urged, could either reconcile her to the way of life he enjoin'd, or oblige her to submit to it with any degree of willingness; and that her tears and intreaties being equally in vain to make him recede from the resolution he had taken, he dismiss'd her from his presence, telling her, in a very angry tone, that he had now done with persuasions, and should take measures to bring her to her duty more becoming his character as a father.

CHAP. III.

The author finds means, tho' with an infinite deal of difficulty, to make a discovery of some part of the unhappy consequences which immediately attended the cruel resolution Flaminio had taken in regard to his daughter.

I went no more to Flaminio's house that day, the greatest part of it being pass'd in transcribing the discourse inserted in the preceding chapter, and getting the impression expung'd from my christaline remembrancer: – I did not fail, however, to repair thither the next morning; – but gain'd nothing by this visit; – Flaminio was abroad, – Isabinda alone in her chamber, and the servants, from whose glib tongues I might have expected something would transpire, were all busied in their several occupations, and seem'd to think of nothing out of their own sphere.

I had never yet attempted to see how Lysimor brook'd the late delays had been given to his intended nuptials, so now took it into my head to go; – a servant, who was carrying out a wig-box, gave me an opportunity of slipping into the house; – I found the old gentleman with a letter in his hand, which seem'd to excite in him very great emotions; – but as he had just finish'd the perusal as I enter'd the room, and was putting it into his pocket, I could not possibly know any thing of the contents; – I was not, however, long unsatisfied; – Lysimor was return'd from a morning walk he had been taking, and enter'd a few moments after; – he appear'd in little better humour than his father, and, when he had paid the usual salutation, – spoke in this manner:

Lysimor. Certainly, sir, something very extraordinary must have happen'd to occasion this sudden change both in Flaminio and his daughter; – I have been to enquire of her health this morning after being disappointed of seeing her last night, and have a second time been deny'd access.

Father. I could have told you that, if I had known you had been there; – I have just received a letter from Flaminio, – see what the old coxcomb writes.

With these words he drew the letter he had been reading from his pocket and threw it on a table, – Lysimor snatch'd it up with the greatest eagerness, and found the contents as follow:

Sir,

An over-ruling fate deprives me of the honour of your alliance, and disposes of my daughter in a different manner from what I once intended; – I must therefore intreat your son will make no future visits at my house, nor take any steps to traverse those designs which I am oblig'd to pursue in relation to Isabinda.

As for yourself, sir, I hope you will impute this alteration in my conduct to what it really is, – an unavoidable necessity, and not to want of respect in him, who in all things else would readily subscribe himself,

Sir,
      Your most humble, and
            obedient servant,

                          Flaminio.

Surprise and resentment now seemed to strive which should be most predominant in the countenance of Lysimor; – he stampt, – bit his lips, – paused a while, then spoke.

Lysimor. This must be madness, – no man in his senses could possibly act thus. – What, – after expressing the highest satisfaction in the intended union between our families, – after the warmest professions of respect to you, sir, and of love to me, to affront both in so gross a manner, without the least cause given on our part; – tis unaccountable, – tis monstrous; – but I cannot think Isabinda shares in her father's frensy.

Father. Whatever she does, it behoves you not to think on her at all; – sooner would I have my family extinct, and my name perish to eternity, than have a branch of that stem grafted on a tree of mine; – and I should be sorry to find you mean-spirited enough to retain a wish that way.

What reply Lysimor would have made I know not, for the old gentleman was call'd hastily out of the parlour to one who waited for him in another room. – Lysimor, when alone, fell into a deep musing, – in which he sigh'd and frown'd alternately, and seem'd divided between his love and his resentment; – but whatever his thoughts were, he had not opportunity to indulge them; – a servant presented him with a letter, which he said was brought by a porter, who desired it might be given to his own hands, and waited for an answer.

Lysimor no sooner saw the characters on the superscription than the late paleness in his cheeks was converted into the most lively red; – he broke the seal with trembling impatience and found it contain'd these lines:

Dear Sir,

MY father, in an unaccountable caprice, tears me from your arms, and is resolute to make me a nun; or rather a martyr of me. – Prayers and tears are ineffectual to move him from his purpose, – I have try'd both in vain, and it is by flight alone I can avoid a fate more dreadful to me than all I can suffer by abandoning his protection; – if you have compassion, – I must not now say love, – assist me in my escape: – I have made no intimacies, – have no confidants on whom I dare rely in this distracting exigence, and there remain not four and twenty hours between me and the impossibility of averting the doom that threatens me: – I am at present a close prisoner in my chamber, and to-morrow, early in the morning, am to take coach for Dover, thence to embark for Dunkirk, under the care of a person whose vigilance I cannot hope to elude, and who is not to quit my sight one moment till I am, beyond redemption, lodged within the walls of a convent. – A girl lately taken into the house, pitying my distress, has promised to get this convey'd to you, and also to grease the hinges of the street door, that I may go out with less noise when the family are all in bed, which I believe will be pretty early, as my father is too much out of humour to see any company; – if you will take upon you the trouble to wait for me at the end of our street, next the square, between the hours of twelve and one, and conduct me to some place where I may be secreted till the search, which doubtless will be made after me, is over, I shall endeavour to earn a subsistence by such ways as I am capable of and fortune shall present: – if you ever truly loved me, you will not think this request too presuming, but rather be sorry for the sad accident that compels me to make it – I beg a line, in answer to this, may inform me what I have to depend upon from your good nature, and what hope remains,

For the forlorn,

And most wretched

ISABINDA.

The lover appear'd extremely touch'd with this melancholy epistle, and when he had finish'd threw his arms across his breast, and cry'd out,

Lysimor. Poor Isabinda, – what dæmon has taken possession of her father's brain! – but I should be even yet more cruel to refuse the assistance she implores. – No, – love, honour, and generosity forbid it; – whatever shall be the consequence I must, – I will defend her from the fate she dreads.

He then call'd his footman, and bid him order the person who had brought this letter to wait for an answer at some distance from the house, lest his father should happen to see him, and be inquisitive from whom, and on what business he came.

Having given these instructions, he ran hastily up into his chamber, where I follow'd, and saw him sit down to his buroe and write in these terms:

TO ISABINDA.

My for ever dear ISABINDA,

WHatever are my sufferings in this unexpected turn of our affairs, I cannot be wholly unhappy while I know you have had no part in the inflicting them. – Why do you unkindly make that a request, which you ought to be convinced you might command from my affection? – I have devoted myself entirely to your service; and no change of circumstances can ever make me withdraw a heart attracted by so much beauty, and confirm'd in its choice by so much merit. – Yes, my charming Isabinda, I am unalterably yours; and you may depend upon my love and honour for every thing you either do, or shall hereafter stand in need of: – I shall employ this day in procuring a proper place for your reception; and shall anticipate the hours you mention to watch for your enlargement, which I pray heaven to facilitate, and bring you safe to the arms of,

My dearest Isabinda,

Your ever faithful and

Most constant adorer,

LYSIMOR.

He had but just dispatch'd this when his father came into the room, and with a voice and air vastly different from what he had a few minutes before assumed, spoke to him in these terms:

Father. I believe, son, I have interrupted your dressing; – but no matter, – I bring you news to console you for the loss of your late mistress; – my old friend, mr. Countwell, the banker, has been with me; – his fair charge, Emilia, comes to town next week, and he has offer'd, for a small premium, to make up a match between you; – he assures me she is a most lovely young creature, – is entirely independent of any one, and has twenty thousand pounds in her pocket, which is more than double the fortune you should have had with the daughter of that fool Flaminio.

Lysimor. I am greatly indebted to your goodness, sir, and to the consideration mr. Countwell has of me; but, sir, you know I have long lov'd Isabinda, and you must give my heart some time to wean itself from its former attachment.

Father. Pshaw, – one woman, like one nail, will drive out the thoughts of another; – your heart must be strangely stupified, if it does not dance to the music of twenty thousand pounds: – remember, son, the estate you are to enjoy at my decease does not amount to quite sixteen hundred pounds per annum; and that I have been obliged to mortgage some part of it, to discharge the debts your extravagant elder brother contracted before he died; – Emilia's fortune will retrieve all. – Well, the breaking off your match with Isabinda is the most lucky thing that could have happen'd.

Lysimor. But, sir, we cannot be sure that the young lady will approve my suit.

Father. Mr. Countwell will manage that, – he is a shrewd man, – he knows what he does, and will undertake nothing without performing it: – you have only to say a few fine things to Emilia, which you know well enough how to do, when once you get Isabinda out of your head.

Lysimor. Sir I shall use my best endeavours to obey you in every thing.

Father. That is well said; – I want no obedience but what is for your own interest, and will leave you to reflect how many charms there are in twenty thousand pounds, and then you will fall in love with the fortune, whether ever you do so with the lady or not.

This conversation being ended, I recollected that I had some affairs of my own to dispatch, and began to think of retiring; but was prevented by Lysimor, who walking in a continued and very hasty motion about the room, obliged me to keep close in the corner where I had placed myself, and not venture to stir left he should rush against me: – at first I was a little vex'd at this confinement; but afterwards rejoiced heartily at it, as it gave me an opportunity of making a discovery which otherwise, perhaps, I should have found much more difficult to attain.

Lysimor, after ruminating for a considerable time, rung the bell for his footman, who, on his entrance, received for his first command to shut the door; – that done, he made no scruple to inform the fellow, who I soon found was in all his secrets, of the concern he was in for Isabinda; – the promise he had given of taking her under his protection; and the vexation he was in to find a proper lodging for her, so that his father might not suspect he had any hand in her escape, nor her own be able to discover where she was concealed.

To this the man, after a pretty long pause, reply'd, – that he had a sister who was a widow, and lived in a very remote and obscure part of the town; – that her house was clean, tho' small; – that her family consisted only of herself, an infant sucking at her breast, and a country girl who did the business of a servant; and added, that if the lady could content herself with so mean an abode, he was certain she might remain there concealed as long as she should think fit.

Lysimor seem'd overjoy'd at this proposal, and bid him go directly to his sister, apprise her of the affair as far as it was necessary, and give her a strict charge to prepare every thing in as decent a manner as she could for the reception of her fair guest.

The fellow went to execute his commission, and I slid softly round the room till I got to the door and follow'd him; but not to the place where he was going; for having already found, by the discourse he had with his master, the name and situation of the street, I had no business to take so long a walk, till something more material than the bare sight of it excited my curiosity.

Lysimor himself, however, was not more punctual to the time appointed by Isabinda than I was to know the issue of this adventure; – it wanted some minutes of twelve when I arrived at the corner of the square, and had but just posted myself under a lamp, when I saw Lysimor come muffled up in his cloak, and attended by his servant.

We had not waited above a quarter of an hour before we saw Isabinda steal out of her father's house, with a bundle under her arm almost as big as herself; – Lysimor, perceiving how she was loaded, made his man hasten to ease her of it; after which she rather flew than ran into the arms of her deliverer, for so she call'd him, – adding, – 'Oh can you pardon the trouble I have given you!' – To which he reply'd, – 'Call not that a trouble which I shall always look upon as the greatest happiness of my life.'

I could hear distinctly little more of what they said to each other, the footman being between us: – they walk'd very fast through the square, and down a street which turned from it, where a hackney-coach waited to receive them, and, as soon as they were enter'd, drove away with all imaginable speed: – I had neither the will nor the power to pursue them, return'd home to reflect at leisure on the passages I had been witness of.

CHAP. IV.

Contains some farther and more interesting particulars of this adventure, and shews that people, by flying from one thing which they think would be a misfortune, often run into others of a nature much more to be dreaded.

Much as I had condemned Flaminio for his bigotted superstition, I could not wholly absolve Isabinda for the step she had taken; – I wonder'd not that she was fearful of being forced into a state of life which few ladies of her years would chuse; but I wonder'd that she was not also fearful of putting herself into the power of a man who loved her, and whom she passionately loved; – she must certainly either not have consider'd the dangers to which she might be exposed, or have depended too much on the strength of her own virtue.

Besides, she could not be so ignorant as not to know that no woman can be made a nun, any more than she can be made a wife, against her will; and a less share of courage than she shew'd in this midnight elopement would have enabled her, on her entrance within the walls of the convent, to declare she had neither call nor inclination to receive the veil, on which neither the abbess nor the bishop of the diocess could have consented to her admission into holy orders.

It is true, that her father might have confined her there a pensioner[69] as long as he thought fit; but as this would not have answer'd his end in devoting her to the service of the church, by way of propitiation for his offenses, there is no doubt to be made but that he would shortly have recall'd her home; – and, perhaps too, been convinced of his folly in attempting a thing so absurd in itself, as well as cruel to his daughter.

I am sensible that many of my fair young readers will be apt to quarrel with me for my animadversions on Isabinda's conduct in this point, and cry out, – if they were in her place they would do the same; – it is very likely, indeed, that they would do so, and full as likely that they would meet with something to make them heartily repent of their inadvertency.

There are others again, who will say, – that they can have no compassion for whatever misfortunes may befal a girl who thus rashly throws herself under the protection of a man not akin to her; but I believe the number of those who are so hard-hearted will be very few, except some profest prudes, who exclaim violently against the least misconduct in public, yet make no scruple of giving themselves the greatest loose in private.

However, as people never were, nor ever will be all of the same way of thinking, it would doubtless have been the most prudent in me, not to incur the ill-will of any, to have conceal'd my sentiments on this matter, and left every one to judge as they pleased: – I have been something too open, I confess, and tho' my disinclination to waste paper will not permit me to blot out what I have already said, I promise to be hereafter more circumspect, and confine myself to the bare recital of such facts as shall come within my cognizance, without pretending to intrude my own opinion on the motives which occasion'd them.

To return, therefore, to the melancholy detail I am now upon; – having little to do with my time the next morning, I went to the house where I knew Isabinda was placed for shelter from her father's power; – I gain'd an easy access, the door being open, as is generally the custom in mean houses: – on my going up stairs I found the unhappy beauty sitting in a very pensive posture, leaning her head against the corner of a cupboard, which I suppose serv'd her for a larder, for I saw a small slice of butter and the remains of a halfpenny roll lying on a coarse earthen plate; frequent sighs issued from her breast, and some tears fell from her lovely eyes: – strange, indeed, would it have been if a young lady, bred up in all the delicacies of life, could have worn a chearful countenance in such a change of situation; – tho' as the fellow had told his master, the room and all the furniture it contain'd was extremely clean, and shew'd the housewifry of the owner, yet nothing could have more the face of poverty.

She seem'd buried, as it were, in a profound contemplation, when the sound of somebody coming up the stairs made her raise her head a little, probably guessing from whom it proceeded, – Lysimor presently appear'd and, on sight of him, a dawn of joy overspread her face; – he ran to her, – embraced her, and said the most tender things, intermix'd with some expressions of concern, that the necessity of her being conceal'd left him not the power of providing a place for her more suitable to her merit and his affection; – she could not now restrain her tears from flowing, which occasion'd the following discourse:

Isabinda. Ah, Lysimor, I beg you will not talk to me in this manner; but rather use all your rhetoric to assist my weak endeavours to suit my humour to my condition: – to be easy, I must forget what I have been, and wish to be no more than what I am.

Lysimor. You never can be other than the most charming and most worthy of your sex.

Isabinda. Alas, I have no longer any pretence to compliments like these; – I have now, as the poet says,

> No name, no family to call my own,
> But am an out-cast, and a vagabond.[70]

As such I must hereafter live; – and that I may lose all remembrance of my former state, I have brought away my jewels and best apparel, for no other end than to dispose of them, and purchase others more conformable to my future circumstances.

Lysimor. Torture not thus a heart to which you are dearer than the vital blood that gives it motion. – Can you believe I would suffer you to part with any of those appendixes to your birth and rank? – no, – I would rather add to them. – Do you not know that my whole fortune is at your devotion?

Isabinda. I must not, sir, accept it.

Lysimor. Why not accept? too scrupulous Isabinda! – But if you are above receiving the tribute of a lover, command whatever you may have occasion for on the score of a brother; – my dear Adario, I know, will readily discharge the obligation.

Isabinda. I am sure he will; and, on that condition, if Providence presents no other way for my support, will not refuse your generous offer.

Lysimor. Think then no more of submitting to any thing unworthy of your character; – I flatter myself our misfortunes are not of long continuance; – that your father will repent him of his cruel resolution, and mine forget the affront offer'd to his family, and we may yet be happy.

Isabinda. I dare not entertain a hope so distant.

Lysimor. You know not how prophetic my passion may prove; – in the mean time I should be glad, methinks, to be made acquainted with the motive that has caused this sudden revolution in our fate.

Isabinda. Tho' I am loth to expose the secrets, I might say the follies, of a father, – yet I can refuse you nothing.

Perceiving now that she was preparing herself to make a detail of those particulars I had heard before, and in a preceding chapter have communicated to the reader, I would not stay to hear a second repetition, but came away and left the lovers together for that time.

From thence I went to the house of Flaminio, where I found, as I expected, every thing in distraction; – messengers running backwards and forwards; – some returning from their fruitless search of Isabinda, – others going to places where they had not before been sent; – and the old gentleman himself so overcome with rage and grief, that he was scarce capable of giving the necessary orders for what he most desired.

Some other adventures, which I shall hereafter publish, then falling in my way, I had no leisure to make a second visit to Isabinda for the space of near three weeks; – but how shall I express my concern for that unfortunate young lady, when on my going thither I found her in the manner I did; and that all the apprehensions I had been in on her account had but too solid a foundation?

When wild desire presides over the heart of man, what is his boasted honour? – what his virtue? – what his regard for the happiness and reputation of the woman he pretends to love? – all shadowy nothing, – vain ideas, which, like the Sybil's words wrote on the leaves of trees,[71] are blown off and scatter'd thro' the air with every gust of passion; – but to proceed,

No obstruction being in my way, I pass'd directly up to Isabinda's chamber; but, finding the door fast lock'd, began to imagine she was either removed or had ventured out to take the air, and was going down again, when I was prevented by the murmuring sound of persons talking within; – I then put my ear close to the key-hole, and easily knew the voices to be those of Lysimor and Isabinda; on which I resolved to wait till the door should be open'd, and in about three or four minutes after the woman of the house came up with two dishes of chocolate and some biscuits on a plate; – she had the key in her pocket, and immediately gave entrance to me as well as herself.

It was now more than past mid-day, yet Isabinda had not left her bed, – Lysimor was sitting on the side of it as lately risen, having both his feet on a chair, without either shoes or slippers: – I was a little surprised at seeing him in this posture, till the chocolate being served, he said to the woman,

Lysimor. Has Jeffery prepared my boots, as I directed last night?

Woman. Yes, an please your honour, – he has so besplash'd them, and made the horse's heels so dirty, that one would swear they had come a journey of twenty miles at least this morning.

Lysimor. That's right; – it would have been ridiculous, after telling my father that I was going on a hunting-match with some gentlemen, to have come home as clean as out of a lady's bed-chamber, and perhaps made the old gentleman suspect some part of the truth: – but go and bid Jeffery bring up the boots.

Lysimor spoke this with a very gay air; but Isabinda hung down her head, and on the fellow's coming in hid her face behind the curtain, nor utter'd a syllable while he was in the room, which was no longer than to equip his master for departure.

Lysimor was no sooner ready, and his servant withdrawn, than he approach'd the bed and began to take his leave of Isabinda with a very tender embrace, accompany'd with some soft words; – she made no other reply for a considerable time than returning his caresses; but at last broke out into these expressions:

Isabinda. Ah, Lysimor, should you forget your vows, – despise the conquest you have gain'd, and leave me to lament my easy faith, how miserable, how abandon'd beyond the power of words to express, would be the condition of your Isabinda!

Lysimor. Unkind and causeless apprehension! – My dearest love, let not the thoughts of such impossibilities disturb your gentle breast; – could I be ungrateful, after being made happy in this proof of your affection, I must be lost to all sense of honour, – unworthy of the name of man, and even to breathe vital air.

Isabinda. Well then, – I must, – I will believe you, – nor repent what I have done; – but tell me, when will you come again?

Lysimor. To-morrow, if I can; – if not, you may depend on seeing me next day; – be assured that every hour will seem an age to me till I renew my joys: – farewel, thou softest, loveliest of thy sex.

He went, but, as I then fancy'd, with more the air of triumph than of real tenderness or respect in his deportment; – Isabinda then call'd for the woman of the house to assist her in rising, and I left the place with a heart full of forebodings for her future fate; indeed I truly pitied the ruin'd maid, and wish'd she never might have occasion to cry out with Monimia in the tragedy:

> How often has he sworn
> Nature should change, the sun and stars grow dark,
> E're he would falsify his vows to me?
> Make haste, confusion then; – sun lose thy light,
> And stars drop down with sorrow to the earth,
> For he is false;
> False as the winds, the water, or the weather;
> Cruel as Tigers o'er their trembling prey:
> I feel him in my breast, – he tears my heart,
> And at each sigh he drinks the gushing blood.[72]

My curiosity having received this painful satisfaction, I imagined not that any farther discoveries, at least that would be material enough to compensate for the trouble I should take, could be made in relation to these lovers, and therefore thought of returning no more, either to the apartment of Isabinda, or to the house of Lysimor.

I should, indeed, have endeavour'd to lose all memory of this unhappy transaction, if the talk of the town had not continually reminded me of it; – every one was full of Isabinda's flight; – few, if any besides myself, were acquainted with the motive of it; and none knew to what place she was retir'd: – and the perfect ignorance people were in on both these scores occasion'd various conjectures, and render'd the wonder much more lasting than otherwise it would have been.

But this was not all; – Flaminio, pierced through with grief and indignation on not being able to find his daughter; and perhaps too with some mixture of remorse for the cause he had given her to leave him, fell into a violent fever, of which he died, after languishing some days.

By his last testament he bequeath'd to his daughter, if ever she should be found, the sum of three thousand pounds, in order, as he caused it to be express'd in the writing, to keep her above the contempt of the world; and likewise, by the smallness of the portion, to keep her in perpetual remembrance of the false step she had taken.

Soon after this I received certain intelligence, that Lysimor was making his public addresses to a fine young lady with a very large fortune; – I doubted not but this was that same Emilia whom I had heard his father so strongly recommend, and was fired with the utmost impatience to see how poor Isabinda would behave on both these events; accordingly I went once more to the house where she had been concealed; but, to my great disappointment, found she was gone from thence; nor could all my search, joined with the assistance of my Invisible Belt, enable me, for some time, to discover to what part of the town or country she was removed.

CHAP. V.

Completes the catastrophe of this truly tragical adventure.

ADARIO had proceeded on his travels no farther than Paris, when the account of his father's death oblig'd him to return to England with all possible expedition: – soon after his coming I made an unseen visit at his house, where I found him, not like most young heirs, exulting in being the entire master of himself and fortune, and contriving in what kind of luxuries he should dispose of both, but full of the most sincere and unaffected sorrow.

He was, indeed, one of those few sons who look on the possession of an estate as no equivalent for the loss of a good parent, such as Flaminio ever had been to both his children, till that fatal caprice which drove his daughter from his protection, – had brought on her undoing, – his own death, – and was the source of other calamities of a yet more dreadful nature, as will presently appear.

The story of Isabinda's elopement, and the uncertainty what fate had since attended her, was a matter of great affliction to this young gentleman; – he loved his sister with a very tender affection, and had hoped to have seen her by this time married to Lysimor; but as his esteem for that friend was no way lessen'd by the match being broke off; and besides, expecting to be better inform'd by him of the particulars of that affair, than he could be by any other person, he was impatient to see him, and I found had sent him that morning notice of his arrival; for a letter, in answer to his message, was deliver'd to him while I was there, the contents whereof were these:

To ADARIO.

SIR,

I congratulate your safe return to England, and should gladly have paid my compliments to you in person, if that honour had not been prohibited by an authority which I must not presume to contend with; – my father, resenting the affront given by yours, which you cannot but have been inform'd of, has forbid me, under the penalty of his eternal displeasure, to converse with any of your family; – he was at home when your servant came, and heard the message you sent deliver'd to me, on which he repeated his former injunction, and exacted a solemn oath of my obedience to it; – you will therefore pardon my not waiting on you, and believe that the discontinuance of our acquaintance will always be extremely regretted by him who is,

With all due respect,
Sir,
    Your most humble and
        Most obedient servant,

                                        Lysimor.

'Alas,' cried Adario, throwing the letter from him as soon as he had read it, 'how cold, how distant is the air of this letter, – how different from those I have been accustom'd to receive from Lysimor! – I find that by one unlucky accident I have at once lost a father, a sister, and a friend.'

This epistle seem'd to increase his melancholy, and he sat in a deep resvery till the entrance of some persons roused him from it, and I quitted the house, perceiving they were only tenants, and came on business relating to the estate, into which I had no curiosity to enquire.

I thought that I had now entirely done with this family; for as Isabinda was not to be found, I expected nothing of consequence could be learn'd either at the house of Lysimor or Adario, so intended to make no more visits to those gentlemen; – chance, however, about five months afterwards, changed my resolution, and threw something in my way which no diligence of my own could ever have attain'd.

As I was going one morning on my Invisible Progression I happen'd to pass by the house of Adario, – he was at the door, and about to step into a hackney-coach which waited for him, when a fellow, who had the appearance of a groom, came running towards him, almost breathless with the haste he had made, and cry'd out, – 'Oh, sir, I have joyful news for you; – I beg your honour will turn back and hear it'. – These words reviv'd all my former curiosity, and, finding Adario comply'd with his servant's request, I follow'd them into the parlour, and was witness of the ensuing discourse:

Groom. Oh, sir, I have seen my young lady.

Adario. What young lady? – Not my sister!

Groom. Yes, indeed sir; – as I was going to fetch the horse your honour sent me for, I saw madam Isabinda looking through the window of a house at the corner of a little lane just by Islington.

Adario. Are you sure it was she?

Groom. As sure as I am alive, sir; – though, poor lady, she is much alter'd, – very thin and pale.

Adario. I fancy you are mistaken; – if my sister were so near London, she would certainly either have sent or come to claim the legacy left her by my father, which I suppose she has need enough of by this time; I am resolved to be convinced notwithstanding. – Do you think she lodges there?

Groom. Yes, sir, for she was all undress'd, and look'd as if she was just out of bed.

Adario. And can you know the house again?

Groom. O, yes, sir; – I took particular notice of it; – there is a pretty big area before it, with a hatch painted brown, and an high tree on each side.

Adario. Well then, – I will only send an excuse to the gentleman I was to meet this morning and go directly thither; – you shall get up in the coach-box and order the fellow where to drive; – but let him stop short of the house, that my sister, if it be she, may not be apprised of my coming before she sees me.

While Adario was calling one of his footmen to send on the message he had mention'd, I ran to the end of the street, went into a narrow dark passage, and pluck'd off my Belt; – then, having recovered the appearance of what I am, a real substance, I popt into an empty coach that had just set down a fare, bid the driver to follow wherever that went which he saw standing at Adario's door.

Both the coaches drove with such speed that we soon reach'd the end of our little journey; – I quitted my vehicle the moment I saw the other preparing to stop; but tho' I made all imaginable haste to put on my Belt, I could scarce have regain'd my Invisibility time enough to have enter'd with Adario, if he had not met with an obstruction in his passage from the woman of the house, who at first deny'd she had any lady lodg'd with her; – then said, she had none of the name he enquir'd for; – on which he reply'd with some heat, – that the lady might have reasons for concealing her real name; – 'But tell her', cry'd he, 'that mine is Adario; – that I am her brother, and must needs see her.' – On this she seem'd somewhat more compliable, and said she would go and acquaint the lady; – accordingly she went up stairs; but Adario was too impatient to wait her return, and follow'd her directly; – I was but one step behind him, and we were both in the room before she could deliver any part of her message.

Isabinda was adjusting something about her dress before a looking-glass; but happening to turn her head just as Adario was within the door, shriek'd out, – 'Oh heavens, my brother!' – and with these words fell back in her chair.

The woman went to fetch some water, – Adario ran to support the fainting fair; but happening to cast his eyes upon the table saw a letter lying there, the superscription of which was in Isabinda's hand, and address'd to Lysimor; – emotions more strong than pity at this time made him quit his sister to examine the contents of this surprising billet, which were these:

To LYSIMOR.

My dear, dear LYSIMOR,

FOR such you are, and ever must be to my fond doating heart; tho' I have too much cause to fear the tender epithet is now no longer pleasing to you. – Ah, Lysimor, how sad is the reverse of my condition! – from seeing you twice or thrice every week, I now see you not once a month; – and even then how cold is your behaviour? – how short your visits? – how cruel is this to one who neither can, nor wishes to enjoy any conversation but yours? – For pity's sake, if not for love, render my life more easy, at least for the present, whatever you do hereafter; – the infant I carry within me simpathises in its mother's anguish, and continually upbraids you with convulsive heavings: – even if your vows of everlasting constancy should be forgot, let some consideration of the unborn innocent, the pledge of our once mutual loves, oblige you to treat with less indifference its unhappy mother,

The ruin'd Isabinda.

P.S. I can no longer bear your absence, else would not have troubled you with this complaint.

What a letter was this to fall into a brother's hands! – Never did I see a man in such distraction. – 'Villain, – villain Lysimor! – wretched Isabinda,' cry'd he out; – then turning towards her; '– but there needed not this proof in thy own hand', added he, 'thy shame is but too visible.'

Isabinda, who by the assistance of the woman was now recovered from her swoon, but not enough to hear what her brother said, threw herself at his feet, and with streaming eyes address'd him in these terms:

Isabinda. Oh, sir, can you forgive my concealing myself from you?

Adario. Would to God that there were equal reason to forgive the cause.

Isabinda, at this instant turning up her eyes, beheld her letter in his hand, and cry'd out with the greatest vehemence,

Isabinda. I am now undone, indeed, – irrecoverably lost to all hope of pardon or of pity! – my shame exposed to him from whom of all the world it should have most been hid.

Adario. Rise, sister, and cease these unavailing exclamations; – your shame will receive no addition by my knowledge of it; – rather, perhaps, be remedied. – But tell, – and tell me truly, – has Lysimor ever promised marriage to you?

Isabinda. A thousand and a thousand times, and bound himself to the performance by the most solemn imprecations.

Adario. Then he is doubly a villain; – and, if you believe him, you are doubly deceived; – he courts another woman.

Isabinda, Indeed, of late, I have suspected this, and often accused him of it; – and he as often has forsworn it.

Adario. Mere words of course: – but say, – have you no testimony under his own hand of the promise he made you, either by letter or by formal obligation?

Isabinda. None, – none, alas!

On this Adario bit his lips, – walk'd two or three times about the room, – then paused and seem'd as if debating within himself in what manner he should behave; at last sat down, and taking the still weeping Isabinda by the hand, endeavour'd to asswage her grief.

Adario. Come, Isabinda, dry your tears; – love and credulity have seduced your innocence; – great has been your fault; – but yet I cannot forget you are my sister, and that you have no friend but me on whom you can depend for consolation: – what is past cannot be recall'd, but it may be redress'd: – be assured you shall one way or other have justice.

Isabinda. Ah, sir, I beseech you proceed not to extremities; – if by my crime you should be involved in any danger or perplexities, it would sink me quite.

Adario. I hope there will be no occasion; – Lysimor was once a man of honour, and may yet return to his first principles: – on this you may rely, – that I shall do nothing rashly nor inconsistent with your interest and reputation.

After this they fell into some discourse concerning the strange resolution Flaminio had taken of sending her to a monastery, the particulars of which the reader being already acquainted with, I shall pass over in silence.

When Adario took his leave, he did it with a great deal of affection; but I was much divided in my thoughts, whether I should stay with Isabinda, or follow Adario home; – the latter seem'd most flattering to my curiosity, as by many tokens I perceived he had something in his head which he was impatient to put in execution.

I was not deceived in my conjectures, – Adario was no sooner in his own house than he flew to his buroe, and without taking any time for deliberation wrote this epistle:

To Lysimor.

Sir,

Conscious guilt, without those commands you seem so zealous in observing, might well make you avoid the presence of a person you have so greatly injured: – when I recommended you to my sister, it was in order to become her protector, – not her undoer; – how cruelly you have abused this confidence, let your own heart remind you; – but I have some hope, how much soever appearances at present are to the contrary, you still intend to do justice to your promises to Isabinda, and the claim she has to your affection: – I need not tell you that you can repair the misfortune you have brought upon her no otherwise than by an honourable marriage; – I am ready to fulfil the agreement made between our fathers on that score, and give my sister the sum of eight thousand pounds, as was then stipulated; – if you comply with this proposal I shall be glad to see you at her lodgings, there to settle every thing; – if not, shall expect you will meet me in another place, and give me that satisfaction which every gentleman has a right to demand when he finds himself ill used: – I attend your determination, and am

Yours, &c.

ADARIO.

He sent this by one of his servants, with a charge to give it into Lysimor's own hands, and wait his answer; – after which, being told dinner was ready, he went down and placed himself at the table, tho' I believe with very little appetite; – for his countenance had upon it all the marks of the greatest inward disturbance, which was not at all lessen'd when his man returned with this from Lysimor:

To Adario.

Sir,

SINCE I find you are so well acquainted with a secret, which, for the lady's sake, I could wish had been inviolably kept, I think myself obliged to deal sincerely with you on the occasion; – you may be assured I can behave to no woman, much less your sister, otherwise than becomes a man of honour; – but marriage is a thing quite out of the question, as I am certain my father never would consent to it: – if any promises on that account ever escaped my lips, I remember nothing of them, and could make them with no other view than to give her modesty an excuse for yielding: – I am sorry, however, for what has happen'd, but you cannot be insensible of the frailties of flesh and blood, and must know, as well as I, that when two young people, who like each other, are much alone together, such accidents will naturally occur. – The resentment you threaten, on my non-compliance with your proposal, appears therefore to me a little unreasonable; – I shall, notwithstanding, be ready to give you the satisfaction you desire, at any time or place you shall appoint.

   Yours, &c.

Lysimor.

All the blood now seem'd to have forsook the heart of Adario to rush into his face; – his lips trembled, – his very eye balls started with excess of passion; – he hesitated not a moment on what he should do, but in this tempest of his mind wrote as follows:

To Lysimor.

Sir,

   I want words to return the insolence and ingratitude of your reply; but have a sword at your service, which I expect you will try the metal of tomorrow morning about seven, in the field behind Montague-house:[73] – as the dispute between us will admit of no witnesses, pray come alone, to

Adario.

Tho' I knew my own dinner waited for me, I could not prevail on myself to go home, till Adario had dispatch'd this billet to Lysimor, and the servant who carried it was come back from that gentleman with a small slip of paper tied up, containing only these words:

To Adario.

Sir,

You may depend that I shall not fail to meet you as desired.

Lysimor.

I now quitted the house of Adario; but after having related the pains I had already taken, I believe nobody will suppose I neglected going the next morning to the field, to see the issue of this combat: – I found Adario was there first; but tho' he waited only a very few minutes for Lysimor, his impatience made him not forbear saluting him in this manner:

Adario. I began to think, Lysimor, that the shame of having done a base action would not suffer you to defend it.

Lysimor. Sir, whatever I dare do, I always dare defend.

Adario. Then, sir, this is no time for words.

Lysimor. I am ready for you, sir.

Here ceased all farther speech between them, and on the part of Lysimor for ever; – on the second push Adario ran him quite thro' the body; – he fell that instant, and expired with only a single groan; – his successful antagonist approach'd the body, and finding life was totally extinguish'd, gave a sigh or two to the memory of a man he once had call'd his friend, then made the best of his way home, in order to provide for his own security, which the likelihood there was of the challenge he had sent to the deceased being found, render'd highly necessary.[74]

The measures he took, indeed, were very prudent; – he sent immediately to hire a post-chaise, which was to wait for him in a street he mention'd, at some distance from that in which he lived; – carry'd no baggage with him, but order'd a servant to follow him with it to Calais; – staid no longer at his own house than to write two short letters; – the one to a gentleman who had been one of the executors of his father's will, which being only on family-affairs need not be here inserted; – the other was to his sister, and contain'd these lines:

To Isabinda.

Sister,

Failing to repair your wrongs by the way I hoped, I have reveng'd them by the death of your seducer, for which I am obliged this moment to leave my native country, perhaps for ever; – I have done what the honour of our family exacted from me; – it belongs to you to regulate your future conduct so as to attone, in some measure, for the errors of the past: – to enable you to do this, you ought to keep in eternal remembrance, that the follies of your fatal passion has not only brought the object of it to an untimely grave, but also drove from all the social joys of life, into an irksome banishment in a foreign land, him who might have been happy, if he had not been

Your brother,

ADARIO.

Thinking, perhaps, he had been somewhat too severe in the above, he added this postscript by way of cordial:

P.S. I shall constantly write to mr. D – n, – he will be able to inform you how to direct for me; – you may be assured I shall receive with pleasure any letters that bring me an account of your welfare, and, in spite of all that has happen'd, to do you every service in my power.

After having sent this, by the groom who had first discover'd the place of her abode, and given some necessary instructions to his other servants, he hurry'd away to meet the post-chaise, and I saw him no more.

As I had truly pity'd Isabinda, I could not forbear going to see in what manner she supported this last dreadful accident; – on my entrance she was in bed, and surrounded by women and physicians; – I gather'd from their discourse, that the surprise and grief she had been in had caused an abortion, accompany'd with fits of a very dangerous nature: – on my next visit, however, I found her youth and the strength of her constitution had got the better of her disease; but though the pains of her body were removed, those of her mind still remain'd; – she was extremely melancholy, – had a thorough contempt for the world, and the thoughts of a monastery were now so far from being shocking to her, that she resolved to fly to one, as the only asylum from censure and from care.

Accordingly, as I was afterwards inform'd, she went, on the re-establishment of her health, to Paris, and enter'd herself into the society of the Benedictine nuns, where I doubt not but she often sees her brother through the grate, as he still continues to reside in that city.

I have now finish'd all the account I am able to give of this melancholy transaction, in which the justice of Providence seems to me to be distinguish'd in somewhat of a peculiar manner; and may serve as a warning to our gay amorous sparks, not to become the seducers of unwary innocence; – especially if they will be at the trouble of reflecting, how the perfidy and ingratitude of Flaminio, to the believing Harriot, was afterwards retorted on his own darling daughter.

CHAP. VI.

Gives the account of an occurrence, no less remarkable than it is entertaining; and shews that there is scarce any difficulty so great but that it may be got over, by the help of a ready wit and invention, if properly exerted.

To make some attonement for my last melancholy recital, to those of my readers who may not care to have their heads fill'd with subjects of too serious a nature, I shall now present them with one more likely to put in motion the risible muscles of the face, than to extort the falling of unwilling tears.

A gentleman, whom I shall call Conrade, had lived to the age of near seventy without ever testifying the least inclination to marriage; – he had been a man of pleasure in his youth, and probably the too great success he then found among the fair had deterr'd him from entering into an honourable engagement with any of the sex; – but there is no account for change of sentiment in this point, – an accident sometimes puts that into our heads which before we never thought of, or perhaps had an aversion to, – as it fell out in the case of the person I am speaking of.

A long friendship had subsisted between him and Murcio, a gentleman, who though not so far advanced in years, had made a better use of his time, – had been married, and was the father of three fine daughters, – two of whom had always lived with him; but the youngest, after the death of his wife, was taken from him, and brought up under the care of an aunt in the country.

The eldest of these ladies being now about to be disposed of in marriage, Conrade received, and accepted an invitation to the wedding; – Melanthe, sister to the bride, was a fine sparkling girl of nineteen; – but whether it were that she appear'd in reality more lovely than usual at this time, or that the mirth and pleasantries common at such solemnities rekindled the long smother'd embers of amorous desire in the breast of Conrade, so it was, that he, who had been in the company of this beautiful maid without ever taking any notice of her charms, now, all at once, became extremely smitten with them, – insomuch that from this moment he resolved on acquainting her father with his new passion, and asking his consent to make his addresses to her; which he did not at all despair of obtaining on the terms he intended to propose.

Murcio had a pretty country-house at a village about ten or twelve miles up the river, where he constantly went every Saturday, and staid till Monday or Tuesday, and sometimes longer; – it was while he was in this retirement that Conrade chose to communicate to him the business he had in his head; – accordingly he went thither, and found him entirely alone; – Melanthe having been prevented from going as she was accustom'd to do, by a violent fit of the tooth-ach; – this our old lover look'd upon as a good omen, being desirous to engage the father in favour of his passion, before he made any declaration of it to the daughter.

He began with saying, that he now repented having lived so long a batchelor; – that having a very large estate, he should be glad of an heir of his own body to enjoy it; – that if he could prevail on a young lady whom he liked to marry him, he would endeavour to attone for the want of youth by all the indulgencies in the power of a fond husband; – and having thus prepared the way, told him, that if he thought proper to bestow his daughter Melanthe on him, he would desire no other fortune than her person; yet would settle a dowry upon her superior to what might be expected if she brought him ten thousand pounds.

It is not to be imagined with what greediness Murcio swallow'd this proposal, – he did not even affect to hesitate, or make the least demur on accepting it; on the contrary, he reply'd, that nothing could afford him a greater satisfaction than such an alliance, and that he doubted not but Melanthe would receive the honour he intended her as a woman who knew her own interest and happiness.

Both parties being equally transported, every thing was immediately agreed upon between them; but Murcio not being able to assure himself that his daughter would so readily comply as he had made the lover hope she would, and fearing that if she should give the old gentleman a rebuff on his first onset, it might discourage him from making a second, and perhaps overturn the whole affair, resolved not to hazard the loss of so advantageous a match by leaving it to her own choice, sent a special messenger to her with a letter, the contents whereof are these:

To Melanthe.

Dear Child,

My worthy friend Conrade has taken a great liking to you, and will make you his wife on such terms as should but little prove the paternal affection I have for you to reject; – be not you less thankful to heaven for so unhoped a blessing than I am; nor, on any foolish pretences, either slight, or seem to slight, the good presented to you. – If you consider the vast advantages of this match, a disparity of years can be no objection: – I say thus much because I would convince your reason, not enforce your action; for I should be sorry to find myself obliged to make use of the authority I have over you in a thing which you ought, and I hope will receive with the same satisfaction I propose it: – know, however, that I have already agreed on every thing for your marriage, – that your future husband is now here, and we shall both be in town either tomorrow or the ensuing day: – I send this on purpose to prepare you to behave towards him in a proper manner, and as it is the absolute command of him who is

Your affectionate father,

Murcio.

I stood behind Melanthe's chair while she was reading this epistle, and never did I see a poor young creature in such terrible agitations; – scarce had she come to the end of the first period before she cry'd out, '– His wife! – his wife! – what terms can the old letcher propose to compensate for the odious title of wife to such a wretch!' – then going a little farther, 'Justly, indeed,' said she, 'does my father suspect my obedience in this point; – death itself would not be so dreadful to me as compliance.' – The more she proceeded, the higher her distraction grew. '– What, fix'd my doom at once!' raved she out; 'at once resolve to cut me off from all the joys of life, and condemn me to everlasting misery! – Is this a parent's love! – oh 'tis most cruel, – most unnatural!'

I know not to what extravagancies she might have been hurry'd, by the sudden rush of grief and despair, if tears now had not afforded their relief; – but tho' they a little soften'd the asperity of her passion, they had not the power to subdue it; her tongue, indeed, ceas'd from exclaiming against her fate; but the agonies of her countenance discover'd how much she inwardly regretted it.

While she was in this distressful and pity-moving situation, the gay, the lively Florimel came in; – this young lady was the most beloved and intimate companion that Melanthe had; – she saw her almost every day, and always enter'd without ceremony; – the seem'd a little surprised at first sight to find her thus, but immediately recovering herself, approach'd her with her accustom'd sprightliness.

Florimel. Heyday, Melanthe, – what in the name of wonder makes you in this pickle? – is your favourite squirrel dead? or has any accident happen'd to your last new peit-en-l'air?[75] or what other misfortune of equal importance has befallen you?

Melanthe. O Florimel! – what would I not give to be in thy condition?

Florimel. My condition! – why what do you find to envy in my condition?

Melanthe. To have no father to controle your actions by an unreasonable exertion of his authority.

Florimel. Why truly, as you say, these old dads are troublesome enough sometimes; – yet, for all that, I should be heartily glad mine were alive again. – But pray what has yours done to make you wish yourself an orphan?

Melanthe. Read that, and see if I have not cause.

In speaking these words she pointed to her father's letter which lay open on the table; – Florimel took it up and read it as desir'd; – on examining the contents, she could not help looking a little grave; but having finish'd, resum'd the discourse with her former vivacity.

Florimel. As sure as I am alive both these old gentlemen are crack'd-brain'd, – the one in thinking of you for a wife, and the other in consenting to give you such a husband.

Melanthe. One would, indeed, imagine they were not in their senses.

Florimel. For my part, I am so astonish'd that I can scarce believe I am awake. – But what will you do?

Melanthe. Nothing.

Florimel. Nothing can come of nothing, as king Lear says in the play.[76] – I am less surpris'd, however, at your stupidity in so perplexing a dilemma, than I am at the folly of those who have involved you in it. – Bless me, what can either your lover or father propose to themselves by such a disproportionable alliance, but horns on the one side, and disgrace to his family on the other.

Melanthe. No, Florimel, it shall never come to that; – I will rather work, or starve, or beg.

Florimel. Look'ye, my dear, neither working nor starving, or begging, as I take it, will agree with your constitution; – something else must be thought on.

Melanthe. What else?

Florimel. Do you think, that when your father comes to know what an implacable aversion you have to this match, he will not be prevail'd upon to recal the promise he has made to Conrade?

Melanthe. Impossible; – I know his temper too well to flatter myself with such a hope: – you might as well think to blow St. Paul's cathedral from its foundation with a single breath, as move him to recede from any thing he has once resolved.

Florimel. Well then, – suppose some way could be contrived to make Conrade himself fly off?

Melanthe. That would be a happy turn indeed; – but, dear creature, how can it be brought about?

Florimel. I have a project in my head that promises fair for it, if you will agree to join in the execution.

Melanthe. You may be sure I shall.

Florimel. It is this: – you must admit a spruce young gallant to lie with you all night; – Conrade must be inform'd of the amour, in such a manner as to make him convinced of the truth of it; and the duce is in him if afterwards he insists on marrying you.

Melanthe. Fye, Florimel; – how can you be so cruel to rally the misfortunes of your friend?

Florimel. No, I protest I am as serious as a judge upon a criminal cause; and would fain have you make the experiment I mention.

Melanthe. What, – would'st thou have me turn prostitute to avoid marriage!

Florimel. No such matter; – I will engage that the gallant I mean shall lie as harmless by your side as an infant.

Melanthe. Prithee do not torture me with such riddles.

Florimel. I shall presently explain them; – the gallant I am speaking of, and who is to be your bedfellow, is no other than my own individual self: – I shall put on a suit of my brother's cloaths, and do not doubt but that when I am dress'd, and equipp'd in all my accoutrements, I shall be a figure handsome enough to make an old man jealous.

Melanthe. Sure never was so wild a scheme; but yet I cannot conceive how it is to be conducted, or which way it can answer the end you propose by it.

Florimel. Lord, – you are strangely dull, or affect to be so; – but I will shew you what I shall write to Conrade, and that my help to enlighten your understanding.

This witty lady waited not to hear what reply her friend would make, but ran to a desk and immediately wrote the following lines:

To HUGH CONRADE, Esq;

SIR,

EVER since I heard of your intended marriage with Melanthe I have been divided in my thoughts, whether the treachery of betraying a secret entrusted to me, or by concealing it expose a gentleman of your character to the worst of mischiefs, would be the most dishonourable action: – the latter consideration has at last prevail'd; and I think it my duty to inform you, that the lady you are about to make your wife has neither heart nor honour to bestow upon you, – both are already disposed of to a person she thinks more agreeable to her years: – not content with the many private assignations she has with him abroad, she frequently makes pretences, when her father goes into the country, to be left at home, where her chamber-maid, who is in the secret, admits this happy lover at midnight, and lets him out early in the morning, before the other servants of the house are stirring, – Murcio being gone to *****, I am well assured it will be in your power to convince yourself of the certainty of this intelligence, by sending any one on whom you can depend to watch about the door, either for the entrance or exit of the favourite gallant: – act as you please, however, – I have discharged the dictates of conscience in giving you this timely warning, and am,

SIR,

Your most humble, tho'

Nameless servant.

This she gave Melanthe to read, and, as soon as she had done, was going to ask her how she approv'd of the contrivance, when the other prevented her by crying out,

Melanthe. Oh the wicked lying letter! – Dear Florimel, if this should be sent, and Conrade should shew it to my father, I believe he would kill me.

Florimel. 'Tis possible he may not shew it; – but if he does, you have only to prepare yourself for a little scolding and swearing; – the worst he can do is to

turn you out of doors; – and then, – to use your own words, it can be but working, starving, or begging.

    Melanthe. Oh, but my reputation, Florimel!

    Florimel. A fiddle of your reputation; – would you hazard nothing to avoid
being tack'd, till death do you part, to such a lump of decay'd mortality as Conrade? – besides, when the affair is all over, and you are once got free from this
cursed engagement, it will be easy, by unravelling the plot, to clear your reputation and reconcile you to your father into the bargain.

    Melanthe. Oh, Florimel, if I was sure of that!

    Florimel. Trust to fortune; – I will lay my life, that if you behave according to
my directions, every thing will go right.

    Melanthe. Well then, – tell me what I am to do.

    Florimel. In the first place, when your father comes home you must seem
to be as well pleased with the match as he would have you be, and pretend that
you are mightily in love with Conrade's estate, whatever you are with the man;
– then, as for the old wretch himself, you have nothing to do but to simper and
look silly when he makes his addresses, and tell him that you are all obedience to
your father's will.

    Melanthe. This is a hard task, and I am a very ill dissembler; – I will try, how-
ever, what I can do: – but Florimel, – there is one thing that neither you nor I as
yet have thought upon; – suppose Conrade should take it into his head to watch
the door himself, and draw upon you in his passion?

    Florimel. What if he does, – I shall have a sword as well as he.

    Melanthe. But not understand so well how to use it?

    Florimel. I don't know that; – but if I can't fight as well, I am sure I can run
much better; – so pray do not be under any concern on my account.

    These fair friends parted not till the night was pretty far advanced; all
which time was taken up with settling some farther particulars in relation to
their design. – Molly, the waiting-maid, was call'd in, and, after a vow of secrecy,
intrusted with the whole affair; – she seem'd a good smart girl, highly proper for
the business she was to be employ'd in, and readily promised her assistance.

    As I was very near as impatient as themselves for the success of this whimsical
enterprize, I went every day to Murcio's house, and found that Melanthe acted
the part she had been taught by Florimel so as to give the utmost satisfaction
both to her father and lover; – who now talk'd of nothing but to have the wedding solemniz'd as soon as the necessary preparations for it could be made.

    Saturday being arrived, I made it my business to enquire whether Murcio was
gone, as usual, to his country seat, and finding he was so, and that Melanthe staid
at home, concluded that this was the day on which the first wheel of the machine
was to be put in motion, therefore hurried away to the house of Conrade, where
I luckily came time enough to see him receive the letter from Florimel.

The wrinkles of this old gentleman's face were greatly agitated while he was reading this epistle: – at first his eye-lids extended themselves, and his brows were elated with surprise, – then were contracted into a frown of anger; – sometimes a sneer of contempt and unbelief lengthen'd the furrows round his wither'd lips; but the attitude of longest duration, was a pensive hanging down of his head, accompany'd with counting the hairs upon his little finger, out of which at last he started, and cry'd to himself, – 'Many reasons may be urged both for and against my giving credit to this story; – but whether built upon truth or malice, I have no need to be at the pains of considering, – the author has pointed out the means of being convinced, and I will take his counsel.'

As I could not be certain that he would continue in this resolution, and much less so, that if he did what the event of it would be, I went by break of day the next morning and posted myself over-against Murcio's house; – in a few minutes after, Conrade came, wrap'd in a cloak, but stood more aloof, yet near enough to see every thing that pass'd; – we had not waited above a quarter of an hour, before the door we watch'd was softly open'd, and a well-dress'd beau rush'd out; – Conrade advanced as fast as his gout would let him, in order, I suppose, to see the face of this invader of his hoped for happiness; but the pretended gallant was too nimble for his pursuit; – but dropt a piece of paper, as if by accident flirted out with his handkerchief; – Conrade immediately snatched it up, and found it was a billet; – the superscription seem'd to have been tore off, but the contents were these:

Dearest of your sex,

My father is gone into the country, and I have made an excuse to be left behind; – come at the usual hour, and Molly will admit you to the arms of

Yours.

I easily perceived that this was a second plot of the young ladies to corroborate the first; and it had all the effect they could wish, and was also productive of something else, which neither of them at that time imagined; as will appear in the succeeding chapter.

CHAP. VII.

*Is a continuance of this merry history, which presents something as little
expected by the reader as it was by the parties concern'd in it; and, if the
author's hopes do not greatly deceive him, will also afford an equal share of
satisfaction as surprise.*

IT is not to be doubted but that Conrade, after having received this double confirmation of Melanthe's transgression, gave over all intentions of becoming her
husband; – yet, by what I could gather from his looks, and some expressions he
let fall, the manner in which he should quit his pretensions was the occasion of a
very great conflict in his mind: – he was a good-natured man, and loth to accuse
this young lady to her father; – yet, to break off a match so far advanced, and
which he had so earnestly sollicited, without assigning any cause for the change
of his resolution, he thought would not only make him appear ridiculous, but
also put a final period to all conversation between him and his old friend; and he
probably continued undetermined in this matter till he found himself obliged
to talk upon it to Murcio himself, who had appointed to come to town the next
day, in order to sign the marriage-writings.

 That gentleman was at home, and having expected him some hours before he
came, began, in a pleasant manner, to reproach his tardiness; to which Conrade
reply'd very gravely, – 'I am, indeed, sir, somewhat beyond my time, yet, I believe,
soon enough for the business which now brings me.' – Murcio seem'd very much
surprised on hearing him speak in this manner; and poor Melanthe, who was
present, well knowing that this alteration in her lover's behaviour was the effect
of the plot concerted between her and Florimel, trembled for the event, and was
no less shock'd at the thoughts how much her innocence suffer'd in his opinion.

 It is uncertain what return Murcio would have made, for the other prevented him from speaking by adding to what he had said before, – that he had
something of a very extraordinary nature, and which required no witnesses, to
communicate to him; on which he made a sign to Melanthe to leave the room,
and she was no sooner withdrawn than Conrade proceeded, tho' not without a
good deal of hesitation, to declare himself in these terms:

 Conrade. Dear Murcio, we have long been friends, and I should be heartily
sorry that what I have to say should occasion a rupture between us; – for my own
part, there is no man living for whom I shall always preserve a greater esteem
than for yourself.

 Murcio. I cannot think, sir, that you have any thing in your mind should give
me reason to regard you less.

 Conrade. Reason is too frequently misled by passion, – I know it by experience, and shall be glad to find yours is more strong; – tho' I confess I have been

to blame, and am sorry things have gone so far: – but, sir, I have consider'd that it is now too late in life for me to think of marriage, especially with so young a lady as Melanthe.

Murcio. This is an odd turn, indeed; – methinks, sir, you should have consider'd this before you made any proposals of that sort, either to me or my daughter. – A treaty of marriage, sir, when concluded on and consented to by both parties, is a thing of too much consequence to be broke off by either, without putting the most gross affront upon the other.

Conrade. Not, sir, when it can be proved that the consummation would be equally inconvenient for both.

Murcio. As how for both? – my daughter has never made the least objection.

Conrade. It may be so; – yet I am well assured she neither does nor ever can regard me with that affection which alone could make either me or herself happy in being united.

Murcio. A mere whim; – a caprice of your own, founded only on the disparity of years; and I am amazed you should think of flying off from your engagement on so shallow a pretence.

Conrade. Perhaps I may have others: – suppose I know she loves another?

Murcio. Sir, I will suppose no such thing; – she love another! – no, sir, she has been bred up in principles too virtuous and too modest, to place her affections on any one, till my commands and the authority of the church make it her duty to do so; and I must tell you, sir, it is base in you to add to the ill usage you are about to give her by traducing her reputation.

Conrade. I scorn the unmanly thought: – be assured I have proofs of what I say.

Murcio. Produce them then.

Conrade. I will, since I find the justification of my own honour depends upon it. – There, sir, – read that, and be convinced.

In speaking this he gave Murcio the letter that had been sent by Florimel, which the other, after having carelesly perused, threw from him, and looking on Conrade with the utmost scorn, said to him,

Murcio. A notable proof, indeed, – there are few people without some enemies; – but this is a piece of scandal too gross, too stupid, and the invention too ill concerted to pass even on the most weak and credulous mind; and seems rather a poor low contrivance of your own, to evade fulfiling an engagement you have taken it into your head to repent of.

Conrade. You are free in your expressions, sir, but I believe it will presently be my turn to retort that contempt you so unjustly treat me with. – Do you know the hand-writing of your daughter?

Murcio. Yes, certainly I do.

Conrade. Then judge of the contents of this, and take shame to yourself for the injurious treatment you have given me.

The reader will easily imagine, that it was Melanthe's little billet he now put into his hands; but no one can conceive, much less am I able to describe the rage, the horror, the distraction, that shook the whole frame of this astonish'd parent, on finding himself no longer able to refuse giving credit to so terrible a misfortune. – 'Death and furies!' cry'd he, 'infamous, abandon'd wretch!' – Then, after loading her with all the foulest names that language could afford, he turn'd to Conrade, – 'Pardon me, dear Conrade,' said he; 'had an angel told me what you did, without this cursed testimony, I should not have believed the story; – but you shall have ample satisfaction; I'll turn this scandal to my family, – this deceiver both of you and me, out of my doors this moment; – never own her, – never see her more, but leave her to the miseries she merits.'

He was running out of the room, and 'tis probable, in the first emotions of his passion, would have done as he had threaten'd, if Conrade had not withheld him; and partly by force, and partly by persuasion, made him sit down while he reason'd with him in this manner:

Conrade. Dear Murcio, compose yourself, and be not rashly guilty of a thing you hereafter may repent of; – consider that the errors of one branch of a family reflect dishonour on the whole; – you have other daughters, who, tho' pure as innocence itself, yet, being of the same blood, may be suspected liable to the same faults; – for their sakes, therefore, rather smother than expose the crime of this fair offender.

Murcio. What! – would you then have me to forgive, encourage, and suffer her to continue in this shameful prostitution under my own roof!

Conrade. No; – but I would have you remember that she is still your child, and that it is your duty, as a father, to use your utmost efforts to retrieve her from perdition, not sink her deeper into it.

Murcio. As how retrieve her! – is she not already lost, – irrecoverably lost to reputation as well as virtue!

Conrade. Not so, I hope; – all yet may be well, if her seducer can be prevail'd upon to repair the injury he has done her by an honourable marriage.

Murcio. A vain expectation.

Conrade. 'Tis worth attempting, at least; – but first you must oblige her to discover the name of this too happy man; for you see, that either by design or accident, the direction to him is torn off the letter.

Murcio. I protest, in the distraction of my thoughts, I had forgot that circumstance; and also to ask you by what means this infamous scrawl came into your possession.

On this Conrade related to him all the particulars he had observed while he had been watching his rival's coming out of the house; and when he had done, in order to encourage Murcio to take the advice he had just given to him, added this description of the supposed gallant:

Conrade. I was very much vex'd that I had not an opportunity of seeing his face; but his back being towards me, and, besides, having the advantage of some twenty paces before me, I in vain endeavour'd to overtake him, but I took great notice of his dress and air, and do assure you he has all the appearance of a man of fashion, and such a one as to whom you could not reasonably have refused your daughter, even if this accident had never happen'd.

Murcio. He should have ask'd her of me then; – but I will call her down, and hear what she has to say. – No, – I cannot, – will not see her; – I know not whether the sight of her might not provoke me to some desperate action.

Conrade. I think it is best you should refrain seeing her, 'till you are more the master of your passion; – but as the affair we have been speaking of admits of no delay, – suppose you write to her.

Murcio. The advice is good. – Oh, what a curse it is to have a disobedient child!

He appear'd in the most bitter anguish of mind while uttering these last words; but, having recover'd himself a little, took pen, ink, and paper, and wrote the following lines:

To MELANTHE.

Thou scandal to my blood and name,

THAT you still live to receive this, thank the gentleman whom you would have wrong'd by carrying pollution to his bed; – he has obtain'd a reprieve for you on this condition, – that you declare the name and quality of your undoer, to the end that I may take such measures as I shall judge proper, to oblige him to do justice to the honour of a family of which you are the only blemish. – Think not to deny your crime, – I have the infamous witness of it under your own hand; but be plain and open in your confession, if you hope ever to obtain mercy either from heaven or

Your offended father,

MURCIO.

After having shew'd this to Conrade, he call'd for the waiting-maid, and with a stern voice and countenance, bid her give that letter to her mistress, and bring him an immediate answer: – I follow'd, and saw with what agonies poor Melanthe read this cruel mandate; – between the fears of what her father's indignation might inflict upon her, and the shame of appearing guilty of a crime her soul disdain'd, she was so much overwhelm'd, that for some minutes she had not power to speak; and when she did, it was only to utter this exclamation:

Melanthe. What will become of me! – oh this vile plot of Florimel's!

Molly. Lord, madam, do not put yourself into this flurry; – you know your father's temper well enough, and could not expect he would be less severe; – but it will be all over in time, and you must resolve to bear it for a while.

Melanthe. I cannot, – will not bear it; – I will go down this instant and disclose all, and clear my innocence!

Molly. Sure, madam, you would not be so mad. – What would you undo all so much pains has been taken to bring about, and be forced to marry Conrade at last?

Melanthe. Was there ever so terrible a dilemma! – what answer can I give to my father!

Molly. Dear, madam, say any thing; – tell him you are in love with the man in the moon, – the Great Mogul,[77] – say any thing but the truth.

Melanthe. How silly am I to ask advice of such a giddy creature! – but I will try what I can do.

With this she turn'd herself towards a table whereon stood a standish, – sat down, – paused a while, then began to write; but had scarce finish'd two lines before she left off, – tore the paper; – mused again, and then began afresh; – the second essay met with the same fate as the former, and so did several succeeding ones, till at last she threw the pen out of her hand, – started up and said,

Melanthe. 'Tis in vain to attempt it, – I cannot write; – can find nothing to say that will abate my father's rage.

Molly. Why then, madam, say nothing, – e'en let him think as he pleases at present; – if you will but pluck up a spirit we shall do well enough; – he will not kill you for his own sake; and as for any thing else you must content yourself to submit to it; – nothing can be so bad as marrying Conrade. – I will go to Florimel presently; if I am so lucky as to find her at home, 'tis ten to one but she puts something into our heads.

Melanthe. Do so; – I wish she were here.

While they were speaking Murcio call'd very loud at the bottom of the stairs for Molly to come down, on which she said:

Molly. Do you hear, madam; – but I must face the storm for fear it should come hither and terrify you worse. – I wish you had as much courage as I have.

She said no more, but ran hastily down into the parlour, where I with no less speed attended her foot-steps, quite impatient to hear how the pert baggage would behave.

Murcio. What is the reason, minx, that I have no answer to the letter you carry'd up?

Molly. Lord, sir, there were somewhat or other in that letter that has frighted my poor lady almost out of her wits; – she does nothing but cry and wring her hands, – it would make your heart ake to see her. – She write an answer! – no indeed, – she is not in a condition to give an answer.

Murcio. If she can't you must, hussey. – Who was that fellow you let out of my house yesterday morning?

Molly. I, sir, – I let out no fellow, not I.

Murcio. 'Tis false; – my friend here, happening to pass through the street at that time, saw him come out.

Molly. Why then, sir, your friend is no better than a pickthank[78] for bringing you such idle stories; and I am not afraid to tell him so to his face. – I say again, I let out no fellow.

Murcio. Was there ever such impudence!

Conrade. Come, come, mrs. Molly, you had better confess the truth, – it will be for the good of your lady, and yourself too.

Molly. Sir, I shall not tell a lye for the matter; – I let out no fellow; – there was a fine gentleman, indeed, that sat up all night playing at cards with my lady, that I let out; – but no fellow I assure you.

Murcio. Well, – and pray mrs. brazenface, what is the name of this fine gentleman?

Molly. Lord, sir, do you think I know the names of all the gentlemen that come to visit my lady? – indeed I am not so impertinent as to ask.

Murcio. No equivocation; – tell me this moment or I shall be your death.

Molly. Bless me, sir, – how can you fright a body so for nothing! – but if you would be my death twenty times over I can say no more than I have done.

Conrade. Dear Murcio, this girl is not worth the passion you are in, – I hope the young lady herself will satisfy you, when once she considers how much it is her interest to do so.

Murcio. Not while she has such a harden'd wretch to encourage her obstinacy. – Hussey, pack up all your trumpery, and get out of my house directly, or I shall provide a place for you in Bridewell.

Molly. Oh, dear sir, I shall not give you that trouble; – there are places enough to be had without your providing.

After she had left the room, and Murcio had vented his passion in two or three hearty curses, he turn'd to Conrade, and, with a tone of voice which express'd the deepest trouble of mind, utter'd these words:

Murcio. You see, my dear friend, that both mistress and maid are alike incorrigible. – What now remains for me to do, either to preserve my family from disgrace, or this degenerate girl from everlasting ruin?

The other, who doubtless condemn'd Melanthe more in his heart than he would let her father know he did, could find nothing to say in her defence; but that he hoped, when the first confusion of this discovery was a little over, she would be brought to reason; and therefore intreated he would allow her some small time to recollect herself.

As the conversation now began to consist only of railings on the one side, and persuasions to moderation on the other, I easily perceived that nothing of importance would be the result, so resolved to leave the two old gentlemen together, and accordingly laid hold of the first opportunity to get out of the house.

CHAP. VIII.

Presents something as little expected by the reader as it was by the parties concern'd in it; and, if the author's hopes do not deceive him, will also afford an equal share of satisfaction as surprise.

BEING very anxious for the situation of poor Melanthe, I fully design'd to make another visit to Murcio's house early the next morning; but I had no sooner got my Tablets clear'd of the impression made on them the preceding day, than some company coming in detain'd me at home till the hour in which I usually dined, and then being told the table was spread, I sat down; but made a very short repast, being always more eager to gratify the cravings of my mind than my sensual appetite.

I came to Murcio's door when Conrade had just alighted from his coach and was stepping in, so I had an easy access, and follow'd him up into the dining-room, where Murcio was then sitting, and express'd the satisfaction he took in seeing him in words to this effect:

Murcio. My dear friend, I am glad you are come to give me your opinion in a thing I am about to do: – my ungracious daughter has given me no answer, – made me no submissions; – I cannot suffer her in my house; and, if I turn her out of it, am in danger of having my whole family scandalized by her behaviour; – I am therefore resolved to send her down to the farthest part of Cornwall, where I have a near kinsman; – I was going to write to him on that occasion when I heard you were here.

Conrade. I flatter myself, sir, that the intelligence I bring will save you that trouble, and the young lady so long a journey: – I have discover'd her favourite lover.

Murcio. Is it possible! – for heaven's sake who, – what is he!

Conrade. One you little suspect, tho' I have seen him often here; – tis Dorimon.

Murcio. Dorimon! – yes, since his return from his travels he visits here sometimes; – his sister, Florimel, and Melanthe were brought up together at the boarding-school, and since they left it have scarce been two days asunder: – but I cannot think Dorimon has been her seducer: – she is neither above his hopes nor below his expectations: – if he had any inclinations towards her, I know of nothing should hinder him from making his honourable addresses. – But what grounds have you for such a supposition?

Conrade. You shall hear: – you know I told you that I did not see the face of the gentleman that came out of your house on Sunday morning; but as I follow'd him a good part of the street I took notice of his habit, which, indeed, had somewhat particular in it, and would have attracted my observation had I seen it on any other person; – it was a dark olive colour'd French barragon,[79] laced with a very rich Point d'Espagne down the seams; – he had also a fine flaxen wig, with a bag[80] and solitair[81] of an uncommon dimension; – I then took him either for a foreigner, or one lately come from abroad; – in the same dress, and as exactly as I saw him then, did I see him within this half hour at the chocolate-house: – I cannot, indeed, swear to the man, but I think may safely do so as to the cloaths; especially as I heard himself say, on some gentleman's praising the suit, and telling him they believed there was not such another in England, that he was pretty sure there was not; for he had bespoke it at Paris, according to his own taste, and it had not been come over long enough for any one to take a pattern by it.

Murcio. I must own that there is a strong probability in what you say; but yet, without a certainty, know not what measures I can pursue.

Conrade. If you will take my advice, – send for him; – I heard him say he should dine at home, – so is scarce gone out; – give some distant hints, at first, concerning a marriage with your daughter; and, according to the answers he makes, you will be instructed how to proceed.

Murcio. It shall be so; – I will not let him see I have any suspicion of my daughter's fault; – and, whether there be any thing between them or not, a proposal of the nature you mention cannot seem strange to him, as our families have always lived together in a perfect harmony and good understanding.

He had no sooner said this than he call'd a servant and sent him with his compliments to Dorimon, and to let him know he desired to speak with him immediately, if not otherwise engaged.

After this the two friends had some farther discourse, concerning what steps the father of Melanthe should take in this affair; when the fellow, who had been sent on the above message, return'd and told his master, that Dorimon said he would not fail doing himself the honour of obeying his commands in a few minutes; on which Conrade took his leave, and Murcio sat down, endeavouring to frame his temper and countenance so as to be suitable to the business he had in hand.

Dorimon appear'd in a short time, and the first compliments being past, Murcio began to open what he had to say, by telling him that he had a great regard for his family; – that he was a fine young gentleman; and that being now five and twenty, he much wonder'd that he had not heard of his addressing some lady on the score of marriage; – to which Dorimon reply'd, that marriage was a thing he had not as yet much thought upon; and that having a sister who took care of the affairs of his houshold, a wife was the less necessary to him. – Murcio then demanded, if he found any averseness in himself to changing his condition in favour of a woman of equal birth and fortune, and who would approve of his pretensions. – Dorimon seem'd a little surprised at these interrogatories; but answer'd in the negative, with this proviso, that the person of the lady were equally agreeable. – Murcio, thinking this reply a proper cue for explaining himself, did so in the following manner:

Murcio. What think you then of my daughter Melanthe?

Dorimon. As of an angel, sir, above my hopes.

Murcio. No fine speeches, Dorimon; – deal sincerely with me. – Do you like her well enough to marry her?

Dorimon. Yes, sir, upon my soul; – and should bless the hand that gave her to me.

Murcio. Sir, I take you at your word, and give you mine that you shall have her, and six thousand pounds, if you think that a sufficient dower.

Dorimon. I do, sir, and though Melanthe is a sufficient fortune of herself, shall accept your offer as a father's blessing, and make a settlement accordingly.

Murcio. Then there remains no more than to get the marriage-articles drawn up, which, if you please, shall be tomorrow morning.

Dorimon. It cannot be too soon. – But, sir, may I not have leave to see the lovely Melanthe, – to throw myself at her feet, and be assur'd she will not regret the happiness you bestow upon me?

Murcio. Oh, sir, you have nothing to apprehend on that account; for, to be plain with you, I design'd her for another; – she rejected the proposal, for which she has been under some disgrace with me; but as I have since discover'd her disobedience was occasion'd by the affection she has for you, I was the more easily induced to pardon it: – she does not yet know that I consent to gratify her inclinations; but you shall have the pleasure of telling her yourself.

He then went to the door and order'd a servant to bid Melanthe come down; after which he turn'd back and said to Dorimon,

Murcio. My daughter will wait on you presently; I know you will excuse my leaving you together, – I have business calls me abroad; but expect to see you tomorrow morning, and shall have a lawyer here.

Dorimon. You may be certain, sir, I shall not fail.

The other said no more, but went hastily away to avoid seeing his daughter; – he had not left the room above half a minute before Melanthe enter'd, but with a confusion impossible to be express'd; – she had expected no other, on being call'd down, than to meet some terrible effects of her father's displeasure; – her eyes, yet red with tears, were now cast down upon the floor, as she advanced with slow and and trembling steps; – nor saw she who was there, till Dorimon sprung forward, and took her by the hand with these words:

Dorimon. Charming Melanthe, how am I transported at the goodness of your father! – how incapable of expressing my gratitude for the permission he has just now given me of telling you how much, how truly I adore you!

Melanthe. Bless me, Dorimon, what is the meaning of all this! – Where is my father!

Dorimon. Gone, to give me the happy opportunity of endeavouring to inspire you with sentiments in favour of my passion, and conformable to his will.

Melanthe. Your passion, and his will! – Certainly, Dorimon, you must either be mad, or I not in my senses. – For heaven's sake explain this mystery!

He was going to reply when his sister Florimel came tripping in, – that young lady having been inform'd by Molly of all that had pass'd at Murcio's house, was extremely impatient to know how her fair friend behaved afterwards on that occasion; – Melanthe no sooner saw her than the flew into her arms, and cry'd,

Melanthe. My dear, dear Florimel, what would I not have given to have seen you last night!

Florimel. I was no less eager to be with you; – but I find that things have quite chang'd their face since then; – I met your father at the door as I enter'd; – the old gentleman seems to be in quite good humour, desir'd me to walk up, and told me I should find you and my brother together.

Dorimon. Ay, my dear sister, we are together, and I hope shall soon be joined to separate no more.

Florimel. Separate no more! as how!

Dorimon. By the solemn and indissoluble ties of marriage; – Murcio, the generous Murcio, has bestowed her on me.

Florimel. What, is it agreed upon!

Dorimon. Absolutely; – to-morrow the articles are to be drawn between us, and there will then be nothing wanting but my angel's consent for the consummation of my bliss.

Florimel. And was this the business on which he sent for you in such haste?

Dorimon. The same.

Here Florimel burst into so violent a fit of laughter as render'd her unable to speak for some time; – in vain Dorimon asked several times over the cause of this extravagant mirth; and it was but by degrees she recovered herself enough to make this reply:

Florimel. I have found out the riddle; – it was I, brother, that have made this match.

Dorimon. You!

Florimel. Yes, with the assistance of that suit of cloaths you have on.

Then, addressing herself to Melanthe, proceeded thus:

Florimel. You must know, my dear, that it was Conrade himself that watch'd me coming out of your house, – I saw him stand perdu[82] under sir Thomas *******'s porch; – he has certainly seen my brother in these cloaths, and, mistaking him for me, has pass'd him upon your father for your supposed gallant.

Melanthe. It must be so, indeed; – there is no other way of accounting for this odd event.

Dorimon was now as much confounded in his turn, as the two ladies had been in theirs, till his sister, having first obtain'd Melanthe's leave, related to him the whole history of their contrivance to break the match with Conrade; – this repetition occasion'd some pleasantry between the brother and the sister; but Melanthe was too much asham'd to bear any great part in it; – her new lover, observing her seriousness, spoke in this manner:

Dorimon. I have got nothing, Florimel, by the account you have given, but the mortification of that vanity Murcio had inspired me with; and dare not now flatter myself that Melanthe will so readily, as I once hoped, acquiesce in the agreement made between us.

Florimel. If she does not all will come out; and if so, Murcio will certainly return to his first engagement to give her to Conrade. – What say you, Melanthe, have you aversion enough for my brother to run so great a risque?

This demand made Melanthe blush excessively; – she paused, – hung down her head; but at last made this return:

Melanthe. So sudden a change in my fortune, might well excuse me from giving a direct answer to such a question: – of this, however, you may be assur'd that I have not courage to disobey my father a second time, and that I love the sister too well to have any aversion to the brother.

On this Dorimon kiss'd her hand with a great deal of warmth, and said many tender and passionate things to her, which, as the reader will easily conceive, I think it needless to repeat; and shall only add, that between the brother and the sister Melanthe was at last prevail'd upon to confess, – that it would be without the least reluctance she should obey her father in the choice he had now made for her.

Tho' there now was little cause to apprehend any disappointment in these nuptials, yet I resolved to see the thing fully concluded on; accordingly I went the next morning to Murcio's house, where I found him very busy with his lawyer; – Dorimon came in soon after, and the writings were presently fill'd up, sign'd, seal'd, and duly executed by both parties: – the lawyer staid no longer than to receive his fees, and he had no sooner left the room, than Murcio spoke to Dorimon in these terms:

Murcio. Well, Dorimon, I think there is nothing now wanting for the making you my son, except the ceremony of the church; and I did not care how soon that also was perform'd; – I do not love to see affairs of this nature kept long in hand;

– besides, you must know, that on my daughter's refusing to marry the person I first proposed to her, I swore in my passion that I would never see her face again till she was a wife.

Dorimon. You may be assured, sir, I shall think every moment an age till I can prevail upon the lovely Melanthe to take that name; and I do not doubt but her knowledge of the vow you have made will very much expedite my wishes.

Murcio. I am going directly to my little country seat, and shall leave you to consult with her about the day; but will write to the rector of ****, who is my kinsman, and desire he will perform the office of tacking you together; – when that is over, would have you both come down to *****, where you may depend on meeting with a fatherly reception.

Nothing farther of any consequence was said by either of them, – Murcio took coach for the country, and Dorimon went to the appartment of his mistress, where strenuously pressing her for the speedy consummation of his happiness, her father's pretended vow serv'd as an excuse for her compliance, and she consented that the wedding should be solemnized on the next Sunday after.

No accident retarded the fulfilling this agreement, and they were married on the day appointed, by the reverend gentleman recommended by Murcio; after which they set out, accompany'd by Florimel, for *****, in order to receive the blessing he had promised to bestow upon them.

As no one of this company had any reason to be discontented at what had happen'd, it is not to be doubted but the goddess of cheerfulness accompany'd them in their little journey; – I say journey, because the sister of Dorimon having an aversion to the water, especially in rough weather, as it was that day, they went in a landau, in complaisance to her; but the subject of their conversation is not in my power to relate, as I had no opportunity of being witness of it.

CHAP. IX.

Contains a succinct account of some farther particulars, in some measure
relative to the foregoing adventure, and, besides, are of too agreeable and
interesting a nature in themselves not to be look'd upon as a rightly judged,
and very necessary appendix.

Having married my two new made lovers, the reader will possibly imagine, that the last act of the play is ended, and that I should now drop the curtain, to prepare for some fresh subject of entertainment; – but he must wait awhile, – I have not yet done with any of my characters; and besides, that there are many things which seem to require a farther explanation, I cannot think of parting with my favorite Florimel without giving her those praises which her wit and good humour may justly claim.

It is not unlikely, indeed, but that there may be some over scrupulous ladies in the world who will be so far from approving the character of this charming girl, that they will highly contemn her for assuming the air and habit of a man, tho' for never so short a space of time; and even rail at Melanthe for consenting to put in execution the stratagem she had contrived for her deliverance from an evil so justly dreaded by her; – such as these will certainly think I have said enough, if not too much on the occasion, and perhaps throw aside the book, and cry they will read no farther: – well, – be it so, – the loss will be entirely their own, – I am pretty confident neither my reputation, nor the profits of my publisher, will suffer by their ill-nature in this point.

It is for the entertainment of the gay, the witty, and the truly virtuous, who, by the way, are never censorious, that these lucubrations are chiefly intended; and if I am so fortunate as to please them, should give myself no great pain what may be said of me by those of the abovemention'd class.

In defiance, therefore, of these fair, or rather unfair critics, I shall proceed in what I have farther to relate concerning the principal subjects of this narrative.

On their arrival at ***** they were received by Murcio with a shew of the greatest satisfaction, yet I, who took care to be there before them, in order to be witness of what should pass at this first interview, could easily perceive that he embraced his son-in-law with more cordiality and less constraint than he did his daughter; – the remembrance of her supposed fault it was that doubtless render'd him unable to treat her with his accustom'd tenderness; – he scarce touch'd her cheek in saluting her, and when he gave her his blessing added, – 'Pray heaven your future conduct may deserve it.'

It could not be otherwise, but that all the company must comprehend the full meaning of these words; but poor Melanthe was so much affected by them, that she burst into a flood of tears, and throwing herself a second time at her father's feet, address'd him in these pathetic terms:

Melanthe. Oh, sir, – I beg, – I beseech you, by all the love you once had for me, to forgive the only act of disobedience I was ever guilty of; – pardon but the aversion I had to the match you first proposed to me, and you will easily absolve the rest.

Dorimon. Yes, sir, – my dear, – my charming wife, is as innocent of every thing that can deserve your blame, as I am from even the most distant wish of violating her purity or dishonouring your family.

Florimel. Ay, ay, – it is poor me that am alone in fault; but since the mischief I have done has been productive of so much good, I scarce doubt of being excused by a gentleman of so much good sense as Murcio. – I have deliver'd your daughter, sir, by my contrivance, from the horrors of a forced marriage; – I have procur'd a wife for my brother, with whom, if he is not the most happy, I am certain he deserves to be the most miserable of all mankind; and I have got you a son-in-law who I hope will merit that honour by his future behaviour.

Murcio, who could not form even the most distant guess at the meaning of all this, look'd sometimes on the one and sometimes on the other, with all the tokens of the utmost amazement, without being able to speak one syllable; which gave Florimel the opportunity of unravelling the whole mystery of the affair, as she had before promised Melanthe to take upon herself to do.

In spite of the little resentment Murcio at first conceived for the trick had been put upon him, he could not forbear smiling within himself at the invention of the contriver; and the wit and spirit with which that young lady talk'd to him upon it, very much contributed to bring him into good humour; but that which entirely reconciled him to the wedded pair, was the consideration that Dorimon was wholly ignorant of the plot till after the marriage was concluded, and the assurance Melanthe gave him, that she was far from any intention to deceive him, but had flatter'd herself with the hope that Conrade would have broke the engagement, without mentioning to him the reasons he had for doing so.

Though to have married his daughter to Conrade would have saved him six thousand pounds; yet the many ill consequences which would probably have attended so disproportionate a match now occurring to his mind, which before he had not thought upon, made him not only contented, but rejoiced that this change of hands had happen'd, and he could not forbear kissing and hugging Florimel for being the chief author of it.

Every one now endeavouring to outvie the other in giving testimonies of their good humour; among the many gay and gallant things said by Dorimon on this occasion, he protested to keep his French cloaths as long as he lived, for a perpetual Memento of the good they had done for him, and never wear them but on the anniversary of that happy day which gave his dear Melanthe to his arms.

On falling afterwards into some discourse concerning the oddness of the accident which had brought about a marriage, so little thought of by either of the parties, yet so agreeable to both, as well as to their friends, Murcio express'd himself in this manner:

Murcio. I cannot help thinking that there is something peculiarly remarkable in this transaction, and looks as if the hand of Heaven had directed the accomplishment, which makes me hope the consequence will make good the old proverb, that

> Blessed is the wooing
> That's not long a doing.[83]

Florimel. I dare almost engage my own life for the mutual happiness of theirs; – their humours are so exactly suited to each other, that neither of them are fit for any body else; and and now I consider on it, am amazed that in the long acquaintance they had together, this business never came into either of their heads till chance put it there.

Dorimon. Nay, sister, I am now convinced, by the transport and the pleasing flutter at my heart, on the offer Murcio made of his daughter, that I was then passionately in love with her, tho' without knowing I was so.

Melanthe. And if you had been as indifferent to me, as I then thought you were, I should not certainly have been so soon and so easily persuaded to be yours.

Murcio. Well, – all things have happen'd for the best, and there is nothing now wanting to complete my satisfaction, but the clearing up Melanthe's innocence to Conrade. – I should be glad he were here.

The word was scarce out of his mouth, when a servant came into the room and informed him, that the person he had mention'd was below, on which he order'd he should be immediately introduced.

The old gentleman, who had heard nothing of what had happen'd, nor seen Murcio since the conversation with him, repeated in a former chapter, had been impatient to know the success of his proposal to Dorimon, and finding he did not return to town as usual, made him this visit at *****, in order to gratify his curiosity.

He had not advanced above half way into the room, when Murcio presented the bride and bridegroom to him; and told him he had been just wishing for him to congratulate the nuptials.

Conrade endeavour'd to compose himself enough to salute them with the accustom'd forms; but as he had not in his heart believed that Dorimon would be preval'd upon to marry Melanthe, tho' he had advised her father to make the experiment, was so much surprised on finding the affair concluded, that he could not forbear testifying it in his looks, as well as by crying out,

Conrade. What married!

Florimel. Yes, sir, – they are married, – the indissoluble knot is tied; – for which all due thanks be given to your fortunate mistake.

Conrade. My mistake, madam; – pardon me if I do not comprehend your meaning.

Dorimon. I believe you do not, sir; – yet it is to your mistaking another for me, that I am indebted for being put in possession of a happiness which otherwise I must have sollicited for a long series of time, and perhaps at last never have obtain'd: – I do assure you, sir, I never presumed to entertain one wish to the dishonour of Melanthe, and was sleeping in my own bed when you imagined me just risen from her arms.

Murcio. He tells you nothing but the truth; – he is innocent, – so is Melanthe; – but here stands her gallant; – here is the author of this enigma.

In concluding these words, which he had utter'd, with the most chearful air he patted Florimel upon her cheek and gently push'd her towards Conrade; but that gentleman was now in such a consternation, that he scarce knew where he was, much less had the power of distinguishing the sense of any thing he either saw or heard, till Florimel related to him, in her sprightly fashion, every particular of that stratagem which had occasion'd the breaking off the intended match between him and Melanthe; – Murcio also, and Dorimon, averring the truth of what she said, he began, at last, to see clearly into the whole affair; – after which Melanthe, with a great deal of modesty and sweetness, address'd herself to him in these terms:

Melanthe. I hope, sir, you will pardon the deception put upon you, as I was constrain'd to pursue so extraordinary a method, to avoid a thing which, in the end, must have been no less disagreable to you than to myself: – I shall always acknowledge my obligation to the generous offer your affection made; but love, sir, is not in our power, – if it were, my gratitude to you, the consideration of my own interest, and the duty owing to my father, would certainly have inspired me with it.

Conrade. Say no more, sweet lady, I am ashamed of my past folly, and only wish you would exert all the influence you have over your witty she-gallant, not to expose this story in print; – I should be sorry, methinks, to see myself in a novel or play.

Florimel. No, no, sir, you need be under no apprehensions on that score, – I would not, for my own sake, have the world know I put on breeches, lest my husband, when I get one, should be afraid I would attempt to wear them afterwards.

This reply of Florimel's set the whole company into a fit of laughter, and would doubtless have been the occasion of many pleasant repartees, if the butler had not that instant given them a summons to the next room, where was a table elegantly spread with every thing suitable to the season; – but as I could not partake with them of any of the delicacies I saw before me, I thought it best to leave the house, so accordingly I slipt out, pluck'd off my Belt, went into a boat, and order'd the waterman to row as fast as possible to London; where being arrived, I contented myself with such fare as my own homely board afforded.

Not many weeks from this adventure had elapsed, before I heard that Florimel was married to a young gentleman who for several years she had loved, and by whom she was equally beloved; – my insatiate curiosity, on this information, led me to enquire into the hidden cause which had so long delay'd the completion of their mutual wishes; and by ways and means too tedious to be here inserted, I at last discover'd it to be such as attracted my highest esteem and admiration.

Dorimon had been a little extravagant in his equipage and way of living while on his travels; – her whole fortune lay in his hands, and if call'd out, which in all probability would have been the case if she had married, he must have been obliged to mortgage some part of his estate for the payment; – it was therefore to save her brother from so great an inconvenience, that this generous young lady had been deaf to all the sollicitations of a beloved lover, and the soft pleadings of her own heart, till Melanthe's fortune coming into the family removed the only impediment to her wishes.

Thus, by the most unseen, undreamt of means, does Providence dispose every thing for the advantage of its favourites: – Florimel, by her wit and contrivance to serve her fair friend, without proposing the least interest to herself, or even imagining she could have any, not only brought about her brother's happiness, but met her own reward in the accomplishment of her felicity.

These two families lived together in the most perfect harmony, and Murcio, who is little less fond of Florimel than of his own daughter, passes most of his time among them; Conrade also is extremely intimate with both, insomuch that it is thought he will, at his decease, divide a good part of his large fortune between them.

End of the First VOLUME.

THE
Invisible Spy.

BY

EXPLORALIBUS.

VOL. II.

LONDON:
Printed for T. GARDNER, at *Cowley's* Head, near St. *Clement's*
Church in the *Strand*.

M,D,CC,LV.

CONTENTS

TO THE

Second VOLUME.

CHAP. V.

CHAP. VI.

CHAP. VII.

CHAP. VIII.

BOOK IV. CHAP. I.

CHAP. II.

CHAP. III.

CHAP. IV.

CHAP. V.

CHAP. VI.

CHAP. VII.

CHAP. VIII.

CHAP. IX.

THE

Invisible Spy.

VOL. II.
BOOK III.

CHAP. I.

In which the author introduces himself to the public by some letters he has received from unrequested correspondents, and the answers he gives to them.

THO' I am very certain of the honour and strict probity of my editor, and believe he employs none, especially in any thing relating to the press, but such whose integrity may be depended upon, yet, I know not how it is, but the title of this work has, by some means or other, taken air, and I perceive has sounded an alarm in the ears of those who blush to be told of what they do not blush to act; for before the first volume was near half completed several letters from different hands were left for me at the Printing-Office; some of which I think it highly proper to insert, as I have no other way of communicating my sentiments to the authors of them, and shall leave it to the public to judge impartially between us.

LETTER I.

To the INVISIBLE SPY.

Mr. INVISIBLE,

I AM a fair enemy, and scorn to cut any man's throat without first telling him I intend to do so: – I therefore send this before the publication of your book, to give you warning not to put any thing into it that may affront the honourable society of Bucks,[84] of which I am not only a member but at present the President. – What if we appear a little terrible to silly people, and sometimes, for sport's sake, overturn a chaise, or jostle an old man or insignificant woman into the kennel,[85] beat the watch, break the windows of houses, or rob the watchmen of their

lanthorns; we look upon ourselves as absolute sovereigns of all public places, and
will not suffer a reprimand from any paultry scribbler of you all; for whatever we
may happen to do, either on the Road, in the Mall, or the Street; – take notice
also, that the least provocation offer'd to any one of us incurs the resentment of
the whole body, and we have unanimously sworn to make a dreadful example
of you if found culpable this way; – hope not to escape, – we shall trace you to
your lurking-hole, – pluck off your case of Invisibility, and hack you into atoms;
– vengeance is the word, – mark that, and tremble how you offend

A Buck.

In answer to this terrible gentleman I shall only say, that tho' I am no friend to
fighting, especially with horned animals, yet I am not coward enough to be so
far intimidated by his menaces as to erace any thing I have once wrote; if therefore he finds nothing in this work concerning the fraternity of which he boasts
being a member, he may assure himself that it is merely because I look on all the
adventures they are engaged in, as too low and too trifling for the entertainment
of my readers.

LETTER II.

To the Author of the Invisible Spy.

Sir,

THERE are a set of men about this town who pick up a pretty tolerable living by inspecting into the secrets of the press; – they are a sort of Spies as well
as yourself, and as Invisible as you can pretend to be; – they find means to steal
the title of every new book long before it is advertised, and almost as soon as the
letters which form it are put together by the compositor, it is by one of those very
useful persons I am informed of the work you have in hand, and being apprehensive that it may contain some things which had much better be conceal'd than
made known, I take the liberty to offer you my sentiments upon it, previous to
the publication, in order that you may make such alterations, as on hearing my
reasons, you shall find necessary and proper.

In the first place, sir, I would have you consider, that whatever is bad either
in the affairs of private families or in national concerns, may possibly be made
much worse, but can never be amended by being exposed; – ill fortune, let it
come in what shape it will, can get nothing by complaints but a short-lived pity;
and when that is over, insults and contempt are sure to ensue: – it is prudence,
therefore, to make a good appearance as long as we can; and, according to the
vulgar adage, let the evil day take care for its self.[86]

It is with great propriety that writers who presume to cavil, and find fault
with the management of those at the helm, are compared to curs barking at the

Moon; for the Ad – m – n, like that planet, secure in its own height, despising all arrows shot from the inferior world, moves on in the same uninterrupted course it has begun, and will continue to do so, except some sudden revolution should happen among the stars, and the disposition of nature be entirely chang'd.

What avails, therefore, all these invectives that from time to time have been thrown out against the ministry? – this presuming to canvas every bill brought into parliament, and grumbling at them after being enacted into laws, since, in spite of all that can be said or wrote, things will be as they are? – The wise of all ages agree, that happiness is seated in content, and if this be true, the good people of England need only think themselves happy, to be so. – This fortunate æra might presently arrive, if the commonality would once cease affecting to be thought politicians, and every one say with mr. Pope,

> In spite of pride, unerring reason's spite,
> One truth is clear, – whatever is, – is right.[87]

But to come to the point; – you must know, sir, I have the honour of a seat in the present parliament, and hope to have the same in the ensuing one; but being conscious of having been pretty strenuous in bringing about some things not very popular, particularly the bill in the relation to the Naturalization of the Jews,[88] I should be glad to have that matter brought as little as possible upon the tapis;[89] – not that I fear being rechosen, – but it will cost me more money; – you understand me; – my constituents will sell their voices at a much higher price; and, it may be, some few of them not be prevail'd upon to sell at all.

I earnestly desire therefore, that if you mention any thing of this affair, it may be wholly in favour of the Israelites; – set up the law of Moses in opposition to the rules of Christianity; – it will be easy for you to prove your argument by quotations out of some ingenious pamphlets publish'd within these few years: – your compliance with this request will oblige me to recommend your book among all my friends, and to do to you every other good office in the power of,

Sir,

Your most humble

and obedient servant,

Judaicus.

I am sorry this gentleman has given himself the trouble to write so long a letter to so little purpose; – I am a very old-fashion'd fellow, I revere the old testament, but endeavour to act according to the precepts of the new, so consequently can be no friend to the profess'd enemies of it: – I shall take care, however, not to offend any member of the honourable house of commons; – I shall be so wise, at least while I keep in remembrance the fate of M—y.[90]

LETTER III.

To the INVISIBLE SPY.

SIR,

I AM shock'd and scandalized beyond measure at your title, and so I believe is every body else that hears it: – What but the very Devil incarnate can have tempted you to assume one so ungracious to all degrees of people? – An invisible Spy! – why, it is a character more to be dreaded than an Excise, a Custom-house or a Sheriff's Officer; – nay, than even a King's Messenger:– human prudence has taught us to elude the scrutiny of all known examiners; but who can guard against what they do not see? – You may be at our very elbows without our knowing you are; – you may explore all the necessary arts and mysteries of our several avocations, without our having it in our power to bribe you to secrecy: – What therefore can you expect, as there is no other way of dealing with you, but to have your book damn'd the first moment of its publication; and to be plain with you, I, who am an author as well as yourself, have already, at the request of some leading men, prepar'd a thing for the press which will effectually do your business? – As a brother of the quill, however, thinking it becoming in me to give you this timely notice, and likewise to advise you to cancel all such pages, as upon a strict examination you shall find may possibly be construed into a libel, – whether the matters they contain are founded either upon truth or fiction; – you know very well, that the one is liable to the same punishment as the other; with this difference only, that the former being the most stinging, is, generally speaking, treated with the most severity; – I have heard some menaces thrown out against you, and sincerely wish you may escape the effects, and meet with no other chastisement for your folly, than what you will receive from the pen of

SCRIBLERIUS.

I shall defer giving my sentiments on my brother author's doughty epistle, till I find myself oblig'd to declare them in an answer to the treatise with which he threatens me, as one trouble will suffice for both.

LETTER IV.

From a lady to the INVISIBLE SPY.

SIR,

SEveral of my acquaintance have taken it into their heads, I suppose not without special information, that there is a book coming out under the title I have prefix'd to this letter; – if there be in reality any such work in the press, I take the liberty of telling the author, that I hope he has more good sense and good manners than to pry into the secrets of our sex, much less to follow the example of a late writer in exposing to the world what he may happen to find in some of our dressing-rooms, cabinets, and private alcoves. – Suppose a woman has the misfortune to like another man better than her husband, – pawns her jewels to pay her debts at play, – or is in the books of her mercer,[91] laceman, and milliner, beyond her utmost ability to clear? – these are all of them foibles which ought to be excused, as they are the fashion, and one should be look'd upon as a creature of the last age to be wholly free from; – so, dear Invisible, I would have you consider, that the want of politeness in your sex is much more ridiculous than the want of chastity and œconomy is in ours: – flattery and homage are the privilege of womankind, and if a father, an uncle, or a brother, assumes to himself the right of correcting any mistakes we are guilty of, we are sure to hate him for it in our hearts; – if therefore there be any one of us whom you would wish to be well with, you must conceal the faults of the rest.

 Yours, &c.

ERRONIA.

I am afraid that I shall have but a very indifferent chance for a place in the good graces of this lady; but as there are others, I hope the greatest number, of an opposite way of thinking, I shall the more easily console myself.

LETTER V.

To the INVISIBLE SPY.

MR. INVISIBLE,

 Nothing is more absurd in effect, than for people to take all opportunities of railing against that which they are continually practising; – the article of gaming is so popular a subject, that tho' you may like the amusement as well as any body, I scarce doubt but to satyrize it makes some part of your lucubrations; but how bold soever you may be with the sweetners[92] and common gamblers, who have no other dependance for their bread, I would have you beware how you meddle with persons of rank and fortune: – if by my address in the turning of a card I win five hundred or a thousand pieces of a fellow who has the vanity to imagine he has as much skill as myself, it is only for the pleasure of circumventing, and then laughing at him, not through the love of lucre: – no, I would have you know, sir, I scorn money, and only put it in my pocket till I can find a proper object to bestow it upon, and the next needy woman of the town I come in company with, toss the fool's pence into her lap; – or perhaps set half a dozen of the poor devils a scrambling for it: – I remember that one night, in very cold weather too, I made a whole covey of them strip naked as they were born, and run galloping the whole length of Pall-Mall after seven or eight hundred moidores[93] I threw out of a tavern window. – If you pretend these are not generous actions you will be thought a silly old Put and your book not worth a farthing. – So no more from

 Yours,

  As I shall find you deserve,

RAKELOVE.

If mr. Rakelove's letter had reached my hands before these volumes were completed, it might have saved me the trouble of exposing the business of cheating at play, by having done it so effectually himself.

LETTER VI.

To the INVISIBLE SPY.

SIR,

I HEAR you are going to set forth a new book, and from the title of it have some reason to apprehend you will be no less bitter in your expressions than some others have been against a nation which desires nothing more than to live in the most perfect concord and amity with yours, I beg leave to expostulate a little with you on that occasion.

I thought you Christians valued yourselves upon acts of benevolence, charity, and good-will to all men; and that to root out the seeds of envy and malice from your hearts was a main part of your religion; – Wherefore then is all this rancour against the Hebrews? – How can you profess the least true regard for Abraham, or any of the Patriarchs, when you grumble to admit their posterity as fellow-citizens within your walls? – How can you place the venerable portraitures of Moses and Aaron in your temples, yet grudge that the people they deliver'd from the house of bondage should share with you in the milk and honey of your land? – What if we crucified the man you worship as your God? – What if we disbelieve and ridicule the miracles you ascribe to him, deny his resurrection, and in our synagogues utter some things which you call blasphemy, our principles, in matters of faith, have no relation to those of loyalty to the king or social conversation with our neighbours? – We can be as good subjects and as merry companions as any Christian of you all; – the want of either of these virtues cannot be imputed to us.

There are many of you, indeed, I believe the greatest number, who put religion quite out of the question, and yet cry out that their rights and properties will be invaded; that when once we have the liberty of being incorporated with you, such numbers of us will flock hither from all parts of the world, that we shall, by degrees, engross all the trade of the kingdom; to which I answer, – that if we should do so, the fault will be wholly in yourselves; – if you work and sell as cheap as we do, you will have the same chance for business; – and as for those who shall be obliged to shut up their shops, they will always find employment among us, either as journeymen or menial servants: – a taylor or a barber would make a good valet de chambre; a merchant, a wine-cooper, a vintner, or a distiller, could not fail of being an excellent butler; – a jeweller, a goldsmith, a mercer, a haberdasher, a woollen or a linnen-draper, would be a spruce footman: – in fine, there is no one person, of any occupation whatever, that might not, if he is not too proud or too lazy, earn his bread under our hospitable roofs.

As you are an author, I must believe you to be a man of sense, and therefore flatter myself that the arguments I have alledg'd will have some weight with you. – I am,

With all due respect,

SIR,

Your most obedient humble servant,

SHIMEI BENZARA.

My answer to Benzara may be found in the return I made to the letter of Judai-cus, so I have only to thank this considerate and beneficent Hebrew for the handsome provision he proposes for the trading part of my countrymen, tho' I hope they never will have occasion to accept it.

LETTER VII.

To the INVISIBLE SPY.

Honour'd sir,

BEING told you are a very extraordinary person, and can see every thing and not be seen yourself, it is likely that chance or design may some time or other bring you to my house; as I live in a genteel part of the town, keep several serv-ants, and am visited by people of the best fashion and repute.

You must know, sir, that I pass for a well jointur'd widow, but in reality was never married in my life, and have no other dependance than the favour of some worthy gentlemen and ladies, who I frequently oblige with a bed at the moderate rate of three guineas per night.

Among the rest of my good customers there are two sisters of distinction, who have each of them their particular favourites, and always meet them at my house; – one of them is married to a man who is as jealous of her as the devil; and if he should get the least intimation of her intrigue, and that I am privy to it, he would blow me up and ruin me for ever.

I therefore beg and beseech you, sir, that if you make any discoveries of this nature, you will not divulge it to any soul in the world, much less not put it into your book; and in return for this favour, be assured that you, and any friend you shall bring with you, shall be welcome to the best appartment in my house, with a hot boil'd chicken and a bottle of wine into the bargain. – I am,

Depending on your honour,

SIR,

Your most devoted

humble servant,

SUSANNA PRIM.

This good gentlewoman's request is come too late to be comply'd with; – she will find, however, if her avocation allows her time for the perusal of these volumes, that I have carefully avoided making any mischief in families.

I have also receiv'd another letter from a young lady, too tedious and too little interesting to be presented to the public, so I shall only give the heads of it, with my opinion on the matter it contains.

She is very pressing with me to clear her reputation, which, as she says, suffers much in the world without being guilty of any real crime; but by the account she gives of herself, even tho' she should be as perfectly innocent in fact as she pretends, and as I hope she is, I can see very little merit in the virtue she so much boasts of, much less expect that any thing I can urge will put to silence the censures she complains of.

When a young woman, well born, genteely bred, and accustom'd in her childhood to converse with persons of condition, can condescend to keep company, and appear in all public places with the meanest and most abandon'd of her own sex, and suffer herself to be treated in taverns by those of the other with whom she had no acquaintance, nor had ever seen before, what can be alleg'd in vindication of her delicacy, her prudence, or her modesty?

She says that her father, in his last moments, put a dagger into her hands, with a strict charge to keep and use it in defence of her chastity if attack'd; but does not add that she ever had any occasion for exerting the heroine in this manner; – so it seems to me that in the numberless dangers she confesses to have provok'd, she must have been indebted for protection merely to chance, or to an uncommon share either of honour, or coldness of constitution in the men with whom she entrusted herself.

Upon the whole, all that can be said in her favour is, that want of thought, the love of pleasure, and variety of company, betray'd her into a conduct she too late sees and repents the folly of, and which will be better retrieved by a future regularity of behaviour than by any vain excuses for the past.

CHAP. II.

Contains the history of a very extraordinary funeral, and also of some other pretty particular occurrences which the author was witness of, in an Invisible visit he made to the most favourite part of the family of a lady of distinction.

I Frequently stroll thro' the town, with my Invisible Belt close girt about me, not always with a view of making any discoveries, but merely to enjoy the freedom of my thought, without being interrupted by the impertinent how-d'ye's of some who might meet and know me by day, and to be safe from the salutation of the stand and deliver, – investors of the street by night, with whom I was no less inclined to engage in combat, than I am to comply with their unreasonable and unjust demands.

In these unmeaning rambles I sometimes stumbled upon adventures no less entertaining than many of those I had sought after, and took so much pains to explore the hidden source of.

I will not, however, pretend to promise that this I am now about to recite is either so improving or so pleasing as several others presented to the public in this work; but be that as it shall happen, – the candid reader will accept of things as they fell under my observation, and content himself with such as are less agreeable, for the sake of those he shall find much more to his taste.

> Even life a kind of chequer-work appears,
> A round of joy, of grief, of hopes, and fears;
> The good, the bad, the wise with patience bear,
> Welcome the former, and the latter dare.
>
> MARSTON.[94]

I was going through a narrow lane one day, and saw a great concourse of the meaner sort of people gather'd together about a little door, which then seem'd to me, and I afterwards found, was the avenue to some stables or coach-house; as I did not imagine that persons of the appearance these were could be assembled on any matter worthy of my attention, I should scarce have stopp'd to make any enquiry into it, if, just as I came near the place where they stood, they had not been join'd by some others, whose interrogatories awaken'd my curiosity.

The first that spoke was a broad ruddy-faced woman, with tatter'd garments, ungirt and loosely flowing, as was her hair, which hung down to her brows; – her heels the length of half a span behind her shoes;[95] and, in fine, every mark about her that denoted her a true devotee to Bacchus, to whom, though it was scarce mid-day, and not the usual time for the performance of his rites, she had been plentifully sacrificing, in such liquor as ladies of her rank are wont of late years to be regaled with; – her words were these:

First Woman. What the devil's to be done here? – Is there any thing to be seen?

To this demand a robust fellow, who by his appearance I took to be a carman or a waggoner, reply'd in these terms:

First Man. Ay, marry, – the finest shew, by report, that ever you saw in your whole life, or may ever see again.

Second Woman. What is it?

Third Woman. Why where have you liv'd, that you have not heard that one of lady Marvell's dogs is dead, and lies in state till the burial?

One of the new comers, on this intelligence, clapp'd her hands and cry'd out:

Fourth Woman. Lord! – Lord! – a dog lie in state; – what will this world come to?

Second Man. To no good I am afraid: – but these quality think they may do any thing; – if it had been a poor man's child, I warrant it might lie above ground, and be sent to the parish for a grave, for any care her ladyship would take about it.

Omnes. Ay, ay, so they might indeed.

An arch wag, who was an apprentice in the neighbourhood, on hearing what was said, thrust himself in among them, and in a sneering voice spoke thus:

Apprentice. Oh fye, you should treat a person of quality's dog with more respect; – besides, I have been told that the deceased was lineally descended, by the side of his dam, from a favourite bitch of Oliver Cromwell's, who was lord protector of England, and that his sire came over from Holland with an officer belonging to the houshold of King William, of immortal memory.

Second Woman. What of all that, I am sure I lived servant in as worthy a family as any at all; – they had a fine dog call'd Cæsar, he was of good king Charles's breed, – every body lov'd him, he was such a gentle good-natur'd creature; – but they made no fuss about him when he died; – he was thrown out upon the dunghil, and there lay till somebody stole him away for the sake of his skin.

I do not doubt but much more would have been said concerning the genealogy of the canine race, if the door had not suddenly been thrown open by a footman in deep mourning, who dismiss'd a great number of those that had been within, and at the same time gave entrance to those who had waited without.

I accompany'd these last, being no less desirous, tho' I believe for very different reasons, of beholding so extraordinary a scene.

A long passage between the stables brought us into a spacious court-yard, which having cross'd, our conductor shew'd us into a magnificent house, and then into the theatre, where the farce I had heard spoke of was exhibited, – the walls of which were lined with black bays, as was also the floor and cieling; – the light of Heaven was entirely excluded thence; but fifty wax tapers, in silver sconces, were placed at an equal distance round the room, with a large lustre in the middle, containing some twenty more, supply'd the absence of the sun: – at the upper end stood a bier, with the coffin of the deceased, both cover'd with black velvet, and on the lid of the latter was fix'd a silver plate with this inscription engraven on it:

CUPID,

Who came into this world April 2, 1749,
And departed September 12, 1753.
He lived beloved, and died lamented,
By
Lady MARVELL.

On one side of the bier, and near the feet of the corpse, sat a woman in deep mourning, holding a white handkerchief close to her face, not to wipe off the tears, but to conceal the disdain with which it was overspread at the office imposed on her.

As we approach'd the bier, the footman, who had been our guide, lifted up the lid of the coffin, and obliged us with a view of the body; and certainly there never was a more truly ridiculous and comical sight than the little black nose of the creature, who was of the Dutch mastiff kind, peeping, as it were, out of a shroud of white Venetian sattin.

It was pleasant enough to behold the different attitudes of the several spectators; – some lifted up their hands and eyes, in token of the utmost astonishment, – others bit their lips and shook their heads, seeming both to despise and be enraged at so egregious a piece of folly and extravagance; while others held the flaps of their coats or their aprons to hide that laughter, which they found it impossible to restrain; and some there were who had their mouths half open, ready to burst into exclamations, had they not been awed by the consideration of the place they were in, and to which it is not to be doubted but that they plentifully gave a loose when they found themselves more at liberty to do so.

The person who had usher'd in this respectable company saw them also out; – on the door being open'd, another cluster press'd for entrance, but were deny'd; – the undertaker's servants, with two mourning coaches and six, were now come, and the funeral procession was order'd to set out for Mary-le-bon, where, as I afterwards heard, Cupid was to be interr'd in a grave dug for him in a field near the pond.

As I was willing to see the whole of this ceremony, I turn'd back into the room, and was immediately follow'd by the footman, on which ensued this discourse between him and the mock mourner:

Footman. Well, mrs. Susan, – the shew is almost over now, and both of us shall soon have done acting.

Susan. It is high time; – for my part, if it were to have lasted longer I must infallibly have given out, tho' I had lost my place by it; – to be confined to sit here for a whole day and a half, as mute as a fish, mourning over a dead dog, and exposed to all the mob in the parish; – sure never was so preposterous a whim.

Footman. I think, indeed, my lady has in this, as Colley says, outdone all her usual outdoings:[96] – however, we have no great reason to complain at the whim, – we have each of us got a good suit of mourning by it.

Susan. That makes some amends, I own.

Footman. Ay, faith; – and I can tell you that poor Catherine has had a much worse time, while she has supply'd your place in waiting upon the living dogs above-stairs, than you have had in pretending to bewail the dead one below.

Susan. As how? – what is the matter?

Footman. Why my lady has done nothing but scold at her all this morning; – she says she heard Pompey howl last night, and she is sure his bed was not made easy; – and that Psyche could not eat her breakfast because it was not brought up in a china bason.

Susan. Oh this is nothing; – don't you remember that her ladyship once threaten'd to turn me out of doors because she catch'd me eating a bit of a shoulder of mutton that was roasted for these plaguy dogs, when we servants had nothing for a whole week together but tough cow-beef.

Footman. That was because her ladyship has that dish at her own table sometimes; – and you know it is an establish'd maxim with her, that for servants to eat of the same victuals their superiors do, makes them sawcy and assuming, – else so many good things would not be kept till they stink rather we should get a taste.

Susan. Hush, – hush; – I think I hear her coming.

The maid was not mistaken, – a rustling of silks proclaim'd her ladyship's approach, – she enter'd that moment, with hasty steps, contracted brows, and all the tokens of ill-humour and discontent; – then, in an imperious tone, spoke to the footman.

Lady Marvell. I hear mr. Grim does not think fit to attend the funeral himself.

Footman. The poor man is not well, it seems, madam, so hopes your ladyship will excuse him, as he has sent four of his best and most solemn looking men to go with the coaches.

Lady Marvell. I suppose the impudent fellow thinks it beneath him to attend the funeral of a dog; – such mean soul'd wretches know not how to make any distinction between the cur of a beggar and the favourite of a woman of quality; – but it is the last burial he shall ever have out of my family, – and so I shall tell him when I pay his bill. – And you, sir, have you taken care that the grave is dug handsome and deep enough, that my poor creature may not be taken up for the sake of his coffin and shrowd?

Footman. Yes, my lady, – I gave orders that it should be two feet broad and nine feet in the earth at least.

Lady Marvell. Gave orders, – gave orders; and what, mr. Jacaknapes, what hinder'd you from going to see if it was done as it ought to be?

Footman. Your ladyship knows I was obliged to attend the door.

Lady Marvell. You have always some pretence or other for not doing as you should; – servants are certainly the greatest plagues in life; – but, as every thing is ready, call in the fellows to screw up the coffin. – No, hold, – I must first take my leave of my poor dear creature; – farewell, my pretty little Cupid: – 'tis a sad thing; – but we must all die. – Susan, as soon as the burial is over, come directly up to your other masters and mistresses; for they have been strangely used these two days: – never was a woman of quality's family so handled: – Catherine is not fit to be dog-maid to a cow-keeper.

Her ladyship went out of the room in speaking these words, and the death hunter's servants were call'd in; – they brought with them a long mourning cloak and hat-band for the footman, – a scarf for mrs. Susan, and gloves for each of them; – as soon as they had fasten'd up the coffin, which I perceived they could not do without laughing, the procession set out, – mrs. Susan bearing the coffin under a velvet pall upon her lap, went in the first coach; – the footman seated himself in the other, and the undertaker's servants walk'd on each side with their hands upon the doors.

A gaping multitude, who could not think of returning to their own garrets or cellars without having been spectators of all that was to be seen, follow'd with a confused noise, grating enough to the ears, but not at all unsuitable to so ridiculous a solemnity.

For my part, my curiosity did not extend so far as to carry me to see monsieur Le Chin deposited in his last receptacle: – it did not, however, stop here; – the truth is, I promised myself with finding something or other in the upper apartments in this house, no less extraordinary than what I had been presented with below; – nor did my conjectures deceive me, as I believe the reader will readily allow, before the conclusion of this chapter.

I was, indeed, a little apprehensive of a disappointment, when, after having search'd two handsome fore parlours, I ascended to the first floor and wander'd thro' several rooms, I could neither see nor hear any one living creature; – but at last the appearance of lady Marvell revived my dying expectations; – she started out from a closet, which I had not taken notice of, at the end of the gallery, and went hastily up another pair of stairs; I pursued her steps with equal expedition, and enter'd with her into a spacious chamber, the furniture of which I shall give a description of to the best of my remembrance.

There were no fewer than fourteen beds of different sizes, the largest not exceeding three feet and a half in height and two in breadth; but all of them extremely neat and fashionable, with curtains, vallens,[97] and bases; each had a mattress, a quilted covering, a pillow and fine holland sheets; – four china soup dishes, full of clear water, were placed at the four corners of the room, and in the middle stood a mahogany table of about two yards long but pretty narrow, and a bench on each side cover'd with the best sort of Dutch matting;[98] – I should have been strangely puzzled to have guess'd the meaning of any one thing I saw here, if the dogs, whose apartment it was, had been absent.

Would one not rather have thought that this was some part of a Lilliputian palace, and these beds intended for the repose of noblemen attending on the king's person, than a kennel for brutes! – but I shall forbear any animadversions of my own at this time, and proceed to relate what happen'd after my entrance into a place which I confess fill'd me with much astonishment.

A maid, whom I soon afterwards found to be the same I had heard mention'd by the footman in his discourse with Susan, was sitting in a low chair, with a large tray before her fill'd with a great number of combs, one of which she was then making use of in smoothing and setting in order the hair of a fine spaniel she held upon her lap; – lady Marvell, seeing what she was about, said to her with great peevishness:

Lady Marvell. A fine time of day, indeed, for what you are about; – my family of creatures ought all to have been spruced up and adjusted three hours ago; – but I suppose you were sleeping in your bed, when you ought to have been waiting on them.

Then drawing a little nearer to her, – and seeing the comb she was using, snatch'd it out of her hand, and struck it into her face with such a force that the blood started out from every pore, crying at the same time:

Lady Marvell. Monster, how dare you touch Hector with this comb?

Maid. Indeed, my lady, they were all here; I did not know any difference.

Lady Marvell. You lye, hussy, and you must have heard that all my dogs have each of them a set of combs to themselves, with their names wrote upon them, – Can't you read, oaf?

Maid. Indeed, madam, I did not see it.

Lady Marvell. Take that then, – you slut, – and that, – and that to clear your sight, and make you remember another time.

These words were accompany'd with blows, first on one shoulder, then on the other, till I believe her own arms aked with the fatigue; – then turning to her dogs, who were crying and yelping all this time, address'd them in these terms:

Lady Marvell. The dear good natured things; – you hate to see me angry, tho' it be in your own cause. – Come hither, Psyche, – you have lost your lover; – but I will get you another Cupid. – Prince, – what makes you so dull this morning? – you don't frisk and caper about as you used do; – I suppose your bed was not made any more than Pompey's; – you look as if you had lain rough all night. – Here is my poor Bully too, – as I live not so much as the black tuft on his tail comb'd out. – Fidell, why do you bark? – you have something to tell me now, if you knew how. – Well, – you have all been sadly managed these two days, since your own maid has been from you. – Come, Cloe, come and kiss your lady: – poh, your mouth is all nasty, that impudent quean has not wash'd your face.

Maid. Indeed, madam, I wash'd every one of them, your ladyship may see the towel yonder is all over wet.

Lady Marvell. The towel, – why, you audacious puss, have you presum'd to wash all their faces with one towel? – get out of my sight, toad, – devil, or I shall break your neck down stairs.

It is likely this was the most comfortable command the poor maid could have received; – she staid not to be bid a second time; – she flew out of the room while her furious lady sent a thousand curses after her.

She was no sooner alone with her dogs, which were thirteen in number, than she began to re-examine them, in hopes, no doubt, of finding some farther matter of accusation against the poor maid; but was interrupted by the sudden coming in of her husband, sir Patient Marvell, who, tho' the best natured man in the world, could not forbear being a little ruffled at the transactions of that morning, and accosted her in this manner:

Sir Patient. I wonder, madam, you will expose yourself in this fashion.

Lady Marvell. Expose myself, sir Patient?

Sir Patient. Yes, madam, both yourself and me too. – You do not know how much you have render'd us the common table-talk of the town.

Lady Marvell. I despise the town and all it can say. – But pray on what occasion?

Sir Patient. How can you ask that question? – Here hath been I know not how many messages sent to enquire after our health. – Undertakers men have been seen to come into the house with bales of cloth, sconces,[99] and other utensils, for a pompous mourning. – What could people think of all this, as we have no children, but that either you or I were dead?

Lady Marvell. Pish, no body could think any such thing: – the little solemnity I order'd for my poor Cupid, was only in the back part of the house; and those who, out of respect to me, came to take their last leaves of the dear animal pass'd through the stables: – he was carry'd out of town by day-light, to be interr'd, and no more than two coaches, with the dog-maid and one footman, assisted at the obsequies.

Sir Patient. Oh, madam, it was ridiculous; – and I must tell you, that the keeping of so many dogs, and in the manner you do, is equally so.

Lady Marvell. Sir Patient, I brought a fortune large enough to keep whatever I please, and in what manner I please; – you have no reason to complain. – What would you say, if instead of dogs I kept a gallant?

Sir Patient. Why really, madam, I know not whether it would make me more laugh'd at, or yourself more censur'd.

Lady Marvell. Mighty well, sir Patient, mighty well indeed; – this is fine treatment for a woman of my unblemish'd virtue; – there are some wives who would not fail to shew you the difference between keeping a few harmless animals and a fellow; and if I refrain from doing the latter, it is as mr. Rowe makes Arbasia tell her tyrant:

> Not that I fear, or love, or reverence thee;
> But that my soul, conscious of whence she sprung,
> Sits unpolluted in her sacred dwelling,
> And scorns to mingle with a thought so mean.[100]

Sir Patient. Virtue has many branches, madam, besides chastity, and I could wish you would remember that the care of not giving offence is not the last among them.

Lady Marvell. I never aimed to give offence, but shall be under no concern about those who take it without cause.

Sir Patient. Well, madam, I hope you will one day consider what you owe to your own character; and also think that it is some part of your duty not to render me unhappy.

He said no more, but as he left the room a deep sigh issued from his breast, at which his lady, however, seem'd as little affected as she had been with his remonstrances; – the moment he was gone she resum'd that discourse with her dogs which his coming had broke off, and which I had already been too much tired with hearing to stay the continuance of, so went directly out of the house, tho' not without a very troubled mind, to have found a lady, who had every requisite to command respect, take a pride in making herself contemptible.

CHAP. III.

Is a kind of a warning-bell to the public, and gives a melancholy, tho' a too common proof, that a person in endeavouring, by unjust or imprudent measures, to avoid falling into an imaginary misfortune is frequently liable to bring on effectually what otherwise might never have happen'd.

OF all the passions which distract the human mind, sure there is none more pernicious in its quality, or more dreadful in its consequences, than jealousy; – it is look'd upon, indeed, as the most certain proof of a strong and violent affection; yet it is such a proof as no one would wish to experience, as it infallibly involves the beloved object in a variety of disquiets, whether innocent or guilty; – nor is the person possess'd of this raging fury less wretched; – so just are these words of mr. Dryden:

> O jealousy! thou raging ill,
> Why hast thou found a place in lovers hearts?
> Afflicting what thou can'st not kill,
> And poisoning love himself with his own darts.[101]

And as the inimitable Shakspear yet more emphatically, in my opinion, expresses it:

> O what damn'd minutes tells he o'er,
> Who doats, yet doubts; suspects, yet strongly loves.[102]

But it is altogether needless to bring any testimonies from printed quotations on this head; – even those who have happily lived free from the direful passion in their bosoms, or never felt the effects of it from those by whom they are beloved, cannot but have seen, among their acquaintance, enough to convince them better of its malignity, than they can be by the pen of any author.

But as jealousy frequently takes possession of the soul by almost imperceptible degrees, the following little narrative may serve as an antidote against its poison, and warn every one, married persons especially, not to give way to its first attacks, lest it should be in time wholly subdued by it.

Cleora had from her very infancy been promised in marriage to the son of a neighbouring gentleman, – about three years older than herself; an inclination for her intended husband grew up with her years, nor was his affection less tender for her, whom he expected would one day be his wife; but when the innocent pair became ripe for the consummation of their mutual wishes, an unhappy dispute happen'd between their parents, which entirely broke off the match at once, and they were forbid to see each other any more.

As I was not at that time acquainted with either of the lovers, I cannot pretend to describe what their young hearts sustain'd in this cruel separation; – it was, doubtless, very grievous to them both at first; – but absence, and variety of amusements, provided for them by their respective parents, in order to dissipate their chagrin, by degrees wrought the desir'd effects: – Leander,[103] for so he was call'd, grew one of the gayest men about the town; and Cleora was so far wean'd from the remembrance of him, that she obey'd her father without reluctance in receiving the addresses of Aristus, who, after the necessary forms of courtship, became her husband.

Few nuptials gave a greater promise of felicity; – the births, – the fortunes of the wedded pair were equal; – their ages perfectly agreeable; – she was not quite nineteen, and he no more than five and twenty; – she was a very lovely woman, – he a most graceful man. – He had adored her to so romantic a height, that it was thought, if he had not obtain'd her, a dagger or a bowl of poison must have been his fate: – she treated him with all the tenderness that could be expected from a virtuous woman by a reasonable man: – they were, in the first months of their marriage, the envy and admiration of as many as knew them.

But alas, how uncertain is the date of human happiness! – When Heaven is not pleased to bestow on us a contented mind; I mean, when we do not ask that blessing and endeavour to acquire it, in vain indulgent fortune lavishes her whole stock of bounties on us; – we repine amidst our plenty, – enjoy nothing we possess, and are wretches because we will be so.

The bridal house, so lately the theatre of joy and pleasure, soon became the cell of gloomy sullenness and black despair; – the eyes of the beautiful Cleora were frequently seen red with weeping; – she ceased to appear at any public place, and received very little company at home; while on the brow of the once cheerful gay Aristus now lower'd a heavy melancholy, and all the indications of a deep inward grief.

Every one saw the change, but none could presently discern the cause; – it could not, however, long be kept a secret; – the servants who waited immediately on their persons were the first who discover'd it, these reported it to the others, and they fail'd not to whisper to as many as they were acquainted with, – that their master was prodigiously jealous of his lady.

The first tokens he gave of this frenzy, as I have been since inform'd, was to debar Cleora from going to the opera, – the play, – the masquerade, and all routs and assemblies, all which places she had been accustom'd to frequent: – she obey'd him, notwithstanding, without murmur or repining; and told him, with a great deal of sweetness, that if those diversions were infinitely dearer to her than ever they had been, she would readily sacrifice all the pleasure she took in them, to that of testifying her love and duty to him.

Not contented with this he proceeded farther, and forbid her to make any visits without him, except to his mother, who lived but in the next street: – and then to let him know, that he might meet her there and bring her home; – hard as this injunction seem'd to her, she comply'd with it, being resolved, if possible, to chase from his mind all those ideas she found he had conceived in prejudice of her discretion, and convince him that she regarded nothing so much as his satisfaction.

What more could woman do, or man expect? – yet all was not enough to make this jealous husband easy: – whenever they were abroad together, if any gentleman happen'd to be in company, the least gallant thing said to her, or complaisance return'd to it by her, immediately set the worm within his brain a madding, and made him, on their coming home, reproach her in terms very unbecoming in him to make use of, and difficult for her to bear with patience; – yet, nevertheless, he still loved her, – loved her to an excess; – but, as the poet says,

> No signs of love in jealous men remains,
> But that which sick men have of life, their pains.[104]

In fine, this behaviour of Aristus engross'd much of the conversation of the town, and various were the conjectures pass'd upon it; – some highly blamed him; – others were apt to imagine there had really been some imprudences on the part of Cleora; and not a few there were among her own sex who, hating her for those very perfections which ought to have excited their esteem, scrupled not to pronounce her guilty of every thing she could be suspected of.

Much was this lady to be pitied, – deprived of all those pleasures to which her youth had been accustsom'd, – ill treated by her husband, – censured by her acquaintance, and secluded from the society of those who might have found means of diverting, if not wholly dissipating her melancholy.

To add to her misfortune, she had no friend near her to whom she might complain; – her father, being a widower, had broke up house keeping soon after her marriage, and was retired with an intent to pass the remainder of his days with her elder sister, who was settled in a far distant county; so that the only person from whom she received any consolation was miss Lucia, the sister of Aristus, a young lady of great good nature, and who believing her truly innocent, used her utmost endeavours to put all chimeras to her prejudice out of her brother's head.

The discourses which continually fill'd my ears about this family, and the different opinions the world had of the manner of their living together, made me resolve to have recourse to my Invisibility, in order to discover which was in the right.

Accordingly I went one day, equipt as usual, with my Belt and Tablet, to make a visit at their house, – Aristus was abroad, but I found Cleora sitting in a very pensive posture in her dressing-room.

I had not been there above two minutes before the waiting-maid came in, and ask'd her lady whether she would be pleased to walk into the next room, or have tea brought in where she was; to which she reply'd:

Cleora. I do not know as yet. – Has any body been here from my sister Lucia?

Maid. No, madam.

Cleora. Well then, get things ready in the drawing-room, – I believe she will be here presently; – she was from home when John went to tell her I desired her company; but as she was expected soon, and must have heard of my message, she would certainly have sent an excuse if any thing had happen'd to prevent her coming.

She had but just given over speaking, and the maid withdrawn to do as she was order'd, than her footman came in and presented her with a letter, which he told her was left for her by a porter, who said it requir'd no answer, and was gone.

I must confess, that on hearing this I was guilty of great injustice to the fair Cleora, and began to be apprehensive that her husband's suspicions were in reality founded on too solid reasons; but I was soon asham'd of my rash judgment, when slipping behind her chair, and looking over her shoulder as she read, I perceived the letter was from miss Lucia, and contain'd these lines:

To Cleora.

Dear SISTER,

Words cannot express how greatly I am troubled, on finding myself oblig'd to send this instead of waiting on you in person; – be assured I love and value your conversation as I ought, and shall no less suffer in being depriv'd of it, Heaven knows for how long a time, than you will do in the knowledge of the cause: – in fine, some idle stories, of which, I dare believe, my brother's unhappy caprice has been the sole occasion, have reach'd the ears of my mamma, and made her think it improper for me to be seen with you, while the world continues to judge of you in the manner it does at present; – she heard of your message to me, and strictly forbid me to obey the summons; – you know too well, my dear Cleora, what duty is owing from a child to a parent, and also how much my father's will has left me in her power, to resent the painful proof I now give of my obedience to her; – I wish, for my own sake as well as yours, that she, my brother, and every one that knows us, were as well convinced as myself of your perfect innocence; but, till that happy time arrives, must content myself with the memory of the many happy hours we have pass'd together, and the hopes of many more yet to come, when once the horrid cloud which now separates us is removed. – Farewell, – that Heaven may send you comfort under your present affliction, and speedily relieve you from it, shall be the constant prayers of her, who is,

> With the greatest sincerity
>> My very dear Cleora,
>>> Your most affectionate sister
>>>> And humble servant,

>>>>>> LUCIA.

P.S. Tho' my mamma intends to talk to you upon this head herself, she would not pardon my giving you any hint of it; for which reason I durst not trust any of our servants to convey this to you, but send it by a strange porter; and beg that, for fear of accidents, you will commit it to the flames as soon as read. – Once more, my dear sister, I bid you, with an aking heart, adieu.

Scarce had she gone through half this epistle before her countenance betray'd the effect it produced; – disdain, – and rage, – and grief, seemed now to have united all their force to raise a tempest in her mind, which immediately broke forth in these and the like exclamations:

Cleora. Deprived of my poor Lucia too, – and on so shocking a pretence! – Good Heaven, for what unknown crime of mine, or of my ancestors, am I link'd into such a family! – Mother and son alike unjust, ungrateful, base, tyrannic! – Have I renounced all the gay amusements of life, – submitted my temper to the will of an imperious husband, and made it my whole study to oblige him, to meet at last with this ungenerous, this barbarous return! – My virtue suspected, my reputation traduced, and my conversation shunn'd as a disgrace! – Oh, tis too much, – too much for human patience to sustain!

It was for some time before she could compose herself enough to finish the perusal of what Lucia had wrote to her; – and after she had done so, relapsed into agitations more violent, if possible, than the former, – with gestures, and a tone of voice which denoted the extremest bitterness of heart, she cry'd out:

Cleora. And must I always bear this usage! – be condemn'd to drag on a life of lasting wretchedness and infamy! – no, I cannot, – will not. – Oh Heaven, who knowest my perfect innocence, send me the means to clear, or to revenge my wounded fame!

Many other expressions of the same nature did her passion vent, till at last, recollecting the request Lucia had made in the postscript of her letter, she snatch'd it hastily from off her toylet and thrust it into the fire, saying at the same time:

Cleora. Poor Lucia, however, must not suffer for her friendship to me.

Aristus being return'd home, was that instant coming up stairs, which being opposite to the room where Cleora was, and the door open, he had an opportunity of beholding this last action, tho' not of hearing the words which accompany'd it; – he flew like lighting to the chimney in order to save the paper, not doubting but it contain'd something that might add fresh fewel to his jealously; but, nimble as he was, the flames were yet more quick, and left not the least part of what he so much wanted unconsumed.

This disappointment, join'd with what he had seen Cleora do, so much inflamed him, that looking on her with eyes sparkling with indignation, he saluted her with this reproach:

Aristus. I perceive, madam, you will be still too cunning for me; – your lovers having so cautious a mistress have little to fear from the resentment of an injured husband; – yet, had I come a moment sooner, I might perhaps have discover'd enough in that paper to have silenced all your future boastings of virtue and fidelity.

Cleora. Oh, sir, you need be under no apprehensions on that score; – the continuance of your base suspicions deserve not that I should be at any pains to undeceive you.

Aristus. No, – 'twou'd be in vain; – too well I know you; – know all your vows and asseverations false as your prostituted heart; – nor can you, – dare you now, attempt to justify yourself, after the glaring proof I have received of your infidelity.

Cleora. What proof?

Aristus. That paper, – perfidious woman; – that paper, whose ashes, if they could speak, would rise in judgment against you; they are, however, silent evidences of your shame and my dishonour.

Cleora. This is madness, or some new pretext to use me ill. – Pray what can the most injurious of your imaginations suggest on the burning of a bit of paper?

Aristus. Did I not observe your countenance while throwing the lewd scrawl into the fire? – Did not your gloating eyes pursue it as you would the fellow from whom it came? – Were not all the marks of guilt and confusion on your cheeks on my approach? – But this is not all; – I was told below that you had just received a letter by a porter: – answer to that, thou hypocrite. – Does it become a married woman, of your rank and circumstances, to receive letters brought by such messengers?

Cleora. A married woman! – say rather, a married wretch; for such are all who have husbands like Aristus.

Aristus. Still you evade the question; – but if you would not deserve to be the wretch you call yourself, – be once sincere, and tell me from which of your pretended admirers that letter came.

Cleora. From none.

Aristus. Perhaps then some female agent, – some sly promoter of your amorous intrigues: – but no equivocations; – explain the whole of this dark mystery, or by Heaven my sword shall rip the secret from your breast.

Cleora. Do, – kill me, – it is the only act of kindness you can shew, and all I now wish to receive from you.

Aristus. So daring in your crimes, – abandon'd creature; – but get out of my sight this moment, lest I be indeed provok'd to do a deed I might hereafter repent of: – much as you have wrong'd me, I should be loth to send your polluted soul to everlasting perdition.

Cleora. Monster! – but to quit your presence is a command I shall always be ready to obey.

It was with an unspeakable haughtiness that Cleora utter'd these words as she flung out of the room. – I am apt to believe, by the amazement Aristus now appear'd in, that this was the first time she had ever testify'd any great marks of resentment for his ill treatment of her; – he stood for some moments in a profound resvery, and when he came out of it, lifted up his hands and eyes to heaven, saying,

Aristus. Good God! nothing but the most perfect innocence, or the most consummate guilt, could inspire a woman with so much boldness. – I know not what to think.

Then folding his arms, again seem'd lost in meditation, which having indulged awhile, the subject of it burst out in these words:

Aristus. If she were innocent, wherefore should she conceal from me the contents of that cursed letter? – No, – 'tis too plain she is guilty; – in vain would my fond heart, that still doats on her, find excuses for her behaviour; – yet it would be some ease to be convinced; but tis impossible, – she has too much art. – How true, O Dryden, are thy words:

> False women to new joys unseen can move,
> There are no prints left in the paths of love:
> All other goods by public marks are known;
> But this, we most desire to keep, has none.[105]

After this he walk'd several times backwards and forwards in the room, then ran hastily down stairs, as I imagin'd, in search of Cleora; but finding he did not, and went out of the house, I also left it too, having an engagement of my own that evening.

CHAP. IV.

In which the reader is requested to expect no more than a continuation of the
same narrative begun in the preceding chapter; and which has in it too
great a multiplicity of incidents to be fully concluded in this.

THE distress in which I had left the beautiful Cleora, and the knowledge I now
had of her innocence, very much affected me, and I must either have chang'd my
nature, or have lost that happy Gift of Invisibility, which enabled me to discover
almost every thing, not to have flown the next morning to the house of Aristus,
in order to inform myself what effects the conversation of the preceding night
had produced.

I truly pitied the unhappy pair, for though Aristus was unjust and cruel in
his suspicions, yet I plainly saw he suffer'd no less in his own mind than what
he inflicted on his much injur'd wife; – especially when I reflected that he was
not guilty through a want of affection for her, but a too violent excess of it; as is
observed by one of our best English poets:

> The greater care, the higher passion shews,
> We hold that dearest, we most fear to lose.[106]

Indeed I soon found, how much more than I could even have imagined, this
offending husband deserved my commiseration; – he was abroad, and Cleora
not yet risen from her bed, when I made my visit, which, as near as I can remember, was somewhat past eleven o'clock; – resolved, however, not to lose my labour
entirely, I had recourse for intelligence to the tatlers of the kitchen, whom,
according to my wish, I found busy in discourse on the very point I wanted.

Some took the part of their master, – some of their lady; and upon the whole,
I found that a second quarrel having ensued after Aristus came home, Cleora
had refused either to sup or sleep with him; but lay in a bed she had order'd to
be prepar'd for her in another room, on which he went not to his own, but continued the whole night walking about the house, and behaved like a man totally
deprived of reason; – I shall relate some few of the animadversions made by these
speculative gentry on this occasion.

Footman. Well, if I were a gentleman like my master, I would not make myself
so uneasy for all the women in the world.

House-maid. Never talk of it, William; – if a man will be jealous of his wife
without a cause, he deserves to suffer.

Cook. Ay faith, Margery, and if he had some women she would soon shew him the difference, and make him jealous for something.

Footman. You may say what you will, but there must be something in it; – 'tis plain he loves her to distraction, and would never be in such passions with her if he did not see things that we know nothing of.

House-maid. You are a censorious fool for thinking as you do; – my lady is as good a woman as ever was born, and I dare say as virtuous; – 'tis nothing but the devil that puts such notions in my master's head; – and 'tis well if some time or other, when he is in these freaks, if he does not do either her or himself a mischief.

Cook. So it is, indeed, Margery; – I met him upon the stairs this morning, and methought he look'd for all the world as if he was going to make himself away.

The footman was just opening his mouth to make some answer when the valet-de-chambre came into the kitchen, and being ask'd if he knew where his master was gone, he reply'd that he did, and that he was gone to wait upon his mother; on which she that had spoke last cry'd out:

Cook. His mother, – he will be much the better for that; – she has a good hand, as I have heard say, at making bad worse; – I remember Sarah that is just gone away overheard her tell my master, that my lady kept too much company, and went too often to the play, and a heap of such stuff; and I believe it is all owing to her that my poor lady is so much confined as she has been of late.

Valet. Hold your tongue, Cook, – she is a very worthy fine old lady, – has seen the world, – is a great œconomist, and nobody can blame her for inspecting a little into her son's affairs; – and it does not become you to talk in this manner of your betters.

Cook. Marry come up, my good essence-bottle; – I warrant you think that your bag-wig and flourish'd ruffles must give laws to the whole family; but I shall talk of whom I please and of what I please, without asking your leave or any body's else, as long as I speak nothing but the truth.

At this instant the footman, on a pretty loud knocking at the door, put his head through the window of the area, and crying, – 'Here is my master,' ran hastily up to give him entrance; – I followed as fast as I could, being more curious to see how Aristus would behave, than to hear what would be the issue of the contest between the Cook and Valet.

I stood close in the corner of an arch in the passage while he pass'd by, and could see nothing in his countenance of that ferocity the servants had been describing; – on the contrary, a perfect composure seem'd to me to sit upon all his features, and left not the least traces of dissatisfaction.

I attended him to a chamber, which, as I afterwards perceived, was the same that Cleora had made choice on for her repose, if it were possible for her to take any, the preceding night; – he knock'd gently at the door, but finding it not readily open'd, retired and went into the dining-room, where he call'd a servant and bid him seek his wife's waiting-maid, and order her to come immediately to him.

The young woman presently appear'd, tho' I easily discern'd not without some tremor of the nerves, expecting, perhaps, to participate in the effects of her master's displeasure; – her countenance, however, grew more assured when he spoke in the most courteous accents, saying,

Aristus. Is your lady awake yet, mrs. Betty?

Waiting-maid. Yes, sir.

Aristus. Then give my compliments to her, – let her know I am come home to breakfast, and ask if she will have the tea served where she is, or in her own dressing-room as usual.

Waiting-maid. Sir, you may be sure I shall be punctual in delivering your honour's commands to her.

Aristus. Say rather my intreaties, mrs. Betty; – for tho' I may be a little out of humour sometimes, as it happen'd last night, yet I cannot think it becoming in our sex to exercise any authority over the ladies.

She said no more, and after making a low curtsy went out of the room, very much surprised at this sudden turn, as indeed was I, after what I had seen and heard; nor was able to determine as yet, whether the extraordinary complaisance he shew'd was real or affected; – I was soon convinced, however, – that it was the former, when the maid return'd with this answer to his message:

Waiting-maid. Sir, my lady desires to be excused; – she has got a violent head-ach, and begs not to be disturbed.

Aristus. Tell her I bring her news that will make her well; – no, – hold, – I will go myself.

With these last words he flew to the chamber, and pushing open the door, which was now unlock'd, found his wife sitting in a very melancholy and dejected posture; – she started up at sight of him, and without giving him leave to speak accosted him in these terms:

Cleora. 'Tis hard that no part of a house, of which I am flatter'd with the name of mistress, can protect me from the insults of a man who certainly married me with no other view than to make me miserable.

Aristus. Oh say not so, – I will soon convince you to the contrary; – nor shall you ever more have cause to fly the presence of Aristus; – I own I have been to blame, have said and done a thousand things that I am asham'd to think on. – But why, my dear Cleora, did you raise my passion to that guilty height? – Why conceal from me the author and contents of the letter which gave me so much pain?

Cleora. It would be easy for me to justify my refusal.

Aristus. I know it would, my angel, full well I know it would; – but I am now let into the secret without your being guilty of a breach of friendship to oblige me.

Cleora. What is it you mean, Aristus?

Aristus. I have been this morning at my mother's, where speaking of our unhappy quarrel, and the motive of it, my sister immediately changed countenance, and after vindicating your conduct with the utmost vehemence, and severely condemning mine, confess'd it was herself had sent that letter to you by a porter, and had desir'd you to burn it as soon as read.

Cleora. Dear Lucia! – oh that the brother had the sister's temper.

Aristus. Brother and sister are equally devoted to you; – if Lucia were Aristus, she would do as Aristus does; and if Aristus were Lucia, he would act like Lucia: – the difference of sexes makes all the difference in our sentiments or behaviour; – her's is a tender friendship, – mine a raging love, which while happy in your possession, trembles at even the most distant possibility of ever being less so.

Cleora. Can it be love that suspects my virtue?

Aristus. By Heaven, my cooler moments have never set you down as capable of wronging me or dishonouring yourself; but when passion rages in the soul, reason has little government over our thoughts or words. – I know I have been much to blame; – but oh, Cleora, forgive a fault occasion'd only by an excess of fondness; – so dear I prize you, that I envy the very air that breathes upon your lips, and wish to grow for ever there and keep out all intruders.

Cleora. But do you consider how wretched this causeless jealousy has made me?

Aristus. Yes, and could tear out my heart for having ever harbour'd the least unjust suspicion of you; yet have I suffer'd torments much greater than was in my power to inflict. – Could you be sensible of the agonies I felt during this last whole cruel night, you must, you would forgive and pity me.

Cleora. Mine have not been less; – yet could I forget all, had my reputation been untouch'd by your ill usage; – you now know the purport of your sister's letter; and can you think it possible for me to support with patience, the being look'd upon by your kindred as a disgrace to the family I am come among?

Aristus. Think not so, my dear Cleora, – my sister was always assur'd of your innocence, and a strenuous vindicater of every thing you did; – my mother never thought worse than that some little inadvertencies in your conduct had wrought me up to the follies I have been guilty on, which she has just now severely chid me for: – they will both wait on you this afternoon, and give you all the proofs in their power of the sincere respect and tenderness they have for you.

Cleora. Well, Aristus, if I could be certain that this was the last trial you would make of my good-nature, I might, perhaps, endeavour to think no more on what is past.

Aristus. If ever I fall back into my former errors despise me, – hate, – think me the worst of men; – no, be assured I am too much asham'd of what I have been, ever to be the like again; and as a proof of the perfect confidence I now have in you, henceforward keep what company you please, I shall prescribe no rules for your conduct, I shall leave all to yourself, and be satisfied that all you do is right.

Cleora. I shall take the less liberty for your granting me so much: – but if you should relapse, remember what a certain celebrated author of our sex says on this occasion:

> We women to ourselves this justice owe,
> That those who think us false should find us so.[107]

She spoke this with so enchanting a smile, that Aristus, tho' not yet quite sure that what he did would be agreeable, could not forbear catching her in his arms, and holding her for some time lock'd in the most strict embrace, – then letting her loose, and looking on her with the extremest tenderness, cry'd,

Aristus. Do you then forgive me?

Cleora. I do.

With these words she threw her snowy arms about his neck, put her face close to his, returning all the endearments he had just before given her; – after which, – that is, as soon as the transport he was in would give him leave to speak, he said,

Aristus. My for ever ador'd Cleora, depend upon it that the whole study of my life shall be to requite this goodness.

Cleora. Treat me but as my actions deserve, – I ask no more: – but come, let us go to breakfast.

With this they went arm in arm into the next room, where mrs. Betty and the tea equipage waited their approach.

I now left this once more happy pair to enjoy the sweets of their reconciliation; and as I doubted not but the contrition of Aristus would be as lasting, as by many indications I had reason to think it was sincere, expected not that any future events, worthy the attention of an Invisible Spy, would happen to call me to their house again.

But, unhappily for the persons concern'd in it, a very few days after convinced me how little I was endow'd with the spirit of prophecy; and also that when once the fatal fire of jealousy has got possession of the mind, tho' it may lie dormant for a while, yet the least wafting of a feather, or even a shadow, is sufficient to give it motion, and kindle the smother'd embers into a blaze.

I was loitering one morning in the Park, the air was serene and not cold, the time of year consider'd, for it was then November; – few people being there, I had an opportunity of indulging contemplation with the wonders of nature, which even in the most barren season affords matter to attract our admiration, and was almost lost in thought, when I was suddenly rouz'd from it by the appearance of Cleora, who, in a rich genteel deshabille,[108] came tripping down the walk, and after looking two or three times round her, seated herself on a bench just opposite to St. James's-house; – my surprise to find a lady of her rank alone in that place stopp'd my farther progress, and engaged me to draw pretty near to her, in order to observe whether chance or any particular motive had brought her hither.

In less time than the taking a pinch of snuff would last, Aristus came as from the palace; – he saw his wife at a distance, cross'd over and came to her, saying,

Aristus. What are you here, my dear, and alone?

Cleora. You see I am, but I did not expect to be pick'd up by a gentleman this morning. – We are well met, however, and if you have no business that requires your haste, should be glad you would give me your company while I stay, which will not be long.

Aristus. With all my heart, – I was only going to the coffee-house; and in return for my complaisance you shall tell me by what accident I find you here thus unguarded.

Cleora. Can one be unguarded where there are so many soldiers? – But you must know I have been among the shops at Charing-Cross and made a great many purchases; – I choose to walk over the Park; – I had William with me, but as I knew the centry would not suffer him to pass through with the things,[109] I sent him home the other way: – when I came hither I found the air so extremely pleasant that I was tempted to sit down and take a little of it, especially as I found nobody here that I thought would take any notice of me: – and now you have the whole history of my morning's transactions.

Aristus. A very concise one; – but suppose, my dear, you had met with any of the Bucks, the Bloods, or the Buffs,[110] how would you have escaped their attacks?

Cleora. Why I would have set my arms akimbo, and look'd as fierce as they: – those sort of 'squires are never bold but to the fearful.

Finding, by their talking together in this gay manner, that they continued in perfect good humour with each other, I thought I had no business to be an evesdropper any longer to their discourse, and was going to quit the place where I had stood, when, just as I had taken it into my head to do so, two gentlemen came down the walk, one of whom, in passing by the bench, stopp'd short, look'd earnestly at Cleora, started, made a low bow, and then went on; – she return'd the salute, but with a confusion impossible to be express'd; – she blush'd, – she trembled through every joint, – her fan fell out of her hand, and she was ready to sink herself upon the seat.

A less observing husband than Aristus must have taken notice of this sudden change; but the alarm it gave his jealous heart was such as compell'd him to be speechless for some moments: – Cleora in vain endeavour'd to recompose herself; all the efforts she made to suppress or to conceal her agitations render'd them but the more violent, and consequently the more visible. – Aristus at last broke silence with these words:

Aristus. You seem disorder'd, madam; – the sight of these gentlemen has had a strange effect upon you.

Cleora. I was a little surprised at the sight of one of them; – but that is not all, – I am not well.

Aristus. I see you are not, either in mind or body; – my coming was unlucky; had I been absent, you would doubtless have retain'd your former gaiety: – but this is no place to expatiate on the cause of your disorder, – I will get one of the soldiers to call a chair, – 'tis fit you should go home.

He waited not to hear what answer she would make, but rose hastily up and spoke to one of those who he saw was not on duty; – the fellow ran to do as he was desired, and presently return'd with a chair: – while he was gone, Cleora had recover'd herself enough to say to Aristus:

Cleora. I perceive you are beginning to entertain sentiments to my disadvantage; – but have patience till we get home, and I shall easily make this matter clear.

As he was putting her into the chair she added,

Cleora. You will follow presently.

Aristus. I shall not be long after you, tho' I believe your own meditations, at this time, will be more agreeable to you than the company of a husband.

I perceived very plainly, by the countenance of Aristus, that a storm was gathering in his breast, which I doubted not but would break forth in thunder; I could not help also being of opinion that there were some appearances on the part of Cleora not much to her advantage; – I thought, however, that the best way to form a true judgment of the accidents of that morning were to see them when they were together, so forbore following either of them, and restrain'd my impatience 'till the hour in which they usually dined, as being the most likely time to find Aristus at home.

On my coming to their house I found the door open, and a footman in a laced livery sitting on a bench in the hall, as waiting for an answer to some message he brought; – I went directly up to the dining-room; – no person being there I pass'd on to Cleora's apartment, and found her writing at her buroe; – a letter lay open before her containing these lines:

To Cleora.

Madam,

I heard not of your marriage till some weeks after it was consummated; and when I did, the hurry of my affairs, being then just going to Paris, prevented my congratulating you upon it; – I return'd to England but three days since, and the first enquiry I made was concerning your health and place of abode; but the answers I received to these interrogatories were mingled with some other informations, which make me not quite sure that a visit from me might not give offence to that happy gentleman who is now your husband; – I would not therefore take the liberty of waiting on you till I had first received your permission; – it is a blessing I ardently long for, but whether proper for you to grant or not, I beg you will believe that I am, With an esteem too justly grounded for change of circumstances to alter,

MADAM,

Your most faithfully devoted,

And most humble servant,

LEANDER.

The answer given by Cleora to the above billet was as follows:

To LEANDER.

SIR,

THAT I still retain a place in your remembrance demands my grateful acknowledgments, and I am sorry to tell you that it is at this distance only I can pay my thanks: – it is easy for me to guess of what nature the informations you mention have been, and think myself obliged so far to confirm the truth of them, as to let you know the favour you intended me is wholly improper for me to receive; and to desire you will attempt no future correspondence of any kind, with her who is no longer mistress of her actions, but who must always preserve in her heart the best wishes for your welfare.

CLEORA.

Having seal'd this she call'd her maid Betty, and bid her deliver it to the man who waited for it; – then took up Leander's letter and read it two or three times over to herself with very disturb'd emotions; – after which she rose hastily from the posture she had been in, whether with a design to burn, or lay it carefully up, I cannot pretend to say, for her husband that instant flew into the room and snatch'd it out of her hand; – she shriek'd, and, in my opinion, very imprudently endeavour'd to wrest it from him; – his stature, as well as strength, being much superior to hers, he held it at arms length and read the contents, in spite of all her weak efforts to hinder it.

Which done he clapp'd it into his pocket, – stamp'd, – bit his lips, – measur'd the room with wild unequal paces, – still as he turn'd darting revengeful glances at the trembling Cleora; – these, and other such like frantic gestures, introduced the following dialogue between them:

Cleora. What is there in that letter can have moved you thus?

Aristus. Was it not sent by him whose sight this morning threw you into such disorder?

Cleora. I was a little surprised at the sudden appearance of a person I had not seen for a long time; but know not that the disorder I was in proceeded from that cause.

Aristus. He knew it did, at least, and I suppose sent you this billet by way of consolation.

Cleora. You put an odd interpretation on his words as well as on my looks. Is this, Aristus, the effect of all those promises you so lately made?

Aristus. When I made those promises I was so weak as to believe there was a possibility of your being faithful; – but I am now convinced of what you are; – know that you are the most vile of women, and I the most accursed of men.

Cleora. You make yourself, indeed, the one, by your unjust and base suspicions; – but no action of mine shall ever prove that I am the other.

Aristus. Death and furies! – did I not meet the villain's servant with a letter from you in his hand!

Cleora. Suppose you did, – I wrote to forbid his coming hither.

Aristus. Yes, and no doubt to appoint a place more convenient for your meeting.

Cleora. 'Tis false; – nor would the man whom your suspicions wrong me with, harbour a thought to the prejudice either of my virtue or my reputation. – No, if you had half his honour or his love I should not be the wretch I am.

Aristus. Then you confess he loves you?

Cleora. He loved me once, and tho' Heaven thought fit to break off our intended union, I believe still preserves an esteem for me.

Aristus. As you for him. – Hell and vengeance! – dare you avow this to my face! – Have I then only the leavings, – the refuse of a beloved rival! – audacious strumpet!

In speaking this he struck her so violent a blow over the face, that the blood gush'd from her nose and mouth, on which she cry'd out:

Cleora. Villain! – there wanted but this to prove the baseness of thy abject soul! – but think not that the name of wife shall make me tamely bear such usage; – no, if the laws of England should refuse to do me justice, I will fly to the remotest corner of the earth, and seek a refuge among the less barbarous Hottentots, rather than live beneath the roof, much less sleep in the same bed with such a monster!

How Aristus would have behaved on this is uncertain, – a servant that moment enter'd the room, and told him that a gentleman, who it seems he had sent for that morning upon business, was now come to wait upon him; – whatever was in the mind of this distracted husband, he had no farther opportunity of shewing it at present, and only giving a furious look at Cleora, and muttering some inarticulate curses between his teeth as he went out, left her to ruminate on what was past.

She no sooner found herself alone than she rung the bell for her maid, who appear'd quite frighted on seeing her lady in such a condition; – the girl's exclamations made her turn to the looking-glass, and the injury that had been done to her beauty, it is probable, gave strength to her resentment, and she resolved to put in immediate execution what she had threaten'd Aristus with doing.

Betty had lived with her before her marriage, and was no stranger to the love had been between her and Leander; the enraged fair one therefore scrupled not to make her the confidant of the motive of this last quarrel with her husband, and the intention she had of quitting him for ever; – then, after considering a little in what manner she should manage this affair, gave the following orders:

Cleora. I would have you take a hackney-coach for expedition sake, and go to mrs. Clip's, the tyre-woman,[111] who cuts my hair, – I know she lets lodgings; if she has any apartment empty, hire it directly; but if her house happens to be full, do not return without procuring one for me in some other; for I am determin'd to go this very afternoon, and shall think every moment an age till I am out of this detested place.

While the maid was gone, Cleora set about packing up her cloaths and jewels, which she did with such adroitness and alacrity, that in less than an hour every thing belonging to her was ready to be sent away; – in a little more than that time Betty return'd, and told her that mrs. Clip's first floor being let she had agreed for the parlours, which she said were very handsome, and she believed her ladyship would approve of, at least till a better apartment could be provided.

Cleora was satisfy'd, – another coach was call'd to carry her, and the maid follow'd in the other with the luggage.

Aristus was all this time abroad, – he went out with the gentleman who had call'd on him, and his absence very much facilitated the execution of his wife's design; for had he been at home 'tis certain that either his love or anger, or perhaps a mixture of both, would have attempted to detain her; but what effects the steps she had taken produced, both on the one and the other, must be left to the succeeding chapter.

CHAP. V.

In which the consequences of Cleora's elopement, in relation both to herself and husband, are fully shewn, and an end put to that suspense which it is highly probable the former pages may have excited in the mind of every interested and curious reader.

I staid some hours at the house of Aristus, expecting to be witness of something extraordinary in his behaviour, when he should be told of the departure of his wife; but he returning not in all that time, I grew weary of the tedious attendance and quitted my post in order to go home; for as to Cleora, I had no thoughts of visiting her in her new apartment 'till next morning.

It not being late, however, I took it into my head to call in at a great coffee-house in my way, and lucky was it for the gratification of my curiosity that I did so; – I found Aristus there, – he was sitting at a table in one corner of the room, some distance from the other company, with paper and a standish before him; – I advanced with all the speed I could towards him, and saw him write the following billet:

To LEANDER.

SIR

YOU are a villain, and have endeavour'd to wrong me in a point too tender to be forgiven: – I need only tell you, that I am the husband of Cleora, to inform you both of what I mean, and what sort of satisfaction my honour demands from you, which I expect you will give me to-morrow morning at seven, in the Artillery-ground, Tothill-fields:[112] – the bearer has orders to wait your answer to

ARISTUS.

This he sent by a porter to the Braund's head in Bond-street, at which house, as I afterwards discover'd, he had with a good deal of pains got intelligence that Leander constantly supp'd every night.

I waited behind Aristus with an impatience, perhaps, not inferior to his own, to see what reply Leander would make to the above, till the porter return'd from him with these lines:

To ARISTUS.

SIR,

THO' your telling me that you are the husband of Cleora cannot make me in the least sensible how I deserve the name of villain, yet I can easily guess at the satisfaction you require, and shall not fail to meet you at the hour and place appointed, in hopes of being better inform'd for what imaginary cause you treat in this manner a person who neither knows or ever had any design to injure you.

LEANDER.

Aristus, after having read this, staid no longer than to drink one dish of coffee; as I perceived he turn'd that way which led to his own house, I could not forbear accompanying him thither; and I believe, by what I have to relate, the reader will think I had no reason to repent the pains I took.

He was no sooner enter'd than he ask'd hastily for his wife, doubtless with an intention to renew his reproaches, and give a vent to some part of the fury he was possess'd of; but never certainly did astonishment work a more strange effect, – on being told by the footman who open'd the door, that she was gone, and the manner in which she went, the sudden shock at once deprived him both of speech and motion, – his face grew pale as ashes, – his eyes were fix'd in a stupid stare, and had he been buried for three days, scarce could he have appeared more the ghost of what he was the moment before.

His deaden'd faculties by degrees reviving, the first use he made of them was to call up all the servants, asking first one, and then another, – why she was suffer'd to depart, – why they did not stop her! – to which they answer'd, that having no order from him they durst not presume so far; – and besides, they knew nothing of her going till they saw the coaches at the door and the port-manteaus carry'd out.

He next demanded to what place she had directed herself to be carried; but both Cleora and her maid having taken the precaution to give no order to the coachmen till they were got some distance from the house, no one of them was able to give him any information, on which he sent them out of the room, not without some curses on their indolence in not following the coaches; – then, thinking himself alone, began to give a loose to the dictates of his despair and rage in these expressions:

Aristus. Then she is lost! – for ever lost to me! for if she should return, my honour, after this, would not permit me to receive her. – Why did I ever marry! – What demon tempted me to become the husband of a woman, whom I knew all mankind who saw must love as well as I! – Yet how secure, how happy did I once think myself in her embraces! – Too bless'd, indeed, had she never given me reason to believe her false! – Heavens! that so fair an outside, such seeming innocence, should be the varnish of a foul polluted mind! – Curse on my fond passion! – curse on her fatal charms! – Oh the deceiver! – the vile hypocrite, while in my arms she languish'd for another! – There is no longer any room for doubt, her flight has proved her guilt. – Revenge is now my sole relief; – she for the present has escap'd my reach; but I will stab her image in Leander's heart. – Oh that it were morning, that I might put a husband's mark upon the lewd adulterer!

While uttering the latter part of this exclamation he flew about the room as if totally bereft of reason; till his spirits, at length exhausted by the violence of his rage, sunk into the contrary extreme, – that of dejection; – he folded his arms, sigh'd, and with tears bursting from his eyes, cry'd out:

Aristus. Oh Cleora! – Cleora! – lovely perfidious wanton, to what hast thou reduced me!

He then threw himself down on a settee, with groans like those which issue from the breasts of men dying in their full vigour; whence, after having lain some time, he started up saying:

Aristus. I will think no more; – to hear of my distractions would but sooth her pride.

He now seem'd a little more composed, and call'd for something to eat; but on its being brought could only mangle a cold chicken, without being able to put one morsel into his mouth, so rose from table and went up to his own chamber, where I did not think fit to pursue him, as having already seen enough to make me know the present disposition of his mind.

It was my full intention, however, to go in the morning to the Artillery-ground, to be spectator of the combat between him and Leander; but was disappointed by sleeping beyond the time they were to meet; – this a little vex'd me, but I consoled myself with the thoughts of being able to hear the event, by calling some part of the day at the house of of Aristus, for I knew not where Leander lived; but my concern for Cleora carrying me first to her lodgings, I there got all the intelligence I wanted.

I found that lady, as I believe, just risen from her bed, for she was in a loose entire deshabille: – she seem'd very pensive, and had the marks of her jealous husband's resentment still flagrant on her lovely face; – Betty was not with her when I came in, but enter'd immediately after, and surprised her with these words:

Betty. Oh! madam, – I have the strangest thing to tell you!

Cleora. What is it?

Betty. Who does your ladyship think I have seen?

Cleora. Nay I know not. – Who, prithee?

Betty. The very footman that brought your ladyship the letter yesterday, and put my master into such a rage; – I was never so confounded in my whole life.

Cleora. Confounded, for what? – Where did you see him?

Betty. In the kitchen, madam: – when I went down, just now, to put on the tea-kettle for breakfast, who should I see there but him talking to mrs. Clip: – his master lodges here in the apartment above.

Cleora. Good Heaven! – was there ever so unfortunate an accident! – to come to lodge in the same house with the man whom at present it most behoves me to avoid! – Do you think he knows you?

Betty. O yes, madam; – your ladyship may remember it was I that took the letter from him and carry'd down your answer: – I warrant he knows me again; but if he did not, I find mrs. Clip has been babling to him about your ladyship, for I heard her mention your name as I was upon the stairs.

Cleora. Sure I was infatuated not to forbid that woman telling any body I was here; – but I must remove immediately; – it would be my utter ruin if my husband, or any of his friends should hear I had lain in this house but one night.

Betty. Very true, indeed, madam, – and as soon as your ladyship has had your breakfast, I will go out and get another lodging.

Cleora. Don't talk of breakfasting, – I will have you go this instant, – I am distracted to think where I am.

Betty. Dear madam, I beg you will not put yourself into such a hurry of spirits, it seems Leander is gone abroad, and these gay gentlemen, when once they go out, seldom return all day: – I will engage your ladyship shall be removed before he knows any thing of your being here.

Cleora. You talk like a fool; – as he went out so early, he is the more likely to come home to dress, – therefore prithee get away, – I would not have him see me here for the world.

Betty, finding her lady so resolute, made no farther delays, but went into the next room and huddled on her capuchin[113] and gloves, which done, she return'd and ask'd what part of the town would be most agreeable to her; – to which Cleora reply'd, – that all situations were alike indifferent to her; but should chuse some one or other of the streets that turn'd out of the Strand, as she must be private for a while, and had fewest acquaintance that way, – and then bid her send mrs. Clip to her.

The maid went out, and mrs. Clip enter'd the room presently after; – Cleora told her the circumstances of her affairs laid her under a necessity of removing from her house, and intreated she would not make mention of her having been there to any one who might enquire for her; – the other express'd a good deal of concern for losing so good a lodger, and assured her of observing secrecy in the point she desir'd.

While they were talking, a loud knocking at the door made mrs. Clip run to the parlour window, and seeing who it was cry'd out,

Mrs. Clip. Bless me! 'tis Leander, – his cloaths are all bloody, and his arm in a scarf! – he has been fighting, that's certain! I thought there were some such thing in hand, by his going out so early this morning; – I beg your ladyship's pardon, I must run and see if he wants any thing I can do for him.

Cleora was too much confounded at the name of Leander, and the condition she heard he was in, to offer to detain her, and after she was gone fell into a profound resvery, which held her for, I believe, not less than half an hour; and perhaps might have done so much longer, if she had not been roused from it by a gentle knocking at the parlour door; – but how greatly was she surprised, when on her calling to the person to come in she saw Leander enter; – she started, – trembled, and with a faultering voice spoke thus to him:

Cleora. Oh, sir, a visit from you is wholly improper at this time!

Leander. I hope not so, madam; since I would not have so far intruded, but to acquaint you with something which it may be convenient for you to know; – I have seen your husband this morning.

Cleora. Oh my foreboding heart! – I dread to ask the consequence of such a meeting!

Leander. You need not, madam, – Aristus is unhurt, and I bear only one slight token of his intent to take my life.

Cleora. Then you have fought!

Leander. It was with the utmost regret I drew my sword against the husband of Cleora; – but be pleased, madam, to peruse this billet, and you will see the necessity that compell'd me to it.

With these words he presented to her the challenge he had received the night before from Aristus; which, as soon as she had look'd over, she return'd to him again, – saying,

Cleora. Unjust Aristus; – but I thank Heaven that nothing worse has ensued!

Leander. Heaven, madam, has indeed alone the praise; since it was not to any superior skill of mine, or to any generosity in my antagonist, that I am indebted for my preservation, but to a kind of miracle.

Cleora. As how; – pray, sir, inform me!

Leander. I know not, madam, whether I can make you sensible how the thing happened, as your sex are ignorant of the terms made use of in the description of such rencounters; – but I will do my best: – When first we met, I would have endeavour'd to reason him out of mistake so injurious to you and his own peace of mind, as well as to myself; but he refused to listen to any arguments I had prepar'd, and flew upon me with the rage of an incensed lion: – by the manner of his fighting, I easily perceived he came with a resolution either to kill or be kill'd; – so as I was desirous of avoiding both the one and the other, I only stood upon my defence and parry'd the pushes he made, tho' in aiming at my breast he several times exposed his own: – the moderation I observ'd but inraging him the more, he attempted to close with me; and in that action I received a wound in my right arm a little above the bend, which hindering me from making any use of that wrist, I shifted my sword into the other hand, saying to him at the same time, 'You see, sir, I am disabled, – we must leave the decision of this affair till some other time.' – 'No,' cry'd he, 'I am not so weak as to lose the advantage I have gain'd.' – On this I retreated some paces, and then redoubling his attacks, the aukward opposition I could now make would not have protected me one moment longer, if in the very crisis of my fate, when the point of his weapon was just ready to transfix me to the earth, we had not fortunately been separated: – some people, whose windows had a prospect of the Artillery-ground, saw the first of our engagement, and making all the haste they could to prevent the threaten'd mischief, arrived in the instant I have mention'd, beat down the sword of Aristus, and placed themselves before me as a shield.

Cleora. How this account has made me shudder! – What then did Aristus do!

Leander. Walk'd sullenly away, pursued by the reproaches of my deliverers till he was out of hearing; and it was with much ado that I prevail'd with them to offer him no farther insults. – But, madam, while I am giving you the history of my ill treatment, I fear it is in your power to present me with a more shocking detail of the cause that brought you hither?

Cleora. It is such a one, indeed, as if the world be not as unjust as Aristus, will easily absolve me for the resolution I have taken of never living with him more; – but it would happen very unlucky for my reputation, should it be known I have seen you even this once; I therefore intreat that after I go hence you will not think of making me any future visits.

Leander. Tho' it is hard to suffer for the faults of another, yet, madam, be assured I shall never desire any thing that may give Aristus a pretence for his ill treatment: – I flatter myself, however, that the remembrance of our former tenderness is not so totally obliterated, but that friendship may subsist between us; – you may, at least, permit me to write to you sometimes.

Cleora. I know not whether even that would not be too much.

Leander. Neither virtue, nor duty to the best of husbands, could set down as a fault the favour I request; and to prevent all misinterpretations of our innocent correspondence, I shall take such precautions as will keep it a secret from all the world.

Cleora. Well, sir, I cannot refuse this proof of your compassion for me, and think I ought not to deprive myself of any innocent consolation under my present affliction; – you may therefore be assured that I shall receive, and answer your letters, with all the satisfaction a woman in my circumstances either can or ought to feel.

He was going to make some reply when Betty return'd from her errand; – she was a little surprised at seeing him there, and said nothing till her lady, impatient to know the success of what she had been about, spoke thus to her:

Cleora. Well, Betty, have you done the business I sent you on?

Betty. Yes, madam, – please to step into the next room and I will give you an account.

Cleora. No, you may tell me here, – I dare trust this gentleman's discretion.

The maid then inform'd her that she had agreed for lodgings at the house of a great taylor, whom she nam'd, in Norfolk-street; – on this Cleora desired Leander to retire, saying she must get herself ready, for she was determin'd to depart immediately; – he offer'd not to oppose her design; but tho' the leave they took of each other now was accompany'd with the greatest respect on his side, and reserve on her's, I could easily perceive that this interview had rekindled in both their hearts those flames of affection they before had felt.

After he had left the room, Cleora's things not having been unpack'd, there needed little preparation for her going; – she sent for mrs. Clip, and made her a handsome present for the trouble she had given her house; but finding her a tatling woman, acquainted her not with that to which she was removing; – I saw both the mistress and the maid, with all their luggage, depart in the same manner they had come; but did not accompany them to their new habitation, as I could not promise myself with finding any thing there as yet worthy of my enquiry.

The discourse of the town afterwards informed me, that Cleora had employ'd a lawyer, and was soliciting either to have her whole fortune return'd, or an annual allowance to the amount of the interest of it: – Aristus was at first refractory to all proposals of this nature; but all his friends, and his mother in particular, joining their persuasions, he at last was prevail'd on to sign articles of a final separation; by which it was agreed that she should have a pension of three hundred pounds a year during his life, and in case he died before her, her whole fortune restored.

I frequently call'd upon Cleora, and found that during this negotiation with her husband she kept her resolution of not seeing Leander; but that affair was no sooner over than he visited her every day, – the consequence of which may easily be guess'd at, and was in a short time proved; for they went to Paris together, and still continue to reside there.

This last action of Cleora's has doubtless given the world room to believe she had not been wrong'd by the suspicions of Aristus; but whoever is of this opinion does her a great deal of injustice, – the Invisible Spy is a witness for her, that her inclinations were virtuous, – her disposition grateful and sincere, and had she been treated with that confidence a good wife ought to have been, no temptations would have had the power to have made her otherwise: – let all husbands therefore beware how they provoke, by ill usage and distrust, the fate they would avoid; – and observe this maxim of the poets:

> He that would keep the fair one true and kind,
> By love must clap a padlock on her mind.[114]

CHAP. VI.

Treats of divers and sundry matters, some of which the Invisible author flatters himself will be very agreeable to the greatest part of the readers, but if, contrary to his expectations, they should happen to be found otherwise, he hopes at least they will be excused on account of others, both past and to come, more entertaining and suitable to his taste.

When my curiosity was not attach'd to the pursuit of any particular adventure, I frequently stepp'd, for the sake of amusement, into one or other of our great coffee-houses; and, indeed, seldom return'd from any of them without bringing home something worthy of my very serious reflections afterwards.

These places, I think, may with propriety enough to be call'd the world in miniature, as they present you with some part of almost every thing that is in it; – the variety of company and of humours one meets there, fill the mind with an agreeable medley, which, when separated and digested by meditation, enlarges the understanding, and gives us ideas which otherwise might perhaps be for ever strangers to us.

The affairs of the army, the navy, the senate-house, the council-board, are here freely discuss'd, and censur'd or approv'd according to the different interests or inclination of the speakers; – our stock at home, our colonies abroad, our commerce with our neighbours, our trade among ourselves, with deaths, births, marriages, and intrigues, are promiscuously treated on; – the courtier, the patriot,[115] the man of business, and the man of pleasure, talk every one on matters relating to his own sphere, and leave you uninformed of nothing.

But it affords a good deal of diversion to a curious observer, when there happens to be in company some country 'squire, who perhaps sees the town but once in half seven years, and knows nothing of what is done in it but what he reads in those few news papers which are permitted to be sent down to the village where he lives; – how he stares, and gapes with his mouth wide open as if he would swallow all he hears, and every now and then asks, – How can this be? – and – How can that be? – and express his honest wonder on being told things which, indeed, without knowing, would scarcely be believed by persons brought up in less simplicity.

But, as much as we town-bred people may laugh at such a one, there is, in my opinion, another species of mortals yet more deserving ridicule: – How often have I seen a fellow almost as ignorant as the seat he sits upon, in every thing but the common occurrences of life, listen with a shew of the greatest attention to an abstruse argument? – give a significant nod at some parts of it, – shrug up his shoulders at another, – sometimes shake his head, – wink with one eye, – seem to debate within himself to which of the orators he should give the preference, and if ask'd any question by a by-stander on the occasion, reply with all the gravity of a philosopher, – 'Sir, I never give my sentiments in these matters.'

Whenever I chance to meet with such a one, I cannot help remembering what the witty Earl of Rochester said in one of his poems:

> When a fool among wise men does silently sit,
> A fool that says nothing may pass for a wit.[116]

Impossible is it to describe folly in all its various shapes; but there is none more preposterous than when it puts on the garb of wisdom, affects to be sententious and austere, and endeavours to hide its ass's ears beneath the veil of deep profundity; – yet nothing is more common than this, as may every day be seen on benches more respectable than those in the places I am speaking of.

But it is very likely that the impatient reader will cry out, – What is all this to the purpose? – and begin to think it high time I should relate something for his entertainment, if not for his improvement; – indeed I cannot positively promise that I shall be able to do either the one or the other, but I will endeavour the best I can; and a candid mind will always allow that there is some merit in a good intention.

Well then, – on the evening of that memorable day in which Dr. Cameron was executed,[117] and the bills for naturalising the Jews and for preventing clandestine Marriages had pass'd the royal assent,[118] I went to a certain celebrated coffee-house at the court end of the town, neither White's nor St. James's,[119] yet I found it as full of company as ever I saw either of them.

The moment I enter'd the room I perceived the important transactions of the day engross'd the discourse of the whole assembly, except among some few striplings, such as the French distinguish by the name of Petit Maitres,[120] but by their dress appear'd belonging to the army; – these I left to adjust their sword-knots and toupees,[121] and advanced where a set of more serious gentlemen attracted my attention.

I found they had been talking of the Marriage-Bill; but whatever arguments had been urged among them, pro and con, either in vindication or disapprobation of it, were all over before I came; and the first thing I heard, and which made me know what had been the subject of their conversation was this:

First Gentleman. I am very sensible, gentlemen, that it does not become us to make objections to any bill in parliament, after it is once enacted into a law: – but I heard of an odd accident happening yesterday, which may serve to shew the consequences that are likely to attend laying such a restriction on the hearts of young people;[122] – if you please I will relate it to you.

Second Gentleman. Pray do, sir.

Third Gentleman. I dare answer it will be a favour to us all.

First Gentleman. You must know, gentlemen, that I am acquainted with an eminent citizen, who has under his guardianship a young lady call'd miss Hasty, a fortune of twenty thousand pounds; – I take him to be a worthy honest man, and one who would faithfully discharge the trust reposed in him; – some business obliging me to call on him this morning, I found him with a countenance full of trouble and confusion; – on my asking him if any misfortune had happen'd in his family, he reply'd, – 'There are few things could give me more concern, – miss Hasty is married, and has thrown herself away in a most strange and unaccountable manner.'

On my expressing some surprise, he related the whole story to me, which I will give you the particulars of, as near as I can remember, in the same manner he told them:

The Marriage-Bill, it seems, had been a great bugbear to this young lady all the time it was depending in parliament, and when she heard it had pass'd both houses, and waited only the royal assent, she took a resolution not to leave it in the power of her guardian to put any constraint upon her inclination; – she had no lover, nor was there any particular person to whom she wish'd to be united for life, yet was determined to be so to somebody or other; – accordingly she went yesterday morning into the counting-house, where my friend's clerk, a spruce young man, sat writing at his desk, – 'Goodmorrow, mr. Cypher,' said she, 'do you not wonder what brings me here so early?' – 'I have not yet had time for wonder, miss,' answer'd he, 'you are but just come in. – But pray what are your commands?' – 'I have a mind to be married,' resumed she, 'will you have me?' – 'Certainly, miss,' said he, 'if I were worthy of that honour.' – 'That is none of your affair,' return'd she, 'if you agree to my proposal throw away your pen and go with me this moment to May-Fair Chapel.'[123] – The young fellow, who imagin'd not she meant any thing more than to rally him, reply'd laughing, – 'With all my heart, miss; but shall we not make my master of our party?' – 'Pish,' cry'd she scornfully, 'I did not think you were such a fool; but remember what I say, you will hereafter repent your not taking me at my word.'

This refusal did not baulk her intention, – she took a hackney-coach directly, made herself be drove very slowly up one street and down another, looking in at every shop she pass'd, till she saw a neat young fellow behind a haberdasher's counter; – here she stopp'd, and beckon'd him to come to her, – which he did, bowing very humbly; but she made him come into the coach, and ask'd him if he were married; – to which question he answering in the negative, she made him the same offer she had the clerk; – the young fellow, who was only a jour-ney-man, having no friends nor fortune to set him up in his business, thought his condition could not be made worse by the venture, and after a short pause consented; – he would have gone back for his hat and gloves but she would not permit him, and away they drove to May-Fair, where they were immediately mar-ried by one of those parsons who officiate there.

When the ceremony was over she sent him home in another coach, telling him she would come in about two hours and claim him for a husband, which she did after having hired handsome lodgings for the consummation of their nuptials.

My friend was surprised when dinner was served up and miss Hasty not at table, and much more so on being told she went out in the morning in a hack-ney-coach, without either her maid or footman to attend her; – night coming on, and she not return'd, he grew very uneasy, – sent to all her acquaintance in search of her, but in vain, nobody had seen her the whole day: – the clerk, on this, beginning to think the offer she had made him was more in earnest than he had believed it, related to his master all the conference that had pass'd between them in the counting-house, on which the honest gentleman was almost out of his wits, – he apprehended the truth of what had happen'd, and that all the measures he could now take would be too late to prevent her ruin.

He told me that no man had ever pass'd a night in greater disquiets than he had the last; – the morning, however, put an end to the suspence he had been in, – she came and brought her bridegroom with her, – told him the motives that had induced her to take the step she had done, and the manner in which she had executed so odd an enterprize; – adding, that it was her glory to have disappointed the legislature, and not left it in the power of any guardian either to dispose of her hand, or restrain her for giving it wherever she had an inclination.

The mischief was now irremedible, advice and reproof were equally in vain, so he answer'd little to the recital she had made him; and she departed with her spouse, taking with her her two servants and all her baggage.

Here the gentleman ended his little narrative, and received the thanks of the company for the trouble he had given himself; – after which one of them said:

Second Gentleman. I do not doubt, indeed, but that the passing this Bill will bring about many such marriages; – I have it confidently affirm'd, that since the bringing it into the house, which I think is not above three months, there have been more couples noos'd in the Fleet, May-Fair, and other private Chapels,[124] than in all the Churches throughout London in a whole Year.

Third Gentleman. That may be; but however unlucky it may prove to some private families, I cannot think it concerns the public in any measure equal to the Naturalization of the Jews; – though, for my part, I am determin'd never to give my vote for any member who supported either.

Here several started up, and cry'd with one voice, – 'Nor I, – Nor I, by Heaven!' – on which another, who I had not heard speak before, reprov'd the warmth they express'd in these terms:

Fourth Gentleman. Hold, gentlemen, – whatever your thoughts are, it seems to me highly impolitic in you to declare them in this public manner; – consider, I beseech you, that if what you say should reach the ears of the honourable house, they might, perhaps, rather than run the hazard of not being rechosen, establish themselves in their seats for seven, fourteen, or one and twenty years, and so on *ad infinitum.*[125]

First Gentleman. What, a perpetual dictatorship! – Tush, – tush, the people would not bear it.

Second Gentleman. No, no, they would not bear it.

Fourth Gentleman. Indeed they would bear that and every thing else; – you are quite mistaken in your fellow-subjects, – they are not what they were in former days; – some few of them, its true, might bounce and bluster a little at first, especially over their cups, but when once the fire of the liquor was evaporated they would cool like a dish of tea, and become as gentle and tractable as lambs.

Third Gentleman. Sir, I have the honour to be entirely of your way of thinking; – the ancient stubbornness of the people of England has been worn off for a long time, – they now know better than to be too strictly tenacious, like their less wise forefathers, of what they call their rights and privileges;[126] – the luxuries of life have taken off all their fierceness, and while they are indulged so far as to be left to play at – *Laugh and lie down,*[127] – will never go to *hard-heads*[128] with any body.

First Gentleman. That is very true in most cases; – but an Election is a thing of a different nature from others; – you do not consider that an Election is a kind of harvest, both in town and country, and a man sometimes gets as much for his vote as enables him to pay his taxes for a twelvemonth.

Second Gentleman. Ay, ay, we shall find no cities, towns, or corporations that will do like the Westminster electors, – set up a candidate, and raise a contribution to bear the expences of his standing.[129]

Third Gentleman. No, – if they did, might like them too be left in the lurch, and laughed at for their pains.

There is no pretending to say how long this dispute would have lasted, or in what manner it would have ended; – the sudden appearance of an uncouth man at the farther end of the room, put a stop to all the conversation, and drew the eyes of the whole company upon him; – he looked wildly about him for some moments, 'till the waiter asking him what he wanted, he answered in accents which shewed him to be Irish.

Irishman. Arra, joy, – I would know of you where I can get to the speech of my coushin Mac Dunder?[130]

Waiter. You have no cosin here, go about your business.

Irishman. Arra, honey, you might give a shivil answer to a poor stranger; – it is not so you would be served if you came to Eireland.

Waiter. I shan't make the trial. – Go, I say, – this is no place for such as you.

Irishman. By my shoul, joy, an honest Eirishman that carries a chair above here did sent me to you, and said you did know my coushin Mac Dunder very well, and could tell me news of him.

On this the pert ill-natured waiter was going to push him out of the house, but a gentleman, either through pity, or for the sake of having some sport with him, called him back with these words:

Gentleman. Come hither, friend, – Who is it you enquire for?

Irishman. For my coushin Mac Dunder; – myself is come all the way from Bullruddre[131] on purpose to see him; – I hear he has got brave trade, and lives as great as the Lord Lieutenant, and it may be he will do something for his poor relashion.

Gentleman. Is mr. Mac Dunder your cousin?

Irishman. Aye, by Crist and St. Patrick, is he, my own ful coushin.

Gentleman. Well then, I'll tell you where you may find him.

Irishman. Bless your sweet face.

Gentleman. At Paris.

Irishman. And where is that place, joy.

Gentleman. Not above a thousand miles hence.

Irishman. Hubbubboo; – and how shall myself get there? – I have but one thirteen-pence piece[132] and two rapparee[133] halfpence in my purse.

Gentleman. You had better not attempt it; for to tell you the truth, I believe he is gone by this time, though much against his will, somewhat farther.[134]

Irishman. If I could have seen him he might have taught me the same trade of gaming that he has got so much by.

Gentleman. What he has got you had better be without; – so, friend, I would advise you to go back to Bullruddre, – and here is something to help bear your charges.

The gentleman then threw him half a crown and turned away, and the poor fellow went out of the house, shaking his head and looking extremely piteous.

The name of Mac Dunder and his late transactions were well known to most of the company, and some discourse concerning him ensued among them, which, in respect to some who have been his associates, I shall forbear to repeat.

I was just thinking to quit this place, and was already at the door, when a hackney-coach stopp'd, and the driver of it alighted from his box, and asked if one mr. Youngly was in the coffee-room; on which the gentleman who owned that name came out and stepp'd to the coach side, where a lady putting out her head saluted him with this reproach:

Lady. How cruel are you to oblige me to this method of seeing you? – I can scarce live a day without you, yet you have suffered me to languish for almost a whole week.

Youngly. I have had business, and could not think a lady, who besides her husband has a plurality of lovers, could want consolation for the absence of one; – mr. Miramour was doubtless in the way to supply my place.

Lady. Ungrateful creature, do you not know that all the love I ever had for him vanished at the sight of you, and that I have never since granted him the least favour? – But come in, – my fool of a husband is secure, and we may pass an hour or two at least together.

Youngly. Impossible at this time, – I have an engagement that I cannot dispense with.

Lady. Well then, shall we meet tomorrow?

Youngly. To-morrow I will; – at the old place, I suppose; – What hour?

Lady. About eight: – But may I depend upon you?

Youngly. You may, I will not fail.

The coach then drove away, and Youngly returned to his company; – but who this lady was, and the effects of her unhappy conduct, must be referred to another chapter.

CHAP. VII.

Presents the reader with a full view of the beautiful and much celebrated
  Sabina, in an impartial description of her person and character, with some
  particulars in relation to her two amours, and the consequences which
  attended this last assignation made with her favourite Youngly.

THAT children do not always behave in the same manner with their parents, is
not so much owing to their being born with different propensities, as to their
education and the company they may happen to fall into, at an age when nature
is most liable to be sway'd by example.

We often see the most virtuous couples unhappy in a degenerate offspring;
but we rarely see good branches sprout from a vicious stock: – an evil disposition
may be corrected by advice, by persuasion and example, and a good one perverted
by the same means; but when a person is so unfortunate as to be descended from
base and wicked parents, is brought up under them, is witness of all their actions,
and have companions of the same cast, it is scarce possible that such a one can
have a mind enriched with any noble, or moral principles.

What other could the once doating deceived Germanicus expect in this marriage with Sabina, than the vexations he has fatally experienced? – Can all the
beauties of her person now make atonement for the blemishes of her mind? –
No, – he rather curses than admires those charms that drew him in, and wishes
himself any thing so he were not a husband.

Yet ask him why he married, he will tell you he married a woman of fortune,
quality, and an uncommon share of beauty; – all this is very true; but a man not
blinded by this passion would have examined by what means the two former
were obtained; and, above all, what sort of disposition was hid beneath the varnish of an outside loveliness.

Was not her Family among the lowest rank, till one of them raised himself to
opulence by actions which ought to have brought him to a Gibbet, and instead
of ennobling his posterity, entailed on them perpetual infamy? – Was she not
trained up under a mother whose bad conduct has been equally notorious? –
Was she not from her most early years soothed in every vanity, pampered in
every luxury, and taught to think that appetites and passions were never given
but to be indulged?

Could Germanicus be ignorant of these glaring truths? – if he were not, yet
rashly ventured on so unpromising a union, who can pity the misfortunes, the
disquiets, the disgrace, it has involved him in?

The many proofs she gave of too warm an inclination before marriage, as also
many of the several amours she had after she became a wife, I shall pass over;
the first that made any great noise in the world was that with Miramour, which

perhaps was chiefly owing to the manner of its commencement, which he thinking himself under no obligation to conceal, has since made no secret of in all
companies, whenever her name happens to come upon the carpet.

This gentleman had a mistress, who, on account of a certain haughtiness in
her temper and behaviour, he call'd Roxana;[135] – he supported her in so genteel
a manner, that had her reputation been equal to her appearance, she might have
been entitled to the best company. – Character, however, was the least thing
consider'd by Sabina in the choice of her acquaintance; – she accidentally met
with this lady at a milliner's, fell into discourse with her, liked her, invited her to
her house, and there soon grew a great intimacy between them.

That Roxana was kept by Miramour was no secret to the town, nor did she
attempt to make any of it to Sabina; – on the contrary, she talk'd freely to her
of many passages in their amorous conversation; but how dangerous is it for
one woman to boast too much of the perfectons of her lover, to another no less
sanguine in her constitution? – Sabina, who had often seen Miramour without
taking any notice of him, now became so fired with the rapturous description
given of him by his mistress, that she instantly became her rival, and languished
to experience in reality that happiness which the other had given her so high an
idea of.

As she never took any thing of this nature into her head without attempting
to accomplish it, and had no regard to decorum in the manner of her doing so,
she sent a billet to him by a porter containing these lines:

To Miramour.

Sir,

If your attachment to the charms of your kept mistress makes you not look
on all the rest of womankind as insipid tasteless creatures, the invitation this
brings you will not be unwelcome; – a woman of quality, young, and in most
men's eyes handsome, has found something in you that excites in her the desire
of a private interview, and to that end will call on you this evening about seven at
White's; – till when must remain,

With a great deal of impatience,

Your Incognita.

The Messenger who carry'd this had strict orders not to tell from whom it
came; – curiosity, however, for it could be call'd no other passion as yet, made
Miramour punctual to the time, nor was Sabina less so; – he had not waited
many minutes before she came; – on his coming into the coach he found her face
entirely hid under her hood, which she told him laughing, he must not expect to
see till they were in a place more proper for him to give her proof how agreeable

it was to him; on this he ordered the coachman to drive to an adjacent tavern, where being shewed into a private room the lady soon threw off her disguise.

He had not enough depended on the character she had given of herself, not to be surprised and transported on finding Sabina in the person of his Incognita; and expressed the sense he had of the honour she did, and the happiness he hoped their meeting would bestow on him, in terms so warm, and so passionate, as infinitely charmed her.

They passed some hours together to their mutual satisfaction, nor parted without an appointment to see each other the next day; but Sabina, not thinking it safe to come often to so public a place as a tavern, undertook to provide a more proper scene for the continuance of their intrigue.

As indolent as this lady is in most other affairs, it must be confessed that no woman was ever more punctual, or more indefatigable in every thing relating to the business of her love; – on consulting with a female acquaintance, who had been often necessary to her on such occasions, she was advised by her to hire a private lodging, by the quarter, in some obscure nook of the town, to which she might retire whenever she had a mind, as it would be always ready, and neither herself nor the friends she should bring with her be taken any notice of.

Sabina highly approving of what she said, the project was put in immediate execution; – the woman took upon herself the accomplishment of what she had proposed, and easily found a place every way suitable for the business it was designed; – the chamber was neat, spacious, and well furnished; – there was a back door to the house, through which any one might slip out in case of any danger of discovery; and the landlady knew perfectly well the decorum that she ought to observe in regard to her guests: – the heroine of this adventure was very much pleased with the accommodation procured for her; and having got this recess, which, according to the French, she used to call her Petit Maison, henceforward never met Miramour at any other place.

But there was one thing I forgot to mention in giving the character of this lady, which is, – the uncertainty of her temper; – she is no less inconstant than she is amorous, and changes her lovers almost as often as she does her garments, and never keeps either till they are worn out; a new friend, like a new fashion, is always charming to her, but a very little time serves to make her equally grow weary of both.

She loved Miramour till she saw Youngly; but there was something in the person and conversation of this last gentleman, that making reason coincide with passion, it is not to be wondered at that she gave him the preference; and a woman of a less mutable disposition might have been easily absolved for transferring her affections to an object so much more worthy than the late engrosser of her heart.

On her first acquaintance with him, she made advances to him which he is too much a man of pleasure to resist from any fine woman; – he returned those of Sabina in a manner which made her think him as much devoted to her as she could wish; and it was not long before she gave him an invitation to drink tea with her at her private apartment, where she told him they might laugh away an hour without interruption.

He took the hint, and flew to the place of rendezvouz, where it is not to be doubted but he found all the welcome he could wish or expect from the obliging fair.

They had many interviews, but Youngly having by some accident heard of her intrigue with Miramour, he not only frequently reproached her with it, but also was far from feeling for her that affection in his heart, which otherwise her beauty might have inspired him with, as the reader will easily believe, by the recital I gave in the last chapter of the conversation he had with her when she called upon him at the coffee-house.

In the mean time, Roxana, who, from the commencement of Miramour's acquaintance with Sabina, had seen him less often than she had been accustomed, and had also some other reasons to suspect a decrease in affection, began presently to imagine that some new face had supplanted her; – she complained to him of his unkindness, but he absolutely denied having given her any cause, and made a thousand excuses for his late behaviour; – but this did not satisfy her, – she was not to be deceived in matters of which she was so good a judge; and convinced that she had a rival, bent her whole thoughts on discovering the person.

By an emissary whom she employ'd to watch Miramour wherever he went, she soon found out the place where he met the object of his new attachment; but as that lady was carry'd into the house in a chair, with the curtains close drawn, was still as far as ever from knowing the face that had undone her.

Upon enquiry among the neighbours, she was inform'd that the house was noted for giving reception to people who liked each other more than they were willing the world should know they did; and this put a stratagem into her head, which was crown'd with all the success she could wish or hope; not only for exploring what at present was a mystery to her, but also for being amply revenged on her fair rival.

The mistress of Miramour knew the town long before she knew him, and was not unacquainted with the customs of such houses; – she went one morning to the governante of this, and after saying that she had been recommended by a person who knew her, told her she should be glad to have a chamber, to which she might sometimes come with a friend, whom it was not convenient for her to see at home: – the old gentlewoman reply'd, that her best room was rented by the quarter, by a lady who came often thither; and that the next, which was the only one she had to spare, the others being occupy'd by herself and family, she fear'd would be too small. – Roxana cry'd, she did not regard how small it was, provided it was otherwise commodious; – on this she was shew'd up to it, and finding it was divided from the other only by a thin wainscot partition, presently agreed for it, giving the old woman so good a premium in hand that she was highly satisfied with her new incumbent.

Having accomplish'd so far of her design, as to get possession of the very next room to that where her lover and his new mistress met, she began to consider, that to go thither alone might raise some suspicious in the woman of the house, and was a little at a loss what man she should take with her and make pass for a gallant, as whoever went he must of necessity be made the confidante of the whole affair; – at last she pitch'd upon the fellow she had employ'd as a spy upon Miramour; – his appearance, indeed, was very mean; but that, she thought, would not be regarded, because there are many fine ladies in town who might be glad of such a place for an interview with their butler or coachman.

Accordingly she went the next day, accompany'd by her pretended gallant; – they were there some time before the hour in which he had told her he had seen Miramour go in, in order to prepare things for a more perfect discovery; – this was done by the young fellow's boring holes through the wainscot in so dexterous a manner, that they could see all over the room without being seen themselves, though they stood close to the orifice: – no one, however, came that night, and the impatient Roxana was obliged to return home as unsatisfied as ever.

The next day she repair'd thither again, attended as before, and met with the same disappointment; but on the third was more successful: – she had not been many minutes in the chamber when a rustling of silks upon the stairs made her know somebody was coming up, on which she ran hastily, without making any noise, to one of the peep-holes; – but how great was her astonishment when she saw Sabina enter; – scarce could she refrain exclaiming aloud against the treachery of a woman, who, after being made her confidant, had robb'd her of the best part of the affections of her lover.

But soon the current of her passion turn'd a different way, when, instead of Miramour, she saw Youngly push open the door and throw himself into Sabina's arms; on which, withdrawing from her post, 'You fool,' cry'd she to her emissary, 'to what a fruitless labour have you exposed me? – it is not Miramour, but Youngly that I have all this while paid you for following. – How could you be so mope-ey'd[136] as to mistake the one for the other?'

'Nay, madam,' reply'd the fellow, 'I am sure I know mr. Miramour, and I will swear that it was him that I saw come into this house, and presently after a lady in a chair, as I then told you.' – ''Tis false,' return'd she; '– but look there and be convinced.'

He then put his eye to one of the crevices; but returning from it in a moment, said, – 'Madam, I see very plainly that the person in the next room is not mr. Miramour, – and one I never saw before; yet am very positive it was mr. Miramour whom I follow'd from his own house to this very door.'

Roxana knew not what to think about this and said no more; but, listening attentively to the conversation within, was presently assured by it that her agent had neither deceived her, nor had been deceived himself.

The reader must observe, that this was the evening ensuing that wherein she had call'd on him at the coffee-house, and the remembrance of the reproach he had then made her at the coach door, occasion'd her to speak to him in this manner, while fondly hanging on his breast:

Sabina. My dear, dear Youngly, I hope you will now believe that I love you above all the world.

Youngly. I know you love me enough to make me happy, and I ought to content myself with the share I have in your affections.

Sabina. Do not talk of a share, – by Heaven you engross me all! – my soul and all its faculties are devoted to you.

Youngly. And yet the letter Miramour accidentally dropp'd in the Park and I took up, flatter'd him with the same assurances you now give me.

Sabina. As I unfortunately play'd the fool with him before I saw you, it was necessary I should break with him by degrees; for to have done it all at once might have made him expose me.

Youngly. You had once, however, a real passion for him.

Sabina. No, – it was all in imagination; – I only fancied I lov'd him: – you must know, that silly vain creature, his kept mistress, was always filling my ears with stories of the violence of his affection for her; and it was more to shew him the difference between such a wretch and a woman of quality, than any extraordinary liking I had to his person, that induced me to grant him the favours I did.

This was enough to let the listening Roxana into the whole of the affair; – it was with much ado she restrained herself from flying into the next room, and returning the contempt thrown upon her by the last words of Sabina; but just as she was at the door, and ready to burst in on the unsuspecting pair, a sudden thought made her turn back, – 'All I can say to this perfidious woman,' cry'd she to herself, 'will avail me nothing: – the wrongs I have received demand a vengeance more complete.'

She then sat down again, and calmly meditating on what she had to do, the fertility of her invention soon supply'd her with the means of repaying, with interest, the double affront Sabina had given both to herself and Miramour, whom it is certain she loved with more sincerity than is commonly found among woman of her profession.

She staid till the lovers took their leaves of each other, and heard an appointment made between them to meet again on the ensuing Thursday.

Having fully perfected in her mind the design she soon after put in execution, she call'd for the woman of the house and said to her, – 'Madam, I know not but some gentlemen may pass an hour or two with me here next Thursday; – they may possibly come before me, but desire you will give them admittance; and, to prevent mistakes, as the furniture of the room is yellow, they shall ask for the key of the yellow chamber.'

The other reply'd, that she might depend on her punctuality in observing her commands; after which Roxana went away: but what she meant by the orders she had given must be left to the next chapter to explain.

CHAP. VIII.

Contains the catastrophe of an adventure, which the author thinks fit to declare is inserted in these lucubrations less to amuse his reader than for the sake of setting in a true light those facts which some people have artfully endeavoured to misrepresent to the public.

ROXANA being now fully furnished with materials for her revenge on Sabina, without exposing her beloved Miramour to the resentment of an injured husband, wrote to the latter the next morning, in words to this effect:

To GERMANICUS.

SIR,

THIS brings you a very ungrateful piece of intelligence; – but, in my opinion, whoever sees a person wronged and conceals it, takes part in the offence, and tho' innocent of the commencement of the crime, is accessary to the continuance of it; – it would certainly be the utmost injustice that you should be the last person to know what concerns yourself alone, and I therefore think it my duty to inform you of what chance has discovered to me.

Your wife, Sir, is false to your bed, and lavishes on mr. Youngly all those favours which you have a right to engross; – the guilty pair meet twice or thrice every week, at a lodging she rents by the quarter for that purpose.

But to say your wife is guilty of so foul a crime is doing nothing, without putting it in your power to prove her so; – the thing is easy, sir, if you will follow my directions; – the lovers have appointed to meet to-morrow about seven at their usual rendezvous, – if you go at that time, or rather before it, to the third house on the left hand in *** lane, on your asking mrs. ****, who is the keeper of this private brothel, and telling her you want the key of the yellow chamber, she will presently conduct you to a room adjoining to that which is the scene of your wife's loose pleasure; – there are holes already bored through the wainscot, through which you may plainly discern all that passes. – It is at your own option, whether you will have any other witnesses of your wife's transgression than your own eyes, and also how to behave towards her after detection. – I have discharged the dictates of my conscience in giving you this information, and am,

SIR,

Your unknown friend.

P.S. Be careful to drop no words that may give the woman of the house the least cause to suspect either who you are, or the motive of your coming.

It is convenient that I should now acquaint my reader, that all I have hitherto related of this story has come to my knowledge entirely by the report of the persons chiefly concerned in it, and without the least assistance from my Belt of Invisibility; – what yet remains to be told I have the testimony of my own eyes and ears to avouch.

The many odd accounts I heard, from time to time, in relation to Sabina's conduct, made me resolve to go one day to the house of Germanicus, in order to satisfy my curiosity with seeing in what fashion this couple behaved to each other.

The lady was abroad when I came, but I found him up in his dining-room, diverting himself with playing on the flute; was soon after rous'd from that amusement by the above letter being delivered to him by his man, saying, it was brought by a fellow who the moment he had put it into his hands vanished like lightning from the door.

The emotions with which he read it were very great, yet much less than might have been expected on such an occasion; – he paused, – then read again, – examined every line with heedful eyes, and seemed extremely divided in his thoughts what credit he should give to the information; – at last said to himself:

Germanicus. If any one had formed this contrivance, through a malicious design of ruining her reputation or my peace of mind, they would certainly have taken other methods, and not by pointing out the place, the hour, put it in my power to prove at once the falseness of the accusation.

After this he threw himself into an easy chair, – leaned his head upon his hand, and in that posture continued musing for a considerable time, – then seeming more resolved, started up and cry'd:

Germanicus. It is easy for me to make enquiry if there be such a house, – if kept by a woman of the name mentioned in the letter, and what character it bears. – Yet why should I do this? – No, it is better to follow the instructions given me, and be at once assured; – it shall be so, – as Shakspear makes Othello say,

> I'll see before I doubt; when I doubt, prove;
> And on the proof there is no more but this;
> Away at once with love or jealousy.[137]

He had scarce done repeating these lines, when Sabina came in singing an Italian air; – Germanicus endeavoured to recompose his countenance; but could not do it so well as not to make her take notice of the change, and ask if he were out of humour; – to which he reply'd:

Germanicus. Out of humour, madam; – no, – I have no cause, – none in the world.

Sabina. I think not, indeed; but men will be peevish sometimes, cause or not cause.

Germanicus. I reserve all my gaiety for to-morrow, – and would have you do so too; – a kinsman of mine makes an entertainment, and has sent an invitation for us to be partakers of it.

Sabina. What to-morrow?

Germanicus. Yes, my dear, to-morrow evening; – so desire you will not engage yourself elsewhere.

Sabina. Indeed I have engaged myself already to lady Gape's assembly.

Germanicus. You have time enough then to send to excuse yourself from going.

Sabina. Indeed I shall not; – I would not disappoint my dear lady Gape for all the kinsmen in the world; but I would have you go, – you may say I am not well, and then my absence cannot be taken amiss.

It was very plain to me, that Germanicus made this pretended invitation only as a trap to discover whether she had really any engagement on her hands that she would not be willing to break; and it is also as little to be doubted, but that her answers very much corroborated the contents of the epistle he had just received.

He forced himself, however, to tell her with a smile, that every thing should be as she would have it, and that he would no farther press her.

Some company presently after coming in, I found there was nothing more to be learned at that time, so took the first opportunity of quitting the house; and went again, the next day in the afternoon, in the hope of discovering something more.

On my arrival, the husband and wife were sitting together in the most seeming amicable manner; – after some little time Germanicus rose up and put on his hat and sword, in order, as he said, to go to his kinsman; on which Sabina, with a great deal of complaisance, said to him:

Sabina. You will not walk sure, my dear; – Have you ordered the Horses to be put to?

Germanicus. No, my dear; I leave the coach for you.

Sabina. There is no occasion, – I always chuse to go to these places in a chair.

Germanicus. That is as you please; – but I shall walk, as I have three or four places to call at in my way to my cousin's; – so farewel, my dear, I hope you will be as merry at the assembly, as I hope to be at the entertainment.

As I imagined Germanicus had something in his head more than I knew of, by his being so hasty to be gone, I followed him close at his heels, and found I had not been mistaken in my supposition; – he went into a tavern, where two gentlemen, whom he had desired to meet him there, waited for him; – the business he had with them, was to communicate the letter he had received from the unknown friend; and after having considered a little on the matter, they both agreed they should all three go together, not only to prevent any indiscreet effects of his rage on the persons who wronged him, in case the affair should prove as the letter had represented; but also to be his witnesses, if he thought proper to bring it before a court of judicature.

They staid till a little before seven, – then went, according to the directions given by Roxana, – found every thing answered the description; – they were shewed up into the yellow chamber; I still accompanied them, and made a fourth person, unfelt, as well as unseen by any of them.

They had not been there above half an hour before Sabina came into the next room, – Youngly soon after joined her; and the much-injured husband and his two friends saw enough, from the peepholes in the partition, to convince them of the truth of that information which had brought them thither.

Difficult was it for Germanicus to restrain his fury on so shocking a spectacle; but his two friends reminding him that there was a much better way for him to shew his resentment, he was at length prevailed on to retire.

They both went home with him, as did myself, resolved to see what farther events this night would produce.

Sabina came not home till near two hours past midnight; – Germanicus ordered that the door should not be opened; but, after her chairmen had knock'd two or three times, went himself to the parlour-window and spoke to her in these terms:

Germanicus. Please, madam, to return from whence you came, or wherever else you shall think proper, – my house shall no longer be the shelter of a prostitute.

Sabina. What! is the man mad! – Sure you have been drinking bad wine to-night.

Germanicus. No, madam, the best I ever drank in my Life, – it has opened my eyes, and shewed me the viper I have so long cherished in my bosom, and now throw off for ever; – but I would not wish you to stay longer in the cold, – you can have no entrance here, and mr. Youngly will doubtless afford you a part of his bed.

With these words he shut the window, and Sabina, finding herself detected, – and that her husband was resolute, ordered her chair from the door; and after some little consideration how to dispose of herself, thought it best to take her husband's advice, and return to the place from whence she came, as it was the only asylum to which she could have recourse at so unseasonable an hour.

In the several visits I afterwards made to Germanicus, I perceived he behaved with much more moderation than some husbands would have done; – Philosophy had taught him to support with patience a misfortune which was irremediable; – he contented himself with taking such revenge as the laws of England have provided in these cases;[138] – Youngly was summoned before a court of judicature, and a penalty inflicted on him for, his offence; but it would have been larger, had it not been proved, by incontestable evidences, that he had not been the first who had seduced Sabina from her marriage vows.

As for the lady, she is now abandoned and despised by both her lovers; and if there be a possibility that any thing can bring her to a just sense of the faults she has been guilty of, it must be the contempt she is treated with by all degrees of people.

End of the Third BOOK.

THE
Invisible Spy.

BOOK IV.
CHAP. I.

In which the Author confesses having been guilty of petty larceny; but hopes
that the fact is of such a nature as will not come under the cognizance of the
law; and also that it merits forgiveness from those into whose hands this
work may fall, as the chief motive for committing it was to oblige the public.

I HAVE been intimately acquainted with Belinda for a considerable time in my
visible capacity, yet never once took it into my head to make her a visit under
the cover of my Belt till her return from Bath this last season; nor perhaps had
done it then, if I had not been told that she suffer'd herself to be conducted to
that place by a certain gentleman whom I thought it highly improper for her
to continue any conversation with, for reasons which I shall hereafter make no
scruple to reveal.

On my entering her apartment I found her very busy with her waiting-maid
in unpacking her baggage, which coming by the waggon, it seems, had arrived in
town but the night before.

As I could promise myself but little entertainment from the assortment
of ribands and jewels, or to the removal from the portmanteau to the Indian
chest,[139] the peit-en-lair, the robe de chambre, the jupe volante,[140] or any other
implement of female finery, I was thinking to quit the place and return at a more
fit season, when the maid pulling out a pretty large sattin bag full of papers,
ask'd, her lady where she would have those writings laid, on which Belinda turn'd
her head that way and reply'd:

Belinda. They are only a heap of letters I received at Bath, of no manner of
consequence, – I have no room for such rubbish; – take them and throw them
all into the fire.

The maid was just going to do as she was bid, but was stopp'd by Belinda, who
suddenly scream'd out:

Belinda. Hold! hold! – I had forgot that one day, in a hurry, I stuff'd two or three letters and poems of Philander's among them; and I would not have one line of that dear witty creature's destroy'd for all the world: – pour them all out of the bag, and look on the names subscrib'd, that I may direct you how to separate the wheat from the chaff.

The maid then threw them all down upon the carpet, and open'd them one by one; – on the first that came to her hands she said to her lady:

Maid. Here is one, madam, from your aunt, lady Careful.

Belinda. Advice for my conduct at Bath: – insipid; – throw it aside.

Maid. One, madam, from your cousin, mrs. Prudence Wishwell.

Belinda. On the same dull subject; – put it to the other.

Maid. One from mr. Tradewell, madam.

Belinda. Oh, that was to recommend a rich merchant of his acquaintance to me for a lover: – nonsense, – as if after having known the court I could ever think of becoming a city dame: – let this wiseacre's epistle keep company with the rest.

Maid. One from mrs. Letitia Vainlove, madam.

Belinda. Silly creature; – she loves a man that has courted her half seven years, yet refuses to marry him, for fear he should afterwards give her cause to love him less: – I shall keep no such stuff by me.

Maid. Oh, madam, here is something from Philander.

Belinda. Give it me, – quick.

The maid having given her the paper, she cry'd out,

Belinda. Oh, the engaging creature! – This was wrote a little before I went down to Bath. – Don't you remember, Sally, that he came one day when I was abroad, – and how vex'd I was when I came home, 'till he sent a messenger quite from the city to me with this little billet?

Maid. Yes, madam, I think I do, and that your ladyship did nothing but quarrel with me because I had persuaded you to go out that day.

Belinda. You must not mind that, Sally; – you know I made you amends next day, by giving you a new set of topknots; – but you shall hear how prettily he writes:

Wrote extempore, from a coffee-house in the city, after being disappointed of seeing the adorable Belinda at her lodgings.

> From Whitehall stairs, whence oft with distant view,
> I've gaz'd whole midnight hours on hours away,
> Blest but to see the roof that cover'd you,
> And watch'd beneath what star you sleeping lay.
> I came, to give my labouring thoughts full scope.
> To love, and your soft charms my all devote.
> To paint my soul, trembling 'twixt fear and hope,
> And speak that passion which my looks denote.

But when I miss'd you, and took boat again,
Scarce could my tongue the proper order give,
Nor my swool'n eyes the starting tears restrain,
While I drove downwards to this busy hive.
Landed at length, I sable coffee drink,
And ill surrounded by a noisy tribe,
Regardless what they say, or do, or think,
I, wrapt in your dear Heaven, my loss describe.

But there is no describing either the transports that your presence gives, or the insupportable anguish of your absence, – both are alike beyond the reach of words, and can only be felt by

The adoring,

PHILANDER.

Maid. He is a sweet gentleman, indeed, madam; – what a pity it is that he is married.

Belinda. So it is, Sally; – but yet I don't know whether I should like him half so well, if that vain thing, his wife, were not so ridiculously jealous of him.

Maid. Sure, madam, she can't be very vain, if she does not think she has merit enough to keep her own husband to herself?

Belinda. You are a fool, and know nothing of the matter; – I tell you she must be vain, and impudently vain too, ever to have expected such a thing.

Maid. Indeed, madam, if ever I marry I should expect it, and be very angry if I found it otherwise.

Belinda. What, I warrant you and your spouse must be like old Joan and Darby in the song;[141] – but I will give you an instance of the folly of Philander's wife: – you must know, that because he is a wit and a poet, she affects to scribble sometimes: – I was there one day and she read over a copy of verses to me, which she told me she had wrote to a lady whom she thought liked her husband but too well; – I knew well enough she meant me, tho' she said another: – I remember nothing of the poem but the two last lines; – but I never shall forget with what an air of imaginary triumph she repeated them, looking me full in the face all the time; – the words were these:

In vain, alas, are all your arts, – since he;
By love, and law, must only live for me.

Philander was present, and gave her a look which shew'd how little he was pleased with her behaviour; and I was told by one of the family, used her very ill upon it after I was gone.

Maid. Yet she often visits you, madam, and is always sending invitations to you to come to her house.

Belinda. She dare do no otherwise, Philander will be obey'd, and she has cunning enough to know it is her interest to seem to do without reluctance whatever he would have her; but I know she hates me in her heart as much as I despise her: – but come, look over the rest of the trumpery, while I lock up this billet in my cabinet.

On this the maid went about examining the other papers, and taking one up in her hand, after having seen the name, cry'd out with some eagerness:

Maid. Oh! madam, here is a letter from mrs. Friendly, – the good-natured gentlewoman that sent her servants to help you out with your things when the fire was at next door, and took such care of them till the danger was over; – What will you have done with this?

Belinda. It is not worth preserving; – 'tis a strange thing, that if people do one a kindness once they think one is obliged to use them civilly ever after. – What more?

Maid. A whole packet of epistles from Selima.

Belinda. Ay, the impertinent creature has given me a long detail of her love affairs, as if I had not enough of that sort of my own to employ my thoughts with.

Maid. One from mr. Worthy, madam.

Belinda. He was my lover once; but I never paid any regard to his affection, and much less to his resentment for the ill usage he pretends to have received from me; – but you need search no farther, – I have found all Philander's letters and poems in this draw, so cram together all you have there and thrust them into the fire.

This sentence was punctually executed, according to the best of the maid's belief; but the poor girl knew not that there was an Invisible Thief, who stood close at her elbow, and while she turned her head another way had the dexterity to preserve some part of the condemn'd cargoe, and slip it into his pocket.

Selima at that time engrossed a good part of the conversation in town; – she was a young woman of no fortune, and few other endowments besides her beauty, of which, in the opinion of most people, she has an uncommon share; though to me there is a certain fierceness in her eyes, and a boldness diffused through all her features, which rob them of that loveliness they would otherwise have; – such as she is, however, she captivated the hearts of two persons who might have carried their addresses much higher without danger of a refusal; – the one is born to a title, and the other possessed of wealth, which when ever he pleases may procure him one; and neither of them can be thought deficient in any of those qualifications which constitute the fine gentleman; – yet Selima was still unmarried; – both her lovers were equally in suspence, and nobody could tell which, or whether either of them would be the happy man.

It is not therefore to be wondered at, that a person of my humour should be extremely desirous of being let into a secret which seem'd so impenetrable, even to those who pretended to be most knowing in other things; nor that I gladly embraced an opportunity which bids so fair for the satisfaction of my curiosity, as the getting her letters into my possession, Belinda having said they contain'd the whole history of this affair.

Behold now my theft; – Belinda's maid had no sooner laid down the packet, by her lady's orders, than I kept my eye constantly fixed upon it, 'till a convenient moment offer'd for conveying it from among the others, which I did with as much adroitness as if I had been bred to the art and mystery of stealing from my cradle.

After this I staid no longer with Belinda, not doubting but I had now about me better materials for my entertainment than any I could expect to be furnish'd with in her apartment, at least for the present.

CHAP. II.

If there be any reader, in this very pious and religious age, that may happen to have too tender and scrupulous a conscience to benefit himself by the receipt of stolen goods, the author thinks it highly necessary to give him this timely notice, that it will be best for his peace of mind to avoid looking either into this or some of the succeeding chapters.

THE distance between Belinda's lodgings and my own seem'd now to to be twice as long as usual, though I believe I measured much fewer paces than ever I had done before, so great was my impatience to be at home and examine the treasure I brought with me.

But as too much eagerness often impedes the accomplishment of our designs, after I got into my apartment I shut myself into a closet; but, in the hurry of my thoughts, had forgot to give orders to my people to say I was from home, to any one that should come to visit me; and I had scarce unloaded my pocket when I was told a gentleman was below and desir'd to speak with me; – this was a person for whom I had a very great regard, and at any other time should have been glad to see, but his company at this juncture I should gladly have dispensed with; – I had no reason, however, to be chagrin'd at the interruption he gave me, as will presently appear.

As soon as the first compliments were over, and we had seated ourselves, he ask'd me if I had heard the news to-day; – I told him I had not seen any of the papers. – 'What I mean,' said he, 'is of too late a date to be got as yet into the public papers; – but I suppose tomorrow they will all be full of it.' – 'Is it of any moment?' cry'd I – 'Not much,' answer'd he, 'except to the parties concern'd. – Selima was married this morning.'

'Selima married!' resum'd I. 'And pray has Dorantes or Vanucius the name of bridegroom?' – 'The former,' reply'd he, 'for which I cannot help feeling some concern.' – 'Wherefore?' demanded I – 'Is it because you do not think him worthy of her?' – 'No, certainly,' said he; – 'and it is possible that she also may be worthy of him. – I blame not the choice he has made of her for the reasons many people do; but for another, which, I think, ought to have had some weight with him.'

'Is it a secret?' cry'd I – 'I shall make none of it to you,' answer'd he. – 'You must know I had the honour of being well acquainted with his father, – he was a person of great sense, honour and probity; – his chief care was to instill the same principles into his son: – among many other excellent precepts he gave him for his conduct in life, one was, not to be tempted with the grandeur of a court; – to avoid going there as much as he could do so with decency; and never to accept of any employment: – now I am very apprehensive that his marriage with Selima will, in a manner, compel him to break through this injunction.'

As I could not well comprehend his meaning in these last words, I desir'd he would be more explicit, and he very readily oblig'd me in his reply, which was to this effect:

'I will tell you,' said he; 'the expences of a marriage bed are very great to persons of quality, especially in an age so luxurious as this; and I much fear that the estate of Dorantes will be found insufficient to defray them, without the assistance of some lucrative employment; – and it is for this reason I could wish he had married a woman of fortune.'

'Perhaps,' return'd I, 'that as Selima brought with her nothing but her person, she will content herself without any of those superfluities which otherwise she would have had a kind of right to expect.'

'You talk like one that knows nothing of the world,' cry'd he; 'people raised from indigence to grandeur, must have a head well stored with wisdom not to grow giddy with the sudden exaltation; Selima is young, gay, and vain to an excess. – Have we not seen her thrust herself into assemblies where she had no pretence to come, and bear a thousand affronts for the intrusion, merely for the sake of boasting afterwards among her acquaintance, that she had been in such and such company, and in such and such places? – Then as to the article of dress, no one certainly was ever more particular and affected.'

'Can it therefore be imagined,' continued he, 'that a woman so passionately fond of shew, and so ambitious of rendering herself conspicuous, should not take all the opportunities of doing so now, when fortune has put it in her power to appear with all those real advantages, which before she could only ape in a tawdry manner? – And can it be supposed that the same love, which induced him to make her his wife, will not also induce him to indulge her in the full splendor of that dignity to which he has raised her; nay, even to humour her in every folly and extravagance her heart may happen to be set upon?'

Tho' I found a good deal of reason, according to appearance, in what my friend had said, yet I suspended my judgment, 'till I should see in what manner this lady had unbosom'd herself to her confidante Belinda, which I was now more than ever impatient to do, and heartily wish'd he would take his leave.

At length he went, and I again retir'd to my closet, after having given proper instructions to prevent a second interruption. – To avoid confusion, I examined the dates of every letter, and shall present them to my readers in the order they were sent.

LETTER I.

To BELINDA, at Bath.

Dear BELINDA,

I received the favour of yours with a double satisfaction; first, as it brought me news of your safe arrival at that agreeable place, and that every thing in it answered your wishes and expectations; – and, secondly, – as it assures me of your friendship by the kind concern you are pleased to express for my welfare.

As to my health, I have quite lost that ugly cough, which so much persecuted me when you left London; – but as to my affairs, they are still in the same fluctuating and unsettled condition as ever; – Dorantes continues his addresses, Vanucius does the same; – How happy might I be if I was loved but by one of them? – but both equally pursuing me, impedes all the good fortune I might enjoy with either, so that I may justly say with the Poet,

Too much plenty makes me poor.[142]

You may remember how much my mamma was transported when Dorantes first declared himself my lover; – Vanucius, tho' not quite dropp'd, was then little regarded either by myself or her; but now the case is altered; – she charges me to treat both with an equal freedom; and, indeed, I think it would be highly impolitic to do otherwise.

The truth is, Dorantes does not come so directly to the point as could be wished; – his courtship is passionate, tender, and full of fire; – he swears I am the idol of his soul, – his earthly goddess, – that he could not live without me, – and that all his hopes are center'd in being one day happy in possessing me; yet, among all these fine speeches, he seldom mentions marriage; and when he does, it is in so slight and evasive a manner as gives me sometimes cause to fear his designs are rather on my heart than hand.

If this should be his intention, and I were weak enough to have fixed my affection on him, how miserable should I be? – but, thank Heaven, I have none of that soft folly in my composition, by which I have seen so many of our sex misled; – my ruling passions are interest and ambition; and I would not hesitate one moment to give myself to Vanucius, if the rank and title of Dorantes did not tempt me to wait a-while the result of his pretensions.

I was yesterday morning in the Mall with Vanucius, Dorantes was walking there with some company; – he changed colour, and seemed in some agitation on meeting us together; – this I looked upon as a good sign; but in the afternoon, when he came to visit me, and I expected he would either have complained of my indifference to him, or reproached me for the public encouragement I had given his rival; he did neither, but behaved the whole time he staid with all the calmness and insensibility of a Stoick.

I must confess I was never more disappointed in all my life, as I had frequently seen him kindle into jealousy on a less occasion, and could not help thinking that the violence of his passion was in a great measure abated, – according to this maxim of mr. Dryden:

> Distrust in lovers is too warm a sun;
> But yet 'tis night in love when that is gone.[143]

On consulting with my mamma, I found she was of the same way of thinking, and it was agreed upon between us, not to suffer ourselves to be trifled with any longer, but that the next time Vanucius made an offer of his hand I should accept it.

But, my dear Belinda, this morning has put a stop to the resolution of last night; – I was scarce out of bed when I received from Dorantes the most passionate billet that ever was dictated by the heart of man, occasioned, as he says, by dreaming he had me in his arms; – if his love be half so impatient to have me there as he pretends it is, he will certainly be now more pressing to make me his own than hitherto he has been.

My next, perhaps, may bring you the decision of my fate; – in the mean time I should be glad to know what is doing at Bath, and what new conquest you have made there; for how much soever you may be envied by some of your acquaintance, be assured that every thing that contributes to your satisfaction will always afford a secret pleasure to her who is,

With the most perfect amity,

Dear BELINDA,

Your affectionate friend

And humble Servant,

SELIMA.

LETTER II.

To BELINDA, at Bath.

Dear BELINDA,

I AM sorry to tell you, that the perplexity of my own affairs has hinder'd me from being inquisitive enough into those of other people, for me to be able to send you the intelligence you request; but as I flatter myself, and you are so good to say that what regards myself will be always most interesting to you, I shall give you a brief detail of what has happen'd to me in relation to Dorantes, since his last kind letter mention'd in my former.

He came the same evening, – the discourse he entertain'd me with was of a piece with his epistle, – all love and transport; – he begg'd I would favour him with my company to the Theatre in Drury-Lane, where he had already sent a servant to keep places in the box; – I consented, and went with him in his chariot, – the play was Romeo and Juliet; – he apply'd all the tender things spoke by the former of these lovers to his own passion, and press'd my hand with a vehemence of fondness, whenever he had an opportunity of doing so unperceiv'd by the audience.

I saw him again the next day, – we were alone together in the dining-room, and my gown being a little more off my shoulder than ordinary, he laid his face upon my bare neck, crying, 'Oh! I could dwell for ever here!' – On this I took courage to say to him, – 'Yet, Dorantes, when once I become your wife, these ardours will perhaps sink into a cold indifference.' – 'No, my angel!' return'd he, 'desire will rather increase by enjoyment of your person; – the sweets contain'd in this dear frame are of too divine a nature ever to satiate.'

In speaking these words he catched me suddenly in his arms, held me to his bosom, and joined his lips to mine with somewhat, I thought, of an unbecoming warmth; – I struggled to get loose, and when I had done so retired some paces from him, and said, with all the haughtiness I could assume, 'Forbear these liberties, sir, till authorised by law to take them;' – he asked my pardon, – apologized for what he had done by the violence of his passion, and then sat down; but appeared more than ordinarily pensive afterwards, – spoke little, and made his visit much shorter than usual.

On my acquainting my mamma with what had passed between us, she did not at all like it, and went directly to her old friend, you know who I mean, to be advised by him how to proceed in a circumstance at once so intricate and critical; – he told her, that my father ought to appear in this business, and that it was his place, and his alone, to demand of Dorantes an explanation of his designs in regard to the courtship he so long had made to his daughter.

My mamma had always been of this opinion; but knowing the indolence of my father's temper, had forbore mentioning it to him; however she now did so; and to engage his compliance, promised to make him a present of a new wig and silver-hilted sword; but all she could say or offer has been ineffectual; – his answer was, – That he did not know how to speak to a person of Dorantes's quality on any such matter; – that he would not interfere in it, and we might act as we thought proper ourselves.

This, you will own, is very vexatious; but there is no turning him out of his own way; – mamma is now resolved, since there is no other remedy, to take the task upon herself, as soon as Dorantes comes to town; – he is at present gone on a hunting-match with some gentlemen, but is expected to return in two days at farthest, and we shall then see the event.

For my part, my spirits are so much fatigued and harrassed with this suspence, that there is but one thing hinders me from putting an immediate end to
it by marrying with Vanucius; – the persons of the men are equal to me; but oh,
Belinda, I am passionately in love with the title of Dorantes, – would to God he
were half as much so with my person, he would not then delay one moment giving me the one in exchange for the other.

The faithful Vanucius, who I have flattered with the belief of not being indifferent to me, is every day soliciting me to fix a time to make him happy, while
Dorantes seems to dally with my expectations; – yet can I not resolve to reward the
constant services of the one, nor to renounce for ever the charming hope of rank,
precedence, the thousand dear appendages of a woman of quality, which the other
has it in his power to bestow on me; – but I will trouble you no farther than to
assure you, that in whatever station my fate shall place me, I shall be ever,

 With the best wishes for your happiness,

  My dear BELINDA,

   Your sincere friend

    And humble servant,

        SELIMA.

P.S. I am highly oblig'd to Philander for the part you tell me he takes in my concerns; – pray be so good as to make my grateful acknowledgments acceptable to
him.

If I took the same pleasure in transcribing, as I did in reading the letters of
Selima, I should not have stopp'd till I had laid them all before the public; but
my pen requires some relaxation as well as my eyes, and I must therefore entreat
the reader will give a small truce to his curiosity.

CHAP. III.

Presents the Reader with the continuance of Selima's Story, as related by her-
self, in several epistles to her friend, in a very natural and affecting manner.

LETTER III.

To BELINDA, at Bath.

Dear BELINDA,

 I would not let this post escape without writing; – what I have now to say
to you, though greatly to the purpose, must be comprised in a few words; – I am
engag'd to go this evening with Dorantes, and some other company, on a party
of pleasure, and I am every moment expecting his landau at the door, so can but

just snatch time to inform you, that my mamma has talk'd to him on the affair in question, – and that his answers have been conformable to our utmost wishes; – yes, I am now convinced that all my apprehensions were groundless, – that he never meant to act otherwise than honourably with me; – he has assur'd both her and myself that every thing shall soon be settled for my future happiness; – rejoice with me, my dear creature, – I have now a heart and head perfectly at ease, and nothing to employ my thoughts, but how to behave becoming of the dignity to which, I flatter myself, a few days will raise me.

Farewel; – the author of my joys is already come, – they call me to receive him, – and I can add no more, than that I am, as ever,

With an unfeigned regard,
Dear Belinda,
Your most humble and
Obedient servant,
Selima.

P.S. Let the length of your next shew you forgive the enforced shortness of this.

LETTER IV.

To Belinda, at Bath.

Dear Belinda,

Little did I expect, and little is it in your power to imagine what I have now to acquaint you with; – so strange a reverse, – so sudden, so shocking a revolution sure never any woman but myself experienced; – but I will keep you no longer in suspence.

I have lost Dorantes, – irrecoverably lost him, – not through any mismanagement of my own, nor any want of affection in him, but through a previous, much worse, and more irremediable accident: – this is the sum of my misfortunes; – I will now relate to you the particulars:

He came to me the other day, and though the salutations he approached me with had their accustom'd tenderness, yet I thought there were somewhat in his countenance, and the whole air of his deportment, very different from any thing I had ever seen in him before: – he had not been in the room many minutes before he told me, that he had something of consequence to impart to me, and desir'd I would order myself to be deny'd to whoever should happen to come. – I readily did as he desir'd; after which he drew his chair close to mine, sigh'd, and looking me full in the face, surpriz'd me with these words:

'My dear Selima,' said he, 'I have deceiv'd you: – have you love enough for me to forgive it?' 'First, let me know the nature of your offense,' return'd I. ''Tis death to me to declare it,' answer'd he; 'yet can it be no longer hid: – I have imposed upon you by a false pretence; – promised what is not in my power to perform; – I cannot marry you.'

Judge, Belinda, of my confusion; – but it is as impossible for you to conceive, as it is for me to describe what I felt in that dreadful moment; – scarce could a thunder-bolt have transfix'd me more; – I had no breath, – no voice, but to eccho part of his last words, – 'Cannot marry! – cannot marry!' cry'd I, and this I repeated several times over.

He seem'd all this time in very great agitations, and after taking one of my hands, and tenderly pressing it to his lips, – 'Heaven knows,' said he, 'how earnestly I desired the union I proposed; – gladly would I resign the one half of those years fate has allotted for my life, to have the other blest with the possession of my Selima, in the way she expects from me; – but, alas! that hope is vain; – the fatal secret is this: – I am already wedded, – my heedless and unwary youth was ensnar'd to give my hand to a creature, who though I never did, nor never will live with as a wife, will not, on any consideration, be prevail'd upon to resign the cursed claim she has to me as a husband.'

Overwhelm'd, as I was, with various passions, I at last assum'd resolution enough to tell him, that he had acted a most ungenerous and dishonorable part in making his addresses to me, knowing himself under so indissoluble an engagement to another. – To which he reply'd, that at first he hoped to have got quit of his unfortunate tye; – and that after he found all the offers he had made to that end were fruitless, the passion he had for me would not suffer him to restrain seeing me, conversing with me, and telling me how much he adored me.

He then made a long harangue on the resistless power of my charms, and the violence of that flame they had inspir'd him with; – swore a thousand oaths that the world to him had nothing in it but myself worth living for; and concluded with a proposal, that since he could not make me his wife, he would settle a thousand pounds a year upon me to be his mistress, – and that it should be at my option either to live publickly with him as such, or to continue with my mamma, and receive his visits in a private manner.

This offer I rejected with more disdain than I had shewn to any of the like nature which had ever been made to me since my first being in the way of temptation; – nor will you wonder that I did do so: – to be courted for a mistress by the very man who had so lately flatter'd me with the hopes of marriage, made me now look upon that as an affront, which before my expectations had been raised to the height they had been, I might perhaps have taken as a proof of his affection.

I ranted, – storm'd, – concealed no part of the spite I was possess'd of; but all I said seem'd to make no great impression on him; – he bore it with a temper which I thought was not at all consistent with the violence of the passion he had pretended; and on his going away calmly told me, that he would make the same proposal he had done to me to no other woman in the world; – that it was no inconsiderable one; and that, as he could do no more, he hoped my cooler moments would represent it as a thing worthy my attention.

Indeed, my dear Belinda, I was half mad, and believe I gave myself some airs not any way becoming in me to a man of his quality. – I met him in the Park this morning, but though he was alone, and I had only Flavia with me, he never offer'd to join us, but pass'd by with a slight bow: – I suppose he resents my behaviour, but it is no matter since he is married.

Vanucius is now my last resource; – if I could persuade the man to purchase a title, he would be full as agreeable to me as Dorantes; – but he is an unambitious creature, and I almost despair of it, I shall try, at least, how far the love he has for me will prevail; – my next will bring you news of what success my endeavours will meet; – till when, I am,

> Even in the midst of my perplexity,
> > Dear BELINDA,
> > > Your very sincere friend,
> > > > And humble servant,
> > > > > SELIMA.

P.S. I thank Philander for the sett of Bath counters[144] he has sent me, but I know not when I shall be in a humour to make use of them. – I was last night at lady Swabler's rout, and play'd so ill that I almost empty'd my purse of a small present my mamma's good friend had made me to buy trinkets for my wedding.

LETTER V.

To BELINDA, at Bath.

Dear BELINDA,

It is almost a sin to disturb the felicity you enjoy with any melancholy accounts; but fresh calamities will always occasion fresh complaints, and while I am giving you a detail of my misfortunes, methinks I am eased of some part of the weight of them: – you may say, indeed, that this is a selfish consideration, and I cannot deny the accusation; but have this to answer in my defence, – however disagreeable the purport of my letters are, they shew, at least, the perfect confidence I have in your friendship and good-nature.

I am apt to think that before I tell you, you will suspect I am also deserted by Vanucius; and tho' I cannot be positive that such a conjecture would be entirely groundless, yet I have little reason to flatter myself with the contrary; – I have neither seen nor heard from him for five whole days, and this morning he set out for Tunbridge, without taking any other leave of me, than sending a slight excuse for not waiting on me before he went.

But this is not all; – a relation of his, who I know has always look'd upon his courtship to me with an evil eye, and had, not long ago, so great a quarrel with him on the occasion, that he was forbid his house, is now so far reinstated in his good graces as to be gone with him to the country; and I do not doubt but will take this opportunity of filling his ears with a thousand stories to my disadvantage, as he has ever done since my first acquaintance with him.

Thus, my dear Belinda, from having, as I thought, my choice of two the best matches in the town, I am likely to lose all hopes of both, and also to fall into the contempt and ridicule of all those flirts who so lately envied my good fortune.

This last circumstance is above all so truly mortifying, that after it I know not whether I shall ever be able to shew my face in any public assembly, but rather take the same pains to conceal myself, as once I did to be conspicuous: – but farewel, the more I reflect on these accidents, the less I am capable of restraining my passion enough to assure you,

With how much sincerity

I am,

My dear Belinda,

Your most devoted,

Tho' unfortunate friend,

Selima.

LETTER VI.

To Belinda, at Bath.

Dear Belinda,

I expected no less from your known goodness, than the consolatory ideas you endeavour to inspire me with; – you would fain persuade me that I have no reason for despair, and that the same beauty which attracted the hearts of Dorantes and Vanucius, will also gain me others of equal estimation; but alas, I have too much experience of myself, and of what the world thinks of me, to entertain so flattering a hope. – You know very well, my dear, that on my first setting up for conquest, I shew'd myself in all public places, and exposed to the view of all who saw me, almost every charm that nature has bestow'd upon me, yet never was address'd on the score of marriage by any but those two whom I have now lost.

Besides, I am now what they call blown upon; – that admiration which my first appearance excited, wears off by my being so often seen, and I begin to be convinced that it was more owing to the peculiarity of my dress and manner of behaviour, than to any real perfections of my person, that I was so much follow'd by a gaping multitude.

You see how I am humbled; and, by what I have said, may perhaps imagine that I have so far done with the pride of life and vanities of the world, as to take up with a little mercer or woollen-draper, if such a one should offer me his hand; but do not harbour so despicable an opinion of your friend; – no, I will never sit behind a compter, or be the wife of one that does; – but I need not make this declaration, – as matters stand I am not likely to be the wife of any body, but still,

> With an inviolable respect,
>> Dear BELINDA,
>>> Your most obliged friend,
>>>> And humble servant,
>>>>> SELIMA.

CHAP. IV.

Contains the Conclusion of Selima's letters.

LETTER VII.

To BELINDA, at Bath.

Dearest BELINDA,

Now may all the Gods of love and wit inspire my pen to describe to you as it deserves, the bless'd reverse in my condition since the last melancholy epistle you receiv'd from me; – I was then plung'd in the lowest pit of deep despair, and am now raised to the highest summit of human felicity: – in a word, I am the contracted spouse of Dorantes; and as soon as the preparations for our wedding can be got ready, shall be the declared ***** of *****.

Methinks I see the surprise I put you in; – you will doubtless cry out, – How can this be! when Dorantes has already confess'd himself the lawful husband of another! – It seems, indeed, a paradox, – yet stands in no need of school-learning to be explain'd, – as you will presently discover.

After the loss of both my lovers, as I then imagined, I scarce did any thing but lie upon the bed and weep for two whole days together; – my father, instead of saying any thing to console my afflictions, added to them by his reproaches; – he told me, – that he knew what it would come to; – that dressing myself up like a Bartholomew-baby[145] would never get me an husband, – and such like stuff, as you know his low way of expressing himself; – but thank Heaven the tables are now turned upon him; and if respect for my mamma did not restrain me, I should return his flouts[146] with interest.

One afternoon, as I was sitting at the window with the sash drawn up, musing on my unhappy fate, I saw Dorantes's chariot come to the door; – while his footman knock'd, he look'd out and made me a very respectful bow; – I was amaz'd, but thought it would be too gross an affront, to a man of his quality, to be denied to him as he saw I was at home; nor had I time for such a thing, if I would have done it; for the maid who open'd the door shew'd him directly up stairs.

On his entrance I assum'd one of those haughty and assur'd airs which vulgar low-bred people are apt to call impudent and sawcy; and with my head half turn'd another way, said to him, – 'I am surprised to see you here, Dorantes, after the conversation you entertain'd me with at your last visit.'

'Oh, Selima,' reply'd he, 'I came not now to repeat the audacity I was then guilty of, nor to offend your modest ears with any future discourses of the like nature; but humbly to beg pardon for the past, and hope that what I have to offer will make some attonement.'

'I do not comprehend your meaning,' return'd I; 'but whatever it may be, cannot think it becomes me to continue any correspondence with a married man, who being so pretended to make his addresses to me on an honourable score.'

'I am not married,' rejoin'd he eagerly, 'and the trial I made of your virtue adds a double lustre to the beauty that first enflam'd me, and I am now much more your slave than ever.'

'Not married!' cried I; – 'Why then did you tell me so?' – 'Pardon the innocent imposition I practised on you,' said he, kissing my hand, – 'I was willing to see in what manner you would resent it; – your behaviour has answer'd to my wish, and I now offer you a hand which I never had one thought or wish to dispose of to any other woman.'

Oh, Belinda, – how did my heart flutter at these words, as Semandra says in the play,

> I took them all, and died upon the sound:
> To the driv'n air my flying soul was fasten'd,
> Each charming syllable he spoke was mine.[147]

The many passionate and endearing things he said to me would not come within the compass of twenty letters; you must therefore, till I have a better opportunity of relating the particulars, content yourself with a brief summary of the whole; – which is this, that he is entirely at liberty to marry me, and is resolved to do so; – that an agreement the same night was made between us for that purpose; and that mamma and her good friend, who luckily happen'd to be with her, were call'd in to be witnesses of it.

Since every thing has been settled thus happily for me, some people have been impertinent enough to assure me, that to their own knowledge Dorantes was really married several years ago, and that his wife is still alive; – but this gives me no manner of concern: – if there be any woman who has a claim of this nature on him, he has doubtless found means to prevail on her to relinquish it, – so I look upon it as none of my affair; – he marries me in the face of the world,

– has promised to present me at court, – and while I enjoy the title of ******* of
******, and the grandeur annex'd to it, shall not trouble myself with any whispers
that may go about the town in relation to the lawfulness or unlawfulness of my
marriage.

It is no inconsiderable addition to my contentment, to hear that you design
to return to town in a short time; I long to see you, and to give you an airing in
my own coach and six, with three flaunting rampant footmen, in rich liveries,
hanging on the back of it: – we shall cut a better figure, Belinda, – than when we
made our little excursions together in a mean dirty hack. – Oh, fortune! – fortune! – dear propitious fortune, how am I bound to praise thee! – But no more
at present, than that I am,

With the greatest good wishes,

Dear creature,

Your most affectionate,

And very humble servant,

SELIMA.

P.S. I need not desire you to tell Philander what has happen'd, – I know you will,
and also that his regard for you will make him participate in the happiness of
your friend. Once more, – adieu.

Here end the letters of this celebrated lady; and, indeed, the picture she has given
of herself in them so much resembles that drawn for her by my old friend, that I
cannot avoid being of his opinion, as to the manner in which we may expect she
will regulate her conduct.

I could not, however, acquit Belinda of ingratitude for the little regard she
seem'd to have for one who was her intimate companion, and so frankly trusted
her with her bosom secrets; – the esteem I once had for her was very much
lessen'd by what I had discover'd of her temper in the Invisible Visit I had made
that morning at her apartments; – and the terms in which she had express'd herself, in relation both to Philander and his wife, gave me a curiosity to see how
that couple lived together.

Tho' I scarce doubted of his being in town, as Belinda was return'd from
Bath, yet I sent privately to his house, in order to be more assured, and finding
he was there, went one morning, imagining that to be the most likely time to
succeed in my design.

I enter'd their house in a lucky moment, – they were together, and deeply
engag'd in a conversation, the beginning of which I cannot pretend to relate; but
what pass'd between them after I came in, will give the reader a sufficient sample
of the disposition both of the one and the other; – it was to this effect:

Philander. So then, you say, madam, that there are some people who pretend to give themselves airs concerning my gallantries with Belinda at Bath?

Wife. You know very well, sir, that the world is apt to talk on such occasions.

Philander. Rot the world; – that impertinent part of it, at least, whom you converse with: – ridiculous; – as if there were any thing wonderful in a man's desiring to be in the good graces of one of the finest women in town.

Wife. They may think, perhaps, that when a married man has such inclinations he ought to be more private in them.

Philander. Private; – humph. – What, they would have the men as great prudes as the women!

Wife. You cannot think it strange, however, that every one believes Belinda, with all the charms you find in her, must be very destitute of admirers, when she encourages the addresses of a man who has no right to offer them.

Philander. Envy, by gad, – mere envy of her power of making universal conquests.

Wife. Scarce so; – a woman who behaves in the manner she does, renders herself rather an object of contempt than envy.

Philander. Look-ye, madam, – you may fancy what you please; but while Belinda has youth, wit, and beauty on her side, she will continue to be the toast of all the polite part of mankind, in spite of whatever malice or jealousy may suggest.

Wife. Indeed, sir, I have no malice to Belinda, nor jealousy of you, and give myself no sort of pain for what may happen between you behind the curtain; – but I do not chuse to be publickly neglected for her sake; – I would have you remember that I am your wife.

Philander. Faith, madam, it is little to your interest that I should remember it.

Wife. Why so?

Philander. Do you not know what a certain great poet, who understood nature better than either you or I, has told us upon this head?

> Who loves to hear of wife?
> That dull insipid thing, without desires,
> And without power to give them.[148]

Wife. Mighty well, Philander; – but certainly a man of this way of thinking ought never to marry.

Philander. Stupid: – Are you so ignorant as not to know a man of fashion marries chiefly for the sake of getting an heir to his estate?

Wife. Then love is quite out of the question?

Philander. Humph. – No, – not absolutely so; – a man generally chuses the woman who most suits his taste at that time, provided her fortune and family be equally agreeable; – but you are not to imagine that the conjugal hoop, like an enchanted circle, must never be leap'd over 'till the spell is ended, which, you know, lasts as long as life?

Wife. And must not then the same latitude be allow'd to the women?

Philander. No, – there are very good reasons to be given for the contrary: – but all this is idle; – since we are upon this topic, let us discuss it like rational creatures; – if we examine our own hearts, and confess the truth, I believe it will be found that my conduct and your discontent proceed from one and the same source, and are widely different from what the world generally ascribes to either: – in fine, madam, it is pride, – mere pride alone, that makes me guilty and you unhappy.

Wife. Pride; – as how?

Philander. I will presently convince you, – the pride of being thought to be well with a woman that half the town runs madding after, makes me fond of appearing in all public places with Belinda; – and it is the pride of engrossing me wholly to yourself that will not suffer you to be easy in seeing another woman preferr'd before you.

Wife. Suppose this to be the case, which I am, however, far from granting, mine would certainly be the most justifiable pride.

Philander. Not at all; – pride is one of the very worst ingredients in the composition of a wife.

Wife. And falshood in that of a husband.

Philander. If you accuse me of falshood, you are, without exception, positively one of the most ungenerous women in the world; – no man could deal more sincerely with a wife than I have just now done with you; and I think you ought to value me for it, and console yourself with the assurance that Belinda will grow stale to me the moment I find she becomes so to the town, – which, to let you into a secret, I believe will be very soon.

Wife. I am very much of your opinion in that point; – but then the ground she loses in your heart, will perhaps be taken up by another, so that my misfortune will receive little abatement by the change of persons.

Philander. As to that, madam, there's no answering for future events; – but whatever happens of this kind, you will always find it the wisest way to be easy; – so, madam, farewel, – I shan't dine at home to-day.

With these words he went away, it is possible to Belinda, or some other engagement of the same nature, which I had no curiosity to pry into; – his wife seem'd more agitated after he was gone, than she had made shew of when he was present; but having sat for some minutes in a musing posture, at length rous'd from it and spoke thus to herself:

Wife. He says true, indeed, – patience is my only remedy; – I may cry and fret myself till I grow so ugly that people will think I deserve the slights he treats me with, and the best I could expect would be the pity of my acquaintance: – Oh! how contemptible a thing is pity! – How mean does the wretch appear who stands in need of it! – I cannot bear the thought! – No, – the world shall never know how miserable I am; – I will tell every body that I discovered the flirt was in love with my husband, and that I put him upon pretending to admire her, on purpose to make her more ridiculous.

The thoughts of this stratagem seem'd to put her into great spirits; – I could perceive her eyes sparkled with the innate satisfaction of her mind, and a dawn of cheerfulness diffus'd itself through all her features. – After a short pause she went on with her soliloquy.

Wife. It shall be so; – her vain coquette airs will give a sanction to what I say, and my speaking of my husband with the utmost tenderness prevent every one from imagining I find myself treated by him with any coldness or neglect. – Oh, Philander, for my own sake I must conceal your faults; – it is a provoking circumstance, however, but I hope I shall have resolution enough to overcome it, and to follow mr. Dryden's advice.

> Secrets of marriage should be sacred held,
> Their sweets and bitter by the wise conceal'd;
> Errors of one reflect on t'other still,
> And when divulg'd proclaim we've chosen ill.[149]

Having now fully satisfied my curiosity, I left this lady to pursue her meditations, and retir'd to my apartment, in order to indulge my own; which, I must confess, afforded me no very pleasing ideas, as I was convinced, by what I had seen and heard, that neither the husband or the wife, or the favourite mistress, had any thing in their characters that could be at all interesting to a person of my way of thinking.

CHAP. V.

Consists chiefly of some reflections of the Author's own on false Taste, – the mistaken road in the pursuit of Fame, and the folly of an ill-directed emulation; to which are added, a few faint sketches taken from the most amiable originals in modern life, and exhibited in the hope of seeing them finish'd by a more able pencil for the improvement of the public.

THE celebrated Monsieur De Bussy[150] tells us, that when we say a man has a fine or true Taste, no more is meant by those words, than that he has a sound judgment, – a clear head, and a nicely distinguishing capacity in judging of what is really worthy and becoming; and what is not so, whether it be in the choice of his amusements, his equipage, his apparel, the furniture of his house, the covering of his table, or whatever else depends on the direction of the will and fancy.

Now, as every thing is best shewn by its opposite, if the definition given us by the French author of the true Taste be just, as I believe most people will allow it is, to think and act contrary to what he describes, is what we call false Taste; but, in my opinion, to think and do always what is wrong, and at the same time imagine that all we think and do is right, is not of itself sufficient to take in the meaning of the phrase in its full extent; – there must also be added an affectation of being singular, – over curious, – over delicate, – over elegant, – somewhat above the common level of mankind: – in fine, the man of a false Taste must not be a fool of Heaven's making but his own.

The late witty Earl of Rochester has presented us with a very picturesque character of the man of false Taste, in the following most excellent and pathetic lines:

> He was a fool thro' choice, not want of wit;
> His foppery, without the help of sense,
> Could ne'er have risen to such an excellence:
> Nature's as lame in making a true fop
> As a philosopher: the very top
> And dignity of folly, we attain
> By studious search, and labour of the brain;
> By observation, council, and deep thought;
> God never made a coxcomb worth a groat:
> We owe that name to industry and arts;
> An eminent fool must be a Man of parts.[151]

A person may be endow'd with great talents, yet, through a false Taste in the manner of displaying them, be render'd ridiculous instead of respectable, and while he aims at attracting universal admiration, become the object of universal contempt.

Hippias is profoundly learned, – is well skill'd in the most useful sciences, and endow'd both by nature and education with every requisite to render him a worthy and beneficial member of society; yet, by some unaccountable oddities of manners and behaviour, he makes himself hated where he might be loved, – despis'd where he might be respected, – and a mere cypher in a world where he might be a figure of the greatest consequence.

He is not at all dissatisfied that every one knows and speaks of him as a man possess'd of a very opulent fortune, yet affects to look down with scorn on all the pleasures, and even innocent amusements it might afford him; and to such an excess does he carry this humour, that whatever is beyond the necessities of nature he treats as luxury and epicurism, vainly imagining that the wearing of a threadbare coat, and a wig that the head it covers scarce remembers ever to have had a curl, or the dining on a cut of coarse boiled beef from a threepeny ordinary, entitles him to the character of a philosopher.

But this ostentatious humility, as I think it may be justly call'd, is not the most unpardonable error into which Hippias is led by his false Taste; – this serves only to make him ridiculous; – but there is another which makes him hateful.

The ambition he has of being reverenced as a stoic, renders him deaf to the dictates of humanity, and wholly insensible of all social feeling for his fellow creatures; – he partakes not in the joys or griefs of even those he calls his friends, nor would lift a finger, move a step, or speak a syllable, either to promote the one or dissipate the other; – the most distressful circumstance has not the power to touch his heart, and if any one knows him little enough to employ his assistance or advice in the extremest exigence, he replies, with a solemn and magisterial air, – that he can say nothing to their complaints; that pity is a passion; and that, by the force of his reason, he has divested himself of all passions of what kind soever.

Thus does Hippias, by indulging one unhappy propensity, forfeit all the love and esteem the qualities he is possess'd of would otherwise attract; – the manner in which he is now look'd upon gives me room to suspect, that whenever he makes his exit from this world he will have an epitaph somewhat like what I read on a tomb-stone in a country church-yard:

> Here *******, stretch'd at his full length is laid,
> Who living, no one lov'd, nor mourn'd when dead.

Numberless are the instances might be given to prove the best capacities may be, and frequently are, perverted by false Taste and misapplication; – as one of our most eminent authors tells us, – the love of Fame is the universal passion,[152] – it is imprinted, in a more or less degree, on every human heart; – those who have great talents are apt to think they can never render themselves sufficiently conspicuous; and those of weaker intellects, yet possess'd of the same vanity, are sometimes so infatuated, as rather than not to make a noise in the world, to do things which may incur a lampoon, since they cannot deserve a panegyric.

A private life, or as they term it, a life of obscurity, is to some people the severest misfortune they can labour under; – they will tell you, that they may as well be out of the world as of no consequence in it; – and few there are who will take the poet's word for a contrary passion.

> Th' unknown, untalk'd of man, is only blest;
> No anxious doubts his peaceful breast annoy,
> From praise and censure equally remote;
> Nor hopes, nor fears, his happiness destroys,
> But safe within himself, himself enjoys.[153]

It is more than barely possible, that some of my witty readers will cry out, – that I have lash'd myself in this remark, and if I were not as fond of being talk'd of as any body else, I should never have presented them with this work; – but I would have these cavillers think a little before they pass such a judgment on me; – however, for fear they should not give themselves the trouble of doing so, as the present age does not seem to care much for thinking, shall give them a very explicit, though short answer:

If I had exhibited these lucubrations with any view of rendering myself popular, I should certainly have pluck'd off my Belt of Invisibility as soon as it had furnish'd me with matter for their entertainment, and appear'd in statu quo, with a long fawning preface in my hand, humbly imploring the approbation of the public on my labours; but as I have resolved to remain in an impenetrable concealment, they must do me the justice to allow that I have the honour to be of the same opinion with the author I just now quoted.

This is all I have to say, – and enough too, I think, to clear me from any imputation of the kind I have mention'd; – so shall now go on with such observations as at present occur on some few of the many branches which sprout forth from that great root of wrong acting, commonly call'd false Taste.

There are people, who, having no peculiarities of their own, affect to imitate those they may see in others, especially if the person they copy after be of a superior rank, or has the reputation of a wit.

These may properly enough be call'd second-hand fools; for they generally take up the follies just when they are left off by the persons they would be thought exactly to resemble; – according to a vulgar adage, – 'The fool will sometimes peep out of the wisest man.' – The least failing in a person of a distinguish'd character is presently adopted by his inferiors till it becomes a fashion.

How justly, therefore, though not the most elegantly, does Michael Drayton express himself when speaking on this subject; – it is a long time ago since I read the old gentleman; but, as near as I can remember, his words are as follow:

> The great, 'tis sure, should first themselves amend;
> For follies of all kinds will still descend:
> What palaces begin, the cottage apes,
> And no degree of men th' infection scapes.[154]

Emulation, however, when well directed, is one of the most noble propensities of the mind; – nothing can be more truly laudable than an endeavour to square our actions by a praiseworthy model; but I am sorry to say that this is not so often the case as every good man would wish it were.

There are some people so unhappy, as to take for a pattern all the bad they can find, and neglect all the good; – and this, too, without design or any untoward inclination, but through mere carelessness; and provided they do something such a one or such a one does, give not themselves the trouble to examine whether what they imitate be a beauty or a blemish; or, indeed, whether it be either, or only a matter of indifference, and altogether unworthy of regard.

And now I am upon this head, I cannot forbear relating an example of the sort I last mentioned; which, though it happen'd some years ago, and is extremely trifling in itself, may serve to shew how little care people sometimes take in their choice of an object for imitation.

A young gentleman of my acquaintance, and who pass'd in the world for a very pretty fellow, either was, or affected to be, because it was the mode, a prodigious admirer of the late deservedly famous sir Isaac Newton; – he had the honour of being known to that truly great man, frequently visited him, and had the opportunity of hearing many things from him, which doubtless were well worthy of being treasured in his memory; – yet I could never find he took particular notice of any thing but this I am now going to repeat.

Sir Isaac had him at his table one day, and happen'd casually to say, that he thought nothing sweeter than a bacon bone; – my friend immediately catch'd up the word, and from that moment made it his own, and on all occasions quoted it; – if any one ask'd him to eat with them he would reply, – 'Yes, if you have any bacon; for, as sir Isaac Newton says, there is nothing sweeter than a bacon bone.' – In fine, he went to no place, – mingled in no conversation, without finding some means to introduce the sweetness of the bacon bone, and repeated the above-mention'd expression so often, and so impertinently, that at last he became the jest of all his companions, who, in derision, call'd him by no other name than the bacon bone.

Ridiculous as this may appear, I can assure my reader, that the gentleman I have been speaking of does not stand alone, but has many parallels in my catalogue of observations on a misguided imitation, as I could easily prove; – but my humour has on a sudden chang'd its vein; and I begin to grow too serious to recite any farther instances of so ludicrous a nature.

Degenerate as we mortals are said to be, and to confess the truth, worse cannot be said of us than we, in fact, deserve; yet even now, in this present equally corrupt and illiterate age, when no encouragement is given either to virtue or to wit, there are not wanting some few illustrious examples of both, whom even an endeavour to copy after would be some merit in the attempter.

See where the noble Altamont stands forth a shining patron of exalted virtue; – dignity in his countenance, – benevolence in his hand, – the strictest justice, honour, and social kindness in his heart; – near him you will always find the chaste and fair Euphemia, his illustrious consort, – a numerous and beauteous offspring, with joyous smiles play round their feet, – Juno and Hymen hover over their heads, and shower continual blessings on the happy pair.

From Altamont and Euphemia, – ye husbands, fathers, learn the duties due to those endearing names; and cease to imagine that to swerve from them is politeness.

Learn you, who languish in a widow'd bed, from Elismonda learn[155] to support the melancholy of your situation as becomes you; – Elismonda, who, tho' as Lee expresses it, in all the full-grown pride of glorious beauty,[156] disdains all overtures for a second marriage, – shuns pomp and ceremony, – nor haunts the court nor public walks, but in her closet ruminates what good is in her power to do, – who most deserves, and who stands most in need of her relief; and all those cares she once employ'd to please the best of husbands are now taken up with acts of piety and soft compassion.

Learn you, fair ramblers after show and hurry, – ye midnight gadders to masquerades and balls, from lovely Amadea learn, the timid modesty that best befits and best secures the honour of a virgin state; – she takes no pains to attract the eyes of the gaping multitude, and rather shuns than covets popular admiration; – she avoids being the first in any new fashion, and never runs into the extreme of it; – goes to no routes, assemblies, or masquerades; – seldom indulges herself even with a play or opera; and when she does, is always accompany'd by some grave relation, whose presence is a check on the impertinence of those whifflers who skip from box to box, saying the same thing to every fine woman they see there; – when she walks in the Park, she makes choice of those hours when the least company are there; and the only public place you are sure to find her in is at Church.

The example of Dorilaus is a noble reprimand to those who suffer themselves to grow old in riots and debaucheries; – early he quitted the levities of youth, – and, as the silver Swan immerging from the stream, shakes off the drops that hang upon its wings; so Dorilaus but dipp'd into the follies of the times, – just tasted the licentious pleasures of the town, – then despised and threw them from him with abhorrence.

Temptations of every kind have since surrounded him, yet has he still remain'd unmov'd, – equally inflexible to the insinuations of luxury and to the bribes of corruption; – steady in virtuous principles, the evil ones at length grew weary of their fruitless labour, and now suffer him to enjoy a calm and undisturb'd repose, in the society of a few select friends, who join with him in commiserating the infatuation and stupidity of an abandon'd and self-ruin'd age.

If there were no cards nor dice in the world, Favonius would be look'd upon as an almost faultless being, and the voice of envy have nothing wherewith to cast a blemish on his name: – it cannot be denied, however, but that Favonius has wit, honour, generosity, affability, and an unaffected sweetness of disposition, – qualifications which would greatly compensate for his love of gaming, if it were not for two considerations, – which are these:

First, That by indulging this unhappy propensity, he lavishes too much of that precious time which might be employ'd in the defence of the liberties of his country, and for the benefit of a commonwealth which stands in the utmost need of so able a friend.

Secondly, That his high character in the world, join'd to an almost general depravity of manners, makes many people ready, and even proud to follow his example in this, the sole error of which he can be accused, while they neglect the least endeavour to imitate any one of the numerous virtues he is master of.

Blush, ye pretended patriots, who wrote and loudly bawl'd for liberty;[157] – who inveigh'd against corruption, only to enhance the market of corruption, and sell your consciences at a dearer rate: – blush, I say, at the awful Camillus! – Camillus, who so long and so strenuously maintain'd the glorious cause he had undertook, 'till deserted, and left almost alone, prudence obliged him to retire, and employ those cares the public were unworthy of, in private benefits on his tenants and dependants.

There are many others of both sexes still living, whose characters would reflect honour on the imitators; and some who, though the world has been so unfortunate as to lose, have left behind them such monuments of their virtues as can never be forgotten; – their memory strikes a damp on guilt, and will eternally be venerated by all the wise and good.

They are now removed from the vices and follies of an age they had not power to reclaim; but, as the divine muse which directed the pen of Herbert truly says,

> In spite of death, the actions of the just,
> Will still smell sweet, and blossom in the dust.[158]

But this is a theme which, tho' perhaps little affecting to the greatest part of my readers, may yet be too melancholy to some others, as well as to myself, I shall therefore dwell no longer upon it, but return to a subject more suitable to the present disposition of the times, which I am not so ignorant as not to know an author ought always to consult, if he regards either his own reputation or the interest of his Bookseller.

CHAP. VI.

Gives a succinct relation of two pretty extraordinary adventures that presented themselves to the Author in a morning ramble; – which accounts, if they are not found altogether so improving as some few readers might desire, have full as good a plea to the approbation of the town in general, – that of being very diverting.

A clear and undisturb'd sky, illuminated with a smiling sun, and perfumed with a thousand odours from the new budding spring, invited me to take the air in Hyde-Park; – I girded my Invisible Belt about me, for the reasons I have already mention'd in a preceding chapter, and also put my Tablets in my pocket, though I had not the least expectation of meeting with any thing in that place which should give me occasion to make use of them.

The sweet solemnity of this solitude afforded me infinitely more pleasure than ever I had found in a crowded Mall; – it inspired me with the most delightful ideas, which indulging, I wander'd for I believe near two hours without meeting with any one object to interrupt my contemplations.

How much longer I might have continued in this agreeable resvery I know not; for I was rous'd from it by the sudden appearance of a gentleman at some distance from me, but who was advancing directly towards the path where I was: – on his approach I stepp'd a little on one side, to prevent his running against me; – he walk'd backwards and forwards with some emotion, – look'd often on his watch, and discover'd many signs of the utmost impatience.

By the cockade in his hat, and some other infallible simptoms I saw about him, I doubted not of his being a military gentleman, and imagin'd that some dispute of honour was that morning to be decided by the point of the sword; but I was soon convinced of my mistake, and that the officer at that time had more of Cupid than of Mars in his head.

I had not been many minutes before a coach came up and stopp'd very near to the place where I stood; – there were three women in it, one of whom, and much the richest dress'd, I presently knew to be the celebrated Lipathea; – the others, as I afterwards found, were her Woman and Nurse; – this, it seems, being the first time of her coming abroad since her bringing into the world a son and heir, to the great joy of that honourable family, – as the News-writers express it.

On sight of the coach the young officer advanced briskly towards it, – Lipathea saw him at the same time, and thrusting out her head, and half her body, with her accustom'd loud laugh, cry'd to him:

Lipathea. So, – my dear punctual Billy.

Officer. More punctual, indeed, than your ladyship; for I have been here this half hour.

Lipathea. Well, well, – come in, – you know I shall recompence your attendance.

With these words the door was immediately open'd, – the two women came out and the officer jump'd in, – after which the coachman was order'd to drive as slow as he could to the Wallnut-tree Walk, and so round to the Ha-ha Wall and back to the same place again.

I had no opportunity to follow them, so was oblig'd to content myself with hearing the discourse that pass'd between the two women who were left behind, – to this end I kept as close to them as I could, with my Tablets in my hand; but the subjects they talk'd on at first were so trifling, that I did not think it worth while to spread them for the impression of their words, 'till all at once the Nurse, lifting up her hands and eyes, burst into this exclamation:

Nurse. Well, – these great folks, they may do any thing! but I wonder her ladyship is not afraid of being met by some one who might tell her husband!

Woman. If such a thing should happen, and he offer to resent it, she would either laugh or fight him out of it.

Nurse. What, do they fight!

Woman. Fight, – aye, mrs. Nurse, and scratch too; but my lady always gets the better.

Nurse. That is likely enough, truly, if they go to handy-cuffs; for she is a good deal the most robust of the two.

Woman. Aye, some people are apt to say they should change sex. – But how can you be surpriz'd at her making this excursion? – Do not you remember that when she had lain-in but ten days, Sam, her favourite footman, conducted the Captain up the back-stairs into her bed-chamber, in the very moment her husband was going into his chariot to take the air after a fit of the gout.

Nurse. Indeed I shall never forget it; – I was quite confounded: – Nurse Dandle too was call'd to shew young master to him, – just as if he had been his father.

Woman. Well, she has fine children, and I believe does not care a pin's point who the world thinks begot them.

Nurse. That's a plain case, or she would never behave as she does.

Woman. It is not our business, however to find fault; for to do her justice, as covetous as she is in other things, she is liberal enough to those who are any way assisting to her pleasures.

Nurse. I believe so; for after the Captain was gone that day she put a broad-piece into my hand, and said he had left it for me. – But hearkye, – I was told for a great secret, that she had an intrigue with my lord Triffli Traffli, – and that he made her the finest presents.

Woman. They need not have told it you for a secret, – all the town knows it, and he is as proud as she is careless of their doing so.

Nurse. How does that matter stand at present then? – Has he forsaken her, or she him?

Woman. Neither, I can assure you; – they are as fond of each other as ever when they are together; but he has lately got into a great employment which takes up his time very much, and he cannot be so often with her as usual, – so that she would be quite mop'd for want of amusement if the Captain were not in the way.

Nurse. Bless me! how times are chang'd! – When I was a young woman there were no such doings; – I have serv'd in many a great family, and nurs'd many a fine lady, but never saw formerly what I have lately seen in this, and some other places, which shall be nameless.

Woman. I have heard, indeed, that people of the last age were very different from what they are now; but we cannot live by the past but by the present, and I would not have you stand in your own light,[159] mrs. Nurse; – my lady talks of recommending you to a certain great person, who will shortly have occasion for one of your profession; but if you seem to disapprove of these things you will spoil all.

Nurse. Nay, for that matter, I, – I can hold my tongue when I find it is for my interest; – I am no babbler, – I will say that for myself; – but thoughts, you know, are free.

This prating woman, who would fain be thought no babbler, now began to run into a long detail of all the particulars she knew, or could remember, that had happen'd in the several families where she had been; but the matters she related being wholly insignificant, and unworthy of record, I shut up my Tablets and gave no farther ear to what she said.

I quitted not the place, however, 'till the lovers return'd from the tour they had been making; – the coach stopp'd, and the Captain was set down near the end of the same path where he had been taken up, and Lipathea beckon'd her two attendants to come in, who by this time, I found, were heartily weary of their promenade.

The well-known character of Lipathea, one would think, should have hinder'd me from being much surprised at any thing she did; yet could I not be an eyewitness of the glaring affront she now put upon her husband, and the modesty of her sex, without being seiz'd with a consternation impossible to be express'd.

My meditations on this adventure had perhaps lasted 'till I came home, if they had not been interrupted by another which fell in my way, and afforded me, in its consequences, more matter for diversion than the former.

Beauty, or what is more than beauty, the power of attraction, is not confin'd to persons of a high station, – nature can exert herself as much in the cottage as the palace, and we sometimes find more real graces under a plain homely coif than under a fine gause cap ornamented with jewels, – as the little incident I am about to rehearse will abundantly evince.

As I was passing through St. James's Park, I met a young woman with a porringer[160] in her hand, sat upon a waterplate, and neatly cover'd with a large earthen saucer; – she advanced with slow and cauteous steps, lest she should spill any part of what she had brought; when she drew near to the Parade, a tall lusty Grenadier stepp'd forth from among his comrades and receiv'd the mess from her, as also a pewter spoon as bright as silver, which she took out of her pocket and presented to him at the same time.

Tho' every thing about her was clean, even to a nicety, yet, as the reader may easily suppose extremely mean; – she had a face, however, that stood in need of no advantages from dress to set it off; – never had I seen a finer pair of eyes, more regular features, or a more soft and delicate complexion; – and to crown all the rest of her perfections, there appear'd not only in her countenance, but in every little motion and gesture, that which, in my opinion, is the very soul of loveliness, a most perfect innocence and simplicity.

I was so much struck at the sight of her, that I could not forbear stopping in order to consider her beauty with more attention, while she stood waiting till the Grenadier, who I found was her husband, had done eating.

I was not, however, the only admirer whom her charms that morning had attracted, – a certain officer of distinction in the army, who happen'd to be walking on the Parade with another gentleman, having beheld her at some distance, quitted his companion and came to the Grenadier, accosting him in these terms:

Officer. So, Grenadier, – you are taking your morning's refreshment; – Is this pretty damsel your wife?

Grenadier. Yes, please your honour.

Officer. She seems very young, you can't have been married long.

Grenadier. About three months, please your honour.

Officer. I hope you use her well; – I dare say she deserves it.

Grenadier. I think she has no reason to complain, sir; – Have you Peggy?

Wife. No, indeed.

Officer. I am glad of it; – I would always have the women used well.

He said no more, but turned upon his heel and walk'd away with a careless air, as if nothing farther than what he had made shew of were in his head; but I perceiv'd he remov'd no farther than the end of the Canal, and kept an observant eye on those he had left behind.

The Grenadier having finish'd his little repast, mingled with some soldiers who were on the Parade, and his wife trip'd out of the Park with much more haste than she had come into it; – the officer, who had never lost sight of her, follow'd, tho' for a while at some distance, and I kept very near him, resolving to see what it was he aim'd at, and what would be the issue of his designs, in case he had any of the nature I suspected.

She went through the Treasury, and when he saw she had enter'd there mended his pace, and coming up with her under the arch'd passage gave her a little slap on the shoulder; – she started and turn'd back, but on seeing him dropp'd a low curtsy, while he spoke thus:

Officer. Well overtaken, my pretty lass; – I wanted to speak with you; – I fancy I have seen you some where or other; – Pray what country-woman are you?

Wife. I was born in Lancashire, – so please your honour.

Officer. I thought so; for I have heard say all the Lancashire girls are very handsome, – And pray what brought you to London?

Wife. The hopes of getting into a good service, please your honour; but not hearing of one presently, and happening to get acquainted with my husband in the mean time, I chang'd my condition.

Officer. You did well; – there is nothing like being your own mistress; – but you country folks are generally afraid of a red coat; – How came you to venture on a soldier?

Wife. I don't know, sir, – it was my fate, I think.

Officer. Well here is something to encourage you to love the army.

With these words he drew a six-and-thirty piece of gold out of his pocket and made an offer of putting it into her hand; but she drew back, either asham'd or unwilling to accept it, and cry'd,

Wife. Oh, sir, I have heard say that women should never take money from the men.

Officer. That is from your mean dirty fellows; but it is ill-manners to refuse any thing given you by your superiors.

He now took hold of her hand, and a second effort obliging her to receive his present, she look'd on it, turn'd it two or three times, and then said,

Wife. Bless me, – what must I do with this great piece of money?

Officer. Oh you will find a use for it; – that pretty face and person of yours require a thousand things that the Grenadier's pay will not enable him to purchase for you: – and now I think on it, – 'tis pity he should continue in that low station; – I have it in my power to raise him, and I will do it, – he shall have a Halbert[161] forthwith; – but I must talk to you a little first upon that score. – Where do you live? – I will come and see you.

Wife. Oh, dear sir, – we have not an habitation fit for your honour to come into.

Officer. No matter for that, – I am not proud, and never scruple to go to any place, how mean soever it be, where I can either do a pleasure to myself or a service to my friends; – therefore no excuses.

Wife. Your honour is very good; – but I do not know how to tell you, for there is no sign near us; – but we lodge up one pair of stairs at a button-maker's, the next door but one to a chandler's shop, in a little alley that turns out of King-street by a green-stall,[162] and is no thoroughfare.

Officer. I shall never find it by this direction, – you shall shew me where it is now?

Wife. Lord, sir, what will the people in the street say, to see me go cheek-by-jole with such a fine gentleman as your honour?

Officer. Well then you shall walk before and I will follow you.

Wife. But, sir, my room is all dirty, – I was just going home to clean it, – now I have carry'd my husband his breakfast.

Officer. I shall not go in, nor visit you 'till after dark, to hinder, as you say, the neighbours from staring at me; – I will come this evening about nine or ten o'clock; – your husband is to be upon duty, but do you take care not to be out of the way; for it is absolutely necessary I should have some discourse with you before I do any thing for him.

Wife. Lord, sir, what business can your honour have with me that he must not know?

Officer. You may tell him afterwards, if you will; – but I won't detain you any longer, – go home and delight yourself with the assurance I give you that your husband shall be made a Serjeant to-morrow, and that I shall use all my interest for his rising still higher; – so that he may come to be a Captain at last.

Wife. A Captain! – oh lae! – I should never have thought of such a thing.

Officer. It all depends upon yourself, and what I have to communicate to you; – so be sure to be at home and alone when I come.

Wife. Yes, please your honour, I would not for all the world be so rude as to disappoint you; – though I am asham'd you should come into such a poor habitation as mine.

Officer. Never mind that, my pretty one, I shall look on nothing in the place but yourself.

While he was speaking this he cast his eyes about, and finding there was nobody in sight, gave her an affectionate kiss upon the cheek, after which she made a low curtsy and turn'd away to go home, blushing all the way she went like the Sun through a gentle shower in an April morning; – he follow'd, as he said he would, 'till he had seen her enter into her little dwelling; nor left the place 'till he had taken sufficient notice of every thing, to be able to remember and know it again.

I was now under a most sensible concern for this poor young creature, – thus likely to be betray'd, not by any inclination to ill but merely through the fear of offending a person above her, – quite ignorant of the snares of the world, and untaught how to resist temptation; she was, alas, just ready to fall into a real fault, by an endeavour to avoid an imaginary one, – as mr. Waller said, tho' on a different occasion,

> Innocence and youth oft makes,
> In artless virgins such mistakes.[163]

Tho' I had not the least doubt but that the young wife of the Grenadier would become a prey to the vicious inclination of her seducer, yet I had the curiosity to see in what manner she would behave on the full discovery of his designs upon her.

Accordingly I went about nine o'clock to the little alley, and posted myself on a bench at a door just opposite to the dwelling of the Grenadier, resolved to go in with the Officer when he should come.

I had not waited above half an hour before he appear'd; – he was muffled up in his cloak; but by the help of a small winking light from an adjacent shop, I easily knew him; – he had taken too much notice of the house to be mistaken in it, and enter'd directly, the door being left open, as I suppose, for that purpose; – I follow'd close behind him, but never had my Invisibilityship been in so much danger as it was now brought into by this adventure.

The Grenadier, it seems, having been inform'd by his wife of every thing that had pass'd between her and the Officer, and more zealous in the defence of his honour, than perhaps some in a much higher station would have been, had prevailed, for some pots of beer, on a brother Grenadier to do duty for him that night, so return'd home before the hour appointed for his rival's approach, and having arm'd himself with a good oaken cudgel, stood on the middle of the stairs ready to give a proper reception to that invader of his rights.

My leader had not advanced above five or six steps of the stairs, when he receiv'd a violent blow on the head, which, together with the surprize it gave him, made him reel back and like to fall on poor Invisible; but I hastily and prudently withdrew to the middle of the entry, and stood aloof to hear, at a more safe distance, what would be the end of this affair.

The Grenadier pursued his strokes, and the Officer, being in no condition to defend himself in that disadvantageous posture, thought it best to make his escape; but not having been accustom'd to such steep winding stairs, fell down to the bottom; – his antagonist, though better acquainted with the passage, in attempting to follow him had the same fate; but being uppermost soon recover'd himself, and catching hold of the Officer by the collar as he was endeavouring to rise, forced him on his knees, and continued buffeting him on the head and face 'till he was cover'd all over with the blood that gush'd from his nose and mouth, as I afterwards perceiv'd.

The Officer made several efforts to draw his sword, and at length did so; but the other finding what he was about, immediately seiz'd it by the hilt, wrested it from him, snapp'd it in sunder with his foot, and threw it over his head. – 'Rascal, will you murder me!' cry'd the Officer. – 'No, no,' reply'd the Grenadier, 'I will only cool your courage, and make you remember running after other men's wives.' – 'Dog, – do you know who I am?' demanded he – 'I only know you for a villain,' said the other, 'that would debauch my wife, and as such I'll use you.' – 'Sirrah,' return'd the Officer, 'I will make you pay dearly for this insolence; – you know well enough that I am ******' – 'you lye,' rejoin'd the other, 'and deserve to be hang'd for taking such a gentleman's name in your mouth; – ****** would scorn to sneek into such a poor hut as this to seduce any man's wife.'

The Grenadier's hands were not idle all this time; but the Officer having at length got upon his feet, they continued wrestling together for some minutes, in which combat the furious husband had much the better, which put me in mind of what mr. Row says in his excellent tragedy of Jane Shore:

> In spite of birth and dignity, a man
> Oppos'd against a man, is but a man.[164]

The Officer now finding himself quite disabled, and being still under the gripe of his unrelenting enemy, call'd vehemently out for help; on which several of the neighbours ran in with lighted candles in their hands, and the entry was presently full of men, women and children; – but never was such a spectacle as this demolish'd Beau. – 'Bless me! what is the matter?' cry'd one – 'What is the matter?' – 'Ask no questions, – here is half a crown for any one that will get me a chair immediately,' said he; and the word was scarce out of his mouth before a cobler ran with all the speed he could to do as he desir'd.

The Grenadier now affected the utmost surprize, and said, – 'All the world should never have made me believe it was your honour; – I protest I took you for a rogue that wanted to come to bed to my wife while I was abroad, and thought I could not use such a one too ill.' – The women, on hearing this, guess'd how the business was, and look'd at one another and grinn'd; – one of them, however, was so charitable as to fetch a wooden bowl of water and a piece of clean rag to cleanse the blood from off his face and garments; – he made use of what she brought, but gave no other answer to what the Grenadier had said than a look full of resentment and confusion.

A chair being brought, he catch'd up his hat and wig, which had fallen off in the scuffle, went into it, leaving behind him sufficient matter to employ the conversation of the whole alley for a long time; – on hearing afterwards the whole truth of the affair from the Grenadier and his wife, every one applauded the conduct of them both, and laugh'd heartily at the disappointment and correction of the lascivious Officer.

For my own part, after I got home, the satisfaction of finding myself safe from the dangers into which my curiosity had brought me, was succeeded by some considerations on the passages I had been witness of, and I could not help being fill'd with the utmost astonishment, that persons endow'd with a liberal education, and from whom much better things might be expected, should, for the sake of gratifying a foolish inclination, the fleeting pleasure of a moment, not only be guilty of the greatest injustice to others, but also of the most abject demeaning of themselves.

CHAP. VII.

Is calculated rather for admonition than entertainment, and therefore is likely to be but little relish'd; – especially as it may happen to give a pretty severe slap on the faces of some who think themselves too great or too wise for amendment.

How vainly do we boast the light of Reason, when we refuse to submit either our wills or actions to the guidance of its direction, when through every stage of life we suffer some darling passion to gain dominion over us, and utterly extinguish that glorious lamp we seem so proud of, and would be thought so eminently to possess above the rest of the creation?

Prodigality is generally the vice of Youth, and Avarice of Age; but tho' both these propensities proceed from a wrong turn of mind, and are diametrically opposite to sound judgment, yet I think somewhat more may be said in excuse of the one than of the other.

The Prodigal lavishes his stores in such things as do a pleasure to himself; and if he squanders away his patrimony in riotous living, and becomes miserable in the end, there are some who profit by his misfortunes; – his money circulates, and the Public suffer nothing by his private ruin.

The Miser, on the contrary, not only denies himself all enjoyment of the goods of fortune, but also withholds them, as much as in his power, from every one else; – he parts with nothing he can get into his clutches, – amasses heaps of treasure, and smiles with a wicked satisfaction to see it lie rusting in his coffers, while numbers of his more worthy fellow-creatures are perishing for the want of it.

Avarice, above all other passions, so takes up the soul that it leaves not the least room for any of the nobler sensations; – love, friendship, pity, and even natural affection, are excluded thence; – the covetous man regards only the gratification of that one sordid view, – all his fears, his hopes, his cares, are center'd there, and he seldom sticks at any thing to obtain it.

Besides, what can be more absurd in itself, than for people to labour with all their might in the heaping riches, which they neither make use of, nor can assure themselves but that the next moment may dispossess them of? and it is remarkable, that the nearer they approach to the time when they can expect no other than to be snatch'd for ever from the idol they have worship'd, they grow the more eager to preserve it.

Strange infatuation, not to be accounted for either by nature or common sense! – Our English Pindar, the inimitable Cowley,[165] has an extreme pretty sentiment on this head; – these are his words:

'Tis madness sure treasures to hoard,
And make them useless as in mines remain,

To lose the occasion fortune does afford,
Fame and public love to gain.[166]

The condition of those children who have the misfortune to be descended from
parents of the humour I am speaking of, can never be too much commiserated,
especially if they happen to be born with notions more just and elevated; – an
instance of which kind I am now going to relate.

A gentleman, whom I shall distinguish by the name of Avario, is sprung from
a very ancient family in the West of England, has a large estate, and might have
been belov'd and respected by his neighbours, if the excessive parsimoniousness
of his disposition did not make him do things which demean his rank, and even
render him contemptible in the eyes both of his equals and inferiors.

He was married in his youth to a lady of birth and fortune; but had no
child by her for near twelve whole years, at the end of which time, however, she
brought a son into the world, which one would imagine should have fill'd the
father's heart with the highest satisfaction; but instead of thanking Providence
for sending him an heir of his own bowels for his estate, he only repined at the
additional expence the new comer must necessarily occasion.

His lady was sensibly afflicted at the little notice he took of the young Clyamon, for so the son of this unworthy father was call'd; but when she reproach'd
him with his unkindness, he only gave her this churlish answer: – That he saw
no cause for any great rejoicing; for he supposed, as she had now began to teem,
he should in a few years have more children than he should be able to maintain.

Clyamon, notwithstanding, grew a very fine boy; but would have had little
to boast of from education, if his uncle by the mother's side, who was exceeding
rich and had no children, had not conceived a more than ordinary affection for
him, and resolved to bestow on him all those advantages which were denied to
him by the niggard disposition of his father.

He told Avario, that if he would trust him with his son he would breed him
as his own, and take care that he should want for none of those accomplishments
which constitute the truly fine gentleman, in case he were capable of receiving
them; 'which,' added he, 'I do not at all doubt of, from the early promise of his
childhood.'

This offer was too agreeable to both the parents not to be readily accepted;
– the father rejoiced at being eas'd of an expence he could not foresee without
regret; and the mother was highly pleas'd to think that her little darling would
now receive a more polite education than she could hope the too great frugality
of her husband would have allow'd him.

Clyamon was about ten years of age when sir Arthur Frankwill, for so this
worthy uncle was call'd, took him under his protection, and carry'd him to a fine
seat he had about twelve miles distance from Avario's: – doubly happy for him

was now this change in his situation; for his mother dying soon after his removal, he would doubtless have been deprived of many indulgences he had hitherto enjoy'd at home; – but which were abundantly made up to him by the tender affection he was treated with by the good baronet.

Sir Arthur, not approving of any of the schools in that part of the country, sent him to Eton, under the conduct of a faithful old servant; – and in that place it was he receiv'd his first rudiments of learning.

The improvements he made there were such as did honour to the masters as well as to his own capacity, in so readily imbibing their instructions; – the accounts those gentlemen gave of him, in their letters to sir Arthur, were confirm'd by their pupil's behaviour whenever the times of breaking up gave him the liberty of going into the country: both uncle and father were surprised on finding the swift progress he made in his learning; – the one was charm'd with the success of his endeavours, and the other quite transported that his son was in a fair way of being possess'd of so many accomplishments without any cost to himself.

Having perfected himself in all he could be taught at Eton, he quitted the school, by his uncle's permission, and return'd to the West; where, after having staid some time to make an acquaintance with the gentry, and take such diversions as the country afforded, his uncle thought proper he should finish his studies at one of the Universities, and for some reasons which he had within himself, made choice of that at Oxford. – Clyamon accordingly went thither at the age of eighteen, and had the good fortune to have for his Tutor a gentleman of deep learning, a keen discernment, and an unprejudiced judgment, who inspired him with such principles of justice and true honour as I believe he will never depart from.

The admonitions of this worthy Tutor, join'd to a natural love of virtue in himself, entirely preserved him from running into any of those excesses which too many of his age are guilty of; – though nothing could be more gay and spirituous, yet every thing he said and did was govern'd by a certain decorum, without seeming to be so.

He could be chearful among the men of his acquaintance, without immorality or prophaneness; – courtly among the ladies, without flattery or insincerity; – respectful to his superiors, and maintain a proper distance to those below him, without pride or ill-nature: – in fine, his character and manners were such as made him highly esteem'd by all the wise and good, and beloved even by those who would not be at the pains to imitate him.

After a stay of about three years at the University he return'd to sir Arthur Frankwill's; for that kind uncle and patron would needs have him continue to look upon his house as his chief home, nor did Avario at all oppose this motion, tho' he was now extremely proud of his son, went often to see him, and would always make him be present at every public assembly or meeting in which he was himself a party.

It is certain, indeed, that never any young gentleman was more happy or more contented in his mind than Clyamon at the time I am speaking of; – he had but one wish beyond what he already posses'd, and that remain'd no longer ungratified than while he forbore to mention it.

He was as well acquainted, as books could make him, with most foreign parts; especially with those kingdoms and states which compose this quarter of the globe; but when he consider'd that the best description cannot but fall infinitely short of the prospect, he was very desirous of being an eye-witness of those things and places he had read of.

Sir Arthur highly approv'd his nephew's inclination to travel; – it seem'd laudable to him, as he had himself often thought it was the only thing wanting to complete his other accomplishments; and one day, as they were talking on that subject, 'My dear Clyamon,' said he, 'the desire you have of seeing the world is truly praise-worthy, and I think you cannot better employ two or three of those years which I hope Heaven has allotted for you, than in visiting the several courts of Europe; – it will enlarge your ideas; and the difference of their manners and policies will, I doubt not, enable you to make such observations as may hereafter be of service to your country.'

'I think,' pursued he, 'that there is no necessity for putting you under the care of any person by way of governor,[167] – you are now arriv'd at years, and I flatter myself, at discretion enough to be trusted by yourself; – as to the rest, you may depend that I shall spare nothing to render the tour you make agreeable to you, and that whatever remittances you shall have occasion for, from time to time, shall be punctually sent to you on a letter of advice.'

This crown'd all the other favours Clyamon had receiv'd from his indulgent uncle; and, it is not to be doubted, drew from him the most grateful acknowledgments: – it was necessary, however, that Avario should be consulted; – the matter accordingly was proposed to him, on which he testified that he was not void of natural affection, by the reluctance he express'd for exposing so deserving a son to the dangers of travelling; but the arguments urged by sir Arthur, and the entreaties of Clyamon, at length prevailed on him to consent.

Clyamon soon made it appear that it was not to gratify a vain unprofitable curiosity, but the laudable ambition of improving his mind, that had made him so desirous of going abroad; – the letters he wrote to his father and uncle, from France, Italy, Sweden, and several parts of Germany, would have been very well worth inserting in this work; but, to the misfortune of the public, I was not then in possession of my wonderful Tablets, and tho' I heard them read more than once, can remember little of the particulars they contain.

This worthy young gentleman had glean'd from every field he pass'd thro' whatever he found capable of increasing the treasures of his mind; and, in somewhat more than two years return'd to England, full fraught, tho' not burthen'd with understanding and an experience far above his years.

I might here entertain my reader with the joy he was receiv'd with by his father and uncle, the compliments made to him by the gentry in that part of the country, and acclamations of the lower sort of people; – but I have no time to waste in such minute particulars, and must proceed to more material circumstances.

Clyamon had no great relish for the country; – he soon grew weary of its amusements; – he lov'd company, and had been accustom'd to a good deal, both at Oxford as well as while he was on his travels, and on account of the great distance between the gentlemen's seats in that country, his uncle's love of retirement, and his father's parsimony, neither of their houses were much frequented: – in fine, he wanted to come to London, – he had never been three whole weeks together in it, and thought he ought to be better acquainted with what was done in the capital of the kingdom.

Sir Arthur was also willing he should be known in a place where the accomplishments he had given him might be render'd more conspicuous; but as he had more than perform'd the part of an uncle, and fully discharg'd him of the promise he had made to Avario concerning his education, he thought it was now high time for that gentleman to take upon him the father, and make a settlement for his son sufficient to enable him to appear in the world according to the estate he was born to inherit.

This proposition was not altogether so pleasing to Avario as it ought to have been; but as he could find nothing to alledge against the reasonableness of it, he only evaded complying with it at present, by some trifling excuse or other, 'till Clyamon, unable to conceal his discontent, sir Arthur press'd more strenuously in his favour than he had done before, and at length, tho' with much difficulty, drew from that niggard parent the scanty sum of fifty guineas.

This was a light loading for the purse of a young gentleman bred in the manner Clyamon had been, and could not be expected to hold out long in so expensive a town as London; – Avario, however, accompany'd it with a promise of letting him have more as soon as he receiv'd money from his tenants, who he pretended had been tardy in their payments of late, and occasion'd his being very much out of cash.

Clyamon could not keep himself from being extremely shock'd at this treatment, from a father who had been at no expence for him since he was ten years old: – sir Arthur was no less chagrin'd, though he concealed it from his nephew, and putting a Bank Bill of fifty pounds into his hand, said to him, – 'My dear Clyamon, I would not have you be disconcerted, – you know your father's temper; but the more he hoards, the more will be your own at his decease; – in the mean time, be assured I will not forsake you, – I will continually urge him on your behalf, and also privately supply you whenever he is deficient; – live therefore like yourself, and be entirely easy.'

These comfortable words, from a mouth on which he knew he might depend, made Clyamon set out chearfully for London; but what happen'd to him after his arrival must be the subject of another chapter.

CHAP. VIII.

Is a continuance of what the former but began; – whoever therefore is not pleased with the porch, had best not venture farther, lest he should meet with something yet more disagreeable within.

THO' Clyamon never had an opportunity of making much acquaintance in this metropolis, and now arriv'd here at a season in which great part of the nobility and gentry retire to their country seats, yet was he soon known, and his conversation courted by those of the best rank who still remained in town.

There were no Operas, indeed, no Plays, no Masquerades to entertain him; but the gardens of Ranelagh, Vaux-Hall, and Mary-le-Bon; or, to speak more properly, the gay company that frequent those places left him no want of any other amusement; – the love of pleasure can never continue ungratified in a town like this, and it is not to be wonder'd at if it sometimes got the better of all Clyamon's discretion; nor, if surrounded with temptations, that he could not always keep himself from giving way to passions which in youth, and a sprightly disposition, are so natural that they scarce deserve the name of faults.

It is not my business to detain the reader's attention with an account of his gallantries with the fair sex, if any of the particulars had come to my knowledge, which I freely confess they did not, – I shall only say that he had no amour which could call his honour in question, bring him into quarrels, or be productive of any other unhappy consequences.

The only mistake in conduct he had any great reason to repent of, he was led into more by the prevalence of example than his own inclination; – he had never been in the least tainted with that epidemic vice, the love of gaming; and rather wonder'd at the pleasure he saw it gave others than desir'd to be partaker of it himself; – yet did he inadvertently suffer himself one evening to engage in a party at that dangerous amusement, which he knew had prov'd so fatal to many of the most opulent fortunes, and utterly unsuitable to a person in his present circumstances.

The persons he play'd with were well experienced, and great proficients in their arts; – they let him win at first some pieces, and this imaginary success luring him to go on, he became at length a loser about seventy pounds, – a trifling sum to a gentleman of his appearance, yet three times more than he, at that time, was master of.

He dissembled his chagrine as well as he was able, but confess'd he had not that sum about him, and would send it the next morning; – on which they told him his honour was a sufficient stake for ten times as much as he had lost, and would fain have prevail'd with him to have play'd on; but he now saw the folly he had been guilty of, so, pretending he had business, took leave of the company, carrying with him a humour very different from what he had brought, and from what he had ever been possess'd of in his whole life before.

Impossible is it to express, as he afterwards told me, how much he was disconcerted at this unlucky event; – he knew it was expected he should promise to send the money the next morning, and by what means he should acquit himself of that promise, and redeem his honour, puzzled him to a degree that made him almost distracted.

He has often protested that he never closed his eyes in sleep during that whole night, but pass'd his restless hours in contriving how to extricate himself from the labyrinth into which he had so foolishly stray'd; – after much revolving in his mind, he at last bethought him of borrowing the sum he wanted of a young gentleman with whom he was extremely intimate, and had a good fortune.

Pursuant to this resolution he rose the next morning more early than he was accustom'd, and went to his friend, who was not yet stirring; but on his saying he had business of consequence to impart to him, was easily admitted to his chamber: – he told him, in few words, what had happen'd, the vexatious situation he was in, and the necessity he was under of borrowing a small sum, 'till he could receive a remittance from the country; – to which the other reply'd:

'Upon my soul, dear Clyamon, I should be glad to serve you on this occasion; – but, faith, it is not in my power at present; – it is not a week ago since I lost five hundred pounds at that damn'd Whist; – and this, with some other demands lately made upon me, have quite drain'd me of all my ready cash; – but I will tell you what I can do for you; – I know a man who has often supply'd me, and several gentlemen of my acquaintance, when they have had a bad run at play; – he has always money by him, and will lend you what sum you please on your advancing a premium; – I will rise this minute and go with you to him.'

Clyamon was highly pleased at this offer, and while the other was dressing reflected within himself how his affairs stood, and that the little presents he had receiv'd from his father and uncle being now almost exhausted, he should soon have calls for more money than his gaming debt, thought it best, since he must borrow, to borrow as much as would supply his expences 'till his father should be prevail'd upon to make him a settlement, which he flatter'd himself would be in a short time.

He communicated his intentions to the gentleman, who approv'd it, and having got himself ready, they went together to old Grub, for so the usurer was call'd.

The wretch was just coming out of his house when they came to it; – on seeing them he turn'd back and conducted them into a little dirty parlour; but, as the discourse that pass'd between them was somewhat extraordinary, I thought it worth writing down, as Clyamon some time after repeated it to me word for word:

Grub. So, my young squire, – 'tis a wonder to see you out of your bed before the sun has run three quarters of his course at least; – I suppose you want a little of my assistance that brings you abroad thus early?

Gentleman. No faith, Grub, not at present; – but I have a friend here that does.

Grub. Your friend is welcome, – I will serve him if I can. – Pray, sir, what can I do for you?

Clyamon. Sir, a present emergency lays me under a necessity of raising two hundred pounds immediately, – if you have that sum by you, this gentleman will inform you who I am, and that I want neither the power nor the will to discharge any obligation I shall enter into on that score.

Gentleman. Ay, ay, Grub, – his note is as good as the Bank of England, – you need not fear your money, – his name is ****, – he is an only son, and heir to near two thousand pounds a year.

Grub. The gentleman has an honest face, indeed.

Gentleman. If you have any scruple, Grub, I will join in the note with all my soul.

Grub. I believe there is no great occasion, – only in case of accidents a collateral security may be necessary.

Gentleman. Well, well, – you shall have it.

Grub. I suppose, sir, you have acquainted the gentleman with the common way of dealing in these affairs?

Clyamon. Sir, I am willing to allow you any interest for your money that you can in reason desire.

Grub. Sir, I am never out of reason with any man; – as to interest, it is quite out of the question, – I shall take no more than what the law allows; – but when we advance money upon a pinch a certain premium is expected.

Clyamon. Please to name it.

Grub. Let me see; – you want two hundred pounds immediately, you say; – it is but a trifling sum, indeed; but too much for a poor man like me to lose; – we who lend money this way run a great risque; – not that I doubt you, nor am unwilling to advance the money; but I think you can do no less than add an odd fifty in the note you make.

Clyamon. How, sir! – fifty pounds for the loan of two hundred, besides the interest.

Grub. Lookye, sir, I would not have you imagine I deal hardly with you; – if you brought me a note on the best tradesman in the city, payable one month after date, I do assure you that I would not discount it a farthing less than twenty per cent. – Consider, sir, I may lie a great while out of my money; – disappointments sometimes happen, and when they do I have not the heart to be severe in point of time; – I scorn to distress a gentleman when I find he has it not in his power to pay, unless I hear he is going out of the kingdom, or to enter into the army, and then, indeed, it behoves me to take care of myself; for you know, sir, the old proverb, Charity begins at home.

Clyamon, in favouring me with the recital of this dialogue, told me that he had not presence enough of mind to keep the shock he felt at so exorbitant a demand from being visible to the Usurer, who looking on him with no very pleasing aspect, said to him,

Grub. I perceive you are disatisfied, sir, and if so, I can keep my money, and you may try to supply yourself at a cheaper rate elsewhere; – for my part, I am at no loss how to dispose of the little I have, – there are enow will be glad to receive it on the terms I offer'd you, and, it may be, not grumble to allow me a better advantage.

Gentleman. Nay, – pshaw, – prithee, Grub, don't be out of humour, – my friend is not accustom'd to these things, and I had not time to inform him before we came.

Grub. Sir, I bear a conscience, and am above imposing on any one; – I am asham'd to think of what is practised at some great Coffee-houses that shall be nameless, where if a gentleman is necessitated to borrow ten pieces he returns twenty for it the next morning, or it may be the same night; – no, – no, – such things are an abomination to me; – I desire no more than a living profit, and whoever does not approve of my conditions is at liberty to reject them; – there is no harm done.

Clyamon. Not in the least, sir, and as this is the first time I ever had occasion to become a borrower, and was utterly ignorant of the methods I should take in such a situation, I may deserve forgiveness.

Thus was poor Clyamon compell'd, by his impatience to discharge his debt of honour, to acquiesce to the excuse made for him by his friend, and comply with the extortioner's demand, – on which Grub was easily brought into temper again, – a note was presently drawn for the sum of two hundred and fifty pounds, and being sign'd by both the gentlemen, the whole sum mention'd in it was deliver'd to Clyamon, who put two hundred pounds into his pocket, and return'd the other fifty to Grub; – this sir, said the wary curmudgeon, I receive as a present from you, and thank you for it.

Clyamon also, in his turn, thank'd him for the favour he had just conferr'd upon him, after which they departed, seemingly with the most perfect good-will towards each other; but it is a truth almost unquestionable, that the lender of this money had infinitely more satisfaction in his mind than the borrower could possibly have.

Dearly, indeed, did he pay for the means of discharging an obligation which his inadvertency had brought him under; – it was, however, of this service to him, that it made him detest high gaming ever since, and careful to avoid all company that might draw him into a second misfortune of the same kind, – as I remember to have formerly read in a very old, and now almost exploded author.

> Wise is the man, who by one error taught,
> No more is in the same temptation caught.[168]

There is a way of refraining from being guilty of indiscreet actions, without affecting to be over wise; – Clyamon had this happy talent, – he knew very well, that for a person of his years to set up for a dictator, instead of reforming his companions would only incur their ridicule; and therefore contented himself with not making a party in the modish vices and follies he was spectator of, without seeming to condemn or be displeased at them.

Conscious that on his first arrival in town he had not taken all the care he should have done to regulate his way of living according to his present circumstances, he began to retrench his expences as much as possible he could, without letting the world see he did so, or sinking too much beneath the character of a gentleman born to inherit the ample fortune he was.

But in spite of this somewhat too late assumed œconomy, he soon found himself in very great necessity for a fresh supply; – he had been in London from the latter end of the month of May to the beginning of October, and had received no remittances from the country since he left it; – all his uncle's remonstrances had not yet prevail'd upon his father to make the proposed settlement on him; the Usurer's loan was quite exhausted, and he had, besides, other small debts to his tradesmen, some of whom had already sent in their bills.

To add to these vexations, Grub visited him almost every day, complain'd he was out of cash himself, and at length grew very importunate, and plainly told him that he could lie no longer out of his money, and that if he did not speedily discharge the note he must take proper measures to force him to it.

In this exigence he wrote a very pressing letter to his father, intreating an order on his Banker in London, but the obdurate Avario only sent him an answer to this effect: – that it was inconvenient for him to break into the sum in the hands of his Banker, – said he must wait awhile, – that he should be in town himself the ensuing November, on the meeting of the Parliament; and that he would then do something for him; – in the mean time bid him live sparingly, and shun all places and company that might draw him into any unnecessary expence.

Poor Clyamon had need enough for all that stock of spirits which nature had endued him with, to enable him to bear up amidst the persecutions of his voracious creditors, and the unnatural behaviour of his father; – he had now no other resource remaining than an application to sir Arthur, but very loth he was to be troublesome to that dear and beneficent uncle, to whom alone he was indebted for what he look'd upon as infinitely more valuable than his being, – his education; and was with much debate within himself, whether it were not better to endure the insults he was exposed to, rather than run the risque of displeasing a patron he had so much cause to love and reverence.

But while he continued thus irresolute in his mind, an accident happen'd which put a final end to all the contention in his thoughts on that score, by presenting him with a misfortune which was the more severe, by its being sudden and unapprehended.

The good sir Arthur Frankwill died, – fate snatch'd him from the world at once, without the least previous warning, and allow'd no time for the making bequests, either to his belov'd Clyamon or any other person, who else he might have thought worthy of a place in his remembrance; – so that leaving no Will behind him, his whole estate, together with all the personal effects he was possess'd of, devolved on a son of his elder sister, as being the first of blood and heir at law, – a gentleman who had always look'd upon Clyamon with too envious an eye to have any sincere friendship for him.

The first account of this misfortune was transmitted to Clyamon in a letter from the abovemention'd kinsman, and contain'd the following lines:

To Clyamon ******, Esq;

Dear Cousin,

This comes to acquaint you with the loss we both sustain by the death of our dear uncle, who departed this life six days ago; – he was seiz'd with an apoplectic fit, out of which he never recover'd, in spite of all the endeavours could be used: – I did not send to desire your company at the funeral, as it would have been a superfluous compliment to him and a great fatigue and expence to yourself, in coming so long a journey; but as I am sensible of the affection he had always for you, I enclose a Bank Bill of twenty pounds for mourning.

I intend to dispose of my uncle's house as soon as I can hear of a purchaser, and am now sending away all the furniture, so can make no invitation to you to come hither; but shall be glad if you pass a few days with me at T –, on your return into the country. – So the hurry I am in at present, permits me to add no more, than that I am,

> With sincerity,
>> Dear sir,
>>> Your affectionate kinsman
>>>> And humble servant,

G. Hawksmore.

It is certain at this time, and indeed almost at any other, there were few things could have happen'd more unfortunately for Clyamon than the death of his uncle, as he had not only lost in him an indulgent parent, a tender friend, and a kind protector, who had promised never to forsake him, but also the only person in the world who had the most influence over his father, and by whose intercession he hoped to have been soon reliev'd from the precarious situation he was at present in.

He had scarce time to recover himself from the first emotions of grief, on the abovemention'd melancholy account, when he receiv'd private intelligence that Grub intended to arrest him, and had even employ'd a Sheriff's officer for that purpose; – he had no way to prevent this affront but by flying for refuge to the Verge of the Court,[169] which he accordingly did, and took a lodging in Scotland-yard; – Grub soon heard of his retreat, – traced him to his asylum, and endeavour'd, by all the means he could, to render it of no service to him; but Clyamon had laid his case before the Board of Green-cloath,[170] and those gentlemen had assur'd him of their protection, till the arrival of his father should discharge this troublesome affair.

The time was now near at hand in which Avario was expected, and he staid not many days beyond it; but his presence rather augmented than put an end to the distress of Clyamon.

That unnatural parent, on finding the condition he was in, flew into the extremest rage, – reproach'd his extravagancies, as he call'd them, in the most bitter terms, – swore he would see him sink under the calamity to which he had reduced himself, rather than give a single guinea to relieve him from it; and even curs'd the memory of the good sir Arthur for having indulg'd him, as he said, in notions so contrary to what he ought to have been inspir'd with; – it was in vain that Clyamon endeavoured to alleviate his fury, – he would harken to no excuses, – be soften'd by no submissions he could make.

One of the gentlemen of the honourable board, on Clyamon's request, urged the defence of that young gentleman in the strongest terms; but Avario for many days continued deaf to all remonstrances in his behalf, and gave no other answer, than that as his son had brought himself into this trouble by his folly, he must endeavour to get out of it by his wit.

This cruel sarcasm, when repeated to Clyamon, made him almost forget the duty of a son, and, as he confess'd to me, ready to burst into exclamations, which he would afterwards have reproach'd himself for having been guilty of uttering, or even thinking of.

Grub, and some other of his creditors, finding they could do no more to him in the place where he was, took their revenge in persecuting him with unceasing clamours, which threw him sometimes into such fits of melancholy, that if he had not been well furnish'd with a great stock of morality and good sense, would doubtless have push'd him on some desperate method to end those misfortunes which he saw no probability of being relieved from.

Avario, in the mean time, notwithstanding his churlish and sordid disposition, was far from being easy in his mind, – the first gust of passion being blown over, the merits of Clyamon rose in opposition to the fault he had been guilty of, and made it, by degrees, seem less; – he could not forbear remembering that he was his son, and such a son as every one who was a father wished his own might copy after.

In fine, nature and reason join'd their forces, and pleaded strongly in the behalf of Clyamon, and almost wrought him to forgiveness; but as often as he reflected how much it would cost to pardon him, and that he could not receive him into favour without the payment of his debts, the thoughts of parting with his money gave a sudden check to his paternal inclinations.

At length, however, some hints which Clyamon dropp'd in one of the many petitionary letters he sent to him, making him apprehensive that the most dreadful consequences might attend the despair of his offending son, he became determin'd to do something for him.

He sent a person to him with ten guineas for his present support, and an offer of making up his affairs, in case he could prevail on his creditors to compound for the one half of what was owing to them; – Clyamon accepted his father's present, trifling as it was, with submission; but could not forbear testifying the utmost disdain at proposing of a composition; for besides being certain it never would be comply'd with, the thing in itself appear'd to him so abject, that he chose to suffer any thing rather than demean himself to mention it.

This refusal put Avario into a second flame; but he soon cool'd again, and after some little conflict within himself, the necessity there was of restoring the liberty of an only son, got the better of his love of money.

Loth, however, to part with his darling pence as long as there was a possibility of keeping them, he found out an expedient to protract the doing a thing so irksome to him, – he communicated his intentions to Clyamon in a letter, which that young gentleman shewing to me afterwards, I found contain'd words to this effect:

To CLYAMON.

SON,

THO' I have been justly irritated against you, first by your extravagances, and since by your late obstinacy, yet I cannot forget I am your father, nor suffer you to sink beneath those misfortunes your folly and disobedience have brought you into; – I have resolved to pay all your debts before I leave London; but as it is not convenient for me to do it sooner, would not have you venture out of the Verge, for fear of bringing yourself into disgrace, and an additional expence on me for your release; – in the mean time am content to allow you two guineas and a half per week, for the subsistence of yourself and servant.

It is expected that we shall be dissolved about the middle of February, when Writs will be issued out for a new Election; and I shall then set you clear in the world and take you home with me; for I do not think it at all adviseable that you should live in this luxurious Town, 'till you are better acquainted with the true value of money than you seem to be at present; – I hope, notwithstanding, that your future behaviour will attone for the errors of the past, and I shall have no occasion to repent the proof I now give you of being

Your affectionate father,

AVARIO.

The joy which Clyamon would have felt, on finding that full satisfaction would be given to the demands of his impatient creditors, was very much abated by the thoughts of being obliged to reside constantly with his father in the country, as the manner in which he knew he must live with the old gentleman would be very disagreeable to his humour, and widely different from what he had been accustom'd to with his uncle.

It also seem'd a little hard to him, that by delaying the discharge of his debts 'till his departure, he should be secluded from all enjoyment of the pleasures and amusements of the town, even while he continued in it; – but he saw into the policy of his father in doing this, and as there was no remedy, endeavour'd to be as contented as possible.

In the answer he gave to his father's letter he express'd himself in terms which were highly pleasing to him, and brought on a perfect reconciliation, as will presently appear, on occasion of an accident which happen'd soon after.

CHAP. IX.

Concludes a narrative which has somewhat in it that will, in a manner, compel those who shall be most offended, to counterfeit an approbation, for the sake of their own interest and reputation.

THO' the greatest intimacy with Clyamon, and a long acquaintance with Avario, made me no stranger even to the minute particulars of the transaction I am relating, I mean, as far as I could be inform'd by the perfect confidence with which I was honour'd by both these gentlemen; yet as no sure dependance can be placed either on what people say of themselves, or the report given of them by others, I should never have ventur'd to speak so positively in many things as I have done, if the gift of Invisibility had not afforded me an opportunity of accompanying them when they thought themselves entirely alone, and of beholding them in those unguarded attitudes which are the best, and, indeed, the only certain discoverers of the inward workings of the human mind.

It was my dear Belt could have alone convinced me that, contrary to the general opinion of the world, it was not ill nature in Avario, or ignorance of what he ought to do, which had hinder'd him from being an affectionate husband, a tender father, a faithful friend, and an indulgent master; but merely his inordinate love of money, and an unaccountable apprehension of being reduced to the want of it, that made him center his whole cares on his bags, regardless of all the ties of blood and nature; and, in fine, render'd him almost incapable of practising any social virtue.

It was by this beneficial present that I became assur'd Clyamon was much more worthy than he took any pains to appear; – that in all serious matters he was steady and unshaken, and in his pleasures decent and well manner'd; and that, young as he was, he had set up a tribunal in his own heart, where Reason presiding as sole judge carefully examin'd all his actions, and whenever any unruly passion had got the start, stopp'd it in its full career, and brought it back to obedience.

Many interesting circumstances, relating to this affair, between father and son, are lost to the public by my having been depriv'd for some time of my Chrystaline Tablets, which had been stolen from me, with several other things of much less, tho' more seeming value, by an unfaithful servant; but the villain, finding, I suppose, that he could make nothing of the Tablets, and looking upon them only as a curiosity which would please no body so much as myself, seal'd them up and caused them to be left for me at a coffee-house; – my joy at getting them again made me forgive the rest of the robbery, and seek no farther after the Thief.

I recover'd my purloin'd treasure just about the time that Clyamon was in the abovemention'd situation; so that what remains to be recited of this narrative will be chiefly taken from the mouths of the persons concern'd in it.

I was one morning in Clyamon's apartment, under cover of my Belt, when a young gentleman of the name of Careless came to visit him; – after exchanging the *bon jour*, and some other customary salutations, Careless began the conversation between them in these terms:

Careless. Where do you think I was yesterday?

Clyamon. I am no conjurer.

Careless. Guess.

Clyamon. It would be a needless trouble; – prithee spare it me.

Careless. Why, faith, in the gallery of the House of Commons.

Clyamon. The House of Commons! – it must be a business of vast importance sure, that could carry a fellow of thy gay sprightly temper into that grave venerable place.

Careless. No, – thank Heaven, business and I are perfect strangers to each other; but I had an hour or two upon my hands, and went thither merely to kill time; – but was never more diverted in my whole life, than to see how some young members, who had got their heads together and were giggling over a copy of verses inscrib'd to Fanny Murray,[171] were put to silence in an instant, and look'd as silly as a school boy under the lash of correction, on the Speaker's crying out with an audible and austere voice, – To order, gentlemen, – for shame – to order.

Clyamon. Methinks, indeed, they might have found a more proper place and time for laughter. – Was my father in the House, pray?

Careless. O yes, and I assure you the old gentleman made as wise a figure as any there; – he said nothing, indeed, but sat as serious as a judge upon a criminal cause, leaning both his hands upon his gold-headed cane, and his chin upon his hands, and listning with great attention to a very long, and I suppose, learned harangue of a leading member.

Clyamon. What was the matter in debate?

Careless. Why, on Ways and Means, how to undo handsomely what they were doing last sessions; – the Jew bill.[172]

Clyamon. Is it like to be repeal'd?

Careless. Nay, I did not stay to hear the end of it; but was told, after I was come out, that the clamours of the people would prevail: – there is doubtless a great ferment among the busy part of the town, – the Court of Requests and Lobby were as full as they could hold of petitioning Christians and remonstrating Jews, the latter of whom, I think, seem to be a little crest-fallen, and good reason they have to be so; for whatever favour they may find within, they are sure to be insulted without doors; – I was half deafen'd as I went down stairs with the noise made by the rabble incessantly bawling out, – No Circumcision, – no Jews, – no Naturalization of Foreigners.

Clyamon. Then I believe there is no great room to doubt of its being repeal'd; for, according to all the accounts I ever read or heard of, whenever the bulk of the people were unanimous in any thing, they were always sure to get the better of the minister.

Careless. It may be so, – and the thoughts of a new election coming on may also possibly contribute a good deal to the complaisance of the Parliament; – but these things are of no sort of concern to you and I. – How do you design to dispose of yourself to day?

Clyamon. I have not yet consider'd.

Careless. 'Tis a glorious morning; are you for the Park? – I come on purpose to ask you.

Clyamon. With all my heart.

Careless. Come along then, – I dare swear the Mall is half full by this time, – let us go and laugh at the great vulgar and the small, – as Congreve says.[173]

Just as they was going out of the room a letter was presented to Clyamon from his father, which he turning back to read I stepp'd behind him, and found it contain'd these lines:

To Clyamon.

Dear Cly,

I have something to impart to you, which is of the utmost consequence to my peace of mind and your future happiness, – be careful, therefore, not to be out of the way to-morrow morning, when I shall call upon you as I go the House; for what I have to propose cannot be settled too soon; – be assured I am impatient to see you make as good a figure in the world as I think you deserve, and that no more is requir'd of you than a just sense of your duty to me, and a regard for what is your own interest, to preserve me always

    Your very indulgent

    And loving father,

                                       Avario.

Clyamon was so transported with the kindness of this epistle, that he could not forbear shewing it to Careless, who, knowing the temper of Avario, had no sooner look'd over than he said:

Careless. I will lay my life upon it, that the old gentleman has found out some rich widow or heiress for you, with whose fortune you may make a figure in the world, and save his own 'till he can keep it no longer.

Clyamon. I hope not so, for as yet I have no inclination to marry; and when ever I do shall like to have a wife of my own chusing.

Careless. You must be cautious, nevertheless, not to venture a second bru-lee[174] with him; for he seems to have set his heart very much upon this business, whatever it is that he has now got into his head.

Clyamon. Deuce take you for putting it into mine; – but I will think no more on it: – if the thing should be as you imagine, I shall have time enough to be uneasy after knowing it; – but come, – 'tis almost two o'clock, – let us away.

With these words they went on their promenade, and I return'd home; where reflecting, as I always did after these excursions, on what I had seen and heard, I could not help being of the same opinion with mr. Careless, as touching the intentions of Avario, and fear'd that poor Clyamon, with all his merit, would be oblig'd to become a prey to some old well jointur'd Jezabel, or rich Dowdy, who ow'd her virginity to her ugliness.

By what I have often freely confess'd, concerning the inquisitiveness of my disposition, the reader will easily suppose I felt no small impatience for the event of Avario's visit to his son; and, indeed, I believe that young gentleman himself could scarce be more anxious.

That I might lose nothing of what should pass between them, I took care to post myself very early in Clyamon's apartment, and it was well I did so, both for the satisfaction of my own curiosity and the emolument of the public; – for Avario came in presently after me.

As they had not seen each other for some time, Clyamon threw himself on his knees, and in that posture thank'd his father for the pardon he had vouchsafed to his offence, as well as for his kind promise he had given for the discharge of his debts: Avario seem'd very much pleased with this submission, raised and embraced him with great affection, and after they were seated reply'd to what he had said in these terms:

Avario. It is a great deal of money, indeed, the folly you have been guilty of will cost me; but it is the first, and I flatter myself will be the last I shall have to complain of, – so we will say no more of what is past; – I came now to talk with you on a subject more agreeable to us both.

Clyamon. I have the greatest reason in in the world, sir, to hope every thing from your goodness.

Avario. Ay, Clyamon, – you are my only son, – you may be sure I have nothing so much at heart as your welfare, and I think I have now hit upon something that will make you as happy as you can wish to be.

Clyamon returning no other answer to these words than a low bow, the old gentleman continued his discourse.

Avario. Your late uncle, sir Arthur, was always teazing me on the score of a constant allowance for you out of my estate, to the end you might be in a manner independent, and I have at length resolv'd to do it.

Clamon. Whatever you are pleased to grant, sir, I shall take care to employ so as to give you no cause to repent your bounty.

Avario. But that is not all, Clyamon; – what I shall do for you will put you in a way of making yourself a much greater man than you would be by what you will enjoy on my decease.

Clyamon. I am not ambitious, sir, but shall readily embrace any laudable means of raising my fortune.

Avario. Why that's well said, and what I have to propose is not only laudable but honourable too: – it is this, – you shall be a Member of the House of Commons.

Clyamon. Sir I should be proud to serve my Country in any capacity; but in this fear my youth and inexperience will be very just objections.

Avario. Tut, – tut, – there are much younger than you in the House, and tho' I say it, of much less understanding too. – As to the forms that are to be observ'd there, I can instruct you in them; – and as to the rest, you will easily come into it of yourself; – therefore no more of such idle scruples: – an over modesty and diffidence of yourself is the worst quality a man that aims to rise in the world can be possess'd of. – I have consider'd on this matter in all its circumstances, before I mention'd it to you; and in order to qualify you for a Member, have resolved to assign over to you five hundred pounds per annum of my estate.[175]

Clyamon. That, sir, is more than I could have presumed to ask.

Avario. I mean, the rents of so much shall be received in your name; – as to the cash, I think it much safer in my own hands than yours; but you shall want nothing that is necessary, and when the business of Parliament calls you to London, give you leave to draw upon me for what sum, or sums, you shall find occasion for in reason.

Clyamon. This, sir, is far from putting me out of a state of dependance.

Avario. You ought not to desire it; – your uncle talk'd foolishly, – very foolishly on this head; and if it had not been for the obligation I had to him on the score of your education, I should have told him so: – a son ought always to be dependant on his father, and I think you have very great cause to be content in being so, as you have experienced the paternal affection I have for you by my readiness to forgive your faults, and to discharge those debts your extravagances had contracted.

Clyamon. Sir, I shall always retain a grateful and dutious sense of all you have done for me; – but, pray sir, since it is your pleasure that I should be a Candidate at the ensuing Election, what Place have you in your eye for me? – I suppose for some Borough.

Avario. No, no, – for our own County.

Clyamon. Then, sir, do you decline standing yourself?

Avario. Yes, Clyamon, – I grow old, and am weary of the fatigue of coming up to London once every year; – I find it very expensive, as well as troublesome; for tho' I board while I am here at a pretty cheap rate, with one that was formerly my servant, yet I know not how it is, money runs strangely away in this town; – besides, I do not think I have been well used, – I have had the honour of representing the County of ****, in three successive Parliaments, and have got nothing by it, – but the honour; – and tho' I have constantly voted on the side of the court, and whenever any Debate of consequence was to come upon the carpet, have always previously attended the Levee of the Minister, to know his will and pleasure; all the recompence I have had, has been sometimes a shake of the hand, a gracious nod, a smile, and, how does my good friend Avario.

Clyamon. You amaze me, sir, – I never imagined a gentleman had any other interest in his Election, than the pleasure of having an opportunity to serve his Country.

Avario. Serve his Country; – a fiddle on the Country; – it would be well worth a gentleman's while, indeed, to cajole, treat, and bribe every little dirty fellow that has a Vote to give, – to spend so much time and money, and, it may be, drink himself half dead into the bargain at his Election, if it were not for the sake of serving himself, instead of the rabble who make choice of him for their Representative; – no, no, – boy, if we had not honour, favour, and preferment in view, our Electors would be obliged to court us to accept their Votes, not we to solicit them.

Clyamon. But, sir, supposing this to be the case, how do you think it possible I should acquire any of those advantages which you say you have fail'd in the pursuit of yourself?

Avario. I'll tell you, Clyamon, – I could only give my bare Vote for or against any Question; – I never had the gift either of speaking or writing; – now I am pretty sure you can do both; and a pathetic speech, or a strong pamphlet are prevailing arguments with the Ministry; – a man that can do these may have any thing, – may make his own price; – so, Cly, it will be your own fault if in a Sessions or two you are not above receiving any assistance from me.

Clyamon. Sir I shall be always ready to exert the little talents I am master of to promote whatever I think is for the good of the Commonwealth.

Avario. Tut, – what have you to do with the Commonwealth? – you are not to set up for a judge of what is for its good or what is not so; – your business is to please the Minister, and to think every thing right he takes upon him to maintain.

Clyamon. But, sir, how is this consistent with my conscience or my honour?

Avario. Idle, – very idle, – I do not like these notions, Clyamon, – they may tempt you to an opposition; – I shall be afraid you are a Jacobite.

Clyamon. Why, sir, are all men of honour Jacobites?

Avario. No; – but this romantic unprofitable honour you talk of, is either Jacobitism or something as bad; – enthusiasm and bigotry. – Is not the Court the source of true honour? – Do not all honours, dignities and promotions flow from thence? – Therefore I say, whoever is against the Court will never rise to honour, or any thing else that is valuable.

Clyamon. A certain right honourable and learned author of the last age has very different sentiments upon this head, – if you will give me leave, sir, I will read to you some part of what he wrote on the subject of Honour.

In speaking these words he took up a book and read this passage out of the late Lord Hallifax's works.

> Not all the threats or favours of a Crown,
> A Prince's whisper, or a Tyrant's frown,
> Can awe the spirits, or allure the mind
> Of him, who to strict Honour is inclin'd.
> Tho' all the pomp and pleasure that does wait,
> On public Places, and affairs of State,
> Should fondly court him to be base and great,
> With even passions, and with settled face,
> He would remove the harlot's false embrace,
> Tho' all the storms and tempests should arise,
> That Court Magicians in their cells devise,
> And from their settled basis nations tear,
> He wou'd unmov'd, the mighty ruin bear;

Secure in innocence, condemn them all,
And decently array'd in Honour fall:
Honour, that spark of the celestial fire,
That above nature makes mankind aspire;
Ennobles the rude passions of our frame,
With thirst of glory, and desire of same,
The richest treasure of a gen'rous breast,
And gives the stamp and standard to the rest.
Wit, strength, and courage are wild dang'rous force,
Unless this soften and direct their course.
Of Honour, men at first, like women nice,
Raise maiden scruples, at unpractis'd vice;
But once this fence thrown down, when they perceive,
That they may taste forbidden fruit and live,
They stop not here their course, but safely in,
Grow strong, luxuriant, and bold in sin:
True to no principle, press forward still,
And only bound by appetite their will;
Now fawn and flatter, while this tide prevails,
But shift, with ev'ry veering blast their sails,
On higher springs true men of Honour move,
Free is their service, and unbought their love.[176]

He was going on, but was stopp'd by Avario, who pull'd him by the sleeve and cry'd out:

Avario. Hold, hold, Clyamon, – enough, – all this is mighty pretty, and sounds well; but you are to consider that it is a great while ago since the noble Lord wrote this Poem; and what was look'd upon as Honour in his days, may probably wear another aspect now; – and 'tis wisdom to conform to the times.

Clyamon. Reason, sir, will still be reason, in all times and ages.

Avario. I do not know that; for they say every age improves in understanding: – but be that as it may, I can answer your quotation with one from another author of great reputation for his wit and learning; – it is this:

– Money is the only Power,
That all mankind falls down before:
'Tis Virtue, Honour, Wit, and all
That men divine and sacred call;
For what's the worth of any thing,
But so much money as 'twill bring.[177]

So you see, Clyamon, that learned men, tho' cotemporaries, are sometimes widely different from each other in their opinions in this point.

Clyamon. The lines you have repeated do not prove it, sir; – I beg you will be pleased to reflect, that the ingenious author of Hudibrass does not utter these sentiments as his own, but puts them in the mouth of his mock hero, a wretch that was in open Rebellion against his lawful King, and are intended as a satire, not an argument.

Avario. Odsheart, boy, thou art in the right, – I never thought of that; – but 'tis no matter what any of them say; – 'tis plain that what is now meant by Honour implies a title, a riband,[178] a pension, a place, or any thing that denotes the favour of the Court to the person who possesses it; – therefore, I say again, – get rid of these prejudices, – sail with the Tide, – keep close with the Minister, and endeavour to make yourself of consequence to him.

Clyamon. Sir, you may be perfectly assur'd that I shall always do my best in the support of every measure which tends to the real honour of his Majesty, and the good of my Country; – and never oppose any which do not oppose the Constitution.

Avario. But you must not examine too scrupulously into these things; – you are to suppose that those who are entrusted with the management of Public Affairs are better acquainted with the Constitution than you can pretend to be; and must therefore take it for granted, that whatever they say or do is right.

Clyamon. But, sir, does not this implicit faith in the judgment of others, and giving up my own entirely, savour somewhat of a slavish submission?

Avario. No, it is only good policy, and look'd upon as such by all who know the world; – indeed, if after your Voting, Speaking, and Writing, they should take no notice of you, it would behove you to pluck up a spirit, and extort that respect to your resentment, which they were not grateful enough to pay to your complaisance; – I shall then give you leave to oppose them in every thing, whether it be wrong or whether it be right.

Clyamon. But would not this changing sides, sir, make me become contemptible to both Parties?

Avario. Not at all; it is a thing too commonly practised to be wonder'd at, and has often had a very good effect when nothing else would do: – Publico, for example; – it was a good while indeed, before they bid up to his price; but he found it necessary at last, and he now enjoys the fruits of his labour.

Clyamon. Yes, sir, and I have heard of many others who have been bought off the same way; but whatever has been done in former administrations, I hope the present will attempt nothing that ought to be opposed.

Avario. No, no, – you are not to suppose they will; unless, as I just now observ'd, they force you to it by neglecting to recompence your services.

Clyamon. According to this, sir, it will be very difficult, if not altogether impossible, for the People to distinguish between those who would defend, and those who would betray and sacrifice the Liberties of their Constituents.

Avario. If the People are betray'd and sacrificed, as you call it, they can blame nobody but themselves. – Why do they take money for their Votes? Why do they, like Esau, sell their birth-rights for a mess of pottage?[179] – When a gentleman buys a County, a Borough, or a Corporation, he has, doubtless, a right to make the most of it he can.

Clyamon. This, sir, is punishing Corruption with Corruption.

Avario. Ay, – is it not just it should be so, – as I remember to have read some where or other?

> This world is all a trick, – then who will dare,
> Among known Cheats to play upon the square?[180]

Lookye, Clyamon, you are a novice in these affairs as yet, but a little time will make them familiar to you; – I do not doubt but I shall hear of your being clos-etted by the great man; and when once you are closetted your business is done; – you will have no farther occasion for my instructions or assistance either; – but I shall say no more at present on that head, – you must think of preparing your-self to set out on your journey to ****, in a day or two.

Clyamon. What, sir, before you go?

Avario. Yes, yes, – we shall not be dissolved so soon as we expected, – I do not believe I shall be able to get down these six weeks or two months; – there have been some odd turns of late; – but no matter, – they are secrets, – and must be kept so; – but it is highly necessary you should begin to make your interest; – you are already known to the greatest part of the gentry, and I am pretty sure that they will all be for you to a man; – but you must cultivate an acquaintance with the Freeholders, – ride about among them, – invite some of the most lead-ing men home, – treat them handsomly, – and make little presents to their wives and daughters, of snuff-boxes, rings, necklaces, and such toys, to please their fan-cies; – I will get a friend of mine to purchase a cargoe of them for you to take down, and will write to my steward to furnish you with what money you shall have occasion for.

Clyamon. Do they know, sir, that you intend to decline standing any more?

Avario. Not yet; but I shall write to-night to inform them of it, and to urge all my friends in your behalf: – I hear your cousin Hawksmore has taken it into his head to offer himself as a Candidate, and tho' he is not beloved, on account of the bustle he made about the Turnpikes,[181] yet the large estate he is now in possession of, by the death of sir Arthur, may give him an influence over some people, – so there is no time to be lost; – I would have you leave London on Monday next; – I have given orders that all your creditors shall be paid their full demands this day, and I think you can have no other business of consequence to detain you here.

Clyamon. None at all, sir.

Avario. Well then, what friends you have to take leave of you may see this afternoon, and come to dine with me to-morrow; – it is Sunday, and you know is a leisure day, and I shall be at home, – tho' I am a boarder, I believe you will be welcome, – or it may be I shall add a dish to the table; – therefore do not fail to come.

Clyamon. You may depend, sir, that this command is too agreeable to me not to be punctually obey'd.

The old gentleman then said no more, but after giving his son a gracious nod went out of the room, with a countenance which denoted the most perfect satisfaction of mind; – Clyamon waited on him down stairs, and I intended to follow as soon as his return should give me an opportunity of going down; but was retarded by mr. Careless, who came in immediately after Avario was out of the house.

This gentleman, who it seems has a sincere friendship for Clyamon, had been extremely impatient, and, indeed, more anxious than could have been expected, from a person of his gay thoughtless disposion, to know the event of the letter he had received from his father, had been come to the house some time, and waited in the parlour till the departure of Avario made it proper for him to appear.

Almost the first Salutation he gave to Clyamon contain'd an entreaty for the satisfaction of his curiosity in this point, which the other very readily comply'd with, in general terms; but had too much discretion to expose his father's mercenary views; or by relating the design he had of making him a Member of Parliament, reveal the motives he had for doing so, or the instructions he had given him for his behaviour after he should be elected.

Mr. Careless, after having congratulated his friend on his being re-establish'd in the good graces of his father, and the honour that was about to recede to him, said a great many pleasant and spirituous things to him, on the occasion of his being likely to become a Member of that august and respectable Assembly.

But the particulars of this discourse, entertaining as it was, I am entirely unable to repeat, my Tablets being already crowded with the preceding dialogue, and all I can remember is, that the two gentlemen, after chatting away an hour, agreed to dine together that day, and to that end adjourn'd to a tavern in the neighbourhood, leaving me at liberty to retire to my own apartment.

I was extremely pleased with finding, by what I had seen that day of Clyamon, that I had not been deceived in the high-raised expectations I had entertain'd of his good sense and probity; and also with perceiving that Avario, in spite of his sordid and avaritious disposition, could not help allowing the merits of a son, whose sentiments and principles were in almost every thing so directly opposite to his own.

The evening of the next day this worthy young gentleman call'd upon me, as he return'd from having pass'd the former part of it with his father; – he was much less reserv'd with me than he had been with mr. Careless, which convinced me he knew how to refrain unbosoming himself to those whose solidity he had cause to doubt, and took a pleasure in being intirely open to those on whom he could depend, that his confidence would not be abused, either by wantonness or neglect.

I am pretty sensible, that on my saying this not a few of my readers will set me down in their minds as a vain presuming fellow, and be apt to cry out against me as if guilty of the very same folly I have, in several pages of this work, with some severity, lash'd in others; but I would have them consider, the only merit I pretend to is a serious humour, which I think is no great boast; and also that there is a justice due from every one to himself, as well as to those he speaks of.

But to return to a subject more interesting than any thing relating to the praise or vindication of myself; – when Clyamon repeated to me the rules prescribed to him by his father for the regulation of his conduct in Parliament, he express'd the little obligation he thought himself under to him on that score in terms the most strong and pathetic; – these are some of his words:

'The love of my Country,' said he, 'I look upon as the first and greatest moral duty of mankind; – and I think I may venture to assure myself, that I never shall be tempted to renounce it on the prospect of any advantage offer'd, in what shape soever.'

I then told him, that I believed the bulk of the People owed the grievances they complained of greatly to the luxury of their Representatives, who having impair'd their estates in the modish excesses of the times, found themselves under a necessity of entering into measures which otherwise they would never have comply'd with. 'Perhaps too,' added I, 'to gratify the ambition of a beloved wife, or prevent the clamour of a turbulent one, may be one reason to which the infringement of public Liberty may be ascrib'd.'

Clyamon listen'd with great attention to what I said, and joining in my opinion, reply'd, that his own observation of some late instances confirm'd the truth of this argument, – 'The first of these excitements,' continued he, 'I have already experienced the danger of through my inadvertency, and shall be wary to avoid the snare in which I have been once entangled; – and as for the other, if ever I marry, shall endeavour to get a wife as near as possible to the description given by the Poet of his mistress;

> A maid
> Who knows not Courts, yet Courts does far outshine,
> In every starry beauty of the mind;
> One who array'd in native loveliness,
> And sweet simplicity, despises art;
> And has a soul too great to stoop to pride,
> With the mean ways by which it aims at grandeur.[182]

With these discourses we pass'd the time he staid; – I have not seen him since, but heard of his safe arrival at ****; – whether he will be elected for that County cannot be determin'd at the time of my writing this; so can only say, that if he is, I doubt not but his character will appear to much more advantage than in the faint sketch I have here been able to give of it.

End of the Second VOLUME.

THE
Invisible Spy.

BY

EXPLORALIBUS.

VOL. III.

LONDON:
Printed for T. GARDNER, at *Cowley*'s Head, near St. *Clement*'s
Church in the *Strand*.

M,D,CC,LV.

CONTENTS

OF THE
Third VOLUME.

CHAP. VI.

CHAP. VII.

CHAP. VIII.

CHAP. IX.

CHAP. X.

BOOK VI. CHAP. I.

CHAP. II.

CHAP. III.

CHAP. IV.

CHAP. V.

CHAP. VI.

CHAP. VII.

CHAP. VIII.

THE

Invisible Spy.

VOL. III.
BOOK V.

CHAP. I.

The author's introduction to this volume consists only of an apology for making
no introduction at all, and his reasons for that omission.

SINCE my setting about this work, I have seen several late treatises that are half
taken up with introductory Prefaces to the publick:[183] – on a serious examination to what end those long discourses were penn'd, they seem to me to have
been occasioned either by one or the other of the following motives:

First, That an author having contracted with his bookseller for a certain
number of sheets, without having well consider'd whether his head be stored
with subject matter to make good his engagement, finds himself under a necessity of filling up the vacant pages by saying something by way of an introduction,
preface, or advertisement to the reader.

Or, secondly, That fearing the eyes of the public will not be sufficiently open
to the merit of his performance; or, perhaps, not have the curiosity even to look
into it at all, he thinks proper to bespeak their favour by a pompous prelude, and
sounds his own praises, like a trumpet at the door of a Puppet-shew.[184]

Now I am too great a lover of liberty ever to bind myself by any such slavish
agreement; the first of these incentives is quite out of the question, and cannot
possibly have any weight with me.

And as to the second, – As a more perfect knowledge of myself, than I perceive some others have, will not permit me to be over vain in any thing I do, so
the indolence of my nature will not permit me to be over anxious for the success.

Besides not having the temptation of the motives aforesaid, I have more
adventures to relate than can be easily crowded into this volume, therefore have
neither time nor paper to spare for an address, which would afford so little satisfaction to myself in the writing, and perhaps less to my reader in the perusing.

It may, indeed, be said, that as I gave some account of myself in the beginning of this work, it would be no more than good-manners to take a decent leave of the public at the end of it; but to this I must have leave to reply, that there is a wide difference between coming and going: – when a man intrudes himself into strange company, it certainly behoves him to tell the business that brought him there; but when he has done that, and has no more to say, I believe every one will allow that it is the best good-breeding to quit the place without ceremony, as I shall do.

CHAP. II.

Contains such matters as, it is highly probable, will be the least pleasing to
those for whose service it is most intended.

THERE is, according to the wise man's phrase, a folly under the sun, which, in my opinion, has as little to be said for it as any one of the many others of the present age, – and that is, – an insatiable inquisitiveness into future events, as if the fore-knowledge of what is to come would enable us either to alleviate or avert the decrees of Providence. – Well does mr. Dryden ridicule this propensity, when he says,

> If fate be not, then what can we foresee?
> And how can we avoid it, if it be?[185]

Yet are all ages, all degrees of both sexes, tainted, more or less, with this epidemic frenzy. – It cannot but afford the most astonishing, as well as melancholy reflections, in a thinking mind, to observe how many impostors, in and about this great town, are maintained by pretending to the art of divination,[186] while the industrious followers of lawful occupations perish for want of due encouragement.

As I was one day on my Invisible Progressions, I accompany'd a mingled crowd of people into a house situated in one of the most obscure parts of the city: – at first I imagined that this was some private chapel, where persons resorted to pay their adorations to the Deity in a manner not authorised by the government;[187] but was soon convinced of my mistake, when, instead of a pulpit and desk, I found the room we came into furnished only with globes and tellescopes, and other implements of a soothsayer and astrologer. – On looking round me these lines of Dr. Garth's came immediately into my head:

> An inner room receives the num'rous shoals
> Of such as pay to be reputed fools:
> Globes stand on globes; volumes on volumes lie,
> And planetary schemes amuse the eye.
> The sage in velvet chair, here lolls at ease,
> To promise future health for present fees:

Then, as from Tripod, solemn shams reveals,
And, what the Stars know nothing of, foretels.
One asks how soon Panthea may be won,
And longs to feel the marriage fetters on:
Others, convinc'd by melancholy proof,
Enquire when courteous fates will strike 'em off:
Some by what means they may redress the wrong,
When fathers the possession keep too long:
Others would know the issue of their cause,
And whether gold can solder up the flaws.[188]

I had not patience to stay to hear what idle predictions this oracle would spout forth, especially as I had no acquaintance with any of those who I saw came to consult him; so took my leave of the deceiver and the deceived, full of indignation against the one, and a pity, mingled with contempt, for the other.

However, as the most learned of all ages have always allow'd that the stars have an influence over the affairs of this sublunary world, it must be confess'd that those men who profess the science of Astrology have the most plausible pretence of any among the various tribes of fortune-tellers, for the impositions daily practised on the credulous part of mankind.

But what can be said in defence of the understanding of those people, who waste their time and money in consulting those abject dealers in futurity! – Creatures who would make you believe they can read the most hidden decrees of fate in the grounds of coffee, tea, chocolate, or powder-blue;[189] nay, even in the dregs of cherry-brandy! – I had often heard much talk of these she-conjurers, but not till I was convinced by the testimony of my own senses, could ever be brought to believe that persons endow'd with a liberal education could descend so far as to listen to their inconsistent prate, much less give credit to what they utter'd.

But so strong is the desire of looking into the seeds of time, especially among the fair sex, that sometimes the most proud, as well as the most nice and delicate, will throw aside all consideration of what they are, or would be thought, and for the sake of being told their fortune, send for, caress, and associate themselves with the very lowest and most dirty wretches in human nature.

Lysetta is descended from a very ancient and honourable house; – she lived, till considerably turned on the wrong side of thirty, without discovering the least inclination for marriage, much less gave any room for the most censorious ever to suspect she encouraged any private gallantries, and the whole tenor of her conduct was such as no one could imagine her capable of harbouring any notions beneath the dignity of her birth and character.

A long acquaintance gave me the privilege of visiting her pretty frequently, and never was deny'd access; – I was one day at her house when she had no other company than a young lady with whom she was extremely intimate; – while we were drinking tea her woman came running into the room, and with a very significant tone of voice said, – 'Madam, the woman you know of is below.' – 'Tis very well,' reply'd Lysetta, 'shew her into my chamber, and bid her stay a little;' – then turning to her friend, they smil'd on each other, – nodded, – winked, and seem'd very big with some secret between themselves.

I found by all this that my presence might very well be spared at this time, so turn'd down my cup after the second dish and took my leave. – As I was going down stairs I heard Lysetta order herself to be deny'd to whoever should come that evening; which convincing me of what I before had reason to imagine, that there was something more than ordinary in hand, I resolv'd, if possible, to fathom the mystery.

Accordingly I went home, popp'd on my Invisible Belt, put my Tablets in my pocket, and return'd with all the speed I could; – a lazy footman lolling against a post, with the door wide open behind him, gave me an easy entrance into the house: – I very well knew the situation of Lysetta's chamber, and went directly thither; – but, to my great mortification, found the ladies had bolted themselves in, and all I could distinguish of what was doing, for some time, was only the hoarse bass of a loud laugh from Lysetta, and the squeaking treble of a shrill te-hee from the other.

I stood centinel, however, at the top of the stair-case, and, at last, was happily relieved, – Lysetta open'd the door, – rung her bell, and call'd to her woman to bring clean cups: – having now gain'd admittance, I soon perceived what they were about; – a coffee-pot upon the table, – the dregs of the liquor it had contain'd pour'd into a bason, – several cups with more figures on the inside than Chinese makers had japan'd on the outside, and the yet recent circles they had left on being whelm'd down on a damask napkin spread on one corner of the table, presently inform'd me they were employ'd in the art and mystery of Dutch conjuration,[190] – properly, indeed, so call'd, as it was first introduced, among many other equally laudable customs, from Holland into England.

The priestess of these farcical rites was a mean habited, ill-look'd woman, and though not old had her nose saddled with a pair of spectacles almost as big as the tops of the cups she pretended to inspect. – She was placed between the two ladies, who seem'd to treat her with the greatest marks of freedom and civility.

Lysetta, I found, had been so complaisant to her friend, as to let her be first served; but it was now her own turn, and fresh cups being brought, and the coffee-oracle having judiciously pour'd the quantity of a tea-spoonful into each, the lady took it into her hand, threw out the liquor three different ways, and whelm'd it on the cloth, turn'd it round as many times, and to close the ceremony, struck it a slight blow on the bottom with her two fore fingers.

All being concluded, the prophetess took up the first with the most solemn air, – look'd stedfastly into it, then on Lysetta, and after having repeated this several times, at last deliver'd her predictions in these terms:

Fortune-teller. I see a ring, madam; – your ladyship will be married.

Lysetta. 'Tis rather a mourning ring; – some of my kindred or friends perhaps may die.

Fortune-teller. I can say nothing as to that, madam, as yet; – but I am positive what I see here is a wedding-ring, for there is a heart just by it, and a little farther there is a great house, with a high wall and a pair of gates; – your ladyship will have some gentleman that has a fine seat in the country; – it looks almost like a castle.

Lysetta. I know nothing of it; – but what else do you see?

Fortune-teller. Here is a man, madam, that seems to bring you money; – here are papers too, I do not know but they may be bills.

Lysetta. Very likely; for I expect my banker here either to-day or tomorrow.

Fortune-teller. Then here is a bundle of something brought to your ladyship's house.

Lysetta. Oh, – that is a new sack I have making; – But is there nothing more?

Fortune-teller. Not in this cup, madam; – but I will look into the next.

Lysetta. Do, for you have told me nothing of any consequence.

Fortune-teller. There is a great deal here, madam, I can perceive already; – here is a gentleman sitting in an easy-chair, leaning his elbow upon the table, and his head upon his hand, and seems to be in a deep study.

Lysetta. Pish, – what's this to me?

Fortune-teller. Yes, madam, it is a great deal to you; for here is your ladyship, and the very same gentleman upon his knees before you; – you turn your head away, and look a little scornful; but he has you by the hand. – Bless me! here you are both together again, – he is talking very earnestly to you; – I never saw any thing so plain; – your ladyship may see it yourself.

In speaking these last words she held the cup to Lysetta, and with a pin pointed out the eyes, the nose, and mouth of the pretended figure; but Lysetta push'd it from her, and said,

Lysetta. I never could see any thing in a cup in my life; – but what sort of man is he?

Fortune-teller. Pretty tall, madam, – well shaped, – very genteel, – has a fair complexion, and somewhat of a languishment in his eyes.

Lysetta. I cannot recollect that I know any man who answers this description.

Fortune-teller. I scarce think you do, madam, at present; but your ladyship may take my word for it, that you will see and be courted by such a one; for here is a figure of three over his head, – it must be either in three days, or three weeks at farthest; – let me consider; – aye, – the moon was at the full yesterday; – this event must happen before she enters into her last quarter; – but the next cup, it may be, will shew it more clearly.

With this she took up the third cup, but had no sooner just look'd it into than she set it down again, clapp'd her hands together, and cry'd out,

Fortune-teller. Bless me! – now I am positive your ladyship will very soon be married; – here is an altar, – and a book upon it, – and a parson, – all as exact as if they were drawn by a pencil.

She then took up the cup again, and perceiving Lysetta began to look a little more serious than she had done, went on in this manner:

Fortune-teller. Well – this is wonderful indeed; – of all the cups I ever turn'd in my life, I never saw any thing like this; – here is your ladyship hand in hand with that same gentleman who I told you was in the other; – I would now swear that your ladyship will be a wife before any one imagines you have any thoughts that way.

Lysetta. I have a very good opinion of your skill, yet am certain you are mistaken in this prediction; for to tell you the truth, I am resolved never to marry.

Fortune-teller. Your ladyship may resolve what you please, but if the stars resolve to the contrary, all your resolutions will come to nothing; – madam, there is no resisting fate, this gentleman is ordain'd to be your husband, and how much so ever you may set yourself against it, the decrees of destiny, are inevitable, and you must submit.

Lysetta. Oh, heavens! whether I will or not!

Fortune-teller. Undoubtedly, madam, – there is no withstanding the superior powers, and those things which we think the farthest removed from us, are frequently the most near at hand; so that design what you will, – resolve what you will, – it is all in vain; your ladyship is ordain'd to be a wife, and the gentleman I see in these cups must be your husband.

Lysetta. You put me in mind of what the poet says,

> The power that ministers to God's decrees,
> And executes on earth what he foresees;
> Call'd providence, or chance, or fatal sway,
> Comes with resistless force, and finds or makes its way;
> Nor kings, nor nations, nor united power,
> One moment can retard th' appointed hour:
> For whate'er we mortals hate or love,
> Or hope, or fear, depends on powers above:
> They move our appetites to good or ill,
> And by foresight necessitate the will.[191]

The young lady, who had done nothing but laugh'd all this time, now first opened her lips to speak, and corroborated the truth of Lysetta's quotation with another of equal authority.

Young Lady. Ay, my dear, as the inimitable charming Cowley tells us in one of his poems:

An unseen hand makes all our moves:
And some are great and some are small;
Some climb to good, some from good fortune fall:
Some wise men, and some fools we call;
Figures, alas! of speech; for destiny plays us all.[192]

Fortune-teller. I am not book-learned; – I cannot pretend to say any thing to these wise men's arguments; but I know my business as well as any she that professes it; – what I say may be depended on, – and I would wager a thousand pounds, if I were mistress of that sum, that lady Lysetta will be marry'd in a very few weeks.

Lysetta. Well, but if such a thing should come to pass, do you think I should be happy in the change of my condition?

Fortune-teller. There is nothing in the cup, madam, that shews the contrary; but I shall be able to tell your ladyship more after you are married.

This answer of the woman so much diverted me, that it was with some difficulty I kept myself from bursting into a loud laughter, which if I had done, the ladies would certainly have been more astonish'd than at any thing had been said to them by the Fortune-teller; – however, this accident did not happen, and I restrain'd the risible muscles so as to make no report that an Invisible guest had been witness to this private conversation.

The cups having been all examined, the prophetess, after receiving a handsome gratuity for her trouble, took her leave, and left Lysetta and her fair companion to reason between themselves on the wonders of her art; – but my Christaline Remembrancer being now quite full, it is not in my power to relate the particulars of their discourse; and can only say, that they both seem'd to give an implicit credit to every thing she had pretended to reveal.

I was very much surprised to find, that persons of good understanding in other things, could suffer themselves to be imposed upon by such stupid stuff; which, I confess, I then believed had no other meaning in it than to get a trifle of money from such who are weak enough to be amused with it; but it was not long before I was convinced of the falsity of my opinion in this point, and that those wretches have sometimes a farther and more wicked design in their pretended prophecies.

CHAP. III.

Presents the Reader with a very foolish adventure of Lysetta's, to which all that
was contain'd in the preceding chapter was only a prelude; with some short
remarks of the author's own on the extreme danger, as well as infatuation,
of consulting Fortune-tellers of any kind, and giving credit to their idle and
absurd predictions.

HAVING discover'd this folly in Lysetta, which before I could never have
imagin'd, I began now to be censorious enough to suspect she might also be
guilty of others, and therefore took it into my head to make her some Invisible
Visits, at those hours in which it was likely her behaviour was most unguarded.

In order to satisfy my curiosity in this point, I went to her house one morning, and found her very busy in looking over some new pamphlets, which had
been just sent her by her bookseller: – as I always thought the most certain way
to form a true judgment of a woman's mind, was in the knowledge of what sort
of reading she was most delighted with, I was glad to perceive that this lady
made choice of only such books as shew'd her neither a wanton or a coquette,
and returned all those which by their titles discover'd the least tendency to prophaneness or obscenity.

After this she took her little ivory folding-stick, and began to open the leaves
of one which she seem'd most impatient to examine; but before she had gone
through half the number of sheets it contain'd, was interrupted by a footman
who presented her with a letter, and said the person who brought it waited for
an answer; – I slipp'd behind her chair while she broke the seal, and the contents
were as follow:

> To the honourable LYSETTA.
> May it please your ladyship,
>
> MADAM,
> I HOPE your goodness will pardon the liberty a stranger takes in writing to
> you; but as I am not so fortunate to be acquainted with any person who can
> introduce me to your ladyship, I am obliged to become my own sollicitor, and
> most humbly request you will allow me the privilege of waiting on you this after-
> noon, if no previous engagement intervenes between me and my desires, having
> something to communicate which is of the utmost moment to the peace of him
> who has the honour to be,
> With the most profound respect,
> MADAM,
> Your ladyship's
> Sincerely devoted and obedient servant,
> ORSAMES.

Lysetta seem'd a good deal confounded on reading this little epistle; and after pausing a while, argued with herself in this manner:

Lysetta. Good God! if this should be the man the Fortune-teller told me of! – she said I should hear or see something of him within three days, and this is but the second since the prediction: – if I was sure he was the person she mentioned, I think I ought not to give him leave to visit me, at least not on his first requesting it. – Yet I should be glad, methinks, to see if he any way answers the description she gave of him; – besides, if I should refuse him, some accident or another would bring us together; for it is certain that there is no such thing as disappointing fate; – Why therefore should I keep myself in suspence? – no, I will see him, and hear what he has to say; – it may be he may come upon some other business than what I imagine, – and then it would be vastly silly in me to avoid him. – Whoever he is, or whatever his designs are, it can be of no prejudice to me to see him once; – he cannot run away with me; cannot have me against my will.

She then call'd her servant, and bid him tell the person who brought the letter, – that she should be at home in the afternoon, and at leisure to be spoke with by any one who had business with her.

The fellow ran down, but had scarce time to deliver the message he was charg'd with before she repented of it, as may be seen by this exclamation:

Lysetta. Lord! what have I done! if he is really the person I take him to be, he must think me strangely forward in so easily granting him admittance.

While she was speaking this she ran to the stair-case with an intent to retract what she had said; but a second thought withholding her, she turned back into the room, and cry'd out,

Lysetta. What a fool I am! – he does not know that I have consulted with a fortune-teller, nor that I have any reason to guess at the business that brings him hither; – Why therefore should I shun him? – What shame can my seeing him reflect upon me? – it will be time enough for me to forbid his visits when he has declared himself my lover.

How long she would have continued in that mind is uncertain; – two ladies came in that instant to desire her company with them to the Park, being a fine clear morning; to which she consenting, I left them to their promenade, and went home, but with a full resolution to return in the afternoon, and see what event the expected interview would produce.

But how greatly was I disappointed? – I had no sooner entered my apartment than I received a letter requiring my attendance at a judge's chambers that same afternoon, at four o'clock, which was the very time in which it was reasonable to suppose Lysetta's new guest would be with her: – the affair I was sent for upon, however, was of too much consequence to be hazarded for the sake of satisfying an idle curiosity; but I do not remember I was ever more vexed in my whole life.

Having dispatched my business, which indeed happened somewhat sooner than I expected, I put on my Belt of Invisibility and went to the house of Lysetta; – I saw a chair waiting, but the door was shut, and I was obliged to stay in the street for a considerable time, I believe not less than an hour, before it was opened for any person, either to go in or out.

I got entrance at last, and passed directly to the dining-room, where I found the person I was desirous of beholding; – on my looking earnestly on him, I saw he had so much the resemblance of the picture drawn for him by the Fortune-teller, that I presently perceived she must be better acquainted with his features than the cups could make her, and that in reality she was a marriage-broker, under the disguise of a coffee-grounds calculator.

He had placed himself very close to Lysetta on a settee, and must have been making a declaration of love to her by the answer she gave just as I came into the room.

Lysetta. Sir, it does not become me to hearken to any professions of this nature, from a person to whose family, fortune, and character I am so an entire stranger.

Orsames. It will be easy for me, madam, to give you full satisfaction in all these particulars; but till I can do so I beg you will permit me, at least, to convince you of my passion.

Lysetta. Tho', sir, there is no room to doubt, either by your appearance or behaviour, but that you are a gentleman and a man of honour, yet I should be glad, methinks, to know some one person with whom you are acquainted.

Orsames. Unfortunately for me, madam, there is not one soul in this town who can give any account of me: – this, perhaps, you will think somewhat odd; but permit me to give you a short sketch of my history, and you will cease to wonder at it.

Lysetta. Then, pray sir, oblige me so far.

Orsames. It is no boast in me, madam, to assure your ladyship that my family is among the number of the most ancient in England, having been settled here long before the conquest, and many of them been bishops, judges, and privy counsellors; but my father, taking some disgust at the measures in a late reign, resolved to quit his native country for ever; and to that end sold the seat of his ancestors, with a very considerable estate in Somersetshire, and carried the purchase money, together with his whole family, to Philadelphia, where he had then a brother, reputed the most wealthy merchant in that place; – it was there, madam, I was born, and am the only surviving issue of my parents, and consequently the sole heir of their possessions, as also of my uncle's, he dying without leaving any child behind him. – I fear I tire you, madam.

Lysetta. No, sir, I beg you will go on.

Orsames. From my very infancy there were somewhat in my nature which could not relish the manners of these Americans, though born among them; – I had read a great deal, and heard much more concerning England, and had always a passionate desire to come to it; but my father, even after my arriving at maturity, would never listen to any intreaties I made him on that score: – after his death, my uncle was no less averse to my removal; but on his demise, finding myself freed from all dependency, and entirely master of my own actions, I left all my effects to be disposed of by a person whose integrity I am well assured of, and taking with me only a thousand guineas, just for present use, embarked in the first ship that sailed for England, where I happily arrived about six weeks since.

Lysetta. But would it not have been better, sir, that you had staid at Philadelphia till your affairs had been settled?

Orsames. Not at all, madam; I have friends there that will manage for me as well as if I were there in person, – besides, an irresistable impulse hurried me to England; – I could not then account for my impatience, but am now convinced it was my guardian angel called me to behold in reality that lovely face I have so often seen in dreams.

Lysetta. What, dream of me!

Orsames. Yes, madam, though so many leagues distant, my spirit has been often with you, – conversed with you, and avowed that flame my mortal part now feels.

Lysetta. Is it possible!

Orsames. True, by Heaven!

Lysetta. And are you certain I am the same you saw in your sleep?

Orsames. I could not be deceived, – the first moment my eyes were blest with your divine presence at the Chapel Royal,[193] I forgot the solemnity of the place, and the pious business that had brought me thither; and as the Poet says,

> When I attempted to say my prayers,
> Began my prayers to Heaven,
> And ended them to you.[194]

Lysetta. 'Tis very wonderful; – but 'tis time enough to talk of these things. – As you have related to me the former part of your life, I should like to know in what manner you intend to regulate the future.

Orsames. That must be submitted to my charming directress; – all my affairs, as well as my heart, must henceforth be at your disposal: – I had thoughts, indeed, of purchasing a small estate, of about fifteen hundred or two thousand pounds a year; – but whether I should put the remainder of my fortune into the public funds, or lay it out on an employment at Court, I had not yet determined.

Lysetta. Oh, by all means buy a place at Court; – the Court is the only Heaven upon Earth.

Orsames. Next to your company I believe it is; and since you approve the thought, shall infallibly pursue it.

Lysetta. Whoever you marry, sir, will doubtless be of my opinion.

Orsames. Ah! do not wrong my faithful heart so much as to imagine it capable of being charmed by any other fair! – No, – if all my love, my services, my prayers, should fail to move the adorable Lysetta, I vow an eternal celibacy.

Lysetta. You men always talk thus when you would impose on the credulity of our sex; – but, sir, it is time alone that is the true touch-stone of sincerity.

Orsames. Madam, it is, and to that, employ'd in my assiduities, and your own goodness, I shall trust the decision of my fate; – therefore, I once more implore your permission to repeat my vows, and pay you the tribute which beauty like yours demands from love like mine.

Lysetta. I will not hear so much of love; – but as you are a stranger in town, and as yet have no acquaintance, I cannot be uncharitable enough to refuse you the privilege of visiting me sometimes.

Orsames. Heavenly creature! but it is in this humble posture I ought to thank your goodness.

With these Words he threw himself upon his knees, and catching hold of both her hands, pressed first the one and then the other to his lips with the greatest appearance of transport; – all which she suffered, nor discovered the least reluctance; – I know not how long he might have continued in this mute courtship, if the sound of somebody at the door had not obliged him suddenly to rise.

It was Lysetta's servant, who immediately entered and presented her with two letters, which had been just left her by the post; – she looked on the superscriptions, then threw them carelesly on the table, without shewing any impatience to examine the contents; but her lover, either thro' politeness, or because he had acted enough of his part for the first time, thought proper to take his leave, saying he would do himself the honour to wait on her the next day.

He was no sooner gone, than she began to give a loose to those agitations which his presence and discourse had occasioned in her mind, and which she had not without great difficulty restrained from being visible.

It was in these terms she expressed herself, which, incoherent as they are, I shall deliver them to my readers, just as I found them the next morning engraved on my Tablets.

Lysetta. Well, this is the oddest accident; sure there was never any thing so astonishing! – let people say what they will, – there is a great deal in the throwing of a cup; – that woman is certainly the devil; – how exactly she describ'd this gentleman. – I have said I would never marry, but if the stars have ordain'd it otherwise, it is in vain for weak woman to resist; and if his fortune be such as he pretends it is, I can see no cause for any one to blame me.

Here she stopp'd, and fell into a little resverie; but soon coming out of it, thus renew'd her ejaculations:

Lysetta. There is nothing in the person nor address of this new lover, but what is perfectly agreeable, – and I believe I shall like him well enough on a little more acquaintance with him; – he seems vastly charm'd with me; but one ought not to build on what the men say on these occasions. – There is something strangely particular, indeed, in his dreaming of me without ever having seen me: – in fine, the more I consider, the more I find the hand of fate is in this business, and I must submit.

After this she seem'd somewhat more composed, and began to read the letters she had received; – I also look'd over them at the same time; but found they were only from relations, of family affairs of no moment to the public, or to the narrative I am reciting.

When I came home, had thrown myself into my easy-chair, and began to ruminate on the extraordinary scene I had been witness of, I knew not whether the base design, which I now plainly perceived had been concerted between the Fortune-teller and Orsames, or the weakness and infatuation of Lysetta in giving credit to their romantic lies, had the most right to engross my amazement.

But when I reflected more deeply on the various impositions I daily saw practised in the world, my wonder ceased, on account either of the Fortune-teller or the Fortune-hunter, and fix'd itself entirely on the simplicity of Lysetta. – It now seem'd not strange to me, that the most illiterate and abject wretches should be endow'd with a natural store of cunning, which, back'd by impudence, renders them capable of forming contrivances to deceive; else how do we so often see common pickpockets and house-breakers circumvent the watchfulness of the most cautious? but then those sort of pilferers rob us when our heads are turn'd another way, or when we are sleeping in our beds; but in listening to Fortune tellers we are defrauded with our eyes broad open, and give, as it were, our own consent to the worst kind of theft, that of stealing away our understanding.

People guilty of this egregious folly, when detected in it, pretend they consult those ridiculous oracles for no other end than merely to divert themselves, without believing, or even remembering afterwards one syllable of the predictions delivered to them – This may, perhaps, at first be true; but there are too many instances which prove that custom, by degrees, turns into earnest what might once be meant but as a jest. – The reason is this:

Those subtle creatures frequently find means, either by emissaries they employ for that purpose, or by insinuating themselves among the servants, to get into the secrets of families, and one real fact, serving to make all they say believed, gives them the power to work the person who depends upon them almost to any point they aim at.

The most pernicious designs have been carry'd on this way. – Husbands have been set against their wives, and wives against their husbands; – parents have been made to disregard their children, and children to forget all obedience to their parents; – the best matches have been broke off, and the most disproportionable ones made: – in fine, there is no kind of mischief but what has happen'd when a Fortune-teller has been bribed by some base person, who has an interest in bringing about such events.

Therefore, as I think there is a law in force against these pretended dealers in futurity,[195] I cannot help saying, that I regret its not being executed with greater punctuality; since the more simple an evil appears, the more dangerous it proves in its effects.

CHAP. IV.

Contains the catastrophe of an affair, which the repetition of ought not to give offence to any one, except the person whose resentment the author will not look upon as a misfortune.

LYSETTA was so strongly persuaded in her mind, that it was her fate to marry Orsames, that she made not the least attempt to check the growing inclination she had for him, but rather thought it a virtue in her to encourage the most tender sentiments for a person ordain'd by Heaven to be her husband.

I made several visits to her, both in my Visible and Invisible capacity, and seldom went without finding Orsames there, and every time more free and degagee[196] than before. – He made so swift a progress in his courtship, that in less than a fortnight he became the Major-Domo[197] of her family, – commanded all the servants, and behaved as if already their master, as indeed he was in every thing except the name.

To add to all this, Lysetta suffered him to conduct her to all public places; – they took the air together in the Mall, Kensington-Gardens, and Hyde-Park, and sat in the same box at the Play-house; he always dined and supped with her, whatever other company were there: – in a word, they were never asunder but in those hours when decency obliged them to be so.

So strange a revolution in the behaviour of Lysetta made a great deal of noise in town; all her acquaintance were surprized; – all her friends and kindred were very much alarmed at it; especially as the person to whom she shewed these extraordinary favours was altogether unknown in the world, nor could they get the least account of him.

Those, who either through a long conversation or affinity of blood, could take the privilege of discoursing with her on this head, did it in a very free manner; but the answers she gave to their interrogatories were far from being satisfactory to them: – when she told them his history as he had related it to her, they treated it with contempt; – some said, – that he was an impostor; – others more modest, that they wished he was not so; – to both which she returned, – that whatever he were, she was certain it was her fate to marry him, and therefore desired that they would give themselves no farther pain on that occasion.

As she was naturally of a haughty, obstinate disposition, it is highly probable that the remonstrances they took the liberty of making to her, rather strengthened than abated her resolution of giving herself to him: – I was at her house one day, under cover of my Invisible Belt, when I heard the following conversation between them:

Orsames. Condemn me not, my angel, for being sometimes melancholy even in your divine presence; – though you have promised to make me one day the happiest of mankind, and I look upon every word of that dear mouth as unfailing as an Oracle, yet when I consider the length of time between me and the consummation of my wishes, the impatience of my passion will not permit me to be gay.

Lysetta. You men are always in such a hurry in every thing you do.

Orsames. Ah, madam, 'tis a dreadful thing to have one's happiness depend on the uncertain winds and waves, it may be yet two months before my effects can arrive from Philadelphia.

Lysetta. And do you call that so long a time?

Orsames. A million of ages in the account of love; and even, according to common calculation, longer than human nature can sustain continual torments; – eight whole weeks, six and fifty anxious days, and as many restless nights; upwards of thirteen hundred hours of tedious expectation; and minutes almost numberless, wasted in pain which might be passed in pleasure, if you would shorten the tremendous date.

Lysetta. What would you have me do?

Orsames. Ah! if you loved, you would not need to be told; but of yourself generously bring the blessed event nearer to my wishes.

Lysetta. You would not have me marry you till your affairs are settled, and things can be done regularly for our mutual satisfaction.

Orsames. I understand you, madam; – the articles of jointure and pin-money,[198] I know, are customary in modish marriages; but the passion you have inspired me with is of too sublime a nature to stoop to such mean forms. – I ask not what your fortune is, but will settle the whole of mine upon you; – your lovely person is all the treasure I am ambitious of preserving; – the rest shall be at your disposal.

Lysetta. That is kind, indeed; but more than I desire or would accept of.

Orsames. Oh! that you had no other fortune than your beauty; – then would the sincerity of my love be proved by endowing you with all that Heaven has made me master of. – Alas! you know not how ardently, – how faithfully I adore you.

Lysetta. Yes, I am vain enough to think I have some share in your affections.

Orsames. Some share! – oh! could you be sensible of the thousandth part of what I feel, pity, if not love, would compel you to ease my throbbing heart of the suspence it labours under, and you would give yourself to my despairing – dying – burning – bleeding passion.

Lysetta. I have already said I will be yours, and now again repeat it.

Orsames. But when, my Angel!

In speaking these words he threw himself upon his knees before her, – burst into a flood of well dissembled tears, and grasp'd her Robe de Chambre with agonies which I cannot but say had much the appearance of reality, while in these terms he prosecuted his design:

Orsames. I have till now supported life but in the rapturous hope of being one day bless'd in your possession: but even hope, by its uncertainty, becomes at last too weak an aid; and soon, very soon, my adorable Lysetta, will you behold your faithful lover a cold breathless corps, unless the balm of your kindness recruits the vital lamp, and gives fresh vigour to my depress'd and breaking heart.

Lysetta. I cannot bear to hear and and see you thus; – rise, sir, – this posture does not become the man whom I intend to make my husband.

Orsames. No, by Heaven, I will never quit your feet without an assurance of my happiness, – Say then, – oh! say! when shall be the blissful day that makes you mine!

Lysetta. Since it must be so, – even when you please. – No, hold, – I had forgot myself.

Orsames. Oh, Heavens, what now!

Lysetta. I promised a reverend clergyman, my near kinsman, that if ever I married he should perform the ceremony; – he is at present out of town, but will return next Sunday, and on the Tuesday following it shall not be my fault if we do not attend him at the Altar.

Orsames. Extatic sound! – may I depend on the performance of this Heavenly promise!

Lysetta. You may, and be entirely easy on that point; take now my hand, as an earnest of my giving it to you in a more solemn manner before a parson: – henceforward I shall look upon myself as yours.

Orsames. Angel! – Goddess! – thus then let me seal the covenant on those charming lips that has pronounced it.

Lysetta. The covenant will not hold good in law without both parties interchangeably sign their assent.

She uttered these words with a most pleasing smile, and at the same time threw her arms about his neck, and returned the passionate salute she had received from him, adding this tender expression:

Lysetta. My dear, dear Orsames, I do not now blush to confess to you, that from the first moment you declared yourself my lover, my heart corresponded with your vows, and told me what would be the event.

He affected too much transport, on hearing her speak in this manner, to be able to make any other reply than kisses and embraces, which, as she was far from repelling, or seeming the least offended at, I know not what advantages he might have taken, on finding her thus soften'd by his artifices, if a sudden interruption had not, happily for her, broke off this dangerous entertainment.

A footman came in, and told her that her aunt, lady Gravelove, was come to visit her; on which she cry'd with some peevishness,

Lysetta. Pish, – Why did you not say I was from home?

Footman. Your ladyship gave me no such orders; but if you please, I will go and tell her that I was mistaken, and that your ladyship went out without my knowing you had done so.

Lysetta. No, no, I must see her; – go and say I will wait on her presently.

Then turning fondly to Orsames, said,

Lysetta. Do you chuse to join company with my aunt; or shall I fetch some book to amuse you with till she is gone?

Orsames. No, my dearest love; – this lady has always look'd upon me with an unpleasing eye, especially of late, therefore will not offend her with my presence; – neither are my spirits enough composed, in the excess of joy you have inspired me with, to read any thing with attention; – so will take a little walk.

Lysetta. Do so; – but I shall expect you back to supper, – my aunt seldom stays longer than to drink tea, and I am sure I shall not press her at this time.

No more was said on either side; – they embraced and parted, – she went into the next room, and he down stairs, in order to go where his business or inclination called him.

As I never believed this fellow was what he pretended, I had taken some pains to discover the truth of his circumstances; but without any success, till it now came into my mind to follow him after he had left Lysetta's house; which I did, resolving not to lose sight him till he should return to her again.

He went directly to Drury-lane, walk'd very fast, and never stopp'd till he came to the entrance of a narrow passage between that place and Wild-street, where he stood still, and look'd round him, as I suppose, to see if any one was near who might know him; for day was not yet quite shut in; – then pass'd a little farther, – look'd about him again, and finding the coast, as he thought, clear, none being in the alley but his Invisible attendant, slipp'd hastily into a little dirty ale-house, where an old woman met him, and told him his friends were all above, on which he ran up stairs and push'd open the door of a room, pretty spacious, indeed, but had otherwise all the signs of beggary and wretchedness about it.

Here we found five or six men, tolerably well habited; but had something in their countenances which made me guess their occupation before they discover'd it by their conversation; for they were no better than a gang of thieves and sharpers, – they were sitting round a table, with a great bowl of punch before them, when Orsames rush'd in, and with a gay air accosted them in these terms:

Orsames. Wish me joy, my lads, – my hearts of steel, – wish me joy; – I have gain'd my point; – all is over, i'faith.

First Man. What, married!

Orsames. No, but as good as married; – the wench and her twelve thousand pounds are as sure to me, as if I had the one in my arms and the other in my pocket; – Tuesday is the day, my buffs.

As he spoke this he drumm'd with his hands upon the table, and roar'd with a shrill voice this scrap of an old ballad:

Orsames.

> On Tuesday morning 'twill be all my care,
> To powder my locks and to comb up my hair:
> Hey, so trim and so smug upon Tuesday.[199]

But I must have more money; by G – d, I have not a single doit[200] left.

Second Man. How! – All the fifty pieces gone already?

Orsames. Ay, faith, and well laid out too; – I shall return it with interest; – you shall all share in the money, and the woman too. – But come, – how stands stock among you?

Third Man. Cursed low: – tho' we have been all out to day we have not collected above thirty pieces, and four gold watches that must be knock'd to pieces, and the cases melted down, or the makers names may betray us.

Fourth Man. The road grows worse and worse every day, I think; – people are either poorer or more cautious than ever they were.

Orsames. But did you get nothing from the four ladies that the Fortune-teller told you were to take the air this morning on Barnes-Common?

Fifth Man. I should have done; but as the devil would have it, just as they were going to pull out their purses, three gentlemen, with fire-arms, came galloping towards us, and oblig'd me to make off without my booty.

Orsames. 'Twas damn'd unlucky.

First Man. One meets with a thousand such disappointments; – for my part I am half sick of the business, and so I believe we are all.

Second Man. Ay, faith; for what with seeing innkeepers, coachmen, fortune-tellers, and other such necessary informers, we have the least part of the profit to ourselves.

Third Man. Ay, – I wish, Orsames, you were once married, that you might set up a gaming-table under the sanction of your lady's name; – gaming is ten times a more profitable, as well as a safer way of thieving.

Orsames. You know it was my bargain, and you may depend upon my honour that it shall be the first thing I will do.

Fourth Man. It will be a joyful day; for since taxes have been so high, and trade so low, such numbers of shopkeepers are obliged to take the road, that we old practioners can scarce get a living by it.

Orsames. Well, well, all this will be over in a short time; – but you must raise me some cash; – I can easily give you an account of the fifty pieces.

Fifth Man. No, no, it needs not; – we know you would not sink upon us.

Orsames. I chuse, however, to do it: – the first article is five guineas to the Fortune-teller, as an earnest of the hundred she is to receive after my marriage with Lysetta: – the second is twenty pounds for a gold snuff-box, which I pretended to have brought from Philadelphia and presented to her ladyship: – the third is about ten more, spent in three several jaunts I made with her to Richmond, Windsor, and Greenwich: – the remainder, you may believe, might well be spent in donations to her servants, board-wages to my own man, – paying my lodgings at two guineas a week, chair-hire, and other such necessary expences.

First Man. You could do no less.

Second Man. Ay, ay, – nothing of all this could have been spared. – But what sum do you demand at present?

Orsames. I believe twenty pieces will defray the whole charges of the wedding, which is all I want; – after them, my boys, I shall have enough for you all.

On this every one turn'd out his pockets, and the sum requested was immediately made up and laid upon the table, which Orsames put into his purse; and then some discourse ensued among this vicious company which I chuse to pass over in silence, as it would be no fit entertainment for the chaste ears of my fair readers.

Orsames staid with them about two hours, and then took his leave in order to sup with Lysetta, as she had desir'd he would; – I accompanied him not thither, but went home to my own apartment, more full of confusion at the discovery I had made than I am able to express.

Tho' I half despised Lysetta for the follies I had seen her guilty of, yet when I reflected on her birth, and the character she had hitherto maintain'd in the world, I could not bear the thoughts of her becoming the victim of the base design concerted against her; and her fortune, reputation, and eternal peace of mind, the prey of such a nest of villains.

My whole study was now fully bent how to snatch this unfortunate lady from that gulph of perdition she was upon the brink of, and so near plunging into.

I was extremely divided in my thoughts what to do on this occasion; to give her any hints concerning the dangers to which she exposed herself and reputation, by encouraging the addresses of a man whose character she was so little acquainted with, I knew would be in vain, as she had rejected all the warnings given her on that score, and refused to listen to the admonitions of her best friends and nearest kindred. – I had it in my power, indeed, to inform her of much more than any of them could even guess at; but then I could not relate the scene I had been witness of without discovering at the same time the secret of my Invisible Belt, which was by no means proper for me to entrust her with.

To acquaint her by letter with what I knew concerning Orsames, and the villanous conspiracy had been form'd to ruin her, I fear'd would be to as little purpose; and doubted not but she would look upon an anonymous intimation only as a piece of malice, and treat it with the contempt it might seem to merit; – as this, however, was the only method which I could take to save her, with any convenience to myself, I resolved to pursue it; and accordingly wrote to her the next morning a full account of all I had been witness of between Orsames and his wicked companions.

I made this letter be left at her house before the time in which she usually got out of bed, to the end she might have leisure to consider the contents, without being interrupted by any company coming in; – as I was desirous of seeing in what manner she would receive this intelligence, I went, under cover of my Belt, and gained entrance just as she had finish'd the perusal.

Her behaviour was such as I had apprehended it would be; – she tore the letter, – storm'd, and cry'd out,

Lysetta. Was there ever so much impudence! – Sure the person that sent this infamous scrawl must have a very mean opinion of my understanding to think I could give the least credit to such a vile aspersion. – Orsames an impostor! a companion for thieves and vagabonds! – ridiculous.

And then again:

Lysetta. This must certainly be a contrivance of some of my wise kindred to break off the match: – I could find in my heart to send for Orsames and marry him this instant, to shew how much I despise their little malice: – but tis no matter, – Tuesday will soon arrive, and that will put an end to all.

I staid a full hour, in the supposition that Orsames would make her a morning's visit; but finding, by some discourse she had with her maid, that she did not expect him, and was making herself ready to go among the shops for things she wanted to buy, I quitted her apartment much disconcerted at the ill success of what I had done.

However, as I had little else to employ my time that day, I went again in the afternoon, Orsames was now there, and two ladies of Lysetta's particular acquaintance: – whether she had mention'd any thing to him of the letter I cannot be certain; but am apt to think she had not; for he appear'd with an alertness, which, by all I could discover, had nothing of constraint in it.

Cards were call'd for, and they were just going to sit down to Whist, when word was brought Lysetta that her cousin, Capt. Platoon, was just arriv'd from Carlisle and come to wait upon her, on which she order'd him to be shew'd up immediately.

Orsames, who I perceived had turn'd pale as ashes on hearing this gentleman's name, now rose hastily from his chair, and said to Lysetta,

Orsames. I have just thought of some business I had to dispatch; – your ladyship must excuse me.

Lysetta. You will not go?

Orsames. The affair that calls me is of consequence; – I cannot stay.

She was going to make some reply, but the Captain came that instant into the room; – while he was paying his compliments to his cousin and the other ladies, Orsames had taken up his hat and was endeavouring to slip out unperceived; but the quick-sightedness of Lysetta prevented him; – she ran to him, and catching hold of his sleeve spoke thus:

Lysetta. You shall not go, at least till I have presented you to my cousin.

Then turning to the Captain said,

Lysetta. This is a gentleman, cousin, whose acquaintance, I believe, you will hereafter think yourself happy in.

On this the Captain advanced with great politeness to embrace the person his fair kinswoman presented to him; but had no sooner fix'd his eyes upon his face, than he started back with the utmost astonishment, and cry'd out to Lysetta:

Capt. Platoon. What is the meaning of this, madam? – Who would you introduce to me?

She was opening her mouth to make some answer; but Orsames, who was drawing as fast as he could towards the door, hinder'd her from speaking, by saying, with a hesitating voice:

Orsames. Madam, – the gentleman does not seem to desire any new acquaintance; – I will wait on your ladyship another time.

In speaking this he got to the top of the stair-case, and 'tis likely would have made but one step to the bottom, if the Captain had not prevented him, by running to him and catching fast hold of him by the collar, dragg'd him back, saying at the same time;

Capt. Platoon. No, rascal, you must not think to leave this place till you have confess'd what devil gave you the impudence to introduce yourself into such company, – and on what villainous design you are thus disguised in the habit of a gentleman.

Orsames. Sir, I don't understand this usage; – you neither know me nor did I ever see you before: – you must mistake me for some other.

Capt. Platoon. Dog, – do you think I am to be deceived by the dress I see you in?

The addressing himself to Lysetta, who stood as motionless as if transfix'd with thunder, went on thus:

Capt. Platoon. Madam, by what means soever this villain has imposed upon you, I do assure you, upon my honour, that two months ago he was a private man in Capt. Cutcomb's company, and drum'd out of the regiment for pig-stealing, and other misdemeanors; for some of which, indeed, he ought to have been hang'd.

On these words Lysetta scream'd out, – 'Oh! Heavens!' – and fell into a swoon; – the Captain seeing this, quitted his prisoner to run with the two ladies to her assistance; and Orsames took this opportunity of making his escape.

Proper means being apply'd, she soon recovered, and the swelling passions which had occasioned this disorder vented themselves in tears; – the Captain appear'd a little impatient to know how she became acquainted with such a wretch as Orsames; but she told him she was not then in a condition to inform him of the particulars – said, she was very ill and must lie down, and desired to see him another time; – on which he took his leave, as did the two ladies, who knowing Orsames had profess'd himself her lover, and the encouragement she had given him, I could perceive smiled within themselves at the discovery.

Thus was Lysetta preserved from ruin, and had no other punishment for her folly than being laugh'd at by those who were privy to the affair: – as for Orsames, I have since met him about town in a very shabby and tatter'd condition; – the gang of villains, his associates, I believe are dispersed, and one of them has made his exit at Tyburn.

CHAP. V.

Treats on various matters, some of which, the author dares venture to assure the public, will hereafter be found not only more entertaining, but also of more consequence than at present they appear to be.

I HAD been told that lady Playfeild's route was an assemblage of the most brilliant and polite persons of both sexes, and tho' I never had any great opinion of these sort of meetings, yet I was tempted to go thither, in order to be myself a witness how far the description that had been given me was consonant to truth. – As I am an entire stranger to her ladyship, and did not care for the formality of being introduced by any one who went there, I chose to make this visit in my Invisible Capacity.

The great number of wax-tapers, the sparkle of the ladies jewels, and the extraordinary beauty of some among them, was dazling to my eyes at first entrance; but I soon found that I had the same fault to find with this as I had done in all other mix'd company I ever saw; – a kind of hurry and confusion, which destroys that solid conversation that is so agreeable when only a few select friends are met together.

It was very near nine o'clock when I went thither, yet there were several who came in after me; – lady Playfeild received all of them with her accustomed politeness; but for a great while there was nothing in the salutations on either side which engross'd my attention so far as to make me spread my Tablets to retain it.

I was, indeed, quite indolent to every thing that was said, till the entrance of lady Allmode gave a little spur to my curiosity; – I had heard much talk of this lady, not only for her being extravagantly fond of every new fashion, but also for a certain peculiarity in her manner of conversation, which made her admired by people of a low education, and as much laugh'd at by those of a superior.

I had been told that she had an utter aversion to plain English; – and so through a contempt for what she called the vulgar way of speaking, that when she talk'd, even on the most common things, she interlarded all she said with the hardest words she could pick out of the Dictionary, and frequently coined new ones of her own, which never were nor scarce ever will be found in any Vocabulary.

Lady Playfeild, I perceived, received her with a great deal of respect; – I was then at some distance, but on finding they were entering into conversation, drew more near, to have an opportunity of hearing and improving myself, by a person of whom so extraordinary a description had been given me.

After the first compliments were over, lady Playfeild addressed herself to her in these terms:

Lady Playfeild. Tho' I am always happy when I see your ladyship, yet now I can scarce forbear complaining of your unkindness in coming without miss Arabella; – I hear she has been in town above a week.

Lady Allmode. I could not have been guilty of so enormous a solecism in good breeding, as not to have brought her to pay her duty to your ladyship, if there had been a possibility in nature to have done it.

Lady Playfeild. I hope miss is well, madam.

Lady Allmode. Perfectly so, madam, as to her health; but such a sight, – such a figure; – a greater metamorphosis than any in Ovid.

Lady Playfeild. What does your ladyship mean?

Lady Allmode. Oh, madam, the remotest corners of the most desart of the three Arabias never produced such a creature, – such a Tramontane,[201] as the Italians elegantly phrase it. – Well, – these people, who live a great way from London, are such absurdians, – such awkwardities. – Would your ladyship believe it, – they sent the girl home in a cap that quite covered the drum of her ears?

Lady Playfeild. That might be to prevent her from catching cold in the stage-coach.

Lady Allmode. Oh, Jupiter! – how am I surpriz'd to hear your ladyship talk in this manner! – as if any one could catch cold with what is the fashion. – But this is not all, – the girl had several new suits of cloaths when she left London, made in the genteelest taste; but my country aunt took it into her head, that either I had allow'd too scanty a pattern, or that she had outgrown them, out of mere goodwill and simplicity, has lengthen'd all her petticoats to such a ridiculous size, that they almost come down to the buckles of her shoes; – I protest one can scarce see whether she has any ancles, much less if she has any calves to her legs.

On this a gentleman who stood pretty near approach'd lady Allmode, and with a tone the most ironical that could be, replied to what she had said in these words:

Gentleman. Your ladyship must excuse the mistake your aunt has made; for I fancy the fashion of going half naked may not yet have reach'd so far as Wales.

Lady Allmode. You certainly speak the rationalii of the thing, sir; – few of these mountaineers regard any thing but loading their tables with provisions, feasting their tenants, paying their debts, standing up for the liberties of their country, and such-like antiquated obsolete customs; – for my part, all my faculties are immerg'd in a profundity of astonishment, to think that my aunt could marry and settle among such aliens to politeness, – such heathens to the laws of good-breeding and the Drawing-Room.

Gentleman. Perhaps, madam, the customs and manners you mention were in vogue at the time of your aunt's marriage?

Lady Allmode. I protest, sir, you have hit upon the solution of this enigma; – it was, indeed, in the reign of queen Ann that she married.

I had seen enough of this fine lady, and did not chuse to have my Tablets crowded with any more of her unintelligible jargon, so retired to another part of the room, where I saw three ladies got together, and seemed very earnest in discourse.

But little was I like to be the better for my near approach, for being on the topic of scandal, each was so full, and so highly delighted with the thoughts of it, that all speaking at the same time prevented me from hearing distinctly what was said by any of them; and all I could gather at last was, that a certain lady of their acquaintance had been caught with her footman; and that her husband contented himself with securing his future honour by an Italian safe-guard.[202]

As I had been informed of the particulars of this story before, the foible of the transgressing fair did not so much engross my meditations as the pleasure those of her own sex seemed to take in exposing it, and I could not help saying to myself with the Poet:

There is a lust in man no charm can tame,
Of loudly publishing his neighbour's shame.
On Eagles wings immortal scandals fly,
While virtuous actions are but born, and die.[203]

But this was a place more proper to collect matter for reflection hereafter, than to indulge it at present; so I pass'd on among the gaming-tables, which were eleven in number, and none of them unoccupy'd.

Here it was pleasant enough to observe the various attitudes of those that play'd; and I think there is not a more sure way of judging people's dispositions than to see them at this diversion; – some of those who swept the stakes received the favours fortune bestow'd on them with an ease and calmness, which shewed that they had not been over anxious whether she smiled or frowned; but there were many more, who snatch'd up the glittering metal with a greediness which sufficiently demonstrated that avarice was the chief excitement to what they did.

As for the losers, it gave me an infinite satisfaction to see the unconcerned behaviour of some few among them; – while others again filled me with a no less sensible disquiet at their impatience: – I was ashamed to find a gentleman of rank and fortune forget all politeness, and sometimes even common decency, to those who had his money in their pockets; and sorry in my heart to see a lady bite her lips, wrinkle her forehead with unbecoming frowns, distort every feature, and disfigure all the charms that nature had bestow'd on her, for the loss of what was not worth half that anxiety to preserve. – 'Good Heaven!' said I to myself, 'if this be the effects of gaming, what madness is it to venture one's peace in that uncertain gulph?'

I remember a saying of old Massenger's, which may be applicable enough on this occasion:

The wise will never put in fortune's power,
That which they cannot lose without repining.[204]

The beautiful Ismena was this night among the number of the unfortunates, but not of the impatients; – I stood behind her chair, and saw her empty a well fill'd purse, and take out of it even the last guinea with a smile; – she was, indeed, a young lady lately come to the possession of a very large fortune, and could not want what she had thrown away; but the same might also be said of Clarinda, who play'd at the same table with her, and had also lost a considerable sum to sir Charles Fairlove, with whom these two ladies had been engaged this whole evening at a Poole at Picquet: – but see the difference, the latter of them rose from the table in a fury, – tore her fan, and cry'd,

Clarinda. Curse the cards, – I will play no more this night, – that I am resolved; – at least not with sir Charles.

Ismena. Nay, madam, we have no reason to be angry with sir Charles, for having done by us what we would gladly have done by him; – for my part, tho' he has stripp'd me of all I had about me, I am as good friends with him as ever.

Sir Charles Fairlove. I hope so, madam, otherwise the good-luck I have had at play would prove the greatest misfortune of my life.

Clarinda. The devil's in the cards to-night, I think; – I never lost at Picquet in my life before, – and now I have thrown away, – I cannot justly say how much, – but I'll see.

She then turned to the table, and pour'd out of a purse what was remaining in it, and having counted the sum went on in the same heat as before.

Clarinda. Yes, – by Heaven I thought so! – no less than six and twenty pieces.

Sir Charles Fairlove. I should be sorry, madam, to give you any disquiet on the score of such a trifle; but I can do not more than offer you a chance for regaining all you have lost; – if you please, I will stake the whole against five of yours.

Clarinda. I should lose that too, I suppose.

Ismena. Venture it, however; – if you lose it I'll be your halves, and send you the money to-morrow morning.

Clarinda. Well then I will make one more essay.

With these words she sat down again; – they play'd; she was the winner, and now appear'd as gay and happy as she had lately been discontented; – sir Charles smiled with some disdain at this reverse in her humour, and turning to Ismena, said,

Sir Charles Fairlove. Now, madam, you must take up the winner.

Ismena. She must give me credit then, sir; you both know I have no stake to lay down.

Clarinda. You must excuse me for that, madam, – it may turn my luck; – besides, one has no heart to play when one does not see the money on the table.

Sir Charles Fairlove. Well then, beautiful Ismena, – I will give you credit; – or if you please, will play upon the square, – my honour against yours.

Ismena. With all my heart, sir Charles.

The ill-nature, the ill-manners, and, indeed, the ingratitude of Clarinda, in refusing to give the credit of a stake at cards, to a friend who had just before offer'd to pay half the losses she should sustain in playing with another, made that young lady as disagreeable in my eyes, as the sweetness of disposition and generosity of the sprightly Ismena made her charming to a much greater degree than ever she had appear'd to me before, – all lovely, as it must be confess'd she is; – but to proceed:

Ismena having accepted the challenge of sir Charles, she cut the cards, and tried once more what chance would do for her; – chance was still against her, and sir Charles again the conqueror. – The game being over, she said laughing:

Ismena. Well, – I may now sing Fortune is my foe, – and content myself, for the remainder of this night, with being an humble spectator of other people's diversion, since I am not in a condition to partake of it myself.

Sir Charles Fairlove. It will be your own fault then, madam, if you are; – I believe I have an hundred and some odd pieces about me, which are all at your devotion.

Ismena. I thank you, sir Charles; but I do not chuse to risque so much as that at one sitting: – I do not care, however, if I become your debtor for twenty pieces.

Sir Charles Fairlove. You do me a pleasure, madam, in accepting any part of the offer I made you; – there is the trifle you mention, if you want more I beg you will command it.

Ismena. No, sir, I am determin'd to play no farther than this, – I am much oblig'd to you for the favour, and will return it to-morrow morning.

She then took up the twenty guineas sir Charles had laid down and put them into her purse; but while she was doing so, he reply'd to her last words in this manner:

Sir Charles Fairlove. There is no occasion, madam, for you to give yourself the trouble of sending this trifle to me, – I have business that will bring me into your neighbourhood to-morrow morning, and if you are so good to permit me that honour, will wait on you about twelve.

Ismena. You may depend, sir, on my being at home.

Clarinda, who had not open'd her mouth all this time, no sooner saw her fair friend receive the money than she laid her hand on hers, and with a gay air said to her:

Clarinda. Now, my dear, I am ready for you, if you please, and willing to venture as much with you as you have borrow'd of sir Charles.

To this Ismena reply'd, with more seriousness than she was wont to put on:

Ismena. No, madam, – I have been very unlucky here, and am resolved to change hands; – I see lady Longmore has given out at the Whist table yonder, – I'll go and take her place.

With these words she rose hastily from her seat and did as she had said, without waiting to hear any thing that might be offer'd to detain her by either of those she had been playing with. – Sir Charles Fairlove follow'd her to the other table, and stood behind her chair till he saw her win more than the sum he had lent her.

On the company's breaking up she look'd round the room for sir Charles, in order, as I suppose, to return the money to him; but if she had any such design he had taken care to prevent the execution of it, by leaving the place some little time before she had done playing.

This action of sir Charles, join'd to some amorous glances I had perceived him to regard her with, made me suspect he had some farther view than mere complaisance in what he had done; but as he was generally accounted a man of honour, and she had an unblemish'd character, I suspended my judgment 'till I should see the event of the visit she had promised to receive from him the next morning.

After I had quitted this scene of gay confusion, as mr. Addison elegantly expresses it,[205] and had time to ruminate on the transactions that evening had presented me with, sir Charles Fairlove and Ismena ran very much in my head, but did not so totally engross my attention as to make me negligent to all others: – I had heard several of the assembly say to each other, that miss Allmode was a most beautiful young creature, and would certainly be the reigning toast of the town if not spoil'd by the affectation of her mother; and this distinct description gave me a curiosity both to see the girl, and in what manner her self-sufficient ladyship behaved towards her.

Accordingly I laid down a plan for my progression the next morning, which was this: – to go to lady Allmode's as early as it was reasonable to suppose she and her daughter would be stirring, and from thence pass on to the apartment of Ismena at the time sir Charles Fairlove had appointed to be there; and then, having fully settled this point in my mind, began to remember that the night was very far advanced, and went to bed, as it is probable some of my readers may find it necessary to do at this time.

CHAP. VI.

Contains such things as are not often to be met with, neither in the one nor the other sex; yet are, or at least ought to be, equally interesting to both.

I ROSE the next morning more early than I had been for the most part accustomed to do, in order to prepare for the two visits I intended to make; but in spite of all the expedition I could practice, I found myself obliged to postpone either the one or other 'till another day.

So much time was elapsed, first in transcribing what I had been witness of at lady Playfeild's, and then in getting the dialogues engrav'd on my Tables expunged by the pure fingers of my yet unpolluted virgin, that when all was ready the clock wanted but a very few minutes of striking twelve.

I hesitated not whether I should go to lady Allmode's or to Ismena; for besides being very much prepossess'd in favour of the latter, I did not doubt of meeting with something of more consequence in her interview with sir Charles Fairlove than I could expect to find in any discourse between lady Allmode and her daughter; – I went thither in a lucky time, – sir Charles Fairlove was just stepping out of his chair when I came to the door, – I followed him up stairs, and Ismena received him with a great deal of gaiety, but accompany'd with an equal air of modesty; – as soon as they were seated, she said to him:

Ismena. Your money was very fortunate to me, sir Charles, I did not lose one guinea after I became your borrower.

Sir Charles Fairlove. Madam, I congratulate myself for being so happy to serve you, tho' on so insignificant an occasion; – but should be better pleased to have it in my power to do so in much greater things.

Ismena. I doubt not of your generousity to persons in distress, and if ever I am reduced to the same exigence again, it is likely may have recourse to the same hand for relief; – in the mean time, sir Charles, permit me to return the favour you have already conferr'd upon me.

In speaking this she drew out her purse and counted twenty guineas on the table, which sir Charles took up and put into his pocket with a very careless air; – saying at the same time:

Sir Charles Fairlove. This trifle, madam, is neither worth your returning nor my receiving, nor should I have ever thought on it, if I had not given you credit on an infinitely more valuable account.

Ismena. Credit! – As how, sir Charles?

Sir Charles Fairlove. Yes, madam, – a debt which I am too impatient to wait long for the payment of, and am now come to claim.

Ismena. You rally well, sir Charles; – but as I cannot comprehend the purport, am not prepared to give an answer.

Sir Charles Fairlove. No, i'faith, madam, you will find me extremely serious; – but sure you cannot be so strangely forgetful as not to recollect what you lost to me last night at play?

Ismena. I lost nothing but what I paid, sir Charles.

Sir Charles Fairlove. Nothing, madam?

Ismena. No, upon my honour.

Sir Charles Fairlove. You have named the very thing, – your honour, madam; – when a lady ventures her honour at a gaming-table, and is so unlucky as to lose, she must expect to pay the forfeit.

Ismena. What do you mean, sir Charles?

Sir Charles Fairlove. My meaning needs no explanation, madam; – you lost your honour to me, and I now demand the immediate possession of what I fairly won, and which if you refuse to yield I have a right to seize.

Ismena. Ridiculous.

Sir Charles Fairlove. Madam, the contempt you treat my pretensions with take not away the validity of them; – what was once your honour is now no longer so, but mine, and at my disposal; – and you would not, sure, go about to defraud me of the good that fortune has bestowed upon me?

With these words he threw his arms about her waist, with a freedom which shew'd he indeed look'd upon her as his own: – she seem'd a little alarm'd at this action, and starting some paces from him, endeavoured to repulse the temerity he was guilty of, by saying to him:

Ismena. Forbear; – this fooling is offensive.

Sir Charles Fairlove. Madam, this coyness is trifling; – I am surprised you will oblige me to have recourse to force for what is so much my due, and I should set a higher value upon if chearfully resign'd. – Come, madam, – I think this way leads to your bed-chamber.

He then catch'd hold of her a second time, and made an offer to bear her into another room; – the grasp he had taken of her was not so strenuous, however, but that she easily disengag'd herself; and having done so, cry'd out with a voice and air full of the extremest disdain.

Ismena. 'Till this action I scarce could think you were in earnest: – base, and presuming man, How dare you entertain thoughts so unworthy of me!

Sir Charles Fairlove. How dare you, madam, hazard on the chance of a game at cards what seems so precious to you?

Ismena. Oh, despicable! – to turn that into a matter of seriousness which you well know was only meant in jest.

Sir Charles Fairlove. We men, madam, take all the advantages we can when we play with a fine woman; and you may be assured I shall not easily be prevailed upon to relinquish those I have gain'd over you.

Ismena. The vain idea will little avail your vile purpose.

Sir Charles Fairlove. You may be mistaken, madam; – the laws of Westminster-Hall, indeed, will scarcely take any cognizance of an affair of this nature; – but those laws by which the polite world are chiefly govern'd, I mean the laws of gaming, will infallibly give it on my side; that pride of your's will be a good deal humbled when you see your stake of honour become the public jest, and all that has pass'd between us the subject of a news-paper.

Ismena. I am confounded! – you cannot certainly be the monster you appear!

Sir Charles Fairlove. I would not wish you, madam, to put me to the proof.

Ismena. Oh, Heavens! – to what has one unguarded word exposed me!

She could not utter this exclamation without letting fall some tears, which I perceived had a great effect on sir Charles, by the change it occasioned in his countenance; – he affected, however, to take no notice of it, and resuming his former boldness went on:

Sir Charles Fairlove. You see, madam, how it is; – you are intirely in my power, and if I cannot have my agreement, I will have my revenge, or at least an equivalent for both.

Ismena. What equivalent! – say, – tell me at once!

Sir Charles Fairlove. You must redeem your forfeit honour by a sum of money.

Ismena. Name it then.

Sir Charles Fairlove. Let me consider, madam, – a woman's honour, as times now are, and beauty renders itself so cheap, will bear but a low price at the market; but as you are well-born, – well accomplish'd, – are extremely handsome, and have more perfections, both of mind and body, than most of your sex can boast of, – I think five hundred pounds is the least I can demand.

Ismena. You shall have it, sir.

With this she ran hastily to a little cabinet that stood in the room, and having taken from thence what she wanted, turn'd again to the table, saying,

Ismena. Those two Bank-bills, sir, contain the sum you mention, – take them, I beseech you, and ease me of your presence.

Sir Charles Fairlove. I must first examine, madam, if they are genuine: – yes they are right; – and now, methinks, 'tis pity to rob you of so much money, – five hundred pounds will purchase five hundred pretty trinkets, and I cannot receive it without feeling some concern.

Ismena. Oh, sir Charles, you need be under no concern on that score; – were it five times the sum, nay my whole fortune, I would gladly give it to be rid for ever both of you and your impudent demand.

Sir Charles Fairlove. Yet, in spite of all this severity, I shall willingly restore these bills on one condition.

Ismena. Sir, I shall make no conditions with you; – therefore be gone and leave me.

Sir Charles Fairlove. Not till you have heard me, madam; – the condition I would stipulate is only this, – that you will make a solemn promise never to play again, except for mere diversion, with some select friends who you are certain will take no ungenerous advantage of you.

Ismena. There is little occasion for me to bind myself by a promise to avoid a thing which I have already proved so mischievous; – the insults I have received from you will make me henceforth detest the sight of cards, and fly the society of all who pursue that dangerous amusement.

Sir Charles Fairlove. It is enough; – my ends are fully answered; and thus, on my knees let me restore your bills, and with them a heart which long has been devoted to you, and never harbour'd a wish to your dishonour.

Never had I known greater anxiety for any thing not relating to myself, or my particular friends, than I did for the issue of this conversation; – I had been extremely scandalized at some part of sir Charles's behaviour; yet, by many indications, could not set him down in my mind for the mercenary villain he affected to be, and was now as much rejoiced to see a likelihood of not having been deceived in my conjectures in his favour, as the reader will presently be convinced.

Ismena, being too much amazed at this sudden turn to make an immediate reply, he went on thus, – still kneeling:

Sir Charles Fairlove. Oh, Ismena; forgive the seeming brutality I have been guilty of; – I counterfeited the libertine, the villain, only to shew you there was a possibility for you to have met with such a one in reality; and assum'd the most odious character, in order to render your's more truly adorable: – the tender passion you inspir'd me with has made me keep a watchful eye over all your actions; – I found you perfect in every thing except a too great readiness to follow the example of others in the destructive love of play; – I know the dangers to which your sex are exposed by it, and that there were many snares spread for your innocence in particular; by this means even last night some there were in company who wanted but the same opportunity I had to behave as I have done, though with far different views. – Oh! pardon, therefore, the only stratagem I could think of to clear your mind of a propensity which might in time have sullied all its brightness.

Ismena. Rise, sir Charles; – the diversity, I might say, indeed, the perplexity of my thoughts hinder'd me, till now, from observing the posture you were in; – pray be seated, sir. – If I may give credit to your words, I am infinitely oblig'd to you for the care you took of my reputation, when you saw it so totally neglected by myself.

Sir Charles Fairlove. No, madam, say not so, – I dare believe you never have fail'd in a due regard for reputation, and am certain that the breath of slander has never presum'd to blast it; and I could not mean to reproach you for any thing that has been, but to warn you against what might be; – an immoderate inclination for gaming in your sex, I take to be the same as an immoderate inclination to drinking is in ours, both are equally intoxicating and destructive to right reason; they make the brain grow giddy, incapable of reflection, or any other pursuit than the darling folly, and they run headlong on, invelop'd in a mist of errors, where fortune, fame, and peace of mind are sometimes irrecoverably lost.

Ismena. Oh, sir Charles, you have open'd my eyes to see that black abyss into which my inadvertency might one day have plunged me.

Sir Charles Fairlove. I know very well, madam, that you wanted only to be reminded of the danger to enable you to avoid it; – the manner in which I have done so may have, perhaps, appear'd too presuming; but I fear'd more gentle methods might not have had the effect.

Ismena. Make no apologies, sir Charles, – I am now convinced you meant me well, and I thank you for it.

Sir Charles Fairlove. If you accept it as a proof of friendship, it may in time engage you to believe that a sincere and tender friendship in a person of my sex to one of yours deserves a softer name, and call it love.

Ismena. We will not cavil about names, but must acknowledge, sir Charles, by what motive soever you have been actuated, the benefit is mine.

Sir Charles Fairlove. How bless'd am I in this confession! – But, charming Ismena, may I not be permitted to wait on you sometimes, and have leave to hope the services I shall hereafter pay you will not be rejected?

Ismena. I flatter myself with being able to regulate my future conduct so as not to give you occasion to offer any of that frightful sort you have done this morning; and if I should relapse into my former errors, could neither expect nor deserve you should take the same trouble for my reformation; – therefore, I think, may safely venture to admit your visits.

She spoke these words with so obliging a smile, that sir Charles could not forbear testifying the transport he was in by imprinting several passionate kisses on one of her hands, after which, looking on her with an equal mixture of tenderness and respect, he said,

Sir Charles Fairlove. Incomparable Ismena! how impossible is it for me to express either what you deserve, or what I feel in a full sensibility of your perfections?

Ismena. I desire you will not go about to express either the one or the other; – the only merit I can boast of is in being so early convinced of my fault, and that I am so is wholly owing to yourself; – for I confess to you, sir Charles, that though it is but lately I have begun to like play at all, yet by conversing with those who seem to have no other way of passing their time, it grew by very swift degrees more pleasing to me; and I believe that it would, in time, have become so habitual to me, that I should have expected the hour of sitting down to cards as naturally as that of sitting down to dinner; – but in the mirror you have presented to me, I now see that to indulge this amusement to an excess, is not only a folly below the dignity of a thinking mind, but also a kind of Scylla or Caribdes,[206] formed by ourselves in the ocean of life, as if on purpose to wreck our fortunes, honour, reputation, and every thing that is dear.

Sir Charles Fairlove. Oh, madam! every word you speak on this occasion thrills me to the very soul; – I am charm'd, – I am ravish'd to find in a person of your sex and years such solid reason. – such an amazing quickness of apprehension.

Ismena. You are relapsing into the panegyric strain; but I will hear no more of it: – you must give me leave to play the Monitor in my turn, – I have been your convert, and you must now be mine; – remember, sir Charles, that to listen to the tongue of flattery is no less pernicious than the folly you have taught me to be asham'd of.

Sir Charles Fairlove. I grant it is, madam; but the just praises of a real virtue cannot cause a blush either in the face of the giver or the receiver.

Ismena. Well, I find you will have the better of the argument, whether the tenet you take upon you to maintain be right or wrong; – therefore to put an end to it, What think you of a turn or two in the Mall this morning?

Sir Charles Fairlove. Madam, I shall be happy to attend you any where.

She then call'd for her capuchin, and little muff, which being immediately brought, sir Charles gave her his hand to to lead her down stairs, and I retired to my apartment.

I had met with nothing a great while that gave me a more sensible satisfaction than to find a lady such as Ismena, in all the pride of blooming youth, beautiful, gay, and surrounded with a crowd of flatterers, bear with so much chearfulness the conviction of her error, and testify so much gratitude to the person to whom she was indebted for her reformation.

The rough method he had taken for this purpose, was so far from raising any resentment in her, after once knowing the motive, that she look'd upon him as her best friend, esteem'd and loved him for it; – conscious that it required no less than such a proceeding to rouse her from that thoughtlessness which alone had made her fall into an error, the danger of which she might otherwise have too late perceived.

I thought that I discovered something in these two accomplish'd persons, that seem'd to me as if Heaven had form'd and ordain'd them for each other, and I soon found that I had not been mistaken; – they are now married with the highest approbation of all the friends and kindred on both sides; and in the opinion of as many as have the pleasure of their acquaintance, bid fair to be one of the most happy pairs that ever enter'd into Hymen's bands.

CHAP. VII.

The Author has been in some debate within himself, whether he should insert
or not, as he is conscious it will be little relish'd by the fashionable genteel
part of his readers; – and what is still worse, can afford neither much enter-
tainment, nor much improvement to the others.

THERE is something very unaccountable in an over-curious disposition; – it makes us eager, impatient, anxious, indefatigable, in prying into things which promise us not the least pleasure in the discovery of when known; – a reader who has not this propensity in his nature, will doubtless think, by what I said of lady Allmode in the fifth Chapter of this Book, that I had already seen enough of her behaviour to keep me from being desirous of seeing more; but this is judging according to the rules of right reason; whereas a person who neglects his own affairs, to find out the secrets of others with whom he has no concern, cannot be supposed to have any.

But as every one is willing to find some excuse or other, even for the silliest things he can be guilty of; and according to the vulgar phrase, put pillows under his elbows;[207] so I thought that in being a spectator of lady Allmode's conduct in her own family, and the manner in which she train'd up her daughter, something might present itself to me that would more than compensate for the time I should expend in going to her house.

How far the public may be of my opinion in this point must be left to the determination of hereafter; for the humour of the present age is so fluctuating and uncertain, that it is an utter impossibility to foresee either what will please or what offend, – as a poet of many centuries ago expresses himself on a parallel occasion:

> – Inconstant still and various,
> There's no to-morrow in us like today;
> This hour we are cloudy, sullen and severe;
> The next, with madding mirth disturb the air.[208]

But all this is foreign to the purpose, and therefore impertinent; – it is enough to say that I went, without repeating the motive that induced me to it; – I shall therefore add no more, but proceed to the success of my visit.

I gain'd an easy access, the door happening to be open just as I reach'd it, to let out a footman in a gay livery, who had come to deliver some message; but was a good deal bewilder'd on my entrance, as I had never been in the house before, and was intirely unacquainted with the situation of any of the rooms; – I judged, however, that as it was morning, her ladyship would probably be above stairs; – on my coming to the top of the stair-case I was as much at a loss as before; – I perceived there were several rooms, but the doors of them all were shut, and I durst not touch the lock of any one of them for fear I should be heard by those who might chance to be within.

The measure of time is always doubled when we wait for an event with impatience; – I remain'd not long, however, in this dilemma, – a servant came running hastily up the back stairs at the farther end of the gallery, with some drinking glasses on a silver waiter in his hand, – I follow'd him into a room where a woman, who by her appearance I guess'd was her ladyship's Abigail,[209] received from him what he had brought, and carried it into an inner-chamber, the door of which she shut after her, but not so suddenly as to prevent my entering with her.

Here I found lady Allmode; but had she appear'd to me in any other place, should never have known her for the same I had seen at lady Playfeild's route, – so vast a difference is it in the power of art sometimes to make.

At the time of my coming in she was under the operation of having her eye-brows shaped with a small pair of pincers, by one of those persons who go by the name of Tyre-women; but, in my opinion, ought rather to be call'd face-menders, since their business is not so much to ornament the head as to rectify the defects of the features: – the important work being over, lady Allmode turn'd to a magnifier that stood upon her toylet, to see if all was right, and having look'd into it, cried out hastily:

Lady Allmode. Oh, mrs. Prim, – sure your eyes are in eclipse to day! – you have left no less than three exuberant hairs on my right brow, and I think arch'd it somewhat higher than the other.

Mrs. Prim. I beg a thousand pardons of your ladyship, but I will presently remedy that error.

Lady Allmode. Do so.

On this the artist employ'd her little instrument for a second essay, – after which lady Allmode look'd in the glass again and said,

Lady Allmode. It is very well now; – but I look wretchedly to day, – and it is no wonder; – What do you think, mrs. Prim, – that careless oaf there put me to bed last night without my Sperma-Ceti mask.[210]

Mrs. Prim. That was a great omission, indeed, madam; – but your ladyship must forgive it, mrs. Pinup does not use to neglect these things.

Pinup. I am very sorry for it, mrs. Prim; – but it was so late when her ladyship went to bed; – and her ladyship was so sleepy.

Lady Allmode. And your foolship was so sleepy too, I suppose. – But that is not all, mrs. Prim, – the creature threw it into some corner or other where Veni got at it, and this morning it was found half devour'd.

Pinup. Your ladyship knows I have almost cried my eyes out about it, – and that I offer'd to bespeak another, and pay for it out of my own pocket.

Lady Allmode. Pay for it, ideot. – But tell me, creature, what attonement can'st thou ever make for these depredations on my countenance? – Here I shall lose a whole day; for 'tis impossible I can think of appearing in public; and do'st thou consider, wench, that a day wasted in private is an age in the life of a woman of quality?

Mrs. Prim. 'Tis very true, madam; – but I dare answer for mrs. Pinup, that she will never be guilty of the like fault again; therefore I beg your ladyship will forgive her.

Lady Allmode. Yes, yes, – I have forgiven her, – and I do forgive her; but she must expect to be told of it sometimes: – if she had lived with some ladies they would have turned her out of doors that instant; – *mais toujours les douceurs du coeur* lay an embargo on my indignation.

Pinup. Your ladyship is all goodness.

Mrs. Prim. There are few such ladies.

Pinup. No, indeed; – and I could tear myself to pieces for having, thro' negligence, offended so sweet a lady.

Lady Allmode. Well, well, – say no more about it; – I am sorry I struck you in the heat of my resentment; – but take the Dresden suit[211] I had on yesterday, and let me see you in it on Sunday.

Pinup. I humbly thank your ladyship.

Lady Allmode. Say no more of it. – Oh, *mon Dieu!* I begin to feel the effects of my disconcertion; – every membrane throughout my whole frame has a pulsation in it; – give me something to take this instant, or I shall faint.

Pinup. I have it ready, madam. – I suppose your ladyship chuses brandy?

Lady Allmode. Aye; – I think brandy is the best composure of the animal faculties: – a little more; – still nearer to the top of the glass; – hold, 'tis very well, I do not love it running over. – Now fill for mrs. Prim. – Pray drink, mrs. Prim, – 'tis right Coniac, I assure you.

Mrs. Prim. I know your ladyship has the best of every thing: – your ladyship's good health.

Lady Allmode. I thank you, mrs. Prim. – But as to the Sperma-Ceti mask, is it not possible for you to get one ready for me before I sleep, – else my face will be a perfect nutmeg-grater by to-morrow morning?

Mrs. Prim. Oh, your ladyship need be under no apprehensions on that score, – I always keep several of these commodities prepar'd, – they want only sprinkling with a little Orange-flower water, to take off the scent; – I will send your ladyship one this afternoon. – But is not your ladyship out of Pearl-powder,[212] you had but one ounce last week?

Lady Allmode. No, nor I do not think of having any more, – it leaves a certain roughness on the skin which is disagreeable; – I will use nothing but Italian pots for the future; – the paste incorporates itself, as it were, with the flesh, and gives a kind of sattiny delicacy to it; – let me have two pots.

Mrs. Prim. Yes, madam. – Has your ladyship any farther commands?

Lady Allmode. Yes, you may send me a box of red for my cheeks; – but do not let it be quite so high-colour'd as the last.

Mrs. Prim. I shall take care to mix it so as to please your ladyship.

In speaking this she was preparing to make her exit with abundance of low curtsies; but lady Allmode would not suffer her to depart without taking another dram.

Lady Allmode. Stay, mrs. Prim, – I must give you a taste of some of my Italian cordials; – I had a fresh chest came in yesterday, with twelve bottles all of different sorts; – Will you have the Rosasoli, [213] La Bergamotta, La Floretta, or La Citroni?

Mrs. Prim. Alack, madam, these rich things come so seldom in my way that I am no judge of them; – but since your ladyship is so good, I shall take a little of any one of them.

Lady Allmode. Fetch La Floretta, Pinup. – You must know, mrs. Prim, that this is a quintessence extracted from the most fragrant flowers the garden of the world affords.

Mrs. Prim. 'Tis extremely fine, indeed, madam; – I never tasted any thing like it.

The good woman was so charm'd with the flavour of this exotic liquor, that to prolong it as much as she could, she sipp'd it like a hot dish of Tea; – lady Allmode perceiving her so delighted, might probably have been induced to give her another glass, if word had not been brought that mr Ruben the Jew was come to wait upon her ladyship, on which the bottles and glasses were hurry'd away, and mrs. Prim took her leave.

The Jew was presently introduced, and received by lady Allmode with the utmost courtesy and affability, and after making him be seated she said to him:

Lady Allmode. You are a great stranger, mr. Ruben; – I have not seen you this long time, and was quite impatient to congratulate you, and the whole Hebrew nation, on the late act pass'd in your favour.

Ruben. Me do most humly dank your ladyship; – we did, indeed, obtain it wid mush greater facility dan we expected, in spite of all de fine promise had been a long time ago.

Lady Allmode. I assure you, mr. Ruben, that I was perfectly transported when I found the bill had pass'd both houses. – I dare say his Grace was very serviceable to you on this occasion.

Ruben. Yes, madam, we are mush obliged to his Grace, as well as to an honourable gentleman in de lower house; but our acknowledgments are chiefly to de good Lord B—ps.[214]

Lady Allmode. True, mr. Ruben; for if they had made any opposition to it, or, at least, any worth mentioning, the rabble would presently have taken it into their heads that their religion was in danger, and made as great a clamour against Judaism as in a former reign they did against Popery.

Ruben, We do not care what dese Skellams[215] tink; – if dey offer to affront us, we fall know how to be revenged: – we have de same law, de same priveledge, as demselves.

Lady Allmode. The vulgar are not to be regarded; – they are no more than moving clods of earth; – but you must own, mr. Ruben, that for the honour of the English nation, the nobility and gentry, those of taste I mean, are intirely on your side.

Ruben. Some of dem have been our good friends indeed; and it is vary true that we have received more favours from de English dan from any nation in de world: – in all de Popish countries, and, indeed, in most of de Protestants one too, ve have been driven from deir cities, and scatter'd like chaff before de vind, – treated as vagrants, and made to vear upon our heads or on our coats, some badge or oder of infamy and contempt; but by dis hospitable act of de Legislature, ve sall be gather'd together like sheep into one fold, and have de liberty to settle and multiply in dis land of plenty.

Lady Allmode. I hope, mr. Ruben, it will prove a second Canaan to you. – But pray what new curiosities does your warehouse afford?

Ruben. It was dat I did come to tell your ladyship; – me have de fine German work for de head-dress, de ruffle and de tippit[216] for de ladies, far exceeding de Dresden; – me have de curious littel pictures for de closet, from Italy, and hand-kerchiefs dat will not lose deir scent with vashing; – den me have some pieces of rich embroidery from Lyons, and gloves from Marseilles; – snuff of de right Batavian[217] manufacture; – Japonees under petticoates, – and oder tings, just imported from all parts of de world.

Lady Allmode. Well, – you Jews are certainly the most charming people upon earth, – you deal in every thing, – Who can deny that you are useful members of a common-wealth? – I will come in a day or two to your warehouse, and rid you of some part of your cargo.

Ruben. Me sall be proud to see your ladyship; – but me must now take my leave, – me am obliged to wait on lady Fantasye, – she did send to speak vid me dis morning.

Lady Allmode. Oh, then I will not detain you; I know her ladyship is a good customer.

Ruben. Pretty well, madam; – she pay me, tho' she do no body else. – Your ladyship's most obedient servant.

Lady Allmode. Your's, mr. Ruben. – Pinup, wait on mr. Ruben down stairs.

The entertainment I had hitherto met with at this lady's had seem'd so insipid to me, that I was in the mind to quit her apartment when mr. Ruben did, and accordingly follow'd him and Pinup out of the room; – but the girl had no sooner shut the chamber door behind her than the goatish Jew turn'd upon her, and before she was aware, catch'd her in his arms and half smother'd her with kisses; – she struggled with all her might, and having broke from him, rubb'd her mouth with her apron, – spit and cry'd,

Pinup. I wonder at your impudence, mr. Ruben, – do you think I would be pull'd and haul'd about by a Jew?

Ruben. Hush, – don't be so angry, mrs. Pinup, – I will give you one pretty ting.

Pinup. Hang your pretty things, and yourself too, – get down stairs, or I will call to some body to shew you out; – the Devil shall wait on you for me.

The Jew said no more, but ran so hastily down stairs, that as Pinup was between us, and the passage we were in very narrow, it was impossible for me to slip by, without being felt either by the one or the other.

Pinup was returning to her lady's chamber, but met her just coming out in order to pass into another room, on seeing her she said to her:

Lady Allmode. I think this girl takes a long time in dressing, – go and see if she is ready, and bid her come to me.

Finding now that there was some probability of my seeing the young lady, which had been, indeed, the chief motive of my going thither, I attended lady Allmode where she went, and placed myself in one corner of the room; where I did not wait above three or four minutes before Pinup, who had gone immediately on her errand, return'd leading miss Allmode.

She seemed to be about thirteen or fourteen years of age; – her face was extremely pretty, and I believe nature had given her a shape no less excellent, if it had not been deform'd by her taylor and mantua-maker;[218] – I need not describe in what manner, since it is enough to say, that every thing about her was in the extremity of the present fashion.

On her approach lady Allmode took her by the arm, – turn'd her round several times, and examined her whole dress from head to foot; – after which, looking very well pleased, she said:

Lady Allmode. Ay, miss, now you look like what you are; – I protest, I scarce knew you for my own child, in the obsolete condition you came from the country. – Are you not highly delighted with yourself?

Miss Allmode. No, indeed, madam, – I think that since 'tis the fashion to have one's cloaths made in this manner, there ought to be as many chimnies in a room as there are chairs.

Lady Allmode. Sure, miss, you are not cold?

Miss Allmode. It would be very strange, madam, if I were not, when my stays are so contrived that the air comes down to the very bottom of my back, and below the pit of my stomach, and my petticoats so short that I am every minute fancying I have tuck'd them up in order to have my legs and feet wash'd; – then as to my ears, I do declare I feel the wind blow from the one to the other, and pierces into my very brain.

Lady Allmode. Oh fye, miss; – this being in the country has spoiled you: – whatever is the fashion is never either too cold or too hot.

Miss Allmode. I must beg your ladyship's pardon; for I am certain this fashion is a great deal too much of both; – the tightness of my sleeves, the load of flounces at my elbows, and the huge semi-circles, as heavy as panniers, hanging on each hip, make some parts of me sweat while all the rest are freezing.

Lady Allmode. Oh hideous! – frightful! – sweat! – what a word is there from the mouth of a fine young lady! – Whenever you have any occasion to complain of too much warmth, you should always say – I perspire: – but I am surprised you should not be charm'd with so becoming a dress.

Miss Allmode. I feel uneasy, and quite uncomfortable, madam.

Lady Allmode. A little use will reconcile you to it. – Without vanity, miss, you are exceeding handsome; – and now I have made you fit to appear in public, the praises that will be given you, and the fine things said on your beauty, will raise such a gaiety *du coeur,* as will make you forget all that you call uncomfortable.

Miss Allmode. I should be glad, madam, if any thing would do that.

Lady Allmode. You must learn to know yourself, miss; – look in the glass; – you have fine eyes, – a very lovely mouth, – a well-turn'd face, – a delicate complexion, good hair: – in fine, you are a complete beauty; – but what is beauty without the possessor understands how to manage it to advantage; – a milk-maid may be a beauty, and no one take any notice of her; – you must practice the art of displaying every charm, and rendering yourself conspicuous.

Miss Allmode. Indeed, madam, I am quite ignorant of these things.

Lady Allmode. I perceive you are, miss; – but that is not your fault; – my formal aunt has never given you any instructions in this point, I suppose; – a few lessons, however, will soon put you in the way to make the most of what nature has bestow'd upon you: – In the first place, miss, you must be sure to thrust out your chin as far as you are able; – when you come into a room always let your chin be the first thing seen of you, – as it were the harbinger of the rest of your person. – Secondly, you must never keep your two hands together, in that stiff country manner you now do, for above the space of a moment; but throw sometimes the one and sometimes the other carelessly back, and lean it on your hip; but when you are speaking, be sure to employ both in gestures that may enforce attention to what you say. – Then, as for your eyes, miss, – you must always keep them broad open, and be sure to have the last look of every one that takes notice of you.

Miss Allmode. Does your ladyship mean the men as well as the women?

Lady Allmode. Undoubtedly, – the men to choose; – a polite woman, and who is fashionably genteel, is never asham'd of any thing she either sees or hears.

Her ladyship was going on with some farther directions concerning the management of the eyes, when she was interrupted by a footman, who came to acquaint her that a person who call'd himself monsieur Le Petit Solee had brought her ladyship a dozen pair of French shoes, – on which she cry'd out in a kind of transport:

Lady Allmode. Oh bring him up! bring him up this minute! – I have been involved in the utmost distress; – I have had nothing but odious English shoes upon my feet for a whole week past.

As I was now heartily weary of my situation, and had no curiosity to see either monsieur Le Petit Solee or his French shoes, I took the opportunity of the door being open, and left this scene of folly and affectation, regretting the time I had thrown away in being there.

CHAP. VIII.

Wherein the wonderful power of beauty, when accompany'd with virtue, is displayd in a very remarkable, as well as affecting occurrence.

VANITY, tho' placed rather among the number of the follies than the vices of human nature, is yet sometimes productive of the very worst we can be guilty of; and the least mischief it does, when indulged to an excess, is to render the person possess'd of it obstinate, proud, impatient of contradiction, deaf to reproof, full of imaginary merit, and apt to despise what is truly so in another.

This weakness, to give it no worse a name, is generally ascribed to the softer sex, who being from their very childhood accustom'd to flattery and praise, are too ready to believe they are in reality the angels and goddesses that they are told they are; but in my opinion it is doing great injustice to the ladies to say they are the only culpable, since we often find men who, without having the same excuse, are no less liable to fall into the same error.

Mutantius is one of the most lovely, most graceful, and most accomplish'd gentlemen of the present age; – he has learning, wit, honour, generosity, and good-nature: – in fine, – he is, both in person and mind, such as might give him a just title to universal admiration, were he but a little less conscious of deserving it, or did not set too high a value upon it.

To render his fine qualities yet more conspicuous, he had the advantages of being descended from a very ancient family, is in possession of an ample fortune both in land and money; – he had not long been arrived at what is commonly called the age of maturity, before several considerable matches were proposed to him; – all the men of his acquaintance, who had sisters or daughters to be disposed of, courted his alliance: – whenever he appear'd, the ladies put on their best looks to engage him; and not a few there were, who could not help betraying by their eyes the secret languishment of their hearts.

Having his choice of so many, was probably the cause that for a long time hinder'd him from attaching himself to any particular object; – he was polite and gallant to all, but made a serious address to none; he would pay his morning devoirs to one, walk in the Mall with another, perhaps dine with a third, drink tea with a fourth, attend a fifth to the play, or some other public entertainment: – in a word, he divided his respects so equally to each, that no one of the fair rivals had much reason either to exult on the power of her own charms, or dread those of her competitors.

The little deity of soft desires would not, however, suffer a man so form'd for love to remain always among the number of the insensibles; – every glance shot from Aristella's eyes was a dart that reach'd his very soul; – all the different graces he had seen in other beauties seem'd now to him to be summ'd up in her, and the passion she had inspir'd him with, made him think her, as the song says,

Fairest where thousands are fair.[219]

Aristella was, indeed, very lovely, and had been well educated; but her father, by gaming and other extravagancies, had reduced his estate to so low an ebb, that when divided between four daughters, which he left behind him at his decease, the income was scarce sufficient to buy them cloaths according to their birth; – two of them, however, were married to tradesmen of good repute in the city, and a third to a gentleman of a small estate in the country; – Aristella, who was the youngest, and the only one unprovided for, lived sometimes with one and sometimes with another of her sisters, and by this means, having few expences besides her dress, was enabled to appear in as genteel a manner as any woman of a moderate fortune could do.

It was at the house of one of her brother-in-law's, who was a linnen-draper, and served Mutantius with Hollands[220] and Cambricks, that she first beheld him; – happening to call there when the master of the shop was abroad, he was desired to walk into the parlour till his return; – Aristella was at work with her sister when he came in; but the latter knowing he was a good customer, threw aside what she was about and received him with a great deal of politeness; – her husband not coming home so soon as he was expected, she made tea, and afterwards order'd wine to be brought.

Mutantius readily accepted the little regale[221] she presented to him, as it gave him the opportunity of feasting his eyes on the charms of her fair sister: – on their entering into conversation the tongue of Aristella lost her nothing of what her eyes had gain'd; and as her beauty had in an instant captivated his heart, so her wit rivetted the chain, and made the conquest sure.

The tradesman at last returning, Mutantius, after having agreed for some things he wanted in the shop, and order'd them to be sent home, took an unwilling leave; but carry'd with him an idea which had afterwards more influence over his mind and actions than he at first imagined.

Love in its beginnings, plays wantonly about the heart, tickling it with flattering images; but having once got full possession there, rules with tyrannic sway, and bears down all before it: – Mutantius indulged the pleasing contemplation of Aristella's beauty 'till he was no longer able to live without seeing her, and for this purpose went again to the linnen-draper's, pretending there were some things he had forgot to bespeak when he was there before.

After having bought those things which the seeming want of had given him an excuse for going thither so soon again, and some previous discourse on ordinary matters, he told the draper that he should be glad to have his wife's advice concerning the trimming of some shirts which were then making for him; – to this the other reply'd, that his wife would think herself honour'd in doing him any service; but that she was at that time unfortunately abroad.

Mutantius was not sorry to hear she was out of the way, and resum'd briskly, – 'Well then, I think it will be equal to me if the young lady who was with her when I had the pleasure of drinking tea here, will do me that favour; – she seem'd, I thought, to have good-nature enough to grant such a request.'

'You mean my sister, sir,' cry'd the draper. – 'I think your wife call'd her so,' answered Mutantius. – 'Yes, sir,' – rejoin'd the former; 'but she is gone down to Kent this morning.' – 'I thought she had lived with you,' said Mutantius. – 'Not constantly, sir,' reply'd he; 'but she has left us now sooner than she would have done, on account of her sister's lying-in.'

It was easy for a man of so much wit, and of so much design as Mutantius now had in his head, to get from the honest unsuspecting draper all he wanted to be inform'd of in relation to the circumstances of Aristella.

As the inclinations of this gentleman, vehemently amorous as they were, had not at present the least tendency to marriage with the young beauty, concerning whose affairs he had been so inquisitive, he was far from being mortified on hearing she had no fortune, and was in a manner dependant on her kindred; nor thought it less conducive to the interest of his passion that she was removed into the country, where he imagined he might find a more easy method of winning her to his desires, than he could have done in town, under the eye of a sister, who, by the little he had seen of her, he perceived to be a woman of great discretion.

He lost no time, but the very next day, attended by one servant, who he knew to be an adroit fellow, posted down to Canterbury, within a quarter of a mile of which city was the house where Aristella at present resided.

Having no acquaintance in that part of the country, he took up his lodging in one of the best Inns, where pretending that it was mere curiosity to see that ancient city, and the fine tombs in the Cathedral, that had brought him thither, several of the neighbouring gentry, as well as townsmen, assured him they should be proud of the honour of accompanying him to all those places which most deserved the attention of a traveller.

Among the number of these hospitable persons, was the brother-in-law of Aristella: – it is easy to suppose that Mutantius made use of all the arts he was master of to insinuate himself into the good graces of a person whose acquaintance was so necessary to his design; and indeed, had not this accident happened, there seemed little probability of his accomplishing them; for Aristella kept so close in the house with her sister, that tho' he had been four days at Canterbury, and taken all imaginable pains to get a glimpse of her, he never yet had been so happy.

Mutantius had something in him no less engaging to the men than enchanting to the women; – he knows how to suit himself to the humour of every one he converses with; – it was therefore not difficult for him to cultivate a friendship with a plain country gentleman, who, free from all guile, was equally free from all distrust.

Beechly, for so he was call'd, had no other fault than loving his bottle a little too well, which Mutantius perceiving, fell in with this foible, and thereby gained his whole heart, – as I remember to have read in a very old treatise, entitled, De Arte Mundi:

> Who would the favour of a patron win,
> With flattering his vices must begin.[222]

Or, as another Author of a more modern date tells us:

> Whate'er we do, we would have others do;
> Proud to be teachers and examples too.[223]

But I beg pardon of my reader for detaining his attention with useless quotations to prove what every one is sufficiently convinced of within himself; and shall now proceed with the thread of my narrative.

These two gentlemen were drinking together very late, – Mutantius had ply'd the other so fast with glasses, that he became more than ordinarily intoxicated; – our lover obliged him to suffer himself to be attended home by his footman, and the next morning sent a polite message to enquire of his health; – Beechly took this so kindly, that he came immediately after to the lodgings of Mutantius, to shew that he was well, and to desire he would do him the honour of dining with him that day.

'My wife,' said he, 'is in the straw;[224] but she has a sister who is at present with us, – a good smart well-behaved girl, and will receive you in the best manner she is able.'

It is not to be doubted but that the heart of Mutantius flutter'd with the most rapturous sensation, on hearing himself invited to come to a place where he was sure of enjoying the company of that fair creature he so much languish'd to behold, and had taken so much pains to pursue.

It is needless to say that he readily accepted so obliging a summons, nor that he rather anticipated than prolong'd the appointed hour of complying with it; – he was met by Beechly at the gate with all imaginable demonstrations of a sincere welcome, and conducted into the parlour, where Aristella, who soon after enter'd, was presented to him.

Whatever emotions Mutantius might feel in approaching to salute her, they were yet inferior to her's in the first surprise of seeing him there; – she had heard her brother Beechly talk of a fine gentleman lately come to Canterbury, and had that morning received orders from him to prepare a handsome dinner for his entertainment; but as she had not heard him mention the name of this new friend, and had no curiosity to ask any thing concerning him, could little expect he was the same she had seen at her other sister's in London.

She had, it seems, from the first interview with him, been possess'd of sentiments in his favour, which, if not altogether so passionate as those she inspired him with, were yet no less soft and tender; but conscious of the vast disparity between their fortunes, she had endeavour'd to check the growth of an inclination, which she thought could only be destructive of her peace, and if ever discover'd, render her ridiculous to the world.

But on this second, and unexpected meeting him again, the stifled wishes of her soul burst out afresh, – a sudden flow of joy rush'd o'er her heart, which, join'd to the surprise she was in, spread a kind of wild, tho' agreeable confusion in her eyes and voice, while she made him those compliments which civility exacted from her to a stranger.

Mutantius, to whose penetrating eyes the change in her countenance was very visible, look'd on it as a happy presage of the success of his design; and the secret pleasure this imagination gave him brighten'd all his air, and added new graces to every thing he said or did, so that poor Aristella became now quite lost in love and admiration.

This day proved, indeed, extremely fortunate to Mutantius; – dinner was no sooner over than Beechly was call'd out to a person who waited to speak with him on some business in another room; – the lover took this opportunity of declaring his passion to his mistress, and relating to her the pains he had taken to get a sight of her; and the answers she made, tho' very modest and discreet, were such as gave him no reason to despair.

Beechly returning broke off their conversation, – he took Mutantius to shew him his gardens, which, tho' not ornamented with statues nor any exotic curiosities, were very pleasant and large; – Mutantius was lavish in his praises on every thing he saw; but above all, his fancy seem'd taken with a long grass walk, and a close arbour at the end of it; – 'If I had such a walk as this in town,' said he, 'I should never trouble the Mall, Vaux-Hall, nor Ranelagh.'

'Since you cannot carry this with you,' reply'd Beechly, 'you shall be extremely welcome to make as much use of it as you think fit while you stay in this part of the world.'

Mutantius thank'd him; but said he was an early riser, and should chuse such a walk chiefly for the sake of meditation in a morning, and that to come at such hours might give too much trouble to the servants.

'I can easily remedy that difficulty, since you make it one,' answer'd the other; 'there is a door that opens behind the arbour into a little field where I keep a cow; – I seldom have occasion to make use of the key, and it is at your service, – so you may come in as early or as late as you please, without disturbing any of my family, or being disturbed by them.'

The lover made a thousand acknowledgments to him for this favour, and received the key, which, in his mind, he look'd upon as a sure passport to all the happiness he wish'd at present to enjoy.

He went the very next morning, taking a book in his hand, to prevent suspicion in case he should be seen, tho' there was no great danger of that, as Beechly kept but two maids and one man servant, who, it might be supposed, had too much business in a morning to ramble in the gardens; but he might reasonably hope to meet with Aristella, who having nothing to employ her time, might probably amuse some part of it in that agreeable place.

It is likely, however, he might have been disappointed for many days together, if fortune had not now befriended him, as she had hitherto done during the course of this adventure.

Aristella was there, indeed, before him, in the same walk, and very near the arbour through which he enter'd; – she had come thither to gather Cinquefoil[225] for her sister, the nurse who attended her being apprehensive of her falling into a fevourish disorder.

'Tis likely she was little less surprised on seeing him in that place, than she had been when introduced to her by her brother; – but as I was not present, and have this part of the story from the report of others, can relate nothing of the particulars of their discourse, and only say in general, that he spar'd no vows nor protestations to convince her of his passion, and that he prevail'd on her to return to him again, after having carry'd in the herbs.

His entreaties, join'd to her own secret inclinations, engag'd her to see him the next day; – this meeting was succeeded by another, that by a third, and so on for several mornings together, – every one of them still more endearing him to her affections; but, in spite of the pleasure she took in his addresses, she could not keep herself from some doubt of the sincerity of his passion, whenever she reflected on the inequality of their fortunes: – one day, expressing herself very emphatically on that occasion he cry'd out, – 'Talk not of fortune, – by Heaven your heart is all I wish!' – this he repeated so often, and so tenderly, that she at last confess'd, – it was already his.

Having brought her to this point, he now thought it proper to let her know the real aim of all his courtship; – he began with telling her, that beauty, such as hers, merited to be set off with all the advantages of dress and grandeur; – that she had wasted too much of her youth on a mean dependance on her kindred; and concluded with the offer of a large settlement, protesting to her at the same time, that he would never marry any other woman, and that she should live in every thing like his wife except the name.

If a dagger had pierced the gentle breast of Aristella, it could not have given her more pain than did this cruel declaration; – for some moments she was unable to make any reply, but burst into a flood of tears, and discovered all the symptoms of the most violent grief; – he endeavour'd to calm this tempest in her mind, by all the arts that love and wit could inspire; – but all was now in vain, – a virtuous pride, by degrees, got the better of her sorrows, and starting from him, she cry'd out, – 'Deceitful and ungenerous man! – but think not that your base desires shall triumph over the weakness I have confess'd for you; – no, – I will never see you more, nor henceforth think of you but with horror and detestation.'

In speaking these words she flew out of the arbour; – rage gave wings to her feet, yet Mutantius would certainly have overtaken her, if the sight of a man, whom Beechly had employ'd to do some work in the garden, had not made him turn back.

He went to his lodgings much disconcerted at this accident, but the knowledge he had of Aristella's affection for him kept him from totally despairing; – he repair'd to the dear arbour the next morning, but no Aristella appear'd; – he went again, but had no better success; – resolved to see her, if possible, he made a visit at the house, and told Beechly in a free manner, that he was come to take a second dinner with him, to which he reply'd with a compliment suitable to the occasion.

Mutantius was again disappointed, – Aristella hearing he was there, sent word to her brother that she had a violent tooth-ach, and desired he would excuse her from coming down; – this drove the lover almost to distraction, – he went home, – wrote to her, and made his footman go, as of his own accord, to chat with the servants, and loyter about the house 'till he should see Aristella and deliver the letter to her.

The fellow found means to execute his commission, – Aristella took the letter on his presenting it to her, and went up into her chamber; but after reflecting a little, would not trust her own heart so far as to read this dangerous epistle, following the Poet's advice.

> The nymph who hears, inclines to sin;
> Who parlies half gives up the town,
> And rav'nous love soon enters in
> When once the out-work's beaten down.[226]

She therefore put it under a cover, and having sealed and directed it, came down and gave it to the man, saying, – 'There's my answer to your master's letter.'

Never had the vanity of Mutantius met with so severe a shock, yet could he not forbear revering the virtue he attempted to destroy; – if before he lov'd, he now ador'd her; and the more he consider'd her perfections, the more he found her worthy to be his wife; – yet, when he thought of marriage, the idea of that state was irksome to him: – he knew that at present he was the idol of the fair, but should cease to be so if once he became a husband: – in fine, he could not bear to lose his darling admiration, yet was equally unable to bear life without the enjoyment of Aristella.

After some debate within himself, his passion, however, got the better of his vanity, and he resolved to marry Aristella; but which way to let her know he meant to do so, seem'd as great a difficulty as any he had pass'd through in attempting to seduce her: – he was convinced she would neither see him nor receive a letter from him, yet, in spite of all this, love fertile in contrivances, put a stratagem into his head, which had the desired effect; – it was this:

Beechly's new-born son had not been yet baptiz'd, on account of the mother's having been more than ordinarily indisposed during her lying-in; – he offered himself to be one of the sponsors at the font, which the other gladly accepted, having already troubled many of his friends on the like occasion; – Aristella could not now avoid his presence, but behaved with so much reserve, scarce ever looking towards him, that a man less conscious of his own merit might have been abash'd. – After some time, when most of the company were engaged in conversation, he found an opportunity to say to her, – 'Madam, I beseech you will forgive the rash proposal I presum'd to make you; – be assur'd I have heartily repented of it, and have now no designs upon you but what are truly honourable;' – to which she reply'd, – 'Sir, I shall never believe a man means me well who has once thought so poorly of me.' – 'I only beg,' resumed he, 'the liberty of entertaining you once more in private, and if what I have then to say does not merit your pardon and your favour I shall leave Canterbury, and perhaps the world, for ever.' – He could add no more at that time, – Beechly call'd to him to pledge him in a bumper to the young Christian; but before they parted he found means to enforce what he had last said, and spoke with so moving an air that she consented to see him the next morning.

The consequence of this interview was a full forgiveness for what was past on the side of Aristella, and on that of Mutantius a solemn vow of making her his wife the moment she consented to be so; but added, that there were some circumstances in his affairs which required their marriage should be kept secret for a time: – to this last article she made no direct answer at present, but the next day, when they met again by appointment, suffer'd herself to be overcome by his persuasions, and promised that every thing should be as he would have it.

In fine, it was at last agreed between them that he should return to London in a few days, and that she should follow as soon as her sister's recovery permitted her to take her leave with decency.

Both these lovers were now in a state of perfect contentment, and each of them observed the promise given to the other with the utmost punctuality; – but what afterwards befel them must be the subject of another Chapter.

CHAP. IX.

*Contains only a continuation of the same narrative, begun in the foregoing
 Chapter, and will not be concluded in this.*

Mutantius having been appris'd, by a letter from Aristella, of the day in which
she should come to town, went in his own coach as far as Greenwich to meet her,
and conducted her to a very handsome and well furnish'd lodging, in one of the
most airy and best streets near Bloomsbury-Square, where he had also provided
a footman and maid-servant to attend her.

She was at first a little scrupulous of putting herself under his protection, till
the sacred ceremony should have united her to him for ever: – he perceived the
apprehensions she was under, and immediately relieved them by renewing his
protestations, that the next morning should make his person as inviolably her's
as his heart had been from the first moment he beheld her, and at the same time
shew'd her a ring and marriage licence, which he had already prepar'd for that
purpose.

He supp'd with her that evening, but when it was over very respectfully
retir'd, to leave her to that repose which he judg'd necessary after the fatigue of
her journey.

I come now to that part of the story which I had an opportunity of being
both an eye and ear witness of: – I was acquainted with the gentlewoman of the
house where Aristella was placed, and happen'd to call there on some business
the very next morning after that young beauty had been brought thither.

My friend told me, among other discourse, that she had lett her lodgings at
a very high rent; but was a little apprehensive that the person they were for was
no better than a kept woman: – on my asking what ground she had for such a
suspicion, she reply'd, – that she had lett her lodgings to a gentleman of fortune,
call'd Mutantius, for the use of a lady whom he brought to take possession of
them the night before, and that he had also hired servants to wait upon her, who
she found knew as little of the person they were to serve as she did.

She farther added, that the lady was extremely young, the most beautiful
creature she ever saw in her life; – and that she could not help thinking it a little odd, that such a one should be under the care of so gay and airy a spark as
Mutantius.

As I was perfectly acquainted with the character of Mutantius, I was a good
deal of opinion that she was in the right; – I advised her, however, to say nothing
till she should see farther into the matter, and not lose so beneficial a lodger on
a bare conjecture.

She approv'd of what I said, and I took my leave, but not to go home, –
what she had told me fill'd me with a curiosity to discover something more of
this affair, so went no farther than the first blind alley I found, where I put on

my Invisible Belt, and returned again just as Mutantius knock'd at the door, – I enter'd with him and follow'd him up stairs; – the sight of Aristella convinced me that the good woman had not been mistaken in the description she gave me of her; – the lovers ran into each other's arms, and Mutantius looking on her with the greatest tenderness spoke thus:

Mutantius. Now, my dearest Aristella, I am come to put a final end to all your doubts either of my love or honour.

Aristella. I am pleased to think that the perfect confidence I have shewn in both gives me some sort of claim to the proof you are now about to give of them, since I must confess myself in every other respect so unworthy of you.

Mutantius. You are worthy of every thing; – but, my dear, you forget that there is another testimony that I expect from you of the regard you have for me.

Aristella. Name it, that my ready compliance may convince you how happy I think myself in every opportunity of obliging you.

Mutantius. It is that you will be content that for some time our marriage may be kept a secret.

Aristella. You know I have already promis'd it.

Mutantius. Yes, – in general terms; – but you have sisters who are very dear to you, and tho' I doubt not of their discretion, I cannot think a secret safe when trusted in so many hands: – Will then your love for me enable you to endure their reproaches for your supposed dishonour, rather than reveal what is inconvenient for me to be made known?

Aristella. The trial is a little severe, but will not last for ever.

Mutantius. No, my dear, a time will come when your innocence shall be fully clear'd, and like the sun, shine brighter after this short eclipse; – till then, may I depend that the name of wife and husband shall be known only between ourselves?

Aristella. You may.

Mutantius. Swear it then.

Aristella. By all that's sacred.

Mutantius. Hold, my dear; – I would have you first understand the full extent of the vow you are about to make; – you swear that no imaginary provocation on my side, nor no unjust contempt nor ill treatment you may meet with from the world, shall ever extort from you a confession that you are my wife, till I myself shall publickly acknowledge you to be so.

Aristella. All this I solemnly swear, and invoke Heaven to bless me as I shall religiously observe it.

Mutantius. Charming, generous creature, and in return, to prevent all future apprehensions in prejudice of my faith or constancy from rising in your gentle breast, if it were possible for me to take a base advantage of the obligation I have laid you under, and make my addresses to another woman on the score of marriage, I here release you from your vow, and leave you at liberty to declare yourself my wife, assert your prior right, and proclaim me for a villain.

Aristella. Heaven forbid it should ever come to that.

Mutantius. No, my Aristella, – there is no danger, I have already rejected greater offers than ever can be made to me again: – to deal sincerely with you, – there has been always in my nature an extreme repugnancy to the name of marriage; the name of husband was irksome to me; – no woman but yourself had ever charms to reconcile me to it; but your beauty, your sweetness, your unaffected modesty, have now inform'd my soul, and by degrees will make me as proud of Hymen's fetters as I should once have been asham'd of them.

Aristella. It shall be my whole study to make them easy to you.

Mutantius. I know it will; – but come, my love, – a coach waits to carry us to church, – that solemn scene which fixes the everlasting happiness or misery of all who approach it in the manner we do.

On concluding these words he took her by the hand and led her down stairs, – I was close behind them when they went into the coach, which was order'd to drive to Clerkenwell; – I presently suppos'd he made choice of this place as there was the least danger of his being seen by any one who knew him.

I follow'd on foot, but came time enough to the church to see Mutantius resign that liberty he had once set so high a value on as to resolve never to part with; – the ceremony of marriage was performed by the curate of the parish, and the clerk officiated as father to give away the bride; – after all was over, Mutantius desir'd their marriage might be register'd, and a certificate of it given to Aristella; – both which were accordingly done.

I now left the new wedded pair to dispose of themselves as they thought fit, and return'd to my apartment in order to ruminate at leisure on an adventure which seem'd to me to have in it many inconsistencies.

To find that Mutantius, after having refused some of the best fortunes and most lovely women in the kingdom, should give his hand to a girl like Aristella, who tho' possess'd of every amiable qualification of the mind, was yet as inferior in beauty as in the goods of fortune; this, I say, afforded much matter of astonishment to me, yet the injunction he had laid her under of keeping their marriage a secret appear'd to me a still greater subject for speculation.

At first I fear'd he did not mean her fair; but when the care he took to have their marriage register'd, and a certificate of it to be deliver'd to her, contradicted that opinion, and I began to think, that as fancy is more prevalent than judgment in the affairs of love, he really thought her worthy of being his wife, and would one day publickly acknowledge her to be such, tho' at present the tenderness he had for her was not strong enough to overcome the vanity of being admir'd by others, which he thought would cease, and he should pass unregarded by the rest of the fair sex, when he should be known to have attach'd himself to one by marriage.

The more I thought on this adventure, the more I was confounded; and the result of all my meditations was, that it must be left to time to unravel the mystery; – I kept, however, a watchful eye on the behaviour of Mutantius, but was little the wiser for the pains I took, as I found he lived in the same gay and gallant manner he had always done in respect to the ladies.

It was about a month, as near as I can remember, after his marriage with Aristella, that a young beauty, call'd Eluatheria, appear'd in town; – the late death of her father had left her mistress of a very large fortune, and with it, what perhaps was not less pleasing to her, the full enjoyment of that liberty, which, during his life, had been much restrain'd.

A new face, without the addition of any extraordinary beauty, is of itself sufficient to draw after it a train of admirers; but Eluatheria had charms, which, join'd to those of novelty, made it not strange that she should soon become the general toast.

The first time Mutantius saw her was at the Playhouse; – he was there with Apamia, – she happen'd to be seated, with two other ladies, in a box just opposite to them; but not knowing who she was, had perhaps taken no notice of her, if Apamia had not indiscreetly mention'd her to him; – I was sitting behind them, and heard this little following dialogue:

Apamia. Do you see Eluatheria yonder?

Mutantius. What! she that makes so great a noise in town? – Pray, madam, which is she?

Apamia. She in mourning just over-against us. – I find her beauty has but little effect on you, that you did not observe her before.

Mutantius. I was too much taken up with what I have more near, madam.

Apamia. Nay, for my part, I can see nothing extraordinary in her; – then she is the most insipid creature in the world; – I have been in her company, and she has not a word to say for herself.

Mutantius. Well, I wonder any man can be charm'd with a woman that has not wit; – one may as well fall in love with a fine picture as with a fine woman without a tongue; but where wit and beauty are united, as in the divine Apamia, all hearts must yield.

Apamia. You flatter me, Mutantius.

Mutantius. No, by Heaven! – you are in reality what the poet says of Corrinna.

All that desire can wish, or fancy form.[227]

All the answer she gave to this was a look full of languishment, accompany'd with a little pat on his shoulder with her fan, and then turn'd from him to observe what was doing on the stage; – but in spite of the fine things he had been saying to her, I easily distinguish'd, from the first mention of Elutheria's name, a certain restlessness in him for a more full view of that celebrated beauty.

He had never been practis'd in the virtue of self-denial, and was not of a humour to put any check on his inclinations, of what kind soever they were; – he soon after made an excuse to Apamia for leaving her a few minutes, telling her he saw a gentleman on the other side of the house whom he must needs speak with.

The person with whom he pretended to have business was seated at the very end of one of the benches in the pit, just under Elutheria's box, so that he could not have thought on a more commodious situation for the gratification of his curiosity.

The play acted that night afforded me little matter of entertainment, and I left it at the beginning of the fourth act: – as I was passing behind the boxes, to go out of the house, I met Mutantius returning to Apamia, but first heard him give directions to one of the orange-women to carry a paper of sweetmeats to the lady in mourning, the next box but one to the stage, with the compliments of a gentleman unknown.

This incident, join'd to some others I had been witness of, made me pity poor Aristella, who tho' married infinitely beyond her hopes in point of fortune, and to one she passionately loved, could not be expected to enjoy a lasting or sincere happiness with a man of so vain, so volatile, and so uncertain a disposition.

A very little time afterwards convinc'd me that Mutantius was not the less general lover for being a husband, – he met Elutheria at the route of a lady of his acquaintance; – she appear'd more lovely to him at this second sight even than at the first, and the sprightliness of her humour gave a double lustre to the graces of her person; – she has, indeed, charms which might inspire the most tender emotions in the heart of any man, – that of Mutantius could not but confess their force, and the liking he had for her, join'd to the ambition of being first in the esteem of a woman who was at present the first in the esteem of most men, made him omit nothing that might conduce to the gratification of that darling passion.

His fine person, – his flowing wit, – his engaging manner of address, had made many conquests without designing it; but here, – where he exerted all his rhetoric, – call'd the dying Cupids to his eyes, and seem'd to breathe nothing but love and soft desire, it is not to be wonder'd at that he stole upon the mind of a young maid, altogether unprepar'd for so dangerous a rencounter.

In fine, she lov'd him, – lov'd and admir'd him to that infatuated degree, that she was proud of doing so, – glory'd in the chains of her too amiable vanquisher, and attempted not to conceal them.

Apamia, who for some months had thought herself the supreme sovereign of his heart, was almost distracted on finding she had so powerful a competitor; – all the inconstancy of Mutantius could not render him less dear to her; – but the charms of her for whose sake she thought herself neglected became so odious in her eyes, that she spar'd nothing which female wit and malice could suggest to blacken her character, and make her appear contemptible to the world.

The unguarded conduct of Elutheria, assisting the envy of her rival, this late celebrated beauty became as much despis'd as she had been once ador'd; but all absorb'd in love and its fallacious joys, she felt not the weight of her misfortune, because she saw it not, 'till Mutantius himself had gain'd his point, and shew'd the world he had bore away the prize so many in vain had aim'd at, open'd her deluded eyes by treating her with a cold indifference and palpable neglect.

But now, – methinks I hear the reader cry out with some impatience, – 'How did Aristella behave all this time? How could she, the lawful wife of this inconstant man, support the share that others had in his affections?' – It is, indeed, impossible for me to say in what manner she would have resented so provoking a circumstance if known to her; but she liv'd too retir'd for this misfortune to reach her ears; – she had, however, other troubles more than sufficient for human fortitude to sustain, but of what nature they were must be left to the next chapter to explain.

CHAP. X.

The catastrophe of this adventure cannot fail of exciting compassion in the breasts of my fair readers, and also afford much matter of speculation to those of the other sex.

THE pursuit of other adventures, which shall be inserted in their proper places before the conclusion of this work, hinder'd me for a long time from going to see in what manner Aristella was treated by Mutantius; but at length, some uneasy reflexions on her account raised an impatience in me to know the certainty of her present state.

Accordingly I went one day to the house where she was lodg'd; but, to my great surprise, found she had made but a short stay there, and had been removed a considerable time before my coming: – on my asking some questions of my friend concerning the reason of it, the good woman answer'd me in these or the like terms:

'The affair was just as I expected,' said she; 'I pity the poor young gentlewoman, indeed, – she has not the looks of such a one; – but I suppose she has been decoy'd by abundance of fair promises: – I wonder, however, that Mutantius, knowing the character of my house, and that I always had people of the best fashion lodge with me, should offer to bring a kept-mistress under my roof; but I was very free with him, – I told him my mind very plainly on the occasion.'

'And pray what answer did he make,' cry'd I, with some impatience, '– when you call'd her a kept-mistress?'

'Very little to the purpose, truly,' resum'd she; 'he only said that she was a gentlewoman, and a friend of his, and as such expected I should treat her civilly; – I told him it was not in my nature to treat any body uncivilly, but that I would encourage no such doings, and therefore desir'd he would provide another lodging for her; – on this he flew into a passion, – told me I was an ignorant foolish woman, and the like; – but I did not regard his bouncing,²²⁸ and as he found I was resolute, took his madam away in a few days afterwards.'

The manner in which this woman spoke made me extremely commiserate the condition of poor Aristella, who, though a lawful wife, was obliged, through the caprice of Mutantius, and the vow she had taken, to endure all the contumely due to a prostitute.

I would have given almost any thing but the secret of my Invisible Belt and Tablets to have clear'd Aristella's innocence in the fullest manner to this scrupulous gentlewoman; but as there was no doing the one without the other, I was compell'd to content myself with getting out of her directions to the place where this much injur'd beauty was removed, resolving to take the first opportunity to see what attonement the behaviour of Mutantius made to her in private, for the injustice he did her reputation in public.

I was so lucky as to find them together the first day I went; but the scene I was witness of, instead of diminishing, very much added to the concern I had carry'd with me, as every good-natur'd reader, on my reciting it, will believe.

Aristella was sitting very melancholy in one corner of the room, – Mutantius in another, with all the marks of discontent and ill-humour in his countenance; – by what follow'd, it appears that she had been speaking somewhat to him in relation to the discovery of their marriage; – I doubt not, by what I saw of her behaviour both before and afterwards, that she express'd herself in very gentle terms on the occasion; but the bare mention of such a thing, to a man of his present way of thinking, was of itself a sufficient offence.

I have already describ'd the posture I found him in; but just as I enter'd the room he reply'd to what she had said, and that reply drew on a conversation which let me into the whole of both their sentiments.

Mutantius. I am sorry to find you have so little regard for me; and, indeed, so little prudence, as whenever I am with you to fall eternally upon a subject which you know is so disagreeable to me.

Aristella. If you lov'd me half so well as you once pretended, it would not be so disagreeable; – and you would, at least, acquaint me with the reasons which oblige me to live in the manner I do.

Mutantius. Perhaps it is not proper for me to reveal them.

Aristella. Oh, Mutantius! – I know not what to think of my condition. – Why did you marry me?

Mutantius. Because I then liked you better than any other woman, and if I do not still continue to do so it is your own fault; – I hate to be teaz'd: – besides, the conditions of our marriage were that it should be kept a secret.

Aristella. Yes, – for a time.

Mutantius. That time will not be shorten'd by your impatience.

Aristella. It may, – for if it last much longer my heart infallibly must break.

Mutantius. Pish, – women's hearts are not of such brittle stuff; – the head is in more danger, when swell'd with senseless pride and vanity.

Aristella. Indeed, sir, I think it would at least become you to be a little more serious on the occasion.

Mutantius. With all my heart, madam, – as serious as you please; – for faith I am not in a humour to be very merry: – seriously then, you seem to me to be one of the most ungrateful, and most unreasonable women under the sun. – Have I not taken you from a mean dependance on your sisters, who I believe could but ill spare the scanty helps you received from them? – Have you not now good lodgings, servants to wait on you, and an allowance sufficient to support you in a fashion beyond what you could ever have expected? – yet all this is nothing in your account.

Aristella. Nothing, when balanced against a life of infamy: – the very servants you upbraid me with despise me while they serve me; – the people of the house treat me but with an enforced civility; – I pass my days as one who was an alien to the world, and had no business in it; – never partake the joys of social conversation, – never visit, nor am visited, and scarce dare venture to breathe the freshness of the open air, lest I should be seen by any who have known me, especially by my sisters, who, mean as you think of them, know how to set a just value upon reputation, and to scorn all the riches of the earth without it.

Mutantius. A very fine catalogue of complaints, truly. – Have you any more to add?

Aristella. Yes, – one thing more, which, with what indifference soever you may now regard me, ought not, methinks, to escape your consideration; – you know I am far advanced in my pregnancy; – perhaps too of a son; and can you support the thoughts, that an infant, born the lawful heir of your estate and name, shall be saluted, on his first seeing light, with the odious title of spurious offspring, – a bastard?

Mutantius. What will he be the worse, – unless you expect to have so wise a child as to know what is said of him as soon as he comes into the world?

Aristella. Oh, Mutantius! – Mutantius! – this is cruel dealing.

She said no more, but wept bitterly; – Mutantius, who it must be own'd has some good-nature, seem'd much mov'd at seeing her thus, and having look'd on her some moments with a great deal of tenderness, bid her come to him; – she obey'd, but advanced with the most sorrowful and dejected air; – he pull'd her to him, – made her sit upon his knee, and kissing away the tears which abundantly stream'd from her lovely eyes down even to her bosom, he spoke thus:

Mutantius. Come, my poor Aristella, do not be so foolish, – you have no cause for weeping, – you know yourself virtuous, – and I know you are so, – and have no need to be afflicted at the mistaken opinion others may have of you, – especially as it is not to last always.

Aristella. If I were certain when this event would happen, even though it were much longer than I hope it will, I should with patience wait.

Mutantius. You must depend for that upon my love and honour; – it is not in my power to assign the very day and hour: – to deal sincerely with you, – I have been a railer at marriage, – have refus'd offers of that nature as much above my expectations as I was above your's, – and I cannot all at once submit to be pointed at for a husband, and hear people laugh and cry out, – that I had thrown myself away; but this, my dear, you may assure yourself, that I will endeavour to get rid of these scruples as soon as possible; – in the mean time, I will give you as much of my company as can be spar'd from business and other attachments which are not to be dispenced with; – I came on purpose to devote this whole day to you, drive me not from you by your discontent; – kiss me, and give me your promise that you will be entirely easy.

She comply'd readily with the first part of this injunction, and said she would do the best to perform the other; – with this he seem'd highly satisfy'd, and bid her ring the bell for a servant to go and order a dinner to be prepar'd for them at an adjacent tavern and sent home; – just as she was about to do as he desir'd, her maid came running into the room and told him that one of his footmen was below, and said he had something of the utmost consequence to deliver to him; – Mutantius, on hearing this, went to the top of the stair-case and call'd the fellow up, who presented him with a letter, saying at the same time,

Footman. From Apamia, sir, – her footman was so pressing to have it deliver'd to your honour, that I promis'd I would endeavour to find you, and bring her ladyship an answer.

Mutantius. You did well.

I stood close behind him while he open'd the letter, and saw it contain'd these lines:

To Mutantius.

Dear Agreeable,

This subpoena demands your presence at a court of Belles and Beaux, to be held in my drawing-room this evening at six precisely; – fail not to come on penalty of forfeiting your character of politeness, nor leave behind you any of those talents which will serve to render the sacrifice we propose to mirth and gayety complete; – you know yourself the life and soul of conversation; your absence, therefore, at this time, would be unpardonable: – if your watch should happen to go too fast, or any other accident make you anticipate the appointed hour, and you come before the rest of the company, you need not apprehend being turn'd back, by

Yours, &c. &c.

APAMIA.

Having read this little billet, he bid his man fly to Apamia and carry her his compliments, with an assurance that he would do himself the honour to be punctual in obeying her commands; – then turn'd into the room and said to Aristella,

Mutantius. I am sorry, my dear, I cannot stay with you as I promised; – some friends desire my company this afternoon, and I cannot possibly excuse myself from complying with their request.

Aristella. You will dine with me, however?

Mutantius. It will be utterly inconvenient for me to do so; – it is now near two o'clock, – I am to meet the company at five, and must new dress; so you will excuse me.

Aristella. When may I hope to see you again?

Mutantius. To-morrow, perhaps, – or next day, – I cannot say exactly when; but I will come soon. – Farewel, – make yourself easy.

In speaking these last words he gave her a slight salute, and went down stairs carelessly humming part of an Italian air, leaving his turtle to moan the absence of her inconstant mate.

By what I had now seen of the behaviour and disposition of Mutantius, I found reason to believe it would be yet a great while before he would bring himself to make a declaration of his marriage, so resolved not to take the trouble of any farther inquisitions, but wait till common fame should give me intelligence of it.

This event, however, happen'd much sooner than I expected; but was brought about by an accident which excited the extremest pity instead of congratulations; – the unfortunate Aristella was not born to enjoy a happiness she so ardently had wish'd for, and so long been made to hope; – death alone had the power to give what life in vain had waited for; and the same breath which told me Mutantius had acknowledged her for his wife, inform'd me also that she was no more.

Aristella, on her leaving the country, was charg'd with letters and some little presents from mrs. Beechly to her two sisters in London; but being hinder'd from executing this commission in person, by the obligation Mutantius had laid her under, she sent what was entrusted to her care by a porter, accompany'd with a little billet from herself; in which she told them, – that an affair of the utmost consequence kept her at present from seeing them, but that she hoped to do so in a short time, and would then acquaint them with the reasons for having absented herself, and begg'd they would entertain no unfavourable thoughts of her conduct in this point.

As she was circumstanced, it was not in her power to have acted otherwise than she did; yet what satisfaction could such a letter as this give to the two sisters? – for a girl, so young and beautiful as she was, to banish herself from her kindred, without acquainting them with the motive of her doing so, or the place to which she was retir'd, had a right to raise in them conjectures of the very worst sort: – they were almost distracted at the thoughts of her supposed ruin, and spar'd no pains to find her out, in order to bring her home, and snatch her from the shame they imagin'd she was involved in.

Fruitless was their search for a long time; but chance, at length, discover'd to them not only where she lived, but also that she was supported by a gentleman; and, in fine, that she was look'd upon as a kept-mistress: – quite transported with grief and rage, they went to the house where she was lodg'd, and the door happening to be open, flew up stairs without any ceremony and burst in in upon her; – the sight of her, for her pregnancy was very visible, added to the passions they were before enflam'd with; – they reproach'd, – they revil'd her in the most bitter terms, while poor Aristella, bound by the fatal oath she had taken, could say nothing in defence of her innocence, but what served to convince them more fully of her guilt.

After having loaded her with opprobrious names, and railed themselves quite out of breath, they left her with the same precipitation they had come, vowing never more to see or think of her as a sister.

Impossible is it for any one to conceive what the soul of Aristella suffer'd in this shocking stroke, – conscious of innocence, yet labouring under all the appearance of guilt; – scandaliz'd, abus'd by those to whom she had been so dear, yet incapable either of defending her wrong'd virtue, or of blaming the severity she was treated with for her suppos'd fall; – every passion that can agitate the human heart at once assail'd, and overwhelm'd her with a variety of anguish; the force of which had such an effect upon her as to cause an abortion that same night, and also to throw her into convulsions, which in a few hours render'd her life despair'd of by all about her.

In her intervals, between those fits which depriv'd her of all sense and motion, she cry'd out for Mutantius, – ask'd where he was, and said she could not die without seeing him; – messengers were immediately dispatch'd to him with this dreadful message; – he came on hearing it, – he seem'd greatly affected at the condition he found her in, but was much more so when he was informed by her maid what it was had thrown her into it; – she was insensible on his entrance, but recovering soon after, and seeing him so near her, catch'd hold of his hand,

and with agonies inexpressible, said to him, – 'Oh! Mutantius, you now will be rid of a tie you have been asham'd to own.' – 'No, by Heaven!' cry'd he, 'Live, live, Aristella, and I will declare to all the world that you are my wife, – my lawful married wife.'

Whether it were this sudden rush of joy, on hearing him speak these words, that was too powerful for her weakness to sustain, or that the lamp of life was wasted by the agonies she had before endur'd, is altogether uncertain, but she expir'd that moment, yielding up her last breath on the bosom of her too late repenting husband.

Love, pity, and remorse, now engross'd all his faculties; – he kept his promise, acknowledg'd her for his wife, had her intomb'd, with the greatest funeral pomp, in his own family vault, and paid all imaginary honours to her memory; whether he will ever relapse into his former vanities it is time alone must shew; – but at present, this once gay thoughtless rover, either is, or affects to be, lost to the joys he lately was so fond of, – behaves with the utmost indifference towards the fair sex, – seldom goes to any public place, – sees but little company at home; and, in fine, seems to be in every thing the very reverse of what he was.

This change, together with the occasion of it, was a terrible disappointment to many a flaunting belle who had plum'd herself on his devoirs; but Apamia and Elutheria were the most deeply affected by it; – both these ladies had, in fact, too liberally rewarded his pretended passion not to be overwhelm'd with grief and spite at the discovery of the deception he had put upon them, and that the heart they had labour'd to engross, and paid so dear a purchase for, had been the right of another before he had ever seen either of their faces.

But Apamia, who, besides a great spirit, had a good deal of the coquette in her nature, got rid of the chagrin more easily than her fair rival had the power to do; – that unhappy beauty, finding herself lost to love as well as to reputation, grew sick of the world, and retir'd into the country, resolving to return no more to a place which had been so fatal both to her honour and repose.

As to the sisters of the unfortunate Aristella, they were seiz'd with the most deep affliction, when they came to know the sad effects their rash resentment had occasion'd; which may serve as a warning to all persons not to be over hasty in censuring actions, the true meaning of which they cannot immediately comprehend.

End of the Fifth BOOK.

THE
Invisible Spy.

BOOK VI.
CHAP. I.

Is dedicated entirely to the Ladies, as it relates an adventure which nearly concerns them to take notice of.

AMONG all the numerous Modes which the wantonness of luxury has of late years introduced into this kingdom for the destroying of time, I know of none more fatal to the virtue and reputation of the female sex than Masquerades; – I mean, as that amusement is at present conducted.

Indeed when a select company of ladies and gentlemen agree among themselves, or are invited by some person of condition, to divert each other in such disguises as their several fancies shall make choice of, as practised in France and some other polite places, the case is widely different; for there, after passing a few hours in music, dancing, and pleasant raillery, according to the characters they assume, the masks are all thrown aside, and every one appears such as he is; – so that none will venture to talk or act beneath a vizard in such a manner, as when he stands reveal'd, will either reflect shame on himself, or give offence to those he has been entertaining; – Masquerades, thus managed, I cannot but allow to be not only innocent but laudable amusements, as they serve to whet the wit and exhilerate the mind.

But here, – sorry am I to say it, – the Masquerade houses may with propriety enough be call'd shops, where opportunities for immorality, prophaneness, obscenity, and almost every kind of vice, are retailed to any one who will become a customer; and at the low rate of seven and twenty shillings, the most abandon'd Courtezan, the most profligate Rake, or common Sharper, purchases the privilege of mingling with the first Peers and Peeresses of the realm, and not seldom affronts both modesty and greatness with impunity.

I perceive, to my very great satisfaction, that there are some Ladies, who, touch'd with a just sense of what is owing to their dignity, are determined not to expose themselves any more in a place where, if no worse ensues, the most licentious freedoms of speech, at least, are often offer'd to the chastest ears, and I am not without hope that the influence of their example will prevail on many others to do the same, so that next season the assemblies at the Masquerade-house will be composed of such only as are fit to herd together.

For the benefit, however, of the unwary, and those who by their small acquaintance in town are ignorant of the usage and customs of those dangerous amusements, it will not be amiss to relate an unhappy adventure which I was witness of, and may serve as a warning to all who are truly innocent and desire to remain so.

Alexis and Matilda were the son and daughter of two gentlemen who lived at a small village near Newcastle upon Tyne; – they had loved each other even before either of them well knew what was meant by the passion, and as their understandings ripen'd, their inclinations increased in proportion: – hope, for some time, gilded the prospect of their mutual wishes; but, when they least expected, a stop was put to the consummation by an unfortunate disagreement happening between their parents.

Alexis was forbid to see Matilda, and Matilda ever to think on Alexis; but these commands had little authority over hearts so fondly enamour'd as theirs; – they form'd the most romantic contrivances to keep alive the flame with which each had inspir'd the other, some of which succeeded so well as to enable them to continue a tender intercourse by letters, and even to gain some private interviews.

It was the father of Alexis who of the two had been the most refractory, and he dying a small time after, the young gentleman found means to reconcile matters so effectually with the parents of Matilda, that they at length consented to give her to him, and completed the happiness of the equally loving and beloved pair.

Matilda, whose every care, and hope, and joy, had all been center'd in her dear Alexis, had nothing now to wish beyond what she was in possession of; and Alexis thought himself so bless'd, that he even defied the power of fortune to give him any cause of disquiet; – fatal security! – How little dependance for the future is there on the present good?

They had not long enjoy'd the sweets of this so-much desir'd union, before Matilda, who had never been in London, express'd some curiosity to see a place she had heard so much talk of; – Alexis, proud to embrace every opportunity of giving her pleasure, immediately took the hint, and told her he was ready to conduct her thither as soon as she should be prepar'd for her departure.

Accordingly they set out from the country, and arriv'd in London about the middle of September; – Alexis took ready furnish'd lodgings, in a handsome house near St. James's, for six months, in which time he thought he should be able to shew Matilda every thing worth her seeing in town.

Alexis had received his first precepts at Westminster school, and having no relations in London, his father requested me, by letters, to call sometimes at the house where he was boarded, and have an eye over his behaviour; – I did so, and the advice I gave him being deliver'd not in a magisterial but friendly manner, the lad conceived a very great affection for me from that time, and has preserved it ever since; – he made me the compliment of a first visit on his coming to town, – told me how happy he was, and begg'd I would be no stranger to the fair person who had made him so.

I accepted the invitation, and went the next day; – on his presenting Matilda to me I was struck with the extremest admiration; for besides a graceful air and shape, a delicate complexion, fine eyes, a set of the most lovely features I ever saw in one face; and, in fine, every thing that could constitute a perfect beauty, there was such a sweet simplicity, – such a chearful unaffected innocence shone through the whole, and brighten'd every grace, that I was in a manner dazzled, and could not forbear crying out with Carlos in the play,

> If the face be the index of the mind,
> She has a thousand treasur'd virtues there.[229]

Alexis was quite transported at the tokens I gave of my approbation of the choice he had made; – the charming Matilda seem'd also highly pleas'd; but I could easily perceive she was not so through the vanity of hearing any praises on herself, but meerly because her dear Alexis was justified in the opinion of one whom she saw he look'd upon as his friend.

But how great soever the satisfaction was which this happy couple received from my behaviour towards them, I think it could scarce exceed what I felt in my own bosom, on finding so perfect a harmony, so uncounterfeited a tenderness, so warm an affection, reciprocally given and paid between two persons united in the manner they were, and whose love was not built on partial inclination, but on the real merits of each other, and confirm'd by the strongest principles of reason, virtue, and morality.

Alexis had never been but once in London since he went from school, and consequently knew but few people in it; as for Matilda, she was entirely a stranger to every body here, – yet both of them having all they wish'd for in each other, neither sought after or desir'd to make any new acquaintance, but kept always together, and never wanted a third person of their party.

As the sole excitement Matilda had to take a journey to London, was to gratify her curiosity with the sight of it, there was no eminent structure or place of note to which she was not conducted by her endearing husband; – he carry'd her to the Royal-Exchange, the Tower, the Cathedral of Paul's, the Palace at St. James's, the Parliament House, and Collegiate Church of St. Peter's, Westminster.[230]

I accompanied them in the last mentioned tour, where, as we were walking and taking a survey of the venerable monuments of the illustrious dead, it pleased me much to observe the particular notice she took, above all others, of the Tomb of that princess of England, who, when her royal consort was wounded by a

poison'd arrow in the Holy Land, and no other means remain'd for his recovery
but by sucking out the venom from the bleeding orifice, willingly undertook the
task, proud to meet an inevitable death to preserve the life of a husband whose
safety was dearer to her than her own.[231]

'How happy was this princess,' said the sweet Matilda, 'in having such an
opportunity of testifying her duty and conjugal affection?' – 'Few women,
madam,' answer'd I, 'would think themselves so, or make the same use of it she
did.' – 'They must then,' return'd she with some warmth, 'have souls little capable
of any sincere tenderness, or of a just sense of what is owing to that mysterious
union, which makes the husband the far better part of the wife.'

Alexis had too much love and gratitude in his nature not to reply to what
she said, in terms which shew'd how deeply he was touch'd with it, and would
doubtless have expatiated much longer upon the theme, if they had been in any
other place.

After having made her better acquainted with every thing in this Metropolis,
than many can pretend to be who have pass'd their whole lives upon the spot, he
went with her to Hampton-Court, Windsor-Castle, Kensington, and the royal
Hospitals of Greenwich and Chelsea, and also to several fine Villas on the banks
of the river; – it would be endless to repeat the various excursions they made, so
I shall only say, that there were nothing omitted to be shewn to her which might
either enlarge her ideas or entertain her fancy.

A new scene of diversions open'd as the winter season came on; – Plays, Operas and Masquerades now began to attract the attention of all who would be
thought polite; – the two first of these amusements Matilda was not altogether
a stranger to, having often seen somewhat like them acted by stroling companies
in the country; but she had not the least notion of Masquerades, and the little
account Alexis was able to give her, making her more impatient to know what
sort of entertainment they afforded, it may be easily supposed, by what has been
already said, that so indulgent a husband would not suffer her to continue long
in suspence; – it may be too, that he had some curiosity of his own to gratify in
this point, having, it seems, never been at a Masquerade himself.

Tickets accordingly were purchased, and masqueing habits hired; – I
happen'd to make a morning visit the day they were to go, and found Matilda
very busy in ornamenting a little Hat and Crook; – the moment I enter'd the
room she told me, with the greatest pleasure in her countenance, that she was to
be at the Masquerade that night, and was to assume the character of a Shepherdess; I reply'd, that she could not take upon her one more suitable to her youth
and innocence: – we then fell into some discourse concerning Masquerades; –
Alexis would fain have persuaded me to accompany them, but I excused myself
in the words of an old blind fidler, who was in the streets when I came in, playing
and singing to his instrument these lines:

In youth when I did love, – did love-a,
Methought it was wond'rous sweet-a;
But now I am old, threescore and above-a,
To be grave is wond'rous meet-a.

'If you have no better excuse than this,' cry'd Alexis laughing, 'it will not serve your turn.' – 'I do not know, indeed, whether it will or not,' reply'd I, 'for when old people affect to be gay, they ought to do it under a mask, to prevent being laugh'd at by the young; – but I have another reason,' added I, 'which will admit of no objection; – I am both to dine and sup with some friends.'

This was, in effect, no false pretence, for I really had an engagement upon my hands, which to comply with, I took my leave of Alexis and Matilda much sooner than I should otherwise have done.

The company I went to breaking up about ten o'clock, which was somewhat sooner than I had expected, it came into my head, in spite of the little liking I ever had to Masquerades, to step in and see how Matilda, who had not been accustom'd to any great assemblies, would behave among such a mingled rout.

In things of small consequence I seldom gave myself the trouble of a second thought, so, pursuing this start of curiosity, I went to a Habit-shop, put on a Domine,²³² and hasted to that babel of hurry and confusion.

It was no difficult matter for me to discover the persons I sought after, as I knew the dresses they were in; – I soon distinguish'd the beautiful Shepherdess, and her husband by the blue Domine I had seen lying on a table in his din-ing-room: – I perceived there were many eyes upon Matilda; for tho' her face was conceal'd, her lovely hair, which with a studied negligence hung in ringlets almost to her shoulders, her alabaster neck, her lovely shape and sprightly air, had somewhat in them sufficiently attractive.

But there was one who above all the rest seem'd particularly attentive to her motions, – he was in the habit of a Huntsman, a character which I afterwards had reason to say to myself suited very well the intentions he had in his head that night: – which way soever Matilda turn'd he took care not to lose sight of her; but as she kept close to Alexis, neither he nor any one else had an opportunity of speaking to her.

I hover'd as near them as I could without being taken notice of, and it gave me a good deal of diversion, to see the surprise this innocent country lady testi-fied at hearing the freedoms with which some people, who seem'd to be perfect strangers, accosted each other; – one incident in particular, which tho' it had nothing extraordinary in it at a Masquerade, appear'd wonderful to her; – it was this:

A Hermit, with more furrows on his vizard than in an acre of plough'd land, and a beard a foot and a half long, mingled with the thickest of the assembly, and leaning on his stick and looking round him, cry'd out with a voice conformable to his decrepid appearance: – 'Vanity! – vanity! – oh vanity of vanities!' This exclamation drew a good deal of laughter, but no reply, 'till a smart lady, dress'd in a Spanish Bonaroba,[233] gave him a slap on the shoulder, and saluted him in these terms:

Lady. Well, – my good father Sanctity, what brings that venerable beard of yours out of your cell at this time of night?

Hermit. I came to warn such wanton minxes as you of your follies; – to warn you of the dangers of the flesh and blood; – to bid you leave off your Jellies, your Eringos, your Ratifee, and your Viper-wine;[234] – to bid you mortify your carnal thoughts, and do penance in cooling herbs and fountain water.

Lady. Pray, is Arbor-Vitæ[235] among your regimen of simples?

Hermit. Yes, I have one root; but I never prescribe it without knowing the complexion and constitution of the person.

Lady. What do you think of mine?

Hermit. First let me know the the Symptoms.

Lady. As how?

Hermit. I will tell you.

With these words he drew her apart from the company, and after a short conversation between themselves, went away together, – at which Matilda, who had lost no part of their behaviour, was so astonish'd that she could not forbear expressing herself to her husband on that occasion in terms which made the Huntsman, and some others who were near enough to hear what she said, laugh heartily at her simplicity and ignorance of the place she was in.

Presently after, a gentleman crossing the room with his mask in his hand, was known to Alexis, who on sight of him cry'd out to Matilda,

Alexis. Look yonder, my dear, – there is mr. Freeman; – I never heard a syllable of his being in town; – I will just step to him and tell him where we lodge; – do you sit here 'till I come back.

He then seated her on a bench, and went hastily after his friend, who had pass'd into another room; – I now doubted not but that the Huntsman would snatch his opportunity of entertaining Matilda, but I lost sight of him in an instant; – he vanish'd, as it were, from the place and I saw him no more; – the fair Shepherdess, however, was not to remain neglected, – I found several were advancing towards her, one of whom was the most grotesque, as well as disagreeable figure I ever beheld;– his stature was far from what could be call'd tall; but the circumference of his carkass exceeded that of any three men in the whole assembly; – his legs look'd like the pillars of a church porch, and when he mov'd, were at such a distance from each other, that a boar of a moderate size might easily pass between them without being incommoded; – he had on the habit of a Turkish Bashaw,[236] which was the worst, indeed, he could have chose; – his huge ears, discover'd by the shortness of his turbant,[237] hung upon his shoulders, as did the wallets under his chin upon his breast: – in a word, he could have no deformity that the dress he was in did not shew to advantage.

This enormous creature had no sooner reach'd the place where Matilda sat, than he threw himself down by her on the bench, and accosted her with language which I should never forgive myself, nor expect to be forgiven by my reader, to repeat; – but I was glad to find, by the whispers of some people behind me, that instead of a gentleman, as I at first took him for, he was no other than a Bully[238] at a certain noted Brothel in Covent-Garden, and was known about town by the name of Lumper-Hammock. – See, ladies, what company you expose your-selves to at a Masquerade; – those, however, who give tickets, and dress up such wretches to make a party among you, deserve little of your favour.

I cannot pretend to say whether this fellow was encourag'd by any other per-son to behave to Matilda in the manner he did, merely to put her spirits into a hurry, or whether he was instigated to it only by his own impudence and brutal-ity of nature; but whatever it might be, the situation of that poor lady was greatly to be pitied; – she mov'd by little and little as far from him as the bench would give her leave; but he still follow'd, and would needs keep close to her and per-secute her with his ribald discourse; – sometimes she got up, and look'd round to see if her husband were coming to her relief; then sat down again, not daring to leave the place for fear of missing him; but all the time shew'd tokens of the utmost agitation of mind.

At length the blue Domine appear'd, on which she started from her seat, and running to him, cry'd, – 'Oh, my dear, I am glad you are come.' – He only reply'd, in a low voice, – 'Ay, ay, – let us be gone;' – and taking her by the hand led her hastily away.

I pleas'd myself with the thoughts of having seen Matilda safe under the protection of her husband, and was equally so that he had discover'd little appro-bation of the Masquerade, by his leaving it at a time when the diversion was at its full height, and more company were coming in than going out.

But the satisfaction I enjoy'd in both these points vanish'd in a moment; – Alexis return'd, – his mask was now off, and he pass'd directly to the place where he had left Matilda, – then started back, – confusion and surprise overspread his face; – he threw his eyes wildly round the room, then ran through every part of it, and without considering how much he exposed himself to the ridicule of that giggling assembly, ask'd first of one and then of another, if they had seen a Shep-herdess in green and silver, and if they knew what was become of her.

This struck me with an infinite concern, as it made me know Matilda had been deceiv'd by the sight of the blue Domine, and in spite of my unwillingness to let him see I had come to a place where I had refused to accompany him, was just stepping forward to inform him of what had happen'd, when a lady hearing his enquiries spoke to him in these terms:

Lady. Sir, the lady I saw with you in the dress you mention, went away a little while ago with a gentleman in a blue Domine, much the same as your own.

Alexis. Oh heavens! – what curst mistake is this!

In uttering this exclamation he flew out of the room like lightning, without staying to thank the lady for the intelligence she had given him; – I follow'd as fast as I could, in order to see what he would do, and found him at the door of the house, encompass'd with Hackney-Coachmen, Chairmen and Link-boys,[239] among whom he was vainly endeavouring to get some account of his lost Shepherdess; – one of them, it seems, had said he saw a lady in the habit he describ'd go into a coach with a gentleman, but could tell nothing either of the figure of the coach or where it was order'd to drive.

It will not be difficult for any one who is a husband, and who loves his wife, to judge of what Alexis must suffer in such a distracting circumstance: – It was very evident to him that his dear Matilda had been carried off, but by whom, or to what place, were things which seem'd altogether impossible for him to discover; and wanting the means either to prevent her ruin or his own dishonour, or to take vengeance on the ravisher for the injury he had done to both, could but fill him with reflections almost equally stabbing as the injury itself: – finding no information could be gain'd in the place where he was, he withdrew from the crowd, as I suppose, to consider what method he should pursue; for he continued in a fix'd posture for the space of two or three minutes at least, leaning against some rails before an adjacent house.

My heart bled for him, and if I had been capable of offering him either advice or consolation, would not have kept at the distance I did; but the accident that had happen'd was without a remedy, and I had often observ'd, that to preach up moderation in the first gusts of passion serve but to inflame it more.

I thought there were no measures he could take that night, yet imagining he had something in his head, was desirous of seeing what event his cogitations would produce, – I therefore laid hold of the opportunity I now had of stepping behind the cover of a hackney-coach in waiting, and girded on my Belt of Invisibility, which I always carried in my pocket, in case any thing should fall in my way to give me occasion to make use of it.

The influence of my valuable gift had but just taken effect, by being warm upon my body, when Alexis rouz'd himself out of the resvery he had been in, and walk'd very fast up the street; – I kept pace with him 'till he came to the house where he lodg'd; – the door being open'd by his own footman, who sat up for him, – 'Is my wife come home?' cry'd he – the fellow answering in the negative, and seeming somewhat surprised at the question, he threw himself into the parlour, saying to himself:

Alexis. How mad a hope did I entertain, that she might have found some means to escape the hands of her ravisher, and been here before me? – No, –

no, – 'tis impossible; – the villain doubtless will secure his prey: – curs'd, curs'd Masquerade, invented by the fiends for the destruction of virtue.

While he was thus speaking he tore off his Domine, with agonies not to be express'd, and stamp'd it under his feet; – then turning to his servant went on thus:

Alexis. William, your mistress is run away with, – stolen from me by some villain in a Domine like my own; – she is lost for ever unless immediately recover'd; – fly this minute to every Tavern and Bagnio[240] you can think on, – describe her habit, – enquire if such a one with a person in a blue Domine enter'd there; – be gone this instant, while I run to a Justice of the Peace, and get a warrant to search in all suspected places.

William. What part of the town, sir, do you think it most likely I shall hear of her?

Alexis. Alas I am as ignorant of that as you; – but all parts must be search'd; – fly then, good William; and, do you hear, ask every Hackney-coachman you meet with if he set any such persons down, and where; – away, I say, – stay not to consider, – a moment may confirm her ruin and my dishonour.

The fellow obey'd without making any farther reply; but, I perceiv'd by his countenance, was not very well contented with the errand he was sent upon; and Alexis went out of the house at the same time he did, in order to have recourse to a Magistrate in this exigence, as he had said he would.

I had no inclination to follow either master or man, on an expedition which promis'd so little success, therefore made all the haste I could to my own apartment, very much fatigued in body, yet much more so in mind, at the unfortunate mistake poor Matilda had fallen into, and which I had all the reason in the world to fear would be attended with the most dreadful consequences.

CHAP. II.

Contains the conclusion of a narrative, which I am certain there is one person in the world who cannot read without being fill'd with the most poignant remorse, unless he is as dead to all sense of humanity as of honour.

THE concern I was under, on account of the accident I had just come from being a witness of, would suffer me to enjoy but little repose the remaining part of that night; – I could not think it practicable that the measures Alexis intended to take, or, indeed, any he could possibly pursue, would enable him to recover his dear Matilda; at least 'till it was too late to save her from dishonour, and trembled for the effects which despair on such an event might probably occasion, both in one and the other.

My impatience to know if Matilda was yet come home, or if the researches of Alexis had gain'd him any information concerning her, made me resolve to go to his lodgings in the morning; but whether I should make this visit in my Visible or Invisible Capacity I was for some time at a loss; – at last it seem'd most eligible to appear in *propria persona*, as if I came only to ask some questions concerning the Masquerade, and how they approv'd of that diversion, as it was the first time they partook of it; and also to take no notice of my being apprized of any thing had happen'd there, unless he related it to me himself, which I did not much doubt of his doing.

On my knocking at the door it was open'd by mrs. Soberton, for so the gentlewoman of the house was call'd; – after a short apology for the trouble I had given her, I ask'd if Alexis or his lady were yet stirring; to which, with a sorrowful countenance and tone of voice she reply'd:

Mrs. Soberton. Oh, sir, the strangest accident, – the saddest misfortune that ever was has happen'd; – I wish you had been here last night, or some good body, to comfort the poor gentleman; for indeed I am afraid he will go beside himself.

I affected a very great surprize on hearing this exclamation, and desir'd she would explain herself, if what she seem'd so full of was no secret; – she then made me this answer:

Mrs. Soberton. A secret; – no, sir, it can be no secret to all the town, much less to one so much a friend to the family as you are: – be pleas'd to walk in and I will tell you all; – I mean, all that is in my power, for Heaven only knows what the end will be.

In speaking these last words she threw the parlour door, which was then half shut, wide open to give me a more commodious entrance; – I went in, and there was sitting by the fire-side an old gentleman who lodg'd in the second floor of the same house; – he was a shrewd man, but no great favourer of the women, as I afterwards found by his discourse.

Mrs. Soberton had no sooner drawn a chair, and oblig'd me to be seated, than she began to tell me that Matilda had been carried off from the Masquerade; – that her husband was in the utmost distraction on missing her; – the means he had made use of to find where she was conceal'd; but that all hitherto had been ineffectual, tho' himself and servant had been half over the town in search of her, with a thousand particulars which I either knew already or could easily guess at; and added, at the close of her long detail, one circumstance which I suppose she thought very material, – that the door of her house had never been shut a quarter of an hour together for the whole night, and that none of the family could get a wink of sleep.

I had scarce time to express the trouble I was in for my friend's misfortune, when the old gentleman took up the word, and said,

Old Gentleman. It is a very ugly accident, indeed, which way soever it came about, and I am heartily sorry for Alexis; – but it shews what vexations men are liable to bring upon themselves by marrying with these gay fine young women.

Mrs. Soberton. I protest you are the saddest gentleman I ever knew in my life, – always against the poor women, – as if we alone were in fault for every thing; – I know there are errors sometimes on both sides; but take it in the general, am very confident that if the men were not more to blame than we are, there would not be so many unhappy marriages: – as for the lady in question, my lodger, I believe there is not a sweeter, better condition'd, and more modest creature breathing, nor one that loves her husband more.

I join'd mrs. Soberton with some warmth in the vindication of Matilda's character; and added, that I knew her incapable of being guilty of any thing to forfeit it; – to which the old gentleman reply'd:

Old Gentleman. It may be as you say, – her inclinations may be perfectly good and virtuous, – God forbid I should harbour any thoughts to the contrary; – but what business had she at the Masquerade? – if women would stay at home, and mind their spinning and their needle, as in former days, none of these mischiefs would happen; but they must be gadding abroad, and provoking temptations they are not always able to resist. – One of our Poets, Outway I think it was, in my opinion, has a mighty pretty sentiment on this matter; – if I remember right his words are these:

> Woman to man first as a blessing given,
> When innocence and love were in their prime:
> Happy a while in Paradise they lay;
> But quickly woman long'd to go astray;
> Some foolish new adventure needs must prove,
> And the first Devil she saw she chang'd her love.[241]

I was too much of the same mind with this gentleman, as concerning Masquerades, to say any thing in the behalf of those entertainments; but urg'd in defence of Matilda's conduct in this point that being a country lady, desirous of seeing every thing in London, and went with her husband, she could not be apprehensive of any kind of danger while under his protection.

He either was, or had complaisance enough to feign himself convinced by the arguments I offer'd; after which I took my leave; but just as I was stepping out of the door I saw Alexis enter, or rather his ghost, for he appear'd more like the shadow than the real substance of my living friend; – he saluted me, however, with his usual freedom and politeness, and when we came into the dining-room embraced me, and began the recital of his misfortune in this pathetic exclamation:

Alexis. Oh, my friend, I am undone! – ruin'd, I fear, for ever! – the author, giver and partaker of all my happiness is lost! – torn from me by some lascivious, some inhuman villain; and him whom yesterday you beheld the most blest of men, you now see the most accurs'd, most wretched and forlorn of all created beings!

He then proceeded to inform me, as well as the distraction of his thoughts would give him leave, of the method he had taken for the recovery of his lost treasure; – how he had pass'd the whole night and that morning in search for her in every place to which he could imagine she might have been carry'd, and that hitherto all his enquiries had been entirely fruitless.

While he was speaking his servant came in, – he ask'd hastily if he had met with any success; to which question the fellow answering in the negative, his agonies redoubled, and never did despair, and rage, and grief, except in the case of suicide, produce more violent effects than what I now beheld in him.

Common compassion and good-nature, without the assistance of that friendship I had for him, would have oblig'd me to make use of my utmost endeavours to asswage his sorrows; though, indeed, the occasion of his distress was of so nice and delicate a kind, as render'd it very difficult to say any thing to the purpose.

Perceiving he had no thoughts of giving over his unavailing rambles, 'till he had gain'd some intelligence concerning her, I told him, that, in my opinion, there was but little probability of benefiting himself by those means; that in an age which paid not much regard either to love or honour, he would only expose both himself and wife to the censures of a sneering town, and perhaps also make the ravisher more careful to conceal his prize.

This seeming to have some weight with him, I added, that I believ'd I could point him out a way which afforded a greater prospect of success than the one he had determin'd to pursue; – on which he cry'd out to me to acquaint him with it.

I then advised him to put an advertisement in one of the Daily Papers, describing the shape and stature of Matilda as near as possible, with all the particulars of the habit she had on, and offering a handsome reward to any one who should give information of the place at which she alighted out of a Hackney-coach, in company with a gentleman in a blue Domine, between the hours of twelve and one at night: – 'This you may do,' said I, 'without mentioning any name, except that of the person to whom such intelligence may be brought; – and 'tis very likely that either the Coachman who carry'd her, or some one who might be about the door where she was set down, or even the servants of the house will, for the sake of the gratuity, make that discovery which all your personal enquiries might not be able to obtain.'

I had no sooner ended than a sudden dawn of chearfulness gleam'd upon his languid face, and to shew how much he approv'd of the thought I had communicated, took pen and paper and immediately wrote in almost the same terms I had express'd it; specifying, at the same time, a coffee-house where the reward should be paid on the requested intelligence being brought.

To keep up his spirits, after the advertisement was sent to the printer, I repeated the hopes I had that the success would answer, – on which he reply'd,

Alexis. Yes, my dear friend, the suspence I labour under is so exquisite a torture, that I would wish to put an end to it, though by the most cruel, the stabbing certainty, – according to the Poet's axiom, that in all misfortunes

To know the worst is some degree of ease.[242]

He could not utter these last words without a sigh which seem'd to rend his very heart-strings; – then starting suddenly from his seat he cry'd out with the extremest vehemence,

Alexis. Oh, Matilda! – my poor Matilda! – what would I not give to purchase an opportunity of revenging thy sad undoing!

Finding now that he was beginning to relapse into his former agonies, I made use of my utmost endeavours to bring him to believe what, indeed, I could not believe myself, – that there was a probability that his wife might in reality suffer no more from this adventure than the fright it must necessarily have put her into; and that as it could not be doubted but that her virtue would resist all the temptations could be offer'd, so the same virtue would also enable her to triumph over the attacks of brutal violence.

I enforced what I said upon this score with all the examples I had ever read of, or at least could remember, in relation to ladies who had the good fortune to make converts of their intended ravishers, and turn what was meant for their dishonour into their glory; and was at length so far successful in this attempt, as to inspire him with a half hope that his dear Matilda might possibly return unviolated.

Having gain'd this point, I prevail'd on him to take some refreshment, which he could not but stand in great need of, as he had neither eat, nor drank, nor slept in so many hours; – at his earnest request I staid with him, and partook what might be more properly call'd a running banquet than a dinner, though, by mrs. Soberton's directions, elegantly enough prepar'd: – after this, nature, who will not be denied her rites, whatever vexations may intervene to rob her of them, spread a certain drowsiness upon his eye-lids, which I perceiving persuaded him to favour, and on my promising him to come again the same evening, or the next morning without fail, he lay down on the bed, and left me at liberty to pursue my inclinations.

As I had now no engagement upon my hands, and had not been at White's Chocolate-house for a considerable time, it was now my full design to go thither, and see what the company were doing; but as I had some very good reasons not to appear in that place, I stepp'd into the first nook I found in my way, and put on my Belt of Invisibility.

I was but just equipp'd, and passing on to my intended rout, when I saw a chair, with the curtains close drawn, stop at a few paces before me; – I should have taken no notice of this, if one of the fellows had not lifted up the top, and told the person in it, that he had forgot whether it were the Red or the Green Lamps; – the answer was given in a voice which I presently knew to be Matilda's; and if I had not so well remember'd, as I did, the accents, I should have suspected it was no other than herself, by her saying, – 'The Two Green Lamps.'

On finding it was she, the reader will easily believe I had more curiosity to see the interview between her and Alexis, than any thing else I could have in my head; – I follow'd the chair 'till it came to the house, and on the door being open'd slipp'd in with it; – on her alighting mrs. Soberton ran out of the parlour, and was beginning to testify her joy at her return, tho' mingled with some demonstrations of surprise to see her in the condition she was, which, indeed, was deplorable enough; – her head without any other covering than a handkerchief tied carelessly over her dishrevell'd hair, – her garments torn, – her eyes swell'd with tears, – every feature distorted, and all the tokens of distraction and despair about her.

She made no answer to what the good gentlewoman said, but, after throwing some money to the chairmen, ran hastily up stairs into the dining-room, where flinging herself on a settee, – she cry'd out, – 'Where is Alexis!' – to which mrs. Soberton, who had follow'd as well as myself, reply'd, – 'Oh, madam, you cannot imagine what trouble both he and all of us have had on your account.'

I know not whether that unhappy lady would have declared to mrs. Soberton any part of what had befallen her or not; for Alexis, who either had not fallen asleep, or was easily awak'd, heard his wife's voice and came flying out of the chamber that instant; – mrs. Soberton, discreetly judging that they might not chuse to have a third person witness of their discourse, went directly down stairs; but the Invisible remain'd, and his wonderful Tablets receiv'd the impression of the following dialogue between them:

Matilda. Oh, Alexis, wherefore did you leave me!

Alexis. Wherefore did you leave the place where I desir'd you should wait for my return!

Matilda. I stirr'd not from it but to follow you, as I then thought.

Alexis. Confusion! – How could you be so mistaken!

Matilda. Alas I had no apprehension of the deception put upon me! – his habit was exactly like yours; – his stature much the same; – he spoke in a low voice; but if he had not, my spirits were in too much agitation at the impudence of a fellow who had just before accosted me, to have distinguish'd the difference.

Alexis. Oh, my torn heart! – But say, – who is the villain that betray'd you! – Where were you carry'd!

Matilda. Alas, – the precautions he took has left me ignorant of both; and all I know is that I am undone.

Alexis. Distraction! – undone, and not know by whom! nor even in what place the horrid deed was perpetrated! – all means for my revenge barr'd up! – Yet perhaps I may be able to discover something, – speak therefore, – tell me in an instant all the particulars of the story!

Matilda. I will, tho' every word I utter will stab me to the soul, and inflict anew the shocks I have undergone.

Alexis. No preparations; – be quick, and answer my demand at once.

Matilda. Have patience then; for while you look so terrible I cannot speak.

Alexis. You cannot think I would hurt you; – speak then, thou wretched woman, and break at once the heart of thy more wretched husband!

Matilda. Oh which way shall I begin! – how end!

Alexis. Keep me not on the rack!

Matilda. Soon as I saw the counterfeit Alexis approach I rose to meet him, and on his bidding me come and stretching forth his hand I gave him mine, glad to find myself conducted from that mingled crowd which I had seen too much of to desire to continue any longer with; – we went into a coach where I began to tell him how I had been affronted by an ugly huge man in a Turkish habit; but he made no answer either to that or any other idle prate I entertain'd him with, 'till the coach stopp'd and he handed me into a house, the entry of which was full of men, who were running backwards and forwards with candles in their hands, and seem'd very busy: – I ask'd where we were going, – he still made no reply; but after a short whisper to one of the fellows led me up stairs.

Alexis. 'Sdeath! – why did you go! – then was your time to have cry'd out for rescue!

Matilda. What, from my husband! – I could not as yet know him from any other than yourself; – I was, indeed, a little surprised at this behaviour; but imagin'd it was owing to some little whim you had taken into your head, on purpose to laugh at my simplicity. – Being warm with having my mask on so long, I pluck'd it off as soon as we got into the room, but he clapp'd it on again; – a man was then just entering with a bottle and glasses in his hand, which having set down on a table he immediately withdrew; – my conducter then bolted the door, and running towards me, said, – 'Now, my angel, I may feast my eye with all that heaven of beauty, which, while beneath a cloud, attracted my admiration, and you behold the man who from this happy moment devotes himself entirely to your charms;' – with these words he took off both mine and his own vizard; – I shriek'd, and surely had fainted with the fright, if an equal proportion of rage had not kept up my spirits.

Alexis. What said he then?

Matilda. A thousand romantic lyes, – such as I have read in Plays and Novels, which I answer'd only with revilings, 'till perceiving my just scorn had no effect upon him I had recourse to tears and entreaties; – told him I was a married woman, – that I had a husband dearer to me than my soul, and by whom I was as much belov'd, and conjur'd him not to detain me nor attempt to violate the sacred rites of marriage.

Alexis. Did not this move him?

Matilda. Oh no, – not in the least, the audacious wretch but laugh'd at this remonstrance, – said that love, like all other appetites, demanded variety; – that I was a fool, and knew not the true interest of my sex, but that he would instruct me better, and make me happy tho' against my will.

Alexis. Execrable Dog! – but go on.

Matilda. You may easily believe, that he who could speak such words would also accompany them with actions of the same nature: – I resisted all I could the indecent liberties he took, – call'd Heaven and Earth to my assistance, but in vain; – I was at last overpower'd: – in the midst of tears, reproaches, swoonings, he effected his brutal purpose, and made me the most miserable of women.

Alexis. Most miserable, indeed! – After this, I suppose, he would have suffer'd you to depart?

Matilda. Can you think me vile enough to continue one moment in the presence of that detested monster, when I was at liberty to leave him! – This, indeed, is cruel. – Oh Alexis! – I hate myself for what I have been compell'd to suffer, – do not you hate me too!

Alexis. No, Matilda, I never can hate you; – but all the hopes of my eternal peace depend on a perfect knowledge of every circumstance.

Matilda. His first pretence of detaining me was to persuade me to moderation; for in those dreadful moments, had the means of death been in my power, I certainly should have committed some desperate deed, either on myself or him: – he feign'd a contrition for following, as he said, the dictates of an ungovern'd passion, and forcing from me a blessing which ought to have been the reward only of long and faithful services; – but soon I found that all these flatteries, – this counterfeited softness had no other aim than to make me as wicked as he had made me wretched, and seduce me to consent to aid his brutal pleasures.

Alexis. Could he have the vanity to imagine you believ'd him?

Matilda. All my spirits had been before exhausted; – I had no voice, no breath to speak; and he, perhaps, interpreted my silence as a half yielding to his will: – he could not well discern how much my looks disdain'd his suit; for tho' it was mid-day, no other light came into the room than what beam'd through two small holes in the window-shutters; – he seem'd very alert, – threw open the windows, – unfasten'd the door, and order'd that something should be got ready to eat; but when the waiter came in to spread the table, he oblig'd me to put on my mask, saying, – 'You see, my dear, how careful I am of your reputation, – I hope you will reward me for it.'

Alexis. The lowest hell reward him! – So then you dined together?

Matilda. Such an attempt would sure have choak'd me; overcome, indeed, with thirst and faintness, I swallowed a little wine mingled with water; but though he forced me to sit by him at the table, I neither could nor would partake of any thing was there; – my refusal, however, nor the sight of my distraction, damp'd not his appetite, he both eat and drank heartily, and having finish'd his repast, pull'd me on his knee and said, – 'By heaven, in spite of all your peevish obstinacy I like you above all the women in the world, and if you will leave your husband and consent to be my mistress, I have the power as well as inclination to support you in a fashion equal to that you live in with the man you are married to, be he of what rank soever.' – I reply'd, with all the resolution I could muster up, that I despis'd his offers as much as I hated himself, and would receive no favours from him but the means of returning to my dear injur'd husband; – on this he paus'd, but still held me fast, and looking earnestly on my face at last spoke thus: – 'Well then, since it is so, and we must part, let us part at least as lovers should do, and if I never must hope to see you more, should be a fool not to make the most I can of the present opportunity;' – with these words he bore me to the bed, and, – oh, Alexis! how shall I repeat it! – triumph'd a second time over the feeble resistance I then had strength to make; – he afterwards used no arguments to win me to forgiveness, but perceiving the day was near closed in, said to me, with a kind of sneer, – 'Madam, you shall be obey'd, – shall go home to the husband you are so fond on;' and then rung the bell for the waiter to call a coach; and when told there was one at the door, tied a handkerchief cross my eyes, I suppose, to prevent my having any knowledge of that scene of my undoing; – he led me down stairs, put me into the coach, and came in himself; but spoke little 'till we stopp'd at a place which I think I have heard you say they call Covent Garden, there set me down, and bid the coachman drive back to the place where we came from as fast as he could, – I pluck'd the handkerchief off my eyes and threw it over my head, my cap and hat being lost in the fruitless struggles I had made; – there were several chairs, I stepp'd into the nearest to me, and was brought home in the deplorable situation you now see me.

Alexis. Oh 'tis too much for man to bear! – Yet one thing more, Matilda, – describe, as near as possible, the features and complexion of this inhuman ravisher.

Matilda. Alas, the horror I was in from the first moment I found myself in the power of a stranger hinder'd me from taking any great notice; – all I can say is, that he had dark eyes, a clear and ruddy skin, and though his behaviour render'd him odious to me, with others I believe he may pass for handsome.

Alexis. Young I suppose.

Matilda. About five or six and twenty, as far as I can judge.

Alexis. Had he the appearance of a man of rank and fortune?

Matilda. Every thing I saw about him, which properly belong'd to himself bespoke him such; – but doubly disguised. – Did you not take notice of an Huntsman at the Masquerade?

Alexis. Yes, and remember he always kept pretty near to us. – Was he the ravisher?

Matilda. The same; – he told me that he had his eye upon me from the first moment I came in, and when he saw you left me, ran and procur'd a Domine as like to yours as he could get, in hopes I might be, as alas I really was, deceiv'd by that fatal habit.

Alexis. 'Tis well; – I may perhaps hunt him.

The eyes of Alexis seem'd to flash fire while he utter'd these words; – after which he stood musing for some time, – then turning to his wife, who still sat weeping in the same posture she had thrown herself into at her entrance, spoke thus to her:

Alexis. Rise, Matilda, retire to your chamber and endeavour to compose yourself to rest.

Matilda. What so early? – 'tis not yet six o'clock.

Alexis. No matter, – your condition requires it, – you have wak'd too long, – therefore pray go.

Matilda. Will you come too?

Alexis. Do not expect me, – I have much to think upon and must be alone.

Matilda. Oh, Alexis! – 'tis as I fear'd, I am now grown loathsome in your sight.

Alexis. No, no, – not so; but there is a fermentation in my mind which must have time to settle, – to-morrow I may be more at ease; – I pray you then to give me liberty this night.

Matilda. Well, you shall be obey'd.

With this she took a candle and withdrew; but with a look and gesture so truly pity-moving, that if a painter had been to draw the picture of Despair he could not have copy'd from an original more striking.

He then call'd for mrs. Soberton, told her his wife had been very much frighted, and was indisposed, so begg'd she would assist her in any thing she might happen to stand in need of, and also that she would order a bed to be got ready for him in another chamber; – she reply'd, with a great many low curtsies, that she would take care his commands should be obey'd, and that she should think nothing in her power too much to serve the good lady.

She said no more, but went out of the room, I suppose, to do what he requested of her; – I was about to follow her, but seeing Alexis put on his wig, which he had pluck'd off when he went to lie down, thought he was going on some expedition which might be worth my taking the pains to explore; – to this end I slipp'd down stairs while he was taking up his sword and hat, – got out of the house before him, – divested myself of my Belt, – became visible, and met him some few paces distant.

I told him I was returning to his lodgings according to my promise, and affected some surprise at seeing him abroad; – he seem'd pleas'd that he had not miss'd me, and repeated, in a few words, the sum of what I have been relating; adding, that he now flatter'd himself with being able to trace out the person who had injur'd him, by the description Matilda had given of him, – and then intreated I would be so good as to accompany him in the search he was about to make; – to which request I readily consented.

I found his scheme was, to enquire among those people who let out dresses for the Masquerade, if any account could be given of a gentleman who the night before had hir'd first the habit of a Huntsman, and afterwards a blue Domine: – the thing, indeed, seem'd feasible enough in itself, though it did not answer expectation. – We went to several shops without receiving the least information; and all we could at last obtain was, that a gentleman, habited like a Huntsman, had come in a very great hurry for a blue Domine, which had not been return'd 'till about half an hour before our coming; – but the name or quality of the person who hir'd it, the woman protested to us she knew nothing of.

Alexis then demanded, somewhat hastily, who it was had brought it back: – she smil'd both at this interrogatory and the manner in which it was made, and reply'd, that she was talking to customers at that time in the shop; but if she had been less engag'd she should scarce have taken any notice; – 'For,' said she, 'provided we have our goods again, and are paid for the use of them, it is not our business to examine any farther.'

Here ended the fruitless search of Alexis; – he had now no shadow of hope for discovering the ravisher but in the advertisement I had persuaded him to get inserted in the News Papers, and his despair became so outragious that it was with much difficulty I prevail'd upon him to go home.

I went with him, fearing if he was left alone in the street he might be guilty of some extravagancy; – it was one of the most fine frosty nights I had ever seen, and while we were knocking at the door he look'd up towards the sky, and, with a voice denoting the extremest bitterness of heart, burst into this exclamation:

Alexis. How many thousand twinkling stars are there, yet not one among them all a friend to me or poor undone Matilda!

I went in with him to the chamber mrs. Soberton had caused to be provided for him, nor would leave him 'till I had seen him in bed; – after which I gave William a caution not to go to sleep, but keep near his master and be attentive to all his motions, in order to prevent any fatal effect of the present distraction of his mind.

I shall not trouble the reader with any account of the anxiety I was in at the condition in which I had left this worthy, though ill-fated pair; – I shall only say, it was such as made me quit my bed very early the next morning, with a resolution to exert my utmost endeavours for the mitigation of their sorrows, and, if possible, to reconcile Alexis to a misfortune which was without a remedy; but, unluckily for my design, a person came to speak with me the moment I was going out; – the business which had brought him very nearly concern'd me, and some papers which I was oblig'd to look over detain'd me 'till almost twelve o'clock.

On my arrival at the place where I so much wish'd to be, I found Alexis just come in before me; – he appear'd with a countenance much more compos'd than the night before, but very pensive and melancholy; – he presently acquainted me, however, with the occasion of his having been abroad; – it was this:

He told me he had pass'd the whole night in considering how he should act in relation to Matilda, and finding it a thing inconsistent with his honour to suffer her to remain in town after what had happen'd, he resolved to send her immediately into the country, and was just return'd from hiring a Post-chaise for that purpose; – the reason he gave for his proceeding in this manner was as follows:

Alexis. She cannot remain here and be shut up, she must appear sometimes; – and who can tell but that in some unlucky minute she may be seen by the very villain who has ruin'd her, and who, either through curiosity or the desire of renewing the gratification of his vicious flame, may discover whose wife she is, and wherever he sees me point me to his lewd companions for the wretch he has made me?

I had nothing to offer in opposition to what he said on this score; for, indeed, I thought it very proper that they should both retire into the country; – so reply'd, that I was glad I had call'd that morning, otherwise I should not have had the opportunity of wishing them a good journey: – to which he hastily rejoin'd, – 'I shall not go.' – 'How!' cry'd I, somewhat surprised, 'do you send away Matilda and stay behind yourself!' – A deep sigh was the first answer he gave; but the testimony of his discontent was presently succeeded by these words:

Alexis. Yes, my friend, – she must go without me; – two days ago nothing was so precious to me as her presence; – I liv'd, indeed, but in her sight; – every glance – every look she gave shot pleasure to my heart; – but now, alas! those happy moments are for ever fled, and I can regard her as no other than the ruin'd reliques of the woman once so dear to me.

It was in vain I represented to him, that as I doubted not but he was perfectly convinced of the purity of Matilda's mind, he ought not to love her less for the violence her person had sustain'd: – he own'd the justness of my reasons, but could not prevail on himself to be govern'd by them; and when I urg'd the cruelty of sending her so long a journey without any companion to alleviate her sorrows, he made me this reply:

Alexis. She does not go alone, – her waiting-maid, who soon after our arrival in town was oblig'd to be remov'd on account of the small-pox, is now quite recover'd, and came home last night; – this girl has attended Matilda for some years, and I know will be very careful of her.

While we were discoursing the chaise came to the door, on which Alexis call'd to have the luggage put in, and his wife to make herself ready: – I ask'd him if he thought it proper I should take my leave of Matilda before her departure; – he reply'd, that it was a ceremony which he believ'd she would gladly be dispensed with from receiving, in her present unhappy situation; – but begg'd I would stay in the dining-room 'till he had dispatch'd this disagreeable affair.

With these words he went out of the room, and I remain'd where I was; – in less than half a quarter of an hour, looking thro' the window, I saw the disconsolate Matilda go out of the house, supported on one side by Alexis, and on the other by her attendant; – I could not see her face, but her motions, and the distracted air with which she threw herself into the chaise, were enough to convince me of the extreme wretchedness of her condition.

Alexis return'd to me in a situation little less pity-moving yet could not my heart altogether absolve him for this last part of his behaviour towards Matilda; – it was now, however, a time to apply rather balms than corrosives to his bleeding and despairing mind; I therefore said every thing in my power which I thought might administer consolation to him; but all my endeavours that way were unsuccessful, and though I staid with him the greatest part of the day, had the mortification to leave him as I found him.

Oh! had the dark unknown beheld the sad effects his wild inordinate desires produced, he surely could not have sustain'd the shock, but must have reveng'd upon himself the mischiefs he had brought upon two worthy persons so lately bless'd, so truly loving and beloved.

CHAP. III.

Consists of some farther particulars relative to the preceding adventure, which came to the Author's knowledge after the departure of Matilda from London; with two letters wrote by that unfortunate lady to her husband in her exile, which it is hoped will not be an unwelcome present to the Public, especially to those who have hearts not utterly incapable of being affected with the woes of others.

I AM very much afraid that Alexis will stand but little justified in the opinion of my fair readers for his conduct towards Matilda; – they will doubtless say, that the love he pretended to have for her had taken but a shallow root in his heart, when it could be shaken by a misfortune which she had no way contributed to bring upon herself.

They will, perhaps, also add, that after she had with so much simplicity, some may think folly too, revealed to him the whole of what had befallen her, it was not only unkind, but highly ungenerous and cruel in him to abandon her to despair at a time when she had so much need of the tenderest compassion and consolation.

I must confess, indeed, that these accusations have the strongest appearance of reason on their side; yet I must take upon me, notwithstanding, to aver, that Alexis in this point was influenced by a principle which is among the things, which tho' we cannot prove to be so, yet we know in fact are so; and how much a paradox soever it may seem to some, Love, when in excess, may, on more occasions than one, produce the same effects as Hate.

I know not whether there are many ladies would like to be loved in this manner; for certain it is, that it was chiefly owing to the too refin'd delicacy of the passion Alexis was possess'd of for Matilda that made them both so greatly wretched; – the thoughts that another, though by force, had revell'd in her charms, depriv'd those charms of all their relish, and sicken'd every wish.

When we have been talking together on this head, often have I heard him, in the utmost bitterness of heart, express himself in these terms:

Alexis. I still adore her mind; – I know it all compos'd of sweetness, innocence, and heavenly truth; – but, oh! the blemish cast upon her person cannot be wash'd off but with the villain's blood; and unless fate allows me the means of doing her and myself that justice, can never look upon her but as the ghost of my once dear wife.

Finding that to prevail on him to live with Matilda as a wife was a thing utterly impracticable, at least 'till time had a little mellow'd the asperity of his resentment, I forbore any farther speech on that head, believing that if a change in Matilda's favour should ever happen, it must come wholly of himself, and not by the arguments of another.

It will be easy for the reader to judge of how little efficacy the persuasions of any friend could be to move him, when those of the tender, the endearing, the so lately ador'd Matilda prov'd in vain, which abundantly appear by the many letters she sent to him after her banishment, two only of which I got an opportunity of transcribing, and here present them to the public as a specimen of the rest.

The first was wrote immediately on her arrival at their country seat, and contain'd these lines:

To Alexis.

My dear, dear Alexis,

I am a sufficient proof that grief is not so fatal as some people would represent it, since I live to tell you I am safely arriv'd at ********; – yes, – I am return'd to that once blissful scene of soft delights, – of pure and virtuous love; – but, oh! that Heaven is fled, a sad reverse supplies its place, and wheresoever I turn my eyes, horrors instead of joys rise to my distracted view!

I remember that when you turn'd me from you, your last words to me were, – be comforted, Matilda. – Alas! you full well know, that without Alexis there is no comfort for Matilda; – your presence is the only balsam can assuage the tortures of my poor burning, bleeding, agonizing heart! – if then, indeed, you wish me less the wretch I am, let me not linger long in a banishment more cruel than death! – quit that detested town, – fly to my relief, and at least join with me in bewailing what is past a remedy.

But, oh! – I have too much cause to fear you have totally withdrawn all your affection from me, and am doubly miserable in a consciousness of being now render'd unworthy to retain it! – yet had sickness, or any other accident, deprived me of that little beauty nature has bestow'd upon me, and made me become lame, or blind, or crooked, I flatter myself you would have lov'd me still; – you would then have pitied and cherish'd me in your bosom; – and sure the misfortune that has befallen me was as far remov'd from my seeking as any of those I have mention'd could possibly be.

I will not, however, anticipate the doom I so much dread, – will not give way to apprehensions distracting to myself, and, I hope, injurious to you; – I know you are generous and just, and will endeavour to assure myself those noble principles, even without the aid of tenderness, will not permit you to hate me, to throw me off for ever, for my person having sustain'd a violence, to which I am persuaded you are convinced my mind was incapable of consenting: – I will believe that you feel all my woes, participate in my anguish, and that my pen ought rather to flow with words of consolation than reproach.

Yet if it is ordain'd that we must both be wretched, let us be wretched together; – let us mingle our tears, and interchangeably eccho back each others sighs; – let us indulge despair, – recal the memory of those blissful hours we once enjoy'd, – compare the present with the past, and join in curses on the base, the inhuman author of our mutual woes!

But whither does my inconsiderate passion lead me! – does it become the love, the tenderness, the duty of a wife, to wish you should partake my ruin! – no, – since I can no longer contribute to your happiness, rather forget, renounce, abandon me for ever! – Yet, oh! 'tis hard; – my brain grows wild on the reflection; – I can proceed no farther. – Pity me, my most dear, my most ador'd Alexis! pity, – oh pity,

The undone,

The lost MATILDA!

P.S. If these distracting lines have any power to move your soul! – if any remains of soft compassion towards me still dwell within your breast, write to me by the first post! – fix, I beseech you, my uncertain fate! – oh that I should live to stand in need of entreaties to hear from you!

When Alexis shew'd me the above, he seem'd all dissolv'd in a flood of love and tenderness; yet I believe the answer he sent to it was dictated in terms not altogether so satisfactory to Matilda as the present disturbance of her mind requir'd.

Here follows the second melancholy epistle of that unfortunate lady.

To Alexis.

My for ever dear, tho' much unkind Alexis,

With what anxiety have I watched the arrival of the post! – how counted the tedious minutes as they glided on! – how trembled between hope and fear on every knock was given at the gate, while in expectation of a letter from you! – at last it came; – but, oh! I am not more at ease!

Wherefore, Alexis, do you keep me in this cruel suspence! – I ask'd no impossibilities of you, – desir'd you not to love me still, – I only begg'd the decision of my fate; and sure that is not a request too much for me to make, or you to grant!

My father, uncles, all my kindred and acquaintance, nay, our very servants, stand amaz'd to see me here without you; – they perceive my alter'd looks, and with officious love enquire into the cause: – all the answer I can make is, – that the air of London not agreeing with my constitution, I hurry'd back before some business you had in town would permit you to return.

These excuses may pass current for a time, but cannot do so long; – I conjure you therefore, by all you have to hope, or fear, or wish, not to expose yourself and me to conjectures which cannot be to the advantage of either of our characters; – pronounce my doom, – say that you will return, and live with me, in all appearance, as before; or scruple not to let me know you have resolved on an eternal separation, that I may retire at once to some dark corner of the world, and shut myself up from pity and contempt.

I know this ought to have been thought upon before you obliged me to remove from London; but both of us were in too much confusion at the time of parting to give our cooler reason any room to operate; – we have since, however, had leisure to reflect on what was proper to be done in our unhappy circumstances; and I flatter myself you will not think me too presuming in being the first to mention it.

Oh, Alexis! imagine not that when I urge you to this eclaircisement,[243] that I am so vain as to sooth my fond heart with a belief that since the dreadful accident has happen'd to me you ever can love me as you have done; – no, I rather expect my sentence will be that of an everlasting banishment; – perhaps it is already sign'd within your breast, and the compassion you have for me alone delays the execution.

If this should be the case, – throw aside that cruel mercy which conceals it from me, I beseech you; – grief and despair has given me fortitude to bear the worst of ills, and sure there can be none half so dreadful to me as seeing you no more; – so much the better for my eternal peace, as it will the sooner rid me of the burden of a hated life; – but I will trouble you no more than to renew my petition of knowing in your next letter what it is you have in effect decreed for

The innocently criminal

MATILDA.

P.S. Your old acquaintance and fellow-collegian, mr. L –, has just now sent to enquire when you are expected down; – he designs, it seems, to set up at the next General Election for the Borough of *******, and greatly depends on the interest he knows you have in that place, – I suppose you will shortly receive a letter from himself on the occasion; – oh may the calls of friendship give weight to those I have mention'd, and influence you to return.

I happen'd to be with Alexis at the time of his receiving this; – he first read it to himself, – then communicated it to me, and when he had finish'd cry'd out with an extraordinary emotion,

Alexis. Poor Matilda! – unhappy charming woman! – with what enchanting eloquence does she plead against herself! – how sweetly labour to oppose what she most wishes to obtain.

As I found the strongest reason in the arguments urg'd in Matilda's letter, I must confess that I was at a loss to comprehend what he meant by speaking in this manner, therefore desir'd he would explain himself, which he immediately did in these terms:

Alexis. O, friend, the more I discover of her merit, the less I am able to forget the violation of her honour; – I must cease to love her as I do, – must bring myself to look upon her with the same indifference that most husbands do upon their wives, before I can support, with any tolerable degree of patience, the thoughts that another has possess'd her.

Thus did he always talk whenever we were alone together, and any mention of his wife came upon the carpet, as it seldom fail'd to do on some occasion or other; – had Matilda known his sentiments, I believe it would be a moot point whether she would not rather have chose a separation than to live with him, after he had reduced himself to such a state of insensibility.

He now, indeed, began to give great indications that he had nothing more at heart than to lose all remembrance, not only of the injury done to Matilda, but of herself also; – by very swift degrees he became the reverse of what he was before his going to that fatal Masquerade; – the pleasures of the bottle, and the conversation of the looser part of womankind, divide too much of his time between them, and he seeks in riots and debaucheries his relief from melancholy.

I am told, however, that he is at present preparing to set out for ******; but what satisfaction can the virtuous Matilda receive from his return thus transform'd, – thus debased in morals and behaviour from the man she had so dearly loved, and who was once so worthy her esteem?

How sad a reverse has a few weeks made in the condition of this lately happy pair! – surely the wretch, for so I must call him, be he of what degree or rank soever, who for the sake of gratifying the fleeting pleasure of a moment has brought this ruin on them, ought never to be forgiven in this world, whatever a sincere contrition, if he is capable of it, may entitle him to in the next.

CHAP. IV.

The Author having found something in his rambles, which he supposes may be of some value to the right owner, to shew his readiness to restore it, condescends to take upon himself the office of a Town-Cryer; – but waves the ceremony of the great O-Yes three times repeated.

HAppening one morning to wake more early than ordinary, I quitted my bed, and the weather being fine, and my humour more inclined to seriousness than gaiety, I took a little promenade, not with the least design or expectation of making any discovery of other people's affairs, but merely to think of my own with more liberty than I could do at home. – I met no living creature in my way except some few birds that perch'd upon the twigs of the yet leafless trees, and in melodious notes chanted forth praises to the approaching spring; – these rather indulging than confounding meditation, I pass'd slowly on by the side of the Serpentine-River, where, as I was bury'd in reflection on things which the reader has no business to be acquainted with, my eyes were attracted with the sight of a white sattin pocket lying just before me, – I suppose it might have been dropp'd from some lady's side the night before; for on my taking it up I found it extremely damp with the dew which always falls in absence of the sun.

I look'd upon this as a lawful prize, and that I had a right to keep it; at least 'till I could find somebody that had a better title; – I therefore tied it up in my handkerchief, and after having finish'd my walk took it home with me, where my impatience did not suffer me to continue long without examining what it contain'd; – I shall give a faithful inventory of all the particulars, reserving only one in petto,[244] in order to prevent being imposed upon by any fictitious claimant.

Money being the chief idol of mankind, I shall give that the preference, and begin with the Purse, which had in it five gold ducats, a leaden French shilling, a bent half-crown, and a medal of the Duke of Cumberland[245] in copper, very curious, but by some accident had been crack'd, and the impression in several parts pretty much erased.

Having look'd over these pieces, I put them carefully back into the Purse whence I had taken them, and then proceeded to a farther scrutiny.

The next thing that presented itself was a very small Pocket-book, which I shall forbear to describe, as well as to make any mention of the several memorandums it contain'd, to any person in the world but to the lady who wrote and shall come to demand them.

There was also a crystal Smelling bottle half full of Sal Armoniac,[246] a tortoseshell Snuff-box rimm'd with gold, and a naked Venus painted on the inside.

But the most valuable part of this cargo, at least according to my opinion, was some papers, – not Bank-Bills, – but letters and other writings more deserving the attention of the public, and which I shall make no scruple to insert, as they gradually fell under my inspection; especially as all of them having been sent under covers, which were not in the packet, the name of the lady to whom they were directed can only be guess'd at.

LETTER I.

MADAM,

I NOW send you the Catalogue you have so often requested of me; but intreat you will be so good as not to let any one soul in the world know you had it from him who has the honour to be,

With the greatest respect,

MADAM,

Your most humble,

And most devoted servant.

The name subscrib'd to this had been torn off, either by design or accident; but the paper which accompany'd it was perfect and entire: – here follows a faithful transcript.

A CATALOGUE *of some very scarce and curious pieces, in Prose and Verse, all wrote by some of the most eminent hands.*

1. THE Art of Pleasing in Conversation. An heroic Poem. – By the E – of C –.[247]
2. An Essay on Power. Wrote originally in High Dutch, and now translated by a person of distinction into English. – Bound in red Turky, finely gilt and letter'd.

3. The Virtues of Carmine, with a Recipe how to prepare it with success, – *probatum est.* – By the C – of C –.[248] Gilt back and letter'd.

4. Patient Grizel. A Poem in six Cantos. – By the real C – of C –.[249] Bound in Calf, very plain.

5. The Politician defeated. A Novel. In three Parts. – By the E – of E –.[250] Stitch'd in blue Paper.

6. The Croaker. A Tragi-comical Farce of one Act. – By L – R –.[251]

7. Cookery improv'd, after the Epicurean stile. – By a Club of Gentlemen. In sheets.

8. The Chaste Maid; or, A new Way to amuse the Town. – A Comedy of three Acts, each sufficient for a Winter Night's Entertainment. – By the facetious H – F –, Esq;[252]

9. Rules to chuse a Wife; shewing the Absurdity of all those generally observed. – By Sir J – C –.[253] In Boards.

10. A philosophical Definition of Card-Craft, – upwards of forty Years compiling – By the very learned and most ingenious Professor Mr. H – e.[254] Stitch'd in gilt Paper.

11. Frugality. A Poem. In nine Cantos. – By the C – of B –.[255] Bound in Vellum.

12. A Collection of Jests and merry Phrases, to keep young Pupils Heads from aching with more laborious Studies. – By a Tutor in the modish Sciences. Finely bound in blue Turky, gilt back and letter'd.

13. Try before you buy. A Poem after the manner of Hudibrass. – By the E – of R– .[256] In Boards.

14. The Charms of Novelty. A Pindaric Essay. – By miss C –.[257] In Sheets.

15. The Pleasures of Matrimony; or, who would not be a Husband. A Farce. – By L – V –.[258] Stitch'd, and very much sullied with often reading.

16. A Dissertation on Flys Eggs. – By the President of a learned Society. In Boards.

17. Laugh and lie down. A Ballad Opera of three Acts. – By L – P –.[259] Stitch'd in blue Paper.

18. An Essay to prove that true Honour is always concomitant with good Sense. – By the E – of O –.[260] Bound in plain blue Turky.

19. Conjugal love. A Pastoral, of one continued Scene. – By the E – of N.[261] Printed on a new Elzevir letter, and neatly bound without tawdriness or affectation.

20. The Patriot. A secret History. – By G – D –, Esq;[262] Bound in clouded Calf.

21. The Double Dealer; or, The Westminster Disappointment. A Farce of two Acts. – By Sir G – V –.[263] Stitch'd in Cap Paper.

22. An Eulogy on Apostacy. – By L – G –.[264] Bound in Calf and gilt back.

23. Love in a Bottle. A Poem, in three Cantos. – By the E – of M –.[265] Stitch'd in blue Paper.

24. Redivivus; or, Old Age and Gallantry reconciled. A humourous Farce of one Act. – By the E – of H –.[266] Stitch'd.

25. An Exhortation to Hospitality to Foreigners, even tho' it should happen to be destructive to the Liberties of the Natives. – By L – T –,[267] as he deliver'd it at the Hay-Market. Bound in the French Taste.

26. Criticisms on the Play of – Rule a Wife and Have a Wife. – By L – P –.[268] In Boards.

27. The Fox weary of Goose-hunting. A Fable. – By the D – of D –.[269] Bound in Parchment.

28. The Lover's Catechism. A new Ballad. – By the celebrated Miss A –.[270]

29. An infallible Remedy for curing the Scotch Itch without Bleeding. – By the D – of A –.[271]

30. The Beauties of domestic Life, illustrated with Examples. A Pastoral Eclogue. – By the D – of B –.[272] Neatly bound.

31. Love levels all; or, A lucky Trip to Bath. An Epic Poem without any Episodes. – By C – B –.[273] Printed on a half worn out letter, but very richly bound.

32. Instructions for a Supplement to Arthur Collins's Peerage of England. – By L – L –.[274] Stitch'd in Marble Paper.

33. Verses in praise of Breeding. – By Miss W –.[275]

34. True Magnificence. An Heroic Poem. – By the D – of M –.[276] Finely bound.

35. Love in a Coach. A true Secret History. – By C – V –.[277] Stitch'd.

36. Second Thoughts best. A Philosophical Treatise, dedicated to a Brother of the Horn. – By Mr. W –.[278] Bound in Sheeps skin.

37. The Triumvirate of Converts; – being a series of Epistles on moral and religious Subjects, which pass'd between L – T –, C – G –, and Mis. C –.[279] In Boards.

38. The Escape. A Satire. Inscrib'd to L – D – M –,[280] by a well-wisher to her Ladyship.

39. A Scheme intended to be offer'd to Parliament for the erecting Stockjobbers into a Corporation, and having a Hall of their own to transact Business in, without going to Exchange-Alley. – By Mr. P –.[281]

40. A Letter sent with a Side of Venison to the celebrated Mrs. J – D –, in the Piazza, Covent-Garden. – By L – T – e.[282]

41. A short Treatise concerning public and private Charities, proving to a Demonstration that the former are of much more Emolument to the Giver than the latter. – By L – E – J –.[283] Curiously bound, with a Register.

42. The Humiliation. A Poem. Address'd to the Inexorables. – By L – G – S
    –.[284] Stitch'd.
43. A Prophecy that Votes for Members of Parliament will fall to no Price at
    the next Westminster Election. – By Sir W – Y –.[285]

Having folded and replaced this Paper in the pocket whence I had taken it, I
proceeded to the others.

LETTER II.

MADAM,

IT must be confess'd that you are endow'd with a courage and resolution
superior to what most of your sex can boast of; but you must give me leave to
say, at the same time, that in these affairs we men run much the greatest hazards;
in case of a discovery, our persons are liable to fall a sacrifice to the resentment
of an injur'd husband, and our fortunes sure to be ruin'd by way of reparation
of his disgrace, – whereas the worst your have to fear is a divorce: – the laws are
favourable to wives, – the portion you brought with you is either return'd, or
an annuity equivalent; – and as for the little shame you sustain by such a pro-
cedure, it is well atton'd for by your being freed from the loathsome caresses of
the man you hate, and at full liberty to pursue your inclinations with him you
love. – Be assur'd, dear madam, I would venture much for the continuance of the
blessing you permit me to enjoy; but I find the intercourse between us begins to
be suspected, and you must therefore pardon me that I yield to necessity, and
refrain any farther meetings with you, at least for the present: – I was yesterday
at Court, and heard some whispers that your jealous coxcomb would soon be
sent abroad; – if such a thing should happen, as I have some pretty good reasons
to believe it will, I shall return with double transport to your embraces, 'till then
prudence obliges me to deny, myself that happiness; but at how great a distance
soever I keep my person, I beg you will do me the justice to believe my heart is
always with you, and that I can never cease to be,

    With the greatest sincerity,
                Dear MADAM,
                      Your most obliged,
                          And most faithfully
                              Devoted servant,
                                  PHILETES.

P.S. I would not have you harbour any unjust suspicions, either of me or your fair
friend, for upon my soul I never had the least design upon her in the way you
mean; and you will find, whenever it is convenient for me to renew my devoirs

to you, that I like no woman better than yourself. – Once more I bid you unwillingly adieu.

LETTER III.

Dear Creature,

YOUR Damon and my Strephon, as we call them, are both with me; – they have found out the most charming place that ever was for us to scamper to, whenever we can delude the eyes of our impertinent gaolers; – if you can find any excuse to get loose from yours, the rendezvous agreed upon is the banks of the Serpentine-river, just after sun-set, whence we are to follow our leaders where they shall please to conduct us. – Lady Fillup has a route to night, – you may tell your tyrant you are going there; but why should I put pretences into a head so much more fertile than my own? – Fail not to come, however, if it be not a thing utterly impossible for human wit to accomplish; but let us know your resolution by the bearer

I am,

> With the most perfect amity,
>> My DEAR,
>>> Your very obedient,
>>>> Humble servant,
>>>>> CORRINNA.

P.S. While I was writing the above, Damon, to shew either his love, or wit, or both, took up a pen and employ'd it in the inclos'd.

> To my Soul's Treasure.

FLY, charmer, fly, – leave homebred cares behind,
With thoughts of coming joys fill all your mind;
Let smiling pleasure wanton o'er your face,
And kindling transports brighten ev'ry grace;
Each vein of mine beats high with love's alarms,
Haste then, and lull me gently in your arms.

I know I am a bad poet, but you will find me a better lover, and that your charms are capable of inspiring me with more fire than all the ladies of Parnassus put together. I am,

> With truth and tenderness,
>> My lovely dear,
>>> Your most passionate,
>>>> And faithful adorer,
>>>>> DAMON.

The letter of Philetes, and that of Corrinna and Damon, being dated on the same day, discover'd to me that the lady who received them was not quite inconsolable for the loss of one lover as she had another in store; and also that she fail'd not to comply with the invitation of Damon, and that she had dropp'd her pocket at the rendezvous appointed by Corrinna.

I make no question but that the inquisitive reader would be glad to know the name and rank of this so much admir'd lady; but as I can do no more, at most, than guess at either, I should be loath to impose my bare and uncertain conjectures upon the public, for fear of a mistake, and being guilty of the worst of wrongs, that of prejudicing the character of an innocent person. – I wish every one would pay as much regard as myself to what Shakespear says on this occasion:

> Good name, in man or woman,
> Is the immediate jewel of our souls:
> Who steals my purse, steals trash: 'tis something, nothing;
> 'Twas mine, 'tis his, and has been slave to thousands;
> But he that filches from me my good name,
> Robs me of that which not enriches him,
> And makes me poor indeed.[286]

Could I have form'd even the most distant supposition to what place Strephon and Damon had conducted their ladies, I doubt not but my curiosity would have carry'd me thither, where my enquiries might perhaps have gain'd me the satisfaction of knowing how much of the night these inamoratos had pass'd together, and in what manner they had been entertain'd; but no mention being made of any thing farther than the place where they were to meet, in Corrinna's letter, I was oblig'd to content myself with what discoveries I had made, and so must the reader also.

I cannot conclude this chapter without an observation which has constantly occurr'd to me whenever anything fell in my way of the kind I have been relating, – which is this: – as the wife has the honour of her husband in keeping, it seems to me a most ungenerous and cruel addition to the crime of wronging his bed, when by public indiscretions she exposes him to that contempt and ridicule which the world, though without the least shadow of reason or justice, is always sure to cast upon the husband of a transgressing wife.

I know very well that people are apt to say, – that when a woman abandons herself to vice she presently becomes utterly incapable of paying any regard to her own reputation, much less to that of her husband; – and that it appears a much greater matter of surprise when they see women, as it must be confess'd many such there are, who, without being criminal in fact, behave in such a manner as to draw on themselves the severest censures.

Though I must allow that this too frequently happens, yet I cannot agree in opinion with those who seem to wonder it should be so, and look upon it as a kind of inconsistency in nature; – I rather imagine that guilt is more likely to inspire circumspection; – a woman who knows herself culpable, I should expect to be very careful not to do any thing in public that might cause suspicion of her being less reserv'd in private; whereas a consciousness of innocence, especially in a thoughtless disposition, may easily render a woman unguarded, and less observant of those decorums, which, tho' not essential to virtue, are doubtless necessary to reputation.

CHAP. V.

Turns chiefly upon the subject of Education, and contains some things which the Author is apprehensive will not be very agreeable to the Female part of his readers, whether of the elderly or the more youthful class, yet may serve as a useful admonition to both.

THE good or the ill fortune of our whole lives chiefly depends on the first bent given to our minds in youth; – impressions made in our early years take a deep root within us, grow up with us to maturity, become part of ourselves, so that they may properly be call'd a second nature, and are seldom, if ever, totally eradicated. – According to one of our English poets,

> Children, like tender osiers, take the bow,
> And as they first are fashion'd, still will grow.[287]

For this reason it is that parents, unless they are very remiss indeed, take so much pride in the education of their children, bestowing on them every accomplishment befitting of their rank and circumstances, and oftentimes more than will well agree with either; – yet all this will not do, – there are some previous steps to be taken, without which all the improvements we can make, from the lessons of the most able masters, will never render us worthy the esteem of others, or truly happy in ourselves, for any length of time.

Pride, and an impatience of control, are the first propensities discoverable in human nature; – if these are humour'd and indulged in their beginnings, which is indeed in our most early years, they will soon become too headstrong and too turbulent to be afterwards restrain'd and subjected to the government of reason, by any methods whatever that can be taken for that purpose;[288] – their first indications should therefore be carefully watch'd, and check'd in every instance.

I smile to think what objections are commonly made, by some over-fond parents, to such a manner of proceeding; – if I am not mistaken these two are the principal; that to curb children too much is apt to break their spirits; and that the world being so full of disappointments, that few people escape them when they come to maturity, it is pity the poor things should know sorrow before their time; – to both which I take the liberty to make this reply:

First, – As to what they call the breaking of the spirit, – that due decorum I would recommend, takes no more of the spirit from the young master or miss than what is necessary to keep them from running into those follies and excesses which, how excusable soever in childhood, render them contemptible in riper years; – as the skilful gardener lops from his tender plant those superfluous branches, which, if suffer'd to continue, would hinder it from growing to perfection.

Then as to the second, – Every one knows the sorrows their little hearts are capable of feeling make no lasting impression on them, – they will cry one moment and laugh the next; – the contradiction they meet with, will only make them sensible that they neither can nor ought to expect they are to have their will in all things; and the trifling disappointments given them will enable them to sustain with fortitude those of more consequence which may hereafter possibly befal them.

A Boy is less liable to the danger of being spoil'd by too much indulgence than a Girl; because he is no sooner taken from the nursery than he is either put apprentice to some trade or calling; or, if of a superior rank, under the inspection of a grave and austere tutor; – that is, when the tender mamma does not interfere, and give orders that no intense studies be imposed upon him, for fear of making his head ach; – but this seldom happens, – her husband, if she has one alive, will not endure his son shall be bred a dunce to please his wife, – whereas he meddles not with the education of his daughters, but leaves them to the direction of their mother.

The good lady, no doubt, is extremely ambitious that her daughter shall be one of the most accomplish'd young creatures in town; – to this end the best masters in their several sciences are employ'd to teach her Music, Dancing and French; – if she is well vers'd in these, – knows how to dress in the most becoming manner, and to give a genteel turn to an invitation on a card, she is look'd upon as complete in every necessary qualification; – for as to any understanding in cookery, pastry, or needle-work, they are consider'd as vulgar things, and below the delicacy of a fine bred lady.

I have the honour to be pretty nearly related, by marriage, to lady Plyant, her late husband being my first cousin; – decency obliges me to visit the widow sometimes; – she is a very affable good natur'd woman, and has, indeed, a greater share of understanding than her too great compliance with the customs of the age will permit her to make shew of.

She keeps a prodigious deal of company, for which reason I see her much less frequently than otherwise I should do; – but happening to pass by her house one day, when no coach nor chair was in waiting there, I ventur'd to knock at the door, and was glad to be told she was alone; – I had not, however, been with her above ten minutes before two or three loud raps proclaim'd the approach of some new guest, and presently after a grave elderly lady was introduced.

Lady Plyant receiv'd her with much politeness and a great shew of friendship, and after the first salutations were over, and we had reseated ourselves, said to her,

Lady Plyant. Dear mrs. Loyter, I have not seen you this age, and have been quite unhappy in the want of you.

Mrs. Loyter. Dear lady Plyant, the loss is wholly mine; – but I have been so embarrass'd; – my poor girl has been extremely indisposed.

Lady Plyant. Bless me! – Miss not well, and I hear nothing of it! – But I hope she is better?

Mrs. Loyter. Perfectly recover'd, madam; – she will have the honour of waiting on your ladyship this evening; she is gone to make about half a dozen visits; but pray'd heartily to find nobody at home, that she might follow me here the sooner.

Lady Plyant. How perfectly kind that was; – well, she is a charming creature; – you are the happiest woman in the world in having such a daughter: – I protest among all my acquaintance I do not know any young lady that comes up to her; – there is something so sweet, – so engaging, in every thing she does.

Mrs. Loyter. She is infinitely oblig'd to your ladyship; – indeed I have taken a great deal of pains with her; for as I have nothing to do with my sons, they being all under their father's management, and I have no other daughter, I should never have forgiven myself if I had not used my utmost endeavours to form her mind so as to make her as agreeable as possible to her acquaintance; and, I thank Heaven, I have been pretty successful in it.

Lady Plyant. Oh, madam, the world must allow you have, – Miss is the darling of every body that knows her.

Mrs. Loyter. The girl has a great deal of good nature, madam, and does not want a genius and capacity to mingle in conversation on almost any subject becoming a young lady to be acquainted with.

I had been upon the wing to take my flight almost from the moment mrs. Loyter came in; but what was said in relation to her daughter determin'd me to stay 'till miss should arrive, in order to be convinced how far her person and behaviour corresponded with the high character had been given of her.

I waited, tho' not without some impatience, 'till abundance more had pass'd between these two ladies on the same subject, and on several other no less trifling, which as I cannot think the reader will be better pleas'd with than I was myself, I shall forbear to insert.

At length miss Loyter appear'd, and I stretch'd my eye-lids to their full extent to take in all the charms I had heard she was possess'd of; – the girl, indeed, was well enough; but I could discover nothing extraordinary about her; nor did her eyes or air give any indications of that sparkling wit her mother seem'd to boast of; but as I thought it unfair to give a verdict on mere appearances, I suspended my judgment on her understanding 'till I had more substantial proofs.

The discourse at first was only on where she had been, – who she had seen, – and how such and such a lady was dress'd; – I found miss talk'd very learnedly on this subject, and therefore was not without hope of hearing something from her equally lively on others of more importance; but none being started I was compell'd to listen to the several animadversions made by these three ladies on caps and flounces, to my very great mortification, as any one who reads this work may easily suppose by what it discovers of my humour.

At last miss happening to say that she had met mrs. O – in one of the visits she had been making, I presently catch'd up the word and said to her, – 'Then, madam, I doubt not but some conversation pass'd which you will do us a favour to repeat, as the lady you mention is perfectly acquainted with public affairs, and reasons upon them very justly.' – To which she made this answer:

Miss Loyter. So they say, sir; but she was just going out when I came in; I was heartily glad of it; for I hate to hear a deal of stuff about things that I know nothing of.

As I had a good share in the ensuing part of this conversation, I shall, to avoid confusion, repeat my own words as if spoke by another person.

Author. Then, madam, you have no relish for politics?

Miss Loyter. No truly, sir. – What business have I with the transactions of kings, and princes, and parliaments? – It makes me sick to hear so much of wars, and treaties, and conventions, and taxes, and grievances, and such nonsense.

Author. I must confess, madam, that the affairs of Europe are a little intricate at present, and may be puzzling to a lady's comprehension; – but I suppose you are well acquainted with the histories of former times.

Miss Loyter. Lord, sir, what have I to do with former times?

Author. Every one, madam, has to do with the annals of the country they were born in.

Mrs. Loyter. These things are quite out of my daughter's way; but for all that I can assure you, sir, she reads a great deal.

Author. It would be pity, indeed, madam, so fine a young lady should be altogether ignorant of books: – I imagine therefore that miss's genius soars to a higher pitch, – the wonders of the creation, so beautifully defined in some treatises of natural philosophy, perhaps are her favourite contemplations; – I make no question but she has read Le Spectacle de la Nature.[289]

Mrs. Loyter. I believe not, sir. – Have you, my dear?

Miss Loyter. Not I, truly; – but I have heard enough of it: – they say that there are four volumes of it taken up with nothing but a description of Trees, and Birds, and Beasts, and Fishes, and nasty Insects.

Author. What do you think, madam, of Fontenelle's Plurality of Worlds?[290]

Miss Loyter. O hang it, – I was never so disappointed in my life; – I thought by the beginning, when I found a gentleman and lady were taking their promenade together by moon-light, that some pretty adventure would have ensued; – but good God, the Author has made them talk of nothing but the Planets and the things that happen in the Sky.

Author. I fancy then, miss, that Romances and Novels are chiefly your taste.

Miss Loyter. I hate Romances, they are too tedious; – as for Novels, I like some of them well enough, particularly mrs. Behn's; – but I know not how it is, the Authors nowadays have got such a way of breaking off in the middle of their stories, that one forgets one half before one comes to the other.

Author. Digressions, miss, when they contain fine sentiments and judicious remarks, are certainly the most valuable parts of that sort of writing.

Miss Loyter. I cannot think so, and I could wish the Authors would keep their sentiments and remarks to themselves, or else have them printed in a different letter, that one might know when to begin and when to leave off.

Author. I presume, miss, you are fond of Poetry?

Miss Loyter. Not very fond; – I can't say I ever read much of it.

Author. Then you can't say whether you give the preference to the ancient or the modern?

Miss Loyter. No, really; – I never thought about the matter.

Mrs Loyter. Sir, my daughter is not so vain as to set up for a critic, tho' I am pretty sure she knows more than she pretends to; – I have heard some good judges allow her to have a very distinguishing taste in some of the Theatrical representations.

Miss Loyter. O I love a Farce or a Pantomime extravagantly; – they are vastly diverting.

Author. Then I suppose, miss, you see Plays merely for the Entertainments which so frequently succeed them?

Miss Loyter. Not entirely so; – there are some Plays I like well enough; but there are others so cramm'd with the words Liberty and Public Spirit, that they are quite surfeiting.

Author. When there is too much of these things, madam, the Licence-Office knows how to correct them.[291]

Miss Loyter. There is Cato,[292] for example, – some people cry it up; but for my part I think it a piece of dull stupid stuff, excepting one scene between Portius and Lucia.

I thought I had now sufficiently founded the genius and capacity of this young lady, therefore ceased to engross her any longer to myself, and soon after took my leave, secretly wondering at the strange partiality of mrs. Loyter in regard both of herself and daughter.

A few hours, however, made me begin to judge somewhat more favourably of these ladies; – 'Tho' mrs. Loyter,' said I within myself, 'is mistaken in believing she has been able to make her daughter pass for a wit, her endeavours, notwithstanding, may have had better success in other accomplishments more essential to her happiness, – she may have made her a good œconomist, and perfectly acquainted with every thing requisite for the well managing a family.'

I had the more reason to imagine that this young lady was train'd up in frugality and good housewifry, as I had been told that mr. Loyter lived to the height of his income, – that he saved no money, – had several sons, the eldest of whom, after his decease, was to run away with the estate; so that it could not be expected the daughter would have any fortune to entitle her to a husband at all suitable to her birth and the appearance she made.

But as I was always willing to be convinced whether my conjectures were right or wrong, I resolved to make an Invisible Visit to this family. – Just as I came to the house, mr. Loyter was going out, and the door being open'd for him I slipp'd in and went up stairs; – the old lady was sitting in the dining-room window with her spectacles on, very hard at work; – breakfast was but just over, as I found by the maid's removing the tea equipage, and Miss was gone up to dress, it seems; for she came down presently after in the same form I had seen her at lady Plyant's; – she ran directly to the great glass in order to examine how her petticoats hung at the bottom, – and then turn'd to her mother, and seeing what she was about said to her,

Miss Loyter. Lord, mamma, have you not done mending my tippet yet!

Mrs. Loyter. Indeed, my dear, it is past mending; – you have torn the lace in twenty places, I believe, with those ugly pins in your stomacher; – I wish you would take more care of your things.

Miss Loyter. Indeed I can't be a slave to my cloaths.

Mrs. Loyter. I would not have you, my dear; – but this vexes me, because it is the only handsome tippet you have; – you must e'en try to coax your father to give you a couple of pieces to buy you another, the first time you find him in a good humour; – for I assure you I have not a single guinea in the world.

Miss Loyter. Well, 'tis a shameful thing one has not money without asking for, when one has a fancy to any thing – But, mamma, can nothing be done with this lace?

Mrs. Loyter. It will never make up again in the shape it is; – but I believe I may contrive to make a handsome tucker[293] out of it.

Miss Loyter. Oh I shall like a tucker of it vastly; – pray, mamma, do it as soon as you can: I must go out and divert myself some where or other.

Mrs. Loyter. Where, my dear?

Miss Loyter. Nay, – I have gone my round of visits twice over since any one of them has been return'd; – I am only going to the next street to lady Lovetoy's, to ask if Miss will take a walk with me in the Park.

Mrs. Loyter. Very well, my dear; but do not stay too long, – your father brings company home to day, and we are to have a great dinner; – mr. Blossom, and his son just come from the University, are to be here, so I would not have you out of the way for the world; – who can tell what may happen!

Miss Loyter. Oh why did not I know that sooner, – I would have had on my new gause cap; – but 'tis no matter, – I will come home time enough to change it.

With these words she snatch'd up her little muff and gallop'd down stairs, leaving her poor mother poring over the breaches she had undertaken to rectify; – presently after a servant maid came into the room, and on mrs. Loyter's demanding what she wanted, made this reply:

Maid. I thought Miss had been here, madam; – I came to desire she would lend a hand to make a crust for the venison, and beat a little spice for the puddings.

Mrs. Loyter. 'Tis a sign, child, you came hither but last night; – my daughter does not know how to make crust.

Maid. O dear, madam, any body may make a little paste to roast a piece of venison in.

Mrs. Loyter. I tell you she knows nothing of cookery, nor I would not have her spoil her hands about it; – but if you will bring me up the pestle and mortar I will beat your spice for you.

Maid. No, madam, – while I am fetching up the things, and carrying them down again, I can do it myself.

The girl said no more, but went out of the room with a countenance which shew'd she was not very well pleased with the family she was come to serve: – I attended not the return of miss Loyter, – my curiosity was now fully satisfied, and I laid hold on the first opportunity I found to quit the house.

Methinks I hear how heartily the gay and witty part of my readers will laugh at the character of miss Loyter; – they will certainly look upon her as a stalking, staring, stupid, noteless creature; a moving piece of mere matter, uninform'd by any soul or spirit, – wholly incapable of deserving praise, and equally insensible of contempt; – 'tis true she appears so, – yet may it not be owning so much to any deficiency of nature in her, as to the mistaken fondness of a mother, who fearing to give her a moment's discontent neglected to rouse the native sluggishness of her faculties by any exercise or employment.

What therefore can be expected from a young person bred in a supine indolence, accustom'd to have her will in every thing, and scarce taught the difference between good and evil, should her whole life long act as chance, or what is as bad, her own undistinguishing fancy shall direct? – Bless all sober and thinking men from a wife of this cast.

CHAP. VI.

The Author expects will make a full attonement to the ladies for the too much plain dealing, as some of them may think, of the preceding chapter.

WOMEN and Wedlock are the common topics of ridicule among men, who, without one spark of genius or capacity, imagine themselves wits, and set up for such; but whatever either they, or some who even have a better way of thinking in other things, pretend to alledge against the sex, it is very evident, and must be confess'd, that nature has endow'd the minds of many women with as great and valuable talents as ever she bestow'd on men.

Numberless are the examples which might be brought from the records both of ancient and modern history, to prove the truth of this assertion, but I shall content myself with mentioning only a few, yet enough to make those unworthy maligners of a sex to which, they know in their own hearts, they are indebted for all the convenience and happiness of their lives, take shame to themselves and blush for what they have said.

Who is so ignorant as not to have heard of the fam'd Cornelia of Rome, – the mother of the Gracchi,[294] – and the wife of Brutus,[295] – the learned Hypatia of Greece,[296] – the Boadicea[297] and the Cartismuda of ancient Britain;[298] – but 'tis needless to look back into such distant times, – the wife of the late Peter the Great of Muscovy,[299] – the imperial heroine of Germany,[300] – Signiora Laura of Italy,[301] – and the present queens of Sweden and the Two Sicilies,[302] are no less public than shining proofs of the capacity of a female mind.

And even here, in this degenerate island, where all wisdom and all virtue have been gradually decreasing for upwards of fifty years, there are not wanting some, I may say many ladies, who in private, and almost obscure life, are possess'd of qualifications that might add lustre to the highest stations.

In fine, – there is nothing more certain, than that if the women, generally speaking, are less knowing than the men, it is only because they are deny'd the same advantages of education, and the mistaken mother lavishes her whole cares in embellishing the pretty person of her daughter, and gives no attention to the cultivation of her understanding.

I am happy in the acquaintance of a lady whom I shall distinguish by the name of Amadea; – she had been married very young to a gentleman whom she tenderly lov'd, but had the misfortune to lose him at the age of twenty-five, and was at the same time the mother of three daughters, the eldest scarce four years old.

The land estate, which was very considerable, descended to the next male heir of the family, and all the personals, with a jointure of four hundred per annum, to the fair widow, and each of her children five thousand pounds.

The first three years of her widowhood she lived the life of a recluse, seldom stirring out of her own house, except to her devotions, or when the necessity of her affairs oblig'd her; – nor did she, with her mourning, throw this reserve entirely off; – tho' it is now full thirteen years since her dear husband's death, she neither visits nor receives visits as formerly, but confines her conversation to those of her kindred, or very long and intimate acquaintance; – never appears at any public diversion, and rejects even the first mention of proposals for a second marriage, though several very advantageous ones have been attempted.

All her cares have been turn'd on the education of her children, and all her pleasures center'd in observing the improvements they made by the instructions given to them; – she had never suffer'd their tender infancy to be frighted with idle stories of spirits and hobgoblins, nor amused with fairy tales; from their most early years she awak'd reason in them, and contriv'd it so, that even the little sports she indulged them in should some way or other conduce to that great end.

As they grew bigger she had masters to teach them music and dancing, the French and Italian languages, and as much of the Latin as was sufficient to make them speak and write English properly; but these politer studies were not to take up all their time, – the œconomy of domestic life she look'd upon as too necessary a qualification not to be well attended to, – some hours in every day were set apart for needle-work; and whenever the table was to be furnish'd with any thing extraordinary, they were sure to be put under the tuition of the cook, and frequently assisted her in those parts of her business which were the most delicate and least laborious.

Thus desirous of enriching their minds with every useful kind of knowledge, it cannot be supposed that books were out of the question, – no, – each of these young ladies takes upon her, in her turn, to read to the two others the whole time they are at work. – Baile's Dictionary[303] may justly be call'd a Library of itself, as it gives a general insight into almost every remarkable occurrence that has happen'd in the world since the creation; and whenever they found any mention made of persons or transactions which gave them a curiosity of being more fully acquainted with the particulars of, she sent immediately to her Bookseller for the history to which that passage referr'd.

But above all other things, this discreet mother was studiously watchful to prevent the pride and little vanities, so incident to human nature, from taking too fast hold of their young hearts; – betimes she taught them, that nothing concerning themselves, except the embellishment of their minds, was worthy their attention; – that all cares relating to dress or person, beyond what cleanliness and decency requir'd, were superfluous and silly, and that every minute wasted at the toylet would rob them of some advantage they might otherwise receive.

I am well aware, that those of my fair readers who have been brought up in a different manner, which, by the way, I fear are much the greatest part, will be apt to cry out against the conduct of Amadea; – they will perhaps say, they wonder the poor girls are not mop'd, and that they must certainly be dull stupid creatures; – but those who think thus need only have a sight of the young ladies to be convinced of their mistake, – nothing can be more lively and spirituous than all the three sisters, – smiles of innocence and joy dwell for ever on their faces, and denote an innate chearfulness and satisfaction, which all those hurrying pleasures, so eagerly pursued by others, have not the power of bestowing.

I made several Invisible Visits to them in their own apartment, and I know very few things capable of giving me a more sincere delight than I took in observing the behaviour of these young beauties, at times when they thought themselves entirely free from all inspection, and had no occasion to put any restraint upon their words or actions.

Never did I find them lolling out of the windows, or consulting their look or motions in the great glass; – never heard them complaining that they were not permitted to be the first in every new fashion; – never wishing to be in the Mall, or any other public place; – never wantonly giggling about love or lovers; – never quarreling with each other, or ridiculing the foibles of their acquaintance.

Sometimes I caught them playing and singing to their instruments, – at others amusing themselves with practising some new dance, and not seldom busily employ'd in needlework for the use of the family; and at the same time making such remarks as occurr'd to them on some passage or other in history: – in fine, I could perceive nothing but what put me in mind of the three Graces, who, according to one of our poets, are actuated but by one soul, and that, – all harmony and sweet contentment.

The truth is, Amadea never makes use of any austerity, – the precepts she gives are only enforced by her own example, and deliver'd in such a manner as to steal themselves upon the mind, and have no need of any compunction from authority; – so that one may truly say,

> Wisdom in her appears so bright and gay,
> They hear with pleasure, and with pride obey.[304]

Happy the children who have such a mother; – happy the mother who has children such as these: – I am persuaded that many examples of this kind might be found, if parents would be at the pains to pursue the same measures Amadea did, and instil into their offspring the principles of virtue and wisdom before they knew what was meant by vice and folly.

CHAP. VII.

Contains the recital of an adventure, which, perhaps, will not be found the less, but the more interesting, for its being not altogether of so singular a nature as some others in this work may have appear'd.

I was one morning taking my Invisible progression into those pleasant fields which lie behind Montague-House, not with the least view of making any discoveries, for I could expect none in that retired place, but merely to enjoy the benefit of the fresh air, which is almost constantly impregnated with various odours wafted from the adjacent gardens.

I had not walk'd many minutes, however, before I heard the tread of some persons close behind me; – I stepp'd aside to let them pass, and saw that one of them was Narcissa, the only daughter of a gentleman who lived in that neighborhood; – the person who accompany'd her was her maid, as I soon after found by the following dialogue between them:

Narcissa. Indeed, Betty, I think Capt. Pike shews but little love to let us be here before him.

Betty. Oh, madam, you should consider that gentlemen in his post are not always masters of their time; – you know he said he came to town on affairs of the regiment, – and something, perhaps, may have happen'd; – but whatever it is that detains him it cannot be want of affection, I am so certain of that, I would pawn my life upon it.

Narcissa. You are very confident, Betty, to offer such security for a man you have never seen but twice in your life.

Betty. If I had never seen him but once, madam, I have seen enough to make me know that he loves you to distraction: – poor gentleman, – if he should not succeed in his addresses I am sure he has reason to curse me.

Narcissa. Curse thee, Betty, – why curse thee?

Betty. He might never have seen you if it had not been not for me. – Don't you remember, madam, how I teaz'd you to go into Jolliffe's shop[305] and buy the last new play; – he was sitting reading when we came in, and I shall never forget how he threw down the pamphlet he had in his hand and stared at you, – and how he sigh'd; – poor soul, he lost his heart from that very moment; – then how he follow'd us into the Park; – and how he trembled when he ask'd your leave to join us?

Narcissa. Pish, – that might be all affectation.

Betty. No, madam, – no such matter; – the tongue may deceive one, but the eyes cannot; – all his looks, while he was talking to you in the Mall, put me in mind of the description Leonora gives of Torrismond in the play:

His very eye-balls trembled with his love,
And sparkled from their casements humid fires;[306]

And then, when you were so good to give him a meeting afterwards in the walk
by Rosamond's-Pond, how tenderly he express'd himself; – for my part, my heart
melted at every word he said.

Narcissa. He can talk moving enough, that's certain; – but yet, Betty, I ought
not to be too hasty in giving credit to a man I know so little of, or what designs
he may have upon me.

Betty. Nay, madam, I think you know as much of him as you can do without
being married to him: – Did not he tell you that his name was Pike, and that he
was a Captain of Colonel *******'s Regiment? – As to his designs, you cannot
doubt of their being honourable, as he begg'd you would permit him to visit you,
and ask your father's leave to make his addresses.

Narcissa. Ah, Betty, I wish such a thing could be, for he is a prodigious pretty
fellow; – but it is impossible, you know my father hates a soldier, – calls them a
pack of locusts, and says they are the bane both of liberty and property; – besides
he has always design'd me for mr. Oakly.

Betty. Ay, madam, and will make you have mr. Oakly too, or lead apes in
hell[307] if you don't take care to prevent it: – you know, madam, a very few days
hence that abominable act will take place which deprives you of all liberty of
chusing for yourself.

Narcissa. Heigh hoe.

Betty. Never sigh, madam, but resolve.

Narcissa. On what?

Betty. To run away from the miseries of a forced marriage; – to exert the
spirit of a true-born Englishwoman, and be your own provider.

Narcissa. How thou talkest!

Betty. I talk nothing but reason, madam; – but here comes one who I fancy
will be able to urge it more effectually.

The person whom she had been so strenuously pleading for now appear'd, –
he was a tall well-made man, and had a good soldierly aspect; but yet I thought
I discover'd something about him that shew'd as if he had not always been
accustom'd to wear the rich cloaths he now had on; – there wanted that easy
freedom in his air, which, in my opinion, chiefly denotes the true-bred gentleman, and I presently set him down in my mind, either for an impostor, or one
whom some lucky chance had elevated far above his birth.

He approach'd Narcissa with a low bow, and after taking hold of one of her
hands and kissing it with the greatest fervency, address'd her in these terms:

Capt. Pike. How miserable have I been, my angel, in being kept thus long
from your divine presence!

Narcissa. I do not doubt, sir, but you have been better engag'd.

Capt. Pike. Cruel supposition. – How can you so far wrong your own transcendent charms, or my profound adoration of them, as to imagine that the whole world has any thing in it which I should put in competition with the blessing I now enjoy? – but the Major of our Regiment is in town, and unluckily sent for me this morning, – we subalterns must obey our commanding officer; but I hope in a few months to be Colonel, and I shall then have leisure to lie eternally at your feet.

Betty. Ah, sir, I am afraid before that time my lady will be obliged to have somebody else lie at her feet.

Capt. Pike. How!

Narcissa. Hold your prating, hussy. – Who gave you the privilege of speaking?

Betty. Madam, the respect I have for you will not suffer me to be silent. – I tell you nothing but the truth, sir; – as soon as this cursed Clandestine Marriagebill takes place, which you know will be next Monday, my lady will be forced to marry a man to whom she has the greatest aversion.

Capt. Pike. Oh Heaven! – so near being torn from all my hopes! – And can you, madam, – can a lady of your delicacy submit to loath'd embraces!

Narcissa. Sir, this foolish wench talks she knows not what; – the act she mentions does not empower my father to drag me to the Altar, – it only hinders me from chusing for myself; – I may live single if I please.

Capt. Pike. Live single! – Heaven forbid that so much youth and beauty should be condemn'd to a cold celibacy! – No, – nature endow'd you not with such superior charms but to bless some man who by his abundant love might make him worthy of them. – Oh that I were the happy he!

Narcissa. Think not of it, Captain, – my father would never give his consent to any one but the person he has made choice of for me, much less would he endure to see me wedded to a gentleman in the army.

Capt. Pike. And have you too that implacable aversion to a sash and croslet?[308]

Narcissa. I will not pretend to say I have; – I think the army our only security in time of war, and the greatest ornament of our country in times of peace.

Capt. Pike. Oh then, if I could flatter myself there was nothing in my person more disagreeable to you than in my function, I should have nothing left to fear.

Narcissa. Yes, indeed, you would, sir, a great deal; for I assure you, if I married you, my father would not give me a groat.

Capt. Pike. Let him keep his dirty trash, – I despise money, – the commission I enjoy at present will keep us above contempt, and I have money in the Bank ready to purchase the first vacant command of a regiment.

Narcissa. Can you imagine I would give myself to a man who has but just begun to tell me that he loves me?

Capt. Pike. My whole life shall be but one continued scene of courtship; – be assured I shall not be the less, but the more, infinitely the more your adorer by being your husband; – oh then be just to my ardent passion, – generously put an end to my despair, and let those divine lips pronounce the happy fiat to my wishes.

Narcissa. Bless me, what would the world say of such a thing!

Capt. Pike. The wise, madam, despise all forms. – Do not kings and princes marry even with those whom they never saw before; – besides, the late proceedings of the legislature lays you under a necessity of coming to a speedy resolution.

Betty. Ay, madam, remember the Act.

Capt. Pike. Ay, madam, consider how soon that fatal Monday will arrive, which takes from you the power of snatching from eternal misery the man who loves you more than life, and would sacrifice every thing for you.

Narcissa. I must confess, Captain, your offering to take me without a fortune demands some gratitude on my part; and if – but no more, – I see a lady yonder whom I would not wish should surprise us in this conversation; this evening you shall know my final resolution. – Where can I send to you?

Capt. Pike. I have an appointment with some young officers this afternoon at Will's Coffee-house, Whitehall, and shall there wait my doom with the most ardent impatience; – but before you pass the irrevocable sentence of my fate, think, – oh think, my life or death depends upon it!

Narcissa. Well, well, – be easy; – but go.

Capt. Pike. I must obey; – may love and all its powers plead for me, and atone for this cruel interruption.

He said no more, but turn'd away as his mistress had commanded, and pass'd on to another part of the field, while she advanced to meet the lady she had mention'd; but Betty, who was heartily vex'd at this accident, could not forbear crying out as they went along,

Betty. I wonder what should bring Marilla here?

The words were either not heard, or not regarded by Narcissa, who, I could perceive by her looks, was little less disconcerted; – she met her friend, however, with a shew of gaiety and satisfaction, and as soon as they came near each other saluted her in these terms:

Narcissa. My dear Marilla, 'tis a wonder to see you in such a place as this; – you used to be an enemy to all solitary walks.

Marilla. So I am still; but I have been at your house and was told you were here, so came in mere good-nature to hinder you from indulging melancholy; but I find I might have spared myself that trouble. – Pray who was that pretty fellow that left you just now?

Narcissa. I know not; – he only came up to us, seeing nobody else in the place, I suppose, to ask which was the nearest way to Great Russel-street.[309]

Marilla. Rather to ask the way to a fair lady's heart who lives not far from Great Russel-street. – Oh, Narcissa, you cannot deceive me; – I could easily perceive, at the distance I was, that he did not part from you with the air of a man who had no other business than to ask such an impertinent question: – besides, I must tell you that you are a very ill dissembler, – your blushes, and the soft confusion in your eyes, declare not only that he is a lover, but also that he is a favour'd one; I know well enough that you met him here by appointment. – Prithee let me into the whole of the secret.

Narcissa still persisted in her first asseverations; but the other seem'd not to give the least credit on that score, and assuming a more serious air than hitherto she had put on, spoke thus:

Marilla. I perceive, my dear Narcissa, I am not thought worthy of your confidence in this point, tho' I am very certain you have not a friend in the world who wishes your happiness with more sincerity than I do.

Narcissa. I believe it, my dear, and am much obliged to you; but you would not have me tell lyes to shew my gratitude.

Marilla. Well, – well, – I shall urge you no farther, and should not have been so impertinent to take any notice of what I saw, but for the transport it gave me to imagine you might now have an opportunity of delivering yourself from the danger of being forced into a marriage with a man whom I have heard you declare so great an aversion for.

Narcissa. And suppose the thing were really as you have taken it into your head to fancy, would you have me disoblige my father by marrying without his consent?

Marilla. Yes, when he will give his consent to no body but one with whom you must be miserable; – for besides the dislike you have to the person of Oakly, his temper is such as would break a woman's heart in two months. – You know I am very intimate with his sister, and cannot avoid seeing such oddities in his behaviour as have made me tremble for you a thousand times.

Narcissa. I cannot think my father will ever go about to compel my inclinations.

Marilla. Oakly is of another opinion; for I can tell you he makes no scruple to say, that if you do not marry him you shall marry no body; – therefore, without diving into the secrets of your heart, let me advise you, my dear creature, not to lose the short time allow'd you, but if you have any offer less disagreeable to you than Oakly, accept it at once, – three days hence it will be out of your power.

Narcissa. But, my dear, what man that is worth having will marry a woman without a fortune?

Marilla. If I were a man I should tell you that your person was a sufficient fortune, and I do not doubt but that there are a great many who would think so; – but you have two thousand pounds left you by your grandmother, independ-

ent of your father, and I dare say that if you were once married, and the thing past
recal, he would forgive it; – consider you are his only daughter, and both your
brothers are provided for, the one by an estate, and the other by good preferment
in the church.

What answer Narcissa would have made I know not, it began to rain very
fast, so that the ladies were oblig'd to mend their pace and make all the haste they
could out of the field; – Marilla took the first chair she met with, saying it would
be dinner-time before she should be able to get dress'd; – Narcissa and her maid
ran home through the shower, and I follow'd, not only to take shelter,but also
to hear the result of the young lady's determination on what had pass'd between
her and capt. Pike.

As soon as they had pluck'd off their wet hats and capuchins, and Narcissa
had a little resettled herself, she said to her maid,

Narcissa. Well, Betty, – this has been an odd morning.

Betty. I hope it will prove a lucky one, madam; but I am glad you did not tell
Marilla any thing of the matter.

Narcissa. She was so pressing that I had half a mind; but when I consider'd
how great she is with Oakly's sister, I thought it was better to keep her in ignorance.

Betty. Much better, indeed, madam – But pray what do you resolve to do in
relation to the Captain?

Narcissa. Why I must e'en have him, I think.

Betty. You made him a kind of promise to send to him.

Narcissa. I did so, and will keep it; – bring me some paper and pen and ink,
– I will write to him this moment, before any company comes in to prevent me.

Betty. You are in the right, madam, – there is nothing like the time present.

The things she call'd for being immediately set before her, I stood at her
elbow and saw her write the following lines:

To Capt. PIKE.

Sir,

I should be guilty of an injustice both to myself and you not to be sensible
of the proof you offer of your sincerity; – I find in it, indeed, all that can be
imagin'd, and much more than could be expected, of love, of honour, and a true
generosity, and hope I shall hereafter stand excused to my father and the whole
world, for taking a step excited by my gratitude, and approv'd of by my reason;
– meet meet therefore to-morrow morning at eight precisely, in the Piazza next
King-street, Covent-Garden, where I will put myself under your protection, and
be conducted by you to whatever place you shall judge most proper for the ceremony which must make me

Eternally yours.

NARCISSA.

Having seal'd this billet she gave it to her maid, with a strict charge to send it by a trusty messenger; on which the girl reply'd,

Betty. Yes, madam, you may depend on the safe conveyance; for I will be the bearer of it myself.

Narcissa. What! – go to a coffee-house!

Betty. Nothing is more common, madam, than for women to send for gentlemen out of a coffee-house when they have any business with them.

What farther chat pass'd between the mistress and maid was too insignificant to be repeated; not, indeed, did I stay to hear much of it, having already gain'd all that was necessary for the present, so shut up my Tablets and retir'd on the first opportunity I found for my leaving the house.

As it was plain to me, however, that Betty was deeply interested in the concession Narcissa had made to the Captain, and I had also some suspicion that he was not in reality the person he pretended to be, I resolved to go in the evening to the coffee-house, and be witness of his behaviour on receiving the letter Betty was to bring.

Accordingly I went and found him there, not as he said, in company with young officers, but sitting alone in a corner of the room with his hat very much flapp'd over his face; – a few minutes after I came in, a waiter call'd aloud to know if one capt. Pike was there, – on which he started up, and, answering to the name, was told a gentlewoman at the door desir'd to speak with him; – he went hastily out and I pursued his steps, not doubting but it was the emissary of Narcissa; – as soon as he saw it was she, he cry'd out in some surprise:

Capt. Pike. What, sister, are you come yourself! – You bring me no bad news, I hope.

Betty. No, no – the best you can expect; – but walk this way, – 'tis not proper to stand here to talk. – For Heaven's sake why did you venture to appoint such a public place as this!

Capt. Pike. No body knows me here, – my Captain never uses this house. – But tell me, how goes our affair?

Betty. Rarely; – she will have you, here is her promise under her own hand.

By this time they were got about the middle of Scotland-yard, where Betty having given him the letter of Narcissa, he stopp'd to read it by the light of a lamp at a gentleman's door, and as soon as he had finish'd cry'd out,

Capt. Pike. This is brave, indeed, and nothing sure was ever so lucky as her fixing to-morrow for our wedding, for the Captain went to Hampstead this morning with a whore he pick'd up in the Park the other night, and will not be in town these two days, so I shall have all that time to myself, and can get at what cloaths and linnen I want. – But, my dear sister, what shall I do with this girl when I have married her? – where must I carry her?

Betty. That is what I came to talk about: – You must take a fine lodging for her by all means, and order a handsome dinner to be provided at some tavern or other; – every thing must be done with a grand air, that she may suspect nothing 'till after you have consummated. – Hah, brother.

Capt. Pike. But, Betty, I have no money; – all will go wrong still if you cannot help me out.

Betty. Nothing would go right if it were not for me; – you may thank God for having such a sister, you might have been a foot-soldier else as long as you lived; – but there is no time to be lost, – I have brought you four pieces, and I believe that will be sufficient for every thing; – go and buy a ring and secure a lodging immediately.

Capt. Pike. You may be sure I shall not fail. – But harkye, Betty, take care she brings the writings of her two thousand pounds and all her jewels.

Betty. Ay, ay, – she shall leave nothing of value behind her I'll engage.

With these words they separated, and I went home, heartily glad that I had made this discovery, and determin'd to save Narcissa, if possible, from the misfortune she was so near falling into, – to which end I sat down to my escrutore and immediately wrote to her father in the following terms:

To JOHN *******, Esq;

SIR,

THE shock I am now about to give you can only be excused by its being done to prevent you from receiving a much greater and more lasting one: – sorry am I to tell you, – yet so it is, – your daughter, the beautiful Narcissa, is on the point of utter destruction; – she has promised, and is resolved to keep her word, to join herself in marriage with a wretch, who, tho' of the most abject rank, in order to seduce her innocence, assumes the character of a gentleman, and calls himself capt. Pike; – Betty, her waiting-maid, is sister to the impostor, and has been the conductress of the whole villainous design; – every thing is prepared for the accomplishment, and to-morrow is the day prefix'd; – but I hope this intelligence will reach you time enough to prevent so irremedible an evil.

I am, Sir
Your unknown well-wisher
And humble servant.

Having sent this away, and fully discharg'd what my honour and my conscience represented as a duty incumbent on me, I flatter'd myself with the expectation of seeing the next day treachery and deceit receive the mortification they justly merited.

CHAP. VIII.

Contains a brief account of the effects that were produced by the good inten-
tions of the Invisible Spy, with some other subsequent particulars.

THO' I had not the least room to doubt but that the information I had given the
father of Narcissa would have all the success I wish'd, yet I could not avoid being
extremely curious to see in what manner the persons concern'd would behave on
this occasion; – accordingly I went to the house the next morning about eleven,
expecting to find that the maid had been turn'd out of doors, the mistress in tears
for her disappointment, and the old gentleman rejoicing in the thoughts of having saved his beloved daughter from undoing herself.

A servant happening to be at the door receiving some shoes from a fellow who
had been just cleaning them, I gain'd an easy access; – finding no body in the lower
floor I went up stairs, but the same solitude reign'd likewise there; – I then proceeded a story higher, and there saw only a servant-maid sweeping out a room,
which, by a toylet being set out, I judg'd was the chamber of Narcissa: – I was
very much surprised to find every thing so quiet in a place where I had look'd for
nothing but confusion, and stopp'd on the stairs to consider what might be the
occasion; when on a sudden I heard the ringing of a small bell, and presently after
saw a footman running hastily up; – I follow'd him where he went, which was into
the chamber of Narcissa's father, who was not yet up, but now call'd for his cloaths;
– as he was putting them on he cast his eyes on the table, and seeing a letter lie
there, ask'd his man – when, and from whom it came; – to which he reply'd,

Footman. Sir, it was left for you last night by a porter; but as you came home
so late I would not disturb you with it.

Father. Give it me.

I was astonish'd on finding that this was no other than the letter I had sent
to him; but more troubled, that by the delivery of it being delay'd, poor Narcissa
had fallen into the trap laid for her; – but if I, a stranger, could be so much
affected, what agony must rend the tender father's heart? – scarce had he gone
thro' the half of what I wrote before he cry'd out, casting at the same time a look
full of despair and rage upon his servant,

Father. Ill-fated wretch! what mischief, what ruin, has thy neglect brought
upon me and my family! – You imagin'd I was drunk last night, I suppose; but
had I been so, here is enough in this dreadful letter to have brought me to my
senses: – but go, – run up to my daughter's chamber, – see if she be there.

Footman. Sir, she went out very early this morning with mrs. Betty, and is not
yet come back.

Father. Nor ever will, I fear: – the intelligence this brings me is too true, I
find. – Run to mr. Oakly and my cousin Johnson's, bid them both come to me

this instant! – fly! – and, do you hear, bring a coach with you; – if I can recover her before consummation, her ruin may be yet prevented.

The fellow went on his errand, and the old gentleman in the mean time stamping, biting his lips, and showing all the marks of an inward distraction, made an end of putting on his cloaths, in order to go in search of his lost daughter when the gentlemen he had sent for should arrive; but I staid not to hear what method would be pursued for that purpose, as thinking it of no moment, and that it would be better to return again in the evening, when I might probably hear what success had attended their endeavours.

The time I chose for going, was as late at night as I thought I might get an opportunity of entering, yet the disconsolate father was but just come home, – his two friends were with him, – they said all they could to alleviate his sorrows, but it avail'd no more than preaching to the winds. – They had found out, it seems, where the marriage was perform'd; after which they went to all taverns, coffee-houses, and other public places which they heard were frequented by officers, to enquire concerning one who call'd himself capt. Pike, but could not receive the least information of any one who bore that name; and all the consolation the old gentleman had for the pains he had taken, was the cruel certainty that his dear daughter was inevitably undone.

Though I saw very little probability of my being able to learn any thing more at this house than I had already done, yet I could not forbear calling constantly there every day, and at last, by this dint of continued application, I became acquainted with the whole melancholy secret of Narcissa's fate, almost as soon as the family knew it themselves.

The pretended Captain had manag'd every thing according to the direction of his sister; – as soon as the ceremony was over, he had conducted his bride to very handsome lodgings, where an entertainment suitable to the occasion was provided; and the poor deluded young lady, seeing nothing but what serv'd to make her satisfied with what she had done, in return for his imaginary generosity made him a present of her two thousand pounds, which was in India Bonds.[310]

Her contentment might, perhaps, have lasted some little time longer than it did, if she had not propos'd waiting on her father, to implore his forgiveness and blessing; on which the impostor, having now got his ends, thinking it needless to continue the deception any longer, confess'd that he was no more than a private man in the army; but told her that he was now treating with his Captain for his discharge, and would purchase a commission with some part of the money she had given him; and added, that 'till these two points were accomplish'd, it would be altogether improper to appear before her father.

Narcissa fell into the utmost distraction on this eclaircisement, – vow'd not to live with a wretch who had put so base a trick upon her, but would go home to her father, who she doubted not but would find means to punish such a flagrant piece of villainy.

He only laugh'd at her reproaches, and said, that as she was his wife she had it not in her choice to leave him. – Betty also now threw off the character of a servant, and, assuming the authority of the sister of her husband, pretended to rebuke her idle prating, as she insolently term'd it.

She found an opportunity, however, of making her escape, and fled for refuge to the house of a near relation, who, on hearing her story, undertook to intercede with her father, which he did so successfully, that the old gentleman forgave and took her again into favour.

All possible measures were taken to set aside the marriage, and compel the impostor to refund the money Narcissa had so unwarily bestow'd upon him; but as he knew the law was too much on his side, having not married her in a false name, tho' under a false character, he carry'd things with a very high hand, would part with nothing, not even the jewels she had left behind, but even threaten'd to commence a process against any one who detain'd her person.

In fine, all that could be done was to get him to sign articles of separation, – after which Narcissa retir'd into the country, where I hear she resolves to waste the whole remainder of her days in a melancholy contrition, for the rashness of her ungovern'd conduct. – So true, though not very elegant, are some lines which I remember to have read in an old poem, call'd, The Card of Fancy;[311]

> When headstrong youth the reins of duty breaks,
> And its own course pursues in desp'rate freaks,
> It certain mischief and destruction seeks.[312]

I must not forget to let my readers known that Marilla is since married to mr. Oakly, with whom, as I am credibly inform'd, she was long passionately in love, and on that motive used the utmost of her endeavours to strengthen the aversion her fair friend had for him.

End of the Third VOLUME.

THE
Invisible Spy.

BY

EXPLORALIBUS.

VOL. IV.

LONDON:
Printed for T.Gardner, at *Cowley*'s Head, near St. *Clement*'s
Church in the *Strand*.

M,D,CC,LV.

CONTENTS

TO THE

Fourth VOLUME.

BOOK VII. CHAP. I.

CHAP. VI.

CHAP. VII.

CHAP. VIII.

BOOK. VIII. CHAP. I.

CHAP. II.

CHAP. III.

CHAP. IV.

THE

Invisible Spy.

VOL. IV.
BOOK VII.

CHAP. I.

The Author, contrary to his expectation, finds himself under a necessity of mak-ing an introductory Preface to this Volume, and at the same time presents the Reader with two letters of a pretty extraordinary nature.

I Have made it my observation, before I had the least thoughts of becoming an Author, that there are two sorts of Readers who particularly distinguish themselves from all the rest, yet, though direct opposites in humour, concur in one point, – that of being eager to see every new book that comes out, and impatient till they get to the conclusion of it; – the one of these affects to be above being pleas'd with any thing he meets with, especially if it exceeds the bulk of a twelve-penny pam-phlet, condemning all beyond as tedious, tiresome, and insipid; – the other with alacrity pursues through every page the catastrophe of the longest work, delighting himself with the expectation of finding something to entertain him.

Methinks I hear, on the publication of these volumes, some one of the former class, with brow contracted and malignant sneer, like Milton's fallen Angel,[313] mutter between his teeth, – 'What does the fellow mean by encumbering us with all this trash? – Who does he think will be at the pains to trudge through such a heap of rubbish?' – While those of the other cheerfully cry out at the beginning of every chapter, – 'I wonder what mr. Invisible has now to present us with!'

But as I had no design or inclination to offend the one, by spinning out these lucubrations by any superfluous interlocutions; so I will not so far dissemble, as to compliment the other with saying, that merely to oblige them I extended the work to the length it is; – much less will I go about to defend myself by the example of a certain modern writer, who has found out the method of wiredrawing whatever matter he takes in hand to such an enormous length,[314] that the eye of remembrance loses all sight of the beginning before it has half reach'd the end.

No, I will be ingenuous, – and confess the truth, – I was mistaken in my calculation; nor 'till the transcripts I had drawn from my Tablets were copied over fair for the press, could have imagin'd they would have employ'd so much paper and time as they in effect have done; and as I propos'd from the beginning not to conceal from the public any part of the discoveries I had made, I persisted in that resolution, without any regard to the number of volumes they might fill up.

This also has been the occasion, that a work which I intended should have made its appearance the latter end of last winter is postpon'd 'till now;[315] which, as an Author, I cannot help looking upon as a double misfortune, for two very good reasons: – in the first place, the facts contain'd in it will be found of a less recent date; and in the next, by being so long in hand some particular passages in it have taken wind, and by that means those who imagine themselves concerned in them are prepar'd to bring the whole performance into contempt.

That this is no idle surmise of my own I am very well convinced, and so may every one else who reads the letters inserted in the introduction to the Second Volume, as well as by two others which have been since left for me at the Printing-Office, and which I shall now take the liberty of presenting to the public; – the first is from a lady, and contains the following lines:

To the gentleman, or whatever he is, who calls himself the INVISIBLE SPY.

Mr. INVISIBLE,

I AM told you are going to publish a kind of scandalous Chronicle of what you, in your great wisdom, may look upon as the foibles of people in genteel life; and that neither birth, beauty, wealth, nor power, are a sufficient defence against so universal a satyrist. – But pray who set you up for a censor of your neighbours actions? – By what rule do you pretend to judge what is deserving reproof, and what is not so? – Wit is the worst authority you can have, – no body now adays pays the least regard to it; – we women like the man who dresses well, can sing a soft Italian air, dance a French Louvre,[316] is complaisant enough to squire us to all public places, and let us win his money at cards. – Those of your own sex also think as little of wit as we do, – they know it is no qualification by which they can expect to succeed either in love or preferment; and therefore, you may be sure, despise in another what they are not possess'd of themselves.

But I also hear that you declare yourself an enemy to Gaming in particular; – and if so, you infallibly ruin yourself with the whole town. – How dull, how sluggishly would life glide on if it were not for that dear diversion? – Dressing and Eating take up but a small part of the day, and Plays and Operas of the evening. – What must become of all our vacant hours? – we should die by dozens of the spleen and vapours for want of employment, if Gaming did not rouze our faculties, keep the passions in a continual flow, and the animal spirits from being subjected to the odious power of sleep and sloth.

If therefore you have presumed to say any thing in opposition to this favourite amusement, erase the invective page, or depend upon it your performance will be cry'd down at every polite table, not only in town but throughout all England. – I would have you know this advice is given by one who has it in her power to be either a very serviceable friend or a most formidable and bitter enemy; – it is in your own choice which of these two you will make of

Yours, &c.

Olimpia.

The other letter is from a member of the last ever memorable parliament, and was sent a few weeks before the writs were issued out for calling a new one. – These are the contents:

To the Author of the Invisible Spy.

Sir,

You cannot but know that a Spy, as soon as detected to be such, is condemn'd by the law of all nations to be carry'd to the first tree and hang'd up immediately. – What then, in the name of common sense, can have induced you to assume a character so obnoxious to mankind, and so dangerous to yourself? – Do you imagine that the natural love people have for intelligence will save you? – no, – if you offend all, you must expect that all will be against you; – but I am charitable enough to hope otherwise, and would fain think you concern yourself only with matters relating to the tea-table and toylet of the ladies, and are more discreet than to meddle with things which ought not to come too much into the heads of the populace.

You understand me, I suppose; – but lest you should not, I will tell you that I should be sorry to find you a dabbler in politics, especially at this critical juncture, when the Parliament is so near being dissolved and a new Election coming on.

I have the honour to be a member of the lower house, and am very sensible that some motions have been made there, which at the time were highly displeasing to the mob; but as most of them seem to be now forgot, and others die away apace, I would not have you scratch an old sore and revive the memory of them.

The Naturalization Bill most of all sticks in the stomachs of the vulgar; – but as I take you for a gentleman and a man of sense, I will reason with you a little upon that affair, and doubt not but to convince you that there never was a Bill better calculated for the true interest of the country, and to make us a great and formidable people.

I shall not need to tire your patience with saying much on the occasion, – the whole sum of this argument, conclusive as it is, may be drawn up in a very narrow compass, – as thus:

Are we not told, in that book which is the rule of our salvation, that we ought to do all the good we can? – Is there any thing more pleasing in the sight of God and the world than acts of hospitality, benevolence and charity? – And can we give a greater proof how much we are endow'd with those noble virtues, than by receiving distress'd strangers into the bosom of our community, and making them partakers of the same rights and privileges that we ourselves enjoy? – This consideration alone would be sufficient to make me, as a good Christian, a zealous advocate for a General Naturalization, without any limitation or exception, whether in regard of Turks, Pagans, Jews, or Atheists.

There are also two other motives which, in my opinion, should make every good commonwealth's man and good subject wish that this bill might be pass'd into a law, – as I shall presently make appear.

First, It must be allow'd that the people of England are, of latter years, extremely indolent; – that the meaner sort of them are lazy, proud, and luxurious, to an excess, chusing rather to steal or beg, than work for moderate wages; – whereas on the contrary, those who it may be suppos'd will come over to take the benefit of such an act are robust in body and humble in mind, – inur'd from their very infancy to want and toil, and accustom'd to hardships, will certainly be glad to sell their labour at a much cheaper rate: – their women may also be an example to ours, and make them less delicate and more obedient; – and how great a blessing such a reformation would be, as the sex at present conduct themselves, I appeal to all fathers, husbands, and masters of families.

Secondly, We want men, – we may want soldiers too, – things least expected often happen; we cannot assure ourselves that the young Pretender may not quit his lurking holes, and once more attempt to disturb us; but if all apprehensions on his score were without foundation, and that as the greatest part of his adherents are destroy'd either by the sword or the halter, all his hopes and endeavours were buried with them; – nay, were the small remains of that family extinct, yet still there never would be wanting a Pretender to the Throne of these Kingdoms; – we all know the late King of Sardinia, as next of blood, enter'd his claim in a Protest against the Settlement of the House of Hanover, and we have no room to think his son would be more passive, if such an opportunity should arrive; [317] – never can we flatter ourselves with being absolutely secure that no other dangers may threaten us from a different quarter.

All these things consider'd, I think it very evident, and you cannot but acknowledge that a General Naturalization would not only be greatly for our honour and convenience, but is also necessary for our safety.

However, as I have before observ'd, the lower class of people having taken it into their heads to imagine that this bill, and several others, were so many attempts to encroach on what they look upon as their undoubted rights and privileges, I should be glad that no mention was made concerning any part of the business transacted in this Parliament; because I am pretty sensible that there are some rustical clodpated fellows who are capable, on the least encouragement from the press, to insult and throw dirt in our faces, instead of giving us their votes.

I should have accompany'd this request with a small present, but really, as things stand, I find all the ready money I can raise will be little enough to stem the torrent of popular resentment; but if you think fit to comply, I shall take an opportunity hereafter to testify my gratitude, and be ready to prove myself,

On all occasions,

SIR,

Your much obliged

Humble servant,

PHILOTEMPO.

The letter of Philotempo had not been inserted without a reply to it, if these Volumes had been publish'd at the time I first intended; but as the Election will be over long before they can possibly make their appearance, and it is likely he may be rechosen, what I would then have said would now, for many reasons, be highly improper.

I must therefore submit to whatever censures either he or any other person shall think fit to pass upon me, – well knowing that to those who are resolved to be offended, all apologies would be in vain, and to those who read with a desire of being pleased, equally unnecessary.

Some, whose impatient thirst for intelligence is not easily satisfied, may perhaps think that in an age so gay, so luxurious as the present, when every day, nay every hour, teems with some fresh adventure, and affords matter for conversation, I might have made a more extensive use of my gift of Invisibility, and that not four, but fourteen Volumes might have been well enough employ'd in the rehearsal of what I had seen and heard; – but those, if any such there are, will find in the close of this work, that if I have omitted many things which doubtless have happen'd worthy remark, it has not been owing to any remissness in me, or a weariness of prosecuting my enquiries, but to an unlucky accident which stopp'd me in my full career, and cut off all farther opportunities of obliging either them or myself.

As this is the last address I shall make to the public, at least while I continue to wear my Belt of Invisibility, I think myself obliged, in good manners, to take my leave, not only of the courteous but also uncourteous reader, – which I now do, – heartily wishing that the one may find in this performance every thing capable of entertaining him, and that the other may be preserved from falling into the spleen or hypochondriac, by discharging on me all the ill-nature he is possess'd of.

CHAP. II.

The Author flatters himself will be no unacceptable present to all those of the fair sex, who are either truly innocent, or would preserve the reputation of being so.

WHEN a young woman, of what rank or degree soever, indulges herself in a too great freedom of conversation with one of a loose and wanton behaviour, she cannot wonder that those who are witnesses of their intimacy should suspect her guilty of the same inclinations; – and that tho' perfectly innocent of the faults of her companion, is made an equal partaker of her shame.

Women, who are either born to, or are reduced by accidents to low and indigent circumstances, excuse themselves by saying, – that the necessity of their affairs compels them to keep an acquaintance with persons who they find it their interest to oblige; – but if this be an insufficient pretence, as certainly it is, since there is no interest which ought to be put in competition with reputation, what can be alledg'd in behalf of ladies of fortune and quality, who have it in their power to chuse their company, and it cannot be supposed would converse with any whose manners they did not approve?

In fine, there is no one error in conduct which, according to my opinion, the sex in general should be more upon their guard against than this; – for tho' some, dazzled with the pomp of show and equipage, may be weak enough to imagine, that to appear in public, or be known to have an intimacy with a woman of a polluted fame, provided she be a person of condition, will bring no blemish on their own characters, or be of any prejudice to their morals, yet that such an intimacy is extremely dangerous to both may be very easily demonstrated.

First, as to character; – If the world should be more silent than it ever was, or ever will be on such occasions, it cannot be expected that a woman, who has thrown off all regard for her own honour, should have any for that of the person she converses with, or would even wish they should be thought possess'd of a virtue she is entirely destitute of herself; – no, – on the contrary, she will rather have recourse to all the wicked artifices she may be mistress of to cast a shade over that brightness which would render her own deformity more conspicuous.

But this is not the worst danger to which an innocent person is exposed by keeping company with a bad woman; – we are told, from an unquestionable authority, that it is hard to touch pitch without being defiled; – and certainly there is nothing more evident, than that vice naturally loses great part of its horrors by becoming familiar to the sight: – the chaste heart, which shudders at the bare repetition of indecent actions, by accustoming itself to be witness of them, ceases first to wonder, and by degrees to detest them; – and though I will not be so uncharitable as to say, that the mind is always corrupted by such a communication, yet I will venture to affirm, that the manners will be so.

I know very well, that the timid modesty I would fain recommend, as the surest guardian of a Virgin's honour, has for many years been exploded; and that since some foreign customs have unhappily been introduced among us, to be capable of blushing is look'd upon by those who pass for models of politeness, as an indication of the want both of wit and good breeding.

This audacity of behaviour being so much the mode, it is not a little difficult to distinguish between those who really pursue the dictates of a licentious inclination, and those who put on a shew of it merely to comply with the example of others; and a person who judges of a woman by what he sees of her in public, runs a very great risque of being mistaken.

Often has my opinion been led astray in this point, even in regard of ladies with whom I was most intimately acquainted, and saw every day; nor did I ever dare to give a character of any one of them 'till my Belt of Invisibility afforded me an opportunity of prying in the secrets of the alcove.

Corisca[318] and Emilia are two celebrated beauties, – they are almost equally follow'd and admir'd by the men; but neither of them were ever jealous or envious of the praises given to the other, and there was once so excessive a fondness between them that they were scarce ever seen asunder: – Corisca has been married some years, – Emilia has not yet been prevail'd upon to part with her liberty; but tho' there is this difference in their circumstances, there has been too much appearance, upon exact similitude, in their humours and constitutions; – I say in appearance; for I have since discover'd that light and darkness are not, in fact, more widely distant.

Corisca, long before she became a wife, was look'd upon as what they call a female rake; – some there were, however, who imputed what she did only to the too great vivacity of her humour, and would not believe her guilty of any real crime; but far the greater number were of a quite different opinion; and, indeed, the little regard she takes of her family since her marriage, – the public contempt with which she treats her husband, and the frequent quarrels she has with him in private, but too much justify the worst character can be given either of her œconomy or her chastity.

Yet notwithstanding all this, there is a certain something in her air, her wit, and her manner of behaviour so engaging to both sexes, that she has always been, and still continues to be, constantly visited by persons not only of the best fortunes, but of the best reputations also, who chuse rather to seem blind to her faults than deny themselves the pleasure of her conversation.

It is, beyond all dispute, a very great pity that a woman so plenteously endow'd by nature with every qualification to shew virtue in its most amiable colours, should, through a strange depravity of principles and inclination, make use of all the fine talents she is mistress of only to varnish over the foul face of vice, and endeavouring to give a pleasing aspect to the deformity of sin and shame.

The beautiful person of Emilia, – her sprightly wit, – her good humour and affability, render'd her the darling of all who knew her; – they beheld with an infinity of concern her intimacy with Corisca, and those, who either by proximity of blood, or a long acquaintance with her, thought themselves privileged to offer their advice, did it in the strongest terms, and spared no remonstrances that might prevail on her to break off so dangerous a communication; – but she was deaf to all could be said to her on this subject: – it was her misfortune to become the mistress of her own actions at too early an age; – what fortune she was possess'd of was in her own hands, and as she was entirely independent on her friends, would not submit to be directed by them.

In justice to this young lady's character, however, I must say, and shall hereafter prove, that there is a fund of honour and virtue in her soul sufficient to have made her look down with contempt and detestation on the conduct of Corisca, and to have oblig'd her, if not to break off all conversation with her, at least not to appear with her in public, or make one in any party of pleasure where she was engaged.

But, alas! the seeds of those noble principles for a time lay dormant in her, choak'd up with the natural levities of youth, and the modish excesses of the age, they had not power to shoot forth into action: – innocently wanton, and indolently gay, she saw not the danger to which she exposed her person and reputation, because she thought not of it, nor gave herself the pains to examine what snares might possibly be spread for her; – but suffering herself to be continually hurried from one amusement to another, never consider'd or reflected on any thing farther than the present satisfaction.

I have been thus particular in describing the character and humour of Emilia, because in the course of my rambles I have found too many others of the same giddy bent, who, without the least propensity to ill, have heedlesly run into actions which have involved their whole future lives in dishonour; – these have reason to pardon this digression, especially as it has not been tedious, and I shall now return to the adventure which occasion'd it.

Among the many Invisible Visits, which for a considerable time together I had made to the apartment of this celebrated Corisca, I happen'd to be there one morning when Favonius and Palamede were with her; – the first of these gentlemen is of a very amorous inclination, and known to be what the world calls well with her; – the other, though gay and lively as Mercury himself, has been restrain'd either through want of inclination to her person, or his friendship to Favonius, from attempting to take any private liberties, and seldom visits her but in his company.

The discourse they were engaged in, when I first broke in upon them, I found was on subjects of too trifling a nature for me to spread my Tablets for the reception, so I shall make no repetition of any things were said 'till the entrance of Emilia, who came in soon after.

The first salutations were no sooner over, than Corisca taking her fondly by the hand spoke thus:

Corisca. Dear creature, this is an excess of goodness in you to come thus early, – I did not expect you 'till dinner time.

Emilia. Indeed, my dear, I never waited on you with so ill a will, nor came on an errand so disagreeable to my inclination; for I have but just time to tell you, that I am deprived of the pleasure I proposed to myself of passing the whole day with you.

Corisca. On what occasion!

Emilia. The most unlucky one that could have happen'd; – an old aunt of mine has taken it into her head to quit her Rookery and Hen-house in the country, and come to stare and be stared at in town; – she arriv'd last night, and sent me word that she must needs see me this morning; – decency obliges me to go, – she is my god-mother, and besides is pretty rich.

Corisca. But cannot you make some excuse to leave her as soon as you have paid your compliments? – I shall have all the world here this afternoon, and would not have you absent upon any score.

Emilia. It cannot be avoided, – she pretends to have a huge fondness for me, and I know will detain me, with a thousand impertinent declarations of it, 'till bed time; – so, my dear, adieu for this whole tedious day; – to-morrow, I hope, will atone for this vexation. – Gentlemen, your servant.

In speaking these last words she turn'd upon her heel and ran out of the room; but not so hastily but that Palamede, with one stride, join'd her at the door and led her down stairs; – in the mean time Corisca, looking on Favonius, said to him:

Corisca. I pity poor Emilia; – the impertinent fondness of an old relation is almost as great a mortification as the sawcy indifference of a young fellow that one likes.

Favonius. The beautiful Corisca, I am sure, can never be in danger of experiencing the latter of these vexations.

To prove the sincerity of this asseveration he closed it with a strenuous embrace, which Corisca return'd; – there was time for no more, – Palamede came back, and Favonius, with a smile, spoke in this manner:

Favonius. By the sparkle in your eyes, Palamede, I should imagine the piece of gallantry you have shew'd to Emilia has been more than ordinarily well received.

Palamede. This and all others I have yet had in my power to treat that lady with have been too trifling to deserve much notice from her.

Favonius. Oh, – every kind glance gives transport to a man in love; – you must know, madam, I have just found out that Palamede is most desperately in love with Emilia.

Corisca. Indeed! – and do you allow the charge, Palamede?

Palamede. Not altogether, madam; – I am not absolutely in love, but confess I think Emilia an extreme fine girl, and have had some very luscious dreams on her account.

Corisca. What hinders you then from making your addresses to her?

Palamede. Why faith, madam, – to confess the truth, I was afraid of not succeeding on the terms I wish'd to do; and as for marriage, the circumstances of my estate require I should make choice of a wife with a much larger fortune than Emilia is possess'd of.

Favonius. You are perfectly in the right, Palamede; – a good fortune with a wife is absolutely necessary for a man of pleasure, as it enables him to make handsome presents and entertainments to those women he may happen to like better.

Corisca. So, Palamede, you durst not ask Emilia the question, for fear of meeting a rebuff from her over-scrupulous virtue.

Palamede. That is indeed the case, madam.

Corisca. Then you are a fool: – not but I believe Emilia is perfectly innocent as yet; – but what is innocence, what is virtue, what is honour, when oppos'd to love and inclination! – Do you not know what mrs. Behn, who must be allow'd to be a perfect judge of nature in our sex, says upon this occasion?

> Oh cursed honour, thou who first did'st damn
> A woman to the sin of shame!
> Honour, who taught lovely eyes the art,
> To wound, and not to cure the heart;
> With love t'invite, but to forbid with awe,
> And to themselves prescribe a cruel law.
> His chief attributes are pride and spight,
> His pow'r is robbing lovers of delight.
> Honour, that puts our words, that should be free,
> Into a set formality!
> Thou base debaucher of the gen'rous heart,
> That teachest all our looks and actions art.
> What love design'd a sacred gift,
> What nature made to be possess'd,
> Mistaken honour made a theft.
> Thou foe to pleasure, nature's worst disease!
> Thou tyrant over mighty kings,

Be gone to princes palaces,
But let the humble swain go on,
In the blest paths of the first race of man,
That nearest were to Gods allied,
And, form'd for love, disdain'd all other pride.[319]

The emphatic accents and graceful manner with which Corisca pronounced these lines, adding to the beauty of the poetry, struck so much upon the hearts of the two gentlemen, that they could not forbear clapping their hands, and crying out several times, 'Encore, – Encore, charming Corisca.' – On which she laugh'd heartily, and reply'd,

Corisca. I want none of these theatrical testimonies of approbation; – I would only convince Palamede, from the unquestionable authority of our English Sappho, that when a woman loves, no considerations are of force to restrain her from acting up to the dictates of her passion.

Palamede. Ay, madam, if I could flatter myself with the hopes of being lov'd by Emilia, I should have nothing to apprehend.

Corisca. I will not pretend to tell you that she is so much in love as not to be able to eat, drink, or sleep for the thoughts of you; but I have heard her say a thousand times over, I believe, that you are, without exception, the prettiest fellow in the whole town, – that you dress the best, – and have something peculiarly agreeable in your air and manner of behaviour; – and on the strength of this, and some other indications I have observed about her, I dare venture to affirm that you are far from being indifferent to her, and that she would be little less pleas'd than yourself with an opportunity of being entertain'd by you in private.

Palamede. Dear madam, you make me the most transported man alive. – But by what means can such a thing be brought about? – some scheme must be laid for that purpose.

Corisca. Nothing more easy; – I have it all in my head already; – she will go any where with me; – we shall be together to-morrow; – you two shall come in as if by accident, and propose going to take the air on the other side of the water; – there is a house the most commodiously situated that can be; – good gardens, good wine, good beds, good every thing: – Favonius is well acquainted with the place.

Favonius. I suppose you mean that kept by mrs. *******.

Corisca. The same. – When we have been there some time, and it begins to draw near the hour proper to think of going home, you shall discharge the coach, and pretend the fellow got drunk and went away without your knowledge; – there will be no possibility of procuring a vehicle to bring us to town, especially at night; – Favonius must be content to do penance with me in loitering about the gardens, or in something or other, 'till morning, while you make the most of your time with Emilia.

Palamede. Excellent, – my charming Machiavel! – But how shall we prevail on Emilia to be separated from her dear Corisca?

Corisca. Leave that to my management; – she shall suspect nothing of the matter 'till she finds herself alone with you, – and then it will be your business to make her satisfied with being so.

Palamede. Kind creature, – where shall I find words to thank this compassion to a suffering lover?

Corisca. Never trouble yourself about thanks, – good actions, they say, reward themselves.

Favonius. As for my part, I shall defer those acknowledgments which your excess of goodness demands from me, both on my own score and that of my friend, 'till to-morrow night, when they shall make part of that agreeable penance I am to perform.

This speech of Favonius paved the way for a conversation conformable enough to the characters of the persons engag'd in it; but I am certain would not be well relish'd by that part of my readers which I am most ambitious of obliging; – I shall therefore close the scene, as indeed I did soon after my Tablets, and quitted the apartments of this fair libertine, in order to retire to my own, and contemplate at leisure on what I had seen and heard.

CHAP. III.

Presents the reader with the catastrophe of an adventure very different from what the beginning may have given him reason to expect.

THO' I had thought myself too well acquainted with the principles and inclinations of Corisca, to be at all surprised at any act of licentiousness she could possibly be guilty of, yet I could not defend my senses from being seiz'd with the extremest shock, on finding she could be base enough to condescend to become the instrument of others pleasures, and betray the innocence of a young lady for whom she had as much friendship as is consistent with a woman of her character, – forgetting all this while what the good old poet, Mr. Philip Massenger, tells us on an occasion similar to this of Corisca and Emilia.

> Virtue and Vice in one sole point agree,
> Each would be glad all like themselves might be.[320]

In ruminating very wisely, as I then imagin'd, on what Corisca had said to Palamede, I must confess I entertain'd suspicions not at all to the advantage of poor Emilia; – I fancied that she had in reality confess'd a passion for that gentleman, and Corisca, in forming this contrivance to bring about a private interview between them, had done nothing but what she was convinced in her own mind would be highly satisfactory to her fair friend.

It was never my custom, however, to place an entire dependence on conjecture, whether of my own or that of another person, so resolved to be as convinced as my Invisible inspection could make me.

Accordingly the next day in the afternoon I girded on my precious Belt and went to the house of Corisca; – Emilia was not yet come, but just as I arriv'd I heard her give orders to refuse admittance to all of her own sex except that lady, and also to all those of the other except Favonius and Palamede.

As I doubted not but I should be able to fathom the whole truth of this affair, by the conversation that would pass between these two ladies while they believed themselves alone together, I was extremely impatient for the approach of Emilia, and equally rejoiced when I saw her enter.

The first salutations they gave each other were such as might be expected from persons who mutually profess'd so warm and tender a friendship; – the subjects they afterwards talk'd upon were not of any consequence; – not one word of Palamede nor the projected tour was mentioned, – on which I absolved Emilia from all blame on this account, and was sorry I had ever wrong'd her.

But the less room I had to condemn, the greater cause I had to pity her, and to detest the cruel plot contrived, and so near being put in execution against her virtue; but I had no time to indulge meditation, – the gentlemen presently came in, – the proposal, as agreed upon between them and Corisca, was immediately made, – the ladies gave a ready assent, – a hackney-coach was order'd to be call'd to the door, and every one seem'd equally on the wing to be gone.

The reader will now perhaps imagine, that it being easy to see into the end of this affair, there was no occasion for any farther enquiries in relation to it, and that curiosity had received its utmost gratification; – but I happen'd to be of a different way of thinking, – I sincerely pitied Emilia, and could not help being desirous to see how she would resent the base artifice practised on her when she should discover it, and also how Corisca would conduct the plot she had contrived.

It was no difficult matter for me to know the house they were going to, both by the description I had heard given of it the day before by Corisca, but also by what I had been told by other people concerning its commodiousness for intrigue, so I no sooner found a hackney-coach was order'd, than I hastly quitted the post I was in, – made the best of my way to the place of rendezvous, – got there before them, – took up my stand at the entrance, – saw them alight, and follow'd them into a well-furnish'd spacious room, to which they were usher'd by a spruce waiter.

Wine and biscuits were immediately served up, and the company, after having refresh'd themselves with this little regale, went to walk in the gardens, which

I found indeed very pleasant, – well laid out into parterres and knots,[321] and larger than I could have imagined; – Favonius led Corisca, and Palamede had Emilia by the hand, who, during this promenade, took the opportunity of entertaining her with many tender speeches, but intermix'd with nothing that the most chaste ear might not have listen'd to without calling a blush upon the face.

I was sorry, however, to observe that she receiv'd what he said with a certain languishment in her eyes which embolden'd him to go on, and made me fear that he had indeed a secret ascendancy over her uncautious, unsuspecting heart.

On their return into the house a table was spread with every thing that could excite the appetite or exhilerate the spirits; – the chearfulness and good humour of the guests gave a double relish to the repast, – wit and sparkling champaign crown'd the board; and tho' the ladies allay'd the too great potency of the one by the assistance of water, yet the other flow'd with no less strength and vigour.

After some hours had been pass'd in the height of gaiety, Corisca on a sudden look'd upon her watch, and assuming a more serious air than she was accustom'd to wear, told the company that it was near one o'clock, and they must think of departing for London; – to which Favonius reply'd,

Favonius. Among all the ridiculous things mankind was ever guilty of, I know none more so than the having set their wits to work to invent a machine, and then submitting to be govern'd by it.

Corisca. There are many other laws, as well as this, by which the silly world have bound themselves to go contrary to the primitive rules of nature and inclination, – indulging by stealth only those pleasures which they were born freely to enjoy; but, however, all these customs, disagreeable as they are to people of real wit and spirit, must in some measure be comply'd with, or the stupid vulgar would presently accuse us of irregularity and indecency.

Palamede. I look upon every one here, madam, to be above the censures of the vulgar, yet I will not pretend to enter into any arguments on that head; and dare answer for Favonius, as well as for myself, that he would not presume to detain you a moment beyond the time you think proper to go.

Emilia. Indeed, gentlemen, I think, and I believe Corisca does so too, that to stay any longer at this time would rather diminish than add to the satisfaction we have hitherto enjoy'd.

Favonius. After such a declaration, madam, any farther pressures to the contrary on our part, might justly be look'd upon as impertinent and troublesome: – it is certainly your province to command, – ours implicitly to obey.

In speaking these last words, he went out of the room with Palamede, as it might be supposed to discharge the reckoning of the house; but in a few minutes return'd, and with a seeming concern in their faces said, – that the coachman, either by having got drunk or mistaking his orders, had gone away soon after he had set them down; – on which Corisca affected to be extremely surprised, and Emilia being really so, they both cry'd out at the same time,

Corisca. This is the oddest accident sure that ever happen'd.

Emilia. Bless me! – which way shall we get home!

Palamede. As for going home, madam, it is a thing quite out of the question; – we have enquir'd, and there is no possibility of procuring either coach, chariot, post-chaise, or any sort of carriage whatever, 'till the morning breaks; – so, ladies, you must content yourselves with being our guests for the remainder of the night.

Corisca. Well, since it is so we must e'en make a virtue of necessity, and divert ourselves as well as we can.

Palamede. It would be an unpardonable vanity in us, madam, to imagine that any thing in our conversation could compensate for the want of your repose; – we will therefore order a bed to be got ready for you two ladies, while Favonius and myself watch the approach of day, in order to provide a vehicle for carrying us to town.

Corisca. No, no, – by no means, – we will all share the same fate; it would be strange indeed, if four people of taste and spirit could not find some way to amuse each other for the space of one night.

While she was speaking a Concert of Flutes, a Hautboy, a Double-Curtal,[322] and some other wind music, on a sudden saluted their ears, – on which she cry'd out,

Corisca. Hark! – music! – if it continues it will very well atone for the loss of a few hours sleep.

Emilia. Nothing ever happen'd so fortunately for me; – I love music as I love my life, especially of this sort.

In speaking this she ran hastily to the window and threw up the sash, in order to hear the several instruments more distinctly; – Palamede follow'd, and they both seem'd absorb'd in a most profound attention for some minutes, which Favonius and Corisca observing, took that opportunity of passing softly behind them and slipp'd out of the room.

Emilia turning her head presently after, with a design, as I suppose, to say something either to the one or the other, was surprised at seeing neither of them there, and cry'd out to Palamede,

Emilia. Bless me! – what is become of Favonius and Corisca!

Palamede. I know not, madam; – perhaps they are gone down into the garden, to be nearer to the music, which seems to proceed from the lower end of the walk.

Emilia. Very likely; – they might have told us, however; – but since it is so we will follow them.

Palamede. With all my heart, madam; – but first permit me to reveal a secret to you which you ought to be told, and my breast has long labour'd with an impatience of discovering.

Emilia. A secret! – What secret can you have with me that would be worth losing one note of this heavenly music to listen to!

Palamede. I hope you will be of another opinion, madam, when I shall tell you that the whole happiness of my future life, and even my soul's eternal peace, depends upon it.

Emilia. You may tell me what you will, but I shall believe nothing of the matter; – so let us rejoin our friends.

It is not so much by what people say, as by the manner in which they deliver themselves, that the sincerity of their words may be guess'd at; and I was heartily glad to find, both by the looks of Emilia and the tone of her voice, that she indeed had more inclination to do as she had proposed, than to stay and suffer herself to be entertain'd by Palamede in the way she might easily perceive he was about to do it.

The discreet intentions of this young lady, however, could avail her but little in her present situation; – Palamede got between her and the door as she was endeavouring to go out, and throwing himself upon his knees before her, and at the same time catching fast hold of both her hands, said to her,

Palamede. No, charming Emilia, I have not so long languish'd for an opportunity like this to let it now escape me! – you must, – you shall hear me. – By Heaven I love you! – love you to the most raging height the passion can inspire! – For many, many tedious weeks, you have been the only object of my nightly visions and waking thoughts, – and –.

He was going on, but Emilia interrupted him by replying in these terms, accompanied with an air full of resentment and confusion.

Emilia. Fye, Palamede, this raillery is impertinent and insipid, – and what I could not have expected to be treated with by a person who has the character of good sense and breeding.

Palamede. Cruelly urged; – oh could you see into my heart you would find it all devoted to you! – devoted to you with a tenderness so perfect as can be equal'd by nothing but the charms that have subdued it. – Frown not, adorable Emilia, nor struggle to get loose; for by all my hopes, never will I quit the grasp I have taken of you, nor rise from the posture I am in, 'till I have convinced you of the sincerity, as well as ardency, of the flame you have kindled in me.

Emilia. Sir, this nocturnal declaration is little consistent with that respect which is always the attendant of an honourable passion. – If you had, indeed, any thoughts of me of the nature you pretend, I am no recluse, and you might have found a more proper season to acquaint me with them.

Palamede. The passion I am inflamed with, is not of a nature to submit to the dull forms observed by vulgar lovers. – Besides, what season can be more fit for love than night, the friend of love? – Turn your eyes towards the window and behold the silver moon, with all the thousand twinkling stars; see how sweet, how mild they shine, with what benevolent aspects they dart their rays upon us; – listen to the melodious sounds you just now prais'd; – will not all these soften your soul, – melt you into pity, and make you think such love as mine deserves some recompence!

Emilia. I'll hear no more; – unhand me, sir, and give me liberty to seek our friends; – or be assured my cries shall raise the house.

He then let go her hands and rose from the posture he had been in; but still kept his back close against the door, while with a half smile, he reply'd to what she had said in this manner:

Palamede. Madam, you are obey'd in part, and if I acquiesce to every thing you demand, it is not to be imagined that you would be one jot less in my power than now; – our friends are too deeply engaged with each other to suffer themselves to be interrupted; and as to the people of the house they know their distance, and are always extremely deaf on these occasions.

On hearing him speak thus she burst into a flood of Tears, and throwing herself into a chair, cry'd out,

Emilia. Oh heavens! – is this possible! – can Corisca be so vile! – am I betray'd! – basely given up by her to infamy and ruin!

On hearing her make this exclamation, he left the place where he had been standing and seated himself near her, – then taking one of her hands and pressing it tenderly to his lips, spoke to this effect:

Palamede. Not so, my angel! – by heaven, the transactions of this night shall be for ever a sacred and inviolable secret! – not even Favonius nor Corisca shall be acquainted with it if you desire the contrary; – I know they will laugh at me, but no matter, – I can bear all that, and much more, to comply with the least request made by my dear Emilia; – oh then be kind, and bless my longing wishes! – let no reluctance damp the coming joys, but yield to share the happiness you give!

The consternation of Emilia, on finding she was exposed to the danger she now was in, by the very woman whom she most had loved, and most believed her friend, had thrown her into so profound a resvery, that I much question whether she heard any part of what Palamede had lately been speaking to her, 'till closing his protestations with a strenuous embrace, she started up, broke from him, and looking wildly round the room she spy'd two swords, which Favonius and Palamede had pluck'd off on their entrance and put in a window, – she snatch'd up one of them, and drawing it out of the scabbard in an instant, held the point to her breast, saying at the same time,

Emilia. Here is at least a refuge from dishonour; – that base woman, who thought to make me as vile as I now find she is herself, shall meet with a disappointment she perhaps does not expect; – if you offer to approach me, or advance one step beyond the spot you stand upon, this goes into my heart!

The amazement, – the shock, – the confusion Palamede was in at this action is altogether impossible to describe; – her words, – her looks, – her voice, – convincing him she was indeed in earnest, he remain'd speechless, – without motion, – his eyes fixed on her in a kind of stupid stare, and seem'd like one transfix'd with thunder, – at length, recovering himself a little, he said to her, in a faultering voice,

Palamede. For heaven's sake, madam, wound not thus my soul by the sight of your despair! – you have no cause! – it is certain that I long have lov'd you, but never had a thought of seducing your innocence; – the plot to bring you hither was not of my contriving; – 'tis true I came into it, as where is the man would not? but be assured I am no ravisher, nor capable of owing my pleasures to brutal violence; – oh therefore throw aside that cruel weapon, or turn the point on me, and if I make the least attempt to offend your modesty bury it to the hilt within my bosom!

Emilia. Sir, I once look'd upon you as a man of honour, and should rejoice to find you could redeem yourself in my opinion.

Palamede. By all that's sacred, not the utmost gratification of my loosest wishes could have given me half the joy as now, to prove myself not wholly unworthy the esteem of such exalted virtue! – Charming Emilia! – perfect in mind as well as form! – in both angelic! – behold me your convert! – The love I had for you is now rarified into adoration! – your virtue, like chemists gold, turns all into itself, and leaves no grosser particles behind! – forgive what is past, and never – never more will I presume to entertain you with discourses less chaste and pure than your own virgin thoughts!

Emilia. May I believe this penitence sincere?

Palamede. You may, by heaven! and when I relapse into my former crime, may infamy, – diseases, – the contempt of the whole world, – your eternal hatred, and every other curse fall on me!

Emilia. Then find some way, if possible, to take me immediately from this place, and conduct me safe to my own apartment.

Palamede. My readiness to obey you, madam, I hope, will prove the integrity of my present intentions, and be some atonement for the past; – it is my happiness to have it in my power to do what you require with much more ease than you imagine; – you shall no longer, beautiful Emilia, be imposed upon; – the coachman, whom we pretended had left us, has only put up at an inn not above forty yards distant from this house; – I suppose he may be gone to bed by this time, as we told him we should not return to London 'till the morning; but I will send and have him roused.

He had scarce made an end of speaking these words, when he rang the bell, and a waiter coming presently up, he gave him the necessary orders for fulfilling the promise he had just given to Emilia; on which that young lady, with the utmost satisfaction in her voice and eyes, cry'd out,

Emilia. This is truly honourable, indeed, – and worthy of yourself.

Something which that instant started into the mind of Palamede, hinder'd him from making any answer, or even, perhaps, from hearing what she said; – he rang the Bell a second time with all his force, and call'd for pen, ink and paper, which being brought, he told Emilia that decency and good manners would not suffer him to depart without taking some notice of the occasion to Favonius, with whom he had always lived in a perfect good understanding, and therefore intreated her permission to write a few lines to that gentleman: – the request was too reasonable not to be complied with, and he sat down and dictated the following little epistle:

To Favonius.

My dear friend,

Things have happen'd very different from what I was made to expect in regard to Emilia: – in fine, – she is not a woman but an angel, – as such I shall always esteem her, and think it my glory to obey every command she is pleased to lay upon me: – the first she has honour'd me with is to remove her hence and conduct her to her own apartment, which I am just now about to do. – I have no opportunity to discharge the music or the expences of the house, so beg you will take the whole upon you, and meet me to-morrow evening at Braund's, where we will sup together and settle that affair. – Make what compliments and excuses you shall think proper for me to Corisca, and believe me,

    With the greatest sincerity,
            Dear Favonius,
                Yours, &c.

                                PALAMEDE.

While Palamede was thus employ'd, it also came into Emilia's head to let Corisca know some part of the resentment she had conceived against her, – accordingly she took another pen out of the standish and express'd herself in these terms:

To Corisca.

Madam,

What the united report of all who know you could never have made me believe, your behaviour this night has not only convinced me of, but also that the tongue of malice can find nothing wherewith to aggravate your real guilt. –

Was it not enough, oh most ungenerous woman! to sink your own honour and reputation in eternal infamy, but you must also endeavour to drag others into perdition with you! – Know, to your confusion, that I happily escaped the snare you had laid for me, and shall reap this benefit by my late danger, as to avoid the company of a person whom to preserve an acquaintance with must in the end have been the ruin of my character, if not of my virtue; for be assured, I shall henceforward be as careful to shun your presence as ever I was eager to come into it. – Here ceases all farther intercourse between us; – may the disappointment of your base designs on me serve as a warning to you not to attempt the like on any other equally inadvertent and uncautious as the

Much deceived

EMILIA.

They had just finish'd, and made up the above billets, when the waiter return'd and told Palamede that he had, tho' not without some difficulty, prevail'd on the coachman to rise, and that before he left the inn he had seen him go into the stable to bring out the horses.

Palamede then gave him the letter he had wrote to Favonius, – saying,

Palamede. Be sure to deliver this to the gentleman who came with us as soon as he shall be stirring, – and let him know I shall send the coach back in the morning.

Emilia also put into his hands her epistle to Corisca, with these words:

Emilia. And let the lady know I left this for her.

The fellow reply'd, that they might depend he would be punctual in discharging the commission they entrusted him with, and then withdrew.

Finding my Chrystaline Tables were now overcharg'd, I was oblig'd to shut them up, so can relate no farther particulars of what conversation pass'd between Palamede and Emilia during the small time they waited for the coach to carry them away; – and can only say in general, that the greatest reserve and distance was observed on both sides: – Emilia, though now perfectly satisfied with the contrition of Palamede, thought it would be imprudent to appear too gay; – and Palamede, fearful to renew her apprehensions, behaved towards her with all the solemnity of a Chinese Mandarin.

On their going down they were met at the bottom of the stairs by the woman who kept this tavern, or rather brothel; who ushering in what she had to say with a low curtsy, told Emilia that she flatter'd herself with the expection of her sleeping there that night, and hoped nothing disagreeable had happen'd to occasion her departure at so unseasonable an hour; – adding, that she should never forgive herself if any thing in her house had disobliged so sweet a young lady.

Emilia answer'd this fawning speech only with a look of contempt; but Palamede told her she need be under no concern on that score, – the lady had no objections to her house, but chose never to sleep out of her own apartment.

No more was said, – they went into the coach and I follow'd on foot; for I had not curiosity enough to make me stay the remainder of the night in that place, for no other purpose than to see how Favonius and Corisca would behave on being told that Palamede and Emilia were gone, and receiving the epistles that gentleman and lady had left for them.

I had a long walk home; but my Invisibility secured me from the danger of any insults, and the satisfaction that rose in my mind, on the noble conquest virtue had gain'd over vice, made the way seem much less tedious.

A few days after I was inform'd, by the report of the town, that Palamede made his public addresses to Emilia: – being willing to be better convinced in the truth of this matter, I made several visits to Emilia's apartment, and found that in fact the thing was as I had been told; – Palamede, who really lov'd Emilia much more than perhaps he was sensible of himself, before this proof she had given him of her virtue, got over that objection which the scantiness of her fortune had before laid in his way; and Emilia, who had liked him as much as Corisca had said she did, gave all the encouragement he could wish to his honourable passion.

I look upon the affair to be now in a manner concluded on, and that a very short time will consummate their mutual wishes, – a catastrophe which I doubt not but every generous reader will heartily rejoice at as well as myself.

Favonius, who is in reality a man of strict honour and good principles, though somewhat too sanguine in his amours, still continues his intimacy with Palamede, and highly applauds his conversion in favour of the fair inspirer of his honourable flame; – Corisca bites her lips whenever the name of Emilia is mention'd, and endeavours all she can to traduce that virtue which she had not the power to destroy; but all she says on that score serves only to shew more plainly her own bad heart; and Emilia, by refraining all conversation with her, has entirely regain'd that esteem and good opinion which she had well nigh lost.

CHAP. IV.

Contains the rehearsal of a conversation which the Author accidentally happen'd to be witness of, and looks upon himself as bound by an indispensible obligation to make public; though perfectly conscious, from his observations of mankind, that there are a very great many of his readers who will labour all they can to bring these pages into discredit.

ONE whom I shall always rank among the number of our best English Authors, tells us in a justly esteem'd poem, that

> Wisdom is still to sloth too great a slave,
> None are so busy as the fool and knave.[323]

How widely different are the pictures drawn of a person whose prudence makes him act and talk with circumspection and reserve? – How various are the representations made of him? – He has almost as many characters as there are speakers of him; – by the abundance one hears of him the judgment is distracted, and there is no forming a right idea of what he truly is.

One can go into no company without hearing some mention made of Lord Honorius, yet one shall seldom find any two people agree in their opinion concerning him, either as to his abilities or principles, whether in religious, moral, or political matters.

He is no follower of the court, yet does not totally avoid going thither; – he professes himself a member of the establish'd church, yet converses freely with those of different persuasions; he listens attentively to the arguments urged by persons of all parties and all sects, without offering any of his own, or giving his opinion, which are wrong or which are right.

For this reason all the zealots, both in religion and politics, brand him with lukewarmness, and say he is a man of an uncertain way of thinking, and has no settled principle of acting.

Some few there are who applaud his moderation, but many more who look upon it as a piece of low cunning, thereby to cover some latent designs he has within his bosom; but of what nature these are I have heard many warm disputes about. – Some will needs have him in the interest of the Pretender, and others that he is secretly a tool of the Ministry: – some have confidently averr'd that they have seen a white rose carry'd into his house on the 10th of June,[324] and others that he has worn a yellow waistcoat on the birth-day of his present Majesty;[325] – as if an innocent flower, or the colour of a piece of silk, were sufficient tokens to shew the wishes of the wearer's heart.

As to his œconomy in private life, he is not at all expensive in dress, equipage, or the furniture of his house, chusing to appear rather below his rank than in any particular to exceed it: – this is frequently attributed to his covetousness, while more favourable judges suppose it to be owing to his contempt of the modish fopperies of the age: – he partakes of all the pleasures of the town, but never pursues them to an excess or with eagerness; – the graver sort of people ascribe this to his discretion, and the more gay to want of spirit and coldness of constitution.

Thus apt are we to form a vain judgment on things we know nothing of; – the heart of man is incomprehensible, unless discovered by himself in some glaring proof either of virtue or vice; – the first he may not have an opportunity to set forth in any conspicuous light, and the the latter he may have artifice and hypocrisy enough to gloss over and conceal. – How impossible then is it to be certain to which of these he is in reality devoted?

Among the variety of descriptions and reports in relation to Lord Honorius, I found, notwithstanding, that it was agreed on by all hands, that though he would not suffer himself to be imposed upon by his tradesmen, yet he always took care their bills should be paid with the utmost exactness and punctuality, and that he never dealt with foreigners, – These articles, however insignificant they may seem to some of those who call themselves the polite world, I confess, gave me such an idea both of his prudence and justice, as made me immediately join with those who spoke the greatest things in his praise in other respects.

But being desirous of penetrating more deeply into the reality of this nobleman's disposition, I resolved to try how my Invisibilityship would serve that end, and accordingly made a visit one morning at his house.

I pass'd through several neat rooms, the furniture of which was rich, and befitting the dignity and fortune of the owner; but had nothing of gaudiness in it. – At last I found the person I went to seek, – he was in a closet within his dressing-room and had a book in his hand; – I was curious to see what was the subject of his meditations, and looking over his shoulder perceived it was the poems of our English Pindar, the celebrated Mr. Abraham Cowley; – the page he was employ'd in on my entrance contain'd, among others, these lines:

> Oh fountains! when in you shall I,
> Eas'd of unpeaceful thoughts myself espy!
> O fields! O woods! when shall I be made
> The happy tenant of your shade!
> Here's the spring-head of pleasure's flood,
> Where all the riches lie,
> That she has coin'd and stamp'd for good,
> To charm the mind as well as eye.
> Pride and ambition here,
> Only in far-fetch'd metaphors appear;
> Here's nought but winds can hurtful murmurs scatter,
> And nought but echo flatter.
> The Gods, when they descended hither
> From Heaven, did always chuse their way;
> And therefore we may boldly say,
> That is the way too thither.[326]

When he came to this part of the poem, he stopp'd and cry'd out with the greatest emphasis,

Lord Honorius. Charming inimitable Cowley! – How just, how truly delicate are all thy notions, and how widely different from those of the age I have the misfortune to live in! – If one may form a judgment, as sure one may, by the writings of seventy or eighty years ago, the genius of Britain was far unlike what it appears at present.

He had scarce finish'd this exclamation, when a servant open'd the door and told him that Sir Whimsy Brainsick was come to wait upon him; – on which he laid aside the book, and went into the next chamber to receive his guest.

After giving and returning the customary salutations of the morning, and having seated themselves, the following dialogue ensued between them:

Lord Honorius. 'Tis a wonder to see you dress'd and abroad thus early, Sir Whimsey; – I think you are commonly in your first sleep after this time.

Sir Whimsey Brainsick. Ay, my Lord, but pleasure must on some occasions give way to business; – I have vast affairs upon my hands at present; – I only snatch'd a moment to take leave of your Lordship, and two hours hence shall set out for the country.

Lord Honorius. On your election, I suppose?

Sir Whimsey Brainsick. No, no, – my Lord Triffli Traffli has secur'd me a borough without my taking the trouble of ever going near it; – my business at present is down at *******, where I have a considerable estate, and, I believe, a pretty good interest; and I have engag'd myself to strain both, as far as they will go, in favour of Sir Crafty Shallowbuggen.

Lord Honorius. Sir Crafty Shallowbuggen! – What then has mr. Worthy, the present member, declined standing?

Sir Whimsey Brainsick. No, no, my Lord, he has not declined; but we are resolved to have him out at any rate.

Lord Honorius. I would not have you deceive yourself, Sir Whimsey, – mr. Worthy is a gentleman who I am told is highly esteem'd by his constituents, and you may be at a great deal of expence to oppose him to no purpose.

Sir Whimsey Brainsick. As to the expence, I don't doubt but it will be made up to me some way or other; – I have my eye upon a place; and, I can tell you, am as good as promis'd either that or a riband.

Lord Honorius. The character I have heard of mr. Worthy makes me sorry so powerful an opposition should be set on foot against him.

Sir Whimsey Brainsick. He has been stubborn, my Lord, very stubborn, – has voted against the Jew and Clandestine Marriage Bills; – and it is not fit the Ministry should be affronted. – Your Lordship, I suppose, is a friend to the Ministry.

Lord Honorius. Sir, I never gave any man reason to believe I was the contrary.

Sir Whimsey Brainsick. No, no, – Your Lordship is too wise; – those who are friends to the Ministry are friends to themselves; – for my own part, if it were not to oblige them I would not give two-pence who had the election at ******, or any where else – But I must beg your lordship's pardon, – I have a thousand things to dispatch, and would not be waited for by four or five gentlemen who accompany me on the same expedition, – so your Lordship's most obedient.

Lord Honorius. Yours, Sir Whimsey, – I wish you a good journey.

With these words they parted, – Lord Honorius saw him to the top of the staircase, and then turn'd back to his closet, saying to himself as he went,

Lord Honorius. What a wild world is this! – How do men toil to bring infamy on themselves, and entail certain ruin on their posterity!

As I thought, by the little sample I had seen, that it was now in my power to make a better judgment of the sentiments of this nobleman than by all I had heard from others, I was following Sir Whimsey Brainsick down Stairs; but on hearing some debate between a plain honest-looking countryman and a spruce footman, who, as I found afterwards, had been but lately taken into my Lord's service, I stopp'd short to listen to the occasion.

I soon perceived that the countryman was desirous of speaking to his Lordship, and the fellow, judging by appearances, thought it too great a presumption, and would fain have turn'd him from the door; but the rustic was not so easily repulsed as the other had imagined; – the first words I could hear distinctly were as follow:

Footman. I tell you, friend, I know not whether my Lord is at home or not; – or if he is, whether he pleases to be visible; – but if you let me know what business you have with him, and from whom you came, I will take care his lordship shall be inform'd, and you may have your answer to-morrow.

Countryman. Goodlack, mr. Skipjack, – who are you? – my Lord is not used to have such malapert[327] fellows about him: – but if I must not see my Lord, pray let me speak to mr. Downright, the gentleman that dresses and waits upon him, – he knows me well enough, and will give me a better answer.

The footman then vouchsafed to call the person he mention'd, and the countryman had the satisfaction to find himself well received, – mr. Downright shook him cordially by the hand, – told him he was glad to see him in London, and ask'd him what business had brought him hither; – to which the other reply'd,

Countryman. In good troth I did not come upon pleasure, – I have business, – very great business with my Lord, and would fain speak to him, – if so be I may have liberty to come into his presence, as you know, mr. Downright, I have done many a good time in the country: – but that mr. Finikin there, with his pig-tail wig, stands as it were like a mud-wall to keep every body off the house.

Mr. Downright. Oh he did not know you, mr. Goodacre; and besides, he has lived in families where nobody without a coach or chair are admitted; – but I will acquaint my Lord you are here, – he is alone, and I am sure will see you.

Countryman. Thank you, mr. Downright; – it is well there are some civil people in this same town.

Mr. Downright then went on his message, – the footman look'd very sheepish and sneak'd away, while the countryman strutted about the hall as great as an emperor, 'till the valet return'd and desir'd him to walk up.

As I took mr. Goodacre for one of my Lord's tenants, and imagin'd he was only come on the score of renewing a lease, or some other country affairs relating to himself, which I had no manner of curiosity to pry into, I was in some debate within myself whether I should stay or go directly out of the house, the door being then open; but a certain impulse, the meaning of which I cannot account for, sway'd me to pursue my first thought, and I turn'd back and accompanied him into the presence of my Lord, from whom he met with a reception not commonly given by persons of quality to a man of his plain appearance, except on particular occasions.

His Lordship made him sit down in a chair very near himself, and, with a smiling countenance and the greatest affability in his voice and air, told him he was glad to see him look so well and hearty, – that he hoped his wife and family enjoy'd the same share of good health, – and then ask'd what business had brought him up to London: – to the former part of these obliging speeches he only answer'd with several low bows; but to the latter reply'd in these terms:

Mr. Goodacre. Why, my Lord, your Lordship knows we are going to have a new Parliament, – and belike there will be a great bustle all over the kingdom about Elections; – and no wonder if there be; – every one makes us such fair promises when they come to ask us for our votes, that 'tis a hard matter to know which we can most depend upon; – we have been served basely, very basely, by some of our representatives, – and it behoves us to be very cautious for the future.

Lord Honorius. Very true, mr. Goodacre, it does so indeed, – and I hope the nation will think so.

Mr. Goodacre. Now as to our borough, – no man could make finer speeches to us, or pretend he had our interest more at heart, than 'Squire Earnly, before he was chosen, yet he no sooner got into the house than he shew'd he did not care a straw for us, – laugh'd at all our petitions and remonstrances, and, I am told, made a merit of it to the Ministry.

Lord Honorius. I am afraid there are too many who have done so. – Does the same gentleman set up again?

Mr. Goodacre. No, my Lord, – he would have no chance for it if he did, – we know him too well, he sees that well enough; – but 'tis thought, however, that he will get in for some place or other.

Lord Honorius. Nothing more likely. – But do you hear who intends to offer himself in his stead?

Mr. Goodacre. Yes, my Lord, – great interest is already making for one Capt. Sashbright; – he is as fine a person, indeed, as the sun shines upon; – but we know nothing of him: – he is recommended by Sir Courtly Jobber, – has brought a power of money down with him; – they went together in Sir Courtly's coach to ******* fair, – bought a many things, and gave them to every body about them; – guineas and broad pieces fly about like hail; – any one, almost, may have them for picking up.

Lord Honorius. So then he may easily carry it, I suppose?

Mr. Goodacre. I cannot tell that, my Lord, – there was a numerous meeting at the Rose about a fortnight ago, and 'Squire Wellwood of the Green was put in nomination, – his family has been settled for a long time at *******, he lives most part in the country, – does a great deal of good among the poor, and is mainly beloved.

Lord Honorius. I know him, mr. Goodacre, – he is certainly a very worthy gentleman.

Mr. Goodacre. Ay, my Lord, – he would have it all to nothing, if it was not for one consideration.

Lord Honorius. What is that?

Mr. Goodacre. The Captain has promised, that if he gets his election he will procure an Act of Parliament for a new Road to be cut,[328] at the Government's expence, from ***** to *****, which your Lordship knows would be a great advantage to our market.

Lord Honorius. A very great one, indeed.

Mr. Goodacre. Ay, my Lord, if we were sure it would be done; – but there lies the query. – Some people will promise any thing to gain their point, and never think of it afterwards. – We all know 'Squire Wellwood to be a noble gentleman, – and so may Capt. Sashbright too, – he may or he may not. – Now we are strangely divided in our opinions, whether we ought to leave the certain good for the uncertain better, – and have at length resolved to be decided by your Lordship.

Lord Honorius. By me!

Mr. Goodacre. Yes, my Lord, we know your Lordship to be a wise man, and a true lover of your country.

Lord Honorius. I have always thought, mr. Goodacre, that to meddle in these things would prove me deserving neither of the one nor the other of the epithets you give me; – every elector ought to give his vote according to the dictates of his conscience, and not suffer himself to be sway'd by any interest or motive whatever; and for a nobleman, or other person of distinction, to attempt, either by menaces or cajolings, to make them act to the contrary, appears to me to be the most gross encroachment on Liberty that can be offer'd.

Mr. Goodacre. But here the case is widely different, my Lord.

Lord Honorius. I grant it is. – You desire my advice as a friend, – not submit to be govern'd by me as a director; – it would therefore be ungenerous, and even cruel, in me to suffer you to be deluded by false pretences, when it is so easily in my power to put you upon your guard against them. – In the first place, you ought to consider that Capt. Sashbright, whatever his character may otherwise be, is an officer in the army, – and as such it is his interest to promote the continuance of a standing army,[329] and consequently of those taxes which are necessary for the support of it. – In the second, Sir Courtly Jobber, who it seems is the person who recommends him, has for a long time, to my certain knowledge, been an agent for the ministry, and is indebted for his title, and the best part of the estate he is in possession of, merely to the good services he has render'd them.

Mr. Goodacre. Ay marry, – these things are worth thinking of indeed: – so I suppose, my Lord, the money he so plentifully throws about is none of his own?

Lord Honorius. Not a doit, – he will be reimburs'd with interest.

Mr. Goodacre. And yet I know not, my Lord, but there may be some among us foolish enough to be inveigled by this bait. – Alackaday! – we country people are ignorant of such practices; – we little think what the great folks in town are doing, and a many there are that would not believe a word of it without good authority. – Oh I wish your Lordship were down at Eggum-Hall at this critical juncture.

Lord Honorius. I will be there, mr. Goodacre, in spite of the aversion I have always had to appear at elections, or to distinguish myself on any occasion; – my love to the place which gave me birth, and good-will to my countrymen, shall overbalance all other considerations; – I will do all I can to strengthen the weak eyes which are in danger of being dazled with Sir Courtly's gold, and shew them the false lustre of his fleeting promises.

Mr. Goodacre. Heaven bless your Lordship! – a noble resolution!

Lord Honorius. When do you return, mr. Goodacre?

Mr. Goodacre. I shall lie but this one night in town, my Lord, and set out be time to-morrow morning.

Lord Honorius. I will not be two days behind you; – in the mean time you may tell them what I say.

Mr. Goodacre. It will be joyful news to some.

There pass'd no farther conversation between them, the honest country-man rose up to take his leave, full of transport at the success of his negotiation; but Lord Honorius would not permit him to depart 'till he had rung the bell for mr. Downright, and given orders that he should be made welcome with the best entertainment the house afforded; – I left him to accept the invitation, and return'd to my apartment, well satisfied in my mind that I was now enabled to form a right judgment of this nobleman's principles and disposition.

CHAP. V.

Presents the reader with the detail of a very remarkable incident, which, I believe, if consider'd with a due attention, there are but few people, especially of the Fair Sex, who will not find themselves enabled to become better members of society by having perused.

A certain sacred writer tells us, that the tongue is an unruly member, and preaches much concerning the government of it;[330] – but I dare not presume to insist too much on his authority, as he has been, with others of his cotemporaries, pretty much exploded for almost half a century; and I might be look'd upon, by my polite readers, as a very old-fashion'd silly fellow to make any mention of him.

But I may venture, without running the risque of being read with a horse-laugh, to quote the words of another very great and learned person of a more modern date, who says, – that the tongue is the most dangerous of all weapons; – that it is capable of destroying all peace, all love, all harmony in the world; – of sowing dissentions among families; of disuniting the hearts of the dearest friends and relations; of ruining the reputation and fortune of whomsoever it is levell'd against; and that even murders and the worst of mischiefs may be occasion'd by it.[331]

That the tongue, when it becomes the instrument of a malicious heart, carries a thousand daggers in it, is a truth which the observation of every one evinces. – But this is not all, – public abuse or private scandal, defamation and detraction, are not the only vices of the tongue, – an unguarded word is frequently productive of the most unhappy consequences, – it wounds, as it were, by chance-medley,[332] and a person may be stabb'd in the most tender part without any intention in the giver of the blow.

A talkative disposition, or, in other words, a passion for repeating every thing one sees and hears, or even guesses at, is extremely dangerous to society; and tho' it is a foible proceeding rather from levity than ill-nature, sometimes produces the same effects; – those guilty of it, perhaps, may mean no hurt; – but, alas! they consider not how far the person to whom they are speaking may be interested in the report they make, and that what they imagine of no moment may stab him to the quick.

Nothing is more common than for people to hurt thus at random, and by their rashness to occasion accidents, which if they foresaw they would be most careful to prevent, – as a poet of the present age emphatically enough expresses it:

> Thinking to shoot my arrow o'er the house,
> I have kill'd my brother.[333]

But this inadvertency, as great a weakness as it doubtless is, has in it somewhat yet more excuseable than to reveal a secret which we are conscious must give the hearer pain. – I confess that this is sometimes done thro' good-will; but then it is a very mistaken good-will in many cases. – If I know a person sustains an injury, and has it in his power to redress the grievance, it is certainly my duty to acquaint him with it; but when the evil is without a remedy, it is infinitely more kind to suffer him to remain in ignorance.

To be well deceived, is almost equal to not being deceived at all, – our happiness consists in the imagination of it; and if we firmly believe ourselves possess'd of what we wish, it is the same thing as being so in reality: – How cruel is it then for any one to draw back the friendly curtain that hides ill fortune from us, and compel us to behold our wretchedness!

Every one who is thus unhappily undeceived may cry out with Bellamira in the play,

> – Ah, cruel friend!
> Why did'st thou wake me from my dream of bliss!
> Why bring me from that scene of fancied joys,
> To one of real anguish, horror and despair![334]

Many unhappy instances of these well-meant ill offices have come to my knowledge since I was in possession of the Gift of Invisibility; – but I shall recite only one of them, which, as it is a very late transaction, and but few people know the real truth of, is at present a matter of much speculation among those who are any way acquainted with the parties concerned, or have even heard their names.

Meroveus and Deidamia were an extreme happy pair, the railers against marriage could find nothing in the conduct of either of them to countenance any sarcasms on that state; – the most tender affection had been the chief, if not the sole motive of the union between them; and the secure and uninterrupted possession of each other, instead of diminishing, seem'd rather to increase their mutual ardour, and the first bridal fondness appear'd in their behaviour after having served a more than seven years apprenticeship to Hymen.

Yet, how on a sudden have we seen all this sweet serenity turn'd into storms and tempests? – Meroveus and Deidamia, who it was thought could not have lived a single week out of each other's presence, are now parted, – according to all probability, – parted, – to meet no more in love.

Besides the many great accomplishments which justified the affection they so long had towards each other, both of them were accounted persons of an excellent understanding and solid sense, – nothing therefore could have more amazed the world than that they should come to this open rupture, even though some little cause of complaint had happen'd either on the one side or the other.

An event so strange, so little dream'd of, put all conjecture to a stand; – people pretended not even to guess what should be the occasion, much less to unravel so great a mystery, – the accomplishment of that work was reserved by fate for the Invisible Spy alone.

The manner in which I made this discovery, I shall relate as concisely, as the conversation which let me into it will admit of.

As I was one day taking a solitary walk on Constitution-Hill, I saw Deidamia leaning on the arm of Eutracia, a lady of birth and fortune, who had been bred up with her at the boarding-school, and ever since been her most intimate friend and companion; – just as they approach'd the place where I was, the following dialogue began between them:

Deidamia. Now for the secret you have to tell me; – methinks I have a more than ordinary impatience to hear it, and we cannot be more retired, – no living soul is near us, and there is no danger of any one coming to interrupt our discourse, as all the world are in the Mall.

Eutracia. I will not keep you long in suspence, my dear; – but first you must answer two or three questions I have to ask you, and then resolve to arm yourself with all the fortitude you are mistress of not to be too much shock'd at what I shall relate.

Deidamia. I cannot conceive that there is any thing, which either you or any one else can tell me, capable of giving me a shock. – But pray, what is it you would know from me?

Eutracia. The town looks upon you as one of the most happy women in it, – is it true that you are really so?

Deidamia. Indeed, my dear, I think myself so; – and if I would labour to be more bless'd, know not how to form a single wish beyond what I possess.

Eutracia. There are many private causes of disquiet, – which prudence obliges us to conceal. – Are you thoroughly convinced of the affection of your husband?

Deidamia. I never had the least cause to doubt it; and the tenderness I have for him is so sincere and delicate, as I think would make me easily perceive a want of it in him. – But wherefore do you ask; – you cannot have any reason to suspect him?

Eutracia. Ah, poor Deidamia!

Deidamia. Why do you sigh, and look so pietously upon me? – some wretch has certainly belyed Meroveus to you.

Eutracia. No; – but one more interrogatory and I have done. – Does he never absent himself without letting you know where he goes? – never lie out of his own house?

Deidamia. Very seldom, and that but lately; – an intimate friend of his makes his addresses to a young lady at Hammersmith, – he frequently desires my husband's company with him, and they sometimes stay all night, when having supp'd there, it is dangerous to return to London, as the roads are now infested.

Eutracia. How easy is it to deceive the innocent. – Meroveus is a villain.

Deidamia. How, Eutracia! – a villain! – Had any other call'd him so, my resentment should have shewn how much I despise so base an accusation.

Eutracia. Alas! – 'tis your own love and honour makes you so tenacious of his, but he is false in both; – and I again repeat the name, – he is a villain, and will put it in your own power to prove him so by the testimony of your own eyes and ears, – provided you promise to give him no previous hints that you have discover'd, or even suspect his perfidy.

Deidamia. But how! – how, Eutracia, is he a villain!

Eutracia. He keeps a mistress, some common wench no doubt; but he adores, – doats on her, – pretends himself her husband, and those nights when you imagine him at Hammersmith, he passes with her.

The tender Deidamia was now so overcome at these words, that her spirits quite forsook her, and she must certainly have fallen on the earth, if they had not happen'd to be very near a bench at the lower end of the walk, where Eutracia placed her; – the keeper of the gate perceiving her condition, was so humane as to run and fetch some water, which being sprinkled on her face soon brought her to herself. – Eutracia, on seeing her fair friend thus agitated, seem'd, and I believe really was, very much concern'd at what she had done; for she could not restrain some tears from falling down her eyes while she express'd herself in these terms:

Eutracia. My dearest Deidamia, if I had not thought you would have received this intelligence with more moderation, you should have been for ever ignorant of it.

The afflicted lady made no reply to these words, but in a few minutes growing somewhat more compos'd, quitted the bench, and leaning on Eutracia, the conversation was renewed in this manner:

Deidamia. Oh, Eutracia! little are you capable of conceiving the agonies this poor distracted bleeding heart sustains! – yet I must know all. – Tell me by what means you got information of this horrid secret, and how you are assured of its veracity!

Eutracia. It was not my intention to conceal any part of it; – but you must determine to listen with calmness to me.

Deidamia. I will.

Eutracia. Well then, – I will tell you all. – I believe you know mrs. Flounceit, my mantua-maker.

Deidamia. I saw her once; – you may remember I was with you when she brought home your last new sack.[335]

Eutracia. That woman, you must know, has an interest with some foreign merchants, and can frequently oblige her customers with some curious things which are prohibited to be sold in public; – she came last Monday, and acquainted me she had several patterns of the most beautiful chints[336] that ever were seen; – I went the next morning in order to see them, and was carried into a back parlour for the sake of privacy; as I was looking over the goods I heard a man call from the top of the stair-case to know if the coach was come; I thought myself perfectly acquainted with the voice, tho' I could not just then recollect whose it was; but presently after saw Meroveus lead a woman cross the garden, at the lower end of which there is a little door that opens into another street; – a pebble, or some such thing, happening to lie in the walk, she stumbled in passing, on which he cry'd out with the greatest tenderness, – 'I hope you are not hurt, my love!' – 'No,' reply'd she briskly, – 'not at all, I cannot receive any prejudice when my guardian angel is so near.' – I was so astonish'd at what I saw and heard, that I had not power to speak, 'till mrs. Flounceit seeing me look earnestly after them, told me they were her lodgers; – that they were lately married; but some reasons obliging them to keep it private, they met each other there only once or twice a week; – 'So,' said she, 'I have very little trouble with them, and they pay me a good rent.' – 'But are you sure', cry'd I, 'that they are man and wife? – it may be an intrigue.' – 'No,' answer'd she, 'they were recommended to me by a gentleman who formerly lodged with me himself, one Sir David Townly.'

Deidamia. Oh heavens! – Sir David Townly! – Why he is the very person my husband pretends he goes with to Hammersmith.

Eutracia. 'Tis likely he may be his confidant in this amour.

Deidamia. Yet still I know not how to think it real, – one man may be like another. – Are you certain it was Meroveus whom you saw?

Eutracia. As certain as that it is Deidamia to whom I am talking. – Did he not lie abroad last Monday night?

Deidamia. He did.

Eutracia. And had he not on a dark-brown velvet coat and a black waistcoat trimm'd with bugles?

Deidamia. He had. – Oh I can no longer shut my eyes against conviction! – the dreadful truth is too glaring to be resisted, and I see myself the most miserable of women!

Eutracia. Do not think so, – rather exert the spirit of an injur'd wife, – detect him in his guilt, shame him to repentance, and make him sue for pardon.

Deidamia. Oh that such love as ours has been should come to this!

Eutracia. All yet may be retriev'd; – your just reproaches may make him loath his past follies, and become more yours than if he never had transgress'd: – the next time he takes his pretended journey to Hammersmith let me know it.

Deidamia. He is gone thither now; – just before you came to call me to the Park he told me Sir David had engag'd his company, and he believ'd he should not return 'till morning.

Eutracia. Well then he shall be met, my dear Deidamia, he shall be met by those he least expects or desires to see; – I will take you in the morning to mrs. Flounceit's, under pretence of bringing her a new customer; – there you will have the same opportunity I had of discovering your husband's guilt, and may act as you shall judge proper on the occasion.

Deidamia. How shall I contain myself! – base – base man! – cruel deceiver of my fond, my unsuspecting heart! – How bear the sight of that vile she! – that infamous deluder of his honour! – that cursed she who has robb'd me of the only treasure I valued upon earth, my husband's love!

Here she burst into the most vehement exclamations; but my Chrystaline Remembrancer being already overcharg'd, I can only say that her behaviour verify'd the words of mr. Nat. Lee, who in his description he gives of the passions of womankind in general, has these lines:

> They shrink at thunder, dread the rustling wind,
> And glitt'ring swords the brightest eyes will blind;
> Yet when strong jealousy enflames the soul,
> The weak will rage, and calms to tempests roll.[337]

The ladies continued their walk 'till Phœbus beginning to withdraw his beams they both thought proper to retire from the approaching dews. – Eutracia, justly apprehending the agitations of her friend would become more violent, if left alone and at liberty to indulge them, offer'd to be her companion that night, which the other gladly accepted, and I saw them take coach together for Deidamia's house, – after which I went home.

CHAP. VI.

Which, according to the Author's opinion, stands in no need of a prelude, as it contains only the sequel of an adventure too interesting to all degrees of people not to demand the attention of every reader.

I was truly concern'd at the injustice which I perceived poor Deidamia sustained, and but little pleas'd with Eutracia, either for the information she had given her of it, or for advising her to detect Meroveus in the manner concerted between them; – indeed, I fear'd that the consequences of such an interview would be only to make the husband become more harden'd in his guilt, and her affliction increase by finding her resentment disregarded.

Few men can bear reproofs, much less reproaches; – if ever they quit a darling folly the reformation must come of themselves: – it must proceed from a consciousness they have done amiss, not from being told so by others; – there is a pride in human nature which disdains admonition, and makes us persist in error, which, if not taken notice of, perhaps in time we might discover to be such, grow ashamed of, and amend.

Besides, remonstrances from a person whom we look upon as any way our inferior, either in point of understanding or circumstances, will be so far from having any weight, that they will rather add to our contempt, and, it may be, raise in us an utter aversion to the giver: – Custom has made the husband so much the head of the wife, that, tenacious of his authority, it is but seldom that he submits to be influenced by her in matters of much less moment to him than his pleasures.

Indeed, when a woman is wrong'd in the manner Deidamia was, it must be confess'd that the shock is greatly trying, and that she has the strongest reason for complaining; – yet will she still find it most prudent to forbear: – love and gentleness are the only weapons by which that sex can hope to conquer, and she who attempts to have recourse to any other only hurts herself. – By seeming not to suspect her husband's vices, she will, at least, oblige him to keep them as private as he can, and also to treat her with all the respect due to her character and the sacred union between them; whereas by growing clamorous and impatient she furnishes him with a pretence to use her ill, and turns the indifference he before had for her into hatred and detestation.

One of our best poets has an observation on this head, which I think is very well worthy of the serious attention of all who are either injured in reality, or imagine themselves to be so, yet find it their interest to preserve an amicable correspondence with the person guilty of the injury; as it is certain that no man detected in the thing which he wishes to to conceal can ever love the person by whom he is detected. – The words of the author I mention'd are these:

> Forgiveness to the injur'd does belong;
> But they ne'er pardon who have done the wrong.[338]

These reflections, together with my impatience to see how Deidamia would support the full conviction of her husband's falshood, so much took up my mind, that it was a considerable time before I remember'd how great an impediment lay between me and the gratification of my curiosity. – Mrs. Flounceit's house was to be the scene of action, and the ladies, during their whole conversation, had made no mention in what street, not even in what quarter of the town, that woman lived: – however, as I supposed her to be a noted woman in her business, I hoped to get over this difficulty, and did so, by sending an emissary to enquire among the mercers, hoop petticoat-makers, and other such people who are employ'd in the equipments of the ladies, and I went not to bed without receiving the direction I stood in need of.

As I knew not the hour in which Meroveus and the partner of his looser pleasures would be preparing to depart, nor that in which Deidamia would be conducted by Eutracia to behold this proof of her misfortune, I took care to go very early to mrs. Flounceit's, and was oblig'd to wait a considerable time before the door happen'd to be open'd to let any one pass in or out; – at last, however, it was so, – I got an opportunity to enter, – went into the back parlour, and posted myself in that corner of it which I thought would be the safest and most commodious.

My patience was not here put to any long trial, – the ladies arrived a few minutes after I came, usher'd into the room by mrs. Flounceit, who placed them on a settee with a great deal of formal compliasance, and then made some apologies, as many people do when they are dress'd as well as they can be, for being in such a deshabille, and not in the order she could wish to receive them.

It was easy for me to perceive, by Deidamia's countenance, how ill she had pass'd the night; – Eutracia also seem'd in some agitation, – though she dissembled it as well as she was able: after having given some slight answer to mrs. Flounceit's compliments, told her she had brought a friend to look over some of her fine things, on which the mantuamaker immediately open'd a large press, and brought out several pieces of chints, with some French brocades and rich Italian silks, – these she spread upon a table, accompanying that action with many praises on the beauty and curiosity of each.

But it was in vain she boasted, – in vain she magnified; – all she said, – as well as the real merit of the goods she exhibited to sale, was wholly lost on Deidamia; – the mind of that afflicted lady was too much bent on those things which she expected to be witness of, to have any eyes or ears for those which were not present to her; – she took up first one piece, and then another, but without seeming to know what she did; and, in fine, had something so distracted in her air and gestures, that Eutracia was obliged to keep mrs. Flounceit in discourse, to prevent her taking any notice of it.

Her behaviour, join'd with my knowledge of the cause, reminded me of mr. Dryden's words, which, if she had been inclined to think of poetry, she might pretty justly have apply'd to her own condition in this crisis:

> Love, justice, nature, pity, and revenge,
> Have kindled a wildfire in my breast;
> I am all a civil war within,
> And like a vessel, struggling in a storm,
> Require more hands than one to keep me upright.[339]

But if she was so little able to support the bare idea of the shock she came on purpose to receive, what must she endure when suspence, and all the remains of hope, were swallowed up in the cruel certainty of her misfortune, and conviction left no farther room for doubt? – The maid of the house came into the room with a chocolate-pot in her hand, and told her mistress that the gentleman and lady above stairs gave their compliments and desir'd the favour of her company to breakfast with them.

Mrs. Flounceit was about to make some answer to this invitation, when Deidamia, not able to contain herself, flew out of the parlour, and directly up stairs, where she found Meroveus and a young woman sitting on the side of the bed they had but lately quitted.

Deidamia had scarce enter'd the chamber when she surpriz'd the guilty pair with these words:

Deidamia. I have a right, sir, to think my company ought to be as acceptable to Meroveus as that of mrs. Flounceit, or any other woman.

Eutracia had follow'd Deidamia as fast as she could, in order, I suppose, to prevent any desperate effects of her present passion, and I was not far behind; but it will be more easy for the reader to conceive the surprise which appear'd in the looks of Meroveus than for me to express it; – he started up, and with a voice which the various emotions of his mind render'd almost unintelligible, said to her:

Meroveus. Confusion! – Deidamia! – Madam, what brings you here!

Deidamia. That is a question which ought rather to be put to you. – I came in pursuit of an ungrateful, too much beloved husband; – you to indulge a lawless flame for an abandon'd prostitute.

Meroveus. Madam, – madam, this does not become you.

Deidamia. Does it become you, sir, to leave your honest home and wife, – make pitiful excuses for your absence, and skulk in corners with a wretch like this, – this abject hireling of licentious wishes!

Mistress. Madam, I would not have you think I am any such person; – I did not know Meroveus was a married man.

Deidamia. 'Tis false, vile creature, you could not know Meroveus without knowing he had a wife; – a wife, who, without boasting, is every way his equal: – but get out of my sight, that I may have liberty to ask my perjur'd husband what he could see in that face of yours to be preferr'd to mine.

On this Meroveus was opening his mouth to speak, but was prevented by mrs. Flounceit, who being astonish'd on the lady's running up stairs, and by the noise she immediately heard above, had hobbled up as fast as her fat would give her leave, and came into the room that moment, – crying as she enter'd,

Mrs. Flounceit. Bless me, what is the matter here!

Deidamia. Perhaps, madam, you are ignorant that your house is made a brothel.

Mrs. Flounceit. Oh my stars! – a brothel! – heaven forbid!

Eutracia. My friend tells you true, indeed; – she is the lawful wife of that gentleman, – they have been married above seven years, – I was present at their wedding, and that woman there is no better than a prostitute.

Mrs. Flounceit. Oh the vile slut! – I wonder Sir David Townly should offer to bring me into this scrape! – he knows very well I never countenance such doings. – Hussy, get out of my house this minute, or I will send for a constable to carry you to Bridewell!

In speaking this she advanced towards the mistress of Meroveus, and was about to push her out of the room; but that gentleman, perceiving her intent, stepp'd between, and with a visage all inflam'd with wrath, said,

Meroveus. Hold, madam, hold; – this lady has put herself under my protection, and I will take care to defend her from all insults whatsoever.

Then turning to Deidamia went on thus:

Meroveus. As for you, madam, – you have only exposed me and undone yourself; – I will never see you more.

He then took his trembling mistress by the hand to lead her down stairs; – Deidamia, in the utmost agony of spirit, follow'd, and catching him by the arm, cry'd out to him,

Deidamia. Oh stay, Meroveus! – you will not, sure, add injury to injury! – stay, I conjure you, and let that woman go!

Meroveus. Stand off, madam, – your touch is now more hateful to me than ever it was agreeable, so leave you to repent the cause.

This cruel rebuff not making her let go the hold she had taken of him, he threw her off with the greatest contempt, and in an instant was out of the house with his dissolute companion, who was, doubtless, as hasty as himself to get from a place where she could expect nothing but affronts.

Deidamia would have pursued her ungenerous husband, perhaps even into the street, had she not been withheld by Eutracia, who endeavour'd to convince her how little it would avail to remonstrate any thing to him while he continued in this humour.

Rage had 'till now kept up the spirits of this unhappy lady; but the objects of it being removed, and the power of reflecting return'd, she sunk into a grief no less immoderate, – she wept, – she wrung her hands, – beat her lovely breast, – she swoon'd several times, and in her intervals of sense could only cry out, – 'Cruel, barbarous Meroveus! – Unfaithful, ungenerous husband! – Good heaven, for what unknown transgression am I become thus miserable!'

Neither Eutracia nor mrs. Flounceit omitted any thing in their power which they thought might serve to give her consolation; but all they could do was insufficient, and it was some hours before she was enough recover'd even to be carried home: – as soon as she was so, Eutracia went with her in the coach, and I walk'd home, touch'd to the very soul at the sight of her distress.

I have already given the reader my opinion concerning the extreme folly of revealing unwelcome secrets to our friends, so shall forbear adding any farther reflections on the head, and proceed, with as much brevity as the story will admit, to the catastrophe of this unhappy adventure.

I went the next morning to the house of Meroveus, and was convinced, by what I heard the servants say among themselves, that he had not been at home that night, which, indeed, I fear'd would be the case. – On my going up stairs I found Deidamia lying on a couch, in a very dejected melancholy posture; – Eutracia was sitting near her, that lady, it seems, having never quitted her since the unfortunate visit they made together at mrs. Flounceit's; but as the discourse between them consisted only of complaints on the one side, and persuasions to moderation on the other, I think it not material enough to be inserted.

I had not been in the room above a quarter of an hour before a servant presented a letter to Deidamia, – it was from her husband, and contained these lines:

To DEIDAMIA.

MADAM,

I AM determin'd to live easy, which I am certain is utterly impracticable for me to do with you, after what pass'd yesterday between us; – what I then said in heat of passion, I now repeat in cool blood, and on the most mature deliberation. – In fine, an eternal disunion must be the consequence of your behaviour, nor should the tongues of angels disswade me from this resolution; – you will do well to bear it with patience, as the misfortune, if it be one, has happen'd entirely thro' your own fault.

To leave you no just reason to complain, I shall order the jointure, settled on you by our marriage articles, to be regularly paid to you as though I were no more; and shall resign to you all the plate, linnen and household furniture, excepting only my books, the India chest and buroe in my dressing-room.

As to our children, – the boy I shall take under my care, – the girl I leave to yours, and shall also add one hundred pounds per annum to the abovemention'd jointure, for her maintenance and education.

Farewel for ever! – As we no more must meet in love, it will be highly improper, and I think could not be very agreeable to either of us, to meet at all, – I shall therefore refrain, as much as possible, going to any of those places you are accustom'd to frequent, – and hope you will have prudence enough to take the same precaution in avoiding me, – especially when I tell you, that it is the only thing in which you can now oblige

Your ill-treated husband,

MEROVEUS.

P.S I shall send to-morrow for the things I mention'd.

My fair readers will be the best judges of what Deidamia felt on finding her husband had taken a resolution which could not but give the most mortal stab both to her love and pride; – she paus'd a little after having read it, then gave it to Eutracia, crying out at the same time with the greatest emphasis,

Deidamia. See there, my dear Eutracia, – this wicked husband is the sole aggressor, yet pretends to be the person who has reason to resent!

That young lady, who was all fire and spirit, could not forbear loading Meroveus with reproaches at the end of every paragraph she read; and when she had finish'd, said to Deidamia,

Eutracia. And how, my dear, do you intend to proceed with this base, this most injurious man!

Deidamia. Indeed I know not.

Eutracia. If I were in your place, I would write him such an answer as should make his ears tingle.

Deidamia. Alas, you know not what it is to be a wife! – but I will write, however.

She then rung her bell for the footman, and ask'd him whether the person who brought the letter waited for an answer; – to which he reply'd,

Footman. No, madam, he only bid me deliver it into your own hands, and told me my master order'd me to come to him about two hours hence at George's coffee-house,[340] and bring some linnen with me.

Deidamia. 'Tis very well; – but do not go 'till I have spoke to you again; – I have a message to send by you.

The fellow assur'd her he would not fail to obey her commands, and withdrew; – after which she sat down to her escrutore, took pen and paper, and began to write in the following terms:

To MEROVEUS.

Cruel and unjust, yet still dear MEROVEUS,

If there needed any other proof than that shameful one I yesterday was witness of, that I am miserable in the total loss of your affection, the letter I have just now received would be a convincing one. – What, – after seven years conjugal tenderness, perfect and sincere on my side, and well dissembled on yours, can you entertain a thought of parting! – Of tearing a family to pieces which has hitherto lived so respectable in the world! – Must I be doom'd to mourn a husband's loss even while that husband lives! – Must my son be bred an alien to his mother, and my daughter a stranger to her father! – O think, Meroveus! and if no consideration of me has any weight, let that of your own reputation, and the interest of our children, prevail on you to alter this cruel resolution! – We may, at least, live civilly together, if not with the same fondness as before this accident. – Yet why should we not! – I am willing to meet you more than half way in love. – You cannot deny but you have wrong'd me in the most tender point: I confess I was too rash in the manner of detecting you; – we both have been to blame; – what is done cannot be recall'd; – but it may be repented of; – let us exchange forgiveness, and endeavour to forget what is past.

There was a time when every little ailment felt by your Deidamia gave equal pain to you! – Oh can you then throw off at once all pity, all humanity, all remorse, for the agonies you cannot but be sensible my poor tormented heart now labours under! – No, – 'tis impossible, – reason, honour and good-nature forbid it! – you will return, accept the pardon I shall with joy bestow; and, in return, vouchsafe me yours. – Let not my hopes deceive me; – I am sure they will not, if you will suffer yourself to reflect seriously on the unhappy consequences that must infallibly attend a separation from her who ever has been, and desires to continue,

With the greatest sincerity,

Your most faithful, and
                    Most affectionate wife,

                                        DEIDAMIA.

This she communicated to Eutracia, who approved of the former part of it, but highly condemn'd the latter, as thinking it too submissive. – Deidamia, however, was of a different opinion, and the footman coming in soon after to know her commands, she seal'd it up and put it into his hands to deliver to his master, bidding him say withal that she was very much indisposed.

After he was gone, the ladies began to enter into some dispute concerning the authority of a husband and the duty that was expected from a wife; – but as I could promise myself no farther information by their discourse on this subject, and besides, remembering I had some business of my own to dispatch, I left the place that instant, not without an intention to return thither the next day.

Accordingly I went in the morning, and found poor Deidamia almost drown'd in tears, and walking backwards and forwards in one of her rooms in a distracted posture; the cause of these fresh agonies I easily perceived by a letter which lay open on the table, – the contents whereof were as follow:

To DEIDAMIA.

MADAM,

I have been in some debate within my mind, whether to answer your epistle in the manner I now do, or not to answer it at all, would be the most effectual means to prevent your giving me or yourself any future trouble; – you find I have pursued the former of these methods, and hope you will have discretion enough not to involve me in a second dilemma on this score.

Be assured that I did not resolve on a final separation without having well weigh'd the consequences attending it, and find them such as can no way come in competition with my peace of mind, without which life would be a curse, – my bed a bed of thorns, – my table a desart, – my house a hell, and every friend that came to visit, a fury to torment me.

See the reverse your jealous folly has occasion'd; – tax me not, therefore, with ingratitude; – a thousand times you have confess'd you thought yourself as happy as a woman could be, and it is certain you were truly so. – During the whole course of the years we lived together you never had the least shadow of a cause to complain of my want either of respect or tenderness: – If I indulged any pleasures, which I imagin'd would give you disquiet, I took care to be very private in them; – Why then did you suffer yourself to be led by an idle curiosity to pry into secrets which the discovery of must give you pain, and possibly prove the total destruction of that love which once you call'd your greatest blessing?

It is doubtless best for both of us, as you rightly enough observe, to forget what is past; but am far from thinking it can be done by the way you mean: – no, to forget can only be accomplish'd by avoiding each other's presence, and ceasing all kind of communication between us, – I shall therefore give orders to my servant to charge himself with no letter or message you may think fit to send, and desire you will assure yourself that this is the very last you ever shall receive from me. – Farewel, I wish you all happiness in any other sphere of life than that you lately lived in with

MEROVEUS.

After having examined this epistle, I listen'd to what pass'd between Eutracia and Deidamia; but tho' I staid 'till my Tablets were crowded, I shall forbear inserting the particulars of these ladies discourse, for reasons which will be hereafter explain'd; and only say in general, that Eutracia would fain have spirited up her friend to resentment and disdain against a husband whom she thought so unworthy of her; that Deidamia's love overcame her sex's pride; and, in fine, that the one argued like a virgin, and the other like an affectionate wife.

Whether Deidamia made any further attempts to move her obdurate husband to a reconciliation I cannot be positive; but believe she did not, for she retired soon after into the country, whence she is but lately return'd, and, whatever her heart may endure, has very much regain'd her usual composure of countenance and behaviour.

CHAP. VII.

*Is somewhat more concise than ordinary, but very much to the purpose, and
will be found not the least worthy of any in the book of being regarded with
attention.*

As during the course of these lucubrations I have been extremely circumstantial in the reports I have made, the reader has a right to be surprised that I omitted the discourse between Deidamia and Eutracia; – I shall therefore, according to my promise, relate my motive for so doing, and flatter myself it is such as will render me perfectly excuseable in this point.

Much about the time of the adventure related in the two preceding chapters, I happen'd to be witness of a conversation, which though between different persons, and on a very different occasion, was still on the subject of marriage, the authority of a husband, and the submission expected from a wife; so seem'd to me to have a certain sameness in it which I thought would be rather tiresome than agreeable to the ear, and for that reason left out the former, and made choice of the latter, as of the two the most interesting.

Two sisters, whose characters I present to the public under the names of Flavia and Celemena, have both of them a tolerable share of beauty, but no other qualification, either natural or acquired, that could entitle them to the hope of an elevated station; – yet, by the benevolent aspect of their happy planets, are they become the brides of Alcandor and Thelamont, persons distinguish'd in the world by their birth and fortune, and still more so by the greatness of their merit.

These nuptials, so astonishing to the town, and which happen'd soon after one another, gave me a curiosity to discover, by the help of my Invisibility, in what fashion the ladies would behave themselves in a sphere of life so altogether new to them, and so little expected, even in their vainest wishes, ever to arrive at.

Flavia was the eldest, and it was to her I made my first visit; – she was in her dressing room, sitting at her toylet, with her waiting-maid behind her, giving the finishing stroke to her head tyre. – Thelamont was also there, and stood leaning his elbow on a buroe, with a good deal of dissatisfaction in his countenance, while she kept looking in the glass, and, without turning her head towards him, said,

Flavia. Prithee, Thelamont, let us talk no more of this stuff, – I am quite sick of it; – I am certainly the best judge of these things, and it is in vain to persuade me, for I will not be contradicted.

Thelamont. You will not then oblige me?

Flavia. Positively no; – not when you intermeddle in these affairs.

Thelamont. Well then, madam, I shall say no more; but must tell you, that I thought I had a right to expect this proof of your complaisance.

With these words he flung out of the room, and she said to herself,

Flavia. Pish; – Was there ever any thing so teasing! – Men are mighty foolish sometimes. – Katherine, bring me my gauze handkerchief.

Maid. Oh, ma'am, did not your ladyship say you would wear your new tippet to-day?

Flavia. Hah. – Yes, – no, – it will shew too much of my neck.

Maid. Oh, ma'am, – your ladyship cannot shew too much of so beautiful a part.

Flavia. That's true; – but I scratch'd one of my breasts with a pin this morning.

Maid. Oh the ugly pin; – I wish I knew which it was, that I might crook it quite double and throw it in the fire.

Just as the maid had express'd her resentment against the weapon that had wounded her mistress, Celemena came into the room, and, after saluting her sister with a freedom suitable to the nearness of their blood and friendship, said to her,

Celemena. What is the matter, my dear sister? – you do not look pleas'd to-day.

Flavia. Umph. – No, – not very well pleas'd; – nor, indeed, much displeas'd.

Celemena. I met Thelamont going out as I came in, – I thought he seem'd more reserv'd than usual, and in a very ill humour.

Flavia. If he chuses to be so, it would be a pity any one should attempt to put him out of it.

Celemena. I hope no misunderstanding has happen'd between you?

Flavia. No, no, – we understand one another pretty well; – I understand that he would fain pretend to take upon him the government of my actions, – and he understands that I will not let him do it; – so we have exchang'd some piquant words this morning, that's all.

Celemena. Have a care, sister, – quarrels in the beginning of marriage promise but little felicity in the continuance of that state.

Flavia. That's true; – but 'tis very provoking when a man will needs interfere in things he has no manner of concern with.

Celemena. Pray what was the subject of your dispute, – if it be not too great a secret?

Flavia. Why you must know he wants me to leave off putting any Carmine upon my cheeks, – calls it nasty daubing, and says I should be a thousand times handsomer without it.

Celemena. I can see nothing extraordinary in this; – there are many men who have an utter aversion to a woman's using any art to her complexion.

Flavia. They may cry out against it; but yet I am sure it is frequently owing to art that they fall so much in love with us; – a little red upon the cheeks gives a sparkle to the eyes, and a lustre to all the features, which otherwise would appear flat and languid; – but they are so foolish as not to consider this; – they like us as they see us altogether, and though they may be sensible we are painted, never once imagine it is to that necessary auxiliary to beauty that we are chiefly indebted for those charms which attract their admiration.

Celemena. Suppose it as you say, which however I am far from allowing to be always the case, Thelamont has now seen you such as nature made you, the night wears off that borrow'd lustre, and the morning shews you what you truly are; and if he approves of you in this light, I know of no other person whom you need be studious to please.

Flavia. I am of a quite different opinion. – Oh the joy of being gaz'd at, and follow'd by a whole crowded Mall.

Celemena. Perhaps to laugh; – but if sincere, a very empty joy, and what a married woman ought not to be too ambitious of.

Flavia. So then you would have me comply with my husband's request?

Celemena. Indeed I would advise you to it: – I am sure if Alcandor express'd a desire that I should cut off my hair, and never let it grow again, though it is the gift of nature, and bestow'd upon me as the greatest ornament of our sex, I would not hesitate one moment to obey him, but be content to wear no other head-dress than a close mob during the whole remainder of my life.

Flavia. Then you are a fool.

Celemena. In this point I do not think I am; – for besides that duty which the law exacts from every wife to her husband, there are other reasons which would oblige me to refuse nothing to Alcandor.

She accompany'd these words with a very significant look, which Flavia observing, order'd her maid, who had been all this time in the room, to withdraw; and, as soon as she was gone, reply'd to what her sister had said in these terms:

Flavia. I know what you would say; – you would infer, that because Alcandor and Thelamont married us without fortunes, we are therefore bound to be their slaves.

Celemena. Not so, – and I dare believe that neither of them will ever require any submissions from us, but such as if we had always been their equals would very well become us to grant.

Flavia. Laird! – what a bustle you make about equals! – Whatever we were before, marriage has made us now their equals; – and for my own part, I shall never submit to do any thing Thelamont requires of me, unless my own inclination happens to concur.

Celemena. But do you apprehend no ill consequences from repeated contradictions?

Flavia. Not in the least; – he cannot unmarry me again; – if he should hate me never so much I must still be maintain'd as his wife, and should give myself no pain about any thing else.

Celemena. Oh, sister, I am amaz'd to hear you talk in this manner! – Have you been married but one month, and can already forget the unhappiness of our single state, – our scanty and precarious dependance, – the difficulties we found to supply ourselves with even the common necessaries of life! – We made, indeed, a kind of tawdry shew when we appear'd abroad; but how was our table pinch'd for it at home. – Present exigencies and future poverty stared us in the face; – and is there no love, no gratitude, due from us to the men who snatch'd us from that scene of misery, and raised us to opulence, grandeur and respect!

Flavia. Pish; – they married us to please themselves, not out of pity to our wants. – But let us have no more of this dull stuff; – you must go with me to mrs. Rakelove's route to-night, – it is the first she has had, and I promis'd her to bring all the company I could.

Celemena. Indeed you must excuse me.

Flavia. For what reason?

Celemena. My dear Alcandor sups at home, and I cannot be abroad.

Flavia. Heavens! – how strangely silly you are grown! – your dear Alcandor sups at home. – What then, he did not marry you to make you a cook! – You do not dress his victuals!

Celemena. No, but he married me to make me a companion at his victuals; and while he continues to desire my presence, as I flatter myself he always will, I shall never form any pretences to be absent.

The face of Flavia grew more red than the carmine had made it, on finding in her sister sentiments so opposite to her own; but was prevented from making any answer by the entrance of a servant, who told her that some ladies were come to visit her, on which she went, accompanied by Celemena, into the dining-room, in order to receive them.

Thus ended the conversation I mention'd, and by it the reader may judge which of these two sisters had the greatest share of prudence, best deserved her good fortune, and was most likely to enjoy a long continuance of it.

CHAP. VIII.

Presents the public with the account of an incident which cannot but be deeply affecting to the youth of both sexes, and no less remarkable in its event than any the Author's Invisibilityship ever enabled him to discover.

AMONG all the various deceptions which are carried on in this great world, I know of none more cruel, and more liable to be attended with the worst of consequences, than those practised in the affairs of love; – yet it is a crime which passes with impunity, and is scarce censured by any but the persons injured by it and their particular friends and confidants.

Even the ladies, generally speaking, for there is no rule without some exceptions, are so little the friends of each other, that we rarely find them taking up the quarrel of their sex in this point; – on the contrary, they are apt to absolve the vow-breaker, and let the whole blame fall on the believer: – a man who has triumph'd over the credulity of an hundred women, sees himself not less respected; and sometimes the number of past conquests shall serve him as a recommendation, and be a means of his attaining new ones.

Perjury is deem'd but a venial transgression in this case; – few think that oaths and imprecations, when dictated by the heat of an amorous inclination, tho' formed in the most binding terms, and utter'd in the most solemn manner, are ever register'd in heaven, – according to the words of the poet, who merrily says,

Jove only laughs when lovers swear.[341]

This vice, as I must take the liberty to call it, is not however wholly confined to the male sex; I am sorry to observe that those of the other, either thro' pride, vanity, or an inconstancy of nature, are sometimes found guilty of deluding their lovers with fallacious expectations.

I hope also to be forgiven by the more discreet part of womankind, when I say that a propensity to such a behaviour is yet less excusable in them than in the men, as a perfect innocence, a sweetness of disposition, and a simplicity of manners are, or ought to be, the distinguishing characteristics of the fair sex.

A young lady, to whom I shall give the name of Syrenia, was endow'd by nature with every requisite to command love and admiration; – she had the finest eyes in the world, – a very regular set of features, fine hair, and a most delicate complexion; – was tall of stature, well shaped, and had somewhat peculiarly attractive in her air and mien. – Fortune had not been altogether so propitious to her; – through the extravagancies of her parents she was left in possession of a very moderate fortune; – it was, however, entirely at her own disposal, and sufficient, with the good œconomy she was mistress of, to support her in a very genteel, though not a grand way of life.

Proposals of marriage had often been made to her by several eminent and wealthy citizens; but she rejected them all, and despis'd the thoughts not only of a shop, but also of all other callings and occupations whatever; – ambition was the predominant passion of her soul, and she had vanity enough to think that her birth, her person and accomplishments were such as might very well compensate for the smallness of her fortune, and entitle her to higher expectations.

She had lived 'till the age of twenty-three without having any offer of the kind she hoped; – but about the expiration of that æra, a young gentleman, call'd Rossano, happening to see her at the house of a relation whom he visited, became violently in love with her, and soon after finding means to get himself introduced, made a declaration of his passion; to which, knowing what and who he was, she gave all the encouragement he could wish, or that was befitting the character of a modest woman.

It would, indeed, have been much to be wonder'd at, if the addresses of Rossano had not been acceptable to her; – he is descended from a very antient and worthy family, has an estate of eight hundred pounds per annum, intirely free from any incumbrance, either mortgage, dowry, or portions to be paid out of it; – his person and behaviour are extremely agreeable; and, to add to all this, has deservedly the reputation of a man of strict honour, and more sobriety than could be expected from his years and the dissoluteness of the present times.

The sincerity and warmth of his affection making him very strenuous in his pressures, and the advantages she found in a match with him rendering her complying, they were beginning to talk of ordering articles for their marriage to be drawn up, when an unexpected accident, relating to his estate, obliged him to go immediately into the country.

Though he proposed to stay but a short time, yet he could not think of being deprived of the sight of his beloved Syrenia, even for a few weeks, without an infinity of grief. – She testified little less regret for this enforced separation; –

their parting was extremely moving, – each seem'd to endeavour to outvie the other in expressions of tenderness; and the only consolation he had was, the repeated assurances she gave him, that wherever he went he carried her heart along with him.

It is highly probable, that the affection she profess'd for him was at that time perfectly sincere, and that she look'd upon the accident which delay'd the celebration of their nuptials as no inconsiderable misfortune to her; but whatever chagrin she might feel at first on this account, it was very soon dissipated, and gave way to ideas of a far different nature.

The motive which brought about so sudden, and so extraordinary a change in her sentiments, I shall relate, as I was afterwards fully inform'd of it by the several conversations I was present at by the help of my Invisibility.

She was one morning in the Park with a lady of her acquaintance call'd Delia, where they were met and join'd by a young officer, brother to Delia, and a gentleman who was with him, and equally a stranger to both the ladies, but behaved towards them with the greatest respect and politeness. – They walk'd two or three turns up and down the Mall, after which the gentlemen took their leave, and Syrenia and Delia went to their respective habitations, without thinking any more of what had pass'd during their promenade.

Little, indeed, could either of them apprehend the consequences of this adventure; – but the next day, pretty early in the forenoon, Syrenia was surprised with a visit from Delia, who came running into her apartment without any ceremony, – crying out as she enter'd,

Delia. Joy to you, my dear; – I come to wish you joy!

Syrenia. Of what! – for I see no other subject of joy than what I always feel on seeing you.

Delia. Me! – no, no, – a thousand such as me are quite out of the question; – but I have the pleasure to congratulate you on the greatest conquest your beauty ever made, or perhaps ever can make!

Syrenia. You are got into a vein of raillery this morning.

Delia. No, upon my honour I never was more serious. – Do you not remember the fine gentleman that was with my brother yesterday in the Mall?

Syrenia. Yes; – you know they join'd company with us.

Delia. His name is Leontine; – he is the eldest son of his father, and heir apparent to three thousand pounds a year: – you saw his person; – for my part, I think nothing can be more agreeable; and my brother tells me he is the most accomplish'd man he ever knew.

Syrenia. Well, – and what is all this to me?

Delia. It is all to you. – It seems he saw you last Sunday at Westminster-Abbey, fell violently in love with you, and would have follow'd to have seen where you lived, but was prevented by some gentlemen of his acquaintance, who that instant laid hold of him and forced him along with them.

Syrenia. 'Tis possible such a one might be there; but I did not take any notice of him.

Delia. That may be, but he took so much of you as not to be able to sleep ever since.

Syrenia. Very romantic, truly. – But pray how came you so well acquainted with the secrets of his heart, who yesterday seem'd an utter stranger to his person?

Delia. I will tell you the whole affair, as my brother last night came and inform'd me of it. – After they had left us they went and dined together at a tavern: – Leontine ask'd a thousand questions concerning your family, – your fortune, and your character; – all which, you may be sure, were answer'd not to your disadvantage: – he then made my brother the confidante of the passion you had inspir'd him with, and intreated him to use his interest with me, as he found I was pretty intimate with you, to engage me to introduce him to you, which I have faithfully promised to do.

Syrenia. What without my consent?

Delia. I hoped to be forgiven; – such an offer, my dear, is not to be rejected.

Syrenia. It is much beyond my expectations, I confess; – but the disparity between our fortunes is too great.

Delia. If he thinks your person an equivalent, it is not your business to make objections.

Syrenia. That is true; – and if I could flatter myself he were really sincere: – but I will consider on it.

Delia. It will be time enough for you to consider when you have heard what he has to say; for I have promised to bring you together this evening.

Syrenia. This evening! – as how!

Delia. As thus: – I invite you to sup with me to-night, – my brother and Leontine shall come in as if by accident; – neither your pride nor your modesty has any thing to scruple; for I assure you I will not let even my brother know that I have previously acquainted you with any thing of the matter.

Syrenia. Well, – on that condition I will come.

Delia. Indeed, my dear, I should think you very much to blame to turn your back on a prospect so highly advantageous; – for though you are well born, – well accomplish'd, – are handsome, and have some fortune of your own, – yet the three first of these, as men now think of marriage, weigh but lightly against what they call the incumbrance of a wife; – and as to the latter, you know, it will not entitle you to a coach and six.

Syrenia. The justice of what you say cannot be denied; – but I would do nothing that should occasion my character being call'd in question, nor would seem too forward, though to promote the highest expectations; – therefore, my dear Delia, remember I depend on your prudence.

Delia. In this you safely may; – I know too well what is owing to my sex, and the cruel aspersions men are apt to throw on our most innocent freedoms, not to be extremely cautious in avoiding giving the least room for censure.

Syrenia. Indeed, my dear, my observation on your own conduct ought to put to silence all my doubts on that score; and whatever is the event of this affair, I shall always gratefully acknowledge your good wishes towards me.

Delia. If it suceeds I shall be a sharer in your good fortune, as nothing gives me a more sensible satisfaction than to have it in my power to contribute to the happiness of my friends: – but I must leave you, – I promis'd to let my brother know whether you could come or not, that he may apprise Leontine of it.

The good-natur'd Delia went away in speaking these words; but I could easily perceive, by the glow on Syrenia's cheeks, how much she was transported with the purpose of her visit; – and was yet more confirm'd of her being so by some disjointed soliloquies she utter'd when she thought there was no witness of what she said.

Syrenia. Three thousand pounds a year, and so fine a gentleman as Leontine! – so handsome, – so polite, – so every thing that is agreeable! – If he is as sincere as Delia imagines him to be, I shall have cause to bless the hour I went to Westminster-Abbey; – or rather, that which carried me to the Park yesterday, without which he might never have known who I was, or where to find me, and should have lost all the advantage my good stars seem to have decreed for me!

Here she ceas'd to speak, other sort of emotions rising in her mind, to which she gave a loose in this exclamation:

Syrenia. It was an unlucky thing I went so far with Rossano, – the poor man loves me to distraction, – he will certainly break his heart when he finds I have forsaken him; – and, it may be, reproach me as the occasion of his death.

On this her countenance seem'd a little disconcerted; but it soon wore off, and after a short pause went on thus:

Syrenia. I am glad, however, that no contract has pass'd between us; the encouragement I gave his passion, and the verbal promises I made him, need be no impediment to my accepting a better offer.[342] – It will be prudence in me, however, not to throw him off, nor give him any room to supect I have less affection for him than I had, 'till I am well assured that Leontine is in earnest.

This was enough to shew me the principle and disposition of Syrenia, both which, indeed, were so little pleasing to me, that I had not patience to stay with her any longer, but quitted her apartment with a contempt, which could she have been sensible of, would no doubt have been her some mortification.

I made one of the company that night at Delia's however; but as it could not be expected, that in a meeting which was to pass for casual, there should be any conversation except on general topics, I reap'd no other benefit by being present, than to be convinced that Leontine, by the glances he took every opportunity of casting at Syrenia, was indeed very much enamour'd, and that she spared no pains to make him more so.

The next day he went with the brother of Delia to visit her, and the succeeding one took the liberty of going thither alone and made a declaration of his passion, which she, having well prepared herself with answers, received in such a manner as neither to reject, nor with too much readiness encourage.

The ice once broke, he prosecuted his addresses with so much vigour and assiduity, that she thought it would be no breach of modesty to give him room to hope he was not altogether indifferent to her; – by degrees, therefore, she became more kind on every visit he made, but did it with caution and reserve, neither by her looks or words forfeiting that character of discretion she so much valued herself upon, – dropping only some hints, as if forced from her, from a fund of tenderness within, which she would fain endeavour to conceal, but had not the power of doing it.

Thus artful in appearing artless, Leontine, though a man of very good sense and penetration, never once suspected she was any other than such as she affected to be, – plain, simple, generous, and incapable of disguising her sentiments.

It is certain, indeed, that her natural cunning was greatly assisted how to proceed on this occasion, by the intelligence she daily received from Delia, to whose brother Leontine made no scruple of disburthening all that pass'd in his heart in relation to his passion for Syrenia.

From this faithful friend she learn'd, that tho' it was not to be doubted but that Leontine was as much in love with her as man could be, yet the great respect and reverence he had for his father would not permit him to think of venturing on a thing of so much consequence as marriage, without having first obtain'd his consent, and approbation of the woman he made choice of for a wife; and that to this end he had already sent two letters to his father, who lived entirely in the country; but the answers he received not being quite so satisfactory as he wish'd, he had wrote a third, dictated in the most passionate and pressing terms.

She could not avoid being under some very uneasy apprehensions on the score of this old gentleman, and also fear'd that the passion Leontine was inspired with might not of itself be strong enough to get the better of that obedience owing from him to a father's will, – she therefore wish'd to interest his good-nature and generosity in her favour, and judged that the surest way to secure his affection was to make him confident of her's.

But the means of accomplishing this was a difficulty she knew not presently how to get over; – to confess by word of mouth she loved him seem'd too great a breach of modesty, especially as his courtship to her had not yet been of any long continuance; and to get him inform'd of it by Delia, she thought would be the same thing, as he would doubtless imagine it was not done without her privity and consent; – besides, she knew not whether that lady would approve of such a step. – Being one day desir'd by him to favour him with a tune on her spinnet, she entertain'd him with an air out of the Opera of Arsinoe,[343] the first in the Italian taste ever exhibited on the English stage, and, in my opinion, has been exceeded by none that have come after it. – The words she sung to her instrument were these:

> Wanton zephir softly blowing,
> Watching, catching, whispering, going,
> Bear in sighs my soul away:
> Tell Ormondo what I feel,
> Tell him how his chains I wear,
> Tell him all my grief and care;
> Gently stealing,
> And revealing,
> More of love than I can say.[344]

But though Leontine extoll'd both the music and the voice which gave it utterance, yet he shew'd no indication of imagining she had any design of flattering his passion in the choice she made of this song; – this making her perceive she must be more explicit, her fertile invention soon presented her with a stratagem, which pleasing her fancy at the same time that it promis'd the success she aim'd it, she put into immediate execution. – It was this:

Having a natural talent for poetry she sat down at her escrutore, took pen, ink and paper, and without being at the pains of much study wrote the following lines:

The breathings of a love-sick heart.

> Wit, manly beauty, every grace combine,
> To deck the youth I love with charms divine.
> But ah! – my too uncautious heart take heed,
> Nor with gay hopes the growing passion feed;
> Wealth's the chief idol that mankind adore,
> The sov'reign power they all fall down before,
> My niggard fortune does that charm deny,
> And love alone will not its wants supply;
> Let me then guard each av'nue to my breast,
> And bar all entrance to this dangerous guest;
> Lest by indulging the presumptuous flame,
> I fall the victim of despair and shame.
> But, oh 'tis vain! – the god of love conspires,
> To aid my Leontine with all his fires,
> Speaks in his voice and sparkles in his eyes,
> And what he sweetly forces, justifies.

'Tis sure determin'd in the book of fate,
I must adore, ev'n tho' he proves ungrate.

This paper, which she wanted him to believe was a sincere confession of the whole secret of her soul, she contrived should fall into his hands in such a manner as should have too much the appearance of chance to be liable to any suspicion of design.

At his next visit, her maid being well instructed by her how to act, ran hastily into the room, and told her that the man whom she had order'd to come for his money was below. – Syrenia affected not to understand what she meant, and cry'd,

Syrenia. What man! – what money!

Maid. Mr. Shapely, madam, – your staymaker.

Syrenia. Oh, – now I remember I did bid him come for his money; – he takes a strange unseasonable time; – people should always come in a morning on these affairs; – however I'll see if I can find his bill, – and do you carry a pen and ink into the parlour, that he may write me a receipt on the back of it.

On this the maid withdrew, and Syrenia open'd a little desk that stood in the dining-room, and beginning to tumble over some writings she had there, as in search of the pretended bill, dexterously slipp'd from among the rest the paper which contain'd the above recited verses, and let it fall to the ground without seeming to observe that any thing was dropp'd; – then saying she had found what she had look'd for, – shut up the desk in a great hurry, – begg'd Leontine would excuse her absence for a few moments, and went down stairs.

She was no sooner gone than Leontine happening to cast his eyes that way saw the paper, and took it up, as I suppose, with no other intention than to deliver it to Syrenia when she should return; but it being purposely folded in such a manner that part of the writing appear'd on the outside, – he must have been strangely incurious indeed, if seeing it a poem, and wrote in his mistress's hand, he had forbore examining it.

Never was any transport more visible than in the countenance of Leontine while reading these delusive stanzas; – his look put me in mind of the poet's words:

Kindness has resistless charms,
All things else but faintly warms;
It gilds the lover's servile chain,
And makes the slave grow pleas'd and vain.[345]

Tho' by the particulars I have been repeating, the reader will easily suppose I was both an eye and an ear witness of them, yet it is utterly impossible for me to describe either the looks or attitude of the one or the other, in the joyous surprise of finding himself, as he imagin'd, thus extremely dear to the only woman to whom he wish'd to be so.

She took care to stay so long below as to give him time to read over, more than once, what she intended for his perusal; it was still in his hands when she return'd, but she seem'd to take no notice of it, and was beginning to apologize for her absence by laying the blame on the impertinence of her staymaker; but Leontine, with a gesture full of rapture, interrupted her, – saying,

Leontine. O, madam, – you must allow me to become an advocate for this honest tradesman, since by his fortunate detaining you I am made the happiest of mankind.

To this, Syrenia affecting not to comprehend the meaning of what he said, reply'd with a smile,

Syrenia. What riddle in this you are about to pose me with? – I am the dullest creature in the world at giving a solution to these things.

Leontine. This paper, madam, wafted to me by the god of love's own hand, has given me the wish'd-for opportunity of proving myself less unworthy of the blessing I aspire to, than your doubts suggest. – No, my charming Syrenia, not all the treasures in the world could add one ray of lustre to the graces of your mind and person, – 'tis those alone I covet to enjoy, and in possessing them shall be more rich than in possessing both the Indies.

While he was speaking Syrenia cast her eyes upon the paper and blush'd excessively; – partly perhaps thro' shame, but more thro' the pleasure which diffused itself thro' all her veins, on perceiving, by the behaviour of Leontine, how well the success of her plot had answer'd to the intention of it.

The well dissembled confusion she was in, was an excuse for her not speaking, and Leontine went on to assure her, in the most tender terms, that no consideration whatever should have the power to oblige him to withdraw that firm affection he now vow'd to her, and that he hop'd a very little time would put a final period to all her apprehensions on that score.

What farther conversation pass'd between them at this time I shall forbear to repeat, as it may be easily guess'd at; and proceed to the conduct of Syrenia in regard to her other lover, who the reader may think I have too long neglected.

The business which call'd Rossano into the country detain'd him there much longer than he had expected, and an unlucky fall from his horse, the very day before he intended to set out for London, occasioned a second delay to his journey; – this absence of his gave Syrenia a full opportunity of entertaining her new lover, tho' she received every post a letter from the former, all which she did not fail to answer with that tenderness which might be expected from a woman who had promised to be his wife; still keeping close to her first maxim, not to give any umbrage to the one 'till she was perfectly secure of the other.

All impediments, however, being at last removed, that gentleman arriv'd in town on the same day that Syrenia and Leontine were engag'd in the manner above recited; – his impatience to see his beloved mistress carried him immediately to her lodgings, – he came while his rival was with her; but her maid, well knowing how improper it was that they should meet, told him her lady was abroad, – on which he went away, saying he would return in the evening, as he knew she was not accustom'd to stay late from home.

He was doubtless much disappointed, but not at all suspicious of the cause, 'till having cross'd the street he happen'd to cast his eyes back upon the house, either by chance, or possibly through fondness of the place which contain'd the idol of his wishes, – Syrenia was sitting in the window and Leontine very near to her: – Rossano had a full view of both; but Syrenia was too earnest in discourse to observe him, tho' he stood motionless on the spot where he was for some minutes. – It seem'd not strange to him that a gentleman should be with her, tho' he could find no way to account why he should be denied access to her but one, which stung him to the soul.

He was more than once tempted by his jealousy, as I afterwards discover'd, to return and demand of the maid a reason for his having been refused admittance; but second thoughts prevail'd, and he went home to deliberate how it would best become him to behave in such a circumstance.

Leontine staid supper, and Syrenia stepping out of the room to give some necessary orders to her maid, was inform'd by her that Rossano had been there and the message he had left: – this greatly disconcerted her; but after a little pause she recover'd herself enough to give these directions:

Syrenia. This is very unlucky, – Leontine will probably stay late; – you must therefore tell Rossano that I am not yet come home, – and that you believe I am gone to the play.

The maid punctually obeying these directions, Rossano only reply'd, – that since it had happen'd so, he would do himself the honour to breakfast with her lady the next morning, – and then departed seemingly well satisfied.

But tho' he forbore giving any indications of his jealousy to this girl, he doubted not but that the second repulse was owing to the same motive the first had been; – resolving, however, to be more fully convinced, he posted his servant, whom he had brought with him for that purpose, under a lamp a few doors from the house where Syrenia lodged, charging him to observe carefully who came in or out, and if he saw a gentleman in black velvet and a bag wig, to follow him wherever he went, find out his name if possible, and bring him an exact account.

Leontine was so much charm'd with the discovery he had made of Syrenia's affection, that he quitted her apartment not 'till the night was very far advanced. – Rossano's servant, however, kept close to his stand, 'till a chair being call'd, he saw the gentleman his master had described go into it; – he follow'd, and as soon as Leontine had enter'd the house where he lodg'd, and the door was shut, ask'd the chairmen if they knew the gentleman they had carried; but they answering in the negative, and he seeing no house open where he might enquire, could learn nothing farther that night; but early the next morning he went again, and had the address to find out all the particulars that could be expected from him.

Rossano was now assur'd not only that he had a rival, but also a rival highly favour'd by his mistress: – the distraction he was in may easily be conceived; but he dissembled it on his first approach to Syrenia, whom he did not fail to visit the next morning, as he had told her maid.

Syrenia, before she was inform'd of it, knew very well, that missing seeing her that night, he would not let another day pass over without coming, had the artifice to tell Leontine she was obliged to go some few miles out of town to see a relation who she heard was dangerously ill.

I am not a person who lives without having some business in the world, yet there are very few things of consequence enough to me to have detain'd me from being a witness of what pass'd in this interview between Rossano and Syrenia, and shall present my readers with it as recorded in my faithful Tablets.

Syrenia no sooner heard he was there than she ran to the top of the stair-case to receive him, and with the greatest shew of tenderness saluted him in these terms:

Syrenia. My dear Rossano, how griev'd have I been for losing the sight of you last night, after having been so long an age of time deprived of it!

Rossano. The misfortune, beautiful Syrenia, was wholly mine; for while I moan'd your absence you doubtless found something to amuse and entertain you. – I heard you were at the play.

Syrenia. I was so; – but what could I find there to compensate for the satisfaction I miss'd by being so unluckily from home!

Rossano. Were you at Covent-Garden?

Syrenia. No; – at Drury-Lane. – But why do you ask?

Rossano. Only for a foolish fancy.

Syrenia. Nay, I may answer myself that question. – I will lay my life you went in search of me; – but I chose to go in a deshabille, and sat on the back bench in Burton's box;[346] – so it was impossible for you to see me.

Rossano. Not so impossible as you imagine, madam: – but I had no need to go to either of the Theatres, – the object I so much languish'd to behold presented itself to me without my taking any pains.

These words occasion'd a visible change in her countenance, – she blush'd excessively, – cast her eyes upon the ground, and had not power to lift them up while she said only,

Syrenia. What is it you mean?

Rossano. There needs no explanation; – the disorder you in vain endeavour to conceal shews but too much how well you are acquainted with my meaning. – Ah, Syrenia, – Syrenia, – how did I once flatter myself with an assurance that your heart was mine, inviolably mine; but now I find my absence has been fatal to me!

Syrenia. Forbear to talk thus; – these suspicions are unjust to me, and cruel to yourself.

Rossano. Why then was I last night turn'd from your door! – Why twice repuls'd, while my more happy rival was allow'd the privilege of entertaining you 'till midnight!

Syrenia. Who tells you this?

Rossano. My own eyes, madam, were my first intelligencers, – I saw you at that window, – saw also your new favourite, and easily judg'd by both your attitudes what was the subject of your conversation; – as to the rest, I was inform'd of it by means to which I afterwards had recourse.

The false Syrenia was now absolutely confounded, – there was no giving the lye to ocular demonstration as to the first part of Rossano's charge against her, but she endeavour'd to avoid the latter, by saying,

Syrenia. Well, sir, I own I was at home, and had order'd myself to be denied; but expected not your coming, or knew you had been here 'till after you were gone: – as for the gentleman you saw with me, 'tis your own jealous fancy alone that makes you regard him in the light of a lover.

Rossano. I grant you did not expect me; but as your servant is no stranger to the footing we are upon, she would certainly have look'd on me as an exception to the general order you had given, if she had not known I was no proper person to join in the company you had above: – besides, you cannot plead ignorance of my second visit, yet I was again turn'd back.

Syrenia. You wrong me; – I protest I never heard of your being here 'till I was going to bed; – think no more therefore of such idle stuff, – this is not discourse for two people who love, and have so long been absent from each other.

Rossano. Ah, Syrenia! – I wish the treatment I have received would allow me to entertain you with any other; – there was a time when I could be as gay, perhaps, as he who now supplants me in your esteem.

Syrenia. Still harping on the same string; – remember what the poet says:

> No signs of love in jealous men remains,
> But that which sick men have of life, their pains.[347]

She had just done repeating these lines when the tea equipage was brought in for breakfast, and Rossano, who I could perceive by his countenance was little pleased with the trifling answers she had made to his reproaches, rose up to take his leave, on which she suddenly catch'd hold of his hand, and with a well counterfeited tenderness in her voice and eyes, said to him,

Syrenia. You will not go and leave me in this humour.

Rossano. Indeed I must; – I have this moment thought of a business that requires immediate dispatch.

Syrenia. Shall I then see you in the afternoon?

Rossano. I cannot promise.

He was half way down stairs while speaking these last words, and though she follow'd him two or three steps, and call'd to him to stay, he turn'd not, nor even look'd back upon her, but went hastily out of the house.

I was resolved to see what was his intent, and accompanied him to the house of that kinswoman where he had first seen Syrenia; – he was beginning to tell her what cause of complaint he had against that lady, but she stopp'd his mouth by saying she was already acquainted with every thing he had to relate, and then proceeded to inform him, that having a friend who lived opposite to Syrenia, she had learn'd that she entertain'd a new lover, who visited her almost every day, and that the neighbourhood believed it would very shortly be a match.

Rossano went from this relation to his his own lodgings, where having vented some part of his rage in exclamations on the levity and ingratitude of woman-kind, he sat down and wrote the following lines:

To Leontine.

Sir,

You have endeavour'd to supplant me in the affection of the woman I loved and am engag'd to marry; – I need not tell you I mean Syrenia; – I expect there-fore you will either resign all pretensions to her under your own hand, or give such satisfaction as one gentleman has a right to demand from another in these cases: – I shall attend you behind Montague-house at eight to-morrow morning, 'till when,

> Yours,

Rossano.

This he sent immediately to Leontine, who happening to be at home return'd an answer by the bearer in these terms:

To Rossano.

Sir,

I own myself a lover of Syrenia, but know nothing of your courtship to her, nor will believe she is under any engagement of the nature you mention, either to you or any other man; and shall be so far from resigning my pretensions, that I will defend them to the last moment of my life; you may therefore rely on my meeting you at the time and place appointed.

> Yours,

Leontine.

Rossano had scarce finish'd reading this billet when a porter brought him a letter from Syrenia, the contents whereof were these:

To Rossano.

My very dear Rossano,

Your behaviour this morning has thrown me into disquiets which might excite compassion in a heart less devoted to me than I flatter'd myself yours was; – I thought the love between us was establish'd on a more solid basis than to be shook by every puff of jealous caprice; – I doubt not but to convince you that yours is no other. – If this is so lucky as to find you at home, or you receive it time enough, I beg to see you this evening; for I cannot bear you should pass another night in such cruel suspicions of

Your faithfully affectionate

Syrenia.

I perceived he was in some dilemma on reading this billet; – he paus'd a while, – then said,

Rossano. My Compliments to the lady, and –

Then paus'd again, and at last cry'd,

Rossano. Tell her I am engag'd this day, but will wait on her to-morrow.

Various reflections seem'd now rolling in the mind of this much abus'd lover; but I left him in them, and contented myself with going the next morning to the field of battle, in order to see how the combatants would behave; – they were both so punctual to the time that it is hard to say which of them was first within the lists. – Rossano, however, having some idea of Leontine, as he had seen him through Syrenia's window, advanced towards him, and said,

Rossano. I guess, sir, you are the gentleman I invited hither?

Leontine. You are not deceived, sir, if your name be Rossano.

Rossano. The same, sir.

Leontine. Mine then is Leontine, and you find me ready to maintain my pretensions to the fair Syrenia.

Rossano. And I to assert that right which a long series of encouraged courtship and mutual vows have given me.

Leontine. This then is the way we must dispute the prize.

Both their swords were already drawn, and Rossano, either through superior skill or better fortune, gave his antagonist a slight wound in the side on the first pass, and on the second a much deeper on the right arm, which occasioning a great effusion of blood, he was obliged to drop his sword, on which the other, imagining the mischief to be greater than it really prov'd, stepp'd hastily towards him with these words:

Rossano. Sir, Though I might expect the justice of my cause would give me some advantage over you, I should be extremely sorry to find it attended with any bad effects, – I beg therefore, as there are scarce any chairs abroad so early, you will give me leave to support you to my lodgings, which are very near, and where you may have immediate assistance.

Leontine accepted the offer, – a surgeon was immediately call'd, and his cloaths stripp'd off in order to have his wounds examined; – that on his side was not at all deep, and that on his arm happening only among a knot of veins, required little more than a tight bandage for its cure: – he was advised, however, to drink some mull'd wine, and then endeavour to compose himself to sleep for a few hours. – Rossano, with a great deal of humanity and politeness, took care to see this injunction perform'd, and on Leontine's requesting it, sent to his lodgings for fresh cloaths and linnen for him to put on when he should awake.

As Rossano was retiring to leave his guest to that repose which was thought needful for him, he saw a paper lying on the floor, which he took up, not knowing but it was something belonging to himself; – but how great was his amazement when he found what it contain'd, – this being the very verses Syrenia had wrote on Leontine, and had fortuitously been shook out of that gentleman's pocket as his cloaths were hastily thrown to the other side of the room.

'Till now, the love he had bore Syrenia kept him from entertaining any worse opinion of her conduct, than that it was the vanity incident to her sex which alone had made her encourage the addresses of Leontine; but this plain proof of her inconstancy gave a sudden turn to his sentiments, and changed at once all the tenderness he ever had for her into contempt and hatred.

Leontine also had some uneasy thoughts on the score of Syrenia; – Rossano seem'd to him to be a man of too much honour to assert a falshood, and began to fear that himself had been deceived in his opinion of that lady's sincerity; – being less inclined to sleep than to be satisfied in this point, he rung a bell which hung by the bedside, on which Rossano, who was no farther than the next room, went in and ask'd how he did; – to which he reply'd,

Leontine. So well that I think I need lie here no longer than 'till my man brings me some clean apparel, that I may rise with decency; – in the mean time, sir, should take it as a favour that you would let me know how far I have been guilty of injustice to you in regard of Syrenia: – in your billet to me you mention an engagement; – if it be so I was perfectly ignorant of it, and at that time imagin'd I had strong reasons for disbelieving, – otherwise I do assure you, sir, not all my passion for that lady should have made me attempt to disunite your loves.

Rossano. Though it may seem ungenerous to boast a lady's favours, as I have no other way to justify my rash proceedings towards you, be pleased to read that letter:

In speaking this he presented to Leontine the letter he had received from Syrenia the day before, which that gentleman had no sooner look'd over than he cry'd out with the greatest surprise,

Leontine. Good heaven! – Why this was dated but yesterday!

Rossano. Yes, sir, and wrote on account of my testifying some jealousy on your being with her the evening before; – but I have now done with that idle passion, and can now resign my claim with as much calmness as I would lately have maintain'd it with eagerness.

Leontine. Is it possible you can be in earnest?

Rossano. Were Syrenia more beautiful than she is, the enjoyment of her person without her heart could give no happiness; and had this paper, which accidentally fell from your pocket in the hurry this morning, happen'd sooner into my hands, I should not have proceeded as I have done.

In speaking this he gave Leontine the paper he had taken up; – the other immediately saw what it was, and receiving it with a smile made this reply:

Leontine. I thank you, sir; but I assure you I am not at all vain of these verses, as they serve only to prove that the lady was willing to be double arm'd, and in case one lover should fail, to be provided with another.

After this they began to enter into a very free discussion on the conduct of Syrenia towards them both; and there now appear'd so much deceit, – mean artifice, – ingratitude and perfidy, as well to the one as to the other, that it is hard to say which of them entertain'd the most despicable notions of her: – in fine, they agreed to resent the impositions she had practised on them in such a manner as some of my fair readers, how greatly soever they may condemn Syrenia, will not perhaps easily absolve them for.

The servant of Leontine being arrived with the things his master had order'd to be brought, that gentleman rose and got himself dress'd, and Rossano in the mean time employ'd himself in gathering up all the letters he had received from Syrenia, and made them up in a large packet, and wrote on the cover,

Amorous billets from a lady, of a very extraordinary character.

They went in two chairs to the house where Syrenia lodged, and the door being open'd rush'd up stairs without any ceremony, and even into the dining-room where she was sitting. – Leontine was the first that enter'd; she rose to receive him; but seeing his arm in a scarf, cry'd out,

Syrenia. Oh, sir, what accident has befallen you!

Leontine. No unlucky one, madam; I have, indeed, received two slight wounds on your account; but I bless the hand that gave them, since they have been the means of curing one of a more dangerous nature in my heart.

She had no time to ask what he meant by these words, – Rossano was now in the room, and rejoined to what the other had said in this manner:

Rossano. My heart is also in a pretty good condition too; – for though I have lost a mistress, I have gain'd a friend, from whom I have reason to hope more sincerity. – You see, madam, two persons together, whom doubtless you wish'd to keep separate, while we had separate interests; but we have now agreed, and as we lately join'd to persecute you with our addresses, now join in the resolution of troubling you no more.

Leontine. I have nothing to add, madam, to what my friend has delivered, but to restore this paper, which can be of no use to me, and may be of some to you, as change but the name the picture may suit some happier man.

Rossano. And I return those letters you have from time to time favour'd me with.

He then laid down the packet, at the same time Leontine did the verses, upon a table. – Syrenia was all this while immoveable as a statue, – she had found from their first entrance that they had compared notes, – that she was exposed, – her arts laid open, and her hopes irrecoverably lost with both; – fain she would have spoke but had not power; and all she could utter at last was,

Syrenia. Mighty well; – so then I am to be insulted.

Rossano. No, madam, your birth and beauty are your protection; and had your mind been equal to either, neither of us, I believe would have broke his chain, or even wish'd to regain that liberty we now have so much cause to triumph in.

Leontine. Come, sir, you see the lady is disconcerted, – let us leave her to meditate on this adventure, it may be of service in some future one.

Rossano. With all my heart. – A good husband to you, madam.

Leontine. I join in the same wish, – Your servant, madam.

They departed with these words, and I staid not long after them, – the sight of Syrenia's despair, how justly soever she had brought it on herself, giving more pain than satisfaction.

End of the Seventh BOOK.

THE
Invisible Spy.

BOOK VIII.
CHAP. I.

Contains a brief detail of such occurrences as presented themselves to the Author's observation in an evening's Invisible ramble thro' several parts of this metropolis.

IT has often been a matter of very great concern to me, and I believe must be the same to every thinking mind, to see how some people are continually hurried and busied about mere trifles, of no manner of consequence to themselves, or scarce to any body else; while all the duties of religion, – all the regard for the welfare of their most particular friends, – all love of country, and even the dearest interests of their own families, are totally neglected.

What judgment can we form of a person of this cast, but that he has a vacuum in his head ready to be fill'd up with the first toy that presents itself, and not being endow'd with a strength of reason sufficient to direct his choice, suffers himself to be engross'd by such things as he finds make most noise in the world, not such as have most relation to his own affairs, either as to fortune or reputation.

Can there be a sight more farcical than for a man who, without any petition to prefer or suit to solicit; in fine, without any call or business whatsoever, is continually cringing at the levee of a minister of state, and when the compliments are paid and the circle is dismiss'd, runs thro' the whole round of his acquaintance, reporting where he has been and what he has seen, sagaciously remarking on every nod, wink, or smile of the great man, and finding mystery even in the tye of his wig, or the loose or strait buttoning his coat?

Another, whose affairs at home perhaps are involved in the utmost perplexities, shall pass the best part of his time among the jobbers in 'Change-Alley, – go from coffee-house to coffee-house, – enquire of every broker he meets with the price of stocks, in which he has no share, or money to purchase any, and be more solicitous in finding out the uses to which the Sinking-Fund[348] is appropriated than for the means of extricating himself out of his present difficulties.

A third values himself much upon being a great connoisseur in politics, – registers all the public papers from year to year, pretends to reconcile all the contradictions they contain, and to discover some latent meaning in every paragraph, and takes more pains to unriddle their imaginary ænigmas than a poor servitor[349] at the university does to translate Perseus[350] for a rich student who pays, and fathers the labour of his brain.

Others have a taste for building, – are extremely curious in ornamenting the structures they cause to be erected with carvings, paintings, and such like superficial beauties; but never once examine how the foundation is laid, or whether the pompous outworks may not be liable to sink very soon into a heap of rubbish. – Some employ their whole cares on the breeding and well managing their horses, hounds, and game-cocks, leaving the education of their sons entirely unregarded.

Impossible is it to enumerate the various trifles with which too many, even among the highest class of life, suffer themselves not only to be amused, but wholly taken up; – but I think, without any danger of being accused of too much severity, one may justly say with Shakespear of such men, that

> The earth has bubbles as the water hath,
> And these are some of them.[351]

In a word, – MUCH ADOE ABOUT NOTHING, – is a play so universally acted in this town, that one can go to very few places without being witness of some scenes of it.

As insignificant, however, as these people may seem by the description I have given of them, and as in effect they really are, they are yet of more consequence to the public than is generally believed, or than they themselves, with all the stock of vanity they are usually possess'd of are capable of imagining; – this, tho' it may be thought a paradox, will be easy for me to make appear, – as thus:

These unjudging creatures, for I have already proved them to be such, are frequently made the tools by which evil and designing men fashion out their ends: – when those in power have any thing on foot, from which they find it necessary to divert the attention of the nation, it is but throwing out some whisper, though of ever so absurd and ridiculous a nature, among the people I am speaking of, and they will immediately ring it in the ears of the populace 'till it becomes the cry, and every argument that truth and reason can alledge is deafen'd with the noise.

It was doubtless by this very means chiefly that Oliver Cromwell and his subtle agents accomplish'd the dreadful work of murder and usurpation; and there have been some instances, of a yet more modern date, which have shewn how far this spirit of enthusiasm has been able to bring about the most astonishing as well as most pernicious events; – events which all good men and faithful patriots have beheld with horror and detestation, though unable to repel the impetuous torrent of a blind, bigotted, and mistaken zeal: – events which we are willing to flatter ourselves will no more spread distraction and devastation through these kingdoms.

A late most excellent poet seems, notwithstanding, to have had some apprehensions of this kind; – in speaking on the topic of national calamities he says very elegantly, though I hope not prophetically,

> Who knows but we may see again what once amaz'd we saw,
> When some black time may come when rage shall grapple law,
> And hush pale justice with dominion's awe? [352]

An experience of many years, join'd with a diligent observation of the world, has convinced me, beyond all doubt, that these inconsiderates, without being sensible of the mischief they do, have been, and daily are, the instruments of propagating the most infamous scandals, gross falsities, and base aspersions on the great and good; as also the most ridiculous and idle stories, invented and calculated by men of more thinking heads, to amuse and divert the attention of the public from what most demands its regard.

A glaring instance of this latter kind now takes up the town, – all mouths are full of it, – all ears are open to it; – but it appears to me that there are few eyes clear enough to discern the secret ground-work of this mountain of absurdities, and on what motive it was erected.

I think it not my province, however, nor shall presume to inform the judgment of any one in this point, but shall only relate a passage I happen'd to be witness of, which every one is at liberty to descant upon as he shall think proper.

Being one day on the other side of the Royal-Exchange, where some business I had there being dispatch'd sooner than I expected, it came into my head to call in at a certain celebrated coffee-house, which I had been told was frequented by a great number of the most eminent and wealthy citizens; but as I had no acquaintance with them, and some other more substantial reasons for not appearing in propria persona, I chose to go in my Invisible capacity.

Pursuant to this resolution I stepp'd into the first obscure alley I could find, and there girded on my precious Belt, which, as well as my Tablets, I seldom went out without taking with me, and then hasted to the place I mention'd.

I found the room very full of company, most of whom were of that sect of dissenters from the establish'd church which are under the denomination of Presbyterians; – I would not here be understood to mean any thing in ridicule of those gentlemen; for I love and revere every man of real virtue and good sense, be he of what persuasion soever.

How far the persons I have just now occasion to speak of answer to either of these characters I will not pretend to say, – let their own words testify, – I shall, according to the phrase of the inspired writer, – set a guard upon my mouth that I offend not with my lips.[353] – But to proceed,

Three or four, who I afterwards perceived were leading men among the sanctified tribe, were engag'd in a very warm dispute with a gentleman who endeavour'd, with a great deal of spirit, to expose the gross absurdities and falshood of a cause they took upon them to maintain, and with a kind of magisterial air attempted to enforce the belief of in others.

The odds appear'd to me at first, I confess, to be a little ungenerous; but I was the more strengthen'd in this opinion when I heard the manner in which they deliver'd their arguments, and that were urg'd in favour of one of the most preposterous and ridiculous complaints that ever engag'd the attention of any men of common sense: – after saying this, I think it is needless to add, it was the affair of Squires and Canning.[354] – As I am utterly unacquainted with the names either of those who defended the cause of the latter, or of him who treated it with contempt, I shall distinguish the one by that of Assertors, and the other by that of Opponent.

The conversation which pass'd on both sides, after I had got a convenient place to post myself, and had spread my Tablets, I shall give the public a faithful transcript of, as taken from those unerring testimonies, and was as the reader will find underwritten.

First Assertor. I am surprised, sir, you should rack your brain for arguments against the cause of helpless innocence and virtue in distress.

Second Assertor. 'Tis barbarous, 'tis cruel. – Where shall we find an object of compassion if Betty Canning is not one? – We know her, sir, – know her to be pure and unpolluted.

Third Assertor. Ay, – She is of our congregation,[355] – has always been a diligent frequenter of the meeting-house, and fervent in her devotions.

Opponent. So because she is of your congregation, it naturally follows she must be chaste and pious; – the lambs of your flock never go astray; – but I forbear to make any reflection on this score, and shall only say, I never shall give credit to a story so full of inconsistencies and improbabilities as this which has been forged by her and her accomplices.

First Assertor. Sir, there is no reasoning against fact; she has sworn to the truth of it before a magistrate, and that magistrate has testified his belief of it.[356]

Opponent. Yes, – the story she told was romantic, – it suited his taste, – he thought it might be a proper subject to work up into a Farce or Puppet-shew, so was willing to promote the credibility of it.

First Assertor. Mere spite and scandal.

Opponent. Not at all; and I doubt not but the imposition will be fully laid open by another magistrate, superior in every degree to him who takes her part.[357]

First Assertor. Sir, it is prophane and impious in him, or you or any man, to espouse the cause of a wicked old hag, – a vagabond, – a gipsey, such as Mary Squires; and a known instrument of libidinous pleasures, such as mother Wells.

Second Assertor. Oh 'tis an abomination to all good men, and every word in favour of those vile wretches smells rankly of the breath of the old serpent.

Opponent. Gentlemen, I have nothing to alledge in defence of these creatures; but that however guilty they may have been, or continue to be, in other respects, they are entirely innocent in this they are now accused of.

First Assertor. No, no, – 'tis impossible.

Opponent. Saying a thing does not prove it to be so; – but give me leave only to offer a few queries, in relation to some of the many inconsistencies in the tale told by that idle wench, Betty Canning.

Second Assertor. Do so, – we shall know how to answer them.

Opponent. First then, – supposing her to have been robb'd in the manner she pretends by two ruffians, – what could induce fellows who live upon the spoil, after having taken from her all they found worth taking, to quit the pursuit of other booty and lose their time in dragging her into the country, only to throw her into the house and then leave her there; for she does not accuse them of making any attempt upon her chastity?

First Assertor. As to that, – it is highly probable they might be fee'd by mother Wells to bring the first young woman they could meet with to her house, in order to be made a sacrifice to her mercenary views, and the lust of some vile fellow.

Opponent. Then they would certainly have chose an object of a more tempting aspect, or would have deserved little for their pains; – but let that pass. – If it were as you imagine, – would any woman, who it is said has long been in practice in the seducing trade, have behaved towards the prey brought into her clutches in the fashion she did to Betty Canning? – Would she not rather have sooth'd the frighted maid, – reviv'd her drooping spirits with good eating and drinking, – promis'd her fine cloaths, and then introduced some man to her, who might have allured her to the sin she aim'd to make her guilty of? – Surely the way to tempt her to be a prostitute was not to lock her up alone in a wild desolate room, without a bed to lie upon, or any other refreshment than a little bread and water; – such usage, one must think, was intended to mortify, not excite a carnal inclination.

First Assertor. Sir, I am grieved, – greatly grieved in spirit, to find you so ignorant of the force of virtue; – I tell you, sir, that the courage and resolution of this pious virgin struck such an awe into the minds of those profligate wretches she was placed among, that they had not the power of putting their wicked designs in execution; – Heaven, indeed, for a trial of her patience, permitted them to distress her helpless innocence, but not to destroy it.

Opponent. Very extraordinary, truly. – But pray, sir, why did this suffering saint remain so long under the roof of such abandon'd creatures, since all accounts agree that in three days, nay in three hours after her confinement, she had the same opportunity of making her escape as at the time she pretends to effect it?

Second Assertor. Her eyes were not open to the means of her deliverance 'till that blessed moment; – it was ordained she should undergo the persecution she did, in order to make her virtue more triumphant over sin and shame.

Opponent. Oh, gentlemen, – these arguments will never be swallow'd any where but in a conventicle.

Third Assertor. Sir, they will always have their due weight with every one but a reprobate.

Opponent. How, sir!

The Opponent was so much incens'd at these words, that he started from his seat and was about to reply with his fist, but some of the more moderate part of the company interposed, and prevented the mischief that might otherwise have ensued: – by their persuasions he sat down again, and the dispute would doubtless have been renew'd, it may be with greater vehemence than before, if a drawer from a neighbouring tavern had not luckily come and told him that two gentlemen, whose names he mentioned, desir'd to speak with him; on which he went away, perhaps to the great satisfaction of the assertors of Betty Canning's cause, who, if he had staid and continued his queries, might probably have been a little puzzled to find answers to them.

During the debate I have been repeating every one in the room kept a profound silence; but afterwards the conversation became general, – several other subjects were started by particular persons, but they were not listen'd to, – the majority seem'd to have their heads so full of Betty Canning that they could scarce think or speak of any thing beside: – 'tis true, indeed, they did not all give credit to her story, yet the positiveness with which they heard it affirm'd made the least credulous divided in their thoughts, and afraid to pass a judgment either on the one or the other side of the question.

The reader will doubtless naturally suppose that it was impossible for me to live in the world, and have any acquaintance in it, without having heard, long before I came to this place, much talk of Elizabeth Canning, – her pitiful distress, – her miraculous preservation and escape, and all the other prodigies of that amazing story.

'Tis true, indeed, I was a stranger to no part of it; – but then my conversation being chiefly among the gay part of the town, I was not much surprised that people who can find very little to employ their thoughts should be fond of a tale which had so much of the marvellous in it; – as children, before they arrive at years capable of being instructed in more solid matters, listen with pleasure to their nurses stories of giants, – fairies, and enchanted castles, – as such I regarded all they said, and thought no further of it.

But when I heard grave citizens, – men of business, – of a sedate department and good understanding in other things, argue with serious countenances on such a heap of wild absurdities, I cannot say whether my astonishment or indignation had most dominion over my faculties; but this I know, that both together destroy'd all the little stock of patience I am master of, and would not suffer me to stay any longer to listen to those insignificant debates which I found were likely to continue among this company.

CHAP. II.

Relates some farther incidents of a pretty particular nature, which fell under the Author's observation in the same evening's Invisible progression.

THOSE turbulent emotions which the scene I had just come from being witness of had rais'd in me, being somewhat quieted by air and walking, I had the curiosity to call in at another great coffee-house, hoping I should find there something to give a turn to the present disposition of my mind.

But I found that the remains of my ill-humour were not to be so soon dissipated as I had imagined. – Here was indeed a vast deal of company, – clerks in public offices, – lawyers, – physicians, – tradesmen, and some few divines, composed the promiscuous assembly; but all were engag'd on the same dirty draggle-tail subject, as one of our news-writers justly terms it, the names of Betty Canning, the Gipsey, and mother Wells, resounded from each quarter of the crouded room, and the cause then depending between these creatures made the whole conversation at every table.

Here I would not be at the trouble of opening my Tablets, easily perceiving that nothing worthy of being recorded in them, or of communicating to the public, was likely to ensue; and also that the smallest part of time I should waste in this company would be paying too dear for any discourses I should hear from them.

Accordingly I left the house after having staid there about seven minutes; but had not reach'd the next street before a confused noise behind obliged me to stand up in the porch of a door 'till the hubbub was pass'd by.

The occasion of this uproar presently appear'd; – it was a poor fellow carried on a bier, with very little signs of life in him, – his face cover'd with blood which issued from his nose and mouth, – his cloaths torn that the naked flesh appear'd in many places; but so deform'd with bruises that it could scarce be known for what it was; – a mix'd rabble of men, women and children follow'd, shouting,

hallooing, and crying, – it was good enough for him, – and that they were glad
he had got his reward.

I was startled at so much inhumanity, for I thought nothing could excuse
such cruel treatment, though I doubted not but the fellow had been guilty of
some atrocious crime; – but I was soon undeceived in this point, and let into the
whole affair.

A tradesman who happen'd to be standing at his shop door, just opposite
to the place where I had taken shelter, stepp'd forward and ask'd what was the
matter, – and by what accident the poor man on the bier was reduced to that
condition he saw him in; – on this several of the mob gather'd about him, and
answer'd his interrogatories in these terms:

First Mob. Ah, sir, he is as arrant a rogue as ever you heard on in your life.

Second Mob. Aye, 'twere no matter if he had been kill'd outright.

Third Mob. No, no, 'tis much better as it is, – I hope to make a holiday to see
him hang'd.

Shopkeeper. But what has he done?

Fourth Mob. Done. sir, you will bless yourself to hear it; – he said that poor
Betty Canning was a perjur'd slut; – that all she had sworn to was lyes; – and
that she deserv'd to be whipp'd at the cart's tail, or pillory'd, or transported to the
plantations; – and a great deal more.

First Mob. Nay, he was beginning to say worse things of her than all this, if his
mouth had not been stopp'd.

Shopkeeper. Then I suppose he has been fighting?

Second Mob. No hang him, – I don't believe he has courage enough to fight;
but he would have run his game on Betty Canning 'till now, for any thing I know,
if a brewer's servant and an honest slaughter-man in Fore-street, and three or
four neighbours of ours in Norton-Falgate, had not all at once fallen upon him
and beat the words down his throat.

Shopkeeper. But was not so many to one odds at football?

Third Mob. There is no minding fair play with such a rascal; – abuse poor
Betty Canning; – why he deserves to have his house pull'd down about his ears.

Fourth Mob. Aye, and so it should, if it were not for his wife and five small
children.

The tradesman said no more but turn'd back into his shop, lifting up his
hands and eyes in token of amazement, and the rabble ran to rejoin their companions, who I could hear still continued insulting and vilifying the poor maim'd
wretch, who was altogether unable to return any part of their abuse.

This shopkeeper appear'd to me to be a more reasonable creature than most
of those I had lately been among; and I should have been glad to have had some
discourse with him concerning this adventure; – but that being impracticable,

as I had no opportunity at present of shaking off my Invisibility, I was obliged to content myself and proceed in my progression.

I had now no design in my head, – no particular course to steer; but as I was entirely free from any engagement that evening, and thought it too soon to go home, I rambled from one street to another for a considerable time, yet without meeting any one thing sufficient to tempt my curiosity to make a farther enquiry into.

Any observing reader may reasonably imagine, that the little satisfaction I had been able to reap in the visits I had made at the two coffee-houses I had been already in, would have hinder'd me from going into another, and indeed I was of that opinion myself; – I soon found I was mistaken however, – and so will he; – I really ventured into a third; but the motive which excited me to do so was this:

As I was passing by I perceived thro' the windows, for then the candles within were lighted up, several gentlemen with news-papers before them, on which they seem'd to be discoursing with each other with a great deal of seriousness and gravity: – as I have naturally an extreme passion for knowing the affairs of the world, those of Europe especially, I thought it highly eligible in me to hear what was said upon them by persons who had the appearance of some understanding in them.

At the first table I came to were six or seven gentlemen, most of whom were some way or other concerned in the British Herring-fishery;[358] but though they talk'd very learnedly on the subject, it suited not my taste, so staid not long with them, but adjourn'd to the next company.

These were merchants, who I found were greatly disconcerted at an article they had been just reading in relation to the strict engagements the French had enter'd into with the Indians, and the daily incursions those miscall'd friends and allies made on the English colonies;[359] – but as I cannot pretend to any skill in commerce, I did not spread my Tablets to receive the impression of their discourse; so can only say in general, that they made very heavy complaints, and cry'd out, that if speedy care were not taken to put a stop to those proceedings, trade must be ruin'd, and our settlements in that part of the world utterly destroy'd.

The third table was fill'd with persons who seem'd to be of no avocation, nor at all interested in any branch of business or public affairs; but talk'd of every thing they had been reading merely as things which afforded matter for conversation. – On my joining them, the magnanimity of the Prussian monarch[360] was the topic; – they extoll'd his wisdom, his bravery, his temperance, his clemency, the encouragement he gave to merit wheresoever he found it, and all unanimously agreed that he was the father of his people, – a blessing to the land he govern'd, – and a pattern to his fellow rulers of the earth.

The just admiration I ever had of this truly great and most amiable prince, – exclusive of that regard due to him as so near a relation to our gracious sovereign,[361] would certainly have kept me at that table as long as the company had continued speaking on so agreeable a subject, if I had not been hurried from it by a propensity, I believe, more or less natural to all mankind, that of being most eager to explore what is hid from us with most care.

I observed at a little table, which was placed at once corner of the room, a good distance from the others, two elderly persons, who seem'd very earnest in discourse on some important and secret affair; – by the winks, the nods, and other significant gestures which accompanied the motion of their lips, I doubted not but that they were profound politicians, and were discussing some extraordinary transaction of the cabinet.

Their heads were pretty close together, and they spoke in so low a voice as to render it impossible to be heard by any one except by each other; – but this precaution had no efficacy when once my wonderful Tablets were display'd, which had this excellent property of receiving the impression of whatever was said within the distance of nine yards, tho' utter'd in the most soft whisper.

On my drawing near to them they seem'd a little impatient for the coming of a person who they expected, and who presently after appear'd; – as soon as he had seated himself the following dialogue ensued:

First Man. Oh, mr. Slycraft, I am glad you are come; – we were beginning to think you long.

Slycraft. I am somewhat beyond my hour, indeed; but I assure you nothing could have made me so but the good of the cause.

Second Man. Your zeal and diligence are not to be doubted; – but let us hear what success have your endeavours met with.

Slycraft. Truly not so much as I hoped; – I do not think there is a more difficult thing in the world than getting people to subscribe; – I have been half the town over and have been able to procure no more than three.

First Man. Then I hope they are fat ones.

Slycraft. Pretty well, as times go; – Credulous Woodcock, Esq; has set his name for twenty guineas.

First Man. Very handsome; – five or six hundred such as he would do the business.

Slycraft. Aye, but where shall we find them?

Second Man. Well, but who are the others?

Slycraft. Why there is mr. Nathaniel Vaingood, – twelve guineas.

First Man. We must take the will for the deed; – he has not above sixty or seventy pounds a year to live upon.

Slycraft. Then there is mr. Simon Goosly, the haberdashers, – ten guineas, but has promis'd to prevail on some friends of his to set their names very generously.

Second Man. I dare say he will do all he can. – But have you seen mrs. Waver?

Slycraft. Yes, but she still desires a little more time to consider; – says, she will enquire farther into the affair, and hear what her friends think of it; and all I could get from her was an assurance, that if she found it proper to subscribe at all she would not set her name for less than an hundred pieces.

First Man. Then we may be pretty certain of her; for I know she will be directed by mr. Cantwell, the Nonconformist preacher, who labours all he can to promote the cause in question.

Second Man. Have you yet found an opportunity of talking with the Orator? [362]

Slycraft. I was with him above an hour, and when I had once convinced him that he should find his account in it, he gave me his word and honour that he would rant and roar 'till his chapel ecchoes in favour of the party.

First Man. That is well; – all engines must be set to work, or the town will grow cool on this business, and begin to renew their clamour against Naturalization of the Jews and Clandestine Marriage bills; – the spirit of the people will have vent on something or another, and you know it behoves us to keep them silent on those scores, – nothing ever did it more effectually than this we are upon; – but it must be kept up for a time: – I could wish, methinks, we had the Westleys[363] on our side.

Second Man. 'Tis a vain attempt, – they are now grown too rich to accept of a small gratuity; and I much question whether their exhortations would answer the expence.

Slycraft. I am of your opinion: – besides, you know there is a person who can influence their congregations as much as any thing they can hear from the pulpit. – But I will tell you what I have done to day, – I have engag'd a clergyman of the establish'd church to write a pamphlet in behalf of the cause we have in hand.

First Man. A clergyman of the establish'd church employ his pen in behalf of such a cause! – Prithee, Slycraft, how did'st thou work upon him? – it must certainly be by some very extraordinary method.

Slycraft. The promise of a small present at first wrought upon his necessities; – but on my telling him who and who were concerned in this business, and the motives which induced them to be so, the hopes of having the pitiful Curacy he now enjoys exchanged for a good fat living, made him wholly ours.

First Man. Admirable!

Second Man. But may we depend upon his secrecy?

Slycraft. Never doubt that, as his own interest is concern'd.

First Man. Hitherto things go pretty swimmingly on our side. – But let me see the subscription book; – I have received five guineas to-day from mr. Obadiah Prim, and must insert his name.

'Till now I was at the greatest loss, as 'tis probable the reader will also be, to know what all this meant, or in whose favour or on what account the subscription they talk'd of was rais'd; but on mr. Slycraft's delivering the book to his friend, I look'd over the shoulder of the latter as he open'd it, and saw in the first leaf, by way of title page, these words wrote in a very fair hand:

A LIST of those worthy Persons

WHO

Have subscribed to the relief

OF

ELIZABETH CANNING.

The names underwritten in this legend were too numerous to be inserted, – I shall therefore only say, that the sum of what was rais'd by their subscription amounted to little less than a thousand pounds;[364] – Monstrous abuse of charity! – Preposterous benevolence! which will hereafter reflect more shame than honour on the bestowers.

My astonishment was greater than I can express; but I had not then time to indulge it. – The book being return'd to mr. Slycraft, he address'd his companions in these terms:

Slycraft. You know, gentlemen, that though it is highly necessary a sum of money should be raised for this girl, to prevent her squeaking, as Virtue Hall[365] has done, yet the intent of those who set us to work was not to make her fortune, but by the strangeness of the story she tells to amuse the populace, and divert their attention from those things which they ought not to be too well acquainted with.

First Man. Very true; and I think it answers the end.

Second Man. Aye, and much better than could be expected.

Slycraft. It has, indeed; but I have been thinking of ways and means to make it do so yet more; – suppose we advertise this subscription in the public papers; – I have drawn up something for that purpose, which I should be glad to have your approbation of?

First Man. By all means; – pray let us see it.

Mr. Slycraft then took a small piece of paper out of his pocket and read these lines:

Slycraft. 'Whereas many well-disposed and compassionate persons, in regard to the severe distresses, cruel usage, wonderful preservation, and miraculous escape of that chaste maid Elizabeth Canning, are inclined to contribute towards her future relief, all such are desired to send what sums they shall think fit to bestow to the following places:'

Slycraft. We shall easily find shops and coffee-houses where the money may be received, if any shall be sent, as doubtless there will be several persons who we have not an opportunity to address. – But that is the least part of the business; – these advertisements will reach the country, – the people there will be curious to know the story, which they shall be inform'd of by ballads and penny books sent down to them. – What do you think of it?

First Man. As of the most excellent stratagem I ever heard of in my life.

Second Man. It is certainly a lucky thought; – the innocent country people will be quite alarm'd, – the young men will talk of nothing but Betty Canning to their sweethearts, and the old men think only to preserve their daughters from the danger she escaped; – all remembrance of what has been done by their superiors will be buried in oblivion, and elections may go how they will.

Slycraft. I wrote the advertisement in a hurry, – just as the thought started into my head, – I am sensible it will admit of some emendations. – Suppose we adjourn to a tavern, where we may consult farther upon it with more privacy than here?

First Man. With all my heart.

Second Man. And mine, as all our expences on this occasion are sure to be reimbursed.

These brethren in iniquity went out of the coffee-house as the last repeated words were spoken, and I had not the least inclination to follow them, nor to hear what farther contrivances would be form'd to impose on the credulous, infatuated, deluded multitude: – indeed I was so thunder-struck at what I had already been witness of, that I could scarce forbear bursting into exclamations, which if utter'd by an unseen mouth must needs have been very astonishing and terrifying to all who had heard them; – I therefore prudently withdrew, designing to attempt no future discoveries that night.

The mean artifices which I found some men, miscall'd the great, make no scruple of putting in practice to gain their ends, fill'd me with an equal share of indignation and contempt; but when I reflected how I had just now seen charity, the noblest of all virtues, perverted and prostituted to reward infamy and vileness, it struck me with a horror which forced from me these or the like words:

'Good God!' said I to myself, 'in an age when numberless, nameless miseries abound, – when all our prisons labour with the weight of wretches confined within their walls, many for small debts which their necessities obliged them to contract, and some by unjust and malicious prosecutions, – while every parish, nay almost every street, affords objects of real distress, – while the remains of the most ancient and honourable families are reduced by the fatal South-Sea scheme,[366] and other more latent public calamities, to the extreamest want shall all these, or any of these, send unavailing petitions to those from whom they might expect redress, while a girl sprung from the lowest dregs of the people, bred up to toil, a drudge, one of the very meanest class of servants, receive donations which she as little knows how to make a proper use of as to deserve! – a girl, who if she had really suffer'd all she pretends to have done, would indeed have had a claim to justice against those who had wrong'd her, but none to the bounties so lavishly bestow'd upon her.'

These kind of meditations would doubtless have accompany'd me to my own door, if they had not been interrupted, as well as my course towards home, by an unexpected accident, which the reader will find faithfully related in the succeeding chapter.

CHAP. III.

Though it appears to be no more than a continuation of the same evening's ramble, yet it presents the reader with an adventure of much more importance to the public than any contained in the two last foregoing chapters.

THE human heart is liable to many bad propensities, which if not timely corrected by reason shoot forth into practice and become vices; – but of these there are two sorts, – the one born with us, and part of our nature; – the other imbibed by the fatal prevalence of example, and rooted in us by custom, which is a second nature.

Those born with us, as the indulging them is attended with some pleasure, urge in their defence the unconquerable desire of gratifying the senses: – the lustful man pleads the warmth of his constitution, and the strong allurements of beauty; – the soul of the ambitious triumphs and exults on every degree of power he gains over his fellow-creatures; – the miser thinks himself happy in counting over his bags, and being master of a thing that will purchase all things else; – and the epicure feels no care, no sorrow, while he is emptying the full-charg'd goblet, and pallating the delicious viand.

But what has the blasphemer, – the profane swearer, or the gamester to alledge in his vindication; – these are crimes in which nature has no part, – nor are the senses any way concern'd in them, as they neither excite nor feel any satisfaction in them; – one might therefore be apt to imagine, that men thus guilty sinn'd merely for the sake of sinning; – but I will not allow myself to think that there are many so impudently daring, – a few distinguish'd persons will serve to bring up a mode, – and every one knows that at present an indiscriminate imitation is the reigning folly of the English nation.

These were reflections which occurr'd to me after I came home, as I was about to transcribe the remaining part of my evening's progress out of my precious Tablets: – I had some farther thoughts on the occasion, but as they might seem more proper for the pulpit than to be inserted in a work of this nature, I shall add no more, but proceed to the narrative of that adventure which gave rise to them.

As I was passing in my way home, thro' a street of no very good repute, two persons from a little narrow alley bolted hastily upon me, to the no small danger of my Invisibilityship, if an agility not very common with me had not that instant enabled me to give a sudden spring, by which I avoided the rush I must otherwise have received.

They went on before me; – the night was extremely dark, – neither moon nor stars to assist the visual ray; but by the help of some candles burning in a shop not yet shut up, I distinguish'd that the one was very richly dress'd, and had much the appearance of a man of fashion; and that the other was a fellow I had often seen on many occasions, and whose character I was perfectly acquainted with.

Scarce is there a greater villain to be found in low-life; – I say in low-life, because should any persons in authority, or dignified with titles, which heaven forbid, ever appear in this nation, to deserve such black denominations, their crimes would, like their ranks, be distinguish'd, and superior to those which the rest of mankind have the power to put in practice, and though placed in an orb too high to be reach'd by the just vengeance of their oppress'd fellow-creatures, would doubtless incur what mr. Addison makes Cato prophetically say in relation to Julius Cæsar, on his endeavouring to subvert the old Roman constitution, and become absolute and perpetual Dictator:

> Sure there are bolts in the right hand of Jove,
> Red with uncommon wrath to blast the Man
> Who owes his greatness to his country's ruin.[367]

But to return to my little knave. – The wretch is now call'd mr. Makeplea, – he was formerly servant to a lawyer whom I employ'd in several affairs I had the misfortune to be engag'd in; – living with that gentleman a considerable time he pick'd up some scraps of law, – and all the terms and phrases of that abstruse science by rote, – knew how to take out a writ, set an officer to work, fill up a bail-bond, and procure evidences in a dubious cause. – With this fund he had the impudence, after his master's death, to pretend he had been his clerk, got himself enter'd as an attorney, and has ever since practis'd as such.

His sole business, however, as may be easily supposed, has always been among the very meanest sort of people, fomenting litigious quarrels, and then making them up, after having drain'd the purses on both sides: – tallymen and usurers, either to get in their weekly payments or to justify their extortions, and harlots to revenge themselves by law on those who call'd their honesty in question, were the chief of his clients, – and the best of those with whom he is accustom'd to converse, the greatest part of his acquaintance being bailiffs and their followers.

I could not therefore avoid being very much amaz'd on seeing him in the company I now did; but my wonder soon ceas'd on hearing, as I was close at their heels, the following discourse between them:

Makeplea. It is very lucky, mr. Coaxum, that I happen'd to be at home when you came; – there are some of the profession who would have scrupled to undertake this business; – but for my part, I am always ready to venture every thing to serve my friends.

Coaxum. My dear Makeplea, you never lost any thing, nor ever shall, by our fraternity; – I know there are some who will sneak their heads out of the collar and leave their lawyer in the lurch.

Makeplea. Aye faith, I narrowly escaped the pillory once; – a vile dog, who, after I had procured him three evidences, pretended a panic in his conscience, threw up his cause, and suffer'd himself to be non suited.

Coaxum. You know we scorn such doings; – and I can tell you this will be a pretty good job to you; – we drain'd the fool's pocket of above an hundred pieces before we plaid upon credit, so that there is enough in bank to make you a handsome present for your trouble.

Makeplea. Well, but concerning this reversion, – I hope he has lost enough to give an air of justice; – that is, a *quantum sufficit*[368] for the making over his estate after the decease of his father?

Coaxum. Upwards of a thousand pounds, – besides a gold watch and a fine diamond ring, which he seems to set a high value upon, – the two last Count Cogdy has agreed to sell him again at a great price; – so that altogether the sum will amount to a sufficient purchase of the reversion of an estate of four hundred a year, – especially as the present possessor is not above fifty years of age, and may live a long time. – Besides, we hear the young fellow is going to be married to a woman of fortune, – so that the deeds may be made redeemable; – we do not regard his dirty acres, – the ready rhino[369] is what we want, and he may pay the money out of his wife's fortune, and be clear of us again.

Makeplea. Oh, then it will be a mortgage rather than a sale. – Who are with him?

Coaxum. Only Count Cogdy, Jack Hazard, and Tom Wheadle.

Makeplea. They cannot be witnesses, as I suppose they are parties concern'd.

Coaxum. We are equal sharers in the booty; but the money was lost wholly to the Count. – However, there will be no want of witnesses, – the landlord of the house and his son will set their hands.

These words brought them to a door, which being open'd at the first knock, by one of the most ill-look'd fellows that ever disgraced human nature, they went through a long dark narrow passage into a back parlour, where I accompany'd them, and was witness of a scene somewhat like what I remember to have seen some years ago in a play of mrs. Centlivre's, call'd the Gamester.[370] – Count Cogdy, as he was call'd, sat leaning his arm upon a table in a careless posture; – Jack Hazard was walking backwards and forwards in the room humming an old tune; – a gentleman, whose name I had not yet heard, had thrown himself across two chairs with all the tokens of despair about him; – Tom Wheadle stood near him, and as we came in was endeavouring to give him some consolation, in these terms:

Tom Wheadle. Prithee, dear Clerimont, do not be thus disconcerted, – I have lost as much as you twenty times over, and have as often recover'd it again, – these things will happen to gentlemen that play; – fortune, indeed, has been against you to-night, but may not always be so, – one lucky hit at another time may bring all back.

Clerimont made no answer, nor seem'd to regard what he said, 'till hearing the name of Makeplea, and Count Cogdy beginning to instruct him in the business he was to do, that unfortunate gentleman started up at once from the posture he had been in, and staring somewhat wildly in the face of Makeplea, cry'd to him.

Clerimont. Are you the fiend who is to convey my soul, that is, my estate, into the regions of eternal darkness, whence it can never, – never more return!

Makeplea. What do you mean, sir!

Count Cogdy. The gentleman is only a little out of humour. – Faith, mr. Clerimont, you do not do well to behave in this fashion; – you have lost some money, indeed, – but you have lost it fairly; – I never take an advantage of any man, and shall be ready to give you your revenge at any time.

Jack Hazard. Aye, I will say that for the Count, that he scorns a mean thing.

Count Cogdy. I believe there is not a more unlucky fellow at play in the world than myself, though I have happen'd to win to-night; – yet, as I said before, I am ready to give mr. Clerimont an opportunity of retrieving all he has lost whenever he pleases: – for my part, I would stake all I am worth against a pair of shoe-buckles, rather than any gentleman should think I impos'd upon him.

Coaxum. No, no, – you are above any such thing.

Jack Hazard. We all know that.

Makeplea. Come, come, gentlemen, – this is doing nothing, – all loss of time, and every moment of mine is precious; – there are two noblemen now waiting for me at the Garter tavern; – pray proceed to the business; – let me know how the deeds I have brought with me are to be fill'd up.

Count Cogdy. I will tell you immediately; – but first I must do justice to this gentleman. – Here, sir, are the watch and ring you stak'd, the value of which, you know, is added to the other sums.

Clerimont put the one in his pocket and the other on his finger with a deep sigh, and the Count went on repeating to Makeplea the substance of what he was to write: – the latter, at the end of every article, demanded of Clerimont whether he agreed to it; – to which he sullenly reply'd,

Clerimont. I do; – I see no other remedy.

The lawyer having dispatch'd his part, Clerimont was desir'd to execute, – that is, to sign and seal; – he did both, but with such a trembling hand and visible distraction of mind that my heart bled for him. – In delivering the writings to the Count he said,

Clerimont. There, sir, – I suppose this is all that is requir'd of me, – and I may now depart?

Count Cogdy. No, no, – we must have a bottle and a bird together, to shew we are still good friends.

Jack Hazard. Aye, and each of us a wench too; – I know where there is a covey of as young, pretty, plump partridges as any in Covent-Garden.

Clerimont. Rot your bottle and your bird and your wenches; – I have done with them, and you, and the whole world for ever.

In speaking these words he snatch'd up his sword and hat and was about to go out of the room; but they all laid hold of him, crying at the same time,

Count Cogdy. Nay, Clerimont, you must not leave us in this humour; – upon my soul no man wishes you better than myself.

Tom Wheadle. We are all your friends, – your very good friends.

Jack Hazard. Dear Clerimont, be persuaded.

Coaxum. Faith we must not lose you so.

He made not the least answer to all this, nor seem'd in the least affected with their pretended kindness; but broke from them and ran directly out of the house. – As for me, I had as little inclination as himself to stay in the company of such blood-suckers; indeed, having never seen him before I was curious to know somewhat more of him, and also how he would behave when alone, and at liberty to ruminate on the misfortune he had plunged himself into, – so follow'd his steps with all the speed I could.

It was not very difficult to keep pace with him; for tho' he gain'd ground of me at first, he soon halted and gave me an opportunity of coming up with him. – Never did man traverse the streets with more disorder'd motions, – crossing the way an hundred times, I believe, within the space of half a quarter of a mile, without having the least occasion to do so: – sometimes he would run as if in pursuit of somebody, and sometimes stand quite still and motionless as a statue; and it was well that the darkness of the night befriended him, otherwise whoever had met him would doubtless have taken him to be mad.

In this fashion he went part of the Strand, and turn'd down one of those streets leading to the water side; – he stopp'd about the middle of it at a door, and had his hand upon the knocker, but a sudden thought coming that instant into his head, he left it without making the signal for admittance, and walk'd slowly to the end of the street, where leaning on a little wall that overlooks the river, he remain'd for some minutes in the most thoughtful and contemplative attitude; – then said to himself,

Clerimont. How profound! – how solemn is this silent scene! – inviting to a certain rest from misery and shame! – Here, within the bosom of this friendly element, may all my follies and misfortunes be hid for ever from the talking world!

I fear'd nothing less would ensue, than that I should see him presently attempt to do as his words had hinted; – I therefore drew as near to him as I could, in order to prevent so sad an effect of his despair. – Here I cannot help remarking what I have often reflected upon since; – that if the thing had happen'd as I expected, and Clerimont had found himself snatch'd from his fate by an Invisible hand, he would doubtless have imagined his preservation owing to the interposition of some Supernatural Being, and reported it as a miracle.

But how he would have acted on such an odd occasion is uncertain; for after a pause, and disburthening himself of some few sighs, he started from the posture he had been in, and cry'd,

Clerimont. No, – it must not be; – I have some business still for life, – revenge on the curst cheat, the villain that has undone me. – Love too, demands something from me; – but by what means I shall repay that mighty debt I know not. – Oh Charlotte! – Charlotte! on how lost a wretch hast thou bestow'd thy heart!

These words were utter'd with a groan which seem'd to cleave his breast, and were the last I heard from him at that time: – he turn'd back, and went hastily to the house where he had first stopp'd, the door was open'd on his knocking, and too suddenly shut again for me to have enter'd with him if I had intended to do so; but the variety of accidents presented to me in this evening's ramble had already sufficiently fill'd my head, and made me glad to retire to my repose.

CHAP. IV.

Relates some passages which, if the Author is not very much mistaken in his conjectures, will draw sighs of compassion from many a tender heart of both sexes.

THE next morning, in running over in my mind the detail of the transactions of the evening before, the vexation I had receiv'd on the score of Betty Canning very much subsided, and I look'd upon the whole thing as below a serious consideration; – I could not help, indeed, retaining some concern that the people of England should be so infatuated as to suffer their thoughts to be led astray and alienated from affairs of the greatest consequence by such an idle story; but as I doubted not but that the imposition she had been guilty of would be detected, though her abettors might perhaps find means to screen her person from the punishment, I became more easy, and resolved to banish as much as possible all remembrance of it.

But my ideas were widely different in regard to poor Clerimont; – as much a stranger as he was to me I was convinced, by what I had seen and heard, that as he had no stock of ready money to prevent the mortgage he had made of his reversion,[371] so I was equally assured, by his despair, that he had no visible means of raising a sum sufficient to redeem it. – His calling on the name of Charlotte with so much vehemence made me also not doubt but that he had some tender attachment, which he fear'd would be broke through by what he had done.

Though I know no vice for which I have a more real contempt than the love of gaming, yet the age of this gentleman, which could not exceed above two or three and twenty, seem'd to me a very moving plea in his behalf, and the graces of his mein and aspect so much interested me in his favour, that I less blamed his inadvertency than compassionated the misfortune it had brought him into.

In fine, – his person and his sufferings had made a very strong impression on me; – he was the first object of my waking thoughts, and my impatience to be better acquainted with his circumstances obliged me to leave my bed some hours before the time in which I was accustomed to do so; – I rose in a hurry, – transcribed what I have been relating, and got the dialogues expunged from my Tablets by the pure fingers of my little Virgin, – then hasted to the house where I had seen Clerimont enter the night before, and which, by the help of some lamps in the street, I had taken sufficient notice of to be able to know again.

The door was luckily open when I came to it; – a servant-maid, who seem'd to have more inclination to hold a gossip's tale than to do the business she was hired for, stood leaning with both her hands upon her mop, very earnest in discourse with one of her own occupation in the neighbourhood; – a few words serv'd to convince me that these wenches were descanting on the affairs of the families they lived in, which, as I was not at present in a humour to pry into, I staid not to hear what was said, but went directly into the house, and up stairs, supposing Clerimont might be lodg'd in the first floor.

I was not deceived, – I found him writing at his buroe in the dining-room, – a letter lay by him directed to Count Cogdy; – this was folded and ready for sealing, so it was not in my power to examine the contents; but his pen, on my entrance, was employ'd on another, which, looking over his shoulder, I saw was dictated in the following terms:

To miss CHARLOTTE ******.

My only dear, and for ever dear CHARLOTTE,

A thousand heart-rending sighs, – a thousand pangs, more terrible than any death can inflict, accompany every syllable of this distracted epistle! – I foresee the anguish it will give you, and feel all the weight of yours added to my own. – Oh, Charlotte! I must see you no more! – that love so long cemented by the utmost proofs of mutual tenderness, and so near being fulfilled in a happy union, must be now broke off at once, – dissolved for ever! – I have renounced all claim to every future good, and justly incurr'd the fate that now attends me! a few short hours will inform you, that I either do not exist at at all, or exist only to be a vagrant! – a wretched exile from father, country, friends, and you more dear than all!

In fine, – my Charlotte, such is the sad necessity to which I have reduced myself, as compels me to do a thing which nature most abhors; – I go this very morning either to kill or to be kill'd, – which of these two shall happen is in the hand of heaven; – each equally tears me from every earthly comfort. – I chose to acquaint you previously with this accident, to the end you may be the less surprised when you shall hear it from the mouth of others. – I can say no more. – Farewel, thou loveliest, best, and dearest of thy sex. – Hate not the memory of

The undone

CLERIMONT.

P.S. As I have render'd myself unworthy of preserving any marks of your affection, I return the ring with which you blest my finger in our happier days. – Accept once more my last adieu; – may endless blessings wait you, superior, if possible, to my woes.

This unhappy gentleman dissembled not in the lines he wrote, – his heart now labour'd with agonies greater than could be express'd with words, and shew'd themselves in every look and gesture.

After having carefully inclosed the ring, and put both that and the letter under a cover, he order'd a chairman to be call'd, and delivering to him both these dispatches, and telling him where they were to be carried, he proceeded to give some farther instructions:

Clerimont. This, to miss Charlotte, you are to leave with her servant, with orders to give it to her lady when she is stirring: – this to Count Cogdy requires an immediate answer, which you must wait for.

The fellow, having assured him that he would be punctual in obeying his commands, went on his errand, and Clerimont continued walking backwards and forwards in the room with a motion extremely discomposed, – then threw himself down on a settee, and presently seem'd buried, as it were, in a profound resvery.

I am pretty certain it was a full half-hour before he exchang'd this fix'd and death-like position for one in a quite contrary extreme; – his looks and gestures now, methought, had somewhat like frantic in them; – he beat his head against the wainscoat, – stamp'd, – and ever and anon burst into the most vehement exclamations, – some of which are these:

Clerimont. How unhappy a creature is man! – the very reason we are so proud of makes us miserable! – the brutes, equally void of passions as of sorrow, neither feel torments here nor dread a future hell! – What will poor Charlotte say on reading of my letter! – How will my father support the story of my fate when it shall reach his ears! – Wretch! wretch that I am, – born to be a curse to all who love me!

The return of the chairman brought him a little to his senses, and he demanded hastily whether he had got an answer from Count Cogdy; – to which the man reply'd,

Chairman. No, sir; – I went there first, but the people of the house told me he was not stirring, nor they believed would be for a great while, so I went on to madam Charlotte's, and left the letter with her maid, as your honour bid me; but I had not got above half the street before her footboy ran after me and said his lady would speak to me, on which I went back with him.

Clerimont. Charlotte already up, – that's strange. – What did she say to you?

Chairman. Sir, she only ask'd where the gentleman was that sent the letter by me, and whether you were alone; – I told her you were at home, and that there was no body with you that I saw; – she said it was very well, and I came away, went again to the Count's, and waited there 'till his own man told me that his master had not been in bed above two hours, and he was sure would not rise 'till twelve or one o'Clock at soonest; said I might leave the letter, and come about that time for an answer; – now as I did not know whether that would be proper, I thought best to bring it back.

Clerimont. You did well; – I shall see him myself.

On this the Chairman laid down the letter on the table, and finding Clerimont had no farther commands for him withdrew. – Clerimont then fell into a second pause, but it lasted not long, and he cry'd out,

Clerimont. Yes, – I will go, – and perhaps 'tis better that he did not see my billet; – he might have found some way to evade the challenge I sent him; but I shall now surprize and force him to accept it.

While he was speaking he stepp'd to the closet and brought out a pair of pocket pistols, with some ammunition to load them with; – he was just beginning to perform that work when the maid of the house came up and told him a lady desir'd to speak with him. – Clerimont turn'd hastily about, but before he had time to speak his fair guest was in the room. – Charlotte, for it was she herself, was very lovely, though extremely disorder'd both in her dress and looks. – On finding how Clerimont was employ'd she thus accosted him:

Charlotte. Oh, Clerimont! – Clerimont! – what means that cruel letter you just now sent me! – Wherefore these dreadful preparations! – tell me, – this instant tell me, or I shall die with apprehension!

Clerimont. Ah, Charlotte! never 'till now unwelcome to my sight, – why in this fatal moment dost thou set before me that angelic form, which serves but to remind me more of the heaven I have lost!

Charlotte. Shock not my soul with this despair, yet cruelly conceal from me the cause! – I have a right to be made the partner of your griefs as well as joys; – speak then, I conjure you, – let me know all!

Clerimont. I cannot!

Charlotte. You love me not if you hide ought from me! – the worst of evils could not give me half the pain as this uncertainty! – Clear then the tempest on your brow, – compose your mind, – remove those murd'rous instruments from my sight, and, – Ha! – what's here!

In pointing towards the pistols she saw the letter directed to Count Cogdy, which she hastily snatch'd up, and went on, saying,

Charlotte. A letter to that infamous villain Count Cogdy! – ah, then I guess what has happen'd, – some cursed gaming quarrel! – Clerimont, I must read this letter.

Clerimont. You may, – it will in part reveal what my tongue has not the power to utter.

Ever since my coming into the room I had been extremely impatient to see the contents of this billet, – so while the lady, with a trembling hand, was breaking open the seal, I slipp'd behind her, and read, at the same time she did, these lines:

To Count COGDY.

SIR,

I REMEMBER that in the midst of my confusion last night you offer'd to give me my revenge whenever I should demand it, which I now do, and expect you will meet me within an hour in the long field behind the bason in Mary-le-bon,[372] arm'd with sword and pistol; for it is not with cards or dice we now must try our skill: – you have left me nothing but my life to lose, and I am impatient 'till I stake it against yours; – come without a second, for I know no gentleman whom I would demean so far as to engage him with any of your infamous associates: – if you refuse to comply with this summons, which does you too much honour, you may depend that the first time I see you, in what place soever it be, I shall make you an example to all scoundrels, cheats, and cowards. – So no more at present from

CLERIMONT.

P.S. Send your answer by the bearer.

Charlotte. Then you would fight! would hazard a life so precious to me, only in revenge for being defrauded of a paultry sum! – Pray how much have you lost?

Clerimont. My all.

Charlotte. Be more explicit.

He then related to her all the particulars of his misfortune, which, as the reader is already acquainted with, would be needless to repeat. – When he had given over speaking, Charlotte, with the greatest serenity and sweetness, said to him,

Charlotte. And is this all that has disconcerted you in so terrible a manner?

Clerimont. What means my Charlotte! – Am I not a beggar, – irrecoverably a beggar!

Charlotte. How can that be, – when you say the writings will be return'd to you on payment of a thousand pounds? and am not I in possession of eight times that sum, which, with myself, you are shortly to be master of?

Clerimont. Plunder my Charlotte! – no, forbid it honour, justice, love! – first let me perish!

Charlotte. Be not so rash; – you must, – you shall accept it.

Clerimont. Charming generous creature! – could I abuse such goodness, I were a villain, meaner, viler far than he that has undone me!

Charlotte. Indeed I will not be denied; and if you persist in this obstinacy, will go myself in person, pay the money and redeem the obligation.

Clerimont. Oh speak not! – think not of such a thing, unless you wish to see me turn against myself one of those weapons I intended for my adversary!

Charlotte. Hold, Clerimont, – forbear to fright me thus! – Just as you spoke a sudden thought started into my head as if there were a way to rid you of this incumbrance without any expence either to yourself or me.

Clerimont. How! – by what miracle!

Charlotte. The project is not yet quite fashion'd in my brain; – but you must come with me to my lodgings, for I dare not trust you with yourself; – as we go perhaps I may be able to bring my scheme to more perfection.

Clerimont. Oh, Charlotte, thy softness quite unmans me!

Charlotte. No 'tis your own despair unmans you; – let me prevail on you to give only some respite to these horrible ideas.

Clerimont. Well, you must be obey'd, – I will defer the execution of my intentions 'till another day.

Charlotte. That's kind.

Charlotte seem'd transported at having won thus far upon him, and a coach being call'd they both went into it; – I listen'd to the directions given where to drive, and eager to know what turn this affair would take, follow'd on foot as fast as I was able.

CHAP. V.

May possibly become the subject of some future Comedy, as there is nothing in
the story that can be objected to by the Licence-Office.

AMONG all the indefatigable enquiries I had so long been making after things
intended to be kept secret, never had my curiosity met with a greater disappointment than it did at the time I am speaking of; – I arriv'd at the house where
Charlotte lodg'd the very moment that the coach which brought that lady and
her lover thither was discharg'd and driving off, and had the mortification to see
the door shut when I was not at the distance of above ten paces from it.

Every present minute however flattering me with the hopes that the succeeding ones would be more successful, I waited, tho' I cannot say with much
patience, the whole time for the space of about two hours, no one having any
occasion, I suppose, either to go out or in; – at last a friendly baker knock'd at
the door, which being open'd, I took the opportunity to slip in while he deliver'd
a loaf of bread to the servant of the house.

I went up stairs, and found the persons I sought for in the dining-room; – but
here, alas, I was a second time disappointed, – the grand consultation between
them was over before my entrance, and what I heard after I came in could not
make me able to form any judgment of the subject they had been upon; – I could
only know that something of great moment had been concluded, as the reader
will easily perceive by the following short dialogue:

Charlotte. You cannot imagine how much you have oblig'd me by this ready
concession; – but I will not detain you lest the villain should be gone out. –
Remember to fix the appointment at seven, or between seven and eight this
evening.

Clerimont. Yes, yes.

Charlotte. By that time I shall be able to get every thing in order, – and you
will see I shall play my part as well as the best actress of them all, – do you only
take care that no unguarded look or word gives the Count any room to suspect
you are less in good humour than you pretend to be.

Clerimont. Fear not, – I shall be cautious not to spoil so good a plot by my
ill performance.

Charlotte. If it succeeds, as I have not the least doubt but it will, the story will
be a subject of mirth for us as lasting as our lives.

Clerimont. And as lasting a subject for my admiration of the wit and contrivance of my dear, dear Charlotte.

Charlotte. Well, well, – defer your encomiums till a more seasonable opportunity; – I long, methinks, to have this business over, and it is high time for you
to begin to set the first wheel of our machine in motion.

Clerimont. I am going. – Adieu, my love.

He accompanied these words with a very tender and passionate salute, then left the room; – tho' I easily perceived that Charlotte had somewhat of great importance to transact in this affair, yet as I could not be in two places at once, I chose to follow Clerimont.

He went directly to the Lodgings of Count Cogdy, and on asking if he were at home was shew'd into a handsome parlour, where, after waiting about a minute and a half, the Count's servant came to him, and said his master had not been long out of bed, and was not quite dress'd, but desir'd he would walk up; – which he did, with his Invisible attendant close behind him.

The Count no sooner saw him enter than he ran to embrace him with a French complaisance, saying at the same time,

Count Cogdy. Dear Clerimont, I am glad to see you.

Clerimont. My dear Count, a lucky morning to you. – I behav'd somewhat oddly last night, and could not be easy 'till I came and ask'd your pardon.

Count Cogdy. Oh, sir, you have it, you have it; – I thought no more of it; – I know 'tis natural for a gentleman to be a little out of humour at first losing his money.

Clerimont. But I was less excusable than you imagine; – for to confess the truth, I had in Bank-bills upwards of two thousand pounds lying in my buroe at home, – so was under no necessity either of playing upon tick or of troubling a lawyer to mortgage the reversion of my estate.

Count Cogdy. Is it possible! – Are you in earnest!

Clerimont. To convince you I am so you shall have the testimony of your own eyes; – see here, Count, – and here.

In speaking this he took out of his pocket-book several bills to the amount of the sum he had mention'd; – the Count stretch'd his eyes broad open, – look'd at the bills, – seem'd much surprised, and said,

Count Cogdy. These are Bank-bills, indeed!

Clerimont. Aye, – I can turn them into ready specie at any banker's in town.

Count Cogdy. Well, I cannot help wondering how a man who had two thousand pounds by him could suffer himself to be disconcerted at the loss of one.

Clerimont. Hang it, – it was not the loss of the money that vex'd me; – but I had got the hyppo,[373] and that damn'd hyppo makes one affront one's best friends.

Count Cogdy. So then I suppose you will redeem your mortgage?

Clerimont. Time enough for that, – But now I think on it, you offer'd me my revenge, and I'll e'en try my chance once more.

Count Cogdy. As how?

Clerimont. Why stake one of these thousands against my mortgage; – so either win the horse or lose the saddle.

Count Cogdy. With all my heart, – whenever you please.

Clerimont. Let it be to-night then.

Count Cogdy. Agreed. – Will you stay and dine with me?

Clerimont. I am engag'd with a young fellow just come to town, and to the possession of a great estate; but I will meet you at night and bring him with me if I can.

Count Cogdy. Do; – I shall be glad of his acquaintance.

Clerimont. We knew one another in the country, he will go any where with me. – But hark'ye, Count, I don't like that house we were in last night, – every thing in it, methinks, has the face of meaness, poverty, and ill-luck; – my young spark is vastly nice, and will be apt to turn up his nose at it; – can't you think of a more agreeable place?

Count Cogdy. I know of several: – the only reason that makes me chuse to go thither so often is because I think it the most safe; – this cursed act of parliament has laid such restriction on us who love play,[374] that it is not every where we dare venture to indulge ourselves in that diversion.

Clerimont. What objection have you to Mixum's, in ***** street?

Count Cogdy. 'Tis a good house, and excellent accommodation. – But don't you know that it was search'd three or four nights ago by a whole posse of constables?

Clerimont. Yes, – but they found nothing of what they came to look for, – therefore the more secure at present, as they will scarce come again in haste.

Count Cogdy. Well then we will meet there if you please. – At what hour?

Clerimont. Seven, or a little after, – if it suits you.

Count Cogdy. Extremely well; – then we shall have the whole evening before us.

He was about to take his leave, and had rose up for that purpose, when Tom Wheadle, Jack Hazard and Coaxum came all together into the room; – they seem'd a little surpriz'd at seeing him there, but saluted him with their usual familiarity.

Jack Hazard. Hah! – dear Clerimont, good morning to you.

Tom Wheadle. Now you look like yourself again; – you were quite another man last night.

Coaxum. Aye faith, – you must expect to be well roasted.

Clerimont. I know I deserve it; but you must defer your sarcasms 'till night; for I am in great haste at present, – so, gentlemen, your servant.

He was going out of the room with these words; but just as he came to the door he turn'd back and said to Count Cogdy,

Clerimont. Be sure, Count, not to forget to bring the writings with you.

Count Cogdy. No, no, – they have never been out of my pocket since you deliver'd them to me last night.

There pass'd no more between them, – Clerimont went hastily down stairs, and I gladly would have follow'd him, but Jack Hazard and Tom Wheadle happen'd to stand between the door and the corner where I had unluckily posted myself, so that it was impossible for me to remove my quarters without running a very great risque of being felt either by the one or the other.

During the short time I was compell'd to stay I heard the following conversation, which I would not trouble my readers with the repetition of, but to shew what monsters of mankind these degenerate wretches are who get their livelihood by gaming.

Coaxum. What does he mean by writings? – sure he is not going to redeem his mortgage!

Count Cogdy. No; but he is going to send a thousand, or 'tis likely two thousand pounds after it. – We have made an appointment to play again tonight.

Jack Hazard. What upon tick?

Tom Wheadle. Phoo, – that is doing of nothing, – the fool has no more estates in reversion to make over.

Count Cogdy. You cannot imagine me so weak as to lose my time with a fellow that has no money nor effects; – no, no, I always go upon good grounds. – I tell you he has two thousand pounds in Bank-bills, – he shew'd them to me.

Jack Hazard. How did he come by them?

Count Cogdy. 'Tis no matter to us how he came by them, we are sure of making them ours before we sleep.

Tom Wheadle. They must certainly be bills his father has intrusted him with, to buy stock either for himself or some of his friends in the country; – the young fellow will hang himself to-morrow, when he reflects on what he has done.

Jack Hazard. Let him hang himself when we have got all he has to lose.

Count Cogdy. Aye, aye, – 'tis best for him and us too that he should put himself out of the way. – But I can tell you better news than this, – he brings a rich young heir with him, one that knows nothing of the world, – a mere sap, – a greenhorn; – there will be fleecing, my boys!

Just as the Count had done speaking some little noise in the street made them all run to the windows, by which means I got the so-much wish'd for opportunity of escaping from my confinement.

When I found myself at liberty I began to consider not only on what I had seen and heard, but also on what I had not seen nor heard; – I was still as much in the dark as ever as to Charlotte's contrivance, and could not keep myself from fretting at the many disappointments I had met with on that account; – I was doom'd, however, to receive yet one more.

Though I doubted not but when the gamesters met the whole would be laid open to me, yet the time seem'd too tedious for my impatience, – I wanted to know the business of the plot before I saw it acted, and set myself to think on the most probable means to accomplish my designs, – accordingly I went to the lodgings of Charlotte, hoping to find Clerimont there, and discover something farther by the discourse they would have together; but to my great mortification perceived the rooms quite empty, excepting a little lap-dog lying on a cushion before the fire.

I had now no other resource than to go home to dinner, which I did, and after having got my Tablets made ready to receive a new impression, diverted myself in the best manner I could 'till the hour arriv'd which enabled me to explore what at present appear'd so mysterious to me.

CHAP. VI.

Will put a final period to the suspense of my readers, in relation to Clerimont and Charlotte.

As precious a thing as time is, and as much as I always knew the real value of it, the hours, methought, moved slowly on 'till the clock struck seven, and told me that I might now hope for the full eclaircisement of an adventure I had already taken so much fruitless pains to explore.

Pretty secure, however, that I should not lose my labour any more on this occasion, I went with great glee and jollity of mind to the house of mr. Mixum, – Count Cogdy and his three Associates came presently after, and were shew'd into the best room, where I accompanied them. – On their calling for wine Mixum came up with it himself to pay his compliments, as not having seen them for a considerable time, and there ensued some discourse concerning the search-warrant that had been granted against the house, – the manner in which those persons who were there had made their escape from the officers, and such like affairs, which not being at all material to my purpose I not regarded, nor spread my Tablets to receive.

Within about half an hour Clerimont and his young friend appear'd; – the first sight of the latter extremely struck me, – I thought I had somewhere seen that face, but when or where, or on what occasion, I could not presently recollect, and it was some minutes before I knew this seeming beau for a real belle; – in fine, that it was no other than Charlotte herself:[375] – she was, indeed, so artfully disguised in all points, that a person much better acquainted with her features might have been deceived; – her cheeks, which had naturally no more red in them than was necessary to preserve her complexion from the character of a dead paleness, were now, by the help of Carmine or Portugal paste, of a high ruddy colour; – her eye-brows, which were of a fine light brown, were now black as jet; and that sweet and modest air, so becoming in the amiable Charlotte, converted into one all bold and rakish.

Clerimont, with a well-dissembled gaiety in his voice and countenance, presented her to the company, telling them he had taken the liberty to introduce a friend, whose conversation he doubted not but would be agreeable to them. – They received her with the greatest politeness and good breeding; – for I must here observe, that tho' these men, either thro' the calamities of the times or their own mismanagement and ill conduct, were reduced to the wretched course they now took for subsistence, they had all of them been endow'd with a liberal education, and knew how to behave like persons of real honour and fashion whenever they found it suitable to their interest to do so.

The glass went round two or three times while they talk'd only on ordinary matters; but our fair Amazon, being impatient, I suppose, to put the finishing stroke to the stratagem she had form'd, started up on a sudden, and said,

Charlotte. Well but, gentlemen, how are we to pass the evening, – I hope in somewhat more agreeable than mere chit-chat? – Clerimont talk'd of play, and I see you have implements ready.

Count Cogdy. Sir, we amuse ourselves that way sometimes, – and if you chuse it shall be ready to oblige you.

Charlotte. Oh by all means; – I love play extravagantly, – the music of a dice-box is to me beyond all Handel's operas and oratorios; – here is more real harmony than in the spheres themselves, and I could dance eternally to the sound.

In speaking these last words she snatch'd up a dice-box, and began to rattle it with all her force; – then sung this catch:

> Away with dull cares,
> That bring on grey hairs,
> Let them fleet with the day,
> And wine, women, and play,
> With jovial delights,
> Engross all our nights.[376]

While the stranger appear'd thus unattentive to every thing, Jack Hazard, who sat next to Coaxum, whisper'd to him,

Jack Hazard. This is a fine sprightly spark; but I fancy we shall make him grow somewhat more grave before we have done with him.

Coaxum. I wonder what could induce Clerimont to bring him, after having lost so much us.

Jack Hazard. Oh, take it for a rule, – when a man begins to find himself undone, he is willing to bring all his acquaintance into the same condition.

They had time for no more, – Charlotte addressing herself to them all in general, said,

Charlotte. Come, gentlemen, – which of you will engage me, – I have some loose pieces in my pocket, which I am ready to throw away, if chance should so determine?

Jack Hazard. Then, sir, I am your man, if you think fit; – for I know the Count has made an agreement to play with Clerimont on a very particular occasion.

Charlotte. Then, sir, I will content myself a while with being a by-stander.

Jack Hazard. You need not, sir, – you see here are more tables than one.

Charlotte. Aye; but I chuse to bet on my friend's side.

Jack Hazard. Nay, as you please for that; – we shall any of us be ready to take you up.

The Count and Clerimont being now in an attitude to play, and the writings laid down on the one side and a thousand pound Bank-bill on the other, Charlotte cry'd out,

Charlotte. What! – paper against parchment! – these are the oddest stakes I ever saw. – Yours, Clerimont, I think, is a thousand pounds?

Count Cogdy. I assure, you, sir, that mine is the full equivalent.

Charlotte. I believe so; – but before you begin you must give me leave to speak a word or two.

Count Cogdy. As many as you please, sir.

Charlotte. It is only this: – you must lose, Count.

Count Cogdy. Must lose, sir!

Charlotte. Aye, sir, must lose.

Count Cogdy. That, sir, will happen as fortune shall decree.

Charlotte. Sir, I stand in the place of fortune, and tell you that you must lose those writings to Clerimont.

Jack Hazard. What means all this!

Count Cogdy. I do not understand you, sir.

Charlotte. I will speak plainer; – your false dice will be of no service to you at this time; – you must willingly return to Clerimont that deed of reversion, which you drew him in to sign as a security for money you had basely cheated him of; – I say willingly, – for if you do not I am come prepar'd with means to force you to it.

Count Cogdy. Sir, I scorn both your words and threats; – I never cheated any man, nor will part with what chance has bestow'd upon me.

Jack Hazard. 'Sdeath, – shall we be bullied by such a prig!

Charlotte. None of your big words, – I have that will silence you; – see here; – the copy of a warrant from Justice Ferrit, to apprehend and bring before him the bodies of George Van Hellmock, alias Count Cogdy, – John Hazard, – Thomas Wheadle, – and William Coaxum; – the original of this is in the hands of persons who, on the least stamp of my foot, will come up and put it in execution.

The gamesters now look'd on each other with all the marks of consternation; but before they had time to make any reply to what Charlotte had said, Mixum, all pale and trembling, came running into the room, and said,

Mixum. Oh, gentlemen, – we are all undone! – three or four constables are at the door, – one of my drawers saw them as he went out to carry a pint of wine to a neighbour's house; and there is a young man below too, who I dare say is a spy, for he does not stay in the room, but walks backwards and forwards in the entry, and looks at every body as they pass by; – so that there is no escaping either one way or other.

Charlotte. He tells you truth; – the person he speaks of is planted there by me, and on my giving the signal will call in his mirmidons; – so that you have nothing for it but to deliver the writings quietly to Clerimont; – if you do this I will instantly go down and send away the officers, under pretence that the information was wrong, and that no gamesters are here.

Count Cogdy. Confusion! – What is to be done!

Jack Hazard. 'Sdeath, Count! – do not part with the writings! – we'll fight our way through them!

Charlotte. Nay then I give the signal.

She advanced towards the door with these words; but Mixum threw himself between, and with the most pity-moving gesture said,

Mixum. Hold, sir, I beseech you! – consider I never offended you! – do not ruin me and my house for ever!

Clerimont. Oh, you will be provided with lodgings in Bridewell, and fare no worse than these worthy gentlemen here, your customers.

Count Cogdy. Well, I did not think mr. Clerimont would have turn'd informer.

Clerimont. Nor did I think I had associated myself with common sharpers, cheats and villains, 'till last night convinced me of it.

Charlotte. These altercations are only loss of time, – the officers will be impatient; – speak, Count, – resolve at once; – Shall I dismiss, or call them to the exercise of their function.

Count Cogdy. Hell and the devil! – What say you, gentlemen?

Tom Wheadle. E'en give up the writings, and the devil go with them.

Coaxum. Aye, aye, give them up.

Jack Hazard. Since there is no remedy I give my vote.

Count Cogdy. Nothing vexes me so much as to be thus outwitted, gull'd, trick'd. – There, mr. Clerimont, take back your mortgage; – but I must tell you, sir, that you have not acted like a gentleman.

Clerimont. I threw off the gentleman when I condescended to play in such company; – a gamester is the lowest and most infamous of all characters; nay the most dangerous too; worse even than a highway robber, – he takes but part, – your plunder, without remorse, the whole fortune of him whom you decoy into your snares; – nor can there be any excuse from your necessities, while we have so numerous a fleet and standing army, which are continually wanting recruits, and refuse none who have health and vigour.

Count Cogdy. Sir, you have got what you wanted, – so pray keep your remonstrances to yourself.

Charlotte. Aye, aye, – advice is lost on such harden'd profligates. – Come, let us go.

Clerimont. I attend you.

Neither Clerimont nor his fair champion said any more, but went directly out of the room; – a volley of curses from the mouths of all these miscreants pursued their steps. – I had no inclination to stay where I was; but just as I pass'd the door I heard Jack Hazard, who was the most violent of the four, say to his companions,

Jack Hazard. It is that saucy pert young Coxcomb that has spirited up Clerimont to do all this; but if ever I meet him in a convenient place I'll pink him, – I'll make a loop-hole in his flesh big enough to let out twenty such puny souls.

I could not forbear laughing within myself at this menace, which, though it shew'd the villainous disposition of the wretch who spoke it, I knew was impossible ever to reach the person it was levell'd against.

The amiable and witty Charlotte kept her promise, and on her coming down stairs gave orders to the young man who waited her commands to send away the constables, – after which she took coach with her lover, attended with as many blessings and good wishes from Mixum as she had been loaded with curses from those above.

As I could expect no more from this adventure than the retributions of Clerimont to his beloved Charlotte for the happy deliverance she had given him from destruction, and which I could easily conceive without hearing, I return'd to my own apartment, in order to get my Tablets made ready for the acquisition of some new discovery.

I must not however, take leave of these lovers without letting the public know that a marriage between them, which had some time before been agreed upon, is now consummated, and that Clerimont, sincerely touch'd with the danger he has escaped, has made a firm resolution never to play but for very small sums, and for those only with persons whose honour and integrity he is well assur'd of.

As for the Gamesters, they still continue to infest this great town, like Satan watching to devour all the prey they can get into their clutches; – if this little narrative may warn any one person to avoid the snare, the pains I have taken to explain it will be well rewarded.

CHAP. VII.

*This the Author has calculated chiefly for the speculation of the serious part of
his readers, and is short enough to be easily pass'd over by the more gay and
unattentive.*

I sometimes make one among the number of visitors to a good old lady, who
being past the enjoyment of all the pleasures of life, except those of conversation,
loves company and keeps a great deal, as her chearful and entertaining manner of
behaviour renders her agreeable even to the youth of both sexes.

It was at her house I first saw mr. Wary, a gentleman of an ancient family, an
affluent fortune, and an extreme good character; but has a certain peculiarity of
humour which deprives him of some part of that respect he could not fail otherwise of attracting from as many as know him.

Whether it be owing to an over diffidence of himself, or of others, it is hard
to determine; that it seems to me that there is a mixture of both in his composition; for he goes not about the most minute and insignificant affair in life,
even to the buying a suit of cloaths, without consulting the whole round of his
acquaintance, never depending on his own judgment, or on the opinion of any
one friend whatsoever; but constantly adhering to this maxim: – that in a multitude of counsellors there is wisdom.

His age at this time does not exceed forty, he has been a widower upwards of
twelve years, yet never had the courage to venture on a second marriage, because
he could find no woman whom every body approv'd of: – he is the father of
one son, a very promising youth, now about thirteen, of whom he is extremely
tender, and so very careful of his education that he would never trust him at any
public school, and has him instructed at home in every thing he thinks necessary he should learn; but it frequently happens that a great deal of time is lost in
providing tutors who seem to him every way qualified for the trust to be reposed
in them.

There was nothing in the character of this gentleman that excited my curiosity to know any thing farther of him than what I did; – indeed I could hope to
make no discoveries worthy of my Invisible inspection, in the family of a person
who had neither wife nor daughter, was not distinguish'd for any particular vice
or virtue, never intermeddled in public affairs, saw little company, and lived in a
very retir'd manner; – therefore I never had a thought of visiting him.

But it often happens that we are sway'd by an unaccountable impulse to
do things which have no meaning in them, nor afford the least prospect either
of pleasure or advantage; and it was in one of these sudden starts that I found
myself hurried into his house, seeing the door open as I casually pass'd through
the street where he lives.

I found him sitting in an easy-chair in his back parlour, with a letter in his hand; but having just finish'd the reading of it as I came in, I had not the opportunity at that time of seeing what it contain'd; – a moment after a servant enter'd, and told him mr. Seewell was come to wait on him, – on which he order'd him to be introduced, and as soon as he was so, said to him,

Mr. Wary. Oh, my good friend mr. Seewell, – you are the most welcome man alive; – I was just wishing for you.

Mr. Seewell. I am glad then I came so opportunely. – But pray on what account am I so happy?

Mr. Wary. Sit down and I will tell you. – You must know I am desirous my son should have a little insight of some branches of the mathematics, and accordingly have been laying out a good while for a proper person to instruct him;[377] – at last I heard of one who they say has very great abilities, and is of a sober character.

Mr. Seewell. That was lucky.

Mr. Wary. Aye, but you have not heard all. – The very next day after I had agreed with him, happening to mention his name to an acquaintance of mine, I was inform'd that he is a Papist, – born and bred a Papist; – on which I presently sent to desire the person who recommended him, to let him know he need not give himself the trouble to come to my house, and also to give him the reasons that induced me to forbid him; for, mr. Seewell, I would rather have my son kept in ignorance all his life, than have his principles tainted with Popery and Jacobitism.

Mr. Seewell. You are very much in the right.

Mr. Wary. Aye, I think I am; – yet for all that I am strangely puzzled, and divided, as it were, in my thoughts; – he sent me a letter this morning, – you shall read it, and then give me your advice what to do.

Mr. Seewell. The best I can you may command.

Mr. Wary then put the letter into his hands, which I read at the same time he did, and found it contained these lines:

To Lemuel Wary, Esq;

Sir,

I cannot forbear being extremely shock'd at the disappointment I have received; but am much more surprised at the reasons you assign for thinking me unworthy the honour of instructing your son in a science which has not the least connexion either with religion or politics. – I shall never be ashamed to own myself a member of the Church of Rome; but am as far from being a Jacobite as you or any one can be, and think it easy to convince you, that my being the one is a sufficient proof that I cannot be the other.

I know that weak minds are strangely carry'd away by mere words; but they cannot long have any influence with persons of understanding; – you, sir, need but give yourself the trouble of a few moments consideration to see plainly how utterly inconsistent it is with the interest of a true Roman Catholic to wish the Pretender, or any of his race, should ever be seated on the throne of these kingdoms.

What, sir, could we hope for from a person who could not favour us, if he were so inclined, without endangering himself; – a person, who, tho' bred in the principles of the Church of Rome, and still professes to adhere to them, yet put his eldest son under the tuition of three of the most zealous enemies of our religion? – I need not tell you I mean the lords Dunbar and Inverness, both of the Kirk of Scotland, and Lascelles, an eminent divine of the Church of England.[378] – What, I say, could we expect, were a revolution ever to happen in favour of that family, which Heaven forbid, but to be deprived of all those privileges the goodness of his present Majesty permits us the enjoyment of, and to be discountenanced even more than the worst of all those numerous sectaries which divide the nation?

Please, sir, to cast a short retrospect on the transactions of the late rebellion; – Were not the heads of Clans, and those of the Nobles who listed under the banner of the young Pretender in Scotland all protestants, the duke of Perth[379] excepted? – Were not those few whom he pick'd up in England Protestants, sons of the Reformation, and most of them of the establish'd Church? – Those of our persuasion neither abetted or any way assisted the Adventurer's undertaking; and sure if our hearts had been affected to his cause, our hands would not have been inactive, our number is not so inconsiderable as not to have done some service; and then, if ever, was the time to have shew'd ourselves; – but our peaceful behaviour at that time ought, methinks, to be a sufficient testimony to the whole world how little we deserve to be stigmatised with the appellation of Jacobites.

Thus much, sir, in relation to my politics; – and as to the other part of your objection, – I do assure you, upon the word of a christian and a man of honour, that I shall never mingle matters of religion in my discourse with any of my pupils.

If, after this declaration, you think me worthy of attending your son, the best of my endeavours shall not be wanting to instruct him in the science

I profess to teach, and in all other things to prove that I am,

With the greatest respect,

SIR,

Your most obedient, and

Humble servant,

P. NEUTER.

Mr. Wary. Well, sir, what do you think of this epistle? – Pray give me your opinion candidly.

Mr. Seewell. Why really, mr. Wary, there are some things in it which cannot be denied; yet I would not advise you, by any means, to put him over your son.

Mr. Wary. Not if I am convinced he is no Jacobite?

Mr. Seewell. What then; – you are convinced he is a Papist, and being such, cannot cordially wish well to any who are Protestants; – the very principles of his uncharitable religion forbid that he should do so; – the Church of Rome looks on what they call the Northern Heresy in a worse light than Paganism; – and though, as he says, they may not desire a change of government in favour of the Pretender, yet they would doubtless be glad to see, not only these kingdoms, but all those where the Reformation has taken place, involved in blood, anarchy and confusion.

Mr. Wary. It is very true, indeed, mr. Seewell; – they have always shewn a spirit of persecution in them.

Mr. Seewell. Hating us as they do, it would be the greatest weakness to imagine they would sincerely contribute any thing towards our making a shining figure in the world; and cannot therefore be looked upon as duly qualified, however able they may be in other respects, for Tutors or Preceptors to our youth.

Mr. Wary. No, no, – I will have nothing to do with him; – I will not be cajoled by his fair pretences.

Here they broke off all farther speech on this subject; and as I found they were beginning to enter on matters which did not seem to me of any consequence, I left them, and took the first opprotunity of going out of the house.

I shall not trouble my readers with any animadversions either on mr. Neuter's letter or the conversation which ensued upon it, but leave every one to judge as he shall think most reasonable.

CHAP. VIII.

Contains such a sort of method for the cure of an amorous constitution, as perhaps there are more ladies than one who will not think themselves obliged to the Author for revealing.

THERE is no resentment so implacable and lasting as that which is occasioned by love converted into hatred by ill treatment; and by the more slow degree this passion rises in our minds, the more virulent it becomes after having once gain'd possession.

Cleanthes, a gentleman of a good family, great worth, and opulent estate, loved to the most romantic excess a young woman, who, excepting a tolerable share of beauty, had no one real charm to recommend her to a person of his character: – she was meanly born, more meanly educated; – she was silly, vain, capricious, and of a reputation not quite unblemish'd.

Yet did he no sooner become acquainted with her than he broke off the addresses he had long made to a lady of great merit and fortune; and in a short time, contrary to all the remonstrances and dissuasions of his friends, publickly married her.

Being a husband made him not less a lover; – his obsequiousness is not to be parallel'd; – his whole study was to please her, every succeeding day brought with it an addition of his dotage of her; – he was always happy in her presence, never easy in her absence; – and, to use Shakespear's expression,

Appetite increas'd by what it fed on.[380]

Aglaura, for so she is call'd, had so little sense of the happiness she enjoy'd, or affection or gratitude for the man who bestow'd it on her, that she presently gave the greatest loose to her too amorous inclinations; – thought of nothing but engaging new admirers, and to that end made advances, which would be shocking to repeat, to every pretty fellow she came in company with, even before the face of her much injur'd husband, who, blinded by his passion, for a long time look'd on all she did as proceeding only from the too great vivacity of her temper.

Had she observ'd the least degree of circumspection in her amours, he would scarce ever have believ'd there was a possibility of her being guilty; – but she took no pains to deceive him, and tho' she knew he lived but in her sight, was scarce ever at home; and, through the want either of artifice or complaisance, gave herself not the pains of making any excuses for her continual rambles.

This made him at last fall into a deep melancholy; yet still he loved her, and could not for a great while prevail on himself to lay any restrictions on her conduct: – all who had any knowledge of the manner in which they lived together, while they highly condemn'd her treatment of him, were ready to despise his lenity and forbearance.

At length, however, the tables were entirely turn'd; – from having been at first the most fond, and afterwards the passive husband, he became, all at once, the most cruel and tyrannic; – he took from her all the jewels and other ornaments he had bestow'd upon her, lock'd her into a garret, suffer'd no one to come near her, except a servant who carried food to her of the coarsest kind, and no more than would just suffice to keep her from perishing.

It cannot be supposed but that so strange an alteration in the behaviour of the late fond, and indeed madly doating Cleanthes, must become the subject of much conversation in town. – A lady of my acquaintance, who is reckon'd to have a pretty taste for poetry, shew'd me a few lines she had wrote extempore on the occasion, which I think may not be disagreeable to my readers. – They are as follow:

On the present Cruelty of CLEANTHES, *to a* WIFE *whom he once loved to as great an excess.*

As tapers languish at th' approach of day,
And, by degrees, melt slow their shine away,
A while they glimmer with contracted fires,
Trembling, unable to relax their spires;
But when the sun's broad eye is open'd wide,
And beams, thick flashing, shoot on ev'ry side,
No more their emulative force they try,
But, struck with radiance, sink at once and die.

So in his heart love long maintain'd its place,
Till full conviction glar'd him in the face,
And forc'd th' unwilling softness to give way
To hate, and rage, and fierce resentment's sway.
Unhappy man!
What wild extremes hurry thy head-strong will? ⎫
What boist'rous passions thy vex'd bosom fill? ⎬
To reason's sacred rules a truant still. ⎭
Whoe'er he be the golden mean foregoes,
Exchanges hop'd-for joys for certain woes.

By all the discourses I heard wherever I went, concerning this affair, I found, that though scarce any one pitied Aglaura, yet almost every one condemn'd Cleanthes, no less for his present ill usage of her, than they had formerly done for the extravagance of his love.

'It is beneath the dignity of a man of sense or honour,' – said one, – 'to treat thus inhumanly a woman, how unworthy soever she may be, who is yet his wife.'

'If she is really guilty of having wrong'd his bed,' – cry'd another, – 'as indeed there is not the least room to doubt, why, on the discovery of her crime, did he not turn her out doors? – why did he not sue for a divorce?'

It is certain that his way of proceeding with her appear'd so odd, that many people were apt to think that her present sufferings were owing rather to a change in his own humour, than to any detection he had made of her falshood: – others, on the contrary, imagin'd he still lov'd her, and that after he had punish'd her a while he would forgive all that was past, and again take her to his bosom.

Various, and widely different conjectures were form'd in relation both to the husband and the wife, at all which I laugh'd in my sleeve, believing, – I dare say with a good deal of reason, – that no one person in the whole world, excepting the Invisible Spy, was at the bottom of this secret; – the means by which I became master of it I shall now acquaint my readers with.

I supp'd one night at the house of an intimate friend at Kensington, and happening to stay there more late than it was judg'd safe for me to go home alone, was very much press'd by him to take a servant with me; – but I, knowing I had a better security about me than any servant could be, rejected his offer, and when I was got a little way from the house girded on my Belt of Invisibility, and walk'd on at my leisure, equally free from danger as from fear.

Foolhardy, as I perhaps was look'd upon for venturing alone through Hyde-Park, on account of some ill accidents had lately happen'd there: – it was not above nine o'clock when I left Kensington, – an hour which I thought too late to make any other visits, and too soon to shut myself up in my own apartment; – therefore, as the night was pleasant and pretty warm, the season consider'd, I saunter'd towards the Serpentine-River, revolving in my mind some part of the conversation I had just been entertain'd with.

Many minutes had not elapsed in this employment before I was disturbed from it by the murmurs of some human voices which I heard at a small distance; – my natural curiosity making me draw nearer to the place whence the sound proceeded, I easily distinguish'd a man of a good appearance holding by the arm a genteel well-dress'd woman, whom he seem'd rather to drag than lead towards the banks of the river; – as these persons were no other than Cleanthes and Aglaura, I shall insert what was said by each of them under their respective names.

Aglaura. Indeed this is mighty foolish, Cleanthes; – I cannot imagine what should make you bring me hither at this time of night.

Cleanthes. Have a little patience, you shall know presently.

Aglaura. I will not stir one step farther 'till you tell me.

Cleanthes. Then you must be forced. – Come, come, – no resistance.

Aglaura. How do I know but you may have a design to murder me!

Cleanthes. No, I have too much regard for myself to go such lengths. – Perhaps, indeed, if you provoke me by your obstinacy, I may chance to spoil that face you are so vain upon. – I can use my sword to other purposes than killing.

With these words he drew his sword, the point of which glittering in her eyes as he pull'd her roughly forwards, frighted her so much that she presently scream'd out,

Aglaura. Ah! – help! help! – Is there no body near to save me!

Cleanthes. Be hush'd; – a second outcry and your nose goes off.

Aglaura. Oh lud! – Oh lud! – Oh lud! – How can you be so barbarous to use me thus only for a little innocent frolic!

Cleanthes. Shameless wretch! – Can you call it an innocent frolic to come to the door of a public coffee-house and send in for your gallant! – Had I not happen'd to be there, – had not these eyes and ears been witnesses of your guilt, you might, and doubtless would have deny'd, forsworn it.

Aglaura. I meant no harm; – I only wanted to rally him a little about something I had heard concerning him.

Cleanthes. Infamous abandon'd prostitute, – have I not an hundred times insisted on your never speaking to that fellow more, nor to that other coxcomb, Le Brune, yet had you not the front to run arm in arm this morning with the one into the Vineyard, in the face of the whole Mall, and at night came in pursuit of the other! – But this is no time for expostulation, – I am convinced of the injury you have done me, and will punish you accordingly. – Come, strip.

Aglaura. Oh lud! – what do you mean!

Cleanthes. You have a raging fever in your blood, which I have bethought me of a more effectual method to cure than all the doctors in Europe could prescribe; – therefore strip, I say.

While he was speaking he began to tear off part of her upper garments; – she struggled, – fell on her knees, – wept, – pray'd, – beseech'd him to forgive her, – vow'd never to offend him more; – but all in vain, he remain'd inexorable to her entreaties, – remorseless to her griefs, and forced her, with his sword pointed to her breast, to pluck off every thing, 'till she was reduced to her birth-day suit, and lay at his feet quite naked, and trembling for the issue of her fate.

The vindictive husband then snatch'd her rudely from the earth, and taking fast hold of both her shoulders plung'd her into the river, keeping her under water 'till she was almost strangled, then suffer'd her to raise her head; but it was only in order to renew her torments, for the moment he found she had recover'd breath he press'd her down again, – so that without being drown'd she felt all the agonies which that kind of death inflicts.

Weary'd, I believe, tho' not glutted, as I afterwards found, with the exercise of his revenge, he threw her on the grass, where she lay for some minutes without motion, and in all appearance without breath; – never had life so much the shew of death; yet was it chiefly fear that had so much overcome her; for she lifted herself up with more agility than I could have imagin'd, on hearing him say,

Cleanthes. The operation is now over, – you may put on your cloaths and prepare for going home.

As much as the fright had seiz'd her spirits, as the cold had benumb'd her limbs, these words enabled her to rear herself and begin to gather up her habiliments, part of which lying scatter'd at some distance, Cleanthes, with a contemptuous air, kick'd nearer to her. – She wrapp'd up her shivering body as well as she could, for I cannot call it dressing, and as soon as she had done, Cleanthes bid her follow him, – which she did, tho' ready to sink at every step she took.

I kept pretty near to them, and found that the coach which brought them thither had, by his orders, waited their return at the Park wall; – he went hastily into it, but poor Aglaura was too feeble to reach the foot stool without the assistance of the coachman: – they drove away, and I went home so much astonish'd at what I had seen, that I had not power to make any reflections on it for some time.

My mind however, grew more settled by a night's repose, and, impatient to know how they would behave to reach other after what had pass'd between them, I went directly to their house; – Cleanthes was up alone and at breakfast. – Soon after my entrance a servant-maid came in and said to him,

Maid. Sir, my lady has call'd for a dish of chocolate, but I would not presume to carry any up without your permission, as your orders last night were so positive that she should be fed with nothing but watergruel and dry bread.

Cleanthes. Why then do you trouble me now? – Do you think I gave orders at night to retract them in the morning? – Be gone, and let me hear no more of it.

The maid withdrew, and I follow'd her to the room where Aglaura was now lodg'd, which was indeed a wretched garret; – she was in bed weeping, but on the maid's repeating the commands of Cleanthes, her tears flow'd faster, – she wrung her hands, – she beat her breast; – but it is more easy for the reader to conceive her despair than for me to express it, – so I shall only say the spectacle was too moving, – I could not bear it, but left the house immediately, and return'd not thither 'till after eight or ten days, in which time the town was appriz'd of the suffering of Aglaura, except the ducking part, and spoke of the strange change of Cleanthes in the manner I have already related.

On my next visit Cleanthes had with him an elderly lady, who I afterwards perceived was his aunt; – she came, it seems, to persuade him to treat his transgressing wife with less severity; – the discourse between them was as follows:

Lady. I am as sensible as you can be of the faults of Aglaura, and the dishonour she has brought upon you; yet, my dear nephew, you demean yourself by using in this fashion a woman who, though unworthy, is still your wife.

Cleanthes. Madam, I can no longer think of her as a wife, nor even as a woman; but as a dog that had bit me! – a serpent that had stung me!

Lady. Put her then out of your house.

Cleanthes. That would be giving her an opportunity of disgracing me more by her prostitutions; – no, since I have not proofs for a divorce I will confine her here 'till I can send her for ever from my sight: – I have already wrote to a tenant of mine in the farthest part of Yorkshire, – he will be in town next week, and take her with him to his house.

The good lady took her leave, after having heard and approv'd this resolution, which, as I have been since inform'd, he put in execution as he had said.

The CONCLUSION.

HERE, O reader! a total stop is put to my endeavours to oblige thee! – nature has baffled all my vain precautions to preserve my little virgin in her native purity: – the woman whom I appointed to attend her, accidentally dropp'd from her pocket the picture of a very lovely youth; – the girl, unfortunately for me, as well as for thee, took it up, was charm'd with it; – sleep renew'd the pleasing image in her mind, and added life and motion to it; – she dream'd that it was her bedfellow, – that it kiss'd, embraced, and lay within their arms; – so that in spite of all my cares, and without ever having seen the substance of a man, she has received an idea of the difference of sexes.

Her pretty fingers no longer have the power to cleanse my Tablets, – the dialogue last repeated remains still unexpunged, and leaves no room for any future impression. – How grievous a disappointment to me! – how terrible a mortification! – but we must all submit to destiny, which compels me now to bid thee eternally adieu! – adieu! – adieu!

FINIS.

EDITORIAL NOTES

1. *some will look upon me as a courtier, – others as a patriot*: The distinction between a courtier and a patriot is derived from the oppositional politics of Henry St John, first Viscount Bolingbroke (1678–1751). Beginning in the 1720s, Bolingbroke sought to forge a new 'country' party opposed to the perceived corruption of the court, here meaning the Walpole administration. In *The Craftsman* (begun 1726) and elsewhere, he argued that the old labels of Whig and Tory were now meaningless, and that political opposition could unite around a Patriot programme driven by a disinterested concern for the good of the nation. For an extended analysis of Patriotism, see R. Harris, *A Patriot Press. National Politics and the London Press in the 1740s* (Oxford: Clarendon Press, 1993); and C. Gerrard, *The Patriot Opposition to Walpole. Politics, Poetry and National Myth, 1725–1742* (Oxford: Clarendon Press, 1994), pp. 3–18 et passim. For a reading of Haywood in terms of oppositional and Patriot politics, see K. King, *A Political Biography of Eliza Haywood* (London: Pickering & Chatto, 2012), esp. chs 4 and 8.

2. *as difficult to discover as the longitude*: The accurate determination of longitude at sea became increasingly important as sea-travel and trade increased. Under the terms of the Longitude Act of 1714, a prize of up to £20,000 was offered to anyone who could provide a reliable method of calculation. A key difficulty was telling the time at sea. The horologist John Harrison (1693–1776) developed and refined marine chronometers between 1735 and 1773, and was eventually awarded the full prize three years before his death.

3. *the ancient Magi of the Chaldeans*: 'Magi' and 'Chaldeans' both denote members of a priestly tribe in western Iran, who became renowned as followers of Zoroaster. They were experts in all types of magical arts, especially astrology. See *The Encyclopedia of Religion*, ed. M. Eliade, 10 vols (New York: Macmillan, 1987), vol. 9, pp. 79–80.

4. *that undiscover'd country, from whose bourn/ No traveller returns*: Hamlet (first performed 1602), IIIi, as cited by Edward Bysshe under 'Futurity' in *The Art of English Poetry*, 2nd edn (1705), p. 160. All further references are to this edition, and abbreviated to *AEP*. Most of Haywood's literary references are drawn from this source. Little is known about Bysshe, including dates of birth and death. He may have been the eldest son of Henry Bysshe of Buxted, a barrister. In 1702 he published *The Art of English Poetry*, with sections on 'Rules for making English Verse', 'A Dictionary of Rhymes', and 'A Collection of the most natural, agreeable, and noble thoughts ... that are to be found in the best English poets'. The latter are organized under headings such as 'Jealousie', 'Honour' or 'Man'. In the dictionary of quotations, he draws primarily on Restoration poets and dramatists, especially John Dryden. The *Art of English Poetry* was widely criticized, but also widely used. Samuel Johnson, Oliver Goldsmith and Samuel Richardson owned copies,

with the latter drawing heavily on Bysshe in *Clarissa* (1748–9). (See P. Baines, 'Bysshe, Edward', *ODNB*; and S. J. Bernard, 'Edward Bysshe and "The Art of English Poetry": Reading Writing in the Eighteenth Century', *ECS*, 46:1 (2012), pp. 113–29). Haywood seems also to have drawn on Bysshe's later handbook *The British Parnassus*, published in 1714: see below, n. 27.

5. *standish*: an ink-stand.

6. *hungary-water*: oil of rosemary and possibly other herbs distilled in alcohol, said to have been invented or used by a queen of Hungary.

7. *such a coif as serjeants at law wear*: Until the mid-nineteenth century serjeants-at-law were the highest rank of barristers, from which the judiciary were drawn. They wore a coif, or skull cap.

8. *to see a man jump into a quart bottle ... in the Hay-market*: To demonstrate the 'credulity of the English nation', John Montagu, second duke of Montagu (1690–1749) wagered 100 guineas that he could fill the Little Haymarket theatre if he advertised the appearance on stage of a conjuror who would enter a quart bottle. He won the bet, but when on 16 January 1749 the conjuror failed to appear, the audience wrecked the theatre.

9. *Adept*: originally, a person who had attained knowledge of the secrets of magic, alchemy or the occult.

10. *such a one as Dorinda in Shakespear's Inchanted Island*: Haywood confuses Shakespeare's *The Tempest* (first performed in 1611) with *The Tempest, or The Enchanted Island* (first performed in 1667), an adaptation by John Dryden (1631–1700) and William D'Avenant (1606–68). In the latter, Prospero's daughter Miranda has a sister called Dorinda.

11. *batteldor and shittlecock*: a game played with a small bat and shuttlecock, similar to modern badminton.

12. *Venetian balls*: 'Venetian' was another term for a domino, or loose cloak worn with a mask covering the upper part of the face, when the wearer was not taking on a particular character; so a ball at which such would be worn.

13. *those gaming-houses ... under the protection of the great*: The law relating to gaming was primarily aimed at preventing the lower ranks from play. Under Henry VIII, a statute decreed that 'no Manner of Artificer or Craftsman or any Handicraft or Occupation, Husbandman, Apprentice, &c. shall play at the Tables, Tennis, Dice, Cards, Bowls, &c. out of Christmas under the penalty of 20s', and the keeping of a house for the purposes of gaming was against the law. Under Charles II and Anne, laws aimed at protecting the landed gentry restricted losses that could be incurred at play, but the wealthy could still play for ready money. (See also below, n. 371). Members of Parliament openly ran gaming parties and claimed parliamentary privilege. White's and Almack's (later Brook's) were the pre-eminent gentlemen's clubs where gambling took place. See D. Miers, *Regulating Commercial Gambling. Past, Present and Future* (Oxford: Oxford University Press, 2004), pp. 20–39.

14. *Julius Cæsar or Severus*: Gaius Julius Caesar (100–44 BC) and Lucius Septimius Severus (AD 145/6–211), both of whom undertook military campaigns in Britain.

15. *virtuoso*: a collector of antiquities or curiosities. In the late-seventeenth and early-eighteenth centuries, the term was usually applied pejoratively.

16. *levee*: a reception of visitors on rising from bed, usually by royalty or a person of distinction.

17. *the route of a woman of quality*: a rout (or route) was a fashionable gathering or *soirée*.

18. *St. James's-park, Kensington-gardens ... and Mary-le-bon*: fashionable locations in London.
19. ruelle: the space or passage between the bed and the wall, or the side of the bed next to the wall. It could also signify the area around the bed where a lady of fashion held morning receptions.
20. *the king was lately return'd from visiting his German dominions*: Both George I (1660–1727) and George II (1683–1760) made regular and lengthy visits to the Electorate of Hanover. The practice reinforced the widespread belief that the monarchy would put the interests of Hanover, a recently formed state, before those of Britain.
21. *Hanover had given back our statesmen*: British diplomats and those eager for preferment, or keen to prove their loyalty, visited Hanover in the reigns of George I and George II. (See J. Black, *The British Abroad. The Grand Tour in the Eighteenth Century* (Stroud: Sutton, 1992), pp. 59–60).
22. *With wondrous art ... truth with lyes*: The first line is probably Haywood's own; part of the second is borrowed from Bysshe's citation of John Dryden's translation of Virgil's *Aeneid* (1697), book 4, l. 271: 'With Court Informers haunts and Royal Spies,/Things done relates, not done she feigns; and mingles Truth with Lyes'. The lines are given as an example of poor scansion in the heroic couplet, in 'Rules for Making English Verse', chap. I, section ii, *AEP*, p. 9.
23. *Hoyle's method of playing the Game of Whist*: *A Short Treatise on the Game of Whist. Containing the Rules of the Game* (1742), by Edmond Hoyle (1671/2–1769). The book was subsequently expanded to include other games, and went through ten editions by 1750.
24. *Bridewell*: a prison.
25. *committed to durance vile, as Hudibras says*: The phrase in *Hudibras* (Part I, dated 1663; Part II, 1664; Part III, 1680) by Samuel Butler (1613–80) is 'durance base' (part I, canto iii, l.995).
26. *a small sum requir'd of me ... on account of a bastard child*: By an act of 1576, it was ordered that bastards should be supported by their putative fathers. The father was expected to contribute towards laying-in and maintenance expenses. See *Bastardy and its Comparative History*, ed. P. Laslett, K. Oosterveen and R.M. Smith (London: Edward Arnold, 1980), pp. 75, 105.
27. *Grace was in all her steps ... dignity and love*: John Milton, *Paradise Lost* (1667), Book VIII, ll. 488–99; also cited under 'Beauteous' by Edward Bysshe, *The British Parnassus*, 2 vols (1714), vol. 1, p. 98.
28. *As if that faultless form ... must forgive*: The lines may be Haywood's own. They also appear in *The History of Betsy Thoughtless* (1751), ch. 40.
29. *take every thing for gospel that they find in the Gazette*: the *Daily Gazetteer*, founded in 1735 to promote Sir Robert Walpole's administration, or as the first issue put it: 'To vindicate Publick Authority from the rude insults of base and abusive Pens' (Monday, 30 June 1735). By 1754 it was no longer a ministerial organ.
30. *The king ... since his return to England*: see above, n. 20.
31. *Spring-garden gate*: a gate into Spring Gardens, which was first a royal and then a public pleasure park, at the North-East end of St James's Park.
32. *Lamia*: In Greek mythology a fabulous monster, supposed to have the body of a woman, who preyed upon human beings and sucked the blood of children.
33. *petite fourberies*: little frauds, or tricks.
34. *carmine*: a red pigment obtained from cochineal.
35. *Probatum est*: something tried and tested, or a recommendation for such.

36. *When I made ... own omnipotence away*: John Dryden, *Amphitryon* (1690), III.i, as cited under 'Gold' by Bysshe, *AEP*, 168.
37. *Many a nymph ... without a feather bed*: Source unidentified.
38. *All this world's noise ... ill-acted comedy*: Abraham Cowley (1618–67), 'The Despair', a poem which appeared in a sequence of 'Love-verses' entitled *The Mistress* (1647), which then appeared in *The Works of Mr. Abraham Cowley* (1668). The collection was reprinted many times in the seventeenth and eighteenth centuries.
39. *Ratifie*: or ratafia, a liqueur made by steeping nuts, fruits or herbs in a sweetened spirit.
40. *a woman need but look down upon her apron-string to find an excuse*: a proverbial expression, dating back to at least the sixteenth century. See P. R. Wilkinson, *Thesaurus of Traditional English Metaphors* (London: Routledge, 2002), p. 623.
41. *the penalty the law inflicts ... to bastardize an honourable family*: Celadon presumably refers to the penalty for adultery. The husband of an adulterous wife could bring a suit against his spouse's lover, and if successful, be awarded damages and costs. See R. Phillips, *Putting Asunder. A History of Divorce in Western Society* (Cambridge: Cambridge University Press, 1988), pp. 227–8.
42. *criminal conversation*: legally, adultery, but also used as a euphemism for any illicit sexual act between a man and a woman.
43. *to bring in a bill of impotency*: Impotence was recognized by the Church courts, and in law, as grounds for divorce. If a marriage had never been consummated it could be annulled. In 1743 the Duchess of Beaufort who, like Marcella, was childless, sued her husband for divorce on grounds of impotence. The Duke submitted himself to, and passed, a virility test, and the Duchess lost her case. (See L. Stone, *Broken Lives. Separation and Divorce in England 1660–1857* (Oxford: Oxford University Press, 1993), 131 ff).
44. *the birthday... the ode / composed by mr. Cibber on that occasion*: Colley Cibber (1671–1757), actor, writer, theatre manager and Poet Laureate from 1730, was called upon to compose celebratory odes on the occasion of the king's birthday. Cibber was closely associated with the Hanoverian monarchy – he met both George and George II fairly frequently – and with leading Whigs. The chief satiric target of Alexander Pope's expanded *Dunciad* of 1742, he was mocked for his vanity and sycophancy.
45. Civet: either the small cat-like creature, or the strong musky perfume obtained from the animal's anal scent glands.
46. *after the Prince's mourning was over*: a reference to the sudden and unexpected death of Prince Frederick Lewis, prince of Wales (1707–51), on 20 March 1751. The Prince was the focus for political opposition from 1737/8.
47. *mantau*: a woman's loose cloak, or an alternative spelling of mantua: see below, n. 218.
48. *point d'espagne*: lacework made, or supposed to be made, in Spain.
49. *not either flower'd in the loom*: not woven into the fabric.
50. *piece-brokers*: those dealing in remnants of cloth for repairing clothes.
51. *St. Clement's church*: the parish church of St Clement Danes at the east end of the Strand. It was associated with High Churchmanship. An altarpiece commissioned from William Kent in 1720–1 was thought by some to represent St. Cecilia and her harp, or Queen Maria Clementina, wife of James II, and her son Prince Charles Edward Stuart. Edmund Gibson, Bishop of London, ordered it to be removed to the vestry in September 1725. (E. E. C. Nicholson, 'The St. Clement Danes Altarpiece and the Iconography of Post-Revolution England', in *Samuel Johnson in Historical Context*, ed. J. Clark and H. Erskine-Hill (Houndmills: Palgrave, 2002), pp. 55–6. See also R. Sharp, 'The Religious

and Political Character of the Parish of St. Clement Danes', in *Samuel Johnson in Historical Context*, ed. Clark and Erskine-Hill, pp. 44–54).

52. *if so, you might have render'd yourself as conspicuous ... character of Iphigenia*: In Greek myth, Iphigenia was the daughter of Agamemnon, sacrificed to appease the goddess Artemis and allow the Greek fleet to sail to Troy. Elizabeth Chudleigh, later Elizabeth Hervey, countess of Bristol (1720–88) caused a scandal when, in May 1749, she appeared in a nearly transparent bodice, dressed as Iphigenia ready for the sacrifice.

53. *robe de chambre*: dressing-gown, or nightdress.

54. *speaking without book*: conjecture. To 'speak by the book' is to speak paying careful attention to the facts.

55. *beneath the rank of right honourable*: beneath the rank of baron.

56. *Le Bris*: perhaps derived from the French verb *briser*, to break, or more pertinently here, to wreck or destroy.

57. *benefice*: an ecclesiastical living.

58. *Fleet-parson ... clandestine marriages*: The area around Fleet prison, known as the 'Liberties of the Fleet' fell outside the jurisdiction of the Church of England, and was notorious as the chief site of clandestine marriages, that is, marriages conducted without banns or licence and away from the home parish of the spouses. Unscrupulous clergy, who might be debtors able to wander within the Rules of the Fleet, would marry couples virtually on demand. It has been estimated that by 1740 around 6,600 marriages a year were being conducted in the Liberties of the Fleet, The Mint, the prison of the King's bench, St George's Chapel, Mayfair, Holy Trinity, Minories or other privileged locations. See R. B. Outhwaite, *Clandestine Marriage in England, 1500–1850* (London: Hambledon, 1995), 28–31 et passim. The practice was ended by the Marriage Act of 1753, sometimes called Hardwicke's Marriage Act, after Philip Yorke, first earl of Hardwicke (1690–1764) and Lord Chancellor from 1737 to 1756. Under the terms of the Act, a marriage had to be a public ceremony conducted in an Anglican church within canonical hours, and with parental consent for those under twenty-one years old.

59. *I lov'd the Precepts for the Teacher's sake*: an adaptation of lines that close *The Constant Couple, or A Trip to the Jubilee* (1699), by George Farquhar (*c.* 1677–1707). The play's main character, Sir Harry Wildair, declares: 'Charming Women can true Converts make/We love the Precepts for the Teachers' sake.'

60. *By no example ... became my snare*: source unidentified.

61. *what age I was ... I could have no relief from law*: The age of consent, and therefore of legal responsibility, was set at ten in 1576, and not raised until the nineteenth century.

62. *recourse to equity*: originally, recourse to general principles of natural justice supplementing statute law, but 'equity' later became a system of rules and precedents in its own right administered by the Court of Chancery.

63. *landau*: a horse-drawn carriage with a folding top.

64. *devoirs*: courteous attentions or addresses.

65. *When fix'd to one ... to ev'ry wave a scorn*: John Dryden, *Tyrannic Love, or The Royal Martyr* (1669), IV, i., as cited under 'Marriage' by Bysshe, *AEP*, p. 251.

66. *'Where there is no modesty, there is little sign of honesty'*: not found in contemporary collections of proverbs, such as Robert Codrington's *Collection of Many Select, and Excellent Proverbs* (1664), John Ray's *Collection of English Proverbs* (1670) or Thomas Fuller's *Gnomologia* (1732).

67. *Short is th' uncertain reign ... nauseates you and parts*: Haywood follows Bysshe's attribution of the lines to playwright and politician Sir Robert Howard (1626–98) in *AEP*

under the heading 'Vicissitude'. They actually come from Dryden's 'Against Pride upon Sudden Advancement', taken from the Italian of Fulvio Testi, in *Examen Poeticum: Being the Third Part of the Miscellany Poems* (1693). The lines read: 'Short is th' uncertain Reign, and Pomp of mortal Pride,/New turns, and Changes ev'ry Day/Are of inconstant Chance the constant Arts,/Soon she gives, soon takes away,/She comes, embraces, nauseates you, and parts'.

68. *like faithful Abraham, I must submit to lay my darling on the altar*: In Genesis 22. i–xviii, Abraham is asked to take his son Isaac and lay him on the altar as a sacrifice. The text was the subject of controversy in the early eighteenth century. See C. Stewart, '*Joseph Andrews* and the Sacrifice of Isaac: Faith, Works and Anticlericalism', *Literature and Theology*, 27:1 (March 2013), pp. 18–31.

69. *a pensioner*: a pensioner could lodge in a convent or monastery for the payment of a sum of money.

70. *No name ... a vagabond*: source unidentified.

71. *the Sybil's words wrote on the leaves of trees*: The Cumaean Sibyl prophesied, in part, by writing on the leaves of oak trees arranged at the entrance to her cave. If the wind blew the leaves away, the prophecy could not be recovered. See Virgil, *Aeneid*, VI, ll. 56–97.

72. *How often has he sworn ... the gushing blood*: a slight adaptation of lines spoken by Monimia, the tragic heroine of Thomas Otway's *The Orphan* (1680), IV, i, cited under 'False', *AEP*, p. 132.

73. *Montague-house*: Montague (or Montagu) House was built between 1675 and 1679 for Baron Ralph Montagu (1638–1709), later first Duke of Montagu. Open fields behind Montagu House were used for duels between 1680 and 1750. (D. Pearce, *London's Mansions* (London: B. T. Batsford, 1986), p. 114).

74. *the likelihood there was ... highly necessary*: The legal position in relation to duelling was clear: a man who killed his opponent in a premeditated duel was guilty of murder. However, the law was often thwarted because the sovereign could, and did, pardon the duellist. (See S. Banks, *A Polite Exchange of Bullets: The Duel and the English Gentleman 1750–1850* (Woodbridge: Boydell Press, 2010), 13ff). Further, 'by the eighteenth century there were groups of powerful, active men operating under a common ethos who were able to propagate in public a vigorous, noisy and even romantic honour culture. ... Opposition was ... fragmented and uncertain' (Banks, *A Polite Exchange of Bullets*, p. 23).

75. *peit-en-l'air*: pet-en-l'air, a short jacket version of the *robe à la Francaise*, which was a gown with a fitted bodice, stomacher, and long, loose pleats at the back. The young wife in William Hogarth's *Marriage A-la-Mode: The Tête à Tête* (c. 1743) is seen wearing a *pet-en-l'air*.

76. *Nothing can come of nothing, as king Lear says in the play*: *King Lear* (first performed c. 1606), I.i.

77. *the Great Mogul*: head of the Muslim dynasty that ruled an empire covering a large part of South Asia from the sixteenth to the nineteenth centuries.

78. *pickthank*: someone who curries favour by telling tales; a flatterer or sycophant.

79. *French barragon*: originally a coarse camlet, but sometimes used to signify a fine cloth of silk or other delicate material.

80. *a fine flaxen wig, with a bag*: a bag-wig, meaning a wig with the back hair enclosed in an ornamental bag.

81. *solitair*: a gemstone, especially a diamond, set by itself.

82. *stand perdu*: stand hidden.

83. *Blessed is the wooing/That's not long a doing*: a proverbial expression dating back to the sixteenth century, if not earlier.

84. *society of Bucks*: Bucks (often twinned with Bloods) were young men operating in gangs, reputedly guilty of rape, drinking, gaming, attacking the nightwatch and acts of vandalism for sport. See 'The Inspector', no. 332, in *London Magazine*, 25 October, 1756: 'these Bucks and Bloods push at every one they meet, affect to have no bowels, laugh at another's calamity, and think it cowardice to fear God'.

85. *kennel*: the gutter.

86. *let the evil day take care for its self*: perhaps derived from Matthew 6:34: 'Sufficient unto the day is the evil thereof.'

87. *In spite of pride … whatever is, - is right*: a misquotation of Alexander Pope (1688–1744), *An Essay on Man* (1733–4), epistle IV, ll. 393–4: 'For Wit's false mirror held up Nature's light;/Show'd erring Pride,-Whatever is, is right'.

88. *the bill in relation to the Naturalization of the Jews*: The Jewish Naturalization Bill passed the Lords on April 16, and the Commons on 22 May 1753. However, after much controversy and popular outcry, it was repealed when Parliament resumed in November. Attitudes to the issue divided along party lines. Tories feared an influx of non-Anglican, non-High Church foreigners, while Whigs had fewer reservations about diluting the comprehensiveness of the sacramental test. Naturalization, as proposed, tacitly extended the principle of toleration to include non-Christians. (See Introduction, pp. xiv–xv; Perry, 31–44 ff; and S. V. Muse, 'Eliza Haywood and the Jew Bill', *Notes & Queries*, 57.1 (2010) pp. 105–8).

89. *upon the tapis*: on the carpet, that is, brought into the open.

90. *the fate of M—y*: an allusion to the imprisonment of Alexander Murray of Elibank (1712–78). See Introduction, p. xvi.

91. *mercer*: a person dealing in fabrics, especially silks, velvets and other fine materials.

92. *sweetners*: here, cheats or sharps, used to draw others into play.

93. *moidores*: Portuguese gold coins current in England and its colonies in the early eighteenth century, each worth about 27 shillings.

94. *Even life a kind of chequer-work appears … Marston*: not found in the works of John Marston (1576–1634).

95. *her heels the length of half a span behind her shoes*: that is, with the heels hanging off her shoes.

96. *as Colley says, outdone all her usual outdoings*: In his address To the Reader which prefaces *The Provok'd Husband* (1728), Colley Cibber said of the actress Anne Oldfield (1683–1730) that 'she *Here Out-did* her usual *Out-doing*', a phrase attracting satiric comment from *Mist's Weekly*, Henry Fielding and others.

97. *vallens*: a valance, meaning either a border of drapery hanging round the canopy of a bed, or around the frame of a bedstead.

98. *Dutch matting*: a type of matting used by cabinet-makers for the packing of goods.

99. *sconces*: ornamental candlesticks, either with a handle or in the form of a bracket attached to the wall.

100. *mr. Rowe makes Arbasia tell her tyrant … a thought so mean*: A slight misquotation of lines from a speech by Arpasia in *Tamerlane* (1701) by Nicholas Rowe (1674–1718): 'Not that I fear, or reverence thee, thou Tyrant:/But that my Soul, conscious of whence it sprung,/Sits unpolluted in its sacred Temple,/And scorns to mingle with a Thought so mean'(IV.i).

101. *Dryden ... And poisoning love himself with his own darts*: John Dryden, *Albion and Albanius: An Opera* (1685), II.ii, cited under 'Jealousie', *AEP*, p. 200.
102. *O what damn'd minutes ... yet strongly loves*: *Othello* (first performed between 1602 and 1604), III. iii., cited under 'Jealousie', *AEP*, p. 203.
103. *Leander*: In Greek mythology, young Leander of Abydos fell in love with Hero, a priestess of Aphrodite, who lived in Sestos on the other side of the Hellespont. Leander swam across the strait every night to visit Hero, guided by a light in her tower. One night, during a storm, the light was blown out, and Leander drowned. When Hero saw Leander's dead body washed up on the shore, she threw herself to her death.
104. *No signs of love ... their pains*: John Dryden, *The Conquest of Granada by the Spaniards* (part I produced December 1670, part II produced January 1671, both published 1672), part 2, III. i., cited under 'Jealousie', *AEP*, p. 200.
105. *Dryden ...But this, we most desire to keep, has none*: Dryden, *The Conquest of Granada*, part 2, III. i., cited under 'Jealousie', *AEP*, p. 200.
106. *The greater care ...we most fear to lose*: Dryden, *The Conquest of Granada*, part 2, III. i., cited under 'Jealousie', *AEP*, p. 199.
107. *We women ... find us so*: source unidentified.
108. *dishabille*: a state of undress, or a casual, or lounging garment.
109. *the centry would not suffer him to pass through with the things*: A Royal Order of January 1703 forbade the sale of goods within St. James's Park, as well as riding on the grass, carts, rude and disorderly people, and beggars. William could be suspected of carrying items to sell.
110. *Buffs*: fellows.
111. *tyre-woman*: a woman who assists at a lady's toilette.
112. *the Artillery-ground, Tothill-fields*: a popular site for duels between Westminster and Millbank.
113. *capuchin*: a hooded cloak or gown.
114. *He that would keep ... a padlock on her mind*: possibly an adaptation of Matthew Prior (1664–1721) in 'An English Padlock': 'Let all her ways be unconfin'd,/And clap your Padlock - on her Mind'.
115. *the patriot*: see above, n. 1.
116. *Earl of Rochester said ... may pass for a wit*: not by John Wilmot, Earl of Rochester (1647–80), but lines from 'A Song of Nothing' in *Merry Drollerie Compleat: or, A Collection of Jovial Poems, Merry Songs, Witty Drolleries, Intermixed with Pleasant Catches* (1691), p. 66. Rochester did write a poem entitled 'Upon Nothing', which Samuel Johnson considered his finest.
117. *Dr. Cameron was executed*: Dr Archibald Cameron (1707–53), physician and Jacobite conspirator, was hanged, drawn and quartered on June 7, 1753. He was involved in the '45 Rebellion and a plot to kidnap the Hanoverian royal family in 1752: the Elibank plot, after Alexander Murray of Elibank (see above, n. 90). He was executed for his part in the former, despite the fact that the Rebellion had long since been subdued. It has been suggested that the Pelham government wanted to protect the identity of their agent Alaistair Macdonald, alias 'Pickle the Spy' (see also below, n. 130) who had kept them informed about the progress of the Elibank plot, and so Cameron was brought to court for his earlier act of treason. (Roger Turner, 'Cameron, Archibald (1707–1753)', *ODNB*).

118. *bills ... had pass'd the royal assent*: not all on the same day, but close in time nonetheless. The Jewish Naturalization Bill passed the Commons on 22 May, whilst Cameron was executed and The Marriage Act received the royal assent on 7 June.

119. *neither White's nor St. James's*: White's club was originally a chocolate-house, and St James's a coffee-house. The latter was associated with the Whigs. See B. W. Cowan, *The Social Life of Coffee. The Emergence of the British Coffeehouse* (New Haven, CT: Yale University Press, 2005), p. 170.

120. *Petit Maitres*: effeminate men, or fops.

121. *sword-knots and toupees*: A sword-knot was a ribbon or tassle tied to the hilt of a sword, and the toupee a periwig in which the front hair was combed up over a pad into a top-knot.

122. *to shew the consequences ... laying such a restriction on the hearts of young people*: In the controversy surrounding the passage of the Marriage Act of 1753, (see above n. 58) there were those who argued that if the young were prevented from marrying at will, debauchery would ensue. It was also argued that the Act was designed to keep wealth in the family by making parental consent a legal requirement, and so represented aristocratic self-interest. In his novel *The Marriage Act* (1754), physician and political writer John Shebbeare (1709–88) dramatized what he saw as the pernicious effects of the Act.

123. *May-Fair Chapel*: see above, n. 58.

124. *noos'd in the Fleet ... other private Chapels*: see above, n. 58.

125. *establish themselves in their seats ... ad infinitum*: A Whig government passed the Septennial Act in 1716, extending the life of present and future parliaments from three to seven years. Most eighteenth-century parliaments thereafter did last for a full seven years, and the Act helped to ensure the dominance of the Whigs.

126. *too strictly tenacious ... of what they call their rights and privileges*: Bolingbroke argued in such writings as *Remarks on the History of England, from the Minutes of Humphry Oldcastle, Esq.,* (originally published in *The Craftsman*, 1730–1) that the history of Great Britain was one shaped by conflict between the prerogative of the monarchy and the spirit of liberty, in which the latter always finally reasserted itself. As Oldcastle puts it: 'British Liberties are not the *Grants of Princes*. They are *original Rights*, Conditions of *original Contracts*, coæqual with *Prerogative*, and coœval with our *Government* ... constantly maintain'd afterwards by that *pertinacious Spirit*, which no Difficulties or Dangers could discourage, nor any Authority abate ...'. The Third Gentleman obviously feels that spirit has been lost.

127. Laugh and lie down: a card game for five people, also known as Laugh and Lay Down, in which players match cards in their hand with those lying face up on the table. The 'laugh' comes from the reaction of other players when one who has no cards left has to throw in their hand. The player left holding cards is the winner.

128. hard-heads: a contest of head-butting.

129. *Westminster electors ... expences of his standing*: In the election of 1749, the candidate Sir George Vandeput (see Introduction, p. xvi) was sponsored by the Independent Electors of Westminster to oppose the Court candidate, Granville Leveson-Gower, Lord Trentham (1721–1803), who, after a recount of votes, ultimately won a narrow victory. During the scrutiny that followed the election, Vandeput received financial support from the Prince of Wales's coterie at Leicester House.

130. *Mac Dunder*: There are at least two possible candidates for the identity of 'Mac Dunder'. One is James Mohr Macgregor (or Drummond, after the proscription of the name Macgregor) (1694/5–1754), who fought on the Jacobite side at Culloden. He was

the son of Scottish folk-hero Rob Roy Macgregor. Having escaped from custody at Edinburgh Castle in 1752, where he was held following a conviction for kidnapping, Macgregor fled to Ireland. From Ireland, Macgregor wrote to William Macgregor of Balhaldy, chief of the Macgregor clan, advising him that he could muster three thousand Irishmen to land in Argyllshire in support of Prince Charles, a message that was passed to the prince. However, it seems likely that he was in the pay of the British government. (See A. Lang, *Pickle the Spy* (London: Longmans, Green and Co., 1897), ch. 10). The other possibility is Alasdair Ruadh MacDonnell (*c.* 1725–61), a government spy with the alias 'Pickle', who betrayed those who plotted to kidnap the Hanoverian royal family in 1752: the Elibank plot, after Alexander Murray of Elibank (see above, n.90). MacDonnell was not definitively identified as Pickle until the publication of Lang's book, though he was suspected by one of Charles's circle as early as 1752. (See F. McLynn, *Charles Edward Stuart: A Tragedy in Many Acts* (London: Routledge, 1988), p. 406).

131. *Bullruddre*: a possible link with Balhaldy, or Ruadh: see above, n. 130.

132. *thirteen-pence piece*: By a proclamation of June 1701, the value of the English silver shilling was fixed at thirteen pence Irish, a rate that lasted for a century.

133. *rapparee*: A rapparee was originally an Irish pikeman or irregular soldier, especially one fighting on the Jacobite side in the Williamite war of 1689–91. The word also came to be used more loosely to signify a rogue or a bandit.

134. *gone by this time ... somewhat farther*: see above, n. 130. Macgregor was in Paris by October 1753, and died there in 1754. In April of 1754, MacDonnell was in Paris.

135. *on account of a certain haughtiness ... Roxana*: Roxane, or Roxana (d. *c.* 310 BC), a Bactrian noblewoman, daughter of Oxyartes, who was captured by Alexander the Great and became his wife.

136. *mope-ey'd*: short-sighted.

137. *I'll see before I doubt ...with love or jealousy*: *Othello*, III.iii, cited under 'Jealousie', *AEP*, p. 201.

138. *such revenge as the laws of England have provided in these cases*: see above, n. 41.

139. *Indian chest*: a fashionable piece of furniture. In 'Epistle to a Lady' (1735), ll. 167–8, Alexander Pope (1688–1744) writes of Chloe that 'She, while a lover pants upon her breast/Can mark the figures on an Indian chest'.

140. *jupe volante*: a flounced skirt, or petticoat.

141. *old Joan and Darby in the song*: Darby and Joan, aged, humble and devoted, appear in a song beginning 'Dear Chloe', in *A Complete Collection of Old and New English and Scotch Songs* (1735).

142. *Too much plenty makes me poor*: an expression derived from Ovid's *Metamorphoses*, III, l. 466: 'inopem me copia fecit': wealth, or plenty, has made me poor. The line is spoken by Narcissus.

143. *Distrust in lovers ... when that is gone*: Dryden, *The Conquest of Granada*, III.i, cited under 'Jealousie', *AEP*, p. 199.

144. *Bath counters*: Bath was a centre for gaming. The counters used for keeping score and as stakes could be ornate objects in their own right, made in Europe and China from materials including ivory, mother-of-pearl and tortoiseshell.

145. *Bartholomew-baby*: a doll sold at Bartholomew Fair in West Smithfield, London. The Fair was held around 24 August, the festival of the Apostle Bartholomew, from 1133 to 1855.

146. *flouts*: jeers or mockery.

147. *I took them all … Each charming syllable he spoke was mine*: a slight adaptation of lines from Nathaniel Lee's *Mithridates, King of Pontus* (first performed 1678), I.i., cited under 'Wooing' by Bysshe, *British Parnassus*, vol. II, p. 978.

148. *Who loves to hear of wife?… without power to give them*: Haywood takes lines juxtaposed by Edward Bysshe under 'Wife' in *AEP*, p. 417. The first line is from Thomas Otway's *The Orphan* (1680),V.i., while the second and third are a slight misquotation of Cleopatra's words in Dryden's *All for Love* (1678), II.i.: 'That dull insipid lump, without desires,/ And without power to give them'.

149. *Dryden's advice … we've chosen ill*: Dryden's *Aurengzebe* (produced 1675; published 1676), II.i., as cited under 'Husband and Wife', *AEP*, p. 198.

150. *Monsieur De Bussy*: possibly Roger de Rabutin, Comte de Bussy (1618–93) who commented on taste, but the work is unidentified.

151. *He was a fool … a Man of Parts*: lines from Rochester's 'A Letter from Artemisia in the Town to Chloe in the Country', cited under 'Fool' by Bysshe, *AEP*, pp. 150–1.

152. *one of our / most eminent authors … is the universal passion*: Edward Young (1683–1765) published a series of verse satires entitled *The Universal Passion* between 1725 and 1728. The poems were revised and collected as *Love of Fame* in 1728.

153. *Th' unknown, untalk'd of man, is only blest … himself enjoys*: The first line is taken from Dryden's *Tyrannic Love, or the Royal Martyr* (1669), III.i., cited under 'Happiness', *AEP*, p. 159. The following lines may be Haywood's.

154. *The great, 'tis sure, should first themselves amend … no degree of men th' infection scapes*: not found in Drayton's work. A four volume *Works of Michael Drayton, Esq.*, was published in 1753, which may have suggested the poet's name to Haywood.

155. *Learn you, who languish in a widow'd bed, from Elismonda learn*: an allusion to the conduct of Princess Augusta (1719–72) after the death of her husband, Prince Frederick, in 1751. She presented herself as a dutiful daughter-in-law to George II, and as a loving wife and mother. She also distanced herself from the political opposition that had formed around the Prince. Augusta tried to engage tutors who would give her sons a moral education, and impressed Earl Waldegrave as 'decent and prudent'. See J. L. Bullion, '"To play what game she pleased without observation": Princess Augusta and the political drama of succession, 1736–56', in *Queenship in Britain 1660–1837. Royal Patronage, Court Culture and Dynastic Politics*, ed. C. Campbell Orr (Manchester: Manchester University Press, 2002), pp. 207–35.

156. *as Lee expresses it, in all the full grown pride of glorious beauty*: not traceable in the works of Nathaniel Lee, unless Haywood is recalling the line: '''Tis beauty calls, and glory leads the way', which closes Act IV of *The Rival Queens; or Alexander the Great, a Tragedy* (1677).

157. *ye pretended patriots, who wrote and loudly bawl'd for liberty*: Many of those who had espoused the Patriot cause failed to act on principle or carry out the promised reforms of parliament when Walpole resigned in February 1742. Walpole himself went unpunished for his alleged corruption. Chief among the apostate Patriots was opposition politician and *Craftsman* writer William Pulteney (1684–1764), who accepted a peerage and retired to the House of Lords as Earl of Bath. In the administration of 1742–4, he and many other previous opposition Whigs voted against a tory motion to repeal the Septennial Act (see above, n. 125). John Carteret, second earl Granville (1690–1763) was in opposition from 1731, and a prominent figure at Leicester House, but in 1742 accepted the position of Secretary of State for the north, and in effect led an administration in which allies of Walpole predominated. A number of opposition Whigs were brought

into the Broad-Bottom administration of 1744–6, with little discernible impact on domestic or foreign policy. Patriots George Lyttelton and, later, William Pitt went on to accept places under Henry Pelham (1694–1754), an 'Old Corps' Whig and a supporter of Walpole. Popular disillusion set in when the old order survived more or less intact.

158. *In spite of death ... blossom in the dust*: not by George Herbert, but an adaptation or misquotation of lines from 'The Glories of our Blood and State', by the lesser-known James Shirley (1596–1666). The lines are: 'Only the ashes of the just/Smell sweet and blossom in the dust'.

159. *stand in your own light*: harm your own interests.

160. *porringer*: a small bowl or basin.

161. *Halbert*: the halbert, or halberd, was a combined spear and battle-axe, but it also, as here, denoted the rank of sergeant.

162. *green-stall*: a vegetable stall.

163. *Innocence and youth oft makes,/In artless virgins such mistakes*: an adaptation of lines from 'To a Fair Lady, Playing with a Snake' by Edmund Waller (1606–87), cited under 'Snake', *AEP*, p. 367.

164. *In spite of birth ... is but a man*: not found in Rowe's *Jane Shore* (1714).

165. *Our English Pindar, the inimitable Cowley*: In the seventeenth and eighteenth centuries, Abraham Cowley was deemed to be one of the chief exponents of the Pindaric ode, after Pindar (*c.* 522–443 BC), a Greek lyric poet. The Pindaric ode was then understood as an irregular form, using a framework of strophe, antistrophe and epode, elevated in style and making extensive use of metaphor.

166. *'Tis madness sure treasures to hoard ... public love to gain*: from Cowley's translation, 'First Nemean Ode of Pindar', cited under 'Riches', *AEP*, p. 342.

167. *putting you under the care of any person by way of governor*: A gentleman usually undertook the Grand Tour between the ages of sixteen and twenty-one, accompanied by a male chaperone, or governor.

168. *Wise is the man ... same temptation caught*: source unidentified.

169. *flying for refuge to the Verge of the Court*: The Verge of the Court was an area originally defined as being within 12 miles of the sovereign's person, wherever that might be. It was subject to the jurisdiction of the Lord High Steward. In the eighteenth century the 'Verge of the Court' commonly referred to the precincts of Whitehall as a place of sanctuary.

170. *Board of Green-cloath*: The counting-house of the royal household headed by the Lord Steward, with control over legal and financial matters within the household.

171. *Fanny Murray*: a prostitute, who 'achieved the pinnacle of her notoriety in the 1740s' (J. Sainsbury, *John Wilkes: The Lives of a Libertine* (Aldershot: Ashgate, 2006), p. 250). She was later the dedicatee of John Wilkes's *Essay on Woman* (1763), an obscene parody of Pope's *Essay on Man* (1733–4).

172. *the Jew bill*: see above, n.88.

173. *the great vulgar and the small, – as Congreve says*: a phrase from *The Old Batchelor* (1693), IV.i., by William Congreve (1670–1729). Congreve's plays were reprinted many times in the eighteenth century.

174. *brulee*: possibly derived from the Scottish or northern dialect word 'bruilliement' or 'brulyiement', meaning a broil or disturbance. A similar usage may be found in Anon., *Woodbury:or the Memoirs of William Marchmont, Esq.*, 2 vols (Dublin: 1781): 'My aunt and Marchmont, on their meeting, to outward appearance, forgot their former *brulée*' (vol. 2, pp. 93–4).

175. *in order to qualify you for a Member ... of my estate*: Under the Qualifications Act of 1711, membership of the House of Commons was restricted to those with an income of £600 per year from real estate for county MPs, and £300 per year from real estate for borough MPs.

176. *Not all the threats ... unbought their love*: from 'The Man of Honour' by Charles Montagu, Earl of Halifax (1661–1715) cited under 'Honour', *AEP*, pp. 186–7.

177. *Money is the only Power ... money as 'twill bring*: a selection and adaptation of lines from *Hudibras* (1663), part III, canto ii, by Samuel Butler (1613–80), cited under 'Money', *AEP*, pp. 262–3.

178. *a riband*: an honour, such as the Knighthood of the Order of the Bath, revived by George I in 1725.

179. *like Esau, sell their birth-rights for a mess of pottage*: Gen. 25: 29–34 recounts how Esau came in faint from working in the fields, and sold his birthright to his brother Jacob for a bowl of pottage.

180. *This world is all a trick ... play upon the square?*: an adaptation of lines from Rochester's 'A Satyre Against Mankind', cited under 'Man', *AEP*, p. 250.

181. *not beloved, on account of the bustle he made about the Turnpikes*: The mid-eighteenth century was an age of 'turnpike mania', with 360 turnpike acts in the 1750s and 1760s. Fifty-two per cent of the total mileage constructed between 1696 and 1836 was authorised between 1750 and 1770. Turnpike Acts created bodies of trustees and gave them authority to finance road improvements by levying tolls and issuing secured bonds, though trustees were forbidden by law from profiting directly from the tolls. Cousin Hawksmore's position in relation to the turnpikes is left ambiguous: he could be either for or against. Generally, improved roads were seen as benefitting the wealthy and improving trade, while unfairly penalising the lower ranks. The establishment of turnpikes provoked riots in the early eighteenth century, and one man was hanged under the Black Act for his attack on the Ledbury turnpike in 1736. (P. Langford, *A Polite and Commercial People. England 1727–1783* (Oxford: Clarendon Press, 1989), p. 392). In January 1750,the Duke of Bedford put forward a bill for the repair of a road between Knotting in Bedfordshire and Market Harborough in Leicestershire, causing the biggest division of the parliamentary session. It was defeated. See Introduction, p. xiv.

182. *A maid/Who knows not Courts ... by which it aims at grandeur*: source unidentified.

183. *half taken up with introductory Prefaces to the publick*: The probable target here is Henry Fielding, whose prefatory chapters were a striking feature of *The History of Tom Jones* (1748–9).

184. *Puppet-shew*: The reference to a 'Puppet-shew' makes the identification of Henry Fielding as Haywood's target (see above, n. 183) almost certain. In March 1748, Fielding launched a satiric puppet show at Panton Lane.

185. *If fate be not ... if it be?*: Dryden and Davenant, *The Tempest*, III. iv., as cited under 'Fate', *AEP*, p. 140.

186. *how many impostors ... pretending to the art of divination*: Fictitious divinations of the real-life fortune-teller, Duncan Campbell (*c.* 1680–1730), gave Haywood the framework for an earlier 'spy' narrative in *A Spy on the Conjurer* (1724).

187. *some private chapel ... not authorised by the government*: a Roman Catholic chapel. Under William III's Act Against Popery (1700), Roman worship was illegal, and a priest saying Mass was liable to perpetual imprisonment. The law was not rigorously enforced.

188. *An inner room ... solder up the flaws*: from *The Dispensary, A Poem* (1699), canto II, by Sir Samuel Garth (1660/61–1719) physician and poet, cited under 'Professor in Astrology and Physic', *AEP*, p. 18.
189. *powder-blue*: powdered smalt, smalt being a finely pulverised glass usually coloured deep blue by cobalt oxide. It was widely used in laundering.
190. *Dutch conjuration*: reading tea-leaves; so called because the Dutch were the first to bring tea from Japan and China at the beginning of the seventeenth century.
191. *The power that ministers ... necessitate the will*: Dryden, *Palamon and Arcite*, book 2, ll. 210–15; 218–21, cited under 'Fate', *AEP*, p. 139.
192. *An unseen hand ... destiny plays us all*: Cowley, 'Destinie', cited under 'Fate', *AEP*, p. 139.
193. *Chapel Royal*: 'Chapel Royal' can denote an institution—the establishment of priests, musicians, and other staff serving the monarch—or Chapels such as those at St. James's Palace or Whitehall, or in its broadest usage, any building in which the king or queen attends a service as sovereign. See D. Burrows, *Handel and the English Chapel Royal* (Oxford: Oxford University Press, 2005), p. 15.
194. *When I attempted ... ended them to you*: source unidentified.
195. *a law in force against ... dealers in futurity*: The Vagrancy Act of 1744 listed fortune-tellers along with beggars and other 'rogues and vagabonds' as vagrants liable to be punished by hard labour or imprisonment.
196. *degagee*: easy, unconstrained.
197. *Major-Domo*: the master of the house.
198. *jointure and pin-money*: Jointure was the wife's sole estate. The allocation of pin-money, a sum allowed to the wife for clothing or other expenses, was described by Joseph Addison in *Spectator* 295, 1712, as being 'of very late Date, unknown to our Great Grandmothers'.
199. *On Tuesday morning ... upon Tuesday*: an adaptation of lines from 'I shall be married on Monday morning', an old English ballad.
200. *doit*: originally, a small Dutch coin worth half an English farthing, later used to denote any very small or trifling sum.
201. *Tramontane*: coming from beyond the Alps: an outsider, a barbarian.
202. *an Italian safe-guard*: In the mid-sixteenth century Italian anatomists identified the clitoris as the seat of female desire. (See P. Findlen, 'Anatomy of a Lesbian: Medicine, Pornography, and Culture in Eighteenth-Century Italy', in *Italy's Eighteenth Century. Gender and Culture in the Age of the Grand Tour*, ed. Findlen, Roworth and Sama (Stanford, CA: Stanford University Press, 2009), p. 223). In 1700 the ecclesiastical jurist Ludovico Maria Sinistrari reinforced the finding when he wrote of a Pavian nun who asked for a clitoridectomy to safeguard her virtue. His work was not translated into English until the nineteenth century, but it is possible that Haywood's obscure allusion looks to this example, or such a practice.
203. *There is a lust in man ... but born, and die*: from the translation of the Ninth Satire of Juvenal by Stephen Harvey (1655–1707), in *The Satires of Decimus Junius Juvenalis ... by Mr. Dryden and Several Other Eminent Hands* (1692), cited under 'Scandal', *AEP*, p. 352.
204. *The wise ... without repining*: not found in the writings of Philip Massinger (1583–1640).
205. *gay confusion, as mr. Addison elegantly expresses it*: from the poem 'A Letter from Italy'(1704) by Joseph Addison (1672–1719).
206. *Scylla or Caribdes*: In Homer's *Odyssey*, book XII, Scylla is the six-headed monster lurking in a cave high up on a cliff, and Charybdis is the whirlpool that faces Scylla across the narrow strait that Odysseus must navigate. Haywood's usage does not capture the sense of being caught between two equally perilous alternatives.

207. *put pillows under his elbows*: to give himself a false sense of security. The expression 'to sew pillows under your elbows' is derived from early translations of Ezekiel 13:18. It is found in Calvinistic preaching in the seventeenth century, which may account for Haywood's sense of its vulgarity.

208. *Inconstant still ... disturb the air*: The first two lines are an adaptation of Dryden's *Cleomenes, The Spartan Hero* (1692), III.i., as cited under 'Man', *AEP*, p. 248. The last two lines are probably Haywood's.

209. *Abigail*: a lady's maid.

210. *Sperma-Ceti mask*: a facial treatment made from the soft fatty substance chiefly found in the head of the sperm whale.

211. *Dresden suit*: 'Dresden' might indicate lace, or another fine material.

212. *Pearl-powder*: a cosmetic powder for whitening or enhancing the skin.

213. *Italian cordials ... the Rosasoli*: Cordials were strong alcoholic waters distilled over herbs or other substances, the fore-runners of modern liqueurs. Rosa solis, or rosolio, probably originated in Renaissance Turin. It was made by distilling spices over quantities of the sundew plant, and was considered an aphrodisiac.

214. *Lord B—ps*: Bishops in the House of Lords.

215. *Skellams*: rascals or scoundrels, derived from the Dutch or German *schelm*.

216. *tippit*: a garment, usually of fur or wool, covering the neck and shoulders.

217. *Batavian*: either from Batavia, an old name for a region of the Netherlands now roughly corresponding to an area around Nijmegen; or Jakarta on the island of Java, which was then known as Batavia, being the *de facto* capital of the Dutch East Indies.

218. *mantua-maker*: originally a maker of mantuas – gowns that could have broad, voluminous skirts – but later, more generally, a dressmaker.

219. *Fairest where thousands are fair*: from the Scottish ballad, 'Tweed-side'.

220. *Hollands*: or Holland cloth, a fine plainwoven linen, especially from the Netherlands.

221. *regale*: feast.

222. *Who would the favour ... his vices must begin*: source unidentified. The lines, like the supposed title, are probably Haywood's.

223. *Whate'er we do ... examples too*: source unidentified.

224. *in the straw*: in child-bed; lying-in.

225. *Cinquefoil*: the potentilla plant, often gathered for medicinal purposes.

226. *The nymph who hears ... out-work's beaten down*: from the song 'Tell me why, my charming fair' by Henry Purcell (1659–95) in the semi-operatic *The History of Dioclesian* (1690). The opera was an adaptation by Thomas Betterton (1635–1710) of John Fletcher (1579–1625) and Philip Massinger's play *Prophetess* (1647).

227. *All that desire can wish, or fancy form*: source unidentified.

228. *bouncing*: blustering.

229. *Carlos in the play ... treasur'd virtues there*: an adaptation of lines spoken by Carlos, a student, in Colley Cibber's *Love Makes a Man: or, The Fop's Fortune* (1735). The original lines are: 'If we may think the eye the window to the mind, she has a thousand treasur'd virtues there.'

230. *Collegiate Church of St. Peter's, Westminster*: the more formal name for Westminster Abbey.

231. *Tomb of that princess ... safety was dearer to her than her own*: A traditional story had it that Eleanor of Castile (*c.* 1244–90) sucked poison from a knife-wound inflicted on her husband Edward I (1239–1307) while in the Holy Land, thus saving his life. Her tomb is in the chapel of St Edward the Confessor in Westminster Abbey.

232. *Domine*: or domino, a loose cloak with a mask covering the upper part of the face.

233. *Spanish Bonaroba*: A bona-roba is a courtesan or prostitute, so Haywood may mean dressed as such.

234. *Eringos ... Ratifee ...Viper-wine*: the candied root of sea holly, served as a sweetmeat and regarded as an aphrodisiac; an alternative spelling of ratafia (see above, n. 39); and a wine to which an extract obtained from a viper has been added, with supposed restorative or invigorating properties.

235. *Arbor-Vitæ*: the popular name of several evergreen shrubs.

236. *Bashaw*: the earlier form of the Turkish title pasha, meaning an officer of high rank.

237. *turbant*: turban.

238. *a Bully*: here, a man hired to protect prostitutes.

239. *Link-boys*: boys who carried torches (links) to light the streets.

240. *Bagnio*: here probably meaning a boarding-house, but can also signify a bath-house or brothel.

241. *Woman to man ... chang'd her love*: Thomas Otway (1652–85), *The Orphan: or, the Unhappy Marriage* (1680), III.i., cited under 'Woman', *AEP*, p. 429.

242. *To know the worst is some degree of ease*: source unidentified. The line may be Haywood's: it appears as the second line of a couplet in *Betsy Thoughtless* (1751), ch. V.

243. *eclaircisement*: to come to an eclaircisement is to come to an understanding or to explain behaviour that seems equivocal.

244. *in petto*: in private, or in reserve.

245. *a medal of the Duke of Cumberland*: Prince William Augustus (1721–65), ennobled as Duke of Cumberland in 1726, was the second surviving son and favourite of George II and his wife Caroline. As commander of British forces, Cumberland routed the Jacobite rebels at Culloden, near Inverness, in April 1746. The suppression of the rebels was brutal. Some 2000 men were hacked to death as they fled, while others were hunted down and summarily executed, earning Cumberland the nickname 'Butcher'. On his return to England he was given a hero's welcome, and a number of medals were struck commemorating the rebels' defeat. In peacetime, however, Cumberland's popularity waned. As ranger of Windsor Forest, he attempted to enforce the forest laws rigorously, preventing even the gathering of firewood from the Great Park. Horace Walpole criticized him in print. The duke sponsored changes in the Army Act in 1749, whereby a refusal to obey orders was made a capital offence. Involving himself in domestic politics in 1749, he opposed his brother Frederick's reversionary interest, and when Frederick died unexpectedly in 1751, aimed to become regent. In the view of the Pelhams, Cumberland's unpopularity made him an unsuitable choice. By the Regency Act of 1751, Princess Augusta would become Princess Dowager Regent if the king died before her son George attained his majority. Cumberland was appointed President of the Regency Council, to which the Princess was answerable, but professed to be very much offended by being denied the Regency. See W.A. Speck, 'William Augustus, duke of Cumberland (1721–1765)', *ODNB*; and Langford, *A Polite and Commercial People*, p. 221.

246. *Sal Armoniac*: the contemporary term for ammonium chloride crystals.

247. *The Art of Pleasing ... E - of C -*: possibly Philip Dormer Stanhope, Earl of Chesterfield (1694–1773), politician. Lord Hervey wrote that Chesterfield 'was allowed by everybody to have more conversable entertaining table-wit than any man of his time', but his parliamentary speeches were always prepared, and 'his manner of speaking was [not] like debating but declaiming' (John, Lord Hervey, *Some Materials Towards Memoirs of the Reign of King George II*, ed. R. Sedgwick, 3 vols (1931; New York: AMS Press, 1970),

vol. 1, p. 71; vol 3, p. 738). In 1774, a collection of letters by Chesterfield was published posthumously, including letters to his illegitimate son. These advised on 'the *Duty*, the *Utility* and the *Means* of pleasing' in conversation and much else besides (*Lord Chesterfield's Letters*, ed. D. Roberts (1992; Oxford: Oxford University Press, 1998), p. 339).

248. *The Virtues of Carmine ... C- of C-*: Maria, Countess of Coventry (*neé* Gunning), (1732–60), who married George William, Earl of Coventry in 1752. She was one of the Gunning sisters whose beauty attracted attention when they arrived in London in 1751. The countess's portrait was painted by leading artists, including Francis Cotes and Gavin Hamilton. Maria wore heavy cosmetics, but during the couple's honeymoon in Paris, her husband forbade her to wear any, and once rubbed rouge off her cheeks in public. (*The Correspondence of Horace Walpole*, ed. W.S. Lewis, W. Hunting Smith and G. L. Lam (London: Oxford University Press, 1960), vol. 20, p. 338).

249. *Patient Grizel ... by the real C- of C-*: 'Patient Grizel' is a proverbial expression for a long-suffering wife, but the 'real C- of C-' is unidentified.

250. *The Politician defeated ... E- of E-*: probably John Perceval, second Earl of Egmont (1711–70), politician. Egmont failed to be elected as an MP on three occasions, but gained a seat in 1741 with the support of Henry Pelham. He crossed to the opposition side almost immediately, and was equally disliked by the ministry and by tories. He became Prince Frederick's chief political advisor, but on the Prince's death in 1751, Princess Augusta (see above, n. 155) distanced her self from her husband's supporters. He was returned as MP for Bridgwater in April 1754. (C. Wilkinson, 'Perceval, John, second earl of Egmont', *ODNB*).

251. *The Croaker ... L- R-*: A 'croaker' is someone who prophesies evil. L- R- is probably Henry Liddell, first Lord Ravensworth (1708–1784), Whig politician. In 1753 Ravensworth brought forward accusations that Andrew Stone (1703–1773), William Murray, later first earl of Mansfield (1705–93), and James Johnson, Bishop of Gloucester (1705–1774), who were involved in the education of the Prince of Wales, had twenty years earlier drunk the health of the 'king over the water'. The matter was investigated by the Cabinet Council in February of 1753, but the accused were vindicated (Langford, *A Polite and Commercial People*, pp. 221–2). See also below, n. 265.

252. *The Chaste Maid ... By the facetious H- F-, Esq*: The 'chaste maid' is the servant Elizabeth Canning (1734–73), whose alleged kidnapping and eventual conviction for perjury caused huge controversy in the early 1750s. (See Introduction, pp. xvii–xviii) Those who disbelieved Canning's version of events were more inclined to believe that she had gone to a lover, and that the story of her abduction was a cover. Canning was convicted of perjury in May 1754 and deported to America.

253. *Rules to chuse a Wife ... Sir J- C-*: According to Horace Walpole, his friend Sir John Chute (1701–76), architect, persuaded Miss Margaret Nicoll (*c*.1735–68), an heiress, to run away from her guardians, proposing to marry her to Walpole's cousin, George Walpole, third earl of Orford (1730–91). She escaped on 4 May 1751. Orford refused her, even though Miss Nicoll was worth more than £150,000. Walpole's uncle, Horatio Walpole (1678–1757) then (allegedly) tried to get her for his third son, Richard Walpole (1728–98), and excluded Chute from seeing her. (See *The Correspondence of Horace Walpole*, vol. 13–14, ii, appendix 1: The Nicoll Affair, pp. 193–233). In March 1753, Margaret married James Brydges, third duke of Chandos.

254. *A philosophical Definition of Card-Craft ... Professor Mr. H-*: see above, n. 23.

255. *Frugality ... C- of B-*: probably Mary Stuart (*neé* Wortley Montagu), Countess of Bute (1718–94), daughter of Lady Mary Wortley Montagu. She married John Stuart, third

earl of Bute, in 1736, and had borne ten children by 1753. One, a son, died a year after his birth in 1741. Chesterfield (see above, n. 247), in his 'Characters' of 1764, wrote that 'Lord Bute and she ... lived eight or nine years in a frugal and prudent manner, in the Island of Bute, which was entirely his own property. ... He proved *a great husband* and had thirteen or fourteen children successively by her, in as little time as was absolutely necessary for their being got and born' (*The Letters of Philip Dormer Stanhope, Earl of Chesterfield*, ed. Lord Mahon, 4 vols (London:1845), vol. 2, p. 470). Bute was part of the Leicester House court, and was appointed one of the lords of the bedchamber by Prince Frederick in 1750. He remained a confidant of Princess Augusta after her husband's death, and became first Lord of the Treasury—effectively prime minister—in 1762.

256. *Try before you buy ... E- of R-*: unidentified.

257. *The Charms of Novelty ... miss C-*: possibly referring to Elizabeth Carter (1717–1806), poet and scholar, who mastered Latin, Greek, Hebrew and a number of other languages. Her *Poems on Several Occasions* was published in 1738. Translations of Crousaz's *Examination of Mr. Pope's Essay on Man* (1738) and Algarotti's *Sir Isaac Newton's Philosophy Explain'd, for the Use of the Ladies* (1739) attracted praise in the *History of the Works of the Learned*. In the 1750s, she worked on translating Horace and Epictetus, with *All the Works of Epictetus which are now extant*, a translation that brought her fame and respect, appearing in 1758.

258. *The Pleasures of Matrimony ... L- V-*: Lady Frances Anne Vane (*née* Hawes), Viscountess Vane (1715–88). In 1735 Frances Anne married William Holles Vane, second Viscount Vane (1714–89), her second husband. In 1736 she eloped with one of her lovers while visiting Paris with her husband, and subsequently engaged in a number of very public affairs. Her scandalous 'Memoirs of a Lady of Quality', possibly revised by John Shebbeare, appeared as ch. 88 of Tobias Smollett's *The Adventures of Peregrine Pickle* in 1751. The 'Memoirs' made her contempt for her husband quite explicit.

259. *Laugh and Lie Down ... L- P-*: For *Laugh and Lie Down*, see above, n. 127. L- P- is probably Laetitia Pilkington (*née* van Lewen) (1709–50), Irish poet and memoirist. The first two volumes of her *Memoirs of Laetitia Pilkington*, which recounted details of her husband's adultery, their divorce on the grounds of her alleged adultery, and subsequent numerous (failed) attempts to seduce her, were published in 1748. According to Pilkington, her would-be lovers frequently became subscribers to the *Memoirs*. She produced a prologue for James Worsdale's ballad opera *A Cure for a Scold*, and wrote an 'operatical farce' called *No Death but Marriage*, performed at Smock Alley in 1738. She criticized Haywood's *The Female Spectator*: 'Mrs *Haywood* seems to have dropped her former luscious Stile, and, for Variety, presents us with the insipid: Her *Female Spectators* are a Collection of trite Stories, delivered to us in stale and worn-out Phrases, bless'd Revolution!' (*Memoirs of Laetitia Pilkington*, ed. A. C. Elias, Jr. (Athens, GA: University of Georgia Press, 1997) 2 vols, vol. I, p. 227).

260. *An Essay to prove that true Honour ... E- of O-*: possibly referring to John Boyle, fifth earl of Orrery (1707–62). Boyle suffered personal tragedy: his father, the fourth earl of Orrery, ostracized him, and his first wife, Lady Henrietta (*née* Hamilton), died after four years of marriage, leaving him with three young children. In the late 1730s and early 1740s, he was an associate of Bolingbroke, a tory, and a Jacobite, communicating with the Stuart court in exile. He later turned to the opposition court of Prince Frederick, but after the Prince's death retired to Italy with his second wife to live more economically. He translated Horace and Pliny, and published a biography, *Remarks on the Life and Writings of Dr Jonathan Swift* (1751). Lady Mary Wortley Montagu described him

as 'a Poet, a Patriot, a Philosopher, a Physician, a Critic, a compleat Scholar, and most excellent Moralist, shineing in private Life as a submissive Son, a tender Father, and zealous Freind' (*Complete Letters of Lady Mary Wortley Montagu*, ed. R. Halsband (Oxford: Clarendon Press, 1965–7), vol. III, p. 56; see also L. B. Smith, 'Boyle, John, fifth earl of Cork and fifth earl of Orrery (1707–1762)', *ODNB*).

261. *Conjugal Love ... E- of N-*: unidentified.

262. *The Patriot ... G- D-, Esq*: probably George Bubb Dodington, Baron Melcombe (1690/91–1762), politician. He served in the Walpole administration from 1724–40, but disappointed by his failure to be given a peerage, moved in and out of opposition circles. By the late 1740s he was close to Prince Frederick, expecting high office when the prince became king. The 'secret History' may refer to the detailed plans that were drawn up at Leicester House, chiefly by Egmont (see above, n. 250), for formalities, parliamentary business and appointments that would follow Frederick's accession to the throne. (See A. N. Newman, 'Leicester House Politics, 1748–1751', *EHR*, 76:301 (1961), pp. 577–89). Princess Augusta (see above, n. 155), had Egmont destroy these papers when her husband died. Alternatively, the 'secret History' could be the diary that Dodington began to compile in 1749, which was not published until 1784.

263. *The Double Dealer ... Sir G- V-*: Sir G- V- is Sir George Vandeput (see above, n. 129). The 'double dealing' refers to the recount that took place in the Westminster election of 1749.

264. *An Eulogy on Apostacy ... L- G-*: probably John Carteret, second earl Granville: see above, n. 157.

265. *Love in a Bottle ... E- of M-*: probably William Murray, later first earl of Mansfield: see also above, n. 250. He came from a Jacobite family, and was brother-in-law of John Hay, Jacobite Duke of Inverness (see below, n. 378). The expression 'bottle Jacobites' denoted those who were prepared to drink a toast to the king in exile, but carried their allegiance no further than that.

266. *Redivivus ... E- of H-*: unidentified.

267. *An Exhortation to Hospitality to Foreigners ... L- T-*: Lord Trentham: see above, n. 129.

268. *Criticisms on the Play of - Rule a Wife and Have a Wife. – By L- P-*: *Rule a Wife and Have a Wife* is a comedy by Beaumont and Fletcher, first performed in 1624 and published in 1640, with a plot where would-be husbands and wives vie for dominance. L- P- is probably Laetitia Pilkington (see above, n. 259).

269. *The Fox weary of Goose-hunting ... D- of D-*: possibly Lionel Cranfield Sackville, first duke of Dorset (1688–1765), politician. He had aspired to go to Ireland as lord lieutenant, and was finally appointed when Walpole dismissed Carteret from the office in 1730. Dorset disappointed Walpole and was relieved of his position in 1737. He was reappointed in April 1750, and chose his third son, Lord George Sackville (1716–85) (see also below, n. 284) as chief secretary. Confrontation over the royal prerogative to use a surplus in the Irish Treasury — the 'Money Bill dispute'—set the crown and members of the Irish parliament at odds in between 1751 and 1754: a period of 'ferment ... a constitutional campaign of great heat and bitterness'(J.C.D. Clark, 'Whig Tactics and Parliamentary Precedent: The English Management of Irish Politics', *HJ* 21:2 (1978), pp. 277; 279). The crisis posed a challenge to the customary method of controlling the Irish commons through patronage, meaning the appointment to crown offices of a Irish Whig élite. A faction of self-styled Patriots led by the speaker Henry Boyle (1682–1764) gained enough support to defeat a money bill on 18 November 1753, and tumultuous scenes followed on the streets of Dublin. Dorset had Boyle and his allies dismissed from

crown offices. He and Sackville left Ireland in May 1754 expecting to return, but the situation in Ireland deteriorated, and the king and his ministers decided to replace Dorset and make terms with Boyle. (See R. E. Burns, *Irish Parliamentary Politics in the Eighteenth Century*, 2 vols (Washington, D.C., WA: Catholic University Press of America, 1990), vol. 2, *1730–1760*, ch. 4).

270. *The Lover's Catechism ... Miss A-*: possibly Elizabeth Ashe, who in July 1751 married, bigamously, Edward Wortley Montagu (1713–76), the only son of Edward Wortley Montagu (1678–1761) and Lady Mary Wortley Montagu. (See R. Halsband, *The Life of Mary Wortley Montagu* (Oxford: Oxford University Press, 1960), pp. 249–50). Montagu left Elizabeth three months later, and was shocked to be asked to contribute to the maintenance of their illegitimate son.

271. *An infallible Remedy ... D- of A-*: Archibald Campbell, third duke of Argyll (1682–1761), Whig politician. At the time of the Jacobite Rebellion, Argyll left Scotland for London, possibly to avoid the suspicion of Jacobitism. He did not return there until after the elections of 1747. Another, possibly more likely, explanation for his hasty departure is that he wanted to avoid the political jealousies created by the part he and his late brother had played in putting down the '15 Rebellion. Both fought in the militia. In 1752 Argyll tried to obtain parliamentary approval for an act that would effectively nationalize Jacobite estates confiscated from the rebels. The estates would then have been improved and developed by a commission established for the purpose. English opponents saw this as a reward for treason, and the Duke of Bedford (see Introduction, pp. xiv–xv and below, n. 272) accused Argyll of protecting the interests of Jacobites who held government offices in Scotland. (A. Murdoch, 'Campbell, Archibald, third duke of Argyll (1682–1761)', *ODNB*).

272. *The Beauties of Domestic Life ... D- of B-*: John Russell, fourth duke of Bedford (1710–71), politician. See Introduction, pp. xiv–xv. Bedford was married twice, first to Lady Diana Spencer (1710–35), and then to Lady Gertrude Leveson-Gower (1718/19–94). His second marriage seems to have been a happy one. Lady Gertrude was interested in politics and had a certain amount of influence on her husband. Bedford devoted time to his estate at Woburn, where the couple enjoyed amateur theatricals. (M. J. Powell, 'Russell, John, fourth Duke of Bedford (1710–1771)', *ODNB*).

273. *Love levels all ... C- B-*: possibly Lady Caroline Brand (*née* Pierrepoint) (1716–53), Lady Mary Wortley Montagu's wealthy half-sister, who in 1749 married the far less well-off Thomas Brand (*c.* 1717–70), MP.

274. *Instructions for a Supplement ... L- L-*: unidentified.

275. *Verses in Praise of Breeding ... Miss W-*: possibly Clementine Walkenshaw (*c.*1720–1802), who became mistress of Prince Charles in 1746. She may have borne him a child in 1747. After discarding her, the prince sent for her again in 1752, much to the dismay of Jacobites who suspected her of being a spy. She had a daughter while with Charles in Liège in October 1753.

276. *True Magnificence ... D- of M-*: possibly an unironic tribute to Sarah Churchill (*née* Jenyns), duchess of Marlborough (1660–1744), who was active in politics for most of her life. Haywood dedicated her anti-Walpole satire *Eovaai* (1736) to the Duchess, and though Sarah was a Whig, she shared many of Haywood's views and allegiances. In 1730 it was rumoured that she was scheming to marry her granddaughter Lady Diana Spencer (see also above, n. 272) to Frederick, Prince of Wales. She supported opposition politicians such as William Pulteney (see above, n. 157), and had family links to the Bedford and Carteret factions. Sarah and her husband Sir John Churchill, Duke of Marlborough

(1650–1722), moved to the palatial residence at Blenheim in 1719, where he died three years later. She was wealthy in her own right, and managed and expanded the Churchill fortune. At her death she had an estate worth over £4,000,000. (James Falkner, 'Churchill, Sarah, duchess of Marlborough (1660–1744)', *ODNB*).

277. *Love in a Coach ... C- V-*: unidentified.

278. *Second Thoughts best ... Mr W-*: unidentified.

279. *The Triumvirate of Converts ... L- T-, C- G-, and Mis. C-*: If 'Mis. C', is Elizabeth Carter (see above, n. 257), then L- T- may be Lewis Theobald (1688–1744), poet, translator and literary editor. Like Carter he translated from Latin and Greek, but it was editing Shakespeare that made his reputation and helped to establish new standards of editorial scholarship. C- G- may be the dramatist and critic Charles Gildon (1665–1724) who translated Persius and Euripides, and published epistolary fiction between 1692 and 1719. He converted from Catholicism and adopted deism for a time before turning to the Church of England. However, the point of Haywood's jibe is unclear.

280. *The Escape ... L- D- M-*: unidentified.

281. *A Scheme intended to be offer'd to Parliament ... Mr. P-*: possibly Henry Pelham (1694–1754), politician, who was responsible for a number of fiscal reforms in the late 1740s and early 1750s, including the repeal of a clause in the City Elections Act of 1725 which had given the Court of Aldermen in London the power of veto over all corporate acts. The so-called Aldermanic Negative was usually seen as being in Whig interests, but it is possible Haywood is referring to this measure. Pelham also opened up the process of bidding for shares in government loans to individual stockbrokers (Langford, *A Polite and Commericial People*, p. 214).

282. *A Letter with a Side of Venison to the celebrated Mrs. J- D- ... By L- T-e*: Jenny Dawson was the madam of a brothel in Covent Garden, but L- T-e is unidentified.

283. *A short Treatise ... L- E- J-*: unidentified.

284. *The Humiliation ... L- G- S-*: possibly Lord George Sackville (see above, n.269). The 'humiliation' could refer to the failure of Sackville and his father to control the Irish Parliament, with the 'Inexorables' being the Irish Patriots. After the Money Bill was rejected on December 1753, Lord George had to leave his chair in front of the House and leave by a back door. Alternatively, G- S- could be George Stone, Archbishop of Armagh (1708–64), who from the Irish House of Lords, allied himself with Lord George Sackville and campaigned against Speaker Boyle. When Boyle was dismissed, Stone, seen as a representative of the hostile 'English interest', became the target of vicious abuse. (See D. O'Donovan, 'The Money Bill Dispute of 1753', in *Penal Era and Golden Age. Essays in Irish History, 1690–1800*, ed. T. Bartlett and D. W. Hayton (Belfast: Ulster Historical Association, 1979), pp. 55–87).

285. *A Prophecy ... Sir W- Y-*: Sir William Yonge (*c.*1693–1755), an ally of Walpole. In 1754, he voted to repeal the Bribery Act of 1727, 'an important statute designed to limit electoral malpractice' (Langford, *A Polite and Commercial People*, p. 717).

286. *Good name ... makes me poor indeed*: *Othello*, III.iii., cited under 'Reputation', *AEP*, p. 339.

287. *Children ... still will grow*: from Dryden's translation of the Fourteenth Satire of Juvenal in *The Satires* (1692), cited under 'Education', *AEP*, p. 110.

288. *if these are humour'd and indulged ... that can be taken for that purpose*: In *Some Thoughts Concerning Education* (1693), John Locke (1632–1704) warned against parental indulgence: '[P]arents, by humouring and cockering [children] when little, corrupt

the principles of nature in their children, and wonder afterwards to taste the bitter waters'(Section 35 ff).

289. *Le Spectacle de la Nature*: *Le Spectacle de la Nature* (1732), an eight-volume work of natural history by the French cleric Noël-Antoine Pluche (1688–1761). The full title in English gives an idea of the work's scope and intention: *Nature Display'd, Being Discourses on such Particulars of Natural History as were thought most proper to excite the Curiosity and form the Minds of Youth.*

290. *Fontenelle's Plurality of Worlds*: Bernard le Bovier Fontenelle (1657–1757), *Entretiens sur la Pluralité des mondes* (1686), an introduction to, and a popularization of, contemporary astronomical ideas.

291. *The Licence-Office knows how to correct them*: After the Licensing Act of 1737, the Lord Chamberlain had the power to censor any plays accepted by the patent theatres. Non-patent theatres were theoretically outlawed, though ways could be found to stage satirical plays without breaking the law. In 1747, the actor and theatre-manager Samuel Foote (1720–77) hit upon the pretext of 'offering tea', while his performance of *The Diversions of the Morning; or, The Dish of Chocolate* (later *The Dish of Tea*) at the Little Theatre at the Haymarket was ostensibly *gratis*. Henry Fielding too charged for refreshments, but not the show itself, at his puppet theatre in Panton Lane.

292. *Cato*: *Cato*, a tragedy by Joseph Addison (1672–1719), first performed in 1713. Addison's highly successful play deals with the death of the republican Cato, who commits suicide rather than submit to the tyranny of Caesar. In a letter to John Caryll (1625–1711), Alexander Pope, who wrote a prologue for the play, described how Whigs and Tories vied with each other to applaud displays of the patriotic virtue of liberty on stage. The political allegiances of *Cato* remain a subject for debate. In the play, Cato's sons Portius and Marcus are both in love with Lucia, daughter of Cato's ally Lucius. Juba, who fights on Cato's side, is in love with his daughter Marcia, though her father has promised her to Sempronius. The presence of romantic sub-plots in the tragedy was attacked by John Dennis, and later Voltaire. A heavily revised version of *Cato* entitled *Cato. A Tragedy. By Mr. Addison. Without the Love Scenes.* was published in 1764, though it did not, in fact, remove the erotic scenes and language, but rather the female characters. See Lisa A. Freeman, 'What's love got to do with Addison's *Cato*?', *SEL*, 39:3 (1999) pp. 463–82.

293. *tucker*: a ruffle stitched round the neck of a gown.

294. *the fam'd Cornelia—the mother of the Gracchi*: Cornelia (d. *c.*100 BC) second daughter of Publius Cornelius Scipio Africanus, wife of Tiberius Gracchus and mother of two famous tribunes, Tiberius and Gaius Gracchus. In Plutarch's *Lives*, she is described as a model of matronly Roman virtue, paying scrupulous care to the education of her children, and ending her days playing host to literary men and kings. She was said to have refused an offer of marriage from Ptolemy after her husband died.

295. *the wife of Brutus*: Porcia, daughter of the republican hero Cato. From 45 BC, she was the wife of Julius Caesar's assassin Brutus, and shared the political ideals of her father and husband. She was said to have inflicted a wound on her own thigh and born the pain to prove she could keep the secret of the planned assassination. According to some sources, she killed herself by eating live coals when she heard of her husband's death.

296. *the learned Hypatia of Greece*: Hypatia (d. AD 415), was the daughter of the mathematician Theon of Alexandria, whose *Commentary on the Almagest* she revised. She was versed in mathematics, astrology and philosophy.

297. *Boadicea*: Boudicca, queen of the Iceni tribe, who led an uprising against Roman forces in the South East of England. Camulodunum (Colchester), Londinium and Verulamium (St. Albans) were all sacked.

298. *Cartismuda of ancient Britain*: Cartimandua, queen of the Brigantes, a tribe occupying northern Britain. Her treaty with Emperor Claudius helped to protect the northern borders of the empire, and keep her in power. In AD 51 she proved her loyalty by handing over the fugitive Caratacus to the Romans.

299. *wife of the late Peter the Great of Muscovy*: Catherine I of Russia (1684–1727), who reigned as Empress from 1725 until her death.

300. *the imperial heroine of Germany*: the Habsburg queen, Maria Theresa of Austria (1717–80), who was also Queen of Bohemia and Hungary. The Habsburgs were originally Austrian Germans, and the empire was an agglomeration of territories, some of which were in Germany. Others stretched from the Netherlands to Italy. Maria Theresa's contested entitlement to the throne was the ostensible cause of the War of the Austrian Succession (1740–8), though the conflict had more to do with princely and imperial ambition. Britain and the Dutch Republic supported Maria Theresa, while Prussia was allied with France and Bavaria. While Maria Theresa might have been a heroine for some, the Haywood of the *Female Spectator* portrayed the queen as ruthless, proud and ambitious, 'wading thro' whole Seas of Blood to reach the Goal' (*The Female Spectator*, in *Selected Works of Eliza Haywood II*, ed. K.R. King and A. Pettit (London: Pickering & Chatto, 2001) vol. 2, book 9, p. 332). The war ended with the Treaty of Aix-la-Chapelle in 1748.

301. *Signiora Laura of Italy*: Laura Bassi (1711–78), Italian scientist. She received a degree (the second woman to do so) from the University of Bologna, and taught at the university. She played a key role in introducing Newtonian physics to Italy.

302. *the present queens of Sweden and the Two Sicilies*: Queen of Sweden in 1755 was Louisa Ulrike of Prussia (1720–82), wife of Adolf Frederick from 1751–71. She brought the French taste to the court, and during her ownership of Drottningholm Palace near Stockholm it was redecorated in rococo style, and the palace theatre was rebuilt. Queen of the Two Sicilies was Maria Amalia of Saxony (1724–60) who married Charles of Bourbon in 1738. 'Two Sicilies' derives from the custom of using the name Sicily for both the island and that part of southern Italy now roughly coinciding with Calabria. She was a cultured woman who patronised the arts: she encouraged her husband to set up a porcelain manufactory in the palace grounds of Capodimonte near Naples.

303. *Baile's Dictionary*: The *Dictionnaire historique et critique*, compiled by the French Protestant scholar Pierre Bayle (1647–1706), which began to be published in 1695. A second revised and enlarged edition appeared in 1702. The *Dictionnaire* was a major work of the Enlightenment, subjecting many biblical and classical figures to critical and historical analysis.

304. *Wisdom in her ... with pride obey*: an adaptation of lines from 'The Man of Honour', in *Poems on Several Occasions* (1715), by Charles Montagu, Earl of Halifax (1661–1715), cited under 'Honour', *AEP*, p. 187. The original lines read: 'When danger calls, and honour leads the way/With joy they follow, and with pride obey'.

305. *Jolliffe's shop*: the shop belonging to John Jolliffe, a bookseller examined during the investigation into the publication of the Jacobite pamphlet 'A Letter from H- G-' in 1749. Haywood was also examined and held in custody.

306. *His very eye-balls ... humid fires*: Dryden, *The Spanish Fryar* (1681), V.i., cited under 'Enjoyment', *AEP*, p. 123.

307. *lead apes / in hell*: in a proverbial expression, the supposed consequences of dying an old maid.

308. *sash and croslet*: British soldiers wore a red sash. The meaning of 'croslet' is a little obscure: in heraldry, it signifies a small cross at the end of a cross, but 'croslet' is also a variant spelling of 'corselet', meaning a piece of defensive armour covering the body.

309. *Great Russel-street*: near the location of the premises at the Great Piazza in Covent Garden where, between 1741 and 1744, Eliza Haywood had a business as a bookseller.

310. *India Bonds*: Bonds issued by the East India Company. They were a popular form of short-term investment for those who wanted easy access to their funds. At mid-century, women constituted a fifth of domestic stockholders in the Company. See H. V. Bowen, *The Business of Empire: The East India Company and Imperial Britain, 1756–1833* (Cambridge: Cambridge University Press, 2006), pp. 32–3.

311. *The Card of Fancy*: Robert Greene's *Gwydonius, The Card of Fancie* (1584).

312. *When headstrong youth ... destruction seeks*: source unidentified.

313. *brow contracted ... Milton's fallen Angel*: The phrase is not found in *Paradise Lost* (1667).

314. *a certain modern writer ... enormous length*: Samuel Richardson (1689–1761), author of *Pamela* (1740), *Clarissa* (1747–8) and *Sir Charles Grandison* (1753–4). Mary Wortley Montagu wrote to Lady Bute in September 1755: 'This letter is as Long and as Dull as any of Richardson's.'

315. *a work which I intended ... postpon'd till now*: The Invisible Spy was published on 12 November 1754, though dated for the following year, as was common at the time. The previous winter would have been that of 1753/4, when Haywood might have supposed that *The Invisible Spy* could influence the spring elections of 1754. A cause for postponement is not known. Haywood's work had been interrupted before, by illness, between 1737 and 1740 (Spedding, 355), and in 1749 (King, *Political Biography*, pp. 162–3).

316. *dance a French Louvre*: The Louvre is described as a slow, majestic dance by Soame Jenyns (1704–87) in his poem of three cantos, *The Art of Dancing* (1729).

317. *the late King of Sardinia ... such an opportunity should arrive*: The late king when *The Invisible Spy* was published was Victor Amadeus II, Prince of Piedmont (1666–1732). He had no claim on the British throne, though his son could have, through the Stuart line. Victor Amadeus II married Charles I's grand-daughter, Anne Marie d'Orléans (1669–1728), and their son, Charles Emmanuel, Duke of Savoy (1701–73), became king of Sardinia on his father's abdication in 1730.

318. *Corisca*: In Giovanni Battista Guarini's (1538–1612) *Il Pastor Fido* (The Faithful Shepherd), published 1589–90, Corisca is the name of the jealous, vengeful woman who schemes to separate the lovers in the play. She is the model for many such female characters in English seventeenth-century drama and beyond.

319. *Oh cursed honour ... disdain'd all other pride*: Aphra Behn (*c.*1640–89), 'The Golden Age', *Poems Upon Several Occasions* (1684), cited under 'Honour', *AEP*, p. 185.

320. *Virtue and Vice ... like themselves might be*: not found in the works of Massinger.

321. *parterres and knots*: level spaces with ornamental flower-beds, and elaborately designed flower-beds.

322. *a Hautboy, a Double-Curtal*: a reed instrument corresponding to the oboe, and another resembling a bassoon.

323. *Wisdom is still ... the fool and knave*: source unidentified.

324. *a white rose carry'd into his house on the 10ᵗʰ of June*: 10 June 1688 was the birthday of James Francis Edward Stuart, the 'Old Pretender', celebrated by Jacobites by the wearing of a white rose.

325. *a yellow waistcoat on the birth-day of his present Majesty*: George II wore a yellow scarf, or sash, as he led the so-called Pragmatic Army, comprising British, Hanoverian and Austrian troops, at the Battle of Dettingen (1743) in the War of the Austrian Succession (1740–8). For Patriots, the wearing of the yellow sash underlined the king's primary allegiance to Hanover. A ballad called 'The Yellow Sash' also commemorated what was seen as the king's cowardice when he called off British troops pursuing the retreating French. (N. Harding, *Hanover and the British Empire 1700–1837*, (Woodbridge: Boydell, 2007) pp. 122–3).

326. *Oh fountains! ... That is the way too thither*: Cowley, 'The Wish', from *The Mistress; or, Several Copies of Love Verses* (1647), as cited under 'Country Life', *AEP*, p. 60.

327. *malapert*: insolent or presumptuous.

328. *an Act of Parliament for a new Road to be cut*: Every new road, and new turnpike trust, required a separate Act of Parliament. See also above, n. 181.

329. *the continuance of a standing army*: Until the enactment of the Bill of Rights in 1689, the power to raise an army lay with the king. The growth of the army under James II, and the authoritarian purposes for which it was used, caused particular anxiety. Under the Bill, the monarch could not keep a standing army in peacetime without parliamentary consent. Opposition to standing armies was one of the main planks of Patriotism, and a cause of divisions in Parliament.

330. *A certain sacred writer ... the government of it*: Church of England cleric Richard Allestree (1621/2–81) published *The Government of the Tongue* in 1674. The work has sections on atheistical discourse, detraction, lying and defamation, scoffing and derision, flattery, boasting, querulousness and obscene talk. It followed on from the huge success of *The Whole Duty of Man* (1657), a work designed to show even the 'very meanest' sort of readers how to behave in this life so as to earn their reward in the next.

331. *another very great and learned person of more modern date ... worst of mischiefs may be occasioned by it*: source unidentified. The thought is a common one, deriving from numerous passages in the Bible that warn against speech fomenting disorder, or scandalous or licentious talk, such as James 3:6–9, or urge discipline of the tongue, as in Psalms 39:1.

332. *chance-medley*: in eighteenth-century law, an act of unintentional homicide in which the killer is not entirely without blame.

333. *Thinking to shoot ... kill'd my brother*: source unidentified.

334. *Ah, cruel friend! ... horror and despair!*: Bellamira: or, *The Mistress* (1687), is the title of a play by Sir Charles Sedley (1639–1701), but the lines are not to be found there.

335. *sack*: a loose gown.

336. *chints*: or chintz, then a colourful painted or stained cotton cloth imported from India.

337. *the words of mr. Nat. Lee ... calms to tempests roll*: a slight adaptation or misquotation of lines by Nathaniel Lee (1645x1652–92) from *The Rival Queens; or, Alexander the Great* (1677), III, i., cited under 'Jealousie', *AEP*, p. 203.

338. *Forgiveness to the injured ... done the wrong*: Dryden, *The Conquest of Granada*, Part 2, I. ii., cited under 'Pardon', *AEP*, p. 325.

339. *Love, justice ... keep me upright*: Dryden, *The Spanish Fryar*, V.i., cited under 'Passions', *AEP*, p. 303.

340. *George's coffee-house*: a coffee-house beside Temple Bar in the Strand, in existence from at least 1723.

341. *Jove only laughs when lovers swear*: A similar expression is found in *Romeo and Juliet*, II.ii: 'At lovers' perjuries/They say, Jove laughs', which is derived from Ovid, *Ars Amatoria*, I. 633: 'Jupiter from on high smiles at the perjuries of lovers'.

342. *the verbal promises I made him ... a better offer*: Before the Marriage Act of 1753 (see above, n. 58), promises to marry exchanged between a man and a woman in private —known as *per verba et praesenti*—could constitute one stage of the marriage process, and were regarded as binding under canon law. Either party could then insist on the performance of the contract, that is, the celebration of the marriage in church, but solemnization was necessary for full rights and responsibilities to arise. See R. Probert, *Marriage Law and Practice in the Long Eighteenth Century* (Cambridge: Cambridge University Press, 2009), p. 35 et passim.

343. *Opera of Arsinoe*: *Arsinoe, Queen of Cyprus* (1705), by Thomas Clayton (1673–1725), was the first full-length English opera in the Italian style, that is, with recitatives instead of spoken dialogue. The libretto, first set in 1676, was by Tommaso Stanzini, translated into English by Peter Motteux (1663–1718).

344. *Wanton zephir ... More of love than I can say*: a slight misquotation of *Arsinoe, Queen of Cyprus* (see above, n. 343), III. ii.

345. *Kindness has resistless charms ... pleas'd and vain*: lines selected from Bysshe's selection from Rochester's 'Give me leave to rail at you', first published in *Poems on Several Occasions* (1680), appearing under the heading 'Kindness', *AEP*, p. 215.

346. *Burton's box*: the middle gallery box at Drury Lane, so-called from the name of its longserving box-keeper. Its screened position made it a popular choice for genteel women who wanted to avoid being seen in the side or front boxes.

347. *No signs of love ... their pains*: Dryden, *The Conquest of Granada*, Part 2, III.i, cited under 'Jealousie', *AEP*, p. 200.

348. *Sinking-Fund*: a fund formed by setting aside revenue to accumulate money at interest for the purpose of reducing the National Debt. A Sinking Fund, devised by Sir Robert Walpole, was launched in 1716. However, the principle of an inviolable Fund was soon abandoned. Rather than paying off the Debt, the Fund could be raided to allow for tax cuts or to finance wars.

349. *servitor*: one of a class of undergraduate members of the Universities of Oxford and Cambridge who received what would now be called scholarships, and could be called upon to perform services for the socially superior commoners.

350. *Perseus*: Aulus Persius Flaccus (AD 34–62), author of poetic satires.

351. *The earth has bubbles ... and these are some of them*: a slight misquotation of Bysshe's quotation from *Macbeth*, I.iii., cited under 'Witch', *AEP*, p. 426.

352. *Who knows but we may see ... dominion's awe?*: a slight misquotation of *Gideon, or The Restoration of Israel* (1720), book I, by Aaron Hill (1685–1750). Hill was a writer, entrepreneur, and in the 1720s, one of the most important figures in London literary life. Haywood was a member of the Hillarian circle—after 'Hillarius', a name given by her to Hill—effectively a salon with Hill at its centre. Other significant Hillarians were Edward Young (1683–1765), John Dyer (1699–1757), David Mallet (c.1705–65), James Thomson (1700–48), Richard Savage (1697/98–1743) and Martha Fowke Sansom (1689–1736). Poems that circulated between Haywood, Hill, Savage and Sansom aspired to an idealized Platonic friendship, with Hill as Muse. However, Haywood satirised Sansom and insulted Savage in *The Injur'd Husband* (1722), and fell out decisively with the Hillarians after the publication of *Memoirs of a Certain Island Adjacent to the Kingdom of Utopia* (1724). (For an account of relationships between Savage, Sansom, Haywood and Hill, see C. Gerrard, *Aaron Hill: The Muses' Projector 1685–1750* (Oxford; Oxford University Press, 2003), esp. ch.4; and K. R. King, 'Eliza Haywood, Savage Love, and Biographical Uncertainty', *RES*, New Series, 59:242 (2007), pp. 722–

39). The lines from *Gideon* cited by Haywood come from Hill's first attempt at his epic poem. He began this work, in the mode of the religious sublime, in 1718–19, and in 1720 published the first two books and a prospectus for later books. He returned to the subject again in the 1740s, and produced a still incomplete second version, *Gideon, or, The Patriot* (1749). Disillusion with self-professed Patriots was by now pervasive (see above, n. 157), and Hill was reluctant even to use the term in his subtitle (Gerrard, *Aaron Hill*, p. 226).

353. *set a guard upon my mouth that I offend not with my lips*: see above, nn. 330, 331.

354. *the affair of Squires and Canning*: see Introduction, p. xvii and above, n. 252.

355. *She is of our congregation*: Opponents of Canning aimed to discredit her case by linking her with Methodists and nonconformists. See Introduction, p. xviii.

356. *she has sworn to the truth of it before a magistrate ... his belief of it*: Henry Fielding, in his capacity as magistrate for Middlesex and Westminster. See Introduction, p. xvii.

357. *superior in every degree to him who takes her part*: Sir Crisp Gascoyne (1700–61), Mayor of London. He took evidence from witnesses who swore that they had seen Squires in Abbotsbury, some 150 miles away from Wells's house in Enfield Wash, at the time of the alleged abduction. Gascoyne examined Virtue Hall, a lodger, who withdrew her earlier confirmation of Canning's story. Gascoyne issued a warrant for the arrest of Elizabeth Canning on 3 March 1753.

358. *British Herring-fishery*: The Free British Fishery Society was founded in 1749 with the aim of challenging Dutch supremacy in herring fishing. Frederick, Prince of Wales, was governor of the Society, and the initiative attracted considerable popular support: ballads and songs were published in celebration of its efforts. In Hogarth's print 'Beer Street' (1751), the utopian vision which contrasts with the horrors of 'Gin Lane' (1751), two fisherwomen are seen reading 'A New Ballad on the Herring Fishery' by the Society's secretary, John Lockman. Opposition politicians associated with Leicester House were keen to identify themselves with the scheme. See Bob Harris, 'Patriotic Commerce and National Revival: The Free British Fishery Society and British Politics, *c.* 1749–58', *EHR*, 114:456 (1999), pp. 285–313.

359. *strict engagements ... the English colonies*: The French representatives of the *Compagne des Indes* saw much more quickly than their British counterparts that trade in India would benefit from involvement in the rivalries of regional princes. To that end, French puppet rulers were installed in the Carnatic (1749) and the Deccan (1750).

360. *the magnanimity of the Prussian monarch*: In the aftermath of the '45 Rebellion, Frederick II of Prussia (1712–86) publicly praised Charles Edward Stuart's generalship, and began favouring exiled Jacobite officers employed in the Prussian service. Chief among these was the Jacobite George Keith, styled tenth Earl Marischal (*c.* 1692/3–1778) who became Prussian ambassador to France in 1751. In the quest for vital foreign support at the time of the Elibank plot, Charles approached Frederick, and at one time it seemed possible that Swedish troops, subsidised by Frederick, might become involved. (See D. Szechi, *The Jacobites: Britain and Europe, 1688–1788*, (Manchester: Manchester University Press, 1994), pp. 114–16).

361. *so near a relation to our gracious sovereign*: Frederick II was the nephew of George II.

362. *the Orator*: John Henley (1692–1756), a dissenting minister known as Orator Henley.

363. *the Westleys*: John Wesley (1703–91), and his brother Charles Wesley (1707–88), founders of Methodism.

364. *the sum ... a thousand pounds*: John Treherne gives the amount collected in 1753 as nearly £300 (Treherne, pp. 38–9).

365. *Virtue Hall*: a witness in the case against Wells and Squires, who withdrew her evidence corroborating Canning's story. See Introduction, p. xvii.

366. *the fatal South-Sea scheme*: Early in 1720, the South Sea Company negotiated with the Stanhope-Sunderland administration to take over 80% of the national debt, which then stood at around fifty million pounds. The company's directors artificially inflated the value of the stock, and a rush to buy shares ensued. At one point, a single share was worth £1,050. New joint-stock companies proliferated in the frenzied atmosphere. A 'Bubble Act' was passed to regularise their formation, and foreign capital began to move abroad. South Sea stock collapsed. Losses were huge and there were many bankrupts. The crash was one of the defining experiences of the early eighteenth century.

367. *Sure there are bolts ... his country's ruin*: The first line may be Haywood's; the second and third are from Addison's *Cato*, I.i.

368. quantum sufficit: an amount that is sufficient.

369. *ready rhino*: ready money.

370. *a play of mrs. Centlivre's, call'd the Gamester*: *The Gamester* (1705) by Susannah Centlivre (*c.*1669–1723).

371. *the mortgage he had made of his reversion*: money raised by using the estate he will inherit as security. Clerimont is in fact protected by law. The Gaming Act of 1710 provided that 'all notes, bills, bonds, judgments, mortgages or other securities' were void if used to pay a gambling debt. (See Miers, *Regulating Commercial Gambling, p.* 28; and Fielding, *An Enquiry*, pp. 96–7). However, a gentleman might see such a debt as a matter of honour.

372. *behind the bason in Mary-le-bon*: The basin at Marylebone was then a large reservoir for York Buildings Waterworks, which supplied waterworks at Buckingham Street and the Strand. A drawing of *c.*1750, attributed to Jean Baptiste Chatelain, show some figures swimming in the basin, and others resting by the water's edge.

373. *hyppo*: a vulgar term for hypochondria, then seen as a disease similar to melancholia. The word began to acquire its pejorative connotation later in the eighteenth century. See J. Darcy, *Melancholy and Literary Biography 1640–1816* (Houndmills: Palgrave Macmillan, 2013), p. 70.

374. *this cursed act of parliament ... us who love play*: the Disorderly Houses Act of 1751. The purpose of the Act was to encourage prosecutions against those keeping 'bawdy houses, gaming houses and other disorderly houses'. By Section 5 of the Act, £10 was to be payable to each of the two householders required to swear an oath before a magistrate as to the nature of the house. The constable who neglected to proceed on such sworn information would be fined £20.

375. *no other than Charlotte herself*: In Centlivre's *The Gamester* (see above, n. 370), Angelica disguises herself as a man and takes part in a card game in a plot to cure her lover, Valere, of his love of gambling, just as Charlotte does with Clerimont.

376. *Away with dull cares ... Engross all our nights*: source unidentified.

377. *some branches of the mathematics ... proper person to instruct him*: an allusion to the controversy surrounding the appointment in November 1750 of George Lewis Scott (1708–80) as mathematics tutor to Prince George. Scott was considered a Jacobite. (See W. P. Courtney, 'Scott, George Lewis (1708–1780)', rev. Alan Yoshioka, *ODNB*).

378. *lords Dunbar and Inverness ... of the Church of England*: James Murray, Jacobite first Earl of Dunbar (1690–1770) and John Hay of Cromlix, Jacobite Duke of Inverness (1691–1740), Dunbar's brother-in-law, were tutors to the young Prince Charles. The Protestantism of the prince's tutors was a vexed issue at the Stuart court in exile in Rome. Charles's mother, Clementina, opposed Murray partly because he was an Episcopalian.

Pope Benedict XIII (1649–1730) objected to a non-Catholic tutor for the prince, and it was rumoured that the young Charles had been taught to laugh at the angelus and despise priests and monks. See McLynn, pp. 17–21. 'Lascelles' has not been identified.

379. *duke of Perth*: either James Drummond, styled sixth earl of Perth, Jacobite third duke of Perth (1713–46), or John Drummond, seventh earl of Perth, Jacobite fourth Duke of Perth (*c*.1714–47), both army officers active in the '45 Rebellion.

380. *Appetite increas'd by what it fed on*: an extract from Bysshe's quotation from *Hamlet*, I.ii., cited under 'Fond', *AEP*, p. 150.

SILENT CORRECTIONS

Book I.

CHAP. I

p. 12, l. 12, those had been bestow'd upon me] those that had been bestow'd upon me

CHAP. II.

p. 17, l. 21, in his heart, his countenance were only smiles] in his heart, in his countenance were only smiles

p. 18, l. 16, .] ?

CHAP. III.

p. 23, l. 22, remind the populous] remind the populace

p. 23, l. 30, revese] reverse

CHAP. IV.

p. 26, l. 22, stiring] stirring

CHAP. V.

p. 34, l. 9, desciption] description

p. 37, l. 17, disappoinment] disappointment

CHAP. VI.

p. 41, l. 24, consin's] cousin's

CHAP. VII.

p. 43, l. 21, proced] procede

p. 47, l. 23, thurst] thrust

p. 52, l. 15, assure me.] assure me

p. 53, l. 41, amasing] amazing

Book II.

CHAP. I

p. 57, l. 8, good humour her] good humour by her

CHAP. II

p. 67, l. 1, *Flainimo*] *Flaminio*

CHAP. III.

p. 71, l. 14, salutaion] salutation

CHAP. V.

p. 82, l. 27, and hear it'] and hear it'.

p. 84, l. 27, unavaling] unavailing

CHAP. VI.

p. 94, l. 40, were] where

p. 95, l. 27, corrobate] corroborate

CHAP. VII.

p. 96, l. 31, Dear,] Dear

p. 97, l. 2, espicially] especially

p. 98, l. 29, retrive] retrieve

p. 99, l. 2, desciption] description

CHAP. VIII.

p. 105, l. 1, Dormion] Dorimon

p. 106, l. 32, disappoinment] disappointment

CHAP. IX.

p. 109, l. 18, would probably,] would probably

Book III.
CHAP. I.

p. 121, l. 24, Israelies] Israelites

Chap. II

p. 126, l. 36, how-d'y's] how-d'ye's

p. 130, l. 16, *Marvel*] *Marvell*

p. 133, l. 7, sir Patient] sir Patient?

Chap. III.

p. 134, l. 24, jealously] jealousy

p. 138, l. 29, immediatly] immediately

p. 139, l. 9, thurst] thrust

CHAP. IV.

p. 144, l. 26, jealously] jealousy

p. 149, l. 7, disorder] disorder?

CHAP. V.

p. 157, l. 3, hunerd] hundred

CHAP. VI.

p. 160, l. 2, married resumed she] married,' resumed she

p. 162, l. 31, Leiutenant] Lieutenant

p. 162, l. 36, face] face.

p. 163, l. 16, puting] putting

CHAP. VIII.

p. 171, l. 12, dinning-room] dining-room

p. 173, l. 22, where-ever] wherever

p. 173, l. 40, irremedable] irremediable

Book IV.

CHAP. I.

p. 177, l. 27, red] read

CHAP. II.

p. 180, l. 31, thurst] thrust
p. 182, l. 11, Deyden] Dryden

CHAP. IV.

p. 190, l. 18, ever,'] ever.'

p. 192, l. 12, admimirers] admirers

p. 192, l. 26, remember it] remember it.

CHAP. V.

p. 195, l. 38, threepeny] threepenny
p. 197, l. 7, furnish'd-me] furnish'd me

p. 197, l. 15, Taste.'] Taste.

CHAP. VI.

p. 201, l. 32, your attendance,] your attendance.

p. 205, l. 10, puting] putting

p. 206, l. 5, for him?] for him.

p. 206, l. 6, Wife,] Wife.

p. 206, l. 15, your honour I I] your honour I

p. 206, l. 28, to he betray'd] to be betray'd

p. 207, l. 31, No, on,] No, no,

CHAP. VIII.

p. 215, l. 36, exhasted] exhausted

p. 217, l. 8, behvoes] behoves

p. 217, l. 13, him.] him,

p. 218, l. 36, waite] wait

p. 220, l. 13, Sotland-yard] Scotland-yard

p. 220, l. 13, assylum] asylum

p. 220, l. 28, softned] soften'd

CHAP. IX.

p. 223, l. 30, *Clyamon]* *Clyamon.*

p. 223, l. 32, spare it me,] spare it me.

p. 223, l. 37, *Careless,]* *Careless.*

p. 228, l. 28, a a] a

p. 229, l. 39, cotemptoraries] cotemporaries

p. 230, l. 8, to him,] to him.

p. 230, l. 23, complisance] complaisance

p. 230, l. 34, your are] you are

p. 233, l. 23, trubulent] turbulent

p. 233, l. 37, as] has

Book V.

CHAP. I.

p. 237, l. 2, EO THE] OF THE

CHAP. II.

p. 242, l. 10, sodder] solder

p. 246, l. 8, *Fortune-teller.,]* *Fortune-teller.*

p. 246, l. 20, *Lysteta]* *Lysetta*

p. 247, l. 13, *Fortne-teller*] Fortune-teller

CHAP. III.

p. 250, l. 37, of of] of

p. 251, l. 6, ancle] uncle

p. 253, l. 18, romantie] romantic

CHAP. IV.

p. 255, l. 24, restless — nights] restless nights

p. 257, l. 21, gone] gone?

p. 259, l. 10, trade lo low] trade so low

p. 262, l. 16, escape,] escape.

CHAP. V.

p. 262, l. 1, choose] chose

p. 263, l. 13, retain it.'] retain it.

p. 263, l. 32, *Playfeild,*] *Playfeild.*

p. 263, l. 38, madam,] madam.

p. 264, l. 34, in discourse.'] discourse.

p. 264, l. 40, safe-guard.'] safe-guard.

p. 267, l. 8, it myself,] it myself.

p. 268, l. 25, to-bed] to bed

CHAP. VI.

p.271, l. 8, bare] bear

CHAP. VII.

p. 280, l. 40, On hideous!] Oh hideous!

CHAP. VIII.

p. 289, l. 27, forgivness] forgiveness

CHAP. IX.

p. 292, l. 23, desier'd] desir'd

p. 294, l. 38, them.'] them.

p. 295, l. 4, ungarded] unguarded

CHAP. X.

p. 296, l. 30, sufcient] sufficient

p. 300, l. 22, guilt] guilt.

Book VI.

CHAP. I.

p. 308, l. 5, what makes] what brings

CHAP. II.

p. 316, l. 12, without,]without

CHAP. III.

p. 325, l. 28, that] than

p. 326, l. 5, dissov'd] dissolv'd

CHAP. IV.

p. 330, l. 31, sitched in blue] stitched in blue

p. 334, l. 11, Spakespear] Shakespear

p. 334, l. 34, utterly] utterly

CHAP. V.

p. 341, l. 29, Loyer] Loyter

CHAP. VII.

p. 352, l. 32, Narcessa] Narcissa

CHAP. VIII.

p. 354, l. 4, counsin] cousin

Book VII.

CHAP. I.

p. 359, l. 1, CONETNTS] CONTENTS
p. 359, l. 3, VOLUMF] VOLUME

CHAP. III.

p. 376, l. 1, which I I] which I
p. 377, l. 31, theroom] the room
p. 379, l. 7, piy] pity

CHAP. IV.

p. 385, l. 34, meataphors] metaphors
p. 386, l. 10, Wimsey] Whimsey
p. 387, l. 4, *Honorius*] Honorius.
p. 387, l. 8, imfamy] infamy

CHAP. VI.

p. 402, l. 1, rest judges] best judges

CHAP. VII.

p. 408, l. 19, maried] married

CHAP. VIII.

p. 411, l. 27, utte stranger] utter stranger
p. 416, l. 23, perusal it] perusal; it
p. 418, l. 35, I am not a person who live] I am not a person who lives
p. 419, l. 27, yourself..] yourself.

Book VIII.
CHAP. I.

p. 430, l. 26, *Assetor*] *Assertor*

CHAP. II.

p. 436, l. 22, you long,] you long.

CHAP. IV.

p. 450, l. 36, kind,] kind.

CHAP. VII.

p. 460, l. 10, three the] three of the
p. 461, l. 6, may good friend] my good friend
p. 462, l. 19, Nobless] Nobles

CHAP. VIII.

p. 465, l. 36, sleve] sleeve

For Product Safety Concerns and Information please contact our EU
representative GPSR@taylorandfrancis.com
Taylor & Francis Verlag GmbH, Kaufingerstraße 24, 80331 München, Germany